blue
rider
press

THE
BOOK
OF
JONAS

THE
BOOK
OF
JONAS

STEPHEN DAU

BLUE RIDER PRESS
a member of Penguin Group (USA) Inc.
New York

blue
rider
press

Published by the Penguin Group
Penguin Group (USA) Inc., 375 Hudson Street, New York, New York 10014,
USA • Penguin Group (Canada), 90 Eglinton Avenue East, Suite 700, Toronto,
Ontario M4P 2Y3, Canada (a division of Pearson Penguin Canada Inc.) • Penguin
Books Ltd, 80 Strand, London WC2R 0RL, England • Penguin Ireland, 25 St Stephen's
Green, Dublin 2, Ireland (a division of Penguin Books Ltd) • Penguin Group (Australia),
250 Camberwell Road, Camberwell, Victoria 3124, Australia (a division of Pearson Australia
Group Pty Ltd) • Penguin Books India Pvt Ltd, 11 Community Centre, Panchsheel Park,
New Delhi–110 017, India • Penguin Group (NZ), 67 Apollo Drive, Rosedale, North
Shore 0632, New Zealand (a division of Pearson New Zealand Ltd) • Penguin Books
(South Africa) (Pty) Ltd, 24 Sturdee Avenue, Rosebank, Johannesburg 2196, South Africa

Penguin Books Ltd, Registered Offices:
80 Strand, London WC2R 0RL, England

ISBN 978-0-399-15845-2

Printed in the United States of America
1 3 5 7 9 10 8 6 4 2

Book design by Michelle McMillian

This is a work of fiction. Names, characters, places, and incidents either are the product of the author's
imagination or are used fictitiously, and any resemblance to actual persons, living or dead, businesses,
companies, events, or locales is entirely coincidental.

While the author has made every effort to provide accurate telephone numbers and Internet addresses
at the time of publication, neither the publisher nor the author assumes any responsibility for errors, or
for changes that occur after publication. Further, the publisher does not have any control over and does
not assume any responsibility for author or third-party websites or their content.

FOR
CLAUDIA
AND
SERAPHINA

THE
BOOK
OF
JONAS

PROCESSIONAL

T hey arrived like a thought, tracing contrails across the deep sky as though writing out their intentions in letters too big to be fully seen from the earth. Or they flowed low and fast over the hills, their great machines arcing silently from horizon to horizon, so fast that they were there and gone before the roar from their engines caught up, screaming the news of their arrival even as they disappeared.

In the village they tried to make sense of it.

The imam said that the Americans were like the lion who had stepped on a thorn, and then went about making a great noise, roaring at the world from his pain. But it would soon pass, he said, when the thorn dried up and fell out, when the pain ebbed, and then tranquillity would be restored.

Younis's father, on the other hand, said that no, this was only the beginning. The planes in the sky were like the first gray dusting of blight on the wheat, which this year might only affect a few sheaves, but which would spread over time, draining the golden crop of its color, rendering it foul and devoid of life.

Most of the villagers tended toward one or the other of these two points of view. But the discussions between them, while occasionally animated, as were most of their discussions, whether about God, or cricket, or livestock, lacked any real vehemence or certainty. The positions staked out were not hard and fixed, but were instead general inclinations to support one side or the other.

Because, in fact, nobody knew what to make of the visitors in the sky. No one could say for sure whether they were a temporary nuisance, as the imam thought, or a harbinger of disaster, as Younis's father said, or even, as a very few dared to profess, brought with them tidings of better days ahead.

So they carried on as usual, bending over their scythes in their fields, or walking the low pastures with their flocks and their dogs. And whenever they spotted a line of smoke, high and pale like the daytime moon, or heard the jets echo from the surrounding mountains, they would look up, and then turn to one another and talk about what it meant as though discussing something large and remote and uncontrollable, like the weather.

INVOCATION

I

What is it like to lose everything?

Younis was first asked this question by a well-meaning development worker, a friendly young man whose specialty was working in war zones. They sat across from each other in cheap plastic chairs beside a bomb-scarred house that served temporarily as a hospital. Just for a chat, he had been told. Just to see if he needed help, to see if he could *be* helped.

"It must be so difficult," said the man, whose face was serene, "to wake up one morning and see that life as you knew it has ended, that so much has been destroyed."

Despite his youth, Younis sensed immediately that the man was trying to get him to do something dangerous. His first instinct was to play it off, to make a grim joke of it—the house was getting old anyway; destruction as a form of camouflage; at least now we don't have to maintain the roof—anything to deflect the course of the inquiry.

But this would not do, he sensed, not with this man who

sat across from him, this friendly man with his placid, expectant face. So how to answer?

Should he talk about his shaking hands, his trembling
limbs, the ringing sound in his ear, his blurred vision? Should
he describe his physical injuries, show him his wounds, the
rudimentary stitches, now nearly ready to be removed, underneath the bandage on his forearm? Should he discuss the
numerous times, after he fled into the mountains surrounding
the village, that he stood at the cliff edge, wind rushing up into
his face, and nearly felt himself take a step off, unconcerned
whether he fell or flew?

Or should he talk about—and this was what he found to
be the odd thing—the blessing of it? The surprise of finding
himself alive, finding himself connected to life. Should he talk
about the days after he ran into the mountains, about feeling
surrounded, even in that barren place, by life? About the plants
that seemed to vibrate with it? Butterflies and rock mice and
ants and caterpillars and snow hare and everything he looked
at, even the stones, seemed alive. On the mountain he once
came face-to-face with a dark falcon riding low on the thermals, wind whooshing through his feathers, and felt one with
him, felt peace, as though just by watching the great bird, just
by following his example, he could stretch his arms and lift his
feet from the ground.

Or should he say that the thing was now part of him,
defined him, founded him, that he could no more describe its
effect than he could describe being born?

What is it like to lose everything, they ask. The question

takes various forms, and that day, sitting in plastic chairs beside a shattered house, he developed his one and only response.

"What is it like to lose everything?" asked the man, the stranger who was there to help.

And Younis fixed him with his pale green eyes and said, "What is it like not to?"

2

He has a memory, or thinks he does.

They are on the train, the old colonial line running alongside the river to the capital. He lies on the wooden, time-polished bench and rests his head in his mother's lap. Thinking he is asleep, she has draped a loose muslin cloth over his head to cut the sunlight that flickers at them through the passing trees. They are going to meet someone, his father, he thinks. Every so often the wind puffs through the open windows and billows the soft cloth, startling him with a strobe of sunshine, like the bright end of a run-out movie reel.

On the station platform, they stand under a broad roof, which is supported by riveted metal beams, and the engine whistles out a last burst of steam. When the fog clears, a man stands as though he has been waiting since the station was built. He is dressed strangely, in Western clothes, jeans and a starched button-down shirt. His face is freshly shaven, and he carries a backpack made of rough canvas. He takes something from one of the pockets, a little square parcel, carefully wrapped in brown paper and tied with twine, and hands it to Younis's mother, who tucks it quickly away into her shift. It is this he remembers, this package, this passing of something important between them. He has so many questions—Why is he dressed this way? Why has he shaved off his beard?—but when he turns back to ask, the man has gone, disappeared into the throng outside the station gates.

Other things must have happened. They may have stayed a time in the capital, he and his mother, lodging in a cousin's whitewashed spare room near the bazaar. Maybe they bought figs and lamb for their supper, and sipped sweet tea purchased from a vendor's cart. Perhaps, when they heard the call to prayer in the evening, they wandered over to the turreted mosque, washed their feet, and knelt down on the worn rugs. Surely at some point they took the train back home, up the river and into the low hills. But if they did any of these things, as they must have done, he can remember none of them.

And it is this that makes him suspicious, makes him wonder: Maybe it didn't really happen. His inability to remember large parts of the experience makes him question all of it: the carefully wrapped parcel, the riveted beams on the platform, the clean-shaven man who should have worn a beard. Maybe it is all just something he heard about or read much later, his imagination filling in the details and making it his own, something he saw one time, something from a film.

3

He changes his name on the airplane. Somewhere over the Atlantic he assumes his new identity. The flight attendant hands out white-and-blue landing cards, and he borrows a ball-point pen from the woman sitting next to him to write out his new name—J-O-N-A-S—in the space provided, right next to the space that gives his age: fifteen. Thus named and dated, he signs the card underneath the paragraph explaining that he waives all his legal rights by doing so—his right to counsel, his right to privacy, his right to oppose deportation. He suspects this will cause trouble; he does it anyway. At customs he will be interrogated for hours, kept in a white room with a veneer-top table and steel folding chairs until someone from the Friends International Assistance Society shows up to bail him out. Or later, at his new school, he will explain to anyone who asks—the math teacher, the English teacher, the assistant principal, the head principal—that legally his new name is a direct translation of his old name, even though he feels intuitively that this is not quite true. He knows that the law and the truth are rarely the same thing.

The plane's motion nauseates him, and in an effort to relieve it, he looks out the Plexiglas oval at the blue void below, the gently curving skyline. Occasionally, he spots an island riding the dark sea, marked by a puff of white cumulus. In the plane, he finds it easy to imagine himself floating between two worlds, two existences, each of them true, but does not yet realize that this is a feeling that will never completely leave him.

The female flight attendant has been joined by a skinny, dark-haired man, and together they wheel the clanking metal food cart down the aisle, passing out foil-covered trays, plastic utensils, and plastic, foil-covered cups of distilled water. The action is polite and efficient. Jonas's meal is chicken and some sort of yellowed rice, which he eats with a voraciousness that seems to embarrass his seatmate, an elderly woman with large eyes and an open face.

The airplane lavatory smells of disinfectant and dry air, and seems to aggravate the ringing in his right ear. A sign on the wall warns him that he may be fined three thousand dollars and sent to jail for damaging or disabling the smoke detector. The notion that a smoke detector might exist in the bathroom of an airplane, much less the impulse to damage or disable it, had not previously entered his mind, but now that it has, he wonders how punishment might be exacted, were he so inclined. He has fifty dollars in his pocket, and a small duffel of clothes in the hold, both of which have been given to him by the society, the combination of which constitutes the entirety of his worldly possessions.

Back in his seat, he looks again at his name, written in block capitals in the demarcated spaces on the landing card, and he underlines it with the borrowed pen. The woman, who is sitting on his left, near his good ear, has fallen asleep. He puts the pen down on the tray table and looks at the long, pale scar running up the dark skin on the back of his arm and under his rolled-up shirtsleeve.

"Where did you get that," the woman beside him had asked. "I fell off a mountain," he had said.

He is beginning to feel claustrophobic in the sealed, pressurized tube. He is tall, constantly mistaken for being older than he is, and his knees knock into the back of the seat in front of him. He can't get comfortable, can't stretch out, and for a moment he fights off a wave of panic. He is surrounded by plastic and metal, which confine him to a predetermined form, a standard that does not comfortably fit him. He pushes his knees again into the back of the seat in front of him, and its occupant shifts, pushing back against him in a kind of warning.

Eventually, a bell dings, and he feels a sinking sensation in his stomach and legs as the plane begins its descent. He fights off another wave of nausea as he folds up his tray table and is told by two different flight attendants to incline his seat. He explains, in nearly panicky tones, that it is broken and that it will not incline, and after this explanation he is left alone.

The ground rises up to meet him, and he feels himself jolted forward, pushes himself into the back of his chair as the plane slows forcefully. When the plane turns from the runway, the gently rolling landscape scrolls past his window like a diorama. How lush, how green it looks! Ivy climbing the massive, broadleafed trees, the atmosphere so thick with humidity that he can see it. And then before he realizes, the plane has rolled up to the gate, and there is a rush for the overhead luggage, and a wafting of heavy, wet air as the door is opened, and they are in the aisles, pushing forward, and he has trouble getting his feet underneath him, trips on a blanket someone has left on the floor, grabs a seat back for support, and it is happening so fast he can't believe it, and he stumbles off the plane and into his new world.

4

The last time he saw his village he was five thousand feet above it.

Sometimes it comes back to him at a word, or a sound, or a scent, and he can see the faint trace of smoke rising toward him like a prayer. From this height he can see the village's broken shell, its careful, jigsaw delineations—yards and orchards and streets—scratched and blurred like a sand castle set upon by a toddler.

Paul tells him that he tends to dissociate.

Jonas goes to see Paul once a week, as he has done since the high school became concerned that he might have been suffering from the results of something traumatic, something they couldn't handle. They suggested that he go see Paul because Paul was someone who knew about these things. Paul had experience. Paul could help him.

Actually, it was slightly more than a suggestion. "We can get a court order," they said, "but we prefer you go voluntarily."

They have been meeting regularly ever since.

During these meetings, they talk about the state of his mental health, which Paul has called, on more than one occasion, "pretty good." Paul has bushy hair and a goatee, and he looks a little bit like a young Karl Marx, an effect amplified by his tendency to explain things in the somewhat dry tones of an economics professor.

"Dissociation is a normal reaction," says Paul. "It's a defense mechanism. And given the circumstances, a certain amount of mental decompensation is probably also to be expected." Paul doesn't seem to understand that this is gibberish until that fact is pointed out to him, and when it is, he tries to make a simplified explanation.

"I know it can feel like touching a hot stove," he says. "Your reflex is to pull your hand away. Your psyche is trying to stem the pain. But to deal with it, to get past it, eventually you are going to have to leave your hand on the stove awhile."

On his desk, Paul has a little silver statue on a marble base. It has sort of a funny shape which is hard to describe, like a wave or an ellipse. Paul tells Jonas that this statue may be used as a focal point, a device to bring him back to the present. It doesn't have to be the statue, he says. It could be anything: a candle, a piece of wood, a lamp, a ball or knickknack, anything, really, but he likes to use this statue because its shape is open to interpretation.

"You are here now," says Paul. "The past is gone, done. Your memories can't physically hurt you. But we need to explore them. We need to understand what happened."

And then they talk.

5

He remembers a conversation, a lecture, voices mixing with the flycatcher's song in the bright courtyard, and his father's friend, the imam, standing tall over him while the early morning sun casts their shadows long over the grass-lined path.

"Now you say it, Younis: 'There is no god but God, and Muhammad is His messenger.'"

"There is no god but . . ."

"Yes. But God, and . . ."

"But why must I say it?"

"Because this is how you become one of the people. A believer."

"Oh. All right. There is no god but . . ."

"Yes."

"But why must I become one of the people?"

"You must become a believer. We are all believers. Your mother, your father. You come from a long line of believers. Now say it, and when you do so, say it earnestly."

"There is no god but . . ."

"Yes, Younis, you may continue. But God. Please."

"But is it really necessary to say it? Can I not be a believer without doing so? Can I simply think it?"

"It is absolutely necessary. You cannot be a believer without reciting the Kalimah. Now please, Younis, continue."

"There is no god but . . ."

"Yes, Younis, please continue."

"But what if I were mute?"

6

He lives with a host family in a large subdivision outside the city. The Martins. Mr. and Mrs. Martin and their two children, whose names Jonas has trouble pronouncing. The girl is called Courtney, although much to her annoyance Jonas usually drops out the n and compresses the vowel sounds, pronouncing her name so that it sounds much like "Cutie." The boy is Addison, which Jonas pronounces "Ad-son."

The evening Jonas arrives in America, he and the Martins eat dinner together. Mrs. Martin has prepared a pair of large roast chickens, each bigger than any chicken Jonas has ever seen, with light brown gravy and golden roasted potatoes and green beans (which have been steamed, she explains, not boiled, because steaming keeps in more of the vitamins) and glazed carrots and warm bread. The five of them sit around the long table in the dining room stacked with crystal and china and silver on what Mrs. Martin calls a "propitious occasion." Cutie and Ad-son sit across from Jonas, and Mr. and Mrs. Martin sit at either end of the table. Mr. Martin says grace.

"Bless this food to our use," he says. While he continues with the prayer, Jonas glances up anxiously to see that Cutie, her head bowed, is snickering, and then Ad-son flinches as though he has been punched or kicked under the table. Mrs. Martin glares at her children, who hastily compose themselves into a picture of reverence.

"And us to thine service," says Mr. Martin.

After grace, Mrs. Martin tells Jonas that they try to eat dinner as a family every night, but that it's difficult, with the children's after-school activities and other interests, and Mr. Martin's frequent need to stay late at the office. She says that they are making a renewed effort to gather together at the end of each day. She says that this is one of the problems confronting American society, the breakdown of the family, the lack of time families spend together, and that they are trying to counter that trend, but that it's difficult, because they are all so busy with other things. She tells Jonas that, aside from their meals in the evenings, the only thing they do consistently as a family is attend church on Sunday mornings, after which, during the season, they try to get back home in time to watch football on television.

"Do you like football?" asks Ad-son, trying to make eye contact with Jonas over the table.

But Jonas is barely aware of it. His mouth had begun watering almost as soon as he walked in the Martins' front door, and the smell of the roasting meat has tortured him for hours, first as they showed him around the massive house, explaining where his bathroom was and how the taps in the shower worked, because they were new and a little bit tricky, and then when they left him alone in his room, a clean, spare room with a single bed, for nearly an hour, where he was supposed to, he didn't know, unpack his meager duffel or make himself comfortable or something. But all he could think about was the food being prepared downstairs.

And so it is some time before he realizes that he has been asked a question.

Jonas becomes aware that the dining room is silent save for his own snuffles and grunts. He has ripped off a large chunk of bread and, together with a slab of chicken breast and half a potato, grasps it all together in his hand, the silver cutlery lying untouched on either side of his dinner plate. His mouth is stuffed full and he wipes a dribble of juice from his chin with the back of his hand. As he becomes aware of the silence, he glances up to see that the Martins have not yet begun eating, but that they are instead all looking at him, staring at him with expressions that range from fascination to pity to disgust, staring at him as though they have just discovered that they are sharing their table with some fierce and alien creature.

7

"Where do you go in your mind?" asks Paul.

Jonas watches his reflection in the silver statue on Paul's desk, leans left and then right to watch his distorted image play in the light. Jonas feels uncomfortable, examined. In an effort to deflect the course of the conversation, he talks for ten minutes about football. American football, which he has found entirely inescapable on television, a weekly tyranny, he calls it. But despite his reservations, he has finally given in and started watching it. He draws contrasts with football as the rest of the world knows it, which, Jonas points out, is actually played with the feet.

"Unless you're a goalie," says Paul, to which Jonas half-heartedly agrees.

Paul has laid out some ground rules. He has given Jonas some forms to fill out, asked some general questions, some of which Jonas has answered, and some of which he has not. He has told Jonas that when they meet, they are in a safe space, that they can talk about anything he wants, that he may feel anger and rage and that that's okay, that part of their purpose is to allow him to access those emotions. He has told Jonas that he is legally obligated to report certain crimes, murder, abuse, but that this is for his own protection.

And he has warned Jonas that any hint of physical violence will not be tolerated, that it will instantly end their meetings, and might even lead to jail.

Then he asks Jonas if he has any questions. Paul looks up from his desk to see that Jonas is staring out the window.

"Where do you go in your mind?" asks Paul.

For a time, Jonas says nothing. He looks around the room, back out the window, at the statue on the desk, at the floor. He avoids Paul's gaze for as long as he is able, trying to think of something to say. Then he has a flash. He latches onto an image from his childhood, a glimpse of a thought which seems to him entirely innocuous, and which has suddenly caught in his mind like a shiny pebble.

"Very well," he says at last, "if you really want to know."

8

Another memory. Heat. Sunlight pours through the open windows and into the irregularly shaped schoolroom, where he is gathered with the other students around the long, thick-grained table set to one end. He draws a picture of a lion on the single sheet of lined paper lying before him on the table. The headmaster is speaking in English, but it is a halting, pidgin English, a distant cousin to the flowing, facile language he listens to on the radio, or practices with his father.

("Where did you learn to speak it," he had once asked after an impromptu lesson, out by the well in the courtyard.

"Bradford," his father had said.)

By contrast, the headmaster's only apparent exposure to a native speaker of English seemed to come from his witnessing, as a young man, a crown customs officer adjudicate an impromptu divorce, an anecdote he repeated often, using it to illustrate both his own superior linguistic abilities and the amorality of the colonialist crown. At some point during the divorce proceedings, one of the parties must have uttered the word "insolent," because this is the headmaster's favorite word to use when describing his pupils. As in, "I tolerate no insolence from any of you," or, "Stop your insolent ways," or occasionally, almost randomly, simply uttered to no one in particular, "Insolent."

The headmaster paces the room, looking at each of them

in turn, and then he notices that one pair of eyes is not turned to meet his.

"What is it upon which you work?" says the headmaster. But the words wash over Younis like a breeze. The lion's mane is coming together on the page in front of him, and with only a few more strokes, a couple of precise pencil lines, he is convinced that he will have the perfect representation of—

Pain. His right ear is grabbed, yanked, twisted, a hard grip on his earlobe, and he suddenly understands that what the headmaster lacks in facility with the English language he more than makes up for in his willingness to swiftly issue corporal punishment.

"I said," says the headmaster, "what is that upon which you work?"

"Ah," says Younis, thinking as quickly as he is able while being lifted bodily from his chair by the ear. "Ah . . . but you did not speak to me!"

At this the headmaster pauses, ever so slightly, reducing incrementally the grip on his ear.

"What?" he says.

"You did not speak to me," says Younis, squinting his eye and resisting the urge to slap at the headmaster's hand, an act he knows will result only in the implementation of more brutal measures. "At least, you did not speak to me directly."

"I did, you insolent boy," says the headmaster, renewing his grip. "I ask you upon what it is you work, and now I see it is upon silly doodlings."

"Yes," says Younis, "but you used the collective 'you.'"

"The what?"

THE BOOK OF JONAS

"The collective 'you.' The 'you' you used was us. All of us."
Younis tries to motion, or nod, or make some kind of gesture
that would indicate the inclusion of his classmates, now gaping
at the proceedings at the far end of the table, but can only roll
his eyes around the room. The vise on his ear relaxes slightly,
but the grip is not completely released. He realizes he must
keep talking. He takes a breath. "When in a group situation,
as we have here, it is necessary for the speaker, that is you,
if speaking to only one member of the group, to identify the
individual to whom he speaks by name or other moniker, so as
to avoid confusion."

The headmaster's eyebrows knit together, as though of their
own will, making his face look, thinks Younis, not unlike that
of a confused puppy. The grip on his ear relaxing still further,
Younis keeps talking.

"It's one of the basic grammatical rules of the English language," he says.

Too late, he realizes that he has gone too far. A brief flash of
pain shocks his head, this time on his left ear as the headmaster smacks his face. But then it is over.

"Insolent child," says the headmaster as he paces to the
front of the schoolroom. "Insolent, unruly boy."

9

He knows little about his new home. The city's name is abbreviated to PIT on the luggage tag that still hangs, six months

after his arrival, from the strap on his duffel, and sounds German to his ear. He imagines it printed in the fractured typeface of old German newspapers. He has seen photos, read some literature. The city is silver, surrounded by water and traversed by bridges. It is home to industry and a sports team whose name sounds familiar, from newspaper articles or radio broadcasts. The society, which has placed him with the Martins, has also enrolled him in a high school, and in a few years can maybe even help him get into the university.

According to a teacher, he lives in the middle of the "rust belt." When he hears the term (which he finds misleading), he pictures himself buckling a flaking iron hoop around his waist. But there is a lot of green space, especially in the suburbs, and the downtown is stainless and tall, but relatively clean, which he is told it did not used to be. Its three rivers, each of them larger than the river next to which he spent his childhood, both bisect and hem in the city. He imagines the boundaries formed by their junction forcing the village, then the town, then the city to grow up rather than out. Underneath the polish is the old city, stone and brick and corniced, pre-Depression confident. Clapboard houses, miners' and steelworkers' houses, lie as though tossed like so many dice onto the surrounding hills, and the university with its towering cathedral looks on from the east.

He strives to adapt to his new life, to understand his place in it. As a welcome present, Mrs. Martin gives him an ornate, leather-bound copy of the Bible, which he keeps on a shelf in his room. For a time, it is his only book.

At the high school, he tries to talk to other students, but they trick him into saying things.

"Hey, Apu," says one of them, blond-haired and cold-eyed, "say, 'Welcome to Quickie Mart.' Say, 'Thank you, come again.'"

He tries to rid himself of the accent, practicing for hours in front of a mirror, but it is hard-wearing, like stone, a singsong abomination.

He gets A's in everything.

He wanders the halls like a ghost.

IO

"Where do you go in your mind?" Paul asks. He wants to explore this. Jonas has told him that often he sees his body, his surroundings, and himself from the outside, objectively. This does not happen all the time, only when he is in a particularly high state of stress or concentration, but that when it does he knows what people are thinking, can feel the energy vibrations in a room, and understands hidden meanings. (Later, when Paul mentions that he is privately skeptical of the existence of God, Jonas says, as mysteriously as he can manage: "Yes. I know.")

II

If he remembers anything, he remembers the book.

He remembers the scratching sound of pencil on paper. He remembers wondering, offhandedly at first, but with ever-increasing interest, what was being written. He remembers the compulsion, the care with which the book was usually guarded.

And he remembers spotting it almost by accident, unaccountably left lying on the ground next to the camouflage backpack, as though it had been casually tossed or dropped in the dust, the color of which nearly matched its worn leather cover, obscuring it to the point that he might easily have missed seeing it in the meek dawn.

Alone for the moment, he glances around, then stoops to pick it up. The leather is creased at the spine, bent and folded over at the corners, worn bare at the edges. It feels dense in his hands. A leather tie wraps the book at its middle, and he gently tugs open the precise knot that holds it closed.

The inside cover is inscribed with a compass rose, next to which is a brief, handwritten dedication in flowing script. The journal is filled with long stretches of text, each separated by half a blank page. Some sections take up multiple pages; some are only one or two paragraphs long. For the most part, the writing is a slanted, hasty scrawl, but occasionally it refracts into neat printing. Penciled-in scratch marks and corrections fill the margins.

He is able to read only the first page. Before he gets a chance to go any further, he hears rocks clattering outside the cave mouth, and realizes the soldier has returned. He quickly closes the book, hastily ties the leather strap with a knot that faintly imitates the original, and puts the book back on the ground next to the pack.

Eventually, he will read the whole thing. At first he will read with passing interest, and then with increasing fascination, and finally with dread. After he reads it, unsure what to do next, he will take the book to the back of the cave and wedge it underneath some rocks, confident that he is the only one who will ever be able to find it again.

But for now, the fear of being discovered forces him to be content with stolen glances and skimmed passages. He knows he is trespassing, that these words were not meant for him. But he is able to convince himself that if he proceeds carefully, respectfully, he will harm nothing, violate no sacred laws. He is allowed to read it, he reasons, because he needs to know whom he is dealing with.

12

You deserve an explanation.

I have had this book with me ever since you gave it to me on my eighteenth birthday. During all that time I have not scratched a hundred words into it. Countless times I have thought of packing it away, or misplacing it, or leaving it behind somewhere. But I kept it. Maybe this is why.

I won't try to justify anything we did, but you should know what happened. Maybe you will read something in the paper. Or maybe you will see a reporter talking into a microphone in the dusty aftermath. Maybe you will think to yourself that the snowy mountains behind him would be beautiful in another context. By then, it will be done. It will feel historical, like a stock-market crash or an election. It will seem inevitable.

But this was not inevitable. We did exactly what we were supposed to do. Maybe that's the horror of it. To call it an accident would be false. To call it a mistake implies that it was unintentional.

What we did stank of intention.

13

"Welcome to America," they say.

It is said often during the two years he stays with the Martins at their large home in the suburbs. They first said it to him when he arrived at their house on a muggy summer afternoon, the duffel slung over his shoulder as he crossed the threshold into a cavernous foyer and a cold blast of conditioned air.

"Welcome to America," they said.

But since then, he is welcomed to America regularly. It becomes a kind of joke.

They say, "Welcome to America," when he expresses astonishment at how friendly everyone is, smiling at him every time he opens his mouth to say anything, smiling at his accent. He is welcomed to America when he comments on the number of church steeples visible in the city and the surrounding towns. He is welcomed to America when he mentions the number of hours the Martins spend sitting passively in front of their television set.

He is welcomed to America when he makes the mistake of saying that he does not like American football, which is all but a second religion in the Martin household. But Jonas says that it's a jerky, start-stop kind of game that lacks rhythm and grace and beauty. He is welcomed to America when the family goes out for fast food one night (slumming it, they call it), and they laugh as Jonas wolfs down four double cheeseburgers in rapid succession, then express concern ("You really think he's okay?") as he spends half an hour vomiting audibly in the bathroom.

He is welcomed to America when he makes any of thousands of observations about his new world: the largeness of the cars, the tallness of the buildings, the neatness of the manicured lawns, the cleanliness of the parks, the skimpiness of the girls' clothing, the enormity of the meals served at restaurants.

For a short time, the Martins welcome him to America anytime he says anything.

One evening Jonas and the Martins walk down Stanwix Street together after a lavish dinner at the Chatham Center, Jonas having eaten triple portions of a succulent roast served from the buffet. A dark figure sits in a doorway off of the sidewalk, legs splayed out in front of him, rattling a paper cup with

a few coins in it. As he has done with the past three such figures they have passed on the street, Mr. Martin pulls a bill out
of his wallet and gives it to Jonas to drop into the man's cup.

"Thank you, sir," says the man.

"You are welcome," says Jonas, suddenly uncomfortable.

"Hey," says the man, "you have a funny accent!"

"Yes," says Jonas.

"Well," says the man, "welcome to America."

14

He remembers that they first came to see him while he was
still in the hospital. It was run by Americans, and he remembers the bright light filtering into his room through curtains
as clean and white as the fresh bandages wrapped around his
forearm. He was hooked up to a tube that they said would keep
him hydrated, and there was a little vase of flowers on a table
next to the bed, brought to him by a smiling army nurse in a
white uniform, who told him only that the flowers had been
sent by friends.

They expressed keener interest in him after they learned he
could speak English. He told them he learned it in school, that
his father spoke it fluently, that he always listened to the BBC,
that he loved American movies.

But good as his English was, he had trouble understanding
their questions. It seemed they asked him his name hundreds
of times, so often that he started giving them different names

each time they asked. "No, you must be mistaken; I am Raul," he would say, or, "I'm sorry, Younis is no longer here. I am Klaus."

They took it as a sign of spirit.

Their questions increased in number and meandered aimlessly, so he simply chatted with them, digressing at will. He chatted amiably about the time of day, the date, the color of the sky, the best way to make couscous, the history of central Asia, animal husbandry, the legends of the constellations, methods to determine whether someone was lying, tips for negotiating with sellers in the market. On these subjects and others he seemed to impress them with his knowledge, or, absent knowledge, his ability to substitute plausible conjecture.

But when they would ask, as they periodically did, about his family, his mother, at least, or his father, the English speaker, for whom they were searching diligently, or his home, so they might better know where to search, he fell silent, studying with rapt attention the coarse weave of the cotton blankets, and refused to speak. They insisted that they were searching everywhere, and that anything he could tell them would be helpful. They pleaded with his silence, but eventually their pleas gave way to the realization, faint at first, but growing with each passing day, that perhaps he remained silent because he knew they would never be found.

15

Jonas finds the Martin children to be a mystery.

Ad-son is a mystery because Jonas rarely sees him. He is the same age as Jonas, and he appears briefly before school, for breakfast, and occasionally at dinner before he disappears into his room for hours on end. Once in a while he says something to Jonas, asks him a question about video games or sports, but these questions are posed in passing. Ad-son seems to remain uninvested in Jonas, unemotional, as though by speaking with him, he is utilizing the scientific method to query a science experiment.

Cutie is a mystery because Jonas does not see her enough. She is two years older, and heavily involved in school activities, cheerleading and gymnastics and something called pep club. Jonas is shocked to find that the Martins allow her to visit with her boyfriend in the living room entirely unsupervised. He is alternately attracted to her and repelled by her, forcing himself not to dwell upon her bare legs or the occasional swear word that escapes her lips when she thinks her parents aren't listening. For a time, he is vaguely concerned about living with a family that allows their only daughter to be alone with a man who is not a blood relative, particularly while wearing such provocative clothing.

Cutie, in turn, seems to regard Jonas with an affectionate, condescending interest, as though he is a puppy that has wandered into her garden. After breakfast one morning, she kisses her mother on the cheek, punches Ad-son in the arm, and then pats Jonas on the head before gliding through the house and out the front door to her boyfriend's waiting car, carried on a cloud of perfume and a toss of blond hair.

Once, when everyone has left the house, he stands in turn at each of the doorways to their bedrooms and tries to place them into context. He does not enter the rooms, in part out of fear of being caught, and in part out of fear of what he might find.

Cutie's room is pink and white, the corners piled with dirty clothes and the shelves punctuated with a smattering of toys left over from a time when she was a younger girl: stuffed animals, a doll or a glittery pinwheel or knickknacks held firm like memories.

Ad-son's room is tidier, but is still filled with stuff, with superheroes and army men, a computer screen on a desk in front of the window, at which he sits for hours a day in front of video games and other mysteries. The walls of both rooms are covered with posters—singers and actors in Cutie's room, and in Ad-son's, football and hockey players and, on the wall next to his desk, a tiny picture of a girl in a bathing suit.

By contrast, Jonas's room is austere, bare-walled, with a simple pine table and chair, both of them labeled with stickers underneath that say, "IKEA," and a small closet, which is empty except for Jonas's several hanging shirts.

"You can change things around however you like," Mrs. Martin had said when she first showed him the room. "We can take you to get some things."

It was said almost in passing, in the midst of the activity

surrounding his arrival, but then the weeks had rolled by, and the promise to "get some things" for the room had been forgotten. Jonas doesn't mind, though. For one thing, he likes the room's clean spareness, and feels that within its space his existence is boiled down to its most basic essence, devoid of the complications of ownership and maintenance.

But the main reason he does not decorate his room is that he feels it would make him too familiar.

Like their rooms, the Martin children announce their identities to the world, inform everyone who cares to know about their every want, dream, proclivity, interest, hobby, or passion. Within a few months, Jonas feels that he knows basically everything there is to know about their lives. For example, he knows that Cutie, although superficially warm and friendly, values her popularity and standing at school above almost anything else, that her greatest fear is losing her status. He knows that Ad-son, while trying to appear cool and aloof and smart, is concerned about where he fits in, about the prospect of living forever in his sister's shadow.

But Jonas lives in a clean white room with a single bed. He strives to keep himself unknowable. He comes to see mystery as an asset. For as much a mystery as he once found the Martin children, he himself remains a far deeper mystery. He enjoys being unfamiliar. Exotic. But he fails to realize that, by declining the opportunity to define himself, he allows others, less interested, more callous, meaner others, to create definitions for him.

16

"Where do you go in your mind?" asks Paul, and Jonas tells him that sometimes he doesn't know, that sometimes he looks up to realize that an hour or more has passed as he sits in the library, or on the edge of his bed, or on a park bench, and that he has no recollection of it.

"Doesn't that worry you?" asks Paul. "How much time do you spend in this way, drifting and unaware, in your head?"

At first Jonas doesn't understand the question. Or thinks that maybe he understands it differently from the way Paul intends it. But then he thinks that he does understand, and his face lights up with comprehension.

"Oh, lifetimes," he says at last. "I have spent lifetimes unconscious."

17

Reluctantly, Jonas remembers that the soldier was called Christopher. When he eventually says the name, he pronounces it precisely, unaccented, as though he has practiced saying it.

"I probably would not have survived without him," says Jonas, looking around the office, out the window, searching for something interesting to comment upon, something to once again shift the conversation. They have been circling this subject for twenty minutes, Paul pushing him for more information, and Jonas reluctant to talk about it.

"Is it not enough," says Jonas, "to know that I have been helped by many people?"

"Why won't you talk about him?"

"There was a doctor," says Jonas. "At the American hospital. She was older than myself, but still young, for a doctor. Let us talk about her. She was wonderful. She helped me. She had smooth hands and fine wrinkles around her eyes, from laughing, and for the time I was there I lived on her smile."

"And yet you can talk about her easily."

"She helped me. I probably wouldn't be here without her, either."

"But you recall her without difficulty. While this other person, this Christopher, you do not like to mention him. Why is this?"

"She was prettier."

When Paul does not respond, but simply looks levelly at Jonas from across his desk, Jonas says, "Is it not enough to know that I survived, that I have been helped along the way?"

"I'm afraid," says Paul, "that it is not."

18

I am no longer certain of much.

I carry a stone around in my pocket. It's hard gray granite. It is pierced by a thin, marbled vein of white quartz. I can feel its rough surface on my palm, but I am consumed by the fear that it will turn to dust in my hand.

Increasingly, I find everything I cling to is fragile.

I remember from an earth sciences class that the white quartz in the stone was formed by something called an igneous intrusion. A crack in the granite let a tiny thread of magma, under pressure, penetrate the rock, where it cooled for years, eventually turning into the white streak running through the gray stone. The streak is like a scar, the molten rock pressed into it like blood.

This is not a rare occurrence, this penetration of solid rock by molten rock under pressure. It happens all the time. Deep in the earth, it is happening right now. Stones like this are not scarce. Just yesterday I walked through a field littered with them. An entire field full of scarred stones. They are abundant. For every diamond in the ground there are probably a million stones like this one. And yet to me, right now, it is the most beautiful thing in the world. The invasion, the pressure. The magma has exploited the injured rock, and has made it beautiful.

When I lie here and cannot sleep, these are the sorts of things I tell myself.

19

Outdoors, Jonas is in charge, at peace. It's late summer, early September, and he walks slowly, reluctantly to school, out of the subdivision and into the lush forest that encroaches from all sides, the sights and smells as if from a tropical island, compared with the desert hills of his childhood. He memorizes their names: the musky scent of Bradford pear, the earthy sassafras, the brilliant rhododendron. Autumn is filled with the deep mystery of fallen leaves, the first sharp whiff of coming frost, lit by curious jack-o'-lanterns, and the winter, foot after foot of snow.

He reads the Bible he has been given. He reads that God created light and darkness on the first day, then that He created the sun, which separates day and night, on the fourth. He reads that man was created before woman, then that they were created at the same time. He reads that God is jealous, and then that He is loving and kind; that man is inherently evil, and then that he is created in God's image; that woman is equal to man, and then that she is subservient. He strives to find in it some direction, some solace from the Book's words, some sense of comfort, but he is instead driven mad by its internal inconsistencies.

The taunting turns physical. Jonas's skinny frame persuades some of the bolder kids that he won't fight back. It's relatively mild at first: stepping on his heels in the hallway to pull off his shoes, overturned plates of food, and when Jonas tells them to stop they just laugh harder.

"Say it again, Apu. 'Stop eet.'"

He shows up late to class. Sometimes he doesn't show up. He finds the schoolwork almost ridiculously easy, and reasons that it is deserving of only part of his time. He spends a whole day in a wooded trace of land between home and school, sitting under a sugar maple. He tracks a deer for a mile in the forest.

The next day he shows up to school as though nothing happened, and the senile old teacher asks for a written excuse, signed by his host parents.

"What excuse," he says, "I was here."

She walks away, looking confused.

Even attending part-time, he gets A's.

20

Where do you go in your mind, Paul asks, and Jonas tells him that sometimes he travels to a meadow with a clear stream running through the middle of it, past a shade tree where a lioness and a gazelle stand looking at each other, a cobalt sky spread overhead. This place is the result of a creativity exercise that was once taught to him by a writing teacher. It was supposed to be a safe place where they could access their inner voice, their muse, but he's not sure that's exactly what it turned out to be.

"It is a mental construct," he says to Paul. "I know it is not real."

21

There is much he cannot remember. In place of these memories, his head is filled with facts. Names, dates, places. He is baffled by what he knows almost as much as by what he does not. For example, he knows that the Empire State Building is nearly fifteen hundred feet tall, that the Declaration of Independence was written in 1776, that the New Deal saved America from communism, that the first World Series was played in 1903. These facts were given to him by the 1980 edition of *The New Book of Knowledge* encyclopedia, which showed up, minus the V volume, in an aid shipment, or maybe with a missionary group, and sat with a smattering of other books—a large English dictionary, the Koran, *A Tale of Two Cities*—in a rough-hewn bookcase at the back of the schoolroom, its row of blue-and-white spines promising enlightenment.

He remembers staying after class to read it, volume by volume, turning the pages right to left as the late-afternoon sunlight slanted through the school window. New York was founded by the Dutch; Gutenberg invented the printing press; the American Civil War was fought to end slavery.

But he is nagged by the suspicion that his brain space is limited, that his mind must toss some things over into the current so that others might be accommodated. It is as though he has exchanged memories for facts, as though whole periods of his childhood have been replaced by lists of questionably useful trivia.

The California gold rush began in 1848; Rosa Parks refused to give up her bus seat; William the Conquerer conquered England; the Mormons founded Utah.

22

The school day begins with a half-hour period known as "homeroom."

It is the period Jonas dreads.

He sits at one corner of the large, desk-filled classroom, as far from the other students as he can get, and prays not to be called upon or otherwise prompted to interact. In the space of only weeks, he has come to fear this half hour more than any other time of the day, an aimless gathering of teenagers that can turn predatory in an instant. The homeroom teacher is an old woman who can barely control her hormone-fueled students. She frequently leaves the room on one ill-timed errand or another, and when she comes back, she seems not to register the hurriedly hushed chaos that has descended in her absence.

Already, Jonas has become a target. He barely comprehends how it happened. The quizzical looks he receives when he says anything, his unusual phrases, his dark complexion, his worn clothes, and then, one morning, the wet splat of a spitball that sticks to his cheek, a hollow ballpoint pen hurriedly tucked out of sight, the muffled snickers of all who witnessed it, and suddenly he has become the outlet for all of homeroom's pent-up aggression.

One day someone invents a game, the object being to see who can hit Jonas with the most spitballs during the brief time the teacher is absent from the room.

Every morning, he sits at his corner desk and remains quiet. He tries to blend into the wall, the Formica desktop, the floor. He attempts to render himself invisible.

And then the old teacher steps out of the room again, and almost instantly Jonas is grabbed from behind, his arms pinned to his sides. A boy's face appears in front of his, freckled and smiling, puckers his lips, and for a horrified instant, Jonas fears he is about to be kissed. And then Jonas feels a long stream of thick spittle running down his cheek. Someone else, someone unseen, spits at him again, but misses his face, and he feels it lodge instead in his hair.

He hears a girl's voice say, "Eww, stop it; that's gross," but his arms remain pinned to his sides. And then, straining, he breaks free of the grip and stands up, his face wet and smelling of other people's mouths. At that moment the old teacher steps back into the room, sees him standing up at his desk, and tells him sharply to sit back down.

"Welcome to America," someone whispers, and the room erupts into laughter.

23

He remembers talking with one of his sponsors, just after he arrived in America. He remembers asking her why they were helping him.

"We are the right hand," she said.

She was the director of the Friends International Assistance Society, the Quaker organization that helped people like him. She was heavyset and wore thick glasses, and she had a kindly face, but tired, her soft brown eyes deep and compassionate. She had just given him the small allowance he could use for "incidental expenses," as they were called, which at this time usually consisted of pizza and bottomless cups of cola. He would meet with her regularly, every few weeks, and she would inquire after his progress, his health, his social adjustment. She would ask about his host family, which the society had found through an interfaith cooperative, and his school, his classes, his friends. He always painted for her a pleasant, sanitized picture, because he felt it would be rude to do otherwise.

He remembers her handing him this little sum of money sealed in a tiny white envelope, and he asked her why she did it, why she helped people like him. She looked at him for a moment from across her cheap metal desk, and then she said, "We are the right hand."

This confused him. "The right hand of what?" he asked. "God?" He was amazed, because this was the kind of thing only

43

zealots thought highly enough of themselves to say, and this woman was no zealot. But she laughed gently.

"No, nothing so bold." She glanced out the window briefly, as though looking for permission to continue; then she looked back to him. "Unfortunately," she said, "our country sometimes has a habit of making a mess with its left hand and cleaning it up with its right. We are the right hand."

24

The kid saved me. I should probably make that point. He showed me the way out. I saw him running down the street out of the corner of my eye, and out of habit I lifted my weapon toward him. I saw that he was running away from me, and I looked around, at what we had just done, and I saw this kid run down an alley, and I followed him. It wasn't logical. There was no reason in it. He could have been leading me anywhere, death trap or salvation, and I didn't care which. You always have choices, but there are times when the split second before you is so starkly illuminated, it becomes clear that everything you are, and everything you are ever going to be, hangs in the balance. And I had one choice to make, which is basically the choice you always have to make in any situation: stay or go.

So I went. I followed him. I didn't care where he led me. And he ducked between some houses and down to the river, and then north along the river. I stayed far enough back that he didn't know I was there, which was pretty easy, because the moonlight seemed to shine

on everything, and I could see him clearly up ahead of me, and the
noise from the river, wide and beautiful and cursed, drowned out
everything else.

25

They share a conversation in the kitchen, in the suburbs, Cutie and Ad-son clearing up after dinner, the clinking of plates and glasses in the sink, the canned echo of laughter from the television in the family room, the low hum of the dishwasher, and Mrs. Martin sitting alone with him at one corner of the kitchen table.

"I'd like to talk to you about something, Jonas," she says, and for a moment he suspects she is on the verge of reaching out to grasp his hand. "Something important."

"Okay."

"You have traveled a long way to come to us, haven't you?"

"Yes."

"And you must have had many difficult experiences. Some horrible things must have happened to you."

"Yes."

"Jonas, did you ever think that perhaps there is a larger plan at work? Did you ever think that maybe you were brought here for a reason?"

"Well, I don't . . . I mean, I'm not sure."

"Jonas, I need to tell you that there is a way to clear away

STEPHEN DAU

all of these horrible experiences. A way to find comfort. A way to be forgiven for all of your sins."

"Yes, well . . ."

"Jonas, I'm going to ask you probably the most important question you will ever be asked."

"Are you?"

"It's the same question I was asked years ago, the same question Mr. Martin was asked, and our children. We have all done this."

"Okay, but . . ."

"Jonas, will you accept Jesus Christ as your personal Lord and savior?"

"My what?"

"Your personal Lord and savior. Will you establish a personal relationship with Jesus Christ?"

"My . . . savior from what?"

"From your sins, of course."

"My sins?"

"Yes, Jonas. Your sins. After all, we are all sinners in the eyes of the Lord."

"But were we not created in His image?"

"That was before. Before we sinned. Now we are all sinners, and must seek His forgiveness by accepting Jesus, whom He sent to die for us, to cleanse us of our sins."

"All our sins?"

"Yes. But we must accept Him first."

"All the sins of all the world?"

"Yes, Jonas."

"Then he must truly have His hands full."

46

26

Where do you go in your mind, Paul asks, and Jonas tells him sometimes he travels someplace else. He goes there in his dreams or in his waking thoughts, but when he is there, he is really there. He stands up high on the southern mountain, the wind blasting up from the far valley below, the first glow of sunrise pale in the east. The smoke, now black and ominous, rises from the burning village, and gunshots echo methodically from the rocks. No, Jonas tells him, this place is real. As real as the pen in your hand, as you note it, as real as the paper and ink. As real as that morning when it comes roaring back to him, standing on the precipice, so scared he can't feel a thing.

And then he's back, the poltergeist fading in the rearview mirror of Paul's silver statue, and he's safe, and maybe he understands a little bit more, and maybe he is ever so slightly wiser.

27

He remembers a clear day on the hill overlooking the village. The rapid, light-handed tapping of metal on stone echoing out over the valley as the mason labors beside a freshly dug grave.

The supine stone, destined to join the chorus of standing rocks which either reach for or point to God, is the same shape, but a shade lighter than its neighbors, which have weathered months or years or centuries and darkened accordingly, their rows on the hillside presenting a graded palette of loss.

He remembers staying in the mosque after prayers, kneeling with his eyes closed while everyone else stood to leave.

"Peace be upon you."

"And upon you."

He remembers the entire village weeping, and his father's angry vows of revenge. He remembers feeling as though there were something overhead, a lens or a prism, an inverted pyramid, serving as a conduit, through which all the world's sorrow was focused.

He remembers how they lowered them into the wounded earth, how they could have been sacks of laundry, or wool rugs wrapped in their protective gauze.

He remembers how, despite his vehement wishes, peace didn't come to him through prayers, or reading the Book, or fiery sermons, all of which served only to cloud his focus. So he learned to wait for it. He would stay a long time, waiting. Forever if he had to, kneeling on the mosque's worn rugs, long after everyone else had left, keeping his eyes closed until he lost track of time, forcing himself to stay, to concentrate through boredom and aching knees and legs fallen asleep, until at last it came, entering his soul with a whisper.

28

When he cannot be outdoors, he escapes the bullying, the interminable host family, the simplistic classes, by hiding away in the high school's library. If the rest of the school is institutional, spartan, coldly lit by fluorescent lights, the library is an oasis of wooden bookshelves and learning, as though built a hundred years earlier. At some point, he comes to realize that this is because it was built years earlier, and while the rest of the school has been recently renovated—shiny, stainless-steel laboratory equipment in the science department, new classrooms filled with sparkling plastic-and-Formica-topped desks, whiteboards instead of chalkboards, a new athletics stadium— the library has undergone no such renovation. Unrefurbished as it is, timeworn and outdated though its shelves and tables and massive card-catalog file are, it is the best-appointed library Jonas has ever seen. As soon as he discovers it, almost by accident one afternoon while wandering the halls, he spends all his free time there.

He reads not only the Bible he has been given, but reads about it, about how it was created. He learns about the Council of Nicaea, where, as far as he can tell, a bunch of priests got together and determined, more or less arbitrarily, what would be included in the Book and what would not. He reads about what was not. He reads about the Apocrypha, the Gospel According to Thomas, and Peter and James. He reads about the Nag

Hammadi manuscripts. He is utterly fascinated by the thought that these writings had survived nearly two thousand years buried in the desert, that they had to be buried so that they might survive.

Often it is dark when he leaves the library, his footfalls echoing from the linoleum floor and institutional green tiles of the hallway. He stays so late that he is nearly locked in the building several times, and has to be let out by the scowling janitor. But he thinks to himself that, with so much he does not know, so much reading to do, this might not be so bad, to be sealed inside such a bastion of knowledge overnight, or for a weekend at the very most.

29

The recruiters came and talked with us in school, and I remember it like yesterday. I wasn't interested. I told them I wanted to do something good. I told them I wanted to help people. I told them I couldn't do it, told them I wasn't interested.

But they told me that there was no better way to do good and to help people. They told me they helped people all the time. Doing good was what they were about. Plus they were going to pay me. Where else could I get paid for helping people? Plus they would pay for my college. Plus, in addition to helping people, and paying me, and paying for my college, they would teach me a skill. I would be helping people, and seeing the world, and earning money, and hav-

ing college paid for, and learning a skill that I could use later to earn money and help people.

In the end, it was a pretty easy decision.

30

He makes it into the news twice.

The first time, he is mentioned within a single sentence, in the form of a number. He is one of eighteen injured civilians. Twelve killed, eighteen injured. When she thinks he is old enough, the director of the Friends International Assistance Society tentatively shows him the newspaper clipping, which she has kept for long enough that it is just beginning to yellow at the edges. The article is short, and he has to read it three times before he realizes that he is not reading about someone else. He catches himself feeling that feeling, that momentary luxury of denial, of thinking, Oh, well, at least there were survivors. He is surprised at how little space the story occupies.

Then he wonders which number he was.

"I think that I was number five," he says. "Of the eighteen."

"Why do you think that?"

"It just feels right."

31

He walks down the high school hallway. It's late in the day, after hours, and Jonas has been in the library since the final bell. He has been reading once again about the Bible. He has become obsessed with it.

He has learned that the original son of God, prince of peace, savior of the world, was Caesar Augustus, that these honorifics were bestowed upon him by the Roman senate. This increases Jonas's admiration for the early Christians, for their acts of defiance, appropriating the emperor's titles to their crucified leader, an act that virtually guaranteed their own executions. And even though Mrs. Martin has told him repeatedly that the Book is the inerrant word of God, that it contains only historical facts, the more he learns, the more he comes to believe that the writings themselves live in metaphor, that they seek not to convey factual information, but to reveal larger truths. He comes to believe that by insisting on taking them literally, Mrs. Martin manages to simultaneously denigrate the scriptures and paint herself a fool.

And so he walks down the hallway after hours, considering the meaning of spiritual truth, the enlightened path, and suddenly there is one of them, the big kid with freckles, standing next to the lockers and laughing with several of his friends.

They have been waiting for him.

"Hey, Apu," says the freckled kid, sneering, and shoves Jonas into the bank of lockers, holds his head against the wall, reaches down to try to do something with his underwear.

Jonas is flooded with despair. Something snaps, something in his mind. Whatever has allowed him to remain passive and afraid snaps like a thread. He feels it, feels the change, as his entire body becomes one single, collective muscle.

He lifts his knee hard into the kid's crotch, grabs a finger and pulls it back, yanking his arm, trips him to the ground. The freckle-faced kid becomes an object, a talisman through which Jonas focuses his rage.

He grabs a textbook from the floor and slams it edgewise down into the face, listens to the bridge of the nose snap, watches twin rivulets of blood flow over the mouth, spreading a red stain on the shirt. The freckled kid lies prone on the ground, holding his face, and Jonas stomps on his knee with both feet, jumps on it up and down, over and over, trying desperately to break the leg. The kid's friends struggle to pull Jonas off, but he breaks free and kicks the freckled kid in the head, opening a gash along the top of his skull.

From nowhere a teacher reaches in and, now with the help of the freckled kid's friends, grabs Jonas and holds him down, pinning his outstretched arms to the ground.

He is assigned to the school psychologist. There are concerns about post-traumatic stress.

The next day he goes and talks with her. He is surprised by what they don't know about him, by his constant need to explain himself in a way they might understand.

"Where did you get that scar," she asks, looking at Jonas's arm.

"I once fought a lion," says Jonas, "and he gave me this."

She is not buying it, but doesn't press the issue. Instead, she asks how he feels.

Eventually, she will tell him that he is fascinating to talk to, that she wants to help, but that her field of expertise does not include him, his "situation," she will call it. But she knows someone, someone good, someone experienced, someone Jonas really needs to see.

"Based on what has happened, we can get a court order," she says. "But I prefer you go voluntarily."

And that's when he starts going to see Paul.

But in the meantime, Jonas is happy to sit in her office and chat, and the conversation gets him out of gym class.

32

Another memory, like a faintly recalled dream. He is walking home from somewhere, across the rough, upturned sod, his breath forming the only clouds under the bright sun. As he approaches the house, his mother comes out the back door carrying a jug of tea and an earthenware cup. He vividly remembers that when she pours the tea, two streams come out: the liquid filling the cup, and the steam drifting up in a hazy mirror image, mingling with their breath.

Later, his father arrives, eclipsing the front door's rectangle of light as he stoops to enter it. He is bearded, and wearing his shalwar, and carrying a large duffel. He has fractured memories of a meal, of his father smoking a pipe at the head of the table. They laugh, but it's an uneasy laugh, as though they know that it is all just temporary.

After dinner, his father disappears into the back room. As his mother clears up, he rises from the table and creeps down the brief passageway, past a low, wooden bench, to peek his head around the corner and look into his parents' bedroom. His father is laying his things out on the floor, shirts and belts, and the plump duffel is open and leaning against the wall. In his memory, the interior of the bag glows as though filled with fireflies, but he knows this is a trick of his mind, looking backward, long after he has peered into it and seen that it is filled with money.

"Hey, get out of here, you little thief!" says his father, laughing. But this is where memory plays another trick. For is it a hearty, honest laugh? Does it not contain some hint of apprehension? Of frustration at the broken secrecy? Of irritation? Of anger? Or perhaps even hidden admiration for his son's stealth, entering the room without being noticed?

It is impossible for him to tell, to look back and see clearly, and each attempt he makes to do so, to clarify his memory, sharpen its lines, results only in further blurring the picture, smudging it like a clumsy child playing with finger paints.

33

The second time he makes the news, a reporter phones him after getting wind of his story. The city has apparently become home to a sizable population of "displaced persons," which has temporarily made it the subject of the national news cycle.

"People would be really interested," says the reporter. "How you came here, how you're making a life for yourself." Noting Jonas's reluctance, the reporter tries to generate a certain level of excitement, and ends up sounding like a game-show host when he says, "After all, you're a success story!"

Jonas wants to ask about all the others, the "sizable population." He wants to scream. He wants to tell him to go to hell.

In the end, he hangs up the phone on him, leaving the article to be written using different sources, other people, before referring obliquely to "countless others who live right here in our own area, some of them too traumatized to speak about their experiences."

This time, he doesn't bother wondering which one he is.

34

The fight lends him an air of credibility, of danger. He is suddenly someone not to be fucked with. He learns of another refugee who attends the school, Hakma, a Kurd, who has lived in America since he was two years old. He does not have Jonas's accent, but shares his dark skin and hair, and they hit it off instantly. Hakma does not remember his brief time as an infant in Kurdistan, but injustice suffuses his soul. They pal around, meeting up after school to walk to one or the other's house and sitting conspiratorially across from each other in the cafeteria.

Students begin to talk to him. Girls seem to like him, mostly, he thinks, because he looks so different from the tow-headed boys they usually know. He has sharp features, which he claims are the product of generations spent in the wind and mountains, pale green eyes, and ink black hair. He learns to cultivate an aura of mystery, of danger, hinting at past experiences and feats without ever coming right out and describing them. Some of his classmates think it is all an act, a reputation built on air and a lucky punch, while others are reverential. He is invited to parties, and often, because he looks older, he is able to buy the beer.

His grades fall.

His teachers describe him as well-adjusted.

35

But there are events about which he refuses to speak.

Paul says, "Maybe you can tell me more about that."

Jonas signals his reluctance in one of two ways: either he

talks purposefully about other things, real things, imagined things, or some combination of the two, or else he is silent, fixing his gaze on the floor in front of him and waiting for the subject to shift of its own volition.

"This is important," says Paul.

"Did you know," says Jonas, taking a quick, deep breath, "that as a young boy I met the Dalai Lama?"

"Really," says Paul.

"Really," says Jonas. "A brave man, Mr. Lama. Very brave. For him to travel to our village, as he did. We were not always particularly tolerant of other perspectives. But he came, paying no heed to the potential danger. He stood out, to be sure, in his red-and-yellow robes, and his shaved head. He was a sight, I can tell you.

"It was the planting season, and I was out in the field, as we all were at that time of year. Mr. Lama, he came walking up the road, up from the river. I do not remember, exactly, whether he came by himself, or whether he was accompanied by others. Now that I think about it, though, I realize he must have had others with him, some sort of retinue. There is a fine line between brave and foolhardy, is there not? Mr. Lama would not have traveled to us alone. That would have crossed the line into foolishness.

"But I remember him, not his accompaniment. He walked up the road in his bright robes and his shaved head, walked right out into the freshly turned field, walked until he stood directly in front of me. And he looked down at me and smiled. Then he said something to me that I will never forget."

"Jonas," says Paul.

"He said, 'Just as the seed you sow today will grow to feed

your village, so shall you, my young friend, grow to nourish the world.'"

"Jonas."

"And then he took my hand in his . . ."

"Jonas."

"And he held it, and . . ."

"Jonas, we were talking about the last time you saw your sister alive."

"Yes," says Jonas, fixing a dull gaze somewhere in the space between them. "Yes. Mr. Lama liked her very much, as well."

36

Another memory: It must have been spring, the gullies filled with meltwater, and they have finished supper. His father stands up and strokes his beard, then goes outside, muttering for Younis to follow. There has been talk all winter. Talk of something big happening, some change, or threat, but he is so young, and it is nearly impossible to reconstruct from the scattered clues of memory. They make their way down to the river, his father several steps ahead, and then they turn onto the river road, walking upstream.

"I'm going to show you something," says his father, "and I want you to remember it."

They walk along the packed stone road, and after an hour they take a break, stooping to drink from a shallow pool near the shore. Out in its middle, the river flows savagely, but it is placid along the bank. The tempest out in the center seems to be totally unconnected to the calm water gently lapping the rocks beside their feet, and yet he can watch a stick or a leaf drifting near the shore, suddenly swept up into the rapids, dancing wildly away.

Eventually they come to one large, flat stone balanced on top of another, forming a distinctive, crooked T shape at the edge of the river, the water roaring around the base.

"See that rock?" asks his father over the river's din, pointing. "Remember that rock. Memorize it, so that you will know it when you see it again."

They turn west, away from the river and toward the mountains, white-capped and imposing. When they come to the base of the foothills, the sun is low in the sky, and his father points to a thin path, little more than a faint wear in the stone and dirt, that leads away and straight up the hill, weaving around a large boulder and disappearing into a hollow in the hills.

His father looks up at the half-formed trail and then down at Younis. "Two hours' walk up this path there is a cave," he says. "If anything ever happens, go there." He looks up again at the mountains, impervious and assured and unconcerned. "I will meet you if I can."

37

The letter, when it arrives, is expected. It is in a thick manila envelope that hints at packets of information enclosed, forms to be filled out and returned. He is happy to receive it, grateful even, but not surprised. Conversations had occurred, things had been arranged, and he had received a phone call the week before, explaining, in congratulatory tones, what was to come.

University of Pittsburgh
Office of Admissions
5413 Fifth Avenue
Pittsburgh, PA 15601

Dear Jonas Iskander,
We are writing to officially inform you that you have been awarded the Nelson A. Atkinson scholarship for the current academic year. As you may know, the scholarship is awarded annually to an incoming freshman from outside the United States who has, in the view of the scholarship committee, overcome significant adversity in his or her quest for higher education.

The scholarship covers the full cost of tuition for the academic year, and includes a stipend to defray the expenses of housing, board, and materials. It is renewable each year, commensurate with satisfactory academic progress.

The enclosed information includes a more detailed description of the scholarship, its provisions and requirements, as well as several forms for you to complete and return. If you have any questions or need any further information, please feel free to contact me.

In the meantime, please accept my heartfelt con-
gratulations and best wishes for a promising academic
career.

Sincerely,
Edith J. Pearl
Dean of Admissions

38

He fills out forms. For everything he needs to do, there seems to be a corresponding form. It began even before he completed the landing card on the plane the day he arrived. It began with a visa application. Then something called a relocation agreement. Then, early on, an application for the health insurance that would eventually pay for his visits with Paul. Some of these forms he completes with the assistance of a volunteer from the Friends International Assistance Society, but quickly his ability to fill them out by himself improves.

There is a residence card application, school admission forms, class enrollment forms, host family questionnaires. Because he receives monetary support, there are tax forms, academic progress reports, something called an "Adaptation Report," which is used, he figures out, to determine his level of social isolation.

Early on, he must complete a form to obtain a social security card. He is mildly surprised to find that it requests the same information that is requested by the form he must complete to obtain a library card, and that they both request the same information as the form he must fill out for a video rental card.

To go to college he must take a standardized test, which he finds to be nothing more than a big, complicated form. Eventually, he will fill out forms to apply for college, then to enroll there, then to apply for an apartment near campus. He fills out more forms for school: emergency contact forms, allergy declarations, vaccination certificates, more insurance forms.

Curious about this peculiar obsession with filling out forms, he does some research in the library. (He does this research on the same day he fills out the form to apply for his library card.) He reads that over the course of a lifetime the average person living in America will spend six months filling out forms. He learns that forms really didn't catch on until the late eighteen hundreds, when the volume of activities people were doing— being born, dying, and getting married the top three—grew so great that the Victorian mind felt the overwhelming need to organize them scientifically. He learns that the form, in its current form, was originally called a formulary, and was invented by an Englishman named Charles Babbage, the same man who invented both an early kind of computer and the cow catcher, a device attached to the front of locomotives to clear debris from train tracks. He learns that Babbage once wrote to Alfred Tennyson to correct two lines from one of Tennyson's poems, which Babbage felt lacked scientific accuracy. This, thinks Jonas, tells you everything you need to know about both the man and the invention of forms.

He will fill out forms to apply for a credit card (he will be denied), to sign up for classes, once he is enrolled in the university, to obtain a bank account, into which his scholarship money is deposited, to reapply for a credit card (accepted this time, with a limit of five hundred dollars, which he will immediately spend on pizza, beer, and a series of baseball games).

Aptly named, the form, he feels. For not only is it orderly in appearance, but it also gives form to that which is hidden. His name, his age, ethnicity, religion, all mental constructs, made manifest through the use of forms. Collected passively, placed on blank lines waiting for answers, the information allows for the efficient counting, sorting, ordering, and categorizing of him, the actual thing the forms represent.

Filling out the forms helps Jonas memorize this information. The ink, usually black, as required by the form, sometimes blue, which Jonas prefers, flows from his pen and into the shapes of the letters and numbers that signify him. Often, after he completes a form, he has the eerie feeling of having just replicated himself, sending off a paper copy that will then live in the files of a cabinet in some warehouse, or be inputted into a computer. To the clerk at the bank or school or business or library or government agency, the form is now him. "Ah, yes," the form says to its reader, "I can tell you all you need to know." He feels dissected and displayed. Worse, he has begun to wonder what all these replicas of himself will get up to, once they are set free.

Nauseated by the thought of filling out yet another form, much less being tested for anything, he refuses to get a driver's license.

39

The first time he sees her, she is surrounded by a field of poppies.

It's their freshman year. They are at a Remembrance Sunday reception in the ornate English classroom in the Cathedral of Learning, to which he assumes they have been invited because of their connections to Commonwealth countries. The wood-paneled room, one of the towering, Gothic building's many nationality-themed classrooms, was built after the war with artifacts rescued from the bombed ruins of the House of Commons, then transported across the Atlantic to be presented to the university as a gift. Something about it, the smell, or the way the light falls on the thick-grained tables, reminds Jonas of his boyhood schoolroom, and he feels as though it had been built especially for him. Tonight it is filled with gray-haired men and women and a smattering of students, all of whom wear the red-paper flowers of remembrance. She is tall and willowy and dark and cuts through the pomp like a thorn. Like a rose.

He stands at the long table filled with hors d'oeuvres and bottled water, speaking with one of the English professors. He watches her peripherally, tracking her red dress and graceful legs. He reaches out to pick up some sort of crab cake or cream puff, stretching his arm out of the sleeve as he does so, and sees the professor to whom he is speaking notice the scar on his forearm. He pulls the sleeve down.

"Climbing a tree as a child," he says. "I fell."

Then, unexpectedly, they are standing next to each other, both of them sipping from their warm bottles of water, looking intently at stained-glass windows bearing the coats of arms of various famous English institutions or people. Her name tag says Shakri.

"India?" he says.

"Delhi," she says. "And you?"

Unlike him, he thinks, she wears her accent beautifully, effortlessly, like wings.

He tells her to guess, like he did, but she gives up after three tries.

Together they tour the room, closely regarding the oak desks, appraising two chairs rescued from Parliament and set in the place of honor at the head of the room, near the fireplace. "What do you want to bet they sat in someone's loo?" says Jonas. "There's an Englishman somewhere chuckling about that."

He tries desperately to think of something else clever to say, something to make her laugh again, but everything he can think of seems contrived or forced. He asks her whether she enjoyed the cream puffs, then silently curses his mouth for allowing such inanity to escape it.

In the end, Shakri herself provides the opening. She asks him, with a forwardness that catches him off guard, whether he doesn't want to just bag it and go for french fries—chips, she calls them—at the O, a local dive known for its french fries.

"Sure," he says, trying to force himself to sound relaxed.

They cross the broad lawn outside the cathedral in the dusky light. He experiences her as a presence walking beside him, a voice. He does not want to look directly at her for fear that he will end up simply staring. So he looks straight ahead as they talk about school, his friends, her family, movies and music, likes and dislikes, and anything else they can come up with, all the mundane details, all the minutiae of existence, but it is really just a pretext to be close to her, an excuse to extend their time, because all he can think is bliss.

40

Absent a nation, he creates his own. There is no initiation, no Pledge of Allegiance, no flag. Just a vague understanding, a discomfited sense of belonging. Hakma the Kurd is the first, and between the two of them, he and Jonas accrete new citizens, they joke, like a ball of tar.

They are different. They are slanty-eyed and dark-skinned. Their names are different. They are Ching Ji and Sinhal and Lhotsu and Thierry, the French kid they mostly just put up with because he pays for everything. They are Trevor from Zimbabwe, or from London, where he added a cockney twang to his southern African dialect of hollowed vowels and soft consonants (speaking, they tease him, like Nelson Mandela would speak if he found work as a chimney sweep). They are James, from Montana, who is someone's roommate and who, as he is frequently reminded, is kept around as the token Yankee, a trapping of respectability, to be traded or sold at any convenient moment. They are interestingly garbed, avant-garde, and nerdy. They listen to diverse music: electronica and funk, jazz and reggae. One of them may be royalty.

They are known everywhere, whether they are welcomed at chic lounges by bartenders who are eager to add a touch of ethnicity to their ambience, or they are the dark kids in the corner, most likely engineering students, who talk funny. Or maybe they are something in between, something more like their classmates, like everyone of a certain age: on their own, confident and self-absorbed and accomplished and immature and cruel and generous and smart and unconcerned and cavalier and sensitive and ambitious, and, and, and.

41

This sticks in my mind.

They tell us to put on our gas masks. They file us into a low, cinder-block hut. They make us stand against the walls. The sergeant enters and closes the door behind him. In the middle of the room is a low, wrought-iron table, and on top of it sits a silver cylinder, like a thermos. Its edges are brown with liquid stains, like coffee. The sergeant twists off the top of the cylinder and drops in several white pellets, releasing a thin haze. Then we are all ordered to take off our masks. None of us wants to do it. But he is yelling at us, telling us we will be court-martialed if we don't.

My eyes tear up as soon as I take off the mask, and I gag on the smoke entering my lungs. We all start coughing up thick gobs of mucus, and our skin burns like it's under a heat lamp. I

*panic, nearly dropping the mask. I think I can see the silhouettes
of people burned onto the walls. Just when I think I am going to
black out, he tells us to put our masks back on. My skin still burns,
but with the mask on, at least I can see clearly and breathe. After
a minute, we are ordered to take off our masks again. This time
we do it quickly, knowing that the faster we get them off, the faster
we will be allowed to get them back on. This done, we file quickly
out of the building and fall into a retching mass on the cool grass
outside.*

42

He soon finds that, except to those in the middle of it, being
in love is the most boring thing, the most incomprehensible
thing in the world.

They dine at a secluded corner table on a red-and-white
paper tablecloth, upon which the food before them either loses
all meaning or becomes their entire existence. Her hands fly
around as she talks, seeming to push the words through the air
in front of her, and he hangs from them like a strand of over-
cooked fettuccini.

She tells him that, were the earth the size of an apple, the
surface would be as smooth as its skin. This bit of trivia feels
vitally important to him, as though it says something fundamental about their lives. He finds it amusing when she tries to
show him the correct way to hold a fork. He tells her that if
you hold your hand at arm's length out to the night sky, an area

of the night equivalent to the space of your thumbnail would contain a million stars, most of which cannot even be seen by the naked eye. By which he means that present between them are infinite possibilities.

And they are only dimly aware that, to an outside observer, someone lacking their interest or enthusiasm or imagination, they are talking a kind of silly code, a special language known only to them.

43

Paul has read an article, and is struck by the coincidence.

Jonas does not want to talk about it.

He was called Christopher.

"That's amazing, don't you think?" says Paul.

Jonas says nothing.

They know only that he was involved. He was called Christopher. And now Paul has read a story in the newspaper. He was from a town not too far away. His mother still lives there.

Jonas looks out the window.

They know he went off to war and that he did not come back. He did not, as they say, make it. But he was there, and he was involved, and maybe, just maybe, says Paul, that is something.

44

The first time Shakri asks him up to her apartment, it is all he can do to keep from bounding up the stairs ahead of her. They have been seeing each other for more than a month, and her sudden forwardness surprises him.

They kiss as she searches for her keys, kiss as she opens the door, kiss as she does not turn on the light. It is as though she has made up her mind. They fumble around over their clothes, awkwardly at first, as though learning the intricacies of sign language, but then with increased fluency, and then one of them suddenly learns how to undo a button, and it is all down-hill from there.

45

Occasionally he is asked: Why America?

Sometimes he gives the long answer. Sometimes he says the question asks him, he feels, a larger question, asks him to place his experience in a global context. Secretly he enjoys this, likes being thought of as part of a movement, although he would never openly admit to this. Instead, he says that he had nothing, and that they came to him and offered him a choice.

Sometimes he mentions the Pakistanis and Indians living

generations deep in Bradford and Manchester, or the Congolese in Brussels, or Algerians and Moroccans in Paris, or Vietnamese throughout California. He has read about them, studied them in school, and even though he feels more alone than he imagines any of these other people must feel, secure as they are in their mobile communities, he tries to place his experience into the frame of these movements, into the complex relationship between victor and vanquished, colonizer and colonized.

A *diaspora*. A sociology professor first used that word to describe him, and he likes it, although he is careful not to reveal the satisfaction he derives from it. He practices using the word casually, in conversation. Diaspora. "As a member of the global diaspora, I feel . . ." And then he is off, propelled by the authority of membership. He likes how it sounds, but mostly he likes the word because of its hints of mystery and power, its implication of choice, all of which are entirely removed when the word "refugee" is used.

Sometimes, though, he doesn't give the long answer. Sometimes he gives the short one. Why America? Because he had a choice. The same choice we always have. Stay or go.

And, given the choice, he went.

46

But the thing is, in all that time, I don't really remember making a decision. I don't remember saying to myself, "Yes, I will do this," or,

"No, I will not do that." They tell you what to do, and you do it. You don't reflect on it. You don't ponder its meaning. You don't explore its ambiguities or consider its consequences. These burdens are removed from you. In theory, these burdens are removed from you.

But you are still human. Eventually, you do reflect on it. The consequences make themselves known. The results of your actions persist. Eventually, you are struck by their meaning. At some point, an accounting is made. Eventually, if you are human, and sane, you examine what you have done.

47

Together, Jonas and Shakri go to movies, to clubs, to parties at the homes of friends and acquaintances. They are seen walking hand in hand across the cathedral lawn after dinner. In public, they are reserved, formal, but they devour each other with their glances. Sinhal claims to have seen them kissing, but is thought to be exaggerating. Trevor catches them on a late Saturday morning at Bart's Café, sitting in the low lounge chairs set around vast coffee tables. Shakri drinks hot chocolate and Jonas tea, while they both read newspapers.

"You two's already like an old married couple," says Trevor as he sits down, forcing himself between them, cheeky and smiling and pulling an earphone out of his ear. "Sitting reading your papers. Me, I don't want a married life till well after thirty!"

Jonas and Shakri look up from their reading.

"We're not married, man," says Jonas.

"Get your feet off the table, Trevor," says Shakri.

48

Paul has read an article about Christopher, but Jonas does not want to hear about it. During a session Paul mentions it, and Jonas does not respond.

The next session, Paul brings it up again. Christopher's mother is called Rose. Rose Henderson. Jonas is not interested. He says only that he is comfortable not knowing, but in reality he feels his stomach tighten each time Paul mentions it.

"You have to admit, it's quite a coincidence," says Paul.

The next session, Paul has brought the newspaper article, which he hands to Jonas like a summons. Jonas doesn't want to look, doesn't want to know, but sees no way to get out of it.

The article takes up most of an inside page, its only illustration being a black-and-white sketch of Rose Henderson. Despite himself, Jonas is transfixed. When he is finished reading it, he reads it again. And when he has read it for the fourth time, he looks up at Paul and says, "Could this . . . I mean, is it possible?" And then he sits silently, looking down at the newspaper in his lap.

Eventually, Paul says, "Would you like to go and talk with her?"

49

Shakri is by far the more dedicated student, planning to follow her family's expected path and go to medical school. She studies for hours at a stretch, biology and chemistry, and a measure of her dedication seems to wear off onto Jonas, who to this point has gotten through school by, as he puts it, "brains and bullshit."

"I go to class," he says, his voice almost a whine. "Do that and you barely have to read anything! We were doing *The Odyssey*, and I only read the last three chapters. Wouldn't you know it; the final exam was just one question: 'Analyze the major themes of *The Odyssey*, referencing only three chapters.' The professor called it the best essay she ever read on the subject."

"She mustn't have read many."

50

On a Saturday afternoon Shakri and Jonas sit in low, open lounge chairs at Bart's. Shakri drinks hot chocolate, which she loves, going through two or three tublike cups of it a day, even in the summer.

Jonas drinks tea. He has kept only a few connections to

the past, and this is one of them. He likes it sweet and strong, and if it is just the right kind—spiced kava, served with a hard sweet the way they do at Bart's—then even the smell of it is comforting. He usually has at least a cup of it a day, more if he drank too much the night before. It's one o'clock, and he's on his fifth cup.

It's a pretty day, autumn and cold, and the sun streams in through the window and highlights Shakri's dark skin and eyes and hair, and Jonas thinks to himself that she really is striking, and he also thinks that maybe he should tell her this. And then he thinks that maybe he shouldn't. He doesn't want to mess anything up by drawing attention to it, does not want to appear fawning or overly demonstrative, refrains from outwardly valuing anything he fears may be taken away. He prefers to appreciate things from a distance.

And then finally he opens his mouth and says: "I was so trashed last night."

"I know," says Shakri, and Jonas avoids her glare by looking studiously out the window. "You passed out cold on my couch. I woke up and you were gone."

He doesn't seem to remember all of this, although he does vaguely remember seeing her, and being surprised to find himself on her sofa with the sun streaming through the window, and then walking home in the early light, not wanting to wake her. The rest of the night, though, is a blur. But there is a detail, an image from the night before that he does remember, that stands out in his mind, and he tells this to Shakri, explains it to her. Then he tells her that you have a choice about how you react to things.

They sit for a while longer in their silence. Jonas is not too distressed by the hangover, and in fact he takes a certain pleasure in the distance it gives him from reality, the tingling fingers, the vague light-headedness, which somehow seems to heighten his other senses. He is fascinated by the intricate dance of waiters to and from the kitchen, the busy clink of plates and glasses in his good left ear, the sunlight falling through the large window and into his sparkling teacup, the hum of conversation and New Agey music. For just a second he thinks that he might be able to hear something out of his right ear, high and distant, like someone whistling, or birds singing on the wind.

"Jonas!" says Shakri, and it is apparent from her tone that this is the second or possibly third time she has called to him.

"Sorry," he says, turning to meet her eyes.

"Over here, man," she says, snapping her fingers up next to her head. "What did Paul say yesterday?"

Jonas thinks back to his session the previous afternoon, which seems a very long time ago. "He said my mental health is surprisingly good."

"He always says that."

"He said I might want to consider not drinking for a while."

"Uh-huh."

"He said I might think about going to see her, this lady, this soldier's mother, thinks it might help me fit things together," he says, realizing even as he does so that to say it out loud is to give shape to something he had wanted to remain formless.

"And what do you think?"

They sit there for a moment, Shakri looking at him ex-

77

pectantly, and then he is certain that in the middle of their silence he can hear something in his deaf right ear, some kind of signal coming through, like strings faintly plucked.

"He said it might give me a sense of closure."

"So you'll do it?"

"I don't know. Maybe."

"I'll drive you, if you want."

"Maybe," he says.

"You should do it."

"I don't know."

The noise fades in and out, the soft, high song, and he turns to look out the windows, convinced he'll see some mysterious musician strumming a sitar, but there is only the street, filled with afternoon light and bustling pedestrians.

51

It was supposed to have been a mellow evening.

Hakma, Trevor, and Jonas take the crosstown bus to listen to jazz on the South Side. They are going to relax. They meet up with a few other people, acquaintances more than friends, who seem to converge every time they go out. Mike, or maybe Mark, from Philadelphia. Luca, who just broke up with his girl-friend. The weekend unfurls like so many weekends among people who might be known to one another by a first name and a single personal detail, these details providing the basis for an evening's lurching conversation, more fluid as the night and the drinks carry on, forgotten by morning until the next weekend, or maybe the next, when the same conversation rolls around again, fresh.

The jazz is modern stuff, which is usually not really Jonas's thing, but the trumpeter is particularly good, playing high and wailing off the piano's depth in unexpected ways, here a mass of unrelated notes, there a perfectly balanced chord progression, unexpected, discordant when they expect harmony, harmonious when they least expect that, alternately keeping them on edge, then lulling them.

They drink. By the end of the set they are convinced that they have just witnessed the future of musical expression: subversive, glorious, embodying all to which music should aspire.

When it ends they cross the street to the Astrid, their conversation loud and animated, and as usual Hakma is talking about Kurdistan. The incarnation of injustice, what the Turks do to us, he says. You just don't understand. Has he ever been there, someone asks, one of the stragglers, obviously, someone who does not yet know this question's inadvisability until he asks it. Yes, says Hakma, and his parents were born there, and his parents' parents, and their blood is his blood, and almost everyone, except for the person who asked the ill-advised question, starts to pay attention to other things, because this is the conversation they have every week, fueled by injustice and rounds of drinks.

The room starts to whirl ever so slightly from the edges, left to right, and Jonas focuses on a knot on the wooden tabletop, only to watch it move slowly to the right, along with the rest of the room, and he has to move his eyes to keep up with it, but he can't get the timing right and his eyes slip past the knot, then move back to try to focus on it again.

Of course *you* understand me, Hakma is saying; *you* are my brothers, my sisters, my comrades against evil, my long-odds risk takers, my fellow freedom fighters. He is really going for it, trying to impress the inapt questioner with the nobility of his plight. Jonas remains silent for much of this conversation. Hakma looks over at him occasionally; they all do, as though looking for permission, or affirmation. Jonas has never spoken directly of his childhood to any of them, but people hear things, divine things from what is left unsaid, and it is widely believed that he holds the trump card in the suit of injustice.

Across the table, Hakma grows louder. They don't get it. Nobody gets it. He raises his voice to a level that seems very loud, but for all anyone knows may simply be appropriate. They have no idea what his people have suffered, goddamned Turks, and he no longer looks around to see whether any of *them* might be present. The uselessness of NATO, and Europe, and America, America the cowardly, America the impotent. They don't know, can't know, can't understand. And then someone comes over, someone big, with a backward baseball cap and very white gym shoes, comes over and tells him to be quiet, to shut the fuck up, and there's some shoving, and the room spins again, and then they're grabbing their coats, and they're hustled out into the yellow-lit street.

Someone has the idea to go to another bar. A better bar. A cooler bar. This bar is loungier, big chairs, low tables, and Jonas sees that the trumpet player they saw earlier is at this bar, and it's a small neighborhood, so he's not really surprised to see him there, tall and skinny and wearing a captain's cap, and his music is playing over the sound system, the same music they had all just heard, but perhaps because of this it strikes them as a thin echo of what they heard live. He knows the bartender, this musician, and they are in the midst of an animated conversation about the music, both of them bopping their heads in time to it.

They all sit down and order beer and resume the conversation, injustice and power, but like the music, it is all getting old for Jonas, thin, and before long he says he's going home. What he really wants to do is go back to Shakri, collapse into her. He gets up and puts on his jacket. Hakma grows quiet. They all shake hands and exchange loose hugs. Trevor drifts off with another friend, and Hakma is left at the table by himself.

Jonas turns around to leave, pulls his coat collar up around his neck. The door opens and he rides out into the cool street on a current of warm air and plaintive trumpet. Once he's outside, he looks back in through the bar's big picture window, and sees the image he will tell Shakri about the next day, while he sits with her sipping tea.

The bar's canned light spills out through the window and onto the street, so it's a little like looking at a giant TV screen. The left side of the bar is awash with people milling about, talking, a series of animated heads and dark clothes, laughing, carrying drinks. On the right side of the barroom is a low table at which Hakma sits alone, lit from above as if by a gentle spotlight, his half-finished beer on the table in front of him, his arms resting on his knees, fingers together, interlaced, his head bowed as if in prayer.

52

Tuesday, September 25 (AP)—Johnstown, Pennsylvania, resident Rose Henderson has only questions, and she wants only answers.

"At first, when they told me he was lost, I thought they just meant lost as in misplaced, like maybe he caught the wrong plane somewhere and he would turn up eventually," she says, referring to her son Christopher, who went missing in action while serving with the Seventh Cavalry Regiment. She speaks with the practiced weariness of someone who has repeated a story many times. "Then, a few weeks later, I got this very official-looking letter that said he had been formally declared missing in action. But they wouldn't say where he was, or how it happened, or why.

"Eventually, we learned a few more things about it," she said recently over a cup of tea in her living room, which has been turned into something of a shrine to her eldest son. A large portrait of him hangs over the mantelpiece, and commendation letters, school trophies, and snapshots are displayed on shelves in a bookcase.

Years later, she says the worst part is not knowing for sure, not having closure. "We were going to hold a memorial service a few years ago, but it just seemed wrong. If there's even a chance he's still alive, however small . . ." At this, Rose's voice trails off, before she is able to take in a breath and continue. "At the same time, I wish there were some kind of end to this."

A spokesman from the Department of Defense, Richard Dominick, refused to discuss the specifics of the case.

In an effort to get more information, she repeatedly contacted her congressional representatives. When she still didn't hear anything, she formed a support group of other military families, many of whom have suffered lost, injured, or killed family members.

"At first it was small, just local. We have a lot of families in the service around here. But pretty soon we were being contacted by people from all over."

The support group, which numbers over one hundred families, calls itself Military Families for Truth. And while they haven't been able to get all the information they believe is available about the loss of Christopher, they have been able to help the families of other soldiers.

"Many of them were misclassified," says Henderson. "Or there was some kind of other clerical error. We're pretty good at getting them to go back and make sure they have told us everything they can, and often, when they look at it again, they realize they can tell us more than they have."

She says that helping other families deal with the loss of their loved ones has helped her deal with her own loss. "He was my first-born son," says Henderson, who is divorced from Christopher's father, and has two younger children who are now grown and live away from home. "The group has brought me up a little," she says. "I was depressed for such a long time, and it helps to know that there are others in similar situations, and that I can help them."

In the meantime, Rose Henderson is still looking for answers. "I don't know if I'll ever learn the whole truth," she says. "But I've got to keep looking."

53

It gets in there, this thought, this way of thinking. They try to plant it, for sure, tend to it so that it grows, foster it, but it is in there to begin with. You're born with it, I suppose, and eventually life takes it out of you. The notion that you're invincible. No fear, they said. They don't want you to have any fear. Those other things, that invincibility, that aggression. They bring it out in you, show you how to do things, try to teach you how not to be stupid, how to protect each other. Protect each other. Be aggressive. Protect each other.

And then one day you find out what that really means.

54

If he has one complaint about Shakri, it is her tendency, in his view, occasionally, not always, but sometimes, to dominate him. At first, he finds it comforting, like a blanket or an old pair of jeans, and he submits himself to it willingly, even eagerly. It shows she cares about him.

She buys him a new shirt as a present, requesting that he wear it out that evening. She has a car, and insists on driving him everywhere—to class, to the store, to the park, to his friends' apartments—even when he wants to walk. He suspects she wants to make sure he is where he says he is.

She says the sight of a cheeseburger makes her physically ill, asks him not to order it, then buys him dietary supplements the next day to compensate for the lost protein. She asks where they are going, purses her lips disapprovingly at his answer, and drives them someplace else.

She talks to him at length about his diet, particularly his drinking, his clothes, his study habits. Once, he comes to see her smelling of cigarette smoke, and she stands over him, hands flying wildly, talking for nearly an hour about cancer, while he tries in vain to tell her it was Trevor who was smoking.

55

The road to Johnstown is built from slabs of grooved cement, laid end-to-end with a small gap between them to accommodate the winter cycle of freezing and thawing. Subsidence tilts the slabs gently away from one another, and driving on the road is like driving over an endless series of roughly laid patios. As usual when he rides in a car, the motion nauseates Jonas, and he diligently regards the scenery to prevent himself from getting sick. The previous winter's black cinders line the road, and a multitude of auto-body shops careen past as they drive, as does the brilliant red-and-yellow foliage of autumn.

"Can you believe we ended up here?" asks Shakri, her accent fluttering in a way that seems to imply she is talking more about herself than about Jonas. He shrugs. Snow flurried across the hills a few days before, but today is unseasonably warm, and he opens his window partway to let in some fresh air.

"I didn't know this was a possibility," he says.

"Could you put your window up?" she says. "I'm cold."

They drive past strip malls and cornfields, churches and forests, low one-floor houses with long, straight driveways and properties well delineated from the surrounding tangle of overgrowth merely by the fact of being mowed, all of it a revelry in the American urge toward expansion. There do not seem to be towns or cities in the usual senses of those words, but only certain areas where there are more buildings and certain areas where there are fewer. Each family has staked out a large section of ground, built a house in the middle of it, and those sections string together, stretching from one built-up area to another, filling up everything, as though everyone everywhere is spreading out their arms in a vast display of ownership.

The hills steepen as they drive closer to Johnstown, and the trees have lost almost all of their leaves at the higher elevation. Piles of snow appear beside the road, which clacks along underneath them like a train track. The houses, white and pink and gray clapboard, crowd the hillside, along with the melting remnants of the unusually early snowfall. Jonas pulls from his pocket a slip of paper with Rose's address and directions scrawled on it, and they exit the highway.

The neighborhood is large, full of large houses set back from the oak-lined streets, large lawns better cared-for than those at the majority of houses they have passed, and large cars sitting in the driveway. Shakri slows the car as they search the mailboxes on the odd-numbered side of the street for number forty-five.

The house sits on a small rise, and it looks perhaps taller than the earth-and-timber houses Jonas remembers from his youth, but of about the same overall area. A massive oak crowds the front yard, and from beside the front door a picture window looks out on the well-kept lawn. Jonas gets out of the car and is struck by how much cooler it is here than in the city.

His heart doesn't start beating quickly until he is walking up to the front door, past the carefully tended shrubs and a light in the front yard made to look like an old-fashioned street lamp. Shakri follows along behind, for once waiting as he makes the first move. He thinks about turning around, getting back in the car, and having her drive him home. But she is a presence behind him, and he realizes that the odds of convincing her to leave are remote. Then he sees the curtain in the large window move, and knows that he has been seen. He walks up to the door, takes a deep breath, and rings the bell.

56

He hears Rose's voice almost before he sees her, the door swinging open and there she is, a tiny woman with a flash of red hair and blue eyes and a sort of sideways smile, not forced, but perhaps strained.

"You must be Jonas," she says, and when he hears her voice he is slightly stunned, both by its volume—such a large sound from such a small person—but also because it is as if he is hearing the original voice for the first time, the accent stronger, a distant echo of the voice he heard long before, high up on a mountain.

"Yes," he says, "Jonas," pitching his own voice almost unnaturally lower, as though doing so will somehow force Rose to adopt a quieter tone, an effort which seems to have the opposite effect.

"Such a nice name!" she booms across the neighborhood, and then she steps out onto the porch and hugs him awkwardly, during which time his arms hang, useless and pinned to his body by her embrace. "And who's this?"

"This is Shakri," he says, watching as Shakri extends her arm to shake hands, only to go wide-eyed and limp during another long embrace.

"Well, that's a pretty name, too!" says Rose, stepping back to look her over. "Fits such a pretty girl. Well, why don'tcha come on in." And she steps aside to let them into the house.

The house is as well cared for inside as the yard is outside, with dark, polished furniture and cream carpets and a tall, ornate grandfather clock in the corner, all of it lit by soft sunlight diffused through thin muslin curtains. The windows are open to the gentle breeze, and when he walks into the living room, Jonas catches his breath.

Over the fireplace is a portrait that dominates the room, nearly the size of the fireplace itself. It *is* him. The face is so familiar but also different, younger and less worn than he remembers it. The crow's-feet have not yet developed around his eyes, and the hair is freshly shorn. He wears a dress blue uniform, and the American flag behind him is so crisp that Jonas can almost see it waving in the cool breeze that puffs in through the open windows. The face looks out at them from its place over the mantel as though presiding over a court.

"Can I get you something to drink?" asks Rose, already on her way to the kitchen to retrieve it. "Water or pop or something?"

"Just some water," says Shakri, but Jonas doesn't say anything. He can't take his eyes off the picture over the mantel. In it, Christopher looks as though he has just graduated from school, maybe in his late teens. It is him, but it's not him at the same time, not Jonas's version of him. It's not the way he remembers him. It's a memory of him, but only one facet, the reality of the picture forcing itself onto everyone's perception, the way it dominates the room. This is not him, Jonas wants to say.

He can't stop looking at it.

When Rose comes back from the kitchen, she carries a plate of cookies and two tall glasses of juice, which she sets down on the coffee table, her hands trembling ever so slightly. Jonas notices that she also has something else. Tucked under her arm is a thick manila envelope.

"When your counselor called to tell me you were coming," she says, "I made this up to give to you." She holds the packet toward him, almost reluctantly. "I don't like to read them anymore, or look at the photos, but they might mean something to you."

Jonas takes the envelope from her and opens it, begins to

look through it, sees that it is full of photocopied press clippings and photographs, but Rose stops him, pushing it closed in his hands. "I'd prefer if you would look at it somewhere else," she says, and she is gentle about it, but firm, so he closes the packet and tucks it under his arm.

At some point Rose notices that Jonas keeps glancing at the portrait over the mantel.

"I practically begged him not to go," she says. "As a mother, you're not supposed to say this, but as soon as he told me, I knew he wasn't coming back." Jonas senses a certain comfort she takes in telling them this, in thinking of it all as preordained. "But that's the way things work out sometimes. Everything happens for a reason. Don't you think so, Jonas?"

They're sitting down now, he and Shakri on the sofa and Rose in a chair across from them, a glass-topped table between.

"I don't know," he says, hesitating as he reluctantly turns his attention away from the picture. "Sometimes I do."

Rose smiles, and it's the most subtle gesture she has made since they arrived. "Tell me," she says, "your counselor, what's his name?"

"Paul."

"Right, Paul. He didn't really give me a lot of detail. I'm— he may have told you—I'm always looking for information. The military is often not too forthcoming."

Jonas is staring at the portrait again, but now he sees that Rose notices, that she recognizes how intently he looks at it, at him, at the portrait of her son, and there is a flash of recognition. She rounds on Jonas, focused. And then she seems to catch herself; not wanting to spook him, easily as she can, she says, gently but firmly, as though handling shards of glass, "Tell me, Jonas"—her voice catches in her throat—"did you know my Christopher?"

The room is bathed in a diffuse glow, the early-afternoon breeze, the grandfather clock ticking away in the corner. Rose's face has been forced into a mask, fixed in place by an endless cycle of yearning and disappointment, a calm exterior laid over a mix of curiosity and something else. Hope.

Jonas hesitates. His mind is a whirl of images and half-remembered events, and he is aware mostly of the necessity of choosing his words carefully, of the importance of the next few moments, of the unbearable weight of both lies and truth. He gathers together his will. Once he begins, he unwinds a story that is, like all stories, a mix of memory and impression. But he does his best to be mindful of his audience, to make it a sensitive story, an appropriate story, and for the hour he takes to tell it, his voice never quavers once.

"Your son saved my life," begins Jonas. And that, at least in part, is the truth.

REMEMBRANCE

I

Something had happened. Something awful.
He remembers the cool night air flowing in through
the open window, the thin woolen blanket keeping the
warmth close to his body. He was young enough that he still
shared a room with his sister, Miriam. But she was not there.
Something had happened.

He remembers armed men running down the street in front
of the house, and his mother wailing. He had been sent to bed
early, told to stay there. And from his pallet on the floor he listened to low voices, his father and brother, occasional shouts
in the street, the arrivals and departures of visitors.

He must have fallen asleep, and it was quiet when he woke.
The cool night air flowed in through the open window, carrying with it the strangely bright light from a crescent moon.
Under the woolen blanket, Younis turned on his side, trying to
get comfortable.

He remembers thinking that the next year, or perhaps the
year after, when his brother had moved out to start his own

family, he would sleep in his own room, now his brother's room, toward the front of the house. But for now he shared a room, a children's room, with his sister, who was not there. Their soft rugs lay against opposite walls, and he felt the cool autumn air streaming in through the window, even as the blanket held close his warmth.

His body warm, his face pleasantly cool, he smelled the faint, lingering scent of woodsmoke high on the air, and then he became aware of an increasingly urgent pressure on his bladder. At first he tried to deny it, and for a moment he contemplated rolling over, pulling the blanket around him, and trying to go back to sleep. Somewhere in the distance a rooster cleared its throat. He wanted to stay in bed, go back to sleep, because he knew that if he got out of bed and into the cold, sleep would have even more difficulty overtaking him when he returned. But then he found the urge was too great to ignore. He braced himself, then pulled back the blanket and allowed the cool air to envelop him, raising gooseflesh on his arms.

He stood up and tugged on his shalwar and kamiz. In the moonlight, he spotted his long, woolen wrap lying in a bundle against the wall, and thought about pulling it over his shoulders for warmth, then reconsidered. He would be gone only minutes, after all, because he was paying only a brief visit to the low earthen hut in the backyard. He strapped on his sandals and walked groggily out through the kitchen, opening the heavy wooden back door as silently as he could manage.

Dew covered the yard's cool grass, and wet his feet as he

crossed, taking practiced steps toward the small outbuilding at the far end of the wall. It was a clear night, with a thin sliver of moon low in the sky, and off to the east the horizon showed the first faint signs of the coming dawn. He wished absently that he weren't so tired, so that he might linger, appreciate it all awhile longer. He entered the outhouse, of habit holding his breath against the acrid smell, pulled the kamiz down slightly, and released his bladder. The rooster crowed again in the distance, and Younis was nearly finished when he heard the noise.

It cut sharply through the clear night, louder and louder. He will never be able to describe it adequately. It sounded like a lot of things: like paper ripping, amplified a hundred times, and overlaying that was the sound of a flag cracking rapidly in a strong wind, and some kind of engine noise, like a scooter with a broken tailpipe, and underneath it all was a low, long whistle, sounding for all the world like the whistle his father made when he called the sheep in from the far pasture. The entire cacophony grew louder and louder, but at the same time, in his memory, extended on until forever.

And then, at the far end of forever was an explosion. But to simply call it an explosion would be like calling the sun a light: literally true but grossly insufficient. It was the crossing of a barrier, a rending of reality. It was light brighter than he had ever seen, and then he was blind; it was louder than imagination, and then he was deaf. He was slammed against the back wall of the outhouse, and then there was nothing.

2

He woke to shouts and more explosions, kept distant by a ringing sound in his right ear. He was still in the outhouse, the walls of which jumped with shadows cast by nearby fire-light, distorted flickers on the wall. He got to his knees and peered out, trying to stretch his arm to support himself, but was stopped short by a stab of pain from his wrist to his shoulder. It felt as though his arm were slowly being torn in two. He clutched at his arm to find that it was wet, and this confused him. He curled the arm to his stomach and pushed himself up to kneel on the earthen floor. He stood weakly and looked down to see large wet patches covering the front of his clothes. His sleeve was ripped almost from the wrist to the elbow, and he moved his arm tentatively, stopping when pain ran up to his shoulder and into his chest. He stumbled out of the outbuilding.

The crescent moon still hung over the horizon, and the eastern sky was not much brighter than it was the last time he looked at it, but everything else was different. His house was gone, in its place a pile of broken stone and burning timbers, the air filled with the charred, pungent smell of smoldering plastic. Flames roared through empty windows in the shattered wall. He considered running back in, took a step forward, then another, but with each step the heat grew exponentially, burning his skin and drying his eyes, until he was barely able even to look at it. He realized he was yelling.

More explosions burst forth from other parts of the village, each preceded by the same nameless sound, and it seemed as though nothing existed in the world except explosions. Younis found himself wondering whether every one of them meant the same thing.

He briefly thought he might be asleep still, in his bed and dreaming it all. The explosions stopped, replaced now by shouts and wails. A diffuse firelight rose and fell all around him, rose and fell, illuminating towering columns of thick black smoke hulking above all the world, fading into the darkness, returning again, massive and dangerous, like monsters disappearing and reappearing from the corners of his bedroom.

Younis moved through it all in a state of hyperawareness, not thinking in the rational sense, but rapidly processing pieces of information, noticing, slowing everything down. He noticed how a small part of the house's back wall, the part farthest away from the outhouse, looked normal, completely unaffected by the carnage around it. He smelled the acrid smell of burning plastic and hair and the sulfur smell of explosives. He noticed that the water well in the courtyard appeared to be untouched, the circular retaining wall pristine, but that something sat on it in flames, as though someone had balanced a burning leg of mutton on the well's lip. Tiny craters pocked the outhouse's mud-brick outer walls, and the courtyard wall buckled in upon itself.

He still held his arm curled up at his stomach, and he

looked down to see that blood dripped off the tips of his fingers and into the dewy grass. He wrapped his forearm in a loose piece of his shalwar, keeping his elbow bent, the fabric wound tightly.

He felt himself go weak, and fought to maintain consciousness. For a moment, he thought he might be able to fly, lift himself off the ground and swoop away toward the hills, where he knew his family awaited him, willing his speedy journey.

The first gunshots came from the south side of the village, sharp, small reports, one or two at a time, like the sound of kindling under an ax. Then a machine gun opened up and the pops came as rapidly as the chain links through the pulley over the well when the bucket was dropped in, the whole chaos of reports moving gradually closer.

Younis ran toward the front gate, which led out onto the street, noticing when he got there that the entire wall beside the gate was now one long pile of bricks that he could have easily stepped over. Despite this, he popped open the latch and let the heavy door swing wide, closing it firmly after he exited.

The street itself was deserted, but he heard the mass of gunfire and shouts moving toward him like a living thing, faster and faster, louder by the second. He turned to go in the opposite direction, and took a single step when suddenly the world opened up all around, the gate and remnants of the wall behind him bursting into chips and splinters and showering him with dust.

The shouts came from everywhere at once, up the street and down, the air around him filling with cracks and whistles. He wanted to lie down, become the earth. He wanted to wake himself up, surround himself with iron and stone, drift away like dust before a windstorm. Instead, he spotted the narrow alleyway between two houses opposite the pile of rubble that used to be his home. He ran across the street and down the alley, the walls barely wide enough for his shoulders to pass through, and into another alley, and then another, all of them familiar and yet completely foreign. And then he was on the road beside the river, the broad expanse of water dark against the growing dawn.

Gunfire echoed again somewhere behind him, but he stopped despite it, suddenly stunned by the river. He probably looked at it for no more than a second or two, but the moment stretches on in his memory, expanding and becoming an event all its own. He was taken in by the beauty of it, by its cold rapids still roiling away, unconcerned by the horror unfolding behind him. For a moment he took in the sound of it, the gentle gurgle closer to shore, a top note underpinned by the deeper, more powerful roar out toward the rushing center. It will never stop, he thought, flowing on and building as it headed south, emptying, finally, into the vast sea, taking with it the water at which he now gazed, as much that night's witness as himself, and yet fallow by comparison, unplanted with its brutality.

He considered jumping into it, letting the rushing water carry him along, whether to safety or not, where he would be silent and invisible in the churning current. He recalled swimming in it during the heat of summer, at the deep pool upstream, the icicles that shot through him when he jumped in from the rocky bank, numbing his legs and arms, bringing his life to the top of his skin, and he realized that in that water, those rapids, he would never survive the journey. And then he wondered whether he wanted to survive, and thought that maybe jumping in would be the best thing after all.

This happened much faster than it takes to describe, only seconds, and later Younis will express his amazement at this, at how quickly everything changes, whether because of a decision you make or the decisions made by others, or just because of chance, and in a moment the entire path of your life, everything you knew and everything you will ever know, is altered. But in those few seconds all he recognized was the need to make a decision and, somewhere deep inside, the importance of his choice.

The gunfire grew louder until it was nearly upon him, and he discovered he was running, only distantly aware of having decided to run, more conscious of the cool morning air blowing his hair, the rush of wind that he was puzzled to find he could hear only in his left ear, and he ran without knowing it, north out of the village, along the river, his legs churning without thought, like the river itself, and he ran down the path toward the hills, toward the mountains, running under the beautiful clear moon, toward the pass, and he ran, unconnected to the world, understanding nothing save the need to run, and he ran, and he was distantly surprised to find, almost offhandedly, that he did not cry, not even a tear.

3

Jonas pauses occasionally, to take a breath, or a sip from his glass of juice, or to gather his thoughts, and when he does, a little gap opens up in the space of the living room. Within these gaps live perceptions rendered undetectable by the telling of the story: the steady ticking of the grandfather clock in the corner, the creak of Rose's wooden chair as she shifts her weight, the echoed shout of a child playing out in the neighborhood, the lengthening shadows in the front yard.

Rose has heard stories like this before. Not this story, of course. This story is different. Each story is different. But all of them share a need to be told, to be heard, and Rose knows how to hear them. She knows that these gaps are important, that they mean something. She knows that often the gaps are nearly as important as the story itself.

And so, despite her growing apprehension, she does not try to fill them. She does not express astonishment, or make meaningless, encouraging sounds. She does not ask questions, does not request clarification. She listens. She gives him her attention, the space to find his words, allows his story to breathe, offers him this measure of grace.

4

The cave his father had described came to mean more in Younis's mind than it actually was. He searched for hours, trying to match his father's instructions to the unfamiliar terrain before him, increasingly tired, weakened by the loss of blood, exhausted, and, finally, desperate. He longed for the cave, longed for all it represented. Its capacity for solace, its ability to shelter grew larger and more mythical with each step he took. He wandered across the empty hills.

Near the rock his father had shown him, balanced unnaturally in the shallow water close to the bank, the path ran away from the river and wove past a low, rocky outcrop before ascending steeply. Into the hills, it leveled out as often as the terrain allowed, but mostly it climbed steeply. The route was clear close to the river, a visible footpath that he easily followed up into the low pastures. But farther into the hills, it traversed stone and gravel, so that he had to search every twenty or thirty steps to be sure he was still walking in the right direction.

Periodically, the route appeared to end abruptly, run straight into a rock wall or stand of brush. He scrambled up the stone face or around the brush, searching above it until he found the barest trace on which to continue, until the trail disappeared again, this time into a deep gully, or a stretch of impenetrable thorns, and he repeated the process, each time hoping that the path on which he resumed his trek was the correct one.

His route trended steeply upward, switching back and forth as it encountered obstacles and sheer faces, sometimes leading right back toward the beginning, twisting around like a noodle dropped on a pile of rocks. And then the trail ended again, in the middle of a vast boulder field, and Younis couldn't find it, no matter how hard he looked.

He slumped to the ground in despair, feeling exposed sitting among the rocks, open to both the sky and the valley far below. He hoped his dark clothes did not stand out against the lighter granite. The ringing in his ear was pronounced, new, and he tried to get rid of it by screwing up his eyes. When that didn't work, he opened them and searched the slope below for any signs of movement, any hint that he might have been discovered. His arm throbbed with an immobilizing pain. Distant, booming thuds echoed from the rocks and seemed to suck away the air. He longed for the cave, to simply be there, to be anywhere that would get him out from under the open sky and off the slope. His head rang as though hit with a mallet. He needed the cave, which he imagined had been custom-built for him, for his shelter, perhaps by his father or his grandfather. His imagination made it a living thing, a rescuer, an active participant in his struggle.

Perhaps he passed out. He lost track of time. Eventually, because he had no choice, he stood. His arm did not seem to be bleeding as much, but he did not dare to look underneath the cloth he kept wrapped around it. He walked around a subtle bend in the hill that did not look like anything at all when viewed from below, but which stretched farther back into a seam in the hillside, its depth becoming apparent only as he entered it. He climbed up what turned out to be a shallow gorge in the rock, mostly hidden from view when seen from below. He surveyed the landscape again. Up the hill, on the other side of this crevice, he saw a flat, shelflike protrusion balanced on the steep slope, and some outcroppings of vegetation, scrub brush and dwarf pine, and farther down the rock were tiny groves of elm and birch, tucked into a hidden part of the mountain.

The sun was descending in the western sky when he stepped around a corner, up over the shallow ledge, and onto a rocky flat, which had a clear view of a large section of the valley. A ledge, but no cave, only the mountainside covered by a heavy layer of dead coarse brush and sage. But as he looked closer, prodded around in the tangle of branches and thorns, he was unable to find the rock wall which the brush appeared to cover. Instead he found that the stone curved inward, and that the vegetation was not well attached, as he first thought, but that it came off in his hand when he grabbed it, revealing a dark recess behind.

Little by little, the branches fell away, revealing a shallow opening about the same depth as the ledge, the ledge itself serving as a kind of threshold. His imagination had turned the cave into a kind of temple, but reality was rougher. He was not disappointed, desperate as he was for any kind of shelter before the approaching night, but at the same time, the shallow depression in the rock wall did not live up to the image he had created in his mind. Judging by the dark burn marks on the ceiling and the packed earth that made up the floor, he concluded that it had been used as a shelter in the past, perhaps during an earlier war.

The sun was sinking quickly, and the temperature began to drop with it. Younis set about as best he could making the cave marginally more habitable, clearing out what brush and stone he could with his good left arm. He was no stranger to sleeping outside, although he usually had a fire during all but the warmest parts of summer. But he carried nothing with him to make a fire, no matches, no flint, and the prospect of spending the night exposed and alone without warmth terrified him.

He pushed away some stones from the cave floor, enough to create a flat area on which to lie, and dragged a fir bough to cover it as a kind of rough pallet. Then he took the dry brush he had pulled from the cave mouth and stacked it up around the rim of the ledge, to prevent the opening from being seen from below. This done, the sun dipping below the horizon, he crawled inside the cave, exhausted, and blacked out.

5

He woke shivering in the dark, the cave mouth edged by the crescent moon's silvery light. His teeth rattled together and his fingers and toes had gone numb. With tremendous effort, he stood up and walked to the entrance of the cave, moving his limbs in an effort to regain some feeling. As he left the cave and walked onto the rocky ledge, he was bathed by the moon, the same wan light that anointed the great valley laid out before him. A thousand visible stars beamed tiny versions of the same pale cast, making everything appear to glow from within. Gradually his limbs, though still cold, regained most of their feeling, and his forearm throbbed. He could clearly see his breath, which seemed to be painted with the same silver sheen. Despite his cold and hunger, he found comfort in the sight of it, precious as the unknowable future, as though the concentrated energy of everything he saw were being focused upon him, standing high up on the mountain, looking out over all the world.

6

Jonas allows this image to linger. He has always liked this detail, this thought: the moonlight, himself looking out on the valley. He is not lying about it, either. At least, no more so than anyone who tells a story. He was there. If anything, it was more dramatic than he describes. But he can't help thinking that maybe he is overdoing it. Perhaps he describes the moonlight once too often. As he watches Rose's face, Jonas becomes concerned that he has gone too far.

The difficulty, he realizes, is inherent in the use of both words and memory. Their imprecision combines to make it nearly impossible for him to tell a true story. Even as he speaks, he is conscious of the fact that it wasn't exactly as he describes. Had he really stopped beside the river that night, looked out into it and thought those things, or had he done that on a previous evening, and then, once again, superimposed one memory on top of another? Does he describe the river accurately, his frantic journey along it, or does he use a sort of verbal shorthand to convey to Rose the general picture, and allow her imagination to fill in the details? Is there any other way to tell her what happened?

Because what Jonas wants, after all, is not simply to describe for Rose a mountain or a cave or his desperation. What he wants is for Rose to feel something, fear or pain or anger or heartache, even if only as a semblance of the emotion he detects within himself, even as he sits in her living room and tells this version of the story. He wants her to know, needs her to know, needs to place it all into context, needs to explain himself, wants her to understand.

So he continues to talk, continues to describe for her how it was, or how he remembers it, or at least how he has convinced himself he remembers it. How scared he was, how angry, how desperate, how alone. And if it comes across as stilted or overwrought, if in his effort to commune with her, conjure for her his reality, he uses commonly held devices, if he describes once too often the strange crescent moon that lit up the world, or his shivering, or the accursed cave in which he was forced to spend the days of his youth, it is in the service of a greater purpose, and he can easily be forgiven.

7

At some point, Younis was woken by convulsions. He lay on his side at the mouth of the cave, legs drawn up and wrapped by his arms. He shivered a little more and closed his eyes, tensing his muscles in an effort to keep away the cold. He shivered again, and moved to stand up, recover some warmth through the motion of doing so. But as he put his hands to the cold earth and began to push himself up, he found that he could not do it, that he lacked the strength to lift his body. He tried again, and again, but found that he could not make himself rise. He tried to open his eyes, but found that he could not, or perhaps, he thought, with a panic suppressed by fatigue, his eyes were open but he could not see anything, or perhaps the world had simply disappeared.

The shivering stopped suddenly, replaced by a distant warmth, and Younis smiled weakly to himself. He drifted in a void, a blackness so complete that a moonless night was like broad daytime in comparison. Images confronted him and then disappeared before he could focus on them, made compelling by his inability to resolve them. He chased after them, trying desperately to focus on something, anything, and a gentle, spinning sensation took hold, rocking him back and forth, lulling him, but simultaneously making it impossible to focus on any one thing, impossible to think, impossible to move. Helpless and exposed, vague visions approaching him from all directions, he gave up trying to focus on them, let them go, and allowed himself to drift.

And then he was back in his village, where everything was as it was supposed to be, his mother walking out to the pasture at the end of the dusty road, carrying naan wrapped in cloth and hot tea, which he took, steaming, in the bright cool air. The sheep surrounded him, and he protected them with devotion, for their wool, for the warmth and the food they provided. He sipped from the earthen bowl his mother handed him, the tea sweetened and faintly spiced, and he looked up into green eyes that so readily mirrored his own. As he looked, her face changed, growing gradually lighter and lighter, as though the sun overhead were drawing itself closer to the earth. He looked around to see that everything grew brighter, less resolute: the pasture, the stone wall, the earth itself fading away, losing contrast in the light. Soon he could see only her most obvious features, her eyes and nose and mouth, her dark hair, and everything else, her skin and wrinkled brow, her arms and hands, grew brighter with each passing moment, until all he could see was light, and nothing else existed. She disappeared into it, disappeared along with everything else, everything he knew, the pasture and the sheep and the hills and the village and even the river itself, the source of all of it, everything he knew, all of it blending into a golden light that was suddenly his entire existence.

8

The light bathed him and he woke, lying on his side beside a crackling fire, covered by a thin blanket, his limbs prickling and stiff as the feeling gradually returned to them, the flame's glow wrestling with the darkness and cold. The smell of cooking food violently ignited his suppressed hunger. Squinting into the flickering light, he could make out only a shadow across the fire, a presence overwhelming the refuge in which he had been so isolated. He closed his eyes, mildly surprised to find that he was not yet dead, then opened them again, tried to focus on the figure opposite him.

"*Salaam aleikum,*" said the figure.

Younis heard the words, clear and accented, oddly pronounced, but was too weak and shocked to respond, and then he lost consciousness again.

"Are you okay? Can you hear my greeting?" said the figure. "I said, 'Peace be with you.'"

Younis rubbed his head, then tried turning to get a good look at the place where the voice came from, but could not move. Gradually he brought the figure into vague focus, adjusting his vision to the harsh firelight. The man was dressed in an odd mix of local and foreign clothes, camouflage fatigues devoid of patches or insignia, a kamiz, and a pakol cap. He gazed levelly at Younis, patiently awaiting his response.

"And also with you," Younis finally replied, weakly. "And you in return? Are you well?" His voice was barely louder than a whisper.

"I am well, sir, thank you," said the man.

"You are English?" said Younis, in English.

"I speak English," said the man.

"Why are you here?"

"I guess I am lost."

9

Younis, his mind addled, tried to force his head clear and strained not just to understand the stranger's English, but to place it. He could not, as it was so dissimilar from the English he had heard his father, or anyone else, speak.

He could feel the strength flowing back into his limbs, spurred by the warmth of the fire, and abruptly he tried to stand.

"If it is not too forward, sir," began Younis, "may I ask where are you . . ." But he stumbled weakly, and fell back down to the earth.

"Have something to eat," said the man, and stepped around the fire, stopping to pick up a shallow pan that had been warming there, and offered it to Younis. "I'm afraid it's not much."

Younis shoveled the food from the pan to his mouth with

his hand. It tasted like beef and some sort of mashed vegetable, but had a plastic taste he could not place. He had to keep himself from throwing it back up out of his empty stomach. The man offered some water from an opaque bottle that faintly carried the same plastic odor.

"Are you from the village down there," asked the man, pointing his thumb over his shoulder in the direction of the valley, toward the bottom of the mountain.

Younis thought first to answer truthfully, and then thought better of it.

"No," he said. "I come from Yokshal, on the other side of the mountain," naming a village he had heard his father speak about occasionally, the home of some distant cousins, or perhaps an uncle.

"Huh," said the man, evidently either unfamiliar or unconcerned with the other village. "We must have come from opposite directions. I came up from the river."

As his eyes became more accustomed to the light, Younis could make out the man's features a little more clearly, filling in the vague outline. He was several days unshaven, with light blue eyes rarely seen in that part of the world. His left forearm was wrapped in a dirty bandage, a mirror image of the wound on Younis's right arm, and a thin cut, just beginning to heal, accented his left cheek and temple. He was well armed, a long rifle propped against a rock beside him, and the hilt of a combat knife protruded from a strap around his thigh.

"How long have you been here?" asked the man.

"I could ask you the same question," said Younis, his voice weak and rasping.

"Here?" said the man, motioning to the ground around him. "About two hours. This part of the world? Nearly a year."

"I don't know how long I have been here," said Younis, slowly gathering his strength. "I fell, injuring my arm, as you can see, and came here to this shelter because I could not walk home. But I have always lived here."

The man looked at Younis coldly, as though measuring his words, then smiled a little half smile and said, nodding at Younis's arm, "I can take a look at that, if you want. I have some supplies with me."

The wind picked up, coursing down the valley and up the steep slope, carrying with it a faint smell, gunpowder and something else, like burning hair. Twenty minutes later, Younis rode a soft cloud of morphine, the roughly stitched wound on his forearm protected from infection by an injection of antibiotics. The morphine bore him up, higher than the mountain, far away from pain or fear or sorrow or loss. How wonderful it would have been to stay on that cloud, to ride on it forever, to drift eternally, untethered. Younis was thinking these thoughts when he fell into the deepest sleep he had ever known.

10

The story, as Jonas tells it, is mostly accurate. If Rose is able to spot what he changes or leaves out, her face gives no indication. But she does not relax, does not even breathe. She waits.

"I woke in a hospital bed," he says, nodding up at the huge

portrait over the mantel, its size directly proportional to the home's grief. "I am sure that's him, but I'm sorry I can't help you any more than that."

The faint background noises—the creaking chair legs, the ticking grandfather clock—grow to fill the room's silence. Jonas sits back in his chair, but Rose remains balanced on the front of hers.

"But," she says, "there must be more."

Jonas says nothing. He bunches his shoulders in what could be a shrug, and bites his lip.

"There must be more," says Rose.

"I wish I could—"

"There must be more. You have to remember something else. I can't believe it. That's it? You just 'woke up'?"

"I know, and I'm very sorry I can't help you more."

"But maybe if you tried. Anything. What was he wearing? How badly was he hurt? Was he scared? Did he tell you anything else? I just can't believe it."

"I wish I could remember something else, something more."

"Yes, anything. Did you see him leave? Did you see where he went? Did he tell you if he had plans?"

"Look, I know how you must feel."

"You have no idea how I feel!" says Rose. "You have no idea what it's like to know that you might never see—" She wipes her cheek quickly with a tissue. "I'm sorry," she says. "Of course you do. I'm sorry. I just, well. I just miss him very much."

The sound of the clock in the corner seems to grow again to fill the room, and when Jonas speaks, he does so almost as much to drown out the sound as anything else.

"There is one thing," he says.

Rose leans even farther forward.

"I just have this image, really. This thing I remember. He had this book that he wrote in, like a diary. Quite a lot. I don't know what he put in it. But he had it. Maybe that is something."

For a long time Rose doesn't say anything. Then, almost reluctantly, she nods. "Thank you," she says. "But really, maybe you'll remember something else. Maybe you'll wake up one morning and think of something. Maybe something will just come to you. You can call me anytime, if it does. I would be grateful."

They talk awhile longer. Jonas thinks that Rose's face looks somehow older than it did when she first opened the door. She asks more questions about his time on the mountain, with her son, but he is unable or unwilling to give any further information, and she leans back, reluctantly, and allows the conversation to drift.

Which it does, meandering around Christopher's early childhood, school and friends, trailing off as its subject ages, closes in on his ultimate fate, which hovers, phantomlike, over the room. Other than seeking to discover what happened to him, Rose does not seem to have any real interest in talking about the military, or Chris's life once he entered it. It is as though the portrait on the wall was taken as his life ended, and the subsequent years turned into hazy recollections and unending sadness.

Jonas and Shakri sense that it is time to leave before anyone states the fact. The sunlight through the windows is golden, the shadows elongated, and they reach an unspoken consensus. Rose hugs them awkwardly to say good-bye as they get up, and again before they go out the door.

And then she is nearly pushing them out into the cool, late afternoon. They stand on the front step, and she holds the door open with her hand across the threshold like a gate, preventing them from reentering the house. She makes it clear they should leave, but at the same time she tells them to come back anytime they want.

COMMUNION

I

For a time, they were little more than rumors spread by children.

The imam argued that, removed as the village was from the capital and its arcane politics, the Americans could have no possible interest in it. The only contact they would ever know would come in the form of the planes seen far overhead. If Younis's father ventured to make a counterargument, that there existed a real and imminent danger, it didn't seem to make an immediate impression.

So when Azar's youngest son, who was no more than ten years old, told his father that he had watched that very afternoon as a patch of reeds along the river moved in an unnatural way, counter to the current and the prevailing mountain wind, it was written off as a figment of the youngster's imagination.

And when Jangi Shah's middle son claimed to have found a boot print in the dew-moistened earth at the base of the rise to the west of the village, he fetched his friends to go and take a look. But one of the boys stepped on it by accident, blurring the impression and making it impossible for anyone else to tell for sure what it was.

Then one evening Ahmand's nephew said that he thought he had glimpsed a parachute falling from the sky on the other side of the river. But when he was questioned further, he conceded that it could have been a kite, or maybe an old plastic bag swept along on the breeze.

In those places where the children gathered, one could perceive, if one cared to listen, in their hushed tones and joking insults, a certain skepticism about what their mothers had told them: that the Americans had come to take away naughty children who did not obey their parents, that they lurked in the dark places between the houses, waiting patiently for those who had been instructed not to go outside after sunset.

But when Ali's teenage daughter came running home at dusk one evening, closing the door quickly behind her, and explained breathlessly that she had seen a lone man stalking in the brush beside the river road, a giant of a man with brilliant blue eyes and a chest like a horse, it was finally conceded that something strange must be happening.

The most probable explanation, it was widely agreed, was that the village was suffering the hauntings of ghosts.

2

Occasionally he hears the voice of his savior.
Usually he tries to ignore it.

It comes to him when he is tired, or drunk, or asleep, or not asleep, simply lying in his bed and unable to turn his thoughts to anything else. He tries to force it to join the chorus in his head, the background noise that reminds him he is alive.

"Perhaps she is correct," says Paul. "Perhaps there is more to the story."

The voice in his head is softly accented by the Pennsylvania hills. It is gentle, and deep, and brings with it the haunted souvenirs of the past: the scent of woodsmoke and reheated rations drifting up a mountain slope, the echo of metal on whetstone as a combat knife is sharpened, the scratching sound of pencil on paper, the crackle and pop of burning cedar, the thin, high tearing noise of another blister pack being opened, another morphine-filled syringe prepared.

"Very well," says Jonas. "Perhaps there is."

With effort, he begins to talk. He tries to get it right, tries to match the words exactly, but has the familiar feeling that he is adding and subtracting, substituting what should have been said for what he fails to remember accurately. He channels the voice as best he can, feels it condense within him and propel out of him, and as he speaks, as this voice speaks through him, he feels himself take a step, as though off a cliff and into the unknown.

3

For a while we were stationed in Uganda. What we were doing there is not important. Weekends, we used to go to the wildlife pre-

serve, just to look around, see the animals. There was an agreement with the government, and we got in free.

So many animals. Animals I had never seen before in real life: giraffes, rhinos, hyenas, lions. The preserve was just a small area of land, and most of the surrounding countryside was being logged or mined. So all these animals were crowded into this little wild area, like ants on a leaf in a rainstorm.

Once, we were driving along and we came upon a woman pulled over beside the dirt trail they used for a road. She's a wildlife biologist, she says, and she's sitting there in her vehicle, staring through binoculars, off into the brush.

"Look at this," she says. I look, and for a long time I don't see anything. She hands me her binoculars. The colors there in the bush, at that time of year, well, there's really only one color, a sort of sand or tan or khaki, just lots of different shades of it, so everything blends together, the earth and the shrubs and the trees and everything, all just the color of the sand. So I'm looking at this, and I don't see anything. I'm starting to get a little frustrated, maybe, because this woman is obviously convinced that something spectacular is there.

"No," she says, "over there, a little to the left."

And then I see it.

There in the underbrush, not fifty yards away, is a lion. It's a lioness, actually, the biologist tells me. She has been watching this lioness for two days.

"A lioness," I said. "Wow, that's great."

"No," she said, "look closer."

And then I think I must have gasped, because standing there right next to the lioness was a little baby gazelle. He was tiny, and so weak he could barely stand, his legs all skinny and sort of quivering, whether from his own weight or fear or both. Every once in a while, the lioness would reach out with one of her huge paws, wrap it around the gazelle, pull him over, and lick his face, just like a dog licking your hand. It seemed like two competing instincts were fighting it out inside of her: her urge to hunt, and her urge to mother. In response, the gazelle would nuzzle up against the lioness's side, maybe not entirely comfortable with the whole situation, but feeling, for a moment, safe.

What had happened, the biologist explained, was that two days previously, the pride's big alpha male had killed both the baby gazelle's mother and the lioness's cub.

"They're heartbroken," she said. "They've adopted each other."

"That's impossible," I said. But there I was, looking at it, unable to convince myself that it wasn't true.

We went back the next afternoon, and they were all still there: the lioness, the gazelle, and the biologist, who stayed there for days. She had never seen anything like it, she said, and she had been studying lions for years. It really affected her. She couldn't think about anything else for weeks afterward, lost her appetite, spent days alone in the bush.

The situation couldn't last. They weren't eating, and sooner or later something had to give.

It ended badly.

But I have never forgotten it. I carry it with me. Somehow, the fact that it ended is not as important to me as the fact that it happened. In a way, they're still there, now that I've seen them,

*set together by chance or fate under the African sun, safe, for the
moment, from the surrounding cruelty, each one's life given meaning by the other's.*

4

As soon as they are back in the car, Jonas glances through the
packet Rose handed to him, and before they are even out of
the neighborhood, he begins to form some initial impressions.
They are copies of articles clipped from newspapers, and letters, or memos, and photographs.

The photographs hold Jonas's most immediate attention.

Some of them are black-and-white, and others have been
reproduced in color, apparently printed using a newer photocopier. They present varying degrees of clarity. Some of them
are more toner smudge than anything else, while others are
tack-sharp. They are interspersed among printed-out e-mail
and official-looking correspondence. Jonas is struck by the
feeling that he has seen them before, if not these exact photographs, then images eerily similar to them. In one photo, a
young Christopher stands with his arm around another soldier
in front of a tank, starkly silhouetted under a blazing sky. There
is a picture of him at some sort of dance or function, in a formal
dress uniform, holding hands with a blond-haired girl who is
nearly as tall as he is. Another shows him mud-spattered and
obviously exhausted, hunched over a picnic table, but managing despite his fatigue to smile up at the camera. Still another

shows him wearing a camouflage uniform, with a large duffel slung over his back, making his way up the ramp of a cargo plane.

5

Rose Henderson pushes the front door closed as Jonas and Shakri leave, then leans against the wooden frame, feeling the cool October breeze through the open living room window. Next to the front door, a tall wooden box that Christopher once dragged home from shop class holds a pair of umbrellas, angled gently away from each other. An old horseshoe, collected during one of the family's innumerable treks through the Pennsylvania countryside, hangs upturned over the doorsill. She feels suffocated as soon as the door is closed, unable to breathe deeply.

The photograph over the mantel. The folded flag on the bookshelf. She is used to them, aware she has gathered these things around her, made the decision to leave them as they were, in view, and as a result they are only occasionally difficult to look at, painful only when she thinks about them too deeply.

But there are the other objects: the boxes of toys and sports equipment hidden away in the basement, out of sight, the school papers and certificates and finger paintings in the attic. And now, to these objects, she adds a list of people. If that which is left in open sight has grown less painful over time, she cannot even think about that which is hidden away.

And then Rose is aware that she has slumped to the floor, that she sits alone in the foyer, pressing her back against the front door.

She spends a few moments trying to gather herself together, rubs her eyes with her hands, is finally able to take a breath, and stands up. She has much to do, she thinks. She grabs a short-handled spade from a bucket next to the sliding glass door that leads onto the back porch and steps into the waning rays of the thin autumn day.

The Henderson property is surrounded by a low stone wall, which Roy Henderson built before their divorce. The wall demarcates a smaller plot around the house, and a larger plot beyond, the back forty, as they always called it, although it is nowhere near so large as forty acres. The back forty is now the domain of overgrown grass, rabbits, and deer. Before he left, Christopher would occasionally mow a section of it, and, with help from the two younger boys, Matthew and Sam, pour down white lime from a large paper bag to mark out a football field or soccer pitch. Then they would stay outside, their footfalls like tiny thunderclaps, until it was so dark they could no longer see.

Rose divides her days by tasks. She writes letters in the morning, attends meetings in the afternoon, or makes phone calls, the important work of organizing the support group occupying more and more of her time. The important work. They always tell her, as if she needs to be told, how important it is. And yet she can't do it all the time, nor all by herself. She has some help, the increasingly complex work now spread among several volunteers. She hears from more and more people who want to get involved, and the group is growing, a fact she finds nearly as tragic as the fact that it exists in the first place.

It wasn't that the two other boys were unaffected, thinks Rose. Not at all. But they were young. And then time passed so quickly, as first Matthew went off to take a construction job outside the state, and then Sam started at college, the first of her boys to do so.

Someone had once told her, insensitively rather than maliciously, that at least she had her other children, implying that when you have several, the loss of one is easier to bear. But Rose knew this for the lie it was. Her other boys were doing well, and she was proud of them, loved them, but everything seemed somehow fainter after Christopher disappeared, and Rose often felt as though she had one foot in the here and now and the other foot somewhere else. Maybe another person would react better, she thinks, and then, with effort, pushes that thought, all the thoughts, away.

Between letters and phone calls and meetings, she takes out her frustration on the weeds in the backyard. She thinks about putting together something for dinner, something light, not really feeling hungry but knowing she has to keep up her strength. The sun is rapidly dropping toward the horizon, its descent chilling the air. Rose thinks about dinner, and something about the light or the crisp fall air reminds her of another dinner, at the end of another fall day not too many years ago.

They ate it around the table in the kitchen. Tacos, she thinks, piled with lettuce and tomatoes in an effort to get her family to eat at least something of the vegetable family. Roughage, she used to call it, before one night when Christopher announced he didn't like the word "roughage" because it sounded like you were going to be attacked by your salad.

After dinner there was still a little light outside, and Christopher wanted to show them something he had learned in soccer practice that afternoon. They filed out through the sliding glass door and into the backyard. It took him a few tries. He got a soccer ball and put it on the ground, placing one foot in front of it and the other behind, and with a scissor motion kicked the ball high into the air, then hit it squarely with his forehead, before kicking it again with his other foot, and they all watched it arc neatly through the autumn air, past everyone, over their heads, and smack into the graceful stone wall. He looked over at his parents and smiled. "Isn't that cool?" he said.

"Yes," said Rose, "that's fantastic."

And for just a moment, she remembers, it was.

6

When we arrived, we told them we were there to help them, but they were ambivalent. It was almost like they were bored. But then we started passing out cash, and they registered the possibilities.

One day we backed the APV up beside the central market. Skeets accidentally pressed the gas instead of the brake, and we hit a merchant's stall. It damaged the wooden booth and the awning. So Jacobs goes over and offers him something to pay for the damages. He accepts it, looks grateful. We could have just driven away. But then the guy in the stall next to him pipes up and says that we hit his stall, too. Sure enough, his awning is knocked over, but Gomez swears the guy kicked it over himself. So what do you do? Jacobs gave him some money, but less than he gave the first guy, and this idiot gets pissed off. Starts talking about how he's going to call the governor.

When they realized how it worked, they started applying leverage. We'd have locals claiming we broke their shit all the time. For a lot of the guys, this is about when their outlook on things started to change.

7

Jonas sits in the front seat, looking through the folder on his lap, which entirely consumes his attention, but Shakri wants to talk. The photocopies of news articles and pictures and letters are spread across his lap. He glances over them, but he has the problem with car sickness. As he tries to read, his stomach turns and he gets nauseous. Shakri is asking him how he feels about seeing Rose, but he doesn't want to talk about it.

He engrosses himself in the contents of the folder. Black-and-white photographs, and letters on official stationery, army stationery, rendered by the photocopier in shades of gray. The late-autumn sun drops steadily, and Shakri is still asking him questions he doesn't want to answer. He starts to sweat. His stomach feels as though it will come up his throat any second. Occasionally he takes a photo out of the pile to show to Shakri, who can't really see what he's trying to show her as she drives, or he tries to read aloud a section of an article for her benefit, anything to divert her attention. But he can't concentrate.

"Pull over," he says.

"What? Why?"

"Pull . . ." And then his stomach opens up and he vomits all over the inside of the car, all over the folder, the photocopies, spewing a partially digested mix of cookies and juice.

"Oh, God . . ." says Shakri, and pulls the car over fast, nearly running into the guardrail in the process. "Why didn't you tell me?"

But he is unable to answer, because he has opened the car door and is spitting the last of his stomach's contents over the buildup of cinders and ash beside the road.

"Why didn't you say something?"

"I tried," he says, breathless, "but . . . so fast."

He is wiping vomit off his chin with his hand, wiping it off however he can, trying not to get any of it on a picture of soldiers gathered in front of a row of sandbags. They pull the damp floor mat out of the passenger side of the car and dump it over the guardrail, down a small ravine beside the highway, where it lands among thousands of cigarette butts, cola bottles, and a pair of white underpants. He salvages as many pages from the packet as he can, scraping vomit off those that can be saved with the edges of those that can't.

"Do you have a paper towel or something?" he asks, and Shakri rummages around for a while in the trunk before holding up a single fast-food-restaurant napkin. He uses it as best he can to wipe down the dashboard, the seat, the armrest, but it is quickly soaked through and useless, and he tosses it over the guardrail, where it lands next to the floor mat.

They get back into the car, which smells, despite their efforts, like ammonia and grape, and pull carefully back onto the highway. Jonas says he is feeling slightly better, and Shakri alternates between asking whether he is okay and concentrating to keep herself from retching.

They drive the two hours back home, bathed in the scent of partially digested hospitality.

8

Jonas remembers the dusty road he walked back home from the schoolhouse, which was set on a hill just outside the village in a whitewashed old colonial building whose original purpose had been forgotten. He remembers being hungry, eager to get home, and the golden begonia lining the road, wild and scattered in the irrigation channels.

As he pushes open the heavy front door, he hears voices, men's voices, rare, but not unknown, a cousin, or an uncle, whose names he has long forgotten, but who were once frequent visitors. His mother is there, cleaning, putting things in order. Maybe she has been cooking, as he hopes, because his stomach has been rumbling in time to his steps. Or is this something else, another fragment recalled from another time?

Is he not combining two different memories again, conflating them into a common past?

There is no way for him to know for sure.

He is more certain about walking into the front room and seeing it transformed, the shock of finding it unfamiliar. Furnishings have been removed, the common items to which he is accustomed, the low table, and the wool rugs and thin pillows, and the ornate silver teapot that usually sits next to the door. All the banal tools of the everyday have been swept away, moved elsewhere.

In their place, groups of men, some of them familiar, some of them complete strangers, sit or kneel or squat on the balls of their feet in small circles of two and three. They huddle around little piles of dark powder heaped on the floor, or beside a stack of short lengths of pipe, or next to a large gray car battery, or over a coil of wire, wound around itself in a loose circle and resting in the corner of the room, sitting on the floor, looking for all the world like a snake.

9

They drive the rest of the way home, and Jonas disappears again into his thoughts. It's dark by the time they get back to the city and park the car. He's feeling much better, he says, but a little tired. They stop by Primanti Bros. on the way home, because Jonas insists on picking up some beer, which he says will help settle his stomach. He holds the packet Rose gave him under his arm, now damp and about three-quarters as full as it was when he received it. He buys a forty-ounce bottle and avoids Shakri's gaze as they walk out into the blue-and-yellow neon, down Forbes to her apartment.

"Is it okay if I take a shower?" he says when they get inside.

"Please," says Shakri.

He takes the oversize bottle of beer with him into the shower, the cold liquid in his throat contrasting with the hot water pouring over his head. He takes another drink. Far from settling his stomach, the beer seems to upset it more, but he manages to force it down.

10

Rose found out only later that it was all a mistake. A bureaucratic problem. While explaining it to her, someone called it a snafu.

Years afterward, at one of the meetings, someone tells her. They are supposed to visit you first, she is told. A real person. Two people, actually, casualty officers, are supposed to come and knock on your door and explain things to you. The letter is supposed to come only later. Or maybe they are supposed to hand you the letter. But at the time, she learns, there were so many, and they couldn't keep up, and they have only so many people trained to do it, and things got done out of order.

"Even for the missing?" she says.

"Even for the missing."

"I got a letter," she says.

The day is frozen in time. She remembers that on the afternoon it arrived in her mailbox, she was baking cookies while Matthew and Sam were out in the back forty, playing football. Or perhaps baseball. Or maybe soccer. Regardless, they were outside, creating whole worlds on a sunny afternoon, while Rose baked cookies in the kitchen. Afterward, whether or not it was true, she swore that she heard the postman drive up before the cookies were finished, but that she did not want to go outside to pick up the mail just then. Not before she finished the cookies, before her sons received them, before they smiled at her with offhanded gratitude.

Later, but not just then.

Rose did not have any particular interest in the people who sent the letter, their biographies, their career paths, their motivations or ideologies. She noticed, in the same way she noticed good wallpaper, the official-looking seal on the corner of the envelope, the fine, ivory parchment. She noticed that the envelope did not have a postmark. And somehow that was when she knew.

At some point before that, she called to her two remaining sons playing in the backyard, to tell them that the cookies were almost ready, but that if they wanted any they would have to come in and wash their hands first.

They had been outside all day. They would talk about it later, with her, with each other. They would talk about how, for a brief moment, Matthew, who had just started at the high school, thought that he might be too old to be out in the backyard playing with his little brother, about how he quickly shrugged aside this thought. Sam would talk about how he knew, just knew, that this time he would be able to throw the ball clean over Matt's head, forcing him to run and get it just as he had been forced to do for about an hour.

When they heard their mother's voice, the boys were torn between eating cookies and continuing the game, but their stomachs quickly won out. They ran in through the sliding glass door that opened onto the backyard, making a show of not tracking dirt inside even as dusty bits of it fell from their shoes.

Rose had made two dozen chocolate-chip cookies. She baked them twelve at a time, on cookie sheets placed one over the other on racks in the oven. The first dozen was nearly done baking when she called to the boys in the backyard, and she deftly formed the second dozen from clumpy balls of dough using two floral-handled tablespoons. As the boys came inside, she pulled the first batch out of the oven with mitted hands, and she reminded them not to get dirt all over the floor.

The two children sat at the kitchen table, each with a glass of milk that she poured from the carton in the refrigerator, and they waited expectantly for her to bring them a large, ivory plate of chocolate-chip cookies. She baked them once every couple of weeks, and when she did there was a minor celebration in the house. Even Roy got excited, and was known to come home from work early, if he could, just to rescue a cookie or two from his voracious sons.

Several years after receiving the letter, Rose will remove one of the five chairs from around the kitchen table. She will not give any explanation, and the missing chair will never be mentioned again.

But for now the bright sun streamed in through the window, and the steam from fresh-baked cookies rose through it. The two boys sat around the kitchen table and bantered, while Rose carried the plate over to them. As she set it down, she heard the mail truck rattle to a stop outside, noticed the silence of its stopping, but she did not go outside to get the mail immediately, did not yet step out into the October sun, did not yet feel its warmth on her arms.

Under the table, one of the boys kicked the other. The other yelled out, and Rose just smiled as she pretended to take back the plate of cookies. Outside, the mail truck abruptly started its engine, drove away down the street, its fading rattle filling the neighborhood with the sound of its mandate. There was a brief moment of silence, until both boys realized that there was no way she would really take back this gift, this memory they would have for the rest of their lives.

II

Jonas hears a knock at the door.

He has lost track of how long he has been in the shower, and Shakri knocks again and asks if he is all right.

"Fine," he says, and fills the empty beer bottle absentmindedly with water from the showerhead. He hears the phone ring, and knows from the tone of Shakri's voice that it is her mother.

Shakri talks to her mother frequently. Her mother, father, and brother are all doctors, as Shakri will be one day. She will be just like her parents, who still live in India, and her brother, in New York.

Photographs of the family—on vacation somewhere exotic and palm-lined, or visiting her once during the winter, gathered around a snowman on a white Pennsylvania day, looking like bundled-up raisins on a sugar-frosted cake, or standing in front of the Taj Mahal, tourists in their native land, or hunched with aunts and uncles and cousins over a board game in a comfortable family room—clutter Shakri's bookshelves and tabletops. When he first visited her apartment, Jonas stood transfixed by the images of Shakri's abundant family. But now he does not really look at them. He finds it too much like staring into a floodlight, the portraits and casual snapshots painting in stark relief his own want.

He keeps a portion of his heart to himself. Although he wants to do more, he finds himself loving her only halfway. He tells himself it is because he is young, too young to freely give away his heart. He tells himself it is because he needs to focus on his studies, or because of his friends, who do not always meet with her approval.

But he suspects there are larger reasons for holding back, reasons related to loss, related to the dangers inherent in loving anything fully, related to the speed with which it might be taken away.

He drinks unthinkingly from the beer bottle, and spits out what he suddenly realizes is warm shower water.

He suspects there are still bigger reasons.

He loves her only halfway. The half he gives basks in it, soaks it up. The half he gives is covered in light. But he knows that there is a part of himself that must never be shown, that could never be loved, an animal part consumed by violence and rage and survival, a part he keeps locked away behind a heavy door.

In part, he loves her only halfway for his own protection, his wounded past, his fragile heart. But mostly he holds back because, deep down, underneath everything, below his thoughts and his movements and even his breath, he hears a knock at that door, low and incessant, and he knows that were it ever opened, were it ever to escape, she would be the first to get hurt.

12

What if you become convinced that, even though you are there to help them, the locals are not only unappreciative, but might actively hate you? What if you start calling all the locals hajjis? What if you start to see them less and less as human beings and more and more as things to be categorized as either very threatening or less threatening? What if your SAW gunner accidentally pops off a round or two in the general direction of a crowd of hajjis who have gathered for some purpose you don't fully understand, but don't like the look of? What if you all start popping off at the slightest provocation? What if you start looking for provocations? What if you start to feel bored when your weapon is silent?

13

For a long time after she received the letter, Rose carried on as though it had never arrived. Her two boys still lived at home, and she was still married. She had activities to keep her busy. She attended PTA meetings. She bought groceries. With perhaps the mildest hint of desperation, she hacked at the weeds that seemed always on the verge of overgrowing the wall in the backyard. She drank coffee with friends.

And when anyone would ask, as they regularly did, whether she had received any news of Christopher, she would smile and say, "Not yet," as though she had just been asked about her tax refund, or a new pair of jeans she had ordered by mail.

And then, at some point, she realized that he was not coming back. Perhaps it was when she went into his room and noticed, as if for the first time, the accumulation of dust on the dresser and shelves. Maybe it was when she looked up from the casserole she had just removed from the oven and realized that his chair at the kitchen table had not been used in years. Perhaps it was the day she saw that the stacks of unopened mail she had been saving for him filled three large boxes.

Not that she accepted his death, per se, merely that she accepted that she would most probably never see him again.

She had been told that once she arrived at the point of acceptance, she would be able to move forward. It would mark a turning point. And they were correct, whoever it was who told her this. It did mark a turning point. But it was not the kind of turning point she had expected. She had come to think of her life as being on hold. She had an inkling that once she reached the point of acceptance, everything could finally begin again. But looking back on it, she realizes that rather than marking the point her life restarted, the day she finally accepted loss marked the point when it all fell apart.

14

You probably know a little bit what it's like. If you've ever shot a gun, even if you've ever used a slingshot, or a bow and arrow, anything like that. You see something out there, a bottle, or a tin can, something far away from you, something that looks to be totally unconnected to you, and you aim at it, pull the trigger, let go of the stone, and the thing you aimed at explodes, disappears.

Now, imagine that times a hundred, times a thousand. We use really big guns. Bombs. Mortars. It's alluring. That's power. Real power. You see a car out there, you see a truck, you see a building, you see a whole fucking village.

Gone.

15

Out of the shower at last, he finds a clean pair of his own jeans and a shirt, left on a previous visit, which Shakri has folded and placed on a stand outside the bathroom. He puts them on, then tells Shakri he's going for a walk.

"Why don't you stay here?" she says.

"I need to think," he says.

And then he's out the door and alone with his thoughts and his footfalls on the rough concrete of the sidewalk.

He feels a pleasant numb sensation in his arms, and out of habit he plays a game with himself in which he tries not to step on the cracks in the battered pavement. Whether from playing this game or not, he has developed a half fear of the cracks, a sort of ridiculous phobia, as though stepping on a crack will open a chasm in the sidewalk through which he will fall. In his mind, the game assumes larger significance.

Stupid, he thinks. Silly thoughts.

And yet he can't help but notice that he is good at it, that he has always been good at it. Good at avoiding pitfalls, avoiding problems, even imaginary problems, like cracks in the cement.

The cracked sidewalk leads Jonas to the house on Adams Street in which Hakma rents a tiny bedroom.

"You look awful," says Hakma.

"Thanks," says Jonas, as he steps into the sparse room that Hakma uses as a bedroom, study, kitchen, and dining room. Over the single bed, Hakma has tacked up a map of the world large enough to take up most of the wall. Large-headed pins protrude from various points on the map's surface, like tiny mushroom clouds. Jonas had once asked whether they marked places Hakma had visited.

"No," Hakma had said. "Each pin is a place where I have a relative."

Close to the geographical center of the map is an oblong circle drawn in thick black marker. The circle takes up portions of Turkey, Syria, Iran, and Iraq, and is labeled "Kurdistan." Hanging on the wall opposite the map is the Kurdish flag, green-and-white-and-red-striped, a bright yellow sun taking up most of the field.

"I called you earlier," says Hakma. "You were out?"

"Yes," says Jonas.

"Where'd you go?"

"Hey, tell me again about your flag."

"Really?"

"Sure."

"Well, as I may have mentioned to you previously, it is made up of three stripes, which, from bottom to top, are green, white, and red, with a large golden sunburst in the middle."

"And tell me again, what do those colors represent?"

"I'm glad you asked. The green stripe represents the land itself, verdant, fertile, the cradle of . . ."

"Is it not mostly desert?"

"It is not. It is verdant and fertile. The white band represents peace, which is what every Kurd wants, the right to live peacefully within the borders of our ancestral homeland."

"Uh-huh."

"And the red band, at the top, represents . . ."

"The blood of the people?"

"The red band represents the blood of the people, their struggle for a homeland free of foreign domination. And the sunburst in the middle is yellow, representing light and power, and it has twenty-one rays, which is important for specific religious reasons."

"What sort of religious reasons?"

"It's, um, the number, twenty-one, is the number of, um, true purity. I think."

"Well, it's a beautiful flag," says Jonas.

"It is beautiful, isn't it?"

"It is."

They stand and look at the flag for what seems to Jonas to be a long time.

"Listen," says Jonas at last, "do you fancy getting a drink?"

"I thought you'd never ask," says Hakma.

They grab their jackets and go out the front door, and the cracked cement sidewalk leads them several blocks farther downtown, to Wilson's, where they find a few more acquaintances already gathered together in a large corner booth.

Trevor carries a pyramid of pint glasses to the faux-wood table, the top of which is already covered with wet rings.

"Here's to Kurdistan," says Hakma, and out of habit, they all raise their glasses and drink.

16

In the photograph's background is a large, square limestone building with ornately carved columns and a frieze over the entrance. It looks almost classically Greek. It is pockmarked with bullet holes, and parts of it, the sharp corners, the most delicately carved figures, lie crumbled around its base. The building is the least noticeable thing in the image, the foreground of which is dominated by a soldier who may be Christopher. He wears dark sunglasses and a uniform of sand-colored camouflage the exact same hue as the shot-up building behind him. His helmet, same color, is emblazoned with sergeant's stripes, and he carries a long gun, pointed down, his finger carefully laid along its side, away from the trigger.

The soldier who may be Christopher looks down at a dark-haired boy who appears to be in his early teens, a tightly wound *lugee* wrapped around his head, and a billowing white cloth around his shoulders, tied on top of a blue-and-white-striped T-shirt. They are obviously talking, the boy looking off into the middle distance, and his hands seem to be absently twirling the fringe of the cloth. The soldier, who stands well over a head taller than the boy, is looking down at him with an earnest expression barely discernible behind his large, nearly black sunglasses. It is as though he is trying to convince the boy of something.

"Do not be afraid," he seems to be saying. "We are here to help."

17

For a time, Rose cursed the sun.

She stayed awake all night. She went to sleep at sunrise and tried to remain unconscious as long as she could. She stopped showering. She stopped taking care of Roy and the two remaining boys. They were also suffering. She knew it. But they could rot for all she cared. No, she thought, that was far too harsh. She didn't mean it. She didn't want to lose them, too. But they required so much, and she simply didn't have the energy to devote to keeping them. It was, she found, no easier to lose one just because you had others.

She made occasional, heartfelt efforts to move on. She joined a bowling league. She didn't know why. A friend had joined, and in a fit of optimism, Rose signed up, too. It was a silly idea. She hadn't been bowling since she was a girl, when the owner of the local bowling lane hosted all-night bowling parties on the weekend, locking the doors so that parents knew where their children would be. She would stay up all night long with her friends. But she remembered that it wasn't about the bowling; it was about just being there, surrounded by everyone. She remembered that it was happy.

She went bowling with the league twice, but couldn't muster the energy for a third outing. It required, she felt, too much.

So she stayed in bed for days. She lay in her room with the curtains drawn. And when the sun dared to filter through them, to brighten the room, she pulled the covers over her head, cursing its audacity for shining on a world in which Christopher wasn't even there to see it.

18

At some point, Jonas passes out. The next morning he wakes up and has no idea where he is. He does not remember the previous night, cannot recall leaving Wilson's, nor what he did afterward.

He sits up with a start, and finds that he is in his own bed, his own room. Rain rattles against the windowpanes. He does not remember finding his way back to his apartment, does not know how he even managed to dig out his house keys and get in the door. His head roars.

Through the fog in his head, he realizes that the phone has been ringing.

He decides he will try something, something he has not tried since he was very young, since he used to go to the mosque, since he happened one day as a child to meet a strange monk in red robes, who taught him how.

He takes the blanket off the bed, folds it into quarters, and places it on the floor. He remembers that he used to stay in the mosque after prayers, sitting on the prayer rugs. He kneels down on the folded blanket, sits back on his calves, closes his eyes. Everyone else was so eager to leave after prayers that they practically ran to put on their shoes, find a football, or run down the narrow streets. But he sat, waiting.

He straightens his back, breathes in, breathes out. He concentrates on his breath. But his head throbs with each heartbeat, and before long his legs have fallen asleep and gone numb, and his stomach rumbles.

Frustrated, he stands up, goes into the bathroom, and takes a shower. He is filled with good intentions. Today will be the day, he thinks. It will be different. He will get some breakfast, and then he will go to the library. There are midterm exams coming up. He will call Shakri, tell her he is all right, tell her where he has been, explain his newfound focus, share with her his determination.

Out of the shower, he sits down on the edge of the bed. His initial burst of energy has worn off. He is tired. His headache has transformed into a dull weakness in his neck and shoulders. The rain beats against the windows, and he is disheartened at the thought of going out into it. He yawns. Perhaps he will rest his eyes, just for a moment. A short nap, and then he will be able to think clearly.

He lies down on the bed, and within minutes, he is fast asleep.

19

Friday, October 7 (AP)—U.S. officials announced today what they called a "highly successful" raid against insurgent targets. The action, which officials say occurred last night, resulted in the deaths of at least fourteen enemy fighters and the capture of ten others, as well as the acquisition of "valuable intelligence information." News on American casualties was not immediately available, although at

least two American soldiers are thought to be among those injured.
A military spokesman promised that further information would be
released in the coming days.

20

And then Rose was angry. The support group was begun out of
anger as much as anything. It felt unjust. Something had been
taken from her, and she had not been compensated. She felt
as though she had been robbed. She wondered almost seriously
whether she could sue.

It started by accident, when she saw an interview on a local
public-access television show with the father of a boy who
had gone off to war and been killed. Friendly fire, it had been
called. He said he was unable to get the whole story, and was
frustrated. He seemed angry, but calm, focused, pointed. When
a caller to the program questioned his patriotism, told him that
he was denigrating the memory of his son by questioning his
mission, he carefully, calmly pointed out that when the caller
had sacrificed one of her own loved ones, she would perhaps
be entitled to that opinion, although he doubted very much
that she would still feel that way, and that, in the meantime,
she could go to hell.

Rose got in touch with him, contacting him through the
TV station. They had coffee. He had been trying to organize
other families, apply some pressure and learn the truth, and
Rose admired that he had given his pain a focus. Roy seemed

to want to pretend that it had never happened, that the hole in their lives could be papered over with work and silence. Here was someone who not only faced tragedy, but used it to reach out to others.

Over dinner, the man explained that he was trying to build a critical mass. "They only respond to pressure," he said. "If they think there is going to be a big stink about it, if they fear for their careers, they will talk. But if they think you are on your own, they try to dismiss you as unstable, or damaged."

Rose made the decision almost without realizing it. It started with a visit to a neighbor, a few blocks over, who had lost a son. The next day she described the visit to the man she had met through the TV show. She described the grief that had filled the room, the overwhelming pain, but also her own sense of pride, of exhilaration at finally doing something.

Before she knew it, she was writing letters to families in other parts of the state, then to her congressman, her senator, the Defense Department, the White House. Soon she was hosting groups in her home. Soon she had a purpose.

21

A few nights later Jonas blacks out again, and when he wakes up he is kneeling on the floor in the hallway outside his apartment, unable to find his keys.

Another time, he blacks out and wakes up in the park by the river, next to the Fourteenth Street bridge, waves gently lapping the shore under a pink dawn. He wakes up in the back of a strange car, parked outside a blue clapboard house, and he gets out of the car and starts walking. He wakes up in the end zone of a football field. Often, relieved, he wakes up in his own bed. To his mild amazement, he never wakes up in a gutter. Once, he wakes up in the crook of a thick tree, his legs straddling the branches, the pattern of the bark imprinted on his cheek. He wakes up in the firm grasp of a large bouncer, moments before being hurtled out through the back door.

These awakenings are enumerated, transformed into stories, to be told and retold, as they all sit around a table somewhere, and raise their glasses, and laugh.

22

And then maybe they plop you down somewhere, give you a mission, like a bite-size chunk, something you can digest. Patrol this area. Or take over that house. Search this ravine. Something you can get your head around, something that sounds simple. Protect this convoy. For that period of time, all of reality is supposed to fit into that mission; those three or five or ten words sum up the entirety of your existence. Recon that village. And it almost always goes pretty well. Not perfect. Never perfect. But usually, you go out and you do your mission and everyone comes home and then you're eating a burger in the food hall.

But let's say one time it doesn't go well. Not well at all. Let's say one time you let your guard down, or your CO gets distracted.

Or maybe nobody screws up. Maybe everyone does exactly what they're supposed to do, exactly the way they're supposed to do it, but you just get outsmarted this time. They lay a perfect trap. Maybe you're in a village and everyone's doing their job the way they're supposed to, and there are women and children around. (Which is supposed to be a good sign, by the way. They tell you to always look to see what the women and children are doing. They're smarter than you, and if they suddenly disappear, you know something's up.)

But maybe they just get the better of you that day. Maybe there are women and children all over the place and despite that, all of a sudden maybe your point man is lying on the ground bleeding from the neck. And maybe you hear those little snaps, like a million tiny flags cracking in the wind, only you know they're not flags. They're bullets breaking the sound barrier as they pass by your head. And then maybe Jacobs goes down, like he's decided to take a nap. And then all of a sudden you are certain of only two things: that you are not invincible, and that you would rather be anywhere in the world except here.

23

The phone rings, and reluctantly Jonas picks it up.

"Hello?" he says.

"Hello, Jonas?" Her voice is eager, nervous, but tries to cover itself with a tranquil veneer.

"Yes," says Jonas.

"It's Rose. Rose Henderson. I just wanted to call and say hi, you know, and to, you know, find out if you might have had a chance to think a little bit more. If you can remember."

"Hi, Mrs. Henderson, hello. Well, I am not really sure what to tell you, ma'am, that I have not already said."

"Oh, well, anything really. Anything. I would be interested in hearing anything."

"Yes, ma'am, I know. You have said that before. And I absolutely promise you, again, that I would call you. If there's anything, I mean."

"I know you will. And I'm really sorry to keep, you know. I don't mean to pester you. It's just, if there's anything."

"I know, ma'am. And believe me, I will. I absolutely will. I promise."

"I know, I know. And really, I want you to know that it could be just anything, you see. It might be something that you don't think means a thing, that maybe doesn't seem very important. And to you maybe it isn't; maybe to you it's just some silly little detail that you wouldn't normally even acknowledge. But to me. Well, it would just mean the whole world to me."

24

He remembers the ruins of a stone fortress on the road outside the village, a caravanserai. They play there, he and his younger sister, Miriam. Miriam the delicate, he remembers, the graceful, transformed in his memories into a glowing presence that trailed him around through childhood. Sometimes, he remembers, his elder brother, Sirhan, came along as well, but not very often.

Later, he will read about them in *The New Book of Knowledge* encyclopedia, the string of inns or rest stations that were built beside roads branching out along the vast network of the Silk Road, stretching from Shanghai to Colombo to Cairo to Vienna.

But as yet he is ignorant of the stone fort's original purpose, and so they are free to turn it into whatever they want it to be: a manor house on a plantation or the royal court in Xianyang, or the Palace of Versailles, or an Aztec pyramid. The pile of rocks is anything they want it to be.

And so it is that one day they find themselves touring the Taj Mahal, or scaling Mount Everest, or climbing the turrets of King Arthur's castle, and they round a corner and there they are, crouched against a low wall, a group of young men, bearded, with long guns slung casually over their shoulders. Sirhan is among them. They smoke something from scraps of rolled-up newsprint, and they stand suddenly when they notice that they have been seen.

Sirhan strides over to them. He stands nearly two heads taller than Younis, and his eyes are deeply bloodshot, the pupils contracted to pinpoints.

"You should not be here," he says, his voice gravelly and low.

Younis is about to say something in response, tease him, or challenge his right to tell them what to do. But then he sees that this person before him, looking like his brother and sounding like his brother, has been replaced by someone else, someone with eager eyes and a hard voice.

Younis reaches down and grabs Miriam's wrist. "Let's go," he says, backing away, unwilling to turn his face from the group of men, unwilling to allow them out of his sight. But Miriam pays no attention, and crouches down to pick up another colored stone she has spotted in the dust.

"I said let's go," says Younis, and yanks her arm, pulling her up to her feet. She cries out, but Younis refuses to let go, moves her so that she stands behind him, and backs them both away from the group of men, some of whom now smile in a way that makes him wish he could move much more quickly.

25

And then it's early November, the first truly cold night of the season, the smell of snow on the air, their breath turning to pale smoke under the street lamps, the welcome warmth of Shakri's apartment, and Jonas punches the wall in her living room.

Her first reaction is to laugh.

He had been out drinking with Hakma at Wilson's, and Shakri met him there and walked with him to her apartment. He had been eager to see her.

During the walk, under bare, shadowed trees half-lit by street lamps, maples and oaks stripped of all but their most tenacious leaves, both of them cold despite walking briskly, because until then the day had been warm and they wore only light jackets, she starts in on him again.

"How much time do you think you spend drinking with

Hakma?" she says. Her face wears the blank and open expression she uses when she is trying to make a point. It is an expression with which he has become familiar.

"Oh, please, just do not start."

"No, really, I want to know."

"Not so much."

"Really? Because I make it to be every night this week."

"I had literature class on Monday night."

"So what are we, Thursday? That's four out of five nights, Jonas. How much money do you think you spend?"

"But Wilson's is cheap."

"You have this tremendous opportunity. Look at what you have been given. You've got—"

"What I've been *given*?"

"You've got the chance to do something amazing, to be an amazing person, and you piss it away in a bar with that angry Kurd."

By this time they have arrived at her apartment. Shakri fumbles through her purse for her keys and finally gets the door open. But the whole time she keeps at him, reminding him of all he is throwing away.

"Look," she says as they walk into her living room. "I know you've had a rough time."

"A rough time?"

She starts to say something else, but Jonas cuts her off.

"What would you know of a rough time? You've had everything handed to you."

"That's not true and you know it! And you also know you can't wallow like this."

He doesn't really know how it happens. He feels the anger
creep up his back, rising in him, an almost physical force, or
something tangible he can touch. He feels it consume him,
blocking out everything else. He feels it. He is momentarily
convinced that Shakri is deliberately bringing it out, seeking
it, wanting it. He convinces himself that it fulfills some need
in her.

The act itself doesn't exist, only its aftermath. Jonas doesn't
even realize what he is doing until he draws back his fist and
punches the wall next to the front door.

To his astonishment, Shakri laughs, albeit a little nervously.

"Oh, no," she says, her accent fluttering. "No, you don't,
you melodramatic git. There is no way I'm going to start living
in a country-and-western song."

He regrets it almost instantly. He has punched a spot on
the wall next to the front door, and realizes only afterward
that he has hit not the dramatically breakable drywall, but the
solid wood of the doorframe. His hand throbs, and he thinks
he may have felt something snap in his wrist. The spot on the
wall shows no sign of having been touched. His anger dissipated, his hand rapidly beginning to swell, he sits down on the
couch.

"I, um . . ." he says, holding his wrist, "I think I really may
have hurt myself."

"You idiot," says Shakri gently. "Let me see."

She sits next to him on the couch and runs her hand down
his arm and over the long, pale scar on his forearm.

"So now I finally know," she says. "I finally know how you
got that."

"You finally know," he says.

"I mean the truth," she says, meeting his eyes. "Right? And not that rubbish about being swept over a waterfall, or falling out of an apple tree, or fighting a lion, or defusing a bomb, or . . . what was that other one, the one you told Trevor?"

"Training accident with a peregrine falcon."

"Yeah, that. How did you ever come up with that?"

She touches his swollen wrist, and he winces at the contact. "That's really swollen," she says.

"I think I might have broken something," he says.

Shakri stands, goes to the closet, and puts on a heavy coat, then hands Jonas his jacket. "Come on," she says. "My friend Mira is on call in the medical center."

"Mira?" says Jonas. "She hates me."

"Yeah," says Shakri. "If it is broken, she will be happy to set it."

Reluctantly, Jonas pulls on his jacket, easing it over his throbbing hand, and in a gust of chill air they are out the door and back into the cold night.

26

Things went downhill fast. After the ambush we didn't care. We got sloppy. We lost something. Inhibitions, I guess. It gets easier; that's for sure. Maybe we lost a little discipline. And then we started losing more guys.

First it was Marin, on point in some village, and he just lay down like he'd decided to take a nap. Then, right after that, Landon tripped an IED and literally disintegrated.

Then a truck ran over Margold. No joke. It's almost funny to think about it, if it weren't so awful. He was on his back underneath the APC, because we thought a tie-rod was broken, and he was checking it, and damn if that rig didn't just roll backward, right over-top of him. Squashed his chest flat, broke his back. We scrambled to lift it off, but there was no way.

Then, back in the zone, we had this big discussion about it. I mean, come on. You go off to war and get killed because a truck you're fixing rolls over you? You could do that in your own back-yard. I had already started thinking it was fate. You showed up and you lived or you died and there was just nothing you could do to alter it. But some of the guys said that they thought it was just chance, all totally random. And we got into it a little. We were pretty upset, which, let's face it, is weird for such a high-brained dis-cussion, fate versus chance, but somebody shoved somebody against a wall, I remember that, and there we were arguing and jabbering about our stretch of bad luck. And someone said it, said, "Well, you know, fuck it. We're cursed."

And everyone went quiet, like a secret that everybody knew but didn't dare say had been spoken out loud. And a couple of guys laughed, but someone else got really angry, said, "Shut up; don't ever say that again."

And it's true. You've got to nip that kind of thing in the bud. But it was too late. It was already out there. A unit gets that kind of thing into its head, that it's cursed, and it's useless. One of two things happens. Either they get mutinous, refuse to go out, or maybe go out and dig in somewhere, refuse to do anything, or else they snap.

We snapped.

27

In the morning, Rose writes letters, often waking before dawn in the cold house and putting a kettle on to boil water for tea before settling into the rocking chair in the large-windowed addition Roy built before the divorce. *Dear Timothy,* she writes, in a graceful, flowing script on a sheet of cream stationery, writing by hand because she is still not entirely comfortable writing on the laptop that sits next to the printer upstairs. *You don't know me, but you served with my son.*

Roy bought her both the laptop and the printer, and checks in on her occasionally, as she does on him. Separated after Christopher disappeared, now divorced, they are friends, of a sort. While Rose had founded the support group, Roy had seemed capable of carrying on as though nothing had happened, and Rose resented him. So she funneled into her work with the group all of the energy and attention that had been squeezed out of the marriage.

Even now, though friendly, they are vaguely wary of each other, each blaming the other in part for the loss of their son, even as they each know how irrational it is to do so.

I am writing because I have organized a group of veterans and their families, anyone who has lost friends or loved ones in the line of duty.

Many of the soldiers and family members she contacts never get back to her, and she is not offended or put off by this. Quite the opposite: She finds it completely understandable, assuming that they want as much distance as possible from the past. But this is the opposite of her own reaction, and that of those who do get in touch with her, those who share a need to be close to others who have had similar experiences.

We are a group of over one hundred family members, friends, and comrades who have lost loved ones.

She never pesters or cajoles, and she is careful not to go on too much about her own loss. Her mission, she feels, is simply to be there, to be in touch, offering to those affected the opportunity for fellowship.

28

Jonas wakes up in pitch darkness to the sound of Shakri's screams.

They are being hunted. He lies on his back, hiding with Shakri next to him. She screams into his ear, his good left ear, so that he can hear nothing aside from her screams. He can't move, can't sit up. They are surrounded. He tries to sit up again and smacks his head against something hard. He tries to keep them alive.

"I don't understand you, Jonas!" Shakri sounds frantic, desperate. "What are you saying?"

It is her voice, but it feels unfamiliar. It is as though she is speaking to someone else, calling him a different name, in a different language, and he registers it merely as a kind of nuisance that threatens to prevent him from doing what needs to be done, and which, more important, threatens to give them away. He is trying to save her, and he needs her to shut up and let him do it.

"Wake up, Jonas, oh, please wake up!"

She is crying now, trying to keep her voice calm, sounding as though she is reasoning with a mugger or a rapist. He wraps his arm around her neck and clasps his hand tightly over her mouth.

He finds that he cannot move his legs, that they feel bound, and he reaches down the length of his thigh with the hand that is not holding shut Shakri's mouth and gropes around to try to figure out what is restraining him.

It feels like bedsheets.

Then he takes a breath. Slowly, he releases his grip on her mouth.

In the darkness, he reaches up, grabs hold of the wooden slats, and pulls himself out from under the bed. He slides out of the sheet and blanket, which have wrapped themselves around his legs. Then he reaches down and tries to help Shakri crawl shakily out, as well, but she pushes away his hands.

He stands beside the bed, his bare chest bathed dimly by the light from the street lamp outside the window, which barely penetrates the darkness of Shakri's bedroom. He is soaked with sweat, and the cool air brings out goose bumps on his arms and legs. He hears nothing but a ringing sound in his good ear. He opens his mouth to say something, then closes it again. When sounds finally emerge from his mouth, they are raspy and forced, his voice catching in his throat.

"I don't . . ." he says. "What happened?" he says. He says, "I didn't mean . . ." and, "Are you okay?"

Shakri is curled fetally on the other side of the bed, practically as far away from Jonas as she can get while remaining in the same room. She holds the side of her head as though in pain, and Jonas suddenly realizes that he injured her as he dragged her underneath the bed. Her body shakes, but she is quiet except for an occasional sob or rapid intake of breath. He crosses the room and sits next to her.

"I thought we were going to be killed," he whispers, and reaches out gently to put his hand on her leg.

"Don't," she says. "Just don't," she says. "Just please don't touch me."

29

What if, a few days later, you find them? What if you find them a week after they kill your point man while you're patrolling some stretch of highway outside some godforsaken village? What if you find them a few days after you lose someone else, vaporized by an IED right outside that same godforsaken village? What if you are absolutely certain that some of the locals know them, know who did it, who it was that killed your friends? What if you then get some intel? What if you get confirmation? What if you suddenly know where they are?

30

The next day it rains, and Rose can do no work in the backyard, so she reads some e-mail she has managed to print out from the computer, or she makes some phone calls, or she stares through the window at the giant drops flooding the small porch outside the front door.

She can still picture them standing there, framed by the doorway, soaking wet, the three of them, clustered around a red wooden wagon, and the thought makes her smile. They wear their dripping, oversize ponchos, their rubber boots as, behind them, the rain turns the front yard to mud.

Christopher had organized them into a team. He and Matthew were supposed to push the wagon and tuck the newspapers behind the subscribers' screen doors, while the baby, Sam, sat in the wagon, pulling papers out from under a folded tarp and stuffing them into plastic bags. But Sam couldn't keep up as the houses rolled by, and then it really started to rain. Though he is still years away from being old enough to drive, Christopher wants to borrow the car. "Just in the neighborhood," he says.

"Come on," says Rose. "I'll drive you."

They make nearly a hundred dollars a week from the paper route, which they split among themselves and spend on toy action figures and slushies and model rockets.

"They should save some of it," says Roy.

"They'll have time to save plenty of money later," says Rose.

They roll the dripping wagon into the garage, load the damp newspapers into the trunk of the car. Matthew and Sam climb into the backseat, and Rose closes the door before whispering something to Christopher, who stands quietly next to the car.

"What were you thinking?" she asks, annoyed despite herself at having to drive them around. She speaks to him as though gently rebuking a confidant. "You know Sam isn't big enough to keep up with you two."

Christopher fixes her with his striking blue eyes. "It was just an idea," he whispers back, before he gets into the car. "I thought it would work, but I was wrong. I'm ready to move past it if you are."

31

Jonas leaves Shakri in thought before he does so in action. He has suspected he would have to. Maybe from the beginning. He has known he must. It is for her own good.

He stops calling. He avoids places he knows she may be. At first he tells himself that it is only temporary, only until he can get himself sorted out.

He knows he owes her an explanation. He considers calling her, talking to her, giving her the chance to convince him otherwise. Partly he wants to tell her why; partly he also wants to be proved wrong. Partly he is afraid of being proved wrong.

He tells himself it's only temporary. He has to work through some things. He tells himself they will get back together after he has had some time, after he gets rid of this thing inside that consumes him. He tells himself that it will be safe for her then, that they will be better than ever. But he fears that none of this is true.

In the end, he picks a time he knows she will not be at home, and he calls and leaves her a message. In the message, he explains to her the reasons he does not contact her: that he is protecting her, that it would not do for her to be with someone like him, that it is not safe, that she does not really know him, that she deserves much better, that he is capable of horrendous things.

32

"What happened to the gazelle?" asks Younis, the wind blowing more gently now, up the mountain behind him. "You know, with the lion, what happened?"

The silence of the night is broken only by the crackling of the fire, the scrape of steel on whetstone, the wind bearing up the slope, and, eventually, by a softly accented voice, almost reluctant to speak.

"Life's cruel sometimes," Christopher says. "It was fast, at least. That was the only good in it."

33

"Here's to Kurdistan," says Hakma, lifting his glass.

"You need a new toast," says Jonas.

It's a Wednesday night, and he is back at Wilson's.

"Never," says Hakma. "I will toast the motherland until the day I die."

Wilson's is empty except for one old guy at the bar, and they sit alone in a booth near the front. The beer looks clear and full, the cold glass in his hand, and he can't wait to taste it.

"Well, then, you need a follow-up."

"Aha," says Hakma. "Nothing wrong with toasting other things after the motherland." He thinks for a moment, and then lifts his glass again. "Here's to my enemies' enemies, who are my friends."

"Very original."

"Got something better?"

Jonas thinks for a moment, raises up his glass, pauses as if in sudden meditation, opens his mouth as if to speak, and then drinks down the entire glass, lifting his hand to order another before it is even completely empty.

The evening settles into a familiar pattern. Condensation from the pint glasses wets rings on the tabletop, and Hakma periodically wipes at them with a soggy napkin. The old man who has been at the bar since before they came in yells something at the bartender, who tells him, in tones gentler than the words, to pipe down or go home. Wilson's is known for nothing if not cheap beer, but when the bartender finally brings their bill, they are stunned by the tab.

"I don't have it," says Hakma.

"Don't look at me," says Jonas.

The room sways gently now that they have stopped talking. Jonas is content to sit there, comfortable in the booth, for the foreseeable future. Then he looks up to see that the bartender has disappeared into the back room, and he is suddenly all action.

"Let's bolt," he says.

Hakma looks at him for a moment, processing the options. "Yeah, okay."

Without even being aware of having made the decision to do so, they're up and out the door like they own it, like it's obvious, and before they really know it they are out into the neon night, rushing down the street through the chill air. Jonas expects shouts or sirens to hit him in the back, but there's nothing, just footfalls and traffic. He feels invincible.

They walk quickly down a side street and head up the hill toward the stadium. Close to the top they pass an apartment building, and Hakma says, "Hey, check this out."

He walks over to the building's side entrance, a glass door with a thin metal bar across the front serving as a handle.

"This is pretty cool. I discovered it a few weeks ago."

The door swings open easily at his push, and they slip into a dim hallway and through a large metal security door, which is also unlocked. Their footsteps echo from the concrete and steel in the stairwell as they climb six floors to the top, where another steel security door opens to put them on the roof.

"I have no idea why they don't lock it," says Hakma.

They step onto the tar-paper roof, cross over to a low brick wall, and hoist themselves up onto the ledge, the street sixty feet below. The entire city is laid out before them, a mass of light divided into three pie pieces by the blackness of the rivers. Everything is lit from below by the streetlights, the buildings shown in stark relief on their sides and dark on their roofs, so that it looks as though someone is shining a dirty yellow flashlight up from below. Packs of students from the university roam up and down Forbes, but up on the roof they are removed from the shouts and laughter, the sounds of traffic and car horns barely touching them. They sit on the ledge awhile, hovering over the glow of yellowed light like gods.

34

The night before we went in, they gathered us in the planning tent around a steel table covered with maps and satellite images and lists of coordinates and frequencies.

They told us this was probably the most hostile village in the entire fucking region. They had found them, they said. They were ninety-nine percent certain. These were the guys who had killed Jacobs. Probably Marin, too. Finally, we had them. They were in this village.

"*Light 'em up,*" *they said. But they didn't know what they were saying.*

They estimated that, after we took the boats up the river, it would take us an hour to hike our way across the plain and over to the rise, two klicks west of the village.

They would be coming in hard, and they wanted to know whether anyone in the village suspected. Observe and report, they said. Radio in anything weird, anything out of the ordinary, they said. And now, in hindsight, I think it's odd that no one questioned it. No one asked how we were supposed to know, after being there for only a few hours, what was weird and out of the ordinary and what wasn't, what was totally normal.

They told us that when the time came, we would go in with the rest.

"*What if we run into contacts?*" *asked Skeets.*

"*Assume hostility,*" *they said.*

"*If we're spotted?*" *I'm not sure, but I think it was Dom who asked this.*

"*Light 'em up,*" *they said.*

It was a phrase we used a lot, and it was said easily, almost casually. But what I think now, what I did not realize at the time, is that for all the people gathered around that table, for all of the planning, and the training, and the money spent on equipment, for all the time that we all spent out there, there wasn't a soul involved who thought about it long enough to know exactly what that meant.

35

"What's that noise?" asks Hakma, and then Jonas hears it, too, the static-click-static of sideband radios, and they rush over to the building's adjacent side, and look over the edge in time to see two men in blue uniforms enter through the same door they did.

"Police," says Jonas, his mind racing. "Just act like you live here." Their plan set, Jonas is surprised to find himself relatively unconcerned as they stand on the roof, waiting, and pleased to find that if he concentrates in just the right way, he can keep the metal door through which the policemen will shortly emerge from drifting out of his field of vision.

"Hi, there, officers," says Hakma, smiling as the policemen come out through the door and onto the roof.

"Hi," says the one in front, a short, balding man who looks to be at least fifty. "What are you doing up here?"

"Oh, just looking at the city," says Jonas.

"Do you live here?"

"Yes, sir."

"Which apartment?"

"Number six, sir."

"Uh-huh. Can I see some identification?"

"Sure."

"Uh-huh. Now, it says here that you live over on Calvert."

"Right. I am actually just here visiting."

"But you said you lived here."

"Well, right, but when you said 'you,' I thought you meant the collective 'you,' not just me. See, you're supposed to designate, if you're talking to a group."

"Uh-huh. And how about you," says the officer, looking hard at Hakma. "And this time, just so there's no confusion, I mean the singular 'you,' as opposed to the collective. Do *you* live here?"

"Well . . ." says Hakma.

Later, as he sits on the cold steel bench in the holding cell at the police station, Jonas will recall how some things seem so clear when you first see them, clouded though your mind may be by fear or alcohol, but when you see them again later, in hindsight, the foolishness of that initial clarity becomes obvious. But the foolishness of what he is about to do is not at all obvious to him at this point. The point at which Hakma is trying to explain his ID situation. The point at which Jonas decides to run.

Too late, he realizes that he has been paying so much attention to the policeman in front of him, the short, bald, out-of-shape-looking man doing all the talking, that he barely notices the policeman behind. In fact, he doesn't really notice him at all until he is trying to run past him, and in one swift motion he kicks Jonas's leg out from under him, and Jonas falls onto the tar-paper roof.

The policeman, who has until now not said a word, bends over Jonas where he has fallen, and finally speaks.

He says, "You're under arrest."

CONFESSION

I

He hears the voice of his savior. It is gentle, and deep, and touched by the lilting music of the Pennsylvania hills.

It is also incoherent. Long strings of muttered words seem to float in the air between them, and Younis has trouble putting them into context.

"Maybe you knew her."

"Knew who?"

"That kid. Was not supposed to go that way."

"Which way?"

"Except that it was."

"Was what?"

"It was designed to happen that way."

The discussion has spun out over the course of an hour, circling and doubling back upon itself, and Younis can find no firm footing in the midst of it. So he sits back and allows the words to dance around him.

"Maybe the south. Maybe the east would have been better. Choppers. We should have used choppers. Skeets was saying that. Should have landed us right there. But the river. First mistake. The goddamned river! Whose Rambo idea was that? Stupid. Poor planning."

The words swirl around him, and at some point, Younis becomes aware that Christopher is looking at him, waiting for a response.

"Do you know what I mean?" says Christopher.

"Sir, I honestly have no idea what you are talking about," says Younis.

Christopher takes a breath. He focuses his attention, and then finally speaks in full and coherent sentences.

"When you do something like what we did, down there in the valley, once you make the decision to do it, it takes on a life of its own. They always tell you that the most important thing is to not make any mistakes. But sometimes, the decision to do it in the first place is the mistake."

Younis doesn't say anything, and turns away from Christopher's stare and looks into the fire.

"Look," says Christopher, pulling the leather journal out of his pack, untying the tie, opening it, and handing it to Younis. "Maybe you should read this."

2

We called her Jezebel, and she was not supposed to be there.

She just appeared. One second there was nothing, just the open field. Then she was there, walking toward us. I hoped that maybe she was a mirage.

We picked that spot, just below the ridge, because it was perfect. It was two kilometers west of the village. It was on a little rise. We came up the river, arrived that morning, and dug our position just as the sky was getting lighter in the dawn. We had our firing sectors laid out, and had everything covered between us and the village.

Then we sat and waited.

Jezebel appeared late in the afternoon.

We had already been ambushed so many times. We had lost three guys. Jacobs had gone down two days before. Some of them wanted payback. We knew they had a house in the village; we knew they used that road. We knew everything we needed to know.

Skeets called her out first. She was about a hundred meters out and wandering in our general direction. How old could she have been? Eight? Younger? Her head was uncovered, and she wore a long white dress that billowed behind her as she walked. In the sun her dark arms and hair stood out against the whiteness. Every few steps, she would stop and look at the ground, and bend down and pick something up, a stone or something, and roll it around in the

179

palm of her hand. Then she would either throw it off to the side, if it didn't meet her mysterious criteria, or she would tuck it into a little cloth bag she wore over her shoulder.

"Vehicles on the road," said Skeets. He was looking through the scope, moving his cheek against the gunstock. "Heading toward us."

We had been briefed. We had been told these were the guys who killed Jacobs. We were reminded of the lack of hard intel, the preciousness of knowledge, the uniqueness of this opportunity. The weight of it pushed down on our shoulders. None of us had slept in thirty-six hours.

And then she was a hundred meters out, directly between us and the village. She bent down again to look at another stone, picked it up, this one meeting her requirements, and she filed it away into her bag. On the road behind her, two white Subarus kicked up the dust.

She was not supposed to be there.

Skeets said, "Gimme the word, sir." His voice sounded strained.

Now she was less than fifty meters from us. She stood up in the field and looked around, off into the distance. I wished she would turn around and walk back to the village. I prayed that I would close my eyes and then open them, and that she would be gone. Instead, she stood for a long time in that no-man's-land between us and the village, as though lost in thought. Then she turned and looked directly at us. She smiled, like she had just glimpsed the exact stone she had been out there looking for that whole time, the one she was looking for, the right size and shape and color, the stone she most wanted in her little canvas sack.

She walked straight toward us.

"Incoming," Skeets said, looking at the road. "We need the order, Chris."

I looked down at him and saw that his trigger hand was shaking, almost imperceptibly, and that he was breathing too fast.

In my mind, I put her odds at about fifty-fifty.

3

Jail is not what Jonas expects. Metal bars do not confine him; food is not some sort of gray slop served on a steel tray. In fact, he's there only for the night, so no food is served at all. He empties his pockets into a wire basket, which is carried nonchalantly away by an obese, uniformed man with a large mole on his cheek. He is allowed to make one phone call before being led into a white room with a heavy door and two long steel benches bolted to opposite walls. Actually, he gathers, it is called a holding cell, which makes it sound almost maternal. The walls are white with dark scuff marks, as though someone wearing black-soled shoes has stutter-stepped across them. Someone has etched the word "smoot" into one wall with a sharp object, the letters sliced thinly into the chipped paint, and a dark splotch stains one corner of the shiny concrete floor. He's just in for the night, he is told again, for his own good, so he can sleep it off. But someone will have to come down and sign him out in the morning.

Other than the steel benches, the room is empty, spinning a little in his vision, filled with only the memory of former residents, the marked-up walls implying carelessness and violence.

"Slow night," says the guard.

For a time he sits on the steel bench and stares at the back of the door. He notices that something is written there, roughly printed at an angle in small, pale letters, written using a blue marker evidently down to its last gasp of ink. Unable to read it from where he is seated, he crosses the room to get a better look. It says, "Jezus died for you're sinz."

Jonas goes back and sits down. The bench is just wide enough to lie down upon, which he does, his head against the hard steel and already starting to ache, and he falls asleep.

4

Rose gathers them together in ones and twos, writing letters and making phone calls, and even, occasionally, despite her unfamiliarity with technology, sending an e-mail. She will act as a facilitator. When they meet her, they will usually be impressed by how big she seems, her personality filling the room, this little woman with the shock of red hair and the booming voice, and the hugs she gives out like Halloween candy.

She is deft in her ability to not allow the conversation

to come around to her own loss. It is not about her, she always says, even though they know that, at least to some degree, it is.

5

He remembers that they came to see him while he was still in the hospital. When they asked him whether he wanted to come to America, he was surprised. He would have to think about it, he said. And he did. He thought about it for days.

He does not remember making the decision. For a moment after he told them yes, he thought that maybe there was a disconnection between his brain and his mouth. He didn't remember actually making the decision, only the act of telling them about it, and he remembers being a little surprised to hear himself saying it. He pictured his mouth making the decision, and the thought made him smile almost imperceptibly, an expression mistaken, at the time, for happiness.

He thinks about it often. Two words, "I'll go," that mark the difference between two paths, two entirely different lives. Words that set in motion a chain of events stretching to fill years. Sometimes he wonders what it would have been like had he said no, as he almost did, balancing on that sharp edge of time in the moment before he opened his mouth, that split second that grows in his mind, stretching as surely as the subsequent events to fill another, different lifetime. Perhaps he'd still be back there, a refugee and not part of a diaspora. Perhaps he'd be dead, left to starve in the street, or left to sell himself, or sell others, or steal and kill.

Or maybe not. Maybe it all would have turned out the same, but by different means. Maybe it all would have happened, the plane ride, the suburban adolescence, the university, Shakri, everything, right up until he was where he found himself right then, as he thought about it, in his present reality, sitting on a steel bench in a jail cell, somewhere in western Pennsylvania.

6

Thursday, October 14 (AP)—U.S. military officials today acknowledged a raid that occurred last week and claimed the lives of two American soldiers. A third U.S. soldier is listed as missing in action. Army spokeswoman Emily C. Walters declined to identify the soldiers pending notification of their families.

One official, who spoke on condition of anonymity, said that the early-morning raid had resulted in the killing of twelve suspected high-level insurgent fighters and the capture of ten others.

Details of the raid were not yet available. Officials estimate that an additional ten to fifteen civilians may also have been killed or injured during the fighting.

The area in which the raid occurred has been described as a lawless border region and a source of consternation to U.S.

military officials because of the insurgents' ability to blend in with the local population and the relative absence of national governing structures.

7

Out of the corner of my eye, I saw her go down. I don't know who shot her. Everybody was popping off like crazy. We were shooting. They were shooting. We were trying to knock out their vehicles before they made it into the village. But we didn't even manage to succeed at that.

I don't know who hit her. I'm pretty sure it was one of ours. Funny thing is, it didn't even look violent. She just fell over. I remember her hair puffed out a little, right before she went down, but that might be my imagination. I don't think I misremember it, though. Not something like that.

It was nothing, really. A blip. At the time. Nothing. For a while, I thought she was going to make it. I thought maybe she had simply had the good sense to get out of the way. It happened so fast. She just fell down. Like she was tired. Like she wanted to take a nap.

8

Like his past, Jonas's future comes to him as a series of images, half dreams that flicker, one to another, as though lit by a strobe. In one, he is married, a hazy female form who may or may not be Shakri, and a child tugs at his pant leg. Then he is walking down a path through the woods, when suddenly he is blocked by a precipitous gorge. Then he is being awarded some kind of prize, or medal, on a podium above a cheering throng. Then he walks down a street in a large city, car horns blaring and a sheen of dirt on his skin. He must cross the canyon, but no obvious method presents itself. He is carried over the heads of the crowd, his name (which name?) chanted as he floats on a tide of hands. A tree has fallen across the gorge, and looks to be a way across. He climbs onto the fallen log and takes a step forward. A wooden ladder appears in the middle of the street, fixed to the ground and stretching so high that he cannot see the top of it, which disappears into clouds above the tall buildings. He is halfway across the fallen tree when he looks down. He grasps the ladder and places his foot on the first rung. Halfway up the ladder he can no longer see the ground. Neither, standing on the fallen tree, can he see the bottom of the chasm. He looks out to see that he is balanced on the rim of a pint glass, beer lapping at its edge like a frothy, golden sea. Vertigo overcomes him, and he cannot take another step. He imagines falling backward into the glass, cleansing himself in it, the pleasant numbing sensation in his limbs and the bubbles tickling his skin. He feels the heady, airy feeling of knowing he could fall, the release of doing so. But although he could do so at any moment, he has not yet fallen. So there he stands, hovering over everything, unable to fall and unable to cross, unable to make the decision to do either.

9

Sometimes Younis wakes on the mountain to a scratching sound. At first, still asleep, he thinks it's a rat clawing at the earth beside his head, searching for morsels. But then, alert, he realizes that it is the sound of pencil on paper. Outside, the wind whistles up the slope past the cave's shallow mouth, and he is surprised he can hear anything above it. But the scratching sound is distinctive, sandpapering his consciousness, dotted by sharp points of punctuation. Younis keeps his eyes closed, listens as the scratching sound fills the cave. Then he opens one eye, just enough to see. Across the fire, Christopher's attention seems entirely occupied by the page before him.

Another time, Younis wakes to a different scratching, this time a longer and sharper sound with a pronounced metallic ring at the end of it, and he looks up to see Christopher hunched next to the fire, a whetstone balanced in one hand, moving his other hand back and forth from the wrist, the long blade of his combat knife flashing occasionally in the flickering light.

Younis notices that when Christopher sharpens his knife, he sits facing him across the fire, the book lying shut next to him on the ground with the pencil tucked inside. But when Christopher writes in his book, everything is reversed. He sits facing away from Younis, the knife either lying on the ground beside him or stuck, hilt up, in the rocky ground.

Younis finds being woken by either of these sounds unnerving. Both actions, the sharpening of the knife and the writing in the book, are obsessive. At one point, Christopher sees that Younis is awake, stops what he is doing, looks over with a half smile, and offers him something to drink, asks about his pain, tells him he has only one dose of morphine remaining.

Younis begins to wonder what is going on. Having arrived, having set up camp, Christopher seems inclined to stay forever. Younis tries to determine how long they have been on the mountain, he drifting in and out of consciousness, Christopher scratching out his defenses. He wonders why Christopher seems so unconcerned about getting back to his unit. He wonders why he has made no effort to get in touch with his comrades. He wonders why Christopher seems not to care whether they ever leave.

And the more he ponders these questions, the less he likes any of the answers he can find.

10

A photograph: Three soldiers stand tall in rising dust that has probably been kicked up by a helicopter's rotor wash. They are covered in Kevlar and strapped with equipment, and they wear dark sunglasses that make them unknowable, showing only their stern mouths. They carry their weapons pointed at the ground, and behind them sits a pile of boxes and large bundles covered by a tightly wrapped tarpaulin. They are waiting for something. Something important, something urgent. They are invincible, human only in the way that robots look human, as if they have been created to look that way, and could easily have been created to look another way if that had suited the purpose of their creator.

Another soldier, a local soldier, sits on a crate in the dust beside them. If the standing soldiers are approximately human, this soldier sitting in the dust is entirely so. He does not wear sunglasses or Kevlar or a stern mouth. He wears a mustache, and his helmet looks to be fifty years old. His face shows clearly under the helmet's broad brim, the bags under his eyes, the wrinkles on his face, and he looks to be wiping from his brow an accumulation of dust and sweat. He seems to be tired. So tired. He seems to just want this whole thing to be over.

II

Rose does not need to raise her voice very much in order to be heard over the murmur of conversation that fills the recreation center. Her distinctive contralto reverberates from the steel folding chairs, the laminated tabletops, the worn Formica tiles, all of it lit from above by hanging fluorescent tubes. She tells those assembled that Pastor McConnell will lead a prayer group later in the afternoon, or that the most recent funding drive has raised a significant amount, or that she has received a letter from Senator So-and-so.

Some of them are already turning gray at their temples, she thinks. Some are losing their hair, like cancer patients. Some are talking continuously, as though trying to expel pent-up emotion in controlled bursts, while others remain mostly silent. A few seem to be totally unaffected.

She will gather them together, first at the church near her home in the Pennsylvania hills, then regionally, renting out moderately sized meeting halls for the occasion, then nationally, in convention centers, as the need for the organization grows in direct proportion to the nation's grief.

She is careful not to talk much about herself at these meetings. If forced, she says only that she has lost her son, biting her lower lip, nodding her head slightly, commiserating fully with someone else she knows has lost at least that much. She feels no need to talk about it, does not want to burden others with her story, but gains strength from their presence, from being connected to them.

Some of the meetings take on an Irish-wake quality, boisterous and laughing back tears. Others are somber. They share in common an underlying stream of activism, of information sharing, of tips about veterans' benefits and job training and education funding, and a subtle segregation between the veterans themselves and those who love them, the former finding one another out and talking in slightly rougher language and at lower registers.

And they also share the events' organizer, a little woman with red hair and a booming voice who calls them together for a moment of silence, or an item of housekeeping, or just to tell them that dinner is being served in the dining hall.

12

He remembers waking up in the firelight. He remembers the dull ache covering the length of his arm. He remembers coughing on woodsmoke. He remembers his legs tingling and numb. He remembers the pain sharpening as he came to. He remembers the figure hunched on the other side of the fire. He remembers hearing one of two noises: the metallic ring of steel on a whetstone, or the rough scratch of pencil on paper. He remembers not knowing which of the two noises he preferred.

13

She was not supposed to be there.

She appeared, gently, across the dusty field. She was not a mirage. We were dug in where we were supposed to be, just like we were supposed to be, two kilometers to the west of the village. But there she was. Poor planning.

Skeets called it out first. "Two hundred meters," he said.

She was rolling a stone around in the palm of her hand. Then she was walking toward us, her long white dress billowing behind her as she walked, reflecting the sun. Then the trucks were on the road, kicking up dust. Then she bent down again and picked up another stone, which she threw off to the side with a laugh.

And then she was a hundred meters out. And then she was fifty. She was not supposed to be there.

I wished she would turn around and walk back to the village, prayed that I would close my eyes and then open them, and that she would be gone. Instead, she smiled and walked straight toward us.

"I need the order, Chris," whispered Skeets.

I saw that his trigger hand was shaking, almost imperceptibly, and that he was breathing too fast, taking in great gulps of air.

It didn't matter, though.

"Light 'em up," I said.

14

"Should we not go?" says Younis again.

But Christopher is not paying attention. He appears unaware that Younis has said anything, or even that he is present. His lips are firmly shut, his eyes squinting in concentration as his hand moves, laboring obsessively.

"Hey!" says Younis.

Christopher looks up, reluctantly, to meet Younis's gaze with blank incomprehension.

"Should we not leave?" Younis says.

"We cannot leave. There is too much to do here."

Younis is amazed by the fact that even while he speaks, even while he is not looking, his hand continues to move, carrying on with its work.

"What, never?" says Younis.

Christopher only continues to stare blankly, and then he winces in unmistakable pain. For a moment, Younis thinks that maybe the question somehow stung him. But then he looks down to see that Christopher has pricked his thumb, and that his pant leg is stained with tiny drops. He quickly grabs some gauze from his pack and wraps it around the thumb.

"Ah, well," he says, once the wound is stanched. "What's a little blood, shed in the common defense?"

15

There is no knock at the door, no buzzer sounding warning; no one asks permission to enter. The holding-cell door simply opens and there is Paul. He wears a rumpled T-shirt underneath a plaid, unbuttoned flannel, and his hair is uncombed.

"You're only the second client I've ever had to visit in jail," he says. "The first one burned down her house. What did you do?"

Jonas sits up and rubs his head. "Nothing," he says, breathing out.

Paul's expression tightens, his lips pursing together, and he turns to leave, saying, "Well, then you can get yourself out."

"No, wait," says Jonas. "I, Hakma, we went into this building up on Fifth, to see the view. They say I was trespassing. Intoxicated publicly. Although we weren't in public, really."

"Where's your friend?"

"I don't know."

"He's not here. But you are, Jonas."

"I tried to run."

Before they are even out of the police station, Paul spells out two conditions that Jonas must meet. They are nonnegotiable if Paul is to continue working with him. If he doesn't oblige, Paul says, he'll wish Jonas all the best and be on his way. The choice is his.

Jonas says that it's all just pointless, that he is unable to comprehend why Paul stands by him. "I'm not worth it," he says. But then, reluctantly, he agrees.

The next evening, Jonas sits to one side of a small circle of people facing one another across a linoleum-floored basement. He knows that he is supposed to say something. He has been listening to them for ten minutes, going around the circle one after another, all saying the same thing. Some of them say it quietly; some share it with voices full of pride, some as though they have just run a great distance.

"Hello, my name is Jonas," he says, and the words come out as they're supposed to, but he thinks it is all ridiculous, stupid. He can barely keep a straight face. He pictures everyone he has ever known laughing at him. It's all so pathetic. But he goes, because he has agreed, and because he knows that several of Paul's other clients are in the group, and that they will tell Paul if he does not.

After the first meeting he says to Paul that it's okay, that he doesn't think he needs to go, tells him he's not that far gone, doesn't really have a problem, tells him it doesn't mean anything to him.

Paul assures Jonas that he does not care.

"It's been one day since my last drink."

"Just keep going," says Paul. "That's the deal."

At the meetings, Jonas always sits in a chair by the door, figuring that from there he can get out quickly if he has to.

16

"Maybe you can tell me what happened the night you left your village," says Paul. "Or maybe you can talk about what happened between then and the time you were found, up in the hills, and taken to the hospital."

Jonas believes himself to be physically incapable of talking about it any further. He feels his stomach clench into a tight ball, his jaw stiffen. There are things Jonas will not talk about. He has developed a skill for deflecting the conversation if it appears to be approaching any of them. He stares at the floor, wishing the moment would go away, vowing to stay silent until it does.

"What else happened, Jonas?"

Almost involuntarily, Jonas tilts his head to the side, as though someone has grabbed the back of his neck and is pinching the muscles together. He feels his face contort slightly, squinting his eye and grimacing his cheek. Once or twice, he opens his mouth to say something, but nothing escapes. The silence drags on, forcing the air from the room.

"What else?" says Paul.

"He saved my life," says Jonas finally, a bare whisper that catches in his throat.

17

Jezebel laid out in that field all day. It was a standoff. Seemed like every person who lived in that village was armed and holed up inside it. They wouldn't come out, so we had to wait for the firepower to go in. And she laid out there in no-man's-land.

She was about forty meters away, and I found that if I set my mind in the right way, I could convince myself that she had simply gotten tired and put her head down for a nap. I could pretend she was going to pop up any minute, awake and refreshed, and laugh her way back home.

I don't know who started calling her Jezebel. We were lying in the dugout, and someone, maybe it was Gordy, nodded his head and whispered, "I'm so tired I could sleep like Jezebel over there." And then someone chuckled. And then we all called her that. She became our mascot. Recon team Jezebel.

Maybe I shouldn't have, but I felt responsible. When the moon came up, I went out to get her. It was this weird crescent moon that seemed to give off more light than it should have. I walked out toward her, and the silver moonlight shone off the rocks and her dress with the same intensity, so that I kept losing sight of her among the field of stones. When I got to her, I bent down to look her over. I couldn't find a wound anywhere. For a second I thought that maybe she really was asleep. Her eyes were closed and she looked peaceful, at rest. Then I saw a tiny, dark dot on her throat. Only when I picked her up I realized there was nothing left to the back of her neck.

I lifted her and carried her as gently as I could back up to our position. The order had come down that we were going to go in, so they were all folding up their kits, hoisting their packs to their shoulders. Turner hacked at the bottom of the shallow dugout with his folding spade to make it deep enough. Probably we shouldn't have, but it felt proper. I stepped down into the pit and placed Jezebel as easily as I could on the floor of it. I put a rock under her head to prop her up a little, but that didn't look very comfortable, so I pulled out my green handkerchief and folded it under her head.

We pushed the dry earth on top of her. Someone whispered that prayer, the one about ashes and dust, because that's all anyone could think of. None of us could remember the whole thing properly, so we mumbled some words to tell her how sorry we were that it had to go the way it did. And then they all filed off, down the ridge, getting ready to go in.

But I stayed there a few minutes, staring at the earth. Something caught my eye in the moonlight, a little flash on the ground, and I bent down and picked up a gray stone with a streak of white quartz in it that reflected the moon.

I still have that stone, here in my pocket. Probably it is not one of the stones Jezebel collected in her little bag that morning, and probably it didn't fall out as we buried her.

But sometimes I pretend that it did.

18

"Maybe we can try something," says Paul. "Something to help you explore this a little more, talk about the rest of it."

They have been sitting for twenty minutes in silence. Jonas feels pinned to his chair like an insect.

"I already have," he says.

"But there's more to it, isn't there?"

Jonas says nothing.

"Isn't there," says Paul again.

"Well, then, maybe you can tell me," says Jonas at last, "because I can't say."

"Okay," says Paul, "if you don't know, maybe you can guess. Sitting here looking at the floor is not going to cut it. Picture yourself up there on the mountain. What's going on? What's there? What do you see? What do you hear? Lots of things might have happened. Maybe you can tell me about those things. Maybe you can tell me what might have happened. Hypothetically."

"I don't know that I can."

"Try."

19

Jonas tells Paul the same thing he told Rose Henderson while he sat in her living room, drinking juice and eating cookies.

A possibility, says Jonas. He says that maybe he left his village. Maybe he was compelled. Maybe he was forced to leave by events upon which he refused to dwell. Maybe he found himself all alone, up on the mountain, huddled in the mouth of the cave his father had told him about months earlier. Maybe he was unable, for a variety of reasons, to decide between living and dying.

And maybe at that moment, Christopher stepped onto the side of the mountain as though descending from a cloud, and built him a fire, and warmed him, and fed him, and stitched him up, and eased his pain. And then, his work done, maybe Christopher stepped back into the void, dissolved back into the air like a thought.

20

Rose runs into them sometimes, usually at a regional meeting, or a national one, because they are spread out across the country. They always seem to already know who she is, and they approach, tentatively, to introduce themselves. I knew

Christopher, they say, and they surround her like a cordon, off to one side of the room, all of them nearly twice her height, and they tell her about her son.

Early on, they tell her, he developed a reputation for being the calm one, the quiet one, the deep one. In the chaos of basic training, the dirty jokes about girls and would-be girl-friends, the rowdy towel-snapping and the occasional fistfights, Christopher always maintained a mellow, almost aloof pres-ence. Even as a noob (a newbie, they explain, as they all were at one time), he seemed to know the score better even than the gunnery sergeant. He suffered the yelling, the physical training, the hazing, with an air of detachment, as though he were watching street theater.

One of them tells her a story, not meant to alarm, he assures her, but this is what Christopher was like.

There was once a mistake made during a live-fire exercise, and a grenade went off much too close to their dugout position, showering them with dirt. In the absolute silence following the explosion, they took a hasty roll call, tallying the living, all present and accounted for, until they came to his name, and there was silence.

"Henderson," they say. "Henderson." They look around.

And when he finally answers, his voice is like the open wind, entirely unconcerned, and possibly even a little annoyed at being compelled to speak. There they were, all freaking out, and then there's this voice.

"Yeah, man," said the voice. "I'm fine." Yeah, man, just like that. And they smile at the memory.

Rose seems happy to meet them, talk to them, seems

touched even by their fumbling efforts to comfort her, and in her desire to not dwell on her own loss, her desire to accommodate them, she refrains from pointing out the irony of hearing from them about the first time, the time when her son came back.

21

Jonas blacks out. He wakes up in a boat, tied to a tree, floating in the shallows of the river, down by the Fourteenth Street bridge. Another time, he wakes up with a shout when a cigarette burns his chest, having fallen from his mouth as he nodded off. He wakes up in someone's living room, the floor covered with people who have not yet woken. He wakes up in front of his television set, his pants bunched around his ankles. He wakes up to a dog licking his face. He wakes up next to nameless girls. He wakes to find himself covered with incomprehensible bruises. He wakes up choking on vomit. He wakes up and has no idea where he is. He wakes up to laughter, still sitting in a booth at the bar, and everyone turned to smile at him, the bright strobe of a camera flash, and it's not until he gets home, stumbles into the bathroom, and looks in the mirror that he realizes that on his face has been drawn the face of a clown.

22

In another photo, a group of soldiers dressed in sand-colored camouflage and weighed down by gear crouch beside a low wall. The sky is overcast, and all of them except one have removed their large, dark sunglasses, which lie strapped on top of their helmets. Behind them, farther down the wall, in the background, a goat stands unconcerned in the dust.

Each of the soldiers looks in a different direction, as though they are each either keeping watch over a different quadrant or have no idea in which direction they should be looking. The soldier in the foreground grips his weapon so tightly that his fingers have turned white at the knuckles. Because they have removed their sunglasses from their faces (all of them except one), their expressions are clearly visible. They look to be on the verge of panic.

23

The sun setting again on the mountain, Younis feels himself caught in a whirlpool.

One moment he fears for his life. He has seen it in Christopher's eyes. He has snapped. He peers from across the fire through a suspicious mask, eyes narrowed to dark slits, glances filled with menace. Younis fears he will not live through the night. He wonders only why it has not been done already.

The next moment he fills with rage. He barely cares whether he lives. For what is his heart now but a hole, what is his life but loss, what is the sum of his entire being but absence? And who is to blame for that?

And the next moment he thinks that maybe they will go their separate ways in peace. After all, one of them saved the other's life. That must count for something. He almost trusts him. They are victims of circumstance, and his own misfortune is theirs shared.

He tries to settle on one interpretation. He searches for an objective reality. He struggles in vain to slow the wheel of conviction spinning uncontrollably in his mind. The more he tries to get a fix on the truth, the more he is dragged in circles, unable to see clearly, unable to stop.

24

At first, Jonas thinks the letter on university stationery is an invitation to another student-faculty function. He opens it expecting to be asked to a reception or a dinner. He is pleased by this, thinks that maybe it's what he needs, a little social interaction with people other than his regular circle. Feeling for some reason that an invitation should be opened properly, rather than simply torn, he goes to the kitchen drawer and, unable to locate a letter opener, pulls out a sharp knife.

Office of the Dean of Students

University of Pittsburgh
1275 Forbes Avenue
Pittsburgh, PA 15601

    We regret to inform you that it has become necessary to place you on academic suspension. You are welcome to apply for readmission to the university following a one-semester absence, during which time you will be required to enroll in remedial classes. Below, you will find information about the remedial classes offered by the university and the procedures for enrolling. Please note that achieving passing grades in these classes is merely a prerequisite for readmission, and they do not in and of themselves convey academic credit.

    If you choose not to enroll in these remedial classes, you will be permanently suspended at the end of the next term. You will then be unable to attend the university for a period of three years, after which time you may reapply, and will be given the same status and consideration as any newly applying student.

    It is also strongly recommended that you seek emotional and/or academic counseling, if you are not doing so already. It has been found that students who are unable to progress satisfactorily with their academic requirements are often affected by underlying personal problems, and that by sorting through these issues it is possible to make a successful return to academic standing. Enclosed please find information about some of the mental health services available, both through the university and in the larger community.

We wish you the best of luck for your continued progress and development. Please do not hesitate to contact our office with any questions you may have concerning this action.

Very best regards,
Roger Mineras
Dean of Students

25

We had orders.

We had orders. We had orders. We had orders. We had orders. We had orders. We had orders. We had orders. We had orders. We had orders.

Those were the guys, they said. Light 'em up.

An order is an order. We could not risk letting them go. I'm sorry it had to go the way it did. I really am. I would change it in an instant if I could. I would go back in time and do it differently. I would ask questions. I would raise objections. I would ask to see the intel. I would pay attention to the nagging sensation in the core of my brain that was trying to tell me that something was wrong. Truly I would.

But we had orders, and they were very clear.
An order is an order.
We had orders.

26

"Hello, my name is Jonas, and I may have a problem. You know. With drinking, I guess."

"Hello, Jonas."

"And, Jonas, how long has it been since you've had a drink?"

"About an hour and a half."

27

In this photo is Christopher, wearing the same uniform, same gun, but he does not wear the dark sunglasses and therefore it is easy to tell that it is him. He looks young. He seems to hold his weapon's weight with difficulty. His body is turned slightly to the right as he walks through the dust, and he looks in the general direction of the camera, but off to the side and down, as though assessing something on the ground to the photographer's right. His expression is determined, but slightly unsure, an expression which strives to betray nothing even as it betrays everything, the expression of a young boy playing poker with grown men.

Behind him, slightly blurred, is a house or mound or hill, some large object, but it is impossible to tell exactly what it is, because it is covered with people sitting, as though in an arena, watching the soldier who has suddenly appeared among them. These people, all of them men, wear beards. Some of them wear tightly wound cloth *lugees* wrapped around their heads, while some of them are bareheaded. To the right side of the picture, in the background, two of these men appear to be talking, whispering. They look to be amused, as though they are quietly making a wager.

28

He has had a recurring thought. A daydream. He tells it to Hakma over drinks.

They have contacted him. He walks down the fluorescent corridor. Travelers rush past him pulling wheeled suitcases or hunched under weighty backpacks. He carries no bag, nothing to hold him up at security, which he has eased through like a leaf floating through rapids. He knows what he is supposed to do. A young woman hurries ahead of him, gripping her child's hand.

"Come on," she says to the unconcerned boy. "They're already boarding."

He steps onto the swift conveyor, adjusting his balance as the belt takes over. He is being pulled along now, set in motion, no longer entirely under his own power.

He doesn't know how they found him, how they knew he was ready.

He finds the bathroom, the one at the far end of the long corridor, the least-used. He waits for everyone to leave, for the bathroom to be empty, a lull. Then he goes over to the trash can, which is stainless steel and set into the wall. He reaches into it, rummages through damp paper towels until his hand strikes something solid, a strap, which he grabs and pulls. It is heavier than he imagined, and he struggles to pull it out of the trash.

He knows what to do.

He hauls it into a stall, locks the door, removes his jacket and shirt, lowers the vest over his shoulders, straps it around his body, heavy as the earth. Then he puts his clothes back on over it.

A voice, commanding and feminine, echoing from the tiled walls, urges him to report unattended baggage. He opens the stall door to see that the bathroom has filled with people, and he is momentarily confused, unable to find the exit. When at last he does, he joins the throng of travelers, of fathers and mothers and aunts and brothers struggling under the weight of luggage and worry, or buoyed by excitement and anticipation, or driven by determined focus, but he feels no connection to any of them, because he is already gone.

29

I thought she might make it. I really did.

I keep replaying it in my mind.

I must have been delusional. I thought something could still happen after the shooting started. I thought there would be a little break, then, a space of time during which she would trip and fall out of the way, or hear her mother calling, or turn around and get out of there at the last moment. She could have bent down to pick up another rock. I don't know, anything. Run light-speed across the field, back to where she came from.

Even now, in my mind, I want to yell at her to get down.

But there was no space of time, no gap. It was instant. I spoke and the guns roared. They continue to roar. I cannot get them out of my head.

She was standing there, curious and vibrant, and then she was a crumpled sack of laundry on the rocks. There was no time for anything, no gust of wind that would blow the bullets off course, no time for angels to descend from the sky and lift her off to safety.

30

Maybe, he tells Paul. Maybe he fled his village, was forced to leave. Maybe he found his way up to the cave his father had told him about. Maybe Christopher saved his life, stitched him up, built him a fire.

But then maybe at some point Christopher started to lose it. Maybe he was crazy. Maybe he thought they needed to move, or realized that they were in the wrong place; maybe he thought they needed to be somewhere else. Maybe he started freaking out because he suddenly realized that he was AWOL on some mountaintop with a wounded hajji.

Maybe Christopher insisted that they pack up, move out. Maybe they rushed to get to the top of some other hill, that hill over there, the one on top of which Christopher suddenly realized they were supposed to be. But maybe, when they got up on top of that one, Christopher realized that it was not the right hill either. Maybe he looked at a map. Maybe this happened a few times. Maybe they were tired. Maybe Christopher started thinking they were supposed to be in a valley, rather than on a mountaintop. That valley over there, and maybe they wandered all over the southern mountains, wandered for days.

Maybe one time it started getting dark while they were out searching around. Maybe the path was difficult, lined with boulders and rocks that were just the right size to trip over, and maybe they were tired. Maybe the trail was narrow, and the mountainside fell away next to it, off into the darkness. Maybe Christopher stepped the wrong way, caught a rock with the side of his boot and tripped, stumbled, fell over the cliff edge. Maybe one instant he was there, and the next he was not. Maybe he dropped without making a sound, silently, like a stone.

31

They tell Rose that he was selfless, that he was always the first to help out. If a noob packed too much gear and struggled over the hills they'd been climbing all morning, it was always Christopher who offered to switch packs with him, carry for him his extra weight. He never seemed to mind cleaning the latrine, or pulling zero-hour guard duty, both of which, he said, gave him time to think. Through anything that came his way, he maintained a Zen-like aura of impregnability. Someone started to call him Yoda, a nickname created in an effort to get to the heart of his calm bearing, and it stuck for a while, but always felt insufficient, cartoony.

One of them, the son of a religious family from Oregon, tells her that he always went to Christopher for advice. His family told him that he should talk only to the chaplain, and he did that sometimes, too, but he always found Christopher to be more real, wise in the same way the chaplain was wise, but street-smart in a way that the chaplain was not.

They tell her they had total confidence in him, both as a soldier and as a person. They tell her he gave them strength. They tell her she could be proud of him, that he was a real credit to her as a mother. They tell her that anyone should be proud beyond words to have had a son like him.

32

He sees two versions of the future. Paul asks him to describe them. One is shadowed, and the other is lit by truth.

"I don't know what to do," says Jonas.

"Do?" says Paul. "You know what you have to do."

"No, I don't."

"Sure you do. You have to start making good choices. You have to establish a track record of positive action."

Jonas looks at the silver statue on Paul's desk, molded into its indescribable shape, like an ellipse, or the melting clocks he once saw in a painting.

"I don't know," says Jonas. "I feel like I'm running out of time."

33

In the foreground, two soldiers, one of them lying prone on the ground, looking down the sight of a sniper rifle supported by a tripod on the earth in front of him. The other soldier crouches beside him, scanning the horizon, a mortar tube slung around his back and the butt of his rifle lodged into his shoulder, ready to come up, ready to be aimed at the slightest provocation. Around them, debris—splinters of wood, stone, mud—covers the damp pavement. In the middle distance stand a series of what may have been houses, the remnants of a wall framing a phantom window the only way to determine what they might have been. And beyond that, in the background, a great mountain range, high and blue in the distance, snowcapped and stunning in its beauty, totally unconcerned by it all.

34

Jonas wakes up and cannot move. He wakes up and sees his dead mother at the foot of his bed. He wakes up floating over the world, totally unconnected and able to see everything, everyone in it. He wakes up and thinks he is dead. He wakes up and wishes he were. He wakes up and then goes back to sleep.

He wakes up wishing that he could be back on the mountain, because at least then he knew the score: Either you lived or you died, and it was all just that simple. He wakes up realizing both that something needs to change, and that he doesn't know how to change it.

Then one day he wakes up knowing deeply in his heart that someday soon he is not going to wake up.

35

The groups Rose helps to organize will grow and change and adapt according to their own needs, in their own time. Friendships will be forged. They will gather at someone's house, or in a bar, or at a football game, huddled before and after around a smoking grill in the parking lot, or at a park on a Saturday afternoon, bringing with them their girlfriends and their wives and their children. They will meet up in pairs or in large groups. They will gather at irregular intervals and in various locations. It will start with a phone call, or a message, or a random meeting on some city street, and they will come together, and they will remember.

In one of these groups, standing loosely around a barbecue, they will remember that the barracks was little more than a cinder-block enclosure with a corrugated metal roof. They will remember that, unbelievably in that godforsaken desert, it was raining when they filed back in, the only rain any of them can remember from the whole tour. Their heads hang down, and they are little more than shadows wrapped in ponchos, which are gradually stripped off and left dripping from nails on the wall, or draped over the ends of steel bunk frames. In silence stark as death, they sit on the edges of their bunks, or on the floor, their legs stretched out in front of them and their backs propped against the wall. Or they just stand, jaws drooping and shoulders slouched.

But this is not quite correct, one of them will say, taking a swig from a bottle of beer, poking at the glowing charcoal. This is not quite the way it was. It was not raining, was it? It rained the day Jacobs got killed. Not only that, but at that time, they did not yet know. It was only the day after they went in, remember, and at that time they hadn't known for sure, thought he might still be out there, hunkered beside a rock somewhere. In fact, one lone voice will say, when they filed into the barracks they were concerned, curious, but optimistic. It was raining, sure thing, but they were not yet in mourning, as they tried to piece together the events, tried to determine where it might all have gone wrong.

36

But we weren't done.

I didn't have time to think much about Jezebel because the second company arrived, and then it was time to go in.

I did not know that we were that capable. We bombed the hell

*out of that place. We had come up the river with great intelligence.
We knew who was there, in the village. They told us they were the
guys who ambushed us, who killed Jacobs.*

*We came up the river, and they told us about the village, about
the bad guys who were in there. The place was crawling with them,
they said. They were all excited about it when they told us. It's a
free-fire zone, they said, so stay aggressive. If you see anyone, odds
are they're muj. We got 'em, they said. They'll never know what
hit 'em, they said. They're there, you know, right where we thought
they'd be. We thought they'd be there and there they were. We
came up the river, which took us most of the night, and then we got
position on them up on this hill. Then there was the standoff all that
afternoon, while we waited for reinforcements.*

We buried the girl in the moonlight, and then we moved out.

*It was all laid out in front of us, the whole thing, just like they
told us it would be. I knew what we could do. Well, I thought I
knew what we could do. Turns out I had never seen them unleashed
like that. They wanted a fight. That river is rough, you know? We
figured that would be the hardest part. But we did it. We got position
on them, up on that rise, all laid out in front of us.*

*I did it. I was on the radio, so it was down to me. I got the sig-
nal, and I started calling ordnance in, and that place just lit up. Just
rained on them. And then we went in, fast. Your heart rate goes up,
and we had to go in hard, but it didn't seem real.*

*Or maybe, when I look back on it now, it seemed so real that
everything else seems fake.*

*A couple of them started shooting back, pretty scattered, but
we lit them up fast. And then we get in, and there's just rubble*

everywhere. By that time, it's just a big debris field, you know. And every once in a while, someone takes a shot at us, but we clear it out quick.

And then we were going down this street, and we came around a corner, and there's . . . It was just broken. Everywhere, rocks and stones and rubble. And over there is a body that just looks like another pile of clothes, and a leg sticking up through the rubble here, but this isn't the worst part. Not by a long shot.

Because I look, and there, in the middle of this, there's . . . in this, I don't know, what used to be a house or something, sitting in between all the stones, there is this little child. He's a toddler. He's holding on to this scrap of blanket or something, and he wasn't even crying. That was the worst part. His face was blank, and he just stared up at us, and there was nothing moving anywhere around him, and he looked right at me. And I remember thinking, as I looked at this kid holding on to a blanket in the middle of that rubble: This is my fault. I did this.

And then they must have regrouped or something, because all of a sudden everything opened up all around us. It was like every man, woman, and child in the place suddenly had a weapon, and they were all aimed at us. I didn't fire another shot, though. I kept my weapon up. Okay, once or twice I shot at a wall around somebody, to scare them, or over their heads.

But the whole time I thought to myself: Fuck this.

That's when I saw the kid. He was older, early teens maybe, and for a long time he just stood there in the street. My first thought when I saw him was, He'd better get himself out of here, or he's done.

And then that's exactly what he did. Just like that. Like I thought it and he did it. He ducked back between two houses, heading east, down toward the river.

And then I thought, Maybe I'd better get myself out of here, too. To my surprise, I followed him.

I just started walking. Made the decision and went down between the same two houses he did. I know it doesn't make sense. None of it makes sense. What if I had followed him down there and a bunch of his friends were there waiting? What if he was sent in there specifically to lure unsuspecting idiots like me back where his brothers could pop them? But that didn't happen.

He was simply trying to get out.

Same as me.

37

The last time he saw his home, he was five thousand feet above it.

Sometimes it comes back to him at a word or a sound. Distantly he hears footfalls and stones clattering. Their muffled voices rise and fall, rise and fall, as he drifts in and out of consciousness, each time their words coming closer and closer before drifting away again in a fog. Something hard pokes him in the ribs.

"Dude's still breathing," someone says.

"Be careful. You never know," says someone else.

He feels a hand on his arm, feels himself being rolled over.

"He's just a kid," says someone. A hand now behind his head, his leg is moved. He is being examined, prodded. The wind whips up the slope, whistling in his ear.

"No way he stitched that up by himself," someone says.

He feels himself lifted from the ground, reaches out with his arm but touches only air. He panics, but it is a distant panic, kept away by the deep haze.

"Whoa, easy there, buddy!" someone says, and then another voice screaming, hard against his head, *"Remain calm. We will help you."*

He tries to clear his vision, and at last resolves the blurry image of two men, one at his head and the other, with his back to him, at his feet. The man at his feet stumbles over something, nearly dropping him onto the rocks, and a distant stab of pain pierces his arm. He hears himself moan.

"Watch it," says a voice. "You're gonna drop him over the edge."

"Easier walk back if I do," says another.

The noise has been there all along, but he becomes aware of it only as it gets louder, through the haze, drowns out the voices, the footfalls, the clattering rocks, the wind. The distant *thump-thump-thump* gets louder and louder until he can feel it, waves of pressure echoing in his head and thudding through his chest, and a violent wind presses down upon every inch of his body.

He feels himself lifted from the world, and then he is a falcon riding high on the thermals, unattached, unhindered, a hundred feet, a thousand feet; he is borne up and away. As the giant bird banks sharply, he is able, for a moment, to bring the earth into focus.

There is the river, rendered tiny and powerless from this odd angle, like a rivulet from an overturned water bucket, and there is the road beside it, and a miniature truck kicking up dust as it careens along in slow motion. He strives to fix his location, struggles to place himself into context, but everything is skewed and unfamiliar.

But when he sees his village, there is no mistaking it. There is the road angling back from the river, and there are the ruins of the caravanserai, where the river road branches apart as it enters the town, and there is the village itself, its streets and houses and fenced-in yards with their orchards. And there is a smoke-blackened house, and there is another, its walls knocked almost casually over, and there is another, still smoldering gently, releasing a single thin tendril of smoke, like a beckoning finger.

And there above it all is Younis, about to pass out again, but conscious for an instant, and aware, and focused, taking it all in, committing the scene to memory, vowing to himself that, if he can recall nothing else, he will always remember this.

38

Monday, November 10 (AP)—The U.S. military has stated that it is investigating a raid conducted last month.

American soldiers apparently believed they were attacking an insurgent hideout in a remote village, and residents of the village claim the Americans killed at least eighteen people. By all accounts, U.S. soldiers arrived before dawn and hit several targets, after an extensive air and artillery barrage.

But beyond that, there appears to be little agreement about what actually happened.

At the first target, the district government offices, they destroyed ammunition, killed four guards, and captured twenty-seven prisoners. But according to some residents, those captured were gunmen loyal to a local politician, plus six people they described as common criminals, pulled out of the local jail. Other residents, however, report that those captured and killed had been inciting violence against international forces for months. While some locals say that the insurgents abandoned the offices weeks ago, others say the building's occupants were heavily involved in insurgent activity.

Another target was a former school building. Armed men were living there, and the U.S. military believes the building had become an insurgent hideout. But once again, locals disagree about who occupied the building. According to some residents and officials, it was actually the headquarters of a local disarmament commission, where officials were collecting weapons from the countryside; others say it was the headquarters of a well-armed insurgent faction.

The morning after the raid, a disarmament commission official says he found vehicles full of bullet holes, gaps blown into the walls, and bodies strewn across three classrooms. Residents say some of the dead men's wrists were bound with plastic handcuffs, evidence that some prisoners were tied up and shot. A U.S. military spokesman disputes this allegation, however, claiming that the prisoners were already dead when soldiers arrived at the location.

At least one source, who spoke on condition of anonymity, reports that the targeted village had been confused with another village some fifty miles away. According to local sources, some families of the dead have already received compensation from the United States—paid in American hundred-dollar bills. It is unclear whether this is true, and, if it is, what criteria were used to distribute this money.

For now, at least, the U.S. military is standing behind its assertion that the government offices and former school building were used by an insurgent operation.

The raid also resulted in the wounding of three U.S. soldiers. The whereabouts of a fourth soldier are still unknown. Several buildings described as private residences were also destroyed, and some inhabitants are still unaccounted for.

Several villagers say the Americans attacked buildings that had become headquarters for two competing political factions. Each faction accuses the other of feeding false information to the U.S. military, tricking the soldiers into destroying its opposition.

Other officials describe the raid not as a conspiracy, but a mistake, suggesting that locals inadvertently gave the American forces flawed intelligence.

Pentagon officials have said thus far that they have received conflicting information about the scope and nature of the operation.

39

I am here by choice. I am ready to accept the consequences of my actions. As I look back, I can see plainly that every choice I have ever made, every action, big or small, was like a single brick in the road leading me here. I will accept responsibility.

I am ready. Tonight I will tell him. He must suspect already. I will tell him, or maybe I will let him read it himself, here, in these pages, where I have laid it out as honestly as I am able. Either way, he should know the truth.

And then everything can either fall apart or hang together, or go whichever way it will.

40

"Hello," he says to the small circle of chairs. "My name is Jonas."

"Hello, Jonas," comes the reply, like a chant. And then a single voice, gentle in the quiet room, says, "And, Jonas, how long has it been since you last had a drink?"

But there is no reply.

The silence stretches on, longer than it seems it should. It grows to encompass the room. Some of those present realize what's going on before others, and they look up. One by one, those gathered in the circle, those whose heads had been bowed as though in thought or prayer, those who had been staring at the walls or the floor, the one or two who held their eyes gently closed, lift their heads to look at the figure sitting in the chair next to the door, his head held in his hands, his body shaking with sobs.

ATONEMENT

I

Occasionally Jonas hears the voice of his savior.
It comes to him when he is unable to turn his thoughts to anything else. The voice he hears is gentle and deep. When he remembers it, he tries to get it right, tries to match the words exactly, but has the familiar feeling that he is adding and subtracting, substituting what should have been said for what he fails to remember accurately.

What should have been said. What he fails to remember.

He is haunted by both.

2

You probably wonder why I want you to read this, why I am telling you all this.

I know who you are. We came to your village, all laid out in the moonlight. We were up on the rise, and then we were like a wave, relentless, effective, crashing down the hill.

I had enough. We snapped. Something snapped. I snapped. And then I followed you here.

I know who you are. I saw you leave. I followed you. I tracked you down the river, watched you turn toward the hills at the balancing rock, chased you up and over the stony slope, looked on as you lost your path and then found it again, lost it and then found it once more.

I watched you. I had to talk to you. I had to explain. I had to make you understand. I had to ask your forgiveness.

And here I lie, prostrate in the dust before you.

Waiting.

3

Jonas wakes in sheets soaked with sweat. He is haunted. He gets out of bed, grabs a T-shirt. He has seen two versions of the future. He gathers together everything he has saved from the packet, every letter, every photocopied photograph, every newspaper clipping, even the envelope itself, labeled in Rose's flowing script in blue ink, labeled "Christopher."

He sees two versions of his future. Then he sees three. Then he sees a thousand, each a slightly distorted reflection of the others, all of them shining back at him like pieces of a shattered mirror.

He goes out into the night. The cold air smells like snow, and his arms prickle in the wind. Picking his path along the cracked cement sidewalk, he makes his way to the park beside the river, next to the railroad bridge on Fourteenth Street.

He has seen himself grown and married, the father of a young child. As he walks to the river, he avoids the cracks in the cement, as though stepping on one of them will open a chasm through which he will fall and be lost. He has seen himself as a criminal, as a murderer, as someone entirely able to rationalize what he has become. He can hear the river before he gets to it, the roar of the rapids out in the middle, seemingly unconnected to the calm, shallow water near the shore. But he knows that a stick or a leaf, floating in the shallows, can be suddenly caught up and taken out and away, into the roaring tempest.

But this is inaccurate. The river is quiet, its flowing volumes of water pouring silent and deep. The yellowed street lamps light his way. To get to the park, he must descend a steep embankment, past a fenced-in cemetery, its standing tombstones pointing toward God. As he struggles near the top of the slope, he trips on a rock, twisting his ankle, and nearly falls over the side, into the river below.

The last time he saw his home, he was five thousand feet above it. He cannot quiet his mind. He has read the Bible he has been given. He has read that God is loving and kind, and then that He is jealous. He has read somewhere else that Jesus died for his sins. He has read that the meek shall inherit the earth, and he does not want any part of it.

The shrill air brings his life to the top of his skin.

He stands with difficulty, takes an agonizing step, his ankle throbbing each time his foot hits the cold ground. He struggles with categories. He can neither place himself into context, nor can he be placed. The usual labels fail. He is a victim. He is a perpetrator. He is a terrorist. He is a refugee. He feels himself placed neatly into boxes. He fights against labels. He is omniscient. He is a criminal.

He has gathered everything together, everything he has, all the physical proof that tells him who he is, who Christopher was, and he takes it all down to the park, next to the bridge, which spans the river pouring dark and wide below. He is a man. He is a boy. He is human. He is an alien.

He wants to burn it, burn everything associated with it, burn his past and send it skyward in a burst of smoke and sparks. He is an arsonist. He is a fireman. He is an archivist. He is a vandal. He has arrived at the park, limping on his twisted ankle, and has placed the sheaf of papers on the ground next to a large boulder before he realizes that he has forgotten to bring any matches.

He is incompetent.

He comes up with another plan. He climbs back up the steep embankment, up to the base of the bridge, climbs the brief stone staircase and grabs hold of the bridge's rusting, cast-iron service ladder. He lives in the buckle of the rust belt. He climbs the ladder and walks out onto a narrow metal catwalk suspended underneath the bridge. He is the product of generations spent in wind and cold. He belongs, secure in his mobile community. He is an outsider. He wonders who has a greater claim to the truth, himself or those who would label him. His darkness is palpable. He skews the demographic.

The rusting catwalk sways under his steps, and he feels each footfall echo through the metal. Maybe he is just like anyone of a certain age. Or maybe he is not. Maybe he is such the product of loss that his soul reeks of it.

He walks on the catwalk out into the middle of the bridge, high over the water. The night is quiet, and he hears the traffic onshore, an airplane passing high overhead, on its way to somewhere else.

He feels the train before he sees it. The rails above him begin to sing with a high-pitched, metallic sound, like the highest note of a chorus of violins, and then he hears what sounds like a hundred flags cracking in the wind, and an engine noise like a broken scooter, and underneath that is a low whistle, like his father calling to the sheep, the whole cacophony getting louder and louder and stretching on until forever. The catwalk jumps and shakes, and the single light on the front of the train's engine lights up the tracks like daytime, so that Jonas can see nothing in the harsh glare. He grips the railing, grips also the packet of papers that tells him who he is. The train passes only feet over his head, shaking the catwalk until his shoes bounce from its surface. He begins to scream, not out of pain or fear or panic, but words, fully formed, screams, enumerates for the world all that has been taken from him, all that he has lost, but finds the words inaudible underneath the roaring train.

And then it is almost instantaneously silent. Subtle noises

return in the wake, the river's gurgle, the traffic on the shore, the distant echo of a tugboat's horn.

Almost as an afterthought, he tosses the sheaf of papers off of the bridge.

As they fly through the air, the pages reflect faintly the meager light from headlights and street lamps onshore. He watches them fly. Many of the pages stick more or less together, forming a relatively solid, plummeting mass, leading the way through the chill air for other individual sheets of paper, which expand, separate from themselves, become a multitude of individual pages, fluttering down, all of them finding their way, eventually, into the pitch-black. They settle silently onto the river's surface, where they remain dimly visible for a time, white sparks floating in the night, until they gradually log with water, and disappear.

4

Someone will buy a round, and someone else will speak up. Remember the river, they will say. Remember how rough it was, the rapids frothy as though a giant blender churned on the riverbed deep below us. Which boat were you in? someone will ask. Oh, that's right, someone else will say, suddenly remembering something he swore at the time he would never forget. And then there was Chris, remember, Henderson in the bow, pointing us through the rapids.

And do you remember that moon, someone will say, that

thin crescent moon slung low in the sky? I have never since seen a moon quite like that one, the way the tiny little sliver of it seemed to light up the whole valley, the whole world, the whole future in front of us, dusted with light.

5

The next morning, Jonas has a plan. He decides that he wants to talk. There is something he knows he must do. His life now revolves around it.

He is suddenly wide-awake, and looks out the window to see that winter has descended like a thick, white duvet. He is out of bed, fighting against the cold of his room. He turns the shower on, hot enough to make him wince, swaying his body under the stream. He is nervous, excited, feels the tension bunch in his stomach and run down his arms to his fingers. He feels himself on the verge of flight.

Outside, he has to concentrate to keep from slipping on the packed snow as his footsteps take him, almost of their own will, to Paul's office.

"All right," says Paul. "Why now?"

"Because there is something I have to do, and it starts with this."

Jonas watches his distorted reflection in Paul's silver statue. He wants to get it out, he says. He has a plan.

But he senses that Paul's energy has subtly changed. He feels it in the room when he arrives. It's nothing overt, at first.

Paul seems a little distracted, that's all. He seems to be marginally less interested in hearing what Jonas has to say, and Jonas assumes that it is because he is thinking about something else.

Nevertheless, Jonas carries on, tells him about the night he left his village, tells him about fleeing into the mountains, about finding the cave, about losing consciousness in the cold and wind, about meeting Christopher there, about how Christopher stitched him up, fed him, built him a fire.

But still he feels that something has changed. Paul wants to hear, he says, wants to know what happened, and still thinks Jonas needs to tell it.

"Then what's the problem?" asks Jonas.

"I'm concerned," says Paul. "I'm concerned about what happened. I'm worried it might be something I have to report. But I'm not sure. I have no experience with this. I have no idea what the law says about this."

Jonas has never seen Paul unable to find his words, or act awkward or ill at ease, and he finds the sight of it troubling.

"Look," says Paul, "let me make a phone call, okay? It shouldn't take too long. I just want to be sure I'm not going to get you into trouble."

And so Jonas is left alone in Paul's office, left alone to contemplate the enigmatic statue on the desk, left to watch his distorted reflection play across its surface.

Paul comes back into the office after a few minutes, but it is Jonas who speaks.

"I've been thinking," says Jonas. "I trust you. This has to come out. You have convinced me of that. This is going to consume me. I don't need a shrink to tell me that." He glances again at the statue on Paul's desk, and thinks to himself that this will probably be the last time he sees it.

"Yes," says Paul, "but as I told you, I am obligated. It's a legal thing. It's not my choice. It may seem arbitrary, I know."

"But what could happen?"

"In reality, I don't know, for sure. Maybe nothing. Maybe they would just come and talk to you. Maybe they would issue a warrant for your arrest. It's hard to tell. They've been taking this stuff pretty seriously lately."

"But it is your choice *when* you tell them, right?"

"Sorry?"

"You don't have to report it today, right?"

"I don't think there is a time . . . I don't know."

"You could give me a few days. You could fill out the form, file the report or make the phone call, or do whatever it is that you have to do, and if anyone ever asks, you could tell them that you did it as soon as you were able. You could do that, right?"

Paul tugs absently at the hair in his goatee, and lets out a long sigh.

"I could," he says at last. "Look, nobody is forcing you."

"I know," says Jonas. "That's why I'm going to do it."

"This makes no sense."

"Don't you see? It's the same thing. You'll be helping me. Forcing me to go. Helping me to do something difficult. Just like Christopher helped me."

"Christopher helped you. You mean when he saved you?"

"No, at the end. When he helped me do it. He knew. He

helped me do it. He knew what would happen, what had to happen. He set it up to happen. He knew."

"He knew what?"

"He knew who I was. He tracked me up there. He set it up to happen."

"Set up what, Jonas?"

"He had to know what I would do. He had to. He just had to."

6

Younis has been lying with his eyes open for hours, lying at the edge of the cave, the dying fire flickering shadows against the rock wall. He has been listening, waiting for Christopher's breath to calm, regularize into the pattern of sleep. He knows now what will happen, what has to happen. He will be purposeful about it. Deliberate. It will be fast. He will grant him that. Speed will be the only good in it.

He knows where the knife will be, honed and hard and cold, its hilt protruding from the rocky soil. He has measured, in his mind, the distance. He is convinced that even Christopher understands what must happen. For has he not told him what to do? Has he not placed the knife in the ground each night, each night slightly farther away from himself and slightly closer to Younis? Does he merely imagine it?

He listens for the breath, the gentle rhythm, the peace. He vows that he will not even wake him. Silently he makes this

promise to both of them. He will be swift, precise. The decision has already been made. There will be no pain, no struggle. Just peace. His own desires are no longer a consideration.
What will happen is what must happen, what is fated to happen. What has been decided.

Afterward, he will roll his body gently off the cliff. He will
scatter some earth after him. He will say a few words, low and
heartfelt, about loss, about God, about how sorry he is that it
had to be this way.

Then he will sit down on a rock and read the book, cover
to cover. He will linger over some passages, and skim through
others. He will place the book gently under a rock at the back
of the cave, confident that he is the only one in the world who
knows where it is.

But for now, he is being pulled along, set in motion, his own
will no longer figuring into it. He listens again for the breath,
calculates his position.

And then—does he imagine it?—Christopher opens his
eyes.

For a moment they see each other, a blink, and Younis hesitates. Within a moment they meet. Younis realizes what he is
about, feels the weight of a moment that will stretch, in his
mind, into an eternity.

And then his eyes are closed.

And then he is motion.

He pops into the air like a gazelle, a blur, silent, focused,
springing to his feet and across the rocky precipice in a single
action, and the knife is exactly where he knew it would be, and
it is in his hand, unsheathed from the earth.

He sees himself as though from the outside, detached, as though it is someone else doing it. And from this place, this disembodied vantage, he sees himself, now a flash, darting across the open space, now merging with the figure prone on the ground, now springing up to stand over him, taut and ready.

And he is surprised by how easy it is, how quiet, how neatly the knife's sharp edge slits his sleeping throat, how simple, like a stone plopping into water.

BENEDICTION

I

One year the group rents out the Carlisle Auditorium in Pittsburgh. The next, they are booked into the Bethel Park Recreation Center. The following year they are given an anonymous donation, which allows them to rent out a portion of the convention center. The group calling itself Military Families for Truth grows, changes, adapts. Other groups take root, sprout up in other parts of the country. The fertile soil of the Southeast, Florida, Georgia, the Carolinas, others in the rocks and scrub of Arizona, Utah, still others under the Northwest rain.

Rose leads a delegation to Capitol Hill, to talk with the representatives in Congress. A member from Michigan introduces himself. He has heard of Rose, and asks her to speak with his colleagues. Loss has come to his state, he tells her, and who is Rose if not loss's spokesperson?

She develops bureaucratic skill. She familiarizes herself with grant applications and donor forums and aid requests. She learns how to advocate for or against legislation, how to submit requests under the Freedom of Information Act, learns who makes the decisions at particular government agencies, and how to most effectively apply pressure to them.

The groups grow, change, merge. Local groups combine into regional groups, which then become national collectives. An umbrella organization is formed, called the Associated Families of Veterans, and Rose is elected its first president.

And yet, despite her tireless efforts, the meticulous attention to detail, it is so often the role of chance or luck that brings her any form of comfort, any sense of closure. An e-mail message, which she now sends and receives proficiently, arrives one day as though from a cloud, or a chance encounter at a meeting or conference, someone who seeks her out, happens across her path.

So it is that Rose finds herself walking across the cavernous expanse of yet another convention center, this one in Denver or Chicago or Albuquerque, her great plume of red hair now streaked liberally with white, walking quickly, purposefully, because she is late to be somewhere else and the place is so big that it takes forever to get anywhere. She sees him from the corner of her eye, peripherally, before she hears his voice.

"Excuse me," he says, and she does not want to be rude, does not want to appear uninterested, but she is late and the appointment is important and . . .

"Excuse me," says the man again, and now Rose sees no way out. She turns to look at him, make contact with him.

"Are you Rose Henderson?" he says as he approaches.

Rose tilts her head back to look up at him. He is balding, his hair cut short in an attempt to cover the fact. He looks to be approaching middle age. He has powerfully built shoulders and arms, but is developing a paunch around his middle.

"I am," says Rose, concentrating on him, now that she has been stopped, giving him her full attention.

"I thought so," says the man. "I've seen your picture. You don't know me, but I served with Christopher."

"Oh," says Rose. "I see. Well, let's . . . let's step over here."

2

Jonas walks down the fluorescent corridor. Travelers rush past him pulling wheeled suitcases or hunched under weighty backpacks. The small sack he carries over his shoulder has floated through security with ease, and his stuffed duffel lies, perhaps already, in the hold of the plane. Despite this, he is convinced that the policemen have been looking at him, regarding him closely. He does not know what Paul has said, whom he has contacted, or even whether, in fact, he has said anything, but he is convinced that it is only a matter of time. A young woman hurries ahead of him, gripping her child's hand.

"Come on," says the woman to the unconcerned boy. "They're already boarding."

He steps onto the swift conveyor, adjusting his balance as the belt takes over. He is being pulled along now, set in motion, no longer entirely under his own power.

He finds the bathroom at the far end of the corridor, conveniently located just across from the gate. Inside, past the row of sinks, the faucets of which are hooked to motion sensors and seem to flow randomly, as though ghosts are washing their hands, he spots the trash can, stainless steel and set into the wall. He pauses, has a thought. He waits for everyone to leave, for the bathroom to empty, a lull, and then he walks over to the trash can. He reaches into it, rummages around.

There is nothing, no nylon straps, no vest, just a trash bag half-filled with damp paper towels. A man walks in and looks at him askance, looks at him with his arm stuck shoulder-deep into the rubbish bin, and he feels foolish. It all comes down to this, he thinks. A choice. The difference between two realities, each of them real, balanced on a knife edge in time.

A voice, commanding and feminine, announces his flight over the public address system, echoing from the tiled walls. The bathroom has filled with people, and he is momentarily confused, unable to find the exit. When at last he does, he joins the throng of travelers, of fathers and mothers and aunts and brothers struggling under the weight of luggage and worry, or buoyed by excitement and anticipation, or driven by determined focus.

When he gets to the gate, he finds that his flight has been delayed. There is some sort of last-minute equipment problem. The irritated crowd, which had just been preparing to board the plane, lets out a collective breath. With nothing else to do, he finds a seat in the waiting area and watches as the passengers huddle around the gate, waiting in the limbo of the airline terminal for time to restart.

He decides he will conduct an experiment. A clean-cut young Indian man wearing a starched dress shirt, the sleeves rolled up to the elbows, gestures urgently as he converses with a disengaged airline representative behind the counter. Jonas was told about it, this experiment, something a monk he once met did whenever he was in public. An overweight couple arrives pushing an overweight toddler in a fragile-looking stroller. Jonas calms his breath, concentrating on nothing more than inhaling and exhaling. He will look each person he encounters in the eyes. To each of them, to every person who meets his gaze, he will wish peace. A tall, thin, elderly gentleman wearing a cowboy hat leans over toward a gray-haired woman who barely comes to his chest, their heads nearly touching, their arms entwined, as they converse in hushed tones. He watches them all as they mill about, or rush to the snack bar to get something to drink, or stare at their laptop screens.

He is unhurried, the swirl of activity surrounding him but not touching him. A dark-skinned gentleman wearing a tan fedora arrives late, carrying a leather briefcase, and approaches the counter, confident, as though it is him for whom everyone has assembled. Jonas regards them inclusively, looking at each as they stand or pass by, male, female, young, old, infirm, healthy, offering to each his attention. Jonas spots a girl about his age, tall, with dark hair and graceful legs, and he stops for a moment, because he thinks that she looks striking and familiar.

Many of them don't see him, are too busy or preoccupied. Some of them see that he is looking at them and look away, at the floor, or at something that has become suddenly interesting. Some of them look up at him and smile.

Mostly, it is the elderly and the children who notice.

3

Through the brightly lit corridors they move, and the cavernous meeting halls, and the convention centers, the high school gymnasiums, the temples, synagogues, and churches. They bustle about or sit and talk among themselves, the wives and children and parents and classmates and friends and girlfriends and comrades. They ask questions, and they provide answers. They mill about, or they rush frenetically. They talk about both the future and the past, starting their conversations with, "What we will do . . ." and "I remember when . . ."

At one of these places, at one of these times, two of them stand temporarily still, apart from the movement and energy around them, and they talk, allowing it all to pass them by, like a river roaring over the rocks.

He is telling Rose about her son, about the strength he drew from him, about how much he meant, about the comfort of his presence, about the last time he was seen alive.

"I remember when," he is saying. "I remember when we were on that rise above the village, before we went in. I looked up, and he was on the hill right there above me. I had just transferred in. It was my first time in combat. The other guys, they were itching for a fight. There was a lot of talk. Talk about payback, revenge. They had lost some guys before I got there. I tried to sympathize, talk a good game, but really I was just scared out of my wits.

"And there he was up above me on the rise, looking out at the valley, at that village in front of us in the moonlight. He was quiet, calm. I think he was always like that. He turned around to look at me. They were all getting themselves angry, worked up. But not him. He didn't think that way. My face must have been so white it shone like that moon. He must have noticed, because he looked down at me with the calm look he had, the one that told you everything was going to be okay, and he patted me on the helmet, smiled a little, like he was resigned to something. It was just one of those moments, one of those things that pass by at the time and you barely even notice it, but then you remember it for the rest of your life.

"That's what I want to tell you. That's why I came here. I remember when I looked at him up on that hill, and the moon was low in the sky behind him, and he reached down and patted me on the helmet, and he nodded at me. And then the radio squawked through our earpieces, and the order came down, and just that fast he was up and over the rise.

"Just that fast. A silhouette, and then he was gone."

RECESSIONAL

I

He changes his name on the airplane. Somewhere over a distant sea, he resumes his old identity. He prints his name—Y-O-U-N-I-S—in the spaces demarcated on the landing card he has been given. In his mind, the landing card increases in significance, becomes something more, a part of the trail of evidence. All this paper, he thinks. All these little ways of telling him who he is.

He goes back. This is the point. As he has done obsessively the entire trip, he shoves his hand into his pants pocket to make sure he still has the scrap of paper, now creased and torn, with Rose's address printed neatly on one side.

And then he imagines himself descending from the bright airplane and into a dry, desert wind that envelops him like a wave. The peaks of the far southern mountains are jagged saw teeth in the distance. Everything is returned to the way it was.

Someone will be there to greet him, a cousin, because his father was unable to make the trip, suddenly called away on some pressing business. But someone will be sent, someone who is happy to see him, and they will drive in a battered white truck up into the hills. They will drive beside the river, the raging torrent in the middle seemingly unconnected to the calm shallows at the edge, but he will know that this is an illusion, that in fact the shallows and the torrent are one.

Despite its inner turmoil, even the river will be happy to see him there, returned.

He will find everything the same. He will see things that are familiar, comforting. The colors, for example, will feel familiar, the red ochre rocks of the foothills, the bleached walls of the houses lining the road. He will be reminded of things he forgot he ever knew. The smells in particular will trigger lucid memories. He will recognize faces, see old friends, be returned to his former self, play in the courtyard with his sister, gratefully receive his mother's tea. He will traverse the upturned sod, wander the low pastures with the flock and the dogs. All that which maintains a hold upon him will lose its grip.

Somewhere over a distant sea he realizes that this is all a fantasy. He will not be greeted by his family. He will recognize little. Perhaps nothing will feel familiar. He will step once again into the unknown.

And so, in the end, he does not change his name. The plane has begun its descent, and the attendants wander the aisles. A bell dings. He feels the sinking sensation in his stomach. He makes a decision. He knows it will cause trouble, but he does it anyway. He glances again at the landing card, at the name printed in black ink, printed in his own handwriting.

And then he tears it up.

2

The parcel arrives unexpectedly in the spring.

It's the first truly warm day of the year, the young leaves and buds only just emerging from the long winter. Rose works in her backyard, spading a hole in the ground large enough to accommodate the sapling that leans on burlap-wrapped roots against the stone wall. Rose thinks that perhaps she is being overly optimistic, planting an oak at her age. She pulls off her gloves and smoothes her graying hair away from her face. Her breath is quickened by her labor, and the earth under her spade looks wounded. She looks around at the new spring leaves' fresh pastels. She hears the mail truck rattle to a halt out front. Reluctant to stop working, she hesitates before she leans the spade against the wall next to the waiting tree, and goes to get the mail.

The parcel is wrapped in brown paper and plastered with green-and-blue stamps and exotic writing. It feels dense and heavy in her hands, the thick paper wrapper crisp and new. Curious, she takes the package inside, sits down at the kitchen table, and begins to remove the wrapping.

She recognizes it instantly.

The book's leather cover is heavily worn at the edges, scuffed and scratched, creased at the spine, and a thin leather tie holds it closed, tied in a precise knot.

It looks, she thinks, like it has been through a war.

Her hand trembles a little as she gently tugs at the knot and opens the front cover. There, beside the compass rose inscribed on the frontispiece, is a brief dedication written in her own flowing script:

> For Chris,
>> On your eighteenth birthday.
>> Because your words are important.
>
>
>> Love,
>> Mom

Rose sits at the kitchen table, her head in her hand, the book open before her. The thin spring sunlight filters in through the window. In the backyard, a young tree leans against an old stone wall, ready to heal the wounded earth. The season is young, the fragile new foliage painting the world pastel. Rose turns the page, begins to read, and is free.

Acknowledgments

The creation of this book has removed any notion I might have held of its being a solo endeavor. I am grateful to so many.

I owe tremendous debts of gratitude to both the world's greatest agent, Henry Dunow, for recognizing what this story could be in its better form, for his unfailing advocacy, and for his willingness to take a chance, and to the world's greatest editor, Sarah Hochman, for her confidence, enthusiasm, and nearly perfect editorial guidance. Tremendous thanks go as well to everyone else at Blue Rider Press and Penguin who have made this book what it is: David Rosenthal, Aileen Boyle, Kate Guadagnino, and Jaya Miceli. Never has an author felt in better hands.

Before there was a book, there was manuscript, and an author thereof, both of which benefited tremendously from merely being in the presence of Bret Anthony Johnston, Amy Hempel, Nick Montemorano, Rachel Pastan, and Brian Morton.

ACKNOWLEDGMENTS

Like many teachers, Judith Vollmer probably had no idea what kind of impact she was making at the time she was making it, but I count her among the reasons I never stopped writing. I am particularly grateful for another of those reasons, my family: Paul Dau, Susan Reed, Michelle Dupuis, and Matthew Dau, for whom the simple fact that I wanted to do something was always reason enough to support it unconditionally, and to my father-in-law, Dr. Zackariya-Marikar, who routinely seems to make anything possible. Special thanks go as well to Tod Goldberg, for offering solid advice, both practical and metaphysical; to my talented and generous Bennington classmates, for their encouragement, enthusiasm, support, and for repeatedly reminding me what can be done with words; and, of course, to Jon Lyons.

And I am always grateful to my daughter, Seraphina, for giving me everything in the world to smile about, and for forgiving Papa the hours spent away, and to my wife, Claudia, who asked me, right after we met, what I wanted to do with my life. I told her that I had wanted to write since I was eight years old, and she said simply, "Then do it." She has not wavered once.

IRAQ:

THE COST OF WAR

IRAQ:
THE COST OF WAR

Jeremy Greenstock

WILLIAM HEINEMANN: LONDON

1 3 5 7 9 10 8 6 4 2

William Heinemann
20 Vauxhall Bridge Road
London SW1V 2SA

William Heinemann is part of the Penguin Random House group of companies
whose addresses can be found at global.penguinrandomhouse.com.

Penguin
Random House
UK

First published by William Heinemann in 2016

www.penguin.co.uk

A CIP catalogue record for this book is available from the British Library.

ISBN 9781785151255 (Hardback)
ISBN 9781785151262 (Trade paperback)

Printed and bound by Great Britain by Clays Ltd, St Ives PLC

Penguin Random House is committed to a sustainable future
for our business, our readers and our planet. This book is made
from Forest Stewardship Council® certified paper.

MIX
Paper from
responsible sources
FSC
www.fsc.org FSC® C018179

For Anne,
who suspected long before I did that Saddam had no WMD

Contents

Foreword

In 2005 I wrote and submitted for publication a book about my involvement, as UK Ambassador to the United Nations and later as UK Special Envoy for Iraq, in the lead-up to the Iraq invasion of March 2003 and in the aftermath on the ground in Baghdad.

In July of that year, Jack Straw, then Secretary of State for Foreign and Commonwealth Affairs, asked me to delay publication until the Ministers involved had left office. He also expressed unhappiness with the concept of Government servants publishing comment on their official work. I therefore withdrew the text from the publishers and cancelled my contract with them. When the Chilcot Inquiry was set up in 2009, I decided to wait until the Inquiry reported before reconsidering publication. Now that the Report is in the public domain, I feel it is a more appropriate moment to re-present my account. While the Iraq story will never be anything but controversial, I hope the passage of time makes my decision to publish less problematic. I offer my apologies to those who disagree.

My main objective in writing this first-hand account had originally been to contribute to the history of the most significant foreign policy issue of the early years of the new millennium, and to attempt some wider lessons for policy-makers in the field of crisis-intervention. The subsequent inquiries in the United States and the United Kingdom, together with a number of books about the Iraq invasion and its aftermath, have largely performed this second function. But the British perspective of what happened behind the scenes at the UN in the lead-up to the invasion and in Baghdad during the Coalition period has not been presented in narrative form. I believe there is still room for a story to be told that sets in a live context the decisions taken and the mistakes committed, and perhaps makes more intelligible the swirl of conflicting considerations that weighed on political leaders at the time.

For this reason I have kept the original text of the 2005 book almost entirely unchanged. Some references to events and personalities have been clarified, to assist memories with the passing of time, and a few passages have been abbreviated where the detail has become unnecessary. But I have resisted the temptation to make any alterations with the benefit of hindsight.

The only new element is the Epilogue, written in the summer of 2016, which tries to summarise the impact of the Iraq saga on the countries involved in it, on the conduct of foreign policy since that time, and on the perception of military intervention as a foreign policy instrument. The second decade of the twenty-first century has brought us a world of much greater openness, equality and complexity, where the attempts of the more powerful nations to exercise their influence have begun to meet strong resistance both from lesser nations and from international public opinion. The use of hard power without an accompanying position of international legitimacy or persuasive justification has become much more difficult, even when a dictator's defiance of the UN security Council's ressolutions presents an argument for action.

The Iraq intervention probably accelerated this trend. It shows the limits of a superpower's freedom of action without severe cost if it fails to gather broad international support. It also underlines the unwisdom of ignoring the force of the precepts set out in the Charter of the United Nations. At the time it seemed that the UN had been gravely damaged by its failure to deal either with Saddam Hussein's contraventions of its resolutions or with the insistence of the United

States, backed by the UK, on the unilateral use of force. But the UN's organs and representatives turned out to have called the situation more accurately than those nations that prioritised their own sovereign prerogative. This truth has not prevented a continuing slide in international affairs towards increasingly subjective and nationalistic decision-making by nation states; and the leading role of the UN in establishing international justice and legitimacy still requires greater promotion and protection. But the strength of the Iraq story as a cautionary tale will continue to stand out as the history of the new millennium evolves.

This book is not an academic treatment of the Iraq story, nor does it qualify as historical research of the subject. I have written my account of things as I saw them, without consulting others who worked much closer to the decision-making centre. It is offered as one individual's view of events for historians to make use of as they see fit, and for readers to gain a more intimate, and I hope understandable, picture of the workings of the UN, of the intricacies of foreign policy decision-making and of the operations of the extraordinary entity set up to govern Iraq after the invasion.

It is also offered with an element of apology to the people of Iraq. The US and the UK helped them to escape the brutality of Saddam Hussein's rule, but failed to ensure that what followed shaped a better life for them and their country. We underestimated the resources required to create a new political structure for Iraq and we miscalculated the steps to a secure and coherent condition for the country. Iraqis too have made mistakes, as any nation will in developing a new system for itself. But the Coalition could have provided them with a better starting-point than the one they inherited on 30 June 2004. I shall follow their future progress with interest and affection, and trust that the next generation will manage to evolve a society of far higher quality than the one that Saddam had produced for them by March 2003.

London, September 2016

Introduction

The story of Iraq is the story of the application of American power. For reach and for superiority above all imaginable adversaries there has never been a power like it. It can deliver destruction anywhere on earth within hours and no combination of other nations or alliances can defeat it. Year by year the military and technological gap between the United States and the rest of the world is growing.

Yet all human power is finite. What happens when power fails to deliver? Iraq is an unfinished story, but its travails have already become a symptom of the limits of power, conventionally defined. The way in which Iraq was chosen as the focus of war and change, and the manner in which it was administered after the 2003 conflict, point to some fundamental realities about the world and its workings which will affect us all if they are not understood in the handling of future problems. That does not just mean that the United States made some significant mistakes. It also means that others have to understand and respect the responsibility they have ceded to the United States to keep the world safe.

The United States likes to have friends, but it also likes to have independent control. Washington has an experience of directing massive power which others can only imagine, and US administrations require decisions on the use of that power to be taken only by Americans. They have an acute sense of duty in serving no one but

1

the American people, whose collective attachment to freedom and individual rights tolerates no interference. Europeans can understand that even if they are frustrated by it.

With globalisation, however, the wheel has turned. The New World is invading the Old as American interests become pervasively global. An overpopulated, under-nourished and culturally divided world, living under a fragile sky, will not always respond to the force of arms or dollars. Iraq may be seen by future generations as a turning-point in US interaction with the rest of the world, because a policy which promised security and justice failed to deliver either. It is as if the two great attributes of the single superpower – protector of freedom and projector of power – are running at cross purposes. Whether this turns out to be an aberration or a trend, we need to know what happened and to see if lessons can be learnt.

As the UK's Ambassador at the United Nations and then Special Envoy in Baghdad, I observed parts of the Iraq saga from close up. I sympathised with the reasons for confronting Saddam Hussein and was as deceived as almost everyone else at the time by his apparent capability in weapons of mass destruction. But I was unconvinced that force had to be used on the March 2003 timing, and disappointed and frustrated by the handling of the post-conflict administration.

These feelings came to a head on the day I left Iraq after seven months of direct involvement with the US-led Coalition's administration of the country. The journey to Baghdad airport is short but scary. Once you have left the artificial safety of the American protected zone on the Tigris's north bank, weaving through the chicane of concrete barriers at the exit point, you rumble over narrow bridges and down a highway where the undergrowth presses in and offers plenty of scope for an ambush. I used to count the minutes to the entrance to the airport security perimeter. My sense of relief that day as the RAF HS 125 spiralled up off the runway and soared out over the Western Desert was very marked. But with it came an equally strong regret at leaving behind a job half done, colleagues in the thick of it and an experience with the people of Iraq as intensive as any in my diplomatic career.

Much has been written, authoritatively and well, about the origins of the decision to use force against Saddam Hussein. But so far no Briton closely involved has offered a version of events. This account does not seek to collate or reinterpret the experiences and perspectives of others. And it cannot draw on the minutes of restricted political and diplomatic exchanges, because they belong to the State. It is a personal attempt to present relevant detail of some significant events and to make sense of some of the more perplexing twists and turns of the story.

What I saw and heard suggests that Iraq took pride of place after 9/11 more because a long-standing desire to remove Saddam became achievable than because security logic made action essential; that the UN negotiations never rose above the level of awkward diversion for the US administration; that the rationales presented for the use of force were exaggerated and inconsistent; that the invasion was a military triumph but failed to achieve international legitimacy; and that the opportunity inherent in the post-conflict administration of Iraq to make the whole initiative broadly acceptable to the watching world was missed through poor policy analysis and inflexible execution.

Iraq dominated the politics of the UN Security Council during my time as the UK's Permanent Representative in New York from July 1998 to July 2003. A huge amount of other work passed across our desks in that period, on Africa in particular, on the Middle East Peace Process most uncomfortably, on the Balkans and East Timor, the International Criminal Court and human rights. But in a committee of high international politics of that kind the most divisive business sets the tone and Iraq was the issue that split the Permanent Members down the middle.

Decisions at the UN in 2002 and 2003 had their roots in the aftermath of the first Gulf War and the confrontation with Saddam in late 1998, but the main political antagonisms lay along a broader fault line than just Iraq. They stemmed from the differing perspectives of the United States and continental Europe on global security and the application of power, with most non-Western countries much more hostile to the US view than to the European one. As Robert Kagan has succinctly described in his essay 'Of Paradise and Power', the United States is inclined to use military and economic power because it has it; whereas the Europeans, who do not, want the use of power to be constrained within inviolable international norms. Each camp advocates a different set of rules accordingly. In practice, when the issue is large enough, the single-minded strength of the former wins over the disparate and half-formed philosophy of the latter – to the extent, that is, that physical power is applicable. Iraq is interesting because it offers clues to the limits of traditional power and illustrates the difficulty of fusing power and legitimacy when the highest stakes are being played for.

Other ingredients became added to this mix: international terrorism, Israel's security, the denial of justice to the Palestinian people, the security of an oil-producing region, the inevitability of the abuse one day of a weapon of mass destruction, and a whole collection of cultural and political rivalries in the world. They produced a cauldron of the most explosive issues. The United States had every right to look to its own capabilities if there was no effective alternative, but not to ignore the legitimate interests of others. While its disdain for the United Nations was overdone, it was also understandable, because from its beginnings the UN has never been able to cope with the most uncivilised or the most determined forms of international disorder. If we are to have an ordered world, US power has to be part of the solution. So does UN collectivism, if US power is to be accepted within a universal framework. One without the other is bound to be insufficient.

I tested that proposition to its limits in the weeks leading up to the decision to attack Iraq on 19 March 2003. The impatience of the United States to deal once and for all with Saddam Hussein was rising, but no one else at the UN, including the United Kingdom, wanted the UN mechanisms for containing Iraq, which had been largely successful over the previous twelve years, to be abandoned at that precise moment. Iraq had defied the United Nations for more than a decade and nobody, least of all his neighbours, had a good word to say for Saddam Hussein. Yet a clear majority of UN members saw little immediate threat to international peace and security and were opposed to the use there and then of brute force to deal with him. The UN Security Council had already lived through the drama of collapsed diplomacy and the bombing of Iraq in late 1998 and failed to see what direct force had achieved. They were just as sceptical in 2003, and even more suspicious of American motives.

This increased suspicion was partly associated with the world's experience up to that point of the administration of President George W. Bush. The early months of 2001 had seen some nervous questions raised in UN corridors: about the handling of the Palestine issue; about the willingness of Washington to contribute to multilateral initiatives, for instance on climate change and the International Criminal Court; about the effect on disarmament if the Anti-Ballistic Missile Treaty were abrogated; about the best way to respond to international terrorism; about the commitment to finance and support the UN itself, when the vexed question of US funding of the UN had only just been resolved by the Clinton administration.

The destruction of the Twin Towers on 11 September 2001 put an immediate halt to all that apprehensive muttering. The pall of dust that hung over a traumatised Manhattan in the following days seemed to alter global sentiment completely. A wave of understanding manifested itself in unanimous support for resolutions condemning the perpetrators and empowering the US and its allies to take forceful action to deal with them. The belief quickly took hold that this was more than just one of those times when differences had to be set aside to express decent human sympathy. It looked like a fresh opportunity to construct a global coalition, with the US on board, against both the forces of violence and the underlying reasons for their emergence.

Our American partners at the United Nations sensed this change of mood and realised its potential. John Negroponte, who had been kept waiting in the wings by the Senate's confirmation processes, was immediately approved for dispatch to New York as US Ambassador, where he capitalised instantly on the responsive momentum he found there. Uninitiated as he was in the curious ways of the United Nations, he soon recognised an atmosphere that seemed to contradict all those warnings in his Washington briefings about the infertility of UN soil for US initiatives. I worked closely with this shrewd and open-minded American diplomat in the months that followed to broaden the scope of international support for British and American policy in the wake of 9/11. We both failed over Iraq.

Well before the election of the new President in November 2000, dealing with Iraq had emerged as a major Republican objective. Amongst the small but capable group of foreign policy planners and thinkers around the Bush campaign, Saddam Hussein was seen as an unresolved challenge to the superpower's interests, a threat to Israel, a supporter of Palestinian terrorism and a possible source of a direct attack on American interests. 9/11 catapulted change in Iraq from wishful thinking into the realm of the achievable. Writers with sources inside the Bush administration have shown, with some credibility, how quickly after the attacks Iraq surfaced as a leading potential target rather than al Qaida or Afghanistan. That was because it was already there, under the surface but set on a loaded spring.

By March 2002, when the realisation began to filter through to New York that an attack on Iraq was a genuine possibility and not just axis-of-evil rhetoric, military planning was well advanced in the Pentagon. Unknown to me at that point, there had already been high-level US–UK discussions about policy options. These exchanges, as they progressed through the summer of 2002, helped to persuade the US President that the UN route was necessary for the construction of an alliance. This was due not so much to the persuasive arguments of Tony Blair and his team – good arguments powerfully expressed by foreign allies are normally not enough to turn an American administration from its preferred course – as to the reality that the UK held the key to wider international support and would not come on board without a basis in international law. Once Colin Powell had won the internal argument, with which I believe the President was instinctively sympathetic, that US unilateralism was bad policy in practice, the multilateral route was given a try.

The effort was less than wholehearted. The US handling of the UN route came across to many observers as an artificial test, not a genuine attempt to find a better way. Powerful voices within the administration pushed for military preparation and derided the capability of the UN. Secretary Powell won time through his skilful negotiation of Security Council Resolution 1441 in November 2002 and the UN inspectors returned to Iraq with President Bush's challenge goading them on to find the missing evidence of weapons of mass destruction. They laboured under repeated accusations, partly true, that Saddam was outwitting them with his techniques of prevarication and concealment. The British Prime Minister pleaded for more time to allow the peaceful route to show its full potential, but Washington saw things differently: the evidence indicated that Iraq possessed WMD; Saddam's uncooperativeness had already been condemned by the UN; to ignore the possibility of an Iraqi link with terrorism after 9/11 might open the door to an even more lethal attack; Saddam was defying the inspectors and the UN system as a whole; US public opinion was likely to support a tough approach. Conclusion: the inspectors would not solve the WMD problem, Saddam remained a danger, war was justified both legally and politically, and it would be a catastrophic error to remain inactive and discover later that the clock could not be turned back.

The UK made one last attempt to avoid war. The only way to do that, as we saw it, was to unite the international community in exerting enough pressure on Saddam to compel him quickly to concede everything the UN had demanded of him. After President

Bush had come to the UN in September 2002, there had been no doubt in my mind that a new resolution was necessary to set a last test for Saddam. The 1991 resolutions had validity in strictly legal terms, but something fresh and clear was needed to convince people that hard action was justified. Suspicion of US motives was rife and the atmosphere in New York had become increasingly tense. I warned London in October that if a new resolution was impossible to secure and the UK wanted to go ahead with military force nonetheless, I would not find it possible to stay in my job in New York. Once Resolution 1441 of November 2002 had been unanimously adopted, the legal situation looked more secure.

I was partly responsible for the idea of a second resolution. It was interpreted by most international observers as an attempt to capitalise on the more threatening articles of 1441 and get the Security Council to authorise the use of force against Saddam Hussein, but the intention was not that crude. The United Kingdom, though committed to fight alongside the United States if military force was to be used, tried to find an instrument for dealing with Saddam and his WMD that would avoid full-scale military action. I was personally convinced that the Iraqi regime was a threat to international order. I believed the thrust of the intelligence about WMD and regularly spoke up in public to warn people of it. But I was deeply uneasy about the start of a conflict which, in the unanimous view of my New York colleagues, was bound to be messy. The second resolution was designed to offer the Security Council an alternative way forward, to deliver clarity and to keep the initiative in US–UK hands.

The negotiations involved a convoluted combination of pressing for support, playing for time and looking for escape routes. Until quite late in the day, I believed that they had a chance of producing an effective alternative: mounting such pressure on Saddam that he would give up without a fight. But, between American apprehension about loss of momentum and French reluctance to be caught rubber-stamping the use of force, the necessary pressure was never generated and diplomacy came to a grinding halt. On 17 March 2003 I walked in front of the microphone outside the UN Security Council in New York and, on instructions from London, announced to a massed and overheated crowd of journalists that the attempt to address the Iraq problem through diplomacy had been terminated and that the United Kingdom reserved the right to consider another way forward. Ambassador John Negroponte, following close behind me, left no doubt as to what that meant for the United States.

It was a bitter moment. After a prolonged, highly charged confrontation over Iraq among members of the Security Council and between world leaders, I was asked to step forward and acknowledge that conflict had beaten diplomacy into second place. Personally, I was not ready to give up the fight. I did not accept that war on this timing was the only option and I dreaded seeing the UK involved in direct responsibility for the state of Iraq, but the American steamroller was engaged in top gear. Saddam Hussein had shown his contempt for the UN and I was fed up with the infighting between the Permanent Members of the Security Council. The acerbity of the differences between the main players was illustrated by the inclusion, on instructions, in my 17 March statement of a sideswipe at the French – 'one country in particular has blocked the way forward' – which was partly deserved but ungracious. The Security Council as a whole was left exhausted and bewildered by the refusal of the United States to allow more time for the weapons inspection process. In the end, however, when the single superpower decides to launch itself forwards, the rest have to stand aside and await events. I picked myself up from the turmoil and wrapped up what business I could, on Africa in particular, in my final months before retirement in July 2003.

There then occurred one of those ironies in life which ought to have been predictable for its perverse intrusion, but which came as a shock nevertheless. I was asked to postpone my departure from Government service and go out to Iraq as the UK Representative. It was Alastair Campbell, the Prime Minister's Communications

Adviser, privately visiting New York in early June 2003 but carrying a message from 10 Downing Street, who first posed the question. I said I had other plans and declined. Two weeks later, the Prime Minister came on the line in person and explained why he wanted me to play the particular role he envisaged. There are times when you do not say no. I agreed to go to Iraq, but for a set period until the end of March 2004, a deadline I had promised my family.

The later part of this book tells some of the story of those months in Baghdad, supporting but often wrestling with Ambassador Paul Bremer and his machine, and skirmishing in the dark, usually without effect, with the veiled authorities in Washington who micro-managed policy on the ground. As in the rest of my account, I cannot provide a comprehensive history of the occupation period. Mine is a partial and subjective view, offered in public because I believe that the Iraq saga is an issue of generational significance. The full story must be reconstructed from a number of perspectives, none of them all-seeing.

The period of Coalition administration in Iraq also deserves study, because success in delivering a better Iraq could have washed out all the controversy of the decision to go to war. Most people in the end accept practical results. The early post-conflict period in Iraq was marked by decisions that were often brave, dynamic and well-intentioned, but sometimes fundamentally flawed. Even the single superpower has to reckon up the expense of less than rigorous analysis and planning. America's righteous indignation collected a massive show of support from the international community in the weeks following 9/11. But, as this account describes, there was a steady progression from sympathy to rejection in the world's reaction to US decision-making. This matters more to long-term US interests than many Americans like to think. The logical disconnect in putting Iraq at the top of the list has carried a cost which Washington has been reluctant to acknowledge. The mistakes made in the implementation of policy resulted in part from the strength of American anger, justified in its origin but misconceived in its application. The costs of war have to include its aftermath, because acceptance of the need for war is linked to a judgement that war has eventually brought about a better state of affairs. In the case of Iraq in 2003, the post-war costs were never planned for or calculated with the same rigour as the war itself.

The team working under Paul Bremer in Baghdad never developed the strength and capacity to deal with the circumstances that evolved. He himself led from the front, learnt some of the lessons of the early American failures and struggled with his own administration to assert the prime importance of judging action by its effect on the ground. He was not always listened to in Washington and was sometimes unjustly loaded with the blame for others' misjudgements. But he could be narrow and over-authoritative and he never made full use of the wisdom he had at his fingertips in the Republican Palace. The capability of the players in the team who possessed Arab world experience and Arabic language skills was rarely exploited, while excessive reliance was placed on young Americans with the right political credentials and excellent academic training, but no experience or understanding of the nature of Iraq.

Bremer and I grew close to a number of senior Iraqis who offered themselves as representatives of their people for this awkward period, but we were a world's distance from many others who had an equal stake in the future of the country but who could not or would not organise themselves to forge a relationship with the powers of temporary occupation. We tried, with considerable success at odd moments, to analyse, forestall and cut down the forces of violence arrayed against us. And we set in place a structure for the political transition of Iraq to a new and freer state, which has stood the test of Iraqi opinion and, so far, of time. But we did not capture the imagination and the hearts of most Iraqis. The security situation became the principal stumbling block and the reasons for that are relevant to our defence against insurgent violence and international terrorism within a much broader context. The lessons from Iraq therefore have a direct application to the interests of a wide range of countries, by no means all of them members of the Coalition that occupied Iraq.

The structure and practice of international diplomacy will have to adjust to the experience of Iraq. What the United States decides to do lies at the heart of almost every international question. Each individual member of the UN wants its own direct and positive relationship with the US. But, collectively, the organised groups of developing states are not persuaded. They rail against US foreign policy choices and vilify what they see as the untouchable arrogance of the single superpower. I was left by the Iraq saga with some sympathy for both points of view, but convinced that the gap between them has to be bridged if the twenty-first century is to witness greater stability than the twentieth. Will the nations of the developing world come to understand that they can benefit from US-inspired freedom and economic dynamism without losing their cultural identity? Is the United States likely to learn from the agonies of this stormy period, and will the experience of the 11 September 2001 attacks and their aftermath bring the American people to understand the limits of hard power? Working with, and sometimes inside, the American machine, I came right up against the extraordinary mix of US strength, generosity, self-righteousness, impatience and blindness. As an ally but a foreigner, I was both invited in and closed out. It was an exhilarating and exasperating experience. Much of the non-American world must feel the same, with exasperation exceeding exhilaration the further you are in spirit from Washington.

If the United States under George W. Bush was the star around which satellite activity in the multilateral field orbited, where has the Iraq explosion left the United Nations? What is this body which so many slickly turn to when they feel outgunned in their capitals, and how has it come to represent the aspirations of such a large proportion of the planet's population when its faults are so familiar and its powerlessness so often exposed? I became an ardent devotee of the UN during my time there, but witnessed its fallibilities from close up. Some things the UN has done well: the restoration of its operational effectiveness after the catastrophes of Somalia, Rwanda and Srebrenica; the success of its work on East Timor; the regeneration of professional competence in the Security Council's peacekeeping decisions on Africa; the increasingly effective response of the development agencies to the millennium call for a new effort on poverty. But these achievements were set into relief, if not dispatched into the shadows, by the dramatic disagreements over Iraq, the collapse of the Middle East Peace Process, the failure to find the funds to match the ambition of development programmes and the weaknesses in executive action and accountability exposed by the investigation into the handling of the Oil for Food programme. As a result, the UN looks weaker and the world seems more polarised, and potentially more violent, than when this saga began.

Part One

1

Generational Change in the Middle East

In my diplomatic career, which included postings in the British Embassy in Washington in the mid-1970s and the mid-1990s, I learnt that there are two areas above all that the United States guards jealously as its own preserves: superpower politics and the Middle East Peace Process. For one reason or another, I constantly found myself butting in on both.

My diplomatic career began and ended in the Middle East, but the middle part was dominated by the great historical event of our age, the collapse of the Soviet Union and the emergence of the United States as the single superpower. Two superpowers presented a choice of champion, fraught with the risk of catastrophic destruction if things went wrong but allowing space for countries on the fringes of this stand-off to play one off against the other and to carve out a niche around and between the poles. The inherent imbalance of a single superpower structure has been obscured, at least from the UK perspective, by the focus since 1990 on the ordering of a free Europe and on the problems and opportunities of globalisation. But it is becoming clear, and not only through the assertions of the President of the French Republic, that the world will not settle down around a single pole. The evidence is mounting that a second superpower is taking shape, in the form of anti-Americanism. If a counter-balance to American power does not develop in a politically structured way from the emergence of a compelling new strength in China, India or any of the other large developing nations, with Russia finding a new role on one side or the other as it sees fit, it could arise from the much more chaotic, asymmetric elements of clashing cultures, failed states and terrorist violence, with or without the horrifying admix of uncontrolled weapons of mass destruction.

The global reach of British interests and its position for the time being as the world's fourth largest economy keep the UK involved in virtually all aspects of geopolitics. The fun of being a British diplomat on the global stage lies in close involvement with the great events of the age without having to bear the ultimate responsibility. The UK's past experience, administrative efficiency and talent for pragmatic analysis earn us a place at the table, but we have long since lost the skills and the resources for projecting real power in great campaigns. If we want to be part of the action, we have to serve with those who have built and retained those assets. It is not just for historical and cultural reasons that we have tended to stay close to the United States.

It was in the Middle East that I cut my diplomatic teeth. My first arrival in the region, a posting in the late summer of 1970 to learn Arabic in Lebanon, coincided with Black September, the suppression by King Hussein of a Palestinian uprising in Jordan. The Palestine Liberation Organization command, together with a large number of Palestinian refugees, moved on to Lebanon to set up 'a state within a state', changing for ever the fragile balance of communities and political forces in that country and laying the foundation for the Lebanese civil war later in that decade. As language students living two thousand feet up the mountain above Beirut, even we could not fail to be aware of the planting of these seeds of strife.

Shortly after our arrival in Lebanon I had the first of many minor car collisions. I was rather taken aback when the other driver leapt from his car and dragged me into a ditch on the side of the road. Four days in foreign territory, I thought, and I was going to have my throat cut for denting a radiator. Then I became aware of the sound of gunfire and the occasional bullet pinging off the rocks around us. It turned out that my imagined assassin was trying to save me from injury: he explained that the death of Gamal Abdul Nasser – President of Egypt, father of pan-Arabism and nemesis of the British and French in the Suez Crisis of 1956 – had just been announced and the people of Lebanon were declaring their grief in time-honoured style by firing their guns into the air.

Learning a language within the region brings the huge advantage of absorption in the local culture. The villagers of Shemlan, for whom the Foreign Office's language school, the Middle East Centre for Arab Studies (MECAS), provided a major economic asset, guarded us conscientiously. Not only were they ready to see off any physical threat, drawing on the massive stash of weapons hidden behind the blacksmith's shop, they also happily participated in the elementary exchanges of greetings and polite enquiries that got the beginner going in Arabic conversation. As mountain people, they were tough, kind and old-fashioned. It was only when we sped down the hill into the lively city of Beirut that we discovered how the French–Arab culture had created new vernacular impulses that could leave even the brightest students floundering.

Our early lessons in local politics were full of Maronite, Orthodox, Druze, Islamic and other distinctions and we expected to come up against these divisions within the Lebanese system, but on arrival at MECAS we learnt that our student community was itself divided into two bitter camps. A long-running spell of the board game Diplomacy had ended in betrayal and acrimony that extended into everyday relationships. They say that the British abroad go to greater lengths than any other nationality to absorb the culture and mannerisms of the local people. I dropped straight into strong supporting evidence of that.

We took our language-learning very seriously, at least during the morning lessons. But Lebanon, Syria and Jordan were there to be explored, with mountains, sea and desert so close together that the sports and pleasures of each could be experienced within a single day.

After eighteen months, our feel and affection for the Arab world, its history and its traditions were running deep, even if we had learnt little of the practical arts of diplomacy. I never spoke Arabic as well again as when I took the final MECAS examination. My next posting took me to Dubai, where a mix of English and Urdu could see you through most situations. Even when I served later in Saudi Arabia as head of the Embassy's Export Promotion section, English was the lingua franca of the merchant class. When I finally returned to a real need for fluency in Arabic, in my wholly unexpected move to Baghdad in my sixty-first year, the rust had bedded in too deep and I could never manage a full business conversation in the language. Nonetheless, those early days at MECAS and my acquaintance with the hard desert culture in the Emirates and in Saudi Arabia left me full of admiration for this remarkable part of the world.

This experience, with natural personal variations, was multiplied through the UK's Diplomatic Service. We Arabists referred to ourselves affectionately as the Camel Corps. Others used the phrase with more suspicion or contempt. The diplomatic world recognised in the British and, for similar historical and professional reasons, in the French an inherited and empirical familiarity with the Middle East region that no other foreigners possessed. Captain William Shakespear would have stood at the side of King Abdul Aziz through the whole creation of the Kingdom of Saudi Arabia had he not been killed in a desert skirmish in 1915. Gertrude Bell, adviser to the British High Comissioner in Iraq, was instrumental in the choice of King Feisal of Iraq in the early 1920s and worked with T. E. Lawrence to bring some form of colonial order to that impossibly fractious territory. My wife's grandfather, William Ashford Hodges, worked as the Egyptian Government's chief architect in the early years of the twentieth century. Colonel Hugh Boustead provided close advice to Sheikh Zayed of Abu Dhabi in the formative years of his transition from local chieftain to internationally recognised President. There are still British advisers at the Court of Sultan Qaboos of Oman.

When I moved on from Lebanon to Dubai in 1972, it was very few years since British diplomats Martin Buckmaster and Julian Walker had placed the territorial markers of the Trucial States in place, creating the internal boundaries for what is now the United Arab Emirates. In my first formal job in a British Embassy, and without an hour of legal training in my background, I became the last Assistant Judge of the Trucial States Court. From genuine pioneer to lowly desk officer, generations of Britons have breathed in the history and the dust of the region. Throughout the Arab world the British were admired, resented, accepted and suspected in equal measure. The Lebanese referred to the language school in Shemlan as the Spy School, since George Blake had passed through its doors, and they claimed they could hear the sound of gunfire up on the roof – in reality not agents practising their marksmanship but the noise of the ball hitting the tin in our echoing squash court. Above all, we are remembered as the progenitors of the Balfour Declaration of 1917, which set the terms for the establishment of the Jewish State in what was then the mandated territory of Palestine.

Successive British Governments have thus acquired a close interest in, and a sharp conscience about, the politics of the Middle East. They see themselves as balanced between the competing demands and arguments of the Israeli and Palestinian peoples. They pay close attention to Israel's right to a secure existence and to her claim to be heard as a democratic partner from a democracy-starved region. But history, relationships, national economic and energy interests make their weight felt on the Arab side as well. The UK is involved across the board, though no longer as a leading power-player. Together with the French, whose government's sympathy for the Palestinians creates a compensating nuance to ours for the Israelis, we constantly annoy the other members of the European Union with our more-knowledgeable-than-thou attitude to Middle East policy discussions. What effect we have on American administrations, whose distaste for our colonial past runs like a red streak through Suez and beyond, is another story. We will come to it in due course.

I remember the feeling of excitement in 1982, when the UK held the Presidency of the European Community for six months and I was working in London on a Middle East desk, when Lord Carrington led the Europeans into the gestation and birth of the European Community's Venice Declaration on the situation in the Middle East. This carefully crafted document, produced without the full approval of the United States, won admiration in many quarters for its balance between the protagonists and for its foreshadowing of the possibility of a Palestinian state. Was this the Holy Grail? Would it mean that I could be a participant in the solution of the Arab–Israel problem? The answer was, predictably, no. The Europeans on their own might develop the ideas, but we could not exert the influence or the power of delivery to see concept through to final result. The Israelis and therefore the Americans – or perhaps it was the other way round: we could never quite make up our minds about this – were not ready for the kind of compromise on territory for peace foreshadowed in UN Security Council Resolution 242 of 1967, which still sets the basis for every negotiation on the peace process in terms of the exchange of territory for peace. The Oslo and Madrid Agreements of the early 1990s, this time with fuller American participation, again raised expectations; and perhaps the Camp David negotiations in 2000 under President Clinton came as close as any detailed set of prescriptions to closing the gap between the two sides. But the antipathies remained – and remain – too strong. The dashing of hope after Camp David led to the extreme bitterness of the second Palestinian intifada, set alight after Ariel Sharon's visit to the Temple Mount in East Jerusalem in September 2000, and the violence has trumped the diplomacy ever since.

The story of Iraq has to be told against the backdrop of the Palestine dispute. The two issues are separate in their political contexts and the Middle East Peace Process has always deserved high-grade attention whatever else is going on in the region, but they are linked in two ways. First, no intervention by the United States in the Middle East was ever going to be accepted by the Arab people unless the central issue governing Arab interaction with the outside world benefited as a consequence. Second, the people of Iraq, whose record of Arab nationalism in the twentieth century is as strong as anyone's, were likely to feel hostile to an American presence on their own soil if the United States was not seen to be contributing to an improvement in the Palestine situation at the same time. Tony Blair saw this clearly and continues to feel it strongly. He argued it out with President Bush on several occasions, not least at their seminal meeting in Crawford, Texas, in April 2002. The President's disinclination to act in practice on a point he accepted in theory was one of the most telling disappointments for the British side in this period. The rest of the UK's foreign-policy-oriented community, in Government, Parliament, the media and the Establishment, felt this keenly. It became one of the criteria by which the Prime Minister's performance on Iraq was judged, as the returns for the UK for its loyal support of the US came to look increasingly thin.

Tony Blair's attempt to keep up the effort on the Middle East Peace Process was not confined to the objective of minimising controversy over Iraq. His policy flowed naturally enough from the legacy of previous British Governments and from the history of the UK's involvement in the Middle East. In the view of most experienced observers of the region, of many objective policy thinkers in the Arab world and of the top experts in international development at the UN, the Middle East is falling behind many other parts of the world in its response to globalisation and in the promotion of its human resources. The Arab–Israel stalemate is part symptom and part cause of this. Arab Governments, it seems, will not devote their full attention to political, social and economic development while the Palestine issue remains as a distraction; and the very difficulty of promoting development sometimes appears to make that distraction welcome.

There were moments when change in Iraq was presented as a potential catalyst for wider change in the Middle East. I never saw evidence of a simple equation in the minds of policy-makers in

London or Washington between an improvement in Iraq and a solution to the Israel–Palestine dispute. The road to Baghdad did not run through Palestine, nor did the road to Arab–Israel peace run through Baghdad. But I recognised, and sympathised with, a line of thought that started with the release of the full talents of the Iraqi people in a freer political system and went on to the spread of reform and opportunity in the wider region, perhaps touching Iran, Pakistan and Afghanistan as well as Egypt, Saudi Arabia and other parts of the Arab world. I never believed that such changes would be achievable through the application of hard power and the insertion of resources from outside. Nor did I think that democracy on the Western model would catch hold in the Middle East. The choices and decisions of the peoples of the region themselves had to be the compelling factor. But as we started to address the task of reconstructing Iraq, I thought that the removal of Saddam Hussein might stimulate a recasting of the mould. For that to happen the Iraqi people would have to have a say in the nature of their government and Iraq's political structure would need to be stable and sustainable. Whether that meant democracy as the top priority remained to be seen. But I felt sure that the outcome in Iraq was bound to exert a broader influence on the region.

2

Iraq Turns Sour

Because of the agonies that Iraq has caused the world in the early years of the twenty-first century, the debate continues over George Bush Senior's decision to end the 1991 Gulf War when he did. Should he not have saved us all the trouble by finishing off Saddam Hussein there and then?

In March 1991 the Iraqi regular army was pulverised. The elite Republican Guard might have defended Baghdad with spirit for a while, but something close to the 2003 outcome was more likely. The terms of the UN's authorisation of military action to reverse the occupation of Kuwait did not extend to the full overthrow of the Iraqi regime and the legality of such a course would have been severely questioned internationally, but the political justification for either could nevertheless have been constructed by the United States, because Saddam Hussein had so blatantly crossed the line by annexing Kuwait. Trampling on a fellow member's sovereignty is the worst sin in the UN book. In my judgement, the outcry would have been containable. In 2003, by contrast, the strict legal case under the corpus of UN resolutions could be made, but the political foundation for the occupation of Iraq was, for the vast majority of international onlookers, unconvincing.

Why then did George H. W. Bush hold back in 1991? The evidence suggests that it was for solid reasons. There was no explicit UN authority for the military overthrow of the Iraqi Government. The war had not been planned that way. The Coalition allies were manifestly reluctant. Above all, the United States was not prepared for the burden of administering the state of Iraq as an occupying power. The planned objective had been achieved and the world's sympathy maintained. It was a pragmatic decision at the time, which the UK Government supported. I played no part in Middle East or UN policy in that period, having taken up a job in London as policy director for the UK's political relationships with Western and Southern Europe, but I remember feeling heartily relieved that the Gulf War stopped when it did.

On 3 April 1991, within a largely willing and supportive Security Council in New York, the harshest sanctions ever imposed on a UN Member State were adopted against Iraq in Resolution 687, until the day when full reparations for the damage done to Kuwait had been paid and all Iraqi weapons of mass destruction had been accounted for. The Security Council resolutions underlying all this (Resolutions 678, 687, 688 and 707 – adopted between November 1990 and August 1991) allowed time for the payment of reparations, but expected WMD eradication to be achieved in weeks or months. Separately, the US, the UK and France proclaimed No-Fly Zones above the 33rd and below the 36th parallels to keep the Iraqi Air Force out of the northern and southern reaches of the country. They calculated that this combination of harsh measures would bring down the Iraqi dictator.

Not for the last time, the analysis in Western capitals proved faulty. During the conflict, the US military and intelligence agencies had renewed contact with Shiite and Kurdish groups within Iraq, as well as with Iraqi external opposition parties, and led them to understand that an uprising against Saddam Hussein would receive the active support of the United States. There was clearly a misunderstanding of what 'support' might mean. Immediately after

Iraq's surrender on 3 March 1991, the Kurds in the north and the Shia in the south initiated a series of urban rebellions, but the United States made no move to help them materially. Perhaps the administration in Washington calculated that Saddam in his weakened state would not be able to contain a general insurrection and his removal might be achieved without incurring a further cost in American lives, resources and political responsibility. If so, they were wrong. Saddam met the threat with an efficiency and a ruthlessness that exceeded even his own previous standards. The challenge seemed to shake him out of the despair of his defeat. The Shiite rebellion in the south was bloodily suppressed by Ali Hassan al-Majid (Chemical Ali), the brutal governor of Kuwait during Iraq's occupation period; and the Kurds were driven into the northern mountains after dozens of towns and villages in southern Kurdistan had been razed to the ground. Hundreds of thousands of Iraqis were killed or imprisoned. The Southern Marshes, the hiding place for large numbers of insurgents, were drained and in the process a unique local civilisation was ruined for ever.

Saddam Hussein must have learnt something from these two US decisions of the spring of 1991, not to finish him off and not to put substantial reinforcements into the insurrection. He could not match American and allied power on the battlefield, but he could survive if his will was stronger. The lesson was learnt on the American side as well, although not until two Presidents later.

It took a few weeks for the weapons inspectors established by Resolution 687 to form themselves into a team and get down to work inside Iraq. Governments using the UN to accomplish their policy aims always tend to overestimate the speed with which results will hit the scorecard. An action team from the International Atomic Energy Authority (IAEA), formed to examine Iraq's nuclear programme, began their preparations on the ground in May. Iraq's chemical and biological weapons programmes were to be investigated by a separate new group, UN Special Commission, UNSCOM for short. It was led in the early years by Rolf Ekeus, a Swedish diplomat with a cool head and extensive disarmament experience. A unit of several hundred UNSCOM weapons experts arrived in June. Their full work programme, however, was not approved by the Security Council until 17 June and by the time the inspectors were ready to start intrusive investigations, the political and psychological circumstances had begun to change. Saddam Hussein had regained confidence in his ability to survive and was determined to make the job of the inspectors as difficult as possible.

For a full understanding of the diplomacy on Iraq in the decade after the Gulf War, it helps to look at some of the detail of Resolution 687. The full text is set out in Appendix A. In layman's language, it required Iraq to surrender or demonstrate the complete destruction of any material relevant to the production or use of a nuclear, chemical or biological weapon; to confine the development of ballistic missiles to a range of no more than 150 kilometres; to allow UN access to all documents and other evidence of WMD programmes; and to foreswear, in legislative terms in line with international treaties, any continuation of or return to such programmes in the future. Iraq's conventional military forces were not to be disbanded or inspected, but Iraq was forbidden from importing, and UN Member States from exporting to it, any military equipment whatever. Crucially for later legal arguments, the resolution made the ceasefire that brought the 1991 military action to an end dependent for its continuing validity on Iraq's full acceptance and implementation of these conditions.

On 6 April Saddam Hussein conceded that Iraq had no alternative but to accept the conditions for the inspection of its unconventional weapons programmes, but when the inspectors arrived in June they soon realised that Saddam was not prepared to respect them in practice. Their experience in the first few months on the ground was peppered with instances of Iraq's 'full, final and complete declarations' needing to be revised when proscribed weapons, almost entirely chemical at this stage, started to be discovered.

While it was assumed during the 1991 Gulf War that Iraq had the capacity to use chemical weapons, because they had been used against the Kurds and in the Iran–Iraq War, the inspectors were shocked to find from their early investigations that Iraq's WMD production during the 1980s had been much more substantial than Western intelligence had calculated. UNSCOM found large stocks of battleground chemical weapons still stored in Iraqi arsenals and discovered that some of these had been deployed to units during the Gulf War but never used. Despite the regime's obstuctiveness, the inspectors achieved significant successes. In the early 1990s Iraq declared to UNSCOM more than 40,000 CW munitions and more than 400 tonnes of bulk agent (mustard, tabun and sarin/cyclosarin). The Iraqis constantly claimed that these submissions demonstrated their compliance with the terms of Resolution 687, but the claim was undermined by regular discoveries of undeclared materials and documents and by the evidence accumulated by UNSCOM and the IAEA of increasingly sophisticated concealment arrangements. Neither did it fit with the sheer mathematics: of the 200,000 CW munitions Iraq claimed to have produced throughout its entire programme, 100,000 had, they said, been used in the Iran–Iraq War and thousands more otherwise disposed of, but large gaps remained in the accounting.

In the nuclear field, the IAEA was confident that Iraq could not conceal an active industrial programme and none was found, but it had to admit that it had underestimated the extent of Iraq's nuclear programme during the 1980s. IAEA inspectors discovered within weeks that Baghdad had gone to extraordinary lengths to hide the evidence that large-scale activity had taken place during and after the Iran–Iraq war. The IAEA's smart and sometimes risky investigations under David Kay, the American expert who later led the search for WMD after the war in 2003, forced Iraq into admitting in June 1991 that it had been experimenting with several different methods of enriching uranium. During the 1990s the inspectors supervised the destruction of more than 50,000 square metres of nuclear-related factory space, some 600 tonnes of specialised metal alloys and around 2,500 items of related equipment, all of which would have helped the speedy establishment of a new programme if Iraq had been allowed the opportunity.

When the inspectors arrived Iraq denied completely that it had developed an offensive biological capability. Gradually, in the following four years, UNSCOM assembled evidence that Iraq had imported relevant equipment, notably bacterial growth media, in unrealistically large quantities for a civilian biotechnology industry. Faced with this, Baghdad acknowledged in July 1995 that it had produced botulinum toxin and anthrax on an industrial scale at their main facility at Al Hakam, disguised as an animal protein factory. When Hussein Kamil, Saddam's son-in-law and a senior member of the regime's executive, defected a month later, the Iraqis had to admit that they had started to fill munitions with biological agents in the late 1980s, but claimed that they had 'obliterated' their programme in the summer of 1991. Even when the regime produced evidence of the destruction, UNSCOM's work over the next three years uncovered the fact that documents, bacterial growth material and facilities had been retained and concealed. The experts were never able fully to account for the biological materials that Iraq had possessed at one stage or another. It was still possible for the inspectors to posit in 2003 that Iraq might have retained 10,000 litres of liquid anthrax.

The realisation that both international experts and the intelligence services had significantly underestimated Iraq's WMD capabilities before the war was not only alarming in itself, it also had a bearing on assessments of the available intelligence between 1998 and 2003, when the inspectors were no longer working actively in the country. Iraq had withheld the truth so often in its official depositions and had gone to such lengths in concealing evidence that no statement it had made since the adoption of Resolution 687 could be trusted without detailed verification. From 1991 the US and others saw it as imperative to prevent Saddam from restoring or enlarging his WMD stocks following the severe reduction in the conventional strength of the Iraqi Army. It was particularly important to ensure that Baghdad could not lay its hands on the ultimate deterrent, nuclear weapons. The effective work of the inspectors had reduced these risks significantly, but not to zero.

The degree to which Iraqi claims and declarations were undermined by subsequent and seemingly accidental discoveries was well illustrated by the episode of the chicken farm. In August 1995 Hussein Kamil decided that he had risked too many quarrels with Saddam's thuggish sons, Uday and Qusay, who were the dictator's principal henchmen and his presumed eventual successors. Together with his brother, who was married to Saddam's other daughter, Kamil took off across the Jordanian border and sought asylum in Amman. For much of the 1980s he had been given responsibility for Iraq's weapons programme as director of the Military Industrial Corporation and knew a considerable amount about WMD developments. While in Amman, he met and talked to representatives of UNSCOM and agents of the US and UK Governments, and filled in various details previously unknown to them, including the fact that Iraq had weaponised biological materials. He also claimed that the regime had destroyed all its chemical and biological stocks in 1991, though this could not be verified. In particular, he provided information on a cache of documents hidden in a remote chicken farm in the empty countryside west of Baghdad, which he claimed would reveal a great deal more about Iraq's past WMD programmes.

The inspectors followed up this lead and found the documents. They contained considerably more detail than previously supplied by Baghdad, in files that Iraq should have surrendered voluntarily. Nothing, however, pointed with absolute clarity to continuing WMD activity and nothing subsequently led to the discovery of undeclared weaponry. After a few months Saddam's daughters grew tired of life in limbo in Jordan, where they and their husbands were tolerated rather than welcomed and could not be sure of full protection. The men re-established contact with Saddam's family, received assurances about their personal safety if they returned, agreed with their wives that the risk was worth it and left Amman for Baghdad. Within days of their return, they were killed on Saddam's orders. Their wives were spared.

The chicken farm episode reinvigorated the search for hidden weapons in Iraq and was publicised enthusiastically by Washington, London and UNSCOM as a considerable coup. From then on the attention of the world's media was more intensively attuned to the threat of Saddam's capacity to cheat on WMD, including now in the biological field. Nevertheless, expert observers of the WMD scene have pointed to some strange features of the story. The farm had been routinely investigated by the inspectors earlier and nothing had been found. So the documents had been moved to the farm within the previous two years. Who had taken them there and why? After Hussein Kamil's defection, no attempt was made to conceal the documents somewhere else. There was some token resistance by the Iraqis when UNSCOM applied to search the farm, but little more than familiar hassle. The value placed by New York, Washington and London on the find did not seem to be matched by Iraqi distress or shame, even though their concealment was unquestionably a contravention of the resolution.

Some observers have concluded that, while Hussein Kamil's defection was embarrassing and the information he offered mostly genuine, the find was not such a great blow to Saddam Hussein. Could Kamil have been knowingly or unwittingly set up? A month earlier, the regime had been forced by UNSCOM's work to concede, after constant denials, that they had been developing a biological programme. Perhaps it was less humiliating for Saddam to have the documents unearthed through treachery than through a submissive response to the United Nations. And it kept alive the image of a powerful Iraq. On their own, the documents and materials discovered could not be taken to demonstrate that Iraq was continuing an active WMD policy in 1995. I myself, in moments of enthusiasm for demonstrating Saddam's guilt, was buoyed up by the evidence of the chicken farm, but I found that most members of the Security Council were reluctant to concede a 'smoking gun' quality to the find or to accept the weight put on it by Washington and London. In retrospect, they were right.

Over the next year or so the inspectors followed up various leads from the chicken farm, but the volumes of concealed materials and papers discovered started to dwindle significantly. With the passage of time from the 1991 War other developments had begun to affect the Iraq issue. George Bush Senior failed to win a second term in 1992 and, although Iraq did not feature as a major electoral theme, Saddam had the satisfaction of knowing that he had outlasted the man who had defeated him. World attention turned to the Balkans from early 1992 onwards and Bosnia became the principal foreign policy concern of the early Clinton years. President Clinton updated the policy from the period of the Iran–Iraq War known as dual containment, through which Iran and Iraq were to be systematically constrained from developing into an out-and-out threat to US interests, preferably without the need for forceful action. The UN Security Council monitored the work of UNSCOM sensibly, but its active agenda became increasingly dominated by the humanitarian and political disasters not only in Bosnia but in Somalia and Rwanda as well. The question of Palestine and Israel, which probably loomed larger in the priorities of the Clinton administration than Iraq, continued to sap the energy and political spirit of the Arab and Islamic worlds and of the United Nations.

Sanctions became an important element in the containment of Iraq. They prohibited the regime from selling its oil freely, from importing any goods or materials of military or technological utility, conventional or unconventional, and from benefiting from the assistance of any other UN Member State for the maintenance of military or WMD activity. There was also, of course, a punitive element in the resolutions which was later to add to the leakage of international sympathy for their implementation. The history of UN sanctions is a chequered one. Many sanctions regimes have failed to implement their full objectives, but most have succeeded in having at least a partial effect on the target country, especially with the passing of time. South Africa in the period of apartheid is a good example. General sanctions tend to affect the wider population as well as the government and partly depend for their eventual effectiveness on the government's incentives for caring for its people and avoiding their adverse reaction. Saddam turned this logic on its head and chose to use the suffering of his people as an instrument to stimulate condemnation of the US–UK approach. Washington and London realised that they were taking a risk, but the comprehensive severity of the Iraq sanctions regime, together with the presumed political weakness of the ruling clique in Baghdad after the Gulf War defeat, led them to believe that Saddam would not last a great deal longer.

Sanctions did indeed take their toll. The Iraqi armed forces never regained their pre-Gulf War capability and Saddam himself became increasingly constrained and frustrated by their effect. Nevertheless, it was the Iraqi population who bore the full brunt of the deprivation. Nutrition and health levels deteriorated sharply. As Baghdad probably intended, the UN, together with the main proponents of sanctions on the Security Council, the United States and the United Kingdom, came to be regarded internationally as being primarily responsible for the deterioration of health standards in Iraq. Human rights organisations began to raise their voices. There were spasmodic minor outbursts within the Iraqi population, but their will to resist Saddam's industry of oppression diminished to a negligible level. The Iraqi dictator was not only surviving but growing increasingly secure, while international sympathy drained away from his Western opponents.

In 1995 Britain and the United States decided that more vigorous action was required on the humanitarian front. They regarded Saddam's cynicism about the effect of sanctions on his people as criminal, but the policy was not working in their favour. They therefore devised a resolution that imposed on the Iraqi Government a series of measures for the provision and distribution of food, medical supplies and other essential goods. Resolution 986, known as the Oil for Food resolution, was adopted on 14 April 1995. It removed the prohibition in Resolution 687 against the export of Iraqi oil, but directed that proceeds from oil sales should be used for the purchase and distribution of essential provisions for the Iraqi people. At first Iraq refused to participate in its implementation, dismissing the Oil for Food programme as an outrageous infringement of national sovereignty. But after a while two factors convinced Saddam that rejection was not in his best interest. First, the propaganda battle, which up to then had been running in his favour, started to turn against him. Second, his advisers and oil market experts began to see the opportunities that the Oil for Food programme offered for scams and pay-offs on the sale of oil and on the contracts for essential supplies.

Once again, Saddam and his close entourage displayed their talent for turning adverse circumstances to their advantage. The major oil companies declined to enter into direct contracts for the sale of Iraqi oil with an untrustworthy regime that could threaten their global reputations. A long list was drawn up of smaller dealers and traders who were prepared to take the risk for short-term profit and to pay a premium back to the Iraqi Government for the business. The UN office running the Iraq humanitarian programme set up a host of monitoring arrangements and worked hard to deliver life-giving supplies to the Iraqi people, but the oversight machinery could not match Baghdad's ingenuity.

The regime's smuggling techniques in both directions – oil out, strategic and luxury goods in – developed on a scale and with a sophistication that only became a real concern in Western capitals after the withdrawal of the inspectors in 1998. In February 2001 the new Secretary of State, Colin Powell, paid his first overseas visit to the Middle East and confronted the Syrian Government with the evidence of their complicity in this illegal trade. Damascus prevaricated, pointing to the parallel activity going on through the

Turkish and Jordanian frontiers. Washington decided that the need to avoid the economic downside for these two friendly countries outweighed its wish to squeeze Syria. In 2002, after the US and the UK had worn down disingenuous Russian and French resistance to a revision of the pricing conditions for Iraqi oil, the Security Council started to squeeze the oil premium down to an acceptable level, but the unchecked flow of goods across the Turkish, Jordanian and increasingly the Syrian borders continued. Other forms of corruption and skulduggery persisted throughout the life of the Oil for Food programme, but at no stage did evidence come the way of the Security Council committee overseeing these arrangements that the UN system itself might have been drawn in. For all the complexity of anything to do with Iraq, we accepted that there was a price to pay to avoid a humanitarian disaster and assumed that the monitoring and auditing systems that the UN had in place, under the overall direction of the Security Council, were adequate for the purpose.

In 1997 Rolf Ekeus stepped down as Executive Chairman of UNSCOM after six exhausting but successful years of skirmishing with Baghdad. He had presided over the destruction of significant quantities of unconventional weapons left over from the 1980s and established a monitoring system that made it extremely difficult for Iraq to continue its WMD programmes except under the tightest conditions of secrecy and concealment. Combined with the regular patrolling of the Iraqi skies in the No-Fly Zones and the systematic scouring of Iraqi territory by satellite cameras, the inspection and monitoring arrangements formed quite an effective containment mechanism. UNSCOM had also developed close informal relationships with American, British and no doubt other intelligence agencies, through the national experts carefully selected and loaned to the UN. The arrangements were not as pure and clean as UN operations like to be, but the US and the UK justified them to themselves as necessary because of the hostility and mendacity of Saddam Hussein's regime.

The new Executive Chairman of UNSCOM was Richard Butler,

until recently the Australian Permanent Representative to the United Nations. Even then he was a controversial figure, larger than life and boisterous in his habits, with a talent for self-promotion which did not always bring him benefit. There was some debate about his suitability, but he was intelligent and determined and had considerable experience of the issues as an arms control negotiator for Australia, a country with a good relationship with the US and the UK on defence and intelligence matters. Madeleine Albright, who had just moved from the US Ambassadorship at the UN to become Secretary of State in Washington, decided to give him US Government backing.

At this point the UN Special Commission was finding the going much harder. Materials and documents that could more readily be unearthed had been dealt with. The Iraqis had, as the tussle with UNSCOM progressed, developed increasingly ingenious concealment techniques. They were also growing immensely irritated with sanctions and repeatedly insisted that they had offered up everything that was required under Resolution 687. Washington and London, however, were not satisfied that Saddam had given up his interest in WMD. The evidence, from both UNSCOM and intelligence sources, confirmed an active and well-staffed concealment programme. Significant amounts of biological and chemical materials, which documentation in UNSCOM's possession showed had existed in earlier years, were still unaccounted for. None of the declarations produced by Iraq to date had turned out to be truly 'full, final and complete'. Saddam's history, character and presumed motivation all pointed to the likelihood that possessing WMD remained a high priority. The investigation process could not be closed until we were 100 per cent sure.

These sharpened attitudes on either side increased the temperature. Butler, who routinely compared Saddam to Hitler, was determined to lead a vigorous inspection regime, but the harassment and obstruction of the inspectors intensified. The Iraqi Government protested loudly that American spies had been included on the inspection teams and refused to allow the inspectors entry into Saddam's offices and palaces – vast complexes dotted all over Iraq, which could have contained any amount of hidden materials. Once the row over the composition of the teams was resolved, with considerable diplomatic fallout (by now France and Russia were beginning to take Iraq's side more overtly), new obstacles were devised by Baghdad. Butler's manner was confrontational. He agitated for UNSCOM's admission to the sensitive sites. Saddam, meanwhile, appeared to be increasingly unconcerned about the consequences of his defiance, confident that nothing the US – and certainly the UN – could throw at him would threaten his grip on power. He saw how difficult it was becoming for his detractors in the Security Council to convince the rest that harsh sanctions and invasive inspections continued to be necessary. The lack of progress in the Middle East Peace Process while Benjamin Netanyahu held the reins in Israel added to the perception of the majority of UN members that the United States and its allies had got their priorities wrong. The prospect of getting rid of sanctions, either through their erosion in practice or through the collapse of the resolutions supporting them, seemed to be within Baghdad's reach.

Yet again Saddam overplayed his hand. After a year when UNSCOM had made very little headway and the international clamour over the humanitarian effect of sanctions was rising, he decided to rattle the cage more loudly. He began again to utter unspecific threats against Kuwait. Then, in October 1997, Baghdad decided to refuse entry to Americans on UNSCOM's inspection teams and expelled those already in Iraq. Washington was outraged and threatened to bomb Iraq. On this occasion, Saddam decided to back down. He retaliated in another way, however, by inviting the international media to Iraq to write accounts of the bitter hardships caused to the Iraqi people by seven years of UN sanctions.

Washington was becoming equally impatient. The indications that Saddam Hussein was a long way from fulfilling his UN obligations were compelling, but the inspection process was beginning to look unproductive and the isolation of Baghdad through sanctions was diminishing. Countries prepared to do business with Iraq, such as Jordan and Egypt, opened up channels of communication under the guise of humanitarian activity. Iraq's more belligerent behaviour in late 1997 took some momentum out of the flow of returning sympathy and generated articles in the American press speculating on possible military action by the United States. Iraqi attempts to shoot down US and UK air patrols increased, triggering firmer responses against Iraqi air defence facilities and related military installations. The Iraqis claimed, without convincing evidence, that these retaliatory attacks frequently killed civilians. The world's press criticised both sides. The atmosphere was becoming thoroughly nasty.

My own work during the 1990s brought me into little contact with Iraq. I was primarily involved with the tortuous efforts to bring peace to the Balkans and during a short spell as Deputy Ambassador in Washington in 1994–5 my main political function was to try to ease the sharp divisions between the US and Europe over Bosnia. As Political Director (senior adviser to the Foreign Secretary on the UK's transatlantic and European policy interests) from 1996 to 1998, I helped to implement some elements of the Oil for Food resolution and kept a general eye on UN and Middle East matters, but the focus of my work was on EU foreign policy and I was some way from the coal-face on Iraq. I absorbed the widespread assumption in Whitehall that Saddam was deceitful and dangerous and saw no reason to question it. Iraqi claims that they were being maltreated by the United States, when Kuwait was still licking its wounds and the UN requirements were so clearly unfulfilled, rang very hollow.

In February 1998, five months before I arrived as Ambassador in New York, Kofi Annan decided to go to Baghdad to see Saddam Hussein. Analysis of events in the UN Secretariat – the Secretary-General's professional staff – suggested that a further rise in temperature would lead to a conflagration. The UN resolutions were not doing the job and the momentum that UNSCOM had built up over the years was dissipating. The Iraqis believed that the United States was determined to wear them down through threats and international pressure, whether or not they conformed to UN requirements. Saddam became increasingly fatalistic from this period onwards, confident in his powers of survival and ready to test his destiny to the limits.

Why did Saddam Hussein risk a crushing invasion of his country when his actual WMD capacity and holdings transpired to have been far lower than was generally assumed? No one on the Security Council during the period leading up to March 2003, and no one within the inspection team itself, claimed that Saddam was implementing the repeatedly underlined and re-clarified demands of the Council. He was in a position to do it if he wanted. He did not. What was he concealing? Materials buried in the ground to which he could return when the storm had passed? Intellectual capability, which could be quickly restored to productive activity at a future date? Or a big sham to give the impression that he was a greater champion of Arab causes than he might otherwise appear? If analysts are right in moving increasingly to this third theory, why did he cling to that line of approach? It left him as the loser in one of history's high-profile gambles, in which the penalty was always likely to outweigh the prize. The answers will be debated for years, because they involve judgements about the mind of one of history's more memorable psychopathic dictators. I never met Saddam, even after his capture in December 2003, but his spirit seemed to be sitting with us in countless Security Council meetings, taunting us with our inability to nail him down. I believe that he was addicted to playing for high stakes, proud of what he had already pulled off, full of his own image of toughness and adamant that he would not compromise on it. So long as he remained a challenge to the superpower he would appear, like Fidel Castro and Slobodan Milosevic, to be a player on the world stage.

Kofi Annan understood that the Iraqi President was raising the stakes and was alarmed. Thirteen months into his first five-year term as Secretary-General, the first to have been appointed from within UN ranks, this charismatic and honourable man was beginning to demonstrate a capacity for inspiring leadership, which the organisation had sorely lacked since the death of Dag Hammarskjold in 1961. After the catastrophic failures of the international community in Rwanda and Bosnia, he was determined to restore the UN's reputation and its capacity to make a difference where it mattered. His political acumen had enabled him to maintain good relationships with both the developed and the developing worlds. He now had to contemplate taking himself where he thoroughly disliked going: into a situation where he could not hope to carry his whole constituency. But if there was a chance to stop the situation in Iraq collapsing into war, he was prepared to take the risk of antagonising some of the UN membership.

Annan spent several hard days in Baghdad negotiating with Saddam Hussein's team, led by the bespectacled, white-haired Tariq Aziz, the Christian Deputy Prime Minister and Iraq's best-known interface with the outside world. Saddam kept himself aloof from the discussions until the final phase. The inspectors had good reason to believe that documents about the WMD programmes, if not actual materials, were concealed in various sensitive sites – presidential palaces and military installations – and that from time to time they were secretly moved between locations. UNSCOM had sometimes been blocked at the entrance of important buildings and had spotted vehicles leaving from the back door before they were allowed in at the front. The Iraqi Government claimed that the dignity of the State would be infringed by unrestricted access to these sites. They also suspected – and later statements by ex-inspectors and other sources corroborated this – that some inspectors were passing on to their governments detailed information about the inner workings of Saddam's administration and the geography of the central areas.

Faced with this stalemate, Annan had a difficult choice. If he insisted on the full rigour of Resolution 687 and its successor resolutions, he could see that Saddam would probably continue to withhold cooperation and that the US and others might resort to 'all necessary measures' (the UN term for military intervention) to force him to comply. The odds would be against the Iraqi dictator, but he appeared determined to break the sanctions regime and would undoubtedly play things very close to the edge. If Annan made compromises in order to keep the inspectors working, he could be accused of being soft on Saddam and of turning himself into a self-appointed interpreter of the Security Council's resolutions. He was also aware that he might even genuinely, be making it easier for Saddam to outwit UNSCOM and develop proscribed weapons.

The Secretary-General therefore insisted on seeing Saddam personally towards the end of the negotiations. He went alone. The President's security people refused to allow the UN team to accompany him, in order to restrict knowledge of where Saddam normally worked. Annan subsequently told me that he was firm with Saddam that the inspectors must not be denied access to any place that could conceivably be suspected of harbouring relevant substance. He agreed to new arrangements outlining how the listed 'sensitive sites' were to be handled and allowing for specified delay times and respectful procedures. Saddam knew enough about the detail to demand a change in the terms in an area which Tariq Aziz had overlooked: he insisted that the neutral diplomats monitoring the entry to 'sensitive sites' must be of senior status and not just token Third Secretaries – another indication of Saddam's preoccupation with status. The Memorandum of Understanding setting all this out was signed on 23 February, without prior reference to the Security Council, and brought back to New York.

The reactions were predictable. The majority of Council members, with France and Russia in the lead, acclaimed the result as a brilliant piece of special-mission diplomacy by Annan and a fair basis for the continuation of the inspections. The United States, which under President Clinton was no less suspicious of Saddam than it would be under President Bush, considered that the Annan memorandum opened up loopholes for the development of unconventional weapons that were now sanctified by the UN itself and thus far harder to challenge than before. But the Americans stopped short of rejecting the result outright.

In a way, both sides were right. Those supporting the memorandum saw that a basis had been laid for the continuation of inspections that would act as a constraint on Iraq's ability to develop real capability in the crucial WMD areas. Those who opposed it concluded that Saddam had won an element of flexibility which, if ruthlessly exploited – as Washington and London tended to assume would be the case – would allow materials, documents and capability to be hidden indefinitely. In either case, sanctions would in all likelihood have to be maintained as a lever on Iraq to keep up a semblance of cooperation, and sanctions carried their own rumbling counter-pressures. The scene was set for the classic dichotomy of approach at the UN that became so familiar over the next five years: passive constraint versus proactive eradication. The dynamic balance between the two was to prove unsustainable.

3

The 1998 Bombing

I arrived in New York in July 1998, hotfoot from my job in London as Political Director in the Foreign Office and devoid of any front-line experience of the UN. As happens to any new ambassador of a Permanent Member of the Security Council, I was dropped straight into the heaving waters of Council discussion. Iraq was the most controversial issue on the agenda.

The Security Council lies at the centre of the institutions that make up the United Nations. It is the place where the raw politics of international affairs are thrashed out and it is the only UN organ whose decisions can have the effect of international law on all Member States. Formed at the birth of the UN in 1945, the Council's arrangements and privileges have been frozen in time. The United States, Russia (as the principal heir of the Soviet Union), China, France and the United Kingdom were invested with Permanent Membership then and retain it now. Any proposed amendment of the UN Charter can be vetoed by any of the Permanent Five. This seemingly immutable structure is deeply unpopular with the rest of the UN members, not least the other ten members of the Council, who are voted in, five each year, for a period of two years only.

The British Ambassador's first duty in the eyes of his Government is to look after UK interests on the Security Council. There are many other important things going on at the UN in New York: development, economic, environmental and human rights issues of huge significance to the world's oppressed and impoverished, together with financial issues of crucial relevance to the Foreign Office's budget. But the political substance of the Security Council agenda catches the headlines and retains the sharpest edge for political leaders in capitals. Woe betide the ambassador in New York who lands a mess on the desks of his bosses back home.

My early appearances in the Council were a steep learning curve. The other four Permanent Member ambassadors had been there for some time. Sergey Lavrov of Russia, the only colleague to precede and outlast me in this global club, was a professional diplomat of outstanding talent with an ability to rip a weak argument to shreds in English or Russian. He was close to Moscow and consistently sensitive to the spirit of his instructions, but he possessed an independent ability to manoeuvre within them which sometimes floored the much less flexible US system. Alain Dejammet of France was personally generous but professionally sharp, and he was not going to give away points to a newcomer. His studious, long-winded style tended to obscure the force of his main points, but he read and assessed everything passing across his desk and it was impossible to get a poorly substantiated argument past him. Bill Richardson, the American, would have given me tremendous help if we had coincided for any length of time, but in the nature of US Permanent Representatives he did not often attend working meetings of the Council and by September he had been promoted to Energy Secretary, leaving a gap that would not be filled at the top level until Richard Holbrooke's arrival a year later. Qin Huasun was a shrewd performer of the old Chinese school, friendly but cautious, his English too poor to engage in corridor negotiation. The range of Chinese active interests during this period was limited to issues closer to home and he gave ground for neither compromise nor spontaneous trouble on Iraq. These four knew their environment and each other well and were curious as to what this new UK product would bring. They were also circumspect. Quite apart from the welcoming instincts of a club to its latest member, they were aware of the self-interest factor: don't make an adversary out of a newcomer until you know how sharp his bite may be.

The ten Non-Permanent Members – or 'elected' members as they liked to call themselves, in a pointed reference to the undemocratic status of the Permanent Five (P5) – were generally a very able group, with occasional stars and the rare individual out of his depth. They represented a wide range of different interests across the continents and, although united in their institutional animosity to the concept of Permanent Membership and thus to any hint of privileged tactics by the P5, took their representative responsibilities seriously and could be moved by the substantive arguments on an issue if their instructions permitted it.

No country tends to send duffers to New York, but the British are respected above all for the capability of the collective team and the UK Mission alongside me represented an impressive resource. Stewart Eldon, my Deputy from September 1998 onwards, knew the inner workings of the UN as I did not and possessed a terrier-like determination to win – as he usually did – every skirmish that came his way. The head of the Security Council section, David Richmond, had a razor-sharp mind, highly developed drafting skills and superb lines of communication to the French; I came to depend on him both in New York and later in Baghdad. The First Secretaries beneath these two, the work-horses of the UK effort, were men and women in their thirties with high-class intellects and independence of spirit who were longing to be given a challenge. Behind this leading edge of quality stood the guiding hand, the on-line support and the solid effectiveness of the Foreign Office in London.

Nevertheless I was nervous. What an ambassador says or does in a diplomatic context can be taken to bind his government and country. He can be denied by his capital, but that does not happen more than once on a major issue without rapid recall. In a bilateral post there is usually time for detailed instructions to be ironed out before a senior diplomat takes up the cudgels on a difficult issue. In New York, and particularly in the Security Council, things can develop fast and unpredictably, and often the best next move is available only for a matter of hours – sometimes minutes. The time difference puts London off-line for half the working day. It can get hairy.

On 15 July 1998 events had not yet wound themselves up to a terminal drama. My staff at the UK Mission, wryly amused at the antics of a new boss, gave me a full brief and sat behind me in the slips to catch the snicks. I would test them to the limits later, but at this point I was all too grateful for their nursery food. I kept very squarely to the agreed line.

It did not take long for Iraq to come up. By July it was clear that Annan's February memorandum had not made things any easier for the inspectors. The Iraqis were claiming that there was nothing further in the WMD category to reveal to the UN, but they offered no proof of the destruction of items unaccounted for from the production records of the 1980s and continued to prevent the inspection team from certifying that buildings and offices that could have harboured evidence were clean. The terms of the memorandum were not so openly breached that the inspectors could claim a foul, but neither was the spirit of Annan's deal being observed in such a way as to give us a chance of closing the files. The US, backed by the UK, argued that this indicated the concealment of proscribed materials or documents. The Russians, French and some others set out the case for coming to terms with the absence of hard evidence and bringing sanctions to an end. The Arab world representative – there is always one on the Council, at this time it was Bahrain – consistently supported a filtered version of the Iraqi view, even if the country in the seat was as anxious as anyone to see the back of Saddam.

Iraq's weapons of mass destruction programmes were divided by the Security Council into four categories: nuclear, chemical, biological and missile technology. At this point the US and the UK were close to recognising that one of the four active WMD files, the nuclear one, could reasonably be closed. A closed file meant that the activity in question could cease to be the subject of proactive investigation by the UN inspectors and could move to a state of 'ongoing monitoring and verification'. The IAEA was ready to present the case for this to the Security Council and the UK would have gone along with a collective Council decision to close the file. It would have indicated that the Council was prepared to play fair by the terms of the 1991 resolutions; it would have reflected the fact that Iraq's ability to develop industrial techniques for constructing a nuclear device was a distant prospect; and it would have offered the Council an opportunity to focus on the other three files – chemical, biological and missiles – which were, in truth, the greater risk. Yet Saddam Hussein's proficiency at deception and concealment was well documented and we did not know what lay hidden.

So it was disturbingly early in my UN experience that I had to make up my own mind where the balance lay. I was of course dependent on London's guidance, indeed its ultimate decision, on where the UK should place itself on the question. To some extent we were all feeling our way with a series of relative judgements: certainty was a luxury we did not often have on Iraq business. And we in New York listened carefully to the UN professionals and to other delegations before we decided where to position ourselves. I was required to offer a view to London on the correct next step.

Margaret Thatcher was not around long enough, in spite of her record-setting tenure of Number Ten, to knock the stuffing out of the character of the Foreign Office and replace it with her brand of absolutism. Our instinct was not to lose friends unless there was no alternative, and it would have required a generational change in British diplomacy to erase that. I like compromise if it serves the longer-term UK interest and feel uncomfortable picking a fight to illustrate a principle. In any case, as the United Kingdom increasingly left the history of empire behind and came to terms with its second-power status, aggressive unilateral diplomacy was increasingly beyond our means. During the course of my thirty-five-year career we moved from a habit of independent decision-making to a much more collective approach and we had to learn the skills that went with this evolution. There is always the risk of being a soft touch, but in a body like the UN Security Council it is preferable to try to keep the group together than to split it on the premise that one side is hugely more right than the other. You have to be doubly sure of your case to succeed with that tactic. It seemed to me that the world's stamina for punishing Iraq for its annexation of Kuwait was beginning to expire; that sanctions were costly and gradually being eroded; that the maintenance of the No-Fly Zones and the occasional bombing of Iraq's military installations were growing ever more unpopular; that the focus on Iraq and the failure to settle the question of Palestine were turning the Islamic and developing worlds against us; and that the facts of the situation on Iraq's nuclear capacity fitted the letter of Resolution 687's conditions for closing a file.

Washington, whose single superpower habits were gradually taking its style of diplomacy in the absolutist direction, was not convinced. The evidence available to those countries consistently gathering intelligence from the inside in Iraq – and that meant only the US and the UK – pointed to a harsh assessment: that Saddam was concealing important material evidence; that he was not cooperating with the inspectors, and that he would take his WMD programme to a concrete conclusion if given half a chance.

Both sides were partially right. Washington set out its arguments in compelling fashion and London listened carefully. But what also counted with me was the value of keeping the Security Council united on the issues that really mattered: preserving the pressures on Iraq to go on giving up its WMD ambitions item by item and maintaining the strength of the powerful resolutions we had behind us. Picking a fight on a non-essential issue appeared to weaken the possibilities for doing that.

In the event, Washington agreed to set a test for Iraq. Resolution 687 of 1991 demanded that Iraq adopt a law to make illegal any activity or attempt to develop WMD in the country. This was transparently a piece of theatre. Saddam could have called for the adoption of legislation to reverse the flow of the Tigris and the vote would have been unanimous. With Stalin and, it sometimes seemed, Caligula for models, Saddam had a free hand when it came to the use of the Iraqi Assembly and paid no need to democratic norms. But 687 had required this new law and Washington was not in the mood to lower the bar. The Americans reminded the Security Council in these July debates that such a law would have to be adopted before the slate could be declared clean for closing the nuclear file.

Saddam declined to play along. I still wonder what might have happened if he had surprised us all and passed the WMD legislation. However meaningless the act would have been, he could easily have taken the step and won momentum towards ending the crippling sanctions on his government and his people. In a sense the test was a revealing one for the attitudes of both the United States and Iraq. Even under the Clinton administration there was not the slightest inclination to let Saddam get away with less than 100 per cent compliance. And Saddam was disinclined to indicate to his real constituency, the Arab masses, that he might not have WMD up his sleeve when it was well known that Israel did. This was Saddam Hussein's fundamental objective through the whole of this sorry period: to appear to be a major power with the capacity to threaten Israel, deter Iran and render himself invulnerable.

Given Saddam's refusal to take the final step, the Security Council was unable to gather the votes to close the nuclear file. The largely neutral members of the Council would have been happy to place themselves at some distance from the US, but not to the point of appearing to swallow a piece of Iraqi nonsense. The Iraqi Government bitterly criticised the decision, blaming the US in particular for its hostility and declaring their doubt that sanctions would ever be lifted whatever Iraq did to fulfil UN resolutions.

So Baghdad had a temper tantrum. The Council would not budge. At the beginning of August 1998 the inspectors tried to conduct a series of searches, some of them in sensitive areas, which were blocked. Saddam refused to see Richard Butler in person. Butler gave up and withdrew UNSCOM. They were not to return for over four months, the longest period of inspector absence since the start of their work in 1991. Saddam, whose motive was to rid himself of both sanctions and inspections if he could do so without giving up his WMD ambitions, had achieved one of his aims. The atmosphere in the Council was distinctly unpleasant when I left for a summer break at the end of July.

When I returned to New York in early September I found that various attempts had been made in August to restore the UN's authority in Iraq and get the inspectors back. A resolution had been adopted, after a wrangle between the Permanent Members, again setting out the requirement for Iraq to cooperate but offering to move forward from intrusive investigation to monitoring mode if Iraq responded. This 'light at the end of the tunnel' approach was to become a feature of the divide in the Council over the next five years. Baghdad maintained that the United States would never concede that Iraq had given up its WMD programmes and constantly reiterated that the US was determined to establish a pretext for an attack. Russia, and to a lesser extent France, thought Iraq had a case and insisted that the Security Council should regularly recall the clause in Resolution 687 which promised an end to sanctions if Iraq complied.

The August resolution nevertheless fell short of constructing a basis for the return of inspectors. Baghdad, having succeeded in getting rid of one of its bugbears – the presence of foreign snoopers on its soil – was not readily going to allow a reversal. The main target in its sights was the end, or at least the heavy erosion, of sanctions. The rhetoric on both sides spilled out into aggression and self-justification.

At this point the idea arose of a 'comprehensive review' of Iraq's progress in meeting the terms of the resolutions. The senior UN Secretariat, anxious to preserve Annan's relevance and authority, pushed the idea hard. They put out feelers to Baghdad without reference to the Security Council and tried to encourage the regime to seize the opportunity of a new assessment. Baghdad played along, spotting an opening for delay and confusion that might deepen the widespread frustration with the hard American–British line. Various parts of the UN system began to devise possible language for the terms of a review. The UK, keen to avoid a further drift towards the use of force and wanting to restore a collective spirit in the Council, took an active interest. Washington thought that it would all be a waste of time, but did not actively block the initiative.

The Presidency of the Security Council rotates around the fifteen members on a monthly basis in English alphabetical order. As it happened, October brought in the UK's turn. Since the United Kingdom and the United States are so closely aligned in the alphabet – only the United Republic of Tanzania is capable of splitting them – it always provoked a groan amongst the disaffected members of the Council when this double Presidency came round on the calendar. The duties of the President are mainly procedural and, because the Chair has to serve the collective will, it offers very few opportunities to affect substantive business beyond occasional manipulation of the agenda. It is a public assignment, with responsibilities towards the membership of the UN as a whole, and the performance of the President is marked throughout the organisation. I had barely served a complete calendar month in New York and I was apprehensive about this early test. The UK Mission rallied round and wrote me a series of full briefs for each meeting, which kept me on the straight and narrow.

No brief, however, could tell me how to prevent the issue of Iraq from collapsing into chaos and recrimination. The US and the UK, with some support from Portugal, were in a clear minority in wanting fierce pressure to be maintained on Iraq through sanctions. The remainder of the fifteen were showing a strong interest in the Secretariat's idea of a comprehensive review. Was I, as President, supposed to serve the clear majority or push my country's line? There was no point in wailing to London about it: for all the UK's promotion of multilateral mechanisms, when it came to hard interest the Government expected their representative to serve its needs.

The first imperative was to try to keep the Council united on any next step. Not only was this the right image for an effective UN; it would also serve US and UK interests to be seen to be sticking with the pack over this period, so long as consensus did not mean that Saddam Hussein could ignore UN pressure. As the UK Presidency got into its stride, the US and UK Missions leant heavily on the so-far undisputed fact that Iraq had not met UN demands. There could be no question of an early release from sanctions. With that established, there was scope for examining what kind of review process might lay the basis for the return of the inspectors. The Secretariat was beginning to set out some recommendations in this respect. The Security Council had not asked for these in any formal sense – the US and the UK would have blocked any move to pass the initiative away from the Council. Most members wanted to hear what the Secretary-General proposed, as his people had been in direct contact with the Iraqis and no one trusted the Americans and British to provide objective guidance. Kofi Annan's team was doing a good job of appearing independent and constructive. This presented a problem for us because their recommendations were likely to be weighted in favour of a move towards ending sanctions. I was being driven into the corner I had hoped to avoid.

Fortunately for my narrow interests, at that moment the Secretary-General's office made a slip. They composed a set of conditions for the holding of a comprehensive review which failed to conform precisely to the terms of previous resolutions. The Secretary-General has a certain degree of tactical flexibility, but the formal decisions of the Council have to be scrupulously respected or some bright spark is bound to pop up and point it out. This time it was my turn; and

I seized the opportunity to try to remove the Secretariat from the implementation process. I persuaded the Council to point out in a carefully drafted letter that it was for them to make the judgement on what would be the proper basis for a review. The Secretariat was stopped in its tracks. I felt uncomfortable at having to be the cause of Kofi Annan's second unsuccessful intervention on Iraq in eight months, but for the time being, the UK's position was protected and the Council had not split.

I handed over the Presidency to the Americans on 1 November with more than a sigh of relief. While I was satisfied that we had not lost the initiative in the Security Council, the underlying trend was not moving in our favour. Kofi Annan's judgement that conflict was not far off, which came out clearly in his private conversations with me, proved more accurate than the compromise position of the Security Council. As October faded out, the Iraqi regime took one step too far in its efforts to shake off international pressure. Having expelled the inspectors from Iraqi territory on 5 August, it now declared that it would cease all cooperation with UNSCOM, even at a distance. Timed by intention or coincidence to come out as the Council was considering the text of a resolution to institute the comprehensive review, this statement hardened the positions of the doubters. President Clinton was focused on the Middle East Peace Process and held no burning ambition to raise the stakes on Iraq to a military level, but a superpower does not like to be challenged. Resolution 1205, adopted on 5 November, established restrictive terms for a review of Iraq's fulfilment of the UN's requirements since 1991 and issued a veiled warning that the patience of the Security Council was wearing thin.

The moment was important because it illuminated a fundamental difference between members of the Council about military intervention, a difference that was papered over on this occasion and again in November 2002, but would tear the organisation apart in March 2003. Those delegations that disliked the increasingly explicit threats of force coming out of Washington made it very clear in their speeches at the horseshoe table before Resolution 1205 was unanimously adopted that they would not agree to the use of force without a further specific Council decision. Sergey Lavrov of Russia, for instance, said:

> We are pleased to note that the draft resolution before us seeks precisely a political solution to the Iraqi problem and contains no language that could be arbitrarily interpreted as some kind of permission to use force. The draft resolution makes it clear that the Security Council, in accordance with its primary responsibility under the Charter for the maintenance of international peace and security, will remain actively seized of the situation.

Many others made the same point, invoking the standard, rather clichéd words about the Council's responsibility for maintaining international peace and security to emphasise that only the Council could authorise the use of force in any foreseeable circumstances over Iraq. But they failed to spot one important factor: the Council had already authorised the use of force against Iraq in the past, an authorisation which had never been rescinded. I deliberately spoke, as did the Americans, after the vote had been taken and I had this different point to make: the first Gulf War was in legal terms left unfinished if Iraq failed to fulfil the requirements of Resolution 687 on complete WMD disarmament. Resolution 1205 in front of us made it clear that Iraq had not fulfilled those requirements. As I put it, in terms agreed with London:

> Certain speakers have given their views on the meaning of this resolution as regards the possible use of force. Let me briefly set out the view of the United Kingdom. It is well established that the authorisation to use force given by the Security Council in 1990 [i.e. Resolution 678, which preceded the Gulf War and underlay Resolution 687 at the end of the war] may be revived

if the Council decides that there has been a sufficiently serious breach of the conditions laid down by the Council for the ceasefire. In the resolution we have just adopted, the Council has condemned the Iraqi decision to cease all cooperation as a flagrant violation of its obligations.

My astute Russian colleague realised immediately what I had done. The United Kingdom, after everyone had voted, was pointing out that the Council had adopted a resolution which, whatever members said about the Council's prerogatives, had not terminated the continuation of the 1991 ceasefire terms approved unanimously by the Council. Sergey Lavrov was angry, as he would have probably recommended a different Russian vote if there had been any question of such an interpretation.

The Iraqis were even angrier. The adoption of Resolution 1205 on 5 November 1998 produced another round of fulminations from Baghdad. Washington replied with similar aggression. The international atmosphere deteriorated rapidly, much to the UK Government's discomfort, and the Security Council remained devoid of fresh ideas. Throughout this period the Americans lacked a senior figure in New York, as it took the administration a full twelve months after Bill Richardson's departure to get Senate confirmation for Richard Holbrooke to be the new ambassador. In the meantime, the US Mission's working team, professional though it was under the shrewd and approachable Chargé d'Affaires, Peter Burleigh, exerted little influence on the White House. President Clinton appeared increasingly determined to stop the rot and the US media began to speculate on preparations for an air strike. The No-Fly Zone patrols moved from occasional responsive strikes to a series of proactive attacks on Iraqi air defence positions. The French Government, which was still in theory a contributor to the maintenance of the Zone at that stage, declined to support this change. Annan tried to restore an atmosphere of calm, but even he had to acknowledge, in his frank and open way, that there might be times when the authority of the UN needed the threat of force to sustain it. Concerned as he was that some members of the Security Council were too inclined to consider the military option, his priority remained to close the gaps between the different UN factions rather than to avoid forceful action at all costs.

None of this appeared to have any effect on Baghdad, whose rhetoric climbed a further degree in aggressiveness, including threats against Kuwait. Saddam's tactic was to provoke maximum division amongst the main international players. The Iraqi Government rejected the terms of Resolution 1205 and showed no interest whatsoever in the return of inspectors. This amounted to defiance not only of the UN but also of the United States, which was publicly demanding Iraqi compliance and just as publicly being snubbed.

President Clinton decided to act. There was much open speculation about his motives, as the Monica Lewinsky scandal was running hard through this period and it was easy for opponents to propagate the general assumption that he was trying to distract domestic US opinion. Yet the superpower's bluff was being called. The US embassies in Kenya and Tanzania had been blown up earlier in the year and the retaliatory strikes on Sudan and Afghanistan had not achieved anything concrete. While no one was attempting to establish a link between Iraq and anti-Western terrorism, Republican critics were beginning to suggest a pronounced disinclination within the administration to do anything. As the weekend of 14–15 November approached, US forces were placed on high alert. The Security Council met on Friday 13 November at the demand of several members who wanted the situation to be brought within the terms of the Council's responsibility for controlling the use of force.

They were too late to have any effect on Washington. The United States issued an ultimatum insisting that Iraq acknowledge their obligation to meet the terms of Resolution 1205 and re-admit the inspectors. The UK did not consider that the time had come for military action and privately counselled restraint, but Prime Minister

Blair, who had stayed closely in touch with President Clinton throughout the escalation, was not going to stand in the way if Saddam Hussein remained obstinate. The UN Secretariat worked overnight and into the weekend to get Baghdad to see the pointlessness of continued defiance. The Security Council met again on the Saturday to examine an apparent message of concession from the Iraqi Foreign Minister. The US delegation did not think it would do the trick. The meeting went on late into the evening and there seemed to be no give between Baghdad and Washington. Tony Blair stayed at his desk throughout this drama, checking the terms of various attempts to bridge the gap. Kofi Annan remained on hand in his office behind the informal consultations room. I was called to the telephone twice to brief the Prime Minister, and the Secretary-General spoke to him close to midnight New York time, 5 a.m. in London. The lines were buzzing between London and Washington. None of this prevented the White House from issuing the order for the US Air Force to start a bombing run soon after dawn in the Gulf.

At that point Saddam Hussein finally decided to change his tune. A written message arrived on Security Council desks at around 1 a.m. on the Sunday morning conceding the return of inspectors. The US bombers were at least an hour into their flight. President Clinton sounded, from reports coming through to the US Mission, very reluctant to undo his decision. The Prime Minister told him that this latest missive changed the legal situation and he could no longer support a strike. Just before the point of no return, the attack was called off.

The episode demonstrated two important things: that the Americans were prepared to follow through with the actual use of force if sufficiently provoked; and that Iraq could, with a huge effort, be made to respond. The concept of a comprehensive review was damaged by this experience, because no one could see how an objective assessment could be implemented in an atmosphere of such constant brinkmanship. The Russians and French in particular remained highly sceptical that any advance was going to be possible.

Nevertheless the Security Council instructed Richard Butler, UNSCOM's Executive Director, to prepare the inspectors for a return. The UN had, after all, used its weight to prevent the outbreak of conflict.

The November crisis thus established the circumstances for the December 1998 attack on Iraq, Operation Desert Fox, which prefigured in so many ways the climax of March 2003. UNSCOM returned to intrusive inspections of Iraqi facilities in the first week of December and carried out some four hundred visits, most of them to sites that had been inspected many times in the past but had to be re-certified as clean. Almost all of these visits went without a hitch, with the Iraqi minders surly but not obstructive. On five inspections, however, directed at targets which the Iraqis were probably not expecting to feature and on which interesting information had recently come in, there was trouble. The Iraqi security forces delayed the team from entering, or were caught moving materials out of the back door. At one place, a Baath Party office, the inspectors were refused access altogether. Butler decided that he could not continue unless he received 100 per cent cooperation. Having established that the US and the UK had no further gems of information to offer him, he ordered the inspectors out. Russia claimed afterwards that the whole thing was a sham orchestrated by Washington to provide an indisputable excuse for a military strike. I saw no direct evidence of a plan to that effect, but Richard Butler knew that unless the Iraqi Government radically changed its approach he would be dragged back into a game of cat-and-mouse which he could not win. He was probably predisposed to cut this exercise short. The Secretary-General, worried about the personal safety of the team, did not demur. By the morning of Monday 14 December all the inspectors had departed, unobstructed by the Iraqis even though they must have known what was bound to follow.

The Security Council majority erupted in anger when they heard that the inspectors, who came under their direct control in policy terms, had been spirited out of Iraq without reference to them. They set up a restricted meeting on 16 December for Butler to come and report to them. This started late in the afternoon and seemed set to continue long into the evening. Ambassador Lavrov of Russia launched an immediate attack on Butler's truthfulness, accusing him of curtailing the inspections in order to provide the United States with a pretext for attacking. Butler had hardly started his response before a messenger came in to whisper something in the Secretary-General's ear and mobile phones began to ring in the meeting room. The Americans and British had started to bomb Baghdad. The Iraqi Government was issuing virulent demands for international protection and an immediate halt to the attack. The meeting broke up in dismay and confusion.

The next day the United States and the United Kingdom were called before an open meeting of the Security Council to explain their actions. Peter Burleigh and I set out the history. My statement traced the story of the blocking and deception of successive inspection teams and of the failure by Iraq over more than seven years to fulfil the terms of the resolutions requiring a complete account of its WMD programmes. They had to be shown that there was a limit. The objectives of the military action were twofold: to degrade Iraq's capability to build and use weapons of mass destruction; and to diminish the military threat which Iraq posed to its neighbours. I also detailed the legal case underpinning the use of force. Resolution 1205 had implicitly revived (I could almost hear the grinding of Ambassador Lavrov's teeth at this point) the authorisation to use force given in Resolution 678 unless Iraq offered full cooperation with UNSCOM. With all other avenues blocked, the United States and the United Kingdom had been left with no alternative if Iraq refused to abandon its WMD programmes.

The bombing stopped, almost as suddenly as it had started, four days later. With relief and resentment flowing in equal measure, the UN and its exhausted Security Council fell into a nervous Christmas break. It was going to be an awful job having to face one another again in the New Year.

4

Picking Up the Pieces

In January 1999 the Security Council returned from its break with a heavy heart. Public recrimination over the mid-December bombing campaign had died down, but no one underestimated the difficulty of returning to discussions of a possible comprehensive review. France, Russia and China, with firm support from Malaysia as a newly elected Non-Permanent Member, became more explicit in their rejection of the US–UK approach and in their determination to find a way of ending sanctions. Russia, in particular, remained virulent about what it perceived as the abuse of UNSCOM's position and the unjustified use of military force.

In an effort to replace endless skirmishing with rational debate, the Canadian Permanent Representative, Robert Fowler, proposed panels of experts to assess Iraq's compliance with different aspects of the Security Council resolutions and make recommendations for next steps. Council members grasped this procedural escape route with relief and appointed their Brazilian colleague, Celso Amorim, a former – and future – Foreign Minister of Brazil, to head the review. With UNSCOM Commissioners acting as its advice bureau, a single panel worked over the following few weeks to produce the not very startling conclusion that, while there was no clear proof that

Iraq was continuing to develop weapons of mass destruction, neither had it fully accounted for its past programmes or met all its obligations under the resolutions. It seemed as though the December breakdown in the Security Council and the four days of intensive bombing had made not the slightest difference to the substance of the debate.

With the recommendations of the review panel sitting heavily on the table in front of it, all fifteen Council members had to find a way of translating the findings into action. This meant drafting a resolution. From April until December 1999, the Council entered into one of the longest negotiations of any resolution in its history. The detailed drafting work had to be done by the delegations of the five Permanent Members, as the rest found themselves unable to act unless the differences between the P5 over the justification for sanctions and over the real depth of Iraq's defiance were somehow resolved. They never were. When Resolution 1284 finally saw the light of day, it failed to unite the Security Council around a single position. The US and the UK, who had done most of the drafting, managed to avoid vetoes by the other three Permanent Members, but China, France, Malaysia and Russia abstained. The Security Council had a new policy at last, but it carried diminished conviction.

1284 established a new mechanism for intrusive inspections in Iraq, to be carried out by a body named the UN Monitoring, Verification and Inspection Commission (UNMOVIC). The resolution, in long and tortuous passages that had driven the negotiators practically to despair, updated and improved the conditions for the continuation of the Oil for Food programme and re-expressed the terms for judging Iraq to have fulfilled all its obligations. Iraq was given no specific deadline by which it had to accept the terms of this resolution, because its proponents assumed that the regime would wish to take advantage of the new terms for escaping from sanctions. That assumption quickly proved starry-eyed. Iraq contemptuously dismissed the new resolution. It stated that it would not work with any UN inspection team and vilified the UN, the US and all those who thought like them for maintaining the sanctions regime under conditions that Iraq said it could not meet when it had already ended all its WMD activity. The stalemate looked set to continue for a good deal longer.

Public attention to all of this was overshadowed by other compelling events in 1999 and the Iraq story would not have featured on many people's list of high-profile issues that year. The Arab–Israel dispute turned progressively more bitter. The violence in East Timor, which had been struggling for twenty-five years to escape from Indonesian strangulation, reached a climax in the summer and the Security Council sent its first overseas mission for years to rein in the Indonesian military and set the territory on the path to successful independence. It was Kosovo, however, that absorbed the energies of the UN and filled international airwaves during the spring and summer. It also generated a further row about the use of force without specific authorisation from the Security Council. Within weeks of the bombing of Iraq, the United States and the United Kingdom similarly confronted President Milosevic of Serbia with the threat of military intervention and, when he did not respond satisfactorily, carried out the threat. The Security Council and its Permanent Members were again badly split. But the outcome was different.

A crisis over Kosovo had been looming ever since the break-up of Yugoslavia. With Slovenia, Croatia and Bosnia now independent, Milosevic's ambition for a Greater Serbia had been cut back to the boundaries of Serbia itself and its southern neighbour Montenegro. Milosevic wanted to be the leader who restored the Serbian province of Kosovo, which was intimately associated with the origins of the Serbian State but was largely populated by Albanian Muslims, to a Serbian majority. The Kosovo Albanians, emboldened by Bosnia's success, harboured their own ambitions for independence. From early 1998 onwards the increasingly violent response of the Kosovo Liberation Army (KLA) to the political pressure from Belgrade gave Milosevic the pretext to move special forces, and later units of the

Serbian Army, into Kosovo to crush resistance. Human rights abuses on both sides, but particularly the deliberate killing of Kosovo Albanian civilians by the Serbs, raised alarm amongst those countries, primarily the United States and the members of the European Union, who had taken on a growing responsibility for the stability of the Balkans since the break-up of the Soviet Union. An intensive period of diplomatic manoeuvring began. It was led by a 'Contact Group' comprising the US, Russia, France, Germany, Italy and the UK, with the principal objective of negotiating a status for Kosovo that would preserve the concept of Serbian sovereignty but remove Serbian political and military control. The UN Security Council debated the issue from time to time, but left the detailed work to the Contact Group.

Over the autumn and winter the diplomacy intensified. The United States, with support from its allies in NATO, became increasingly insistent that force would have to be used against Belgrade if the Serbian Army refused to withdraw from Kosovo. The UN Secretary-General declared on 30 January 1999 that the threat of force was justified if it brought the Serbs to the bargaining table. Five days later the US Secretary of State, Madeleine Albright, set out the American philosophy on the use of force in a public lecture on the 'lessons of Bosnia':

Kosovo is not Bosnia because we have learned the lessons of Bosnia; and we are determined to apply them here and now. We know . . . that the only reward for tolerating atrocities is more of the same. We know that the longer we delay in exercising our leadership, the dearer it will eventually be in dollars lost, in lost credibility and in human lives . . . Finally, we learned in Bosnia, and we have seen in Kosovo, that President Milosevic understands only the language of force. Nothing less than strong engagement from NATO will focus the attention of both sides; and nothing less than firm American leadership will ensure decisive action.

Last-chance talks were held over two extended sessions in February and March 1999 in the chateau of Rambouillet in France, in the hope of reaching a peaceful settlement on the basis of autonomy for Kosovo, policed by NATO troops. Milosevic refused to attend the meetings, but the Kosovo Albanians almost overreached themselves in rejecting a three-year autonomy deal without a guarantee of independence at the end. Eventually they signed up, with the possibility of independence left open. Milosevic refused to sign if it meant the presence of NATO forces on the territory of the Republic of Serbia and on 22 March he rejected any further compromises. The bombing of Serbia began on 24 March.

The Russians had been playing a vital role in the Contact Group, since they exerted the main influence on Belgrade. As supporters of the Serbs and as the only non-NATO member of the Group, they rejected any attempt by the Western allies to underwrite the use of force with Security Council authorisation and drew constant attention to the abuses committed by the KLA. On one occasion towards the end of the Rambouillet negotiations, which the Security Council was following with active interest, I came across Ambassador Sergey Lavrov in the darkened section of the second-floor corridor outside the Security Council and decided to put a proposition to him. If Moscow was so determined to avoid war over Kosovo, why did it not back up the threat of force presented by all the other members of the Contact Group? Surely that was the only way to persuade Milosevic that he had to take what was on offer at Rambouillet? The result would otherwise be both war and a drastic setback for Serbia. Lavrov saw the point at once, as he always did. But he did not think that he could sell this approach to his capital: it would have meant too great a capitulation to US policy. The lines had been drawn.

Moscow's resentment over the opening of the bombing campaign quickly boiled over into the presentation by Russia of a draft resolution in the Security Council condemning the use of force without Security Council authorisation. The Russians struck a chord when they accused the allies of trampling on the Council's responsibility for judging matters of international peace and security by not even bringing the failure at Rambouillet to its formal attention. Lavrov argued with particular virulence, with the Iraq bombing campaign still fresh in his mind, that the US decision to initiate air strikes against Serbia was a further step towards the dissolution of the international security framework. The majority of Council members thought this was taking things a little far, when Milosevic had failed to appear at Rambouillet and the attacks by Serbian forces on Kosovo Albanian civilians were growing in brutality every day. Lavrov's very intensity lost him support, not least after he was challenged in a stinging intervention on the humanitarian disaster by the blunt-speaking Ambassador of the Netherlands, Peter van Walsum. The draft resolution was defeated by a margin of twelve votes to three (Russia, China and Namibia), which had the reverse effect of legitimising the NATO action in the eyes of most members of the international community.

NATO's attack on Serbia went through some agonising phases: early hope of a quick success, subsequent doubt that Belgrade could ever be ground down and eventual, rather surprised, achievement. The Russians, increasingly worried that the continuation of conflict would damage their wider interests, played a significant role in getting Milosevic to capitulate, but they retained strong doubts about the legitimacy of the use of force in such circumstances – together with many others in the UN system and indeed in the US and UK public arenas. On top of the Russians' disgust with the bombing of Baghdad, the action against Serbia reinforced their resistance to the efforts which the UK, Canada and several others began to make to establish guidelines for the international handling of internal human rights abuses within states or by 'rogue' states. The results in Kosovo, though they came at a cost, were broadly regarded with time as excusing the arbitrariness of the military intervention. That was not to be the case with the intervention in Iraq.

*

Following the adoption of Resolution 1284 in December 1999, the UN went comparatively quiet on Iraq. The diplomatic possibilities had been exhausted. In the months that followed, UNMOVIC gradually came into existence in New York, but Iraq showed no interest whatsoever in doing business with it. Lazy thinking set in. The United States and the United Kingdom put a brave interpretation on the achievements of the December 1998 air strikes, but we knew that we had shot an important bolt from our thin quiver of options without doing any real damage to Saddam's position. Just as before, we were going to have to rely on the UN-based sanctions and containment policy to keep the Baghdad regime within bounds. The year 2000 was in any case a Presidential election year in the US, not a time to take further risks on a painful issue. London could do nothing without Washington, because Iraq had no reason to take account of the UK on its own.

I was all too ready to embrace this passive state. With eighteen months of UN experience under my belt, I was looking for ways to improve the effectiveness of the Security Council and needed room to manoeuvre on a broader range of issues. The constant dogfights over Iraq in the Security Council had proved wearing. In personal terms, as someone who did not go looking for confrontation but preferred to work away at building consensus where it was possible, I felt I would be happier getting on to matters such as peace-building and development in Africa, where the parts of the UN machine outside the Security Council could be brought more into play. From the UK viewpoint, we were taking a fair amount of flak for our closeness to the United States over Iraq and it was time to build up some credit with the UN majority. I was all too conscious of the unpopularity of the five Permanent Members of the Security Council. The thinness of the UK's claim still to be one of them in the new millenium would inevitably damage us unless our place was merited by energetic action on behalf of a much wider swathe of the UN membership and in areas of the UN machine that did not rely on the Security Council. I took care to spend time on economic and social matters, on the internal health of the UN system, with NGOs and other agencies, areas where good things were being done, but a huge amount of chivvying and tidying up was needed. Richard Holbrooke, confirmed at last as US Permanent Representative in September 1999 and warmly welcome as an old colleague and sparring partner from Bosnia days, similarly realised that support needed to be earned, even for the superpower. He made a point of forming a relationship with all his opposite numbers, threw himself into the fight against HIV/AIDS and took up the cause of East Timor with the applied vigour that marked him out as exceptional. On Iraq, on the other hand, he deliberately kept his distance, despite my pleas to him to share the heavy lifting.

Africa featured strongly on both our agendas. I was an enthusiast for efforts to try to turn Africa round and soon found myself caught up in the fervour of millennial optimism. The record of the United Nations, government aid agencies and Africans themselves had, over the decades, been dismal. The combination of work within Africa by Africans to establish a new collective spirit of partnership for development and renewed attempts at the UN and in the developed world to raise the amount of help going into Africa promised to change all that. The list of particular conflicts and crises needing attention was too long to address in full: Sudan and Somalia, in particular, were left to fester. The urgent crises in Sierra Leone and the Democratic Republic of Congo dominated our efforts. The Security Council sent new missions to the Great Lakes region and West Africa, the first of them led by Holbrooke. These were intensive, fascinating working visits, engaging over consecutive days several African presidents who we felt had to try harder to cooperate and compromise. Some of the time it worked.

There were reasons other than irrational enthusiasm for the new century to explain why morale at the UN had begun to rise. The setting of new targets for the eradication of poverty, however ambitious, seemed to indicate a collective will at the highest levels to grapple with important things that had been left undone. Later in

2000, in a superb piece of bullying diplomacy by Holbrooke, the contentious business of UN funding was sorted out for the foreseeable future. Human and women's rights started to be handled in a much more pragmatic fashion. Even Fidel Castro came to the UN Millennium Summit to offer Cuban medical help for Africa. Was the UN gloom at last beginning to lift?

There was one issue, however, that never left us alone for long: the Middle East Peace Process. Whenever an incident occurred causing serious Palestinian casualties, the UN majority made their sympathies felt, heavily weighted as they were in favour of the Palestinian cause. Israel's sovereign statehood was accepted in formal terms by virtually all the UN Member States, but the country remained a pariah in their eyes in many practical respects. Although UN resolutions, and particularly Resolution 242 of 1967 crystallising the concept of an exchange of land for peace, still provided the principles for a comprehensive settlement, it was widely recognised that the machinery of the United Nations was incapable of negotiating a solution. Only the United States possessed the influence and the operational capacity to do that, if the right policy prescription could be found.

The Oslo Peace Accords, signed between the Israelis and the Palestinians in 1993, were supposed to lead to the curbing of Palestinian violence in exchange for the phased withdrawal of Israeli forces from parts of the Gaza Strip and the West Bank. But the consequences of Oslo bore down hard on the Palestinian economy and GDP and employment declined sharply in the years that followed. Restraint proved impossible for Palestinian militants and Israeli reactions to their attacks were swift and brutal. Meanwhile the building or enlarging of Israeli settlements in the West Bank and Gaza continued inexorably and unchecked, despite their clearly illegal status under international law. Time and again bitter Palestinian complaints about over-forceful Israeli military measures were brought to the UN Security Council or the General Assembly, often in the form of draft resolutions; and time and again Member

States failed to resolve their differences over the wording or ran into a straight US veto. For the United Kingdom these were always agonising occasions, torn as we were between firm support for Israel's security and insistence on justice for the Palestinians; and we often drove our EU colleagues to distraction as we looked for one more element of balance to set beside the mild but noticeable European bias in favour of the Palestinians.

During the course of 2000 President Clinton decided to make one last effort to resolve the issue before his term expired. After a tortuous series of preliminary negotiations to narrow the gap on territory, security arrangements, return of refugees, the holy places and all the other historically loaded details of the dispute, the President brought the chief negotiators to Camp David in July to thrash out the final terms of a settlement. The attempt came very close to success: for a short while the American team thought that they had done it. The Israelis under Prime Minister Barak were ready to accept arrangements that no one had believed possible at the start; and on the Palestinian side Yasser Arafat seemed just about ready to close a deal. Both leaders realised that they would be taking a huge risk with their domestic constituencies if they signed up: closure would not be possible unless each of them recognised that achieving only a proportion of their aims would be better than no agreement at all. At the United Nations, where for so long we had not dared to hope that the thorniest issue of all was resolvable, the possibility of a new beginning seemed to open up.

Then, at the last moment, Arafat calculated that he was being asked to concede too much. The initiative came to an abrupt halt. Indeed, Camp David did not merely end in failure; having raised and then dashed expectations amongst those most directly affected in Israel and Palestine, it worsened the atmosphere for their co-existence thereafter. The Palestinian side was widely regarded as carrying the greater responsibility for the breakdown, although there had been no guarantee that the prospective agreement could have been implemented if Arafat had put his name to it.

Less than two months later the security situation deteriorated dramatically. The collapse at Camp David was generally regarded as the principal cause, but Palestinian feelings had been building up to boiling point for some time before that. Desperation over their political and economic conditions led the majority of Palestinians to conclude that they could only regain the diplomatic initiative if they raised the cost of stalemate by expending Palestinian lives in an uprising. The Al-Aqsa intifada grew from these roots. Its earliest stages were set in motion by a badly timed decision on Thursday 28 September by the then Israeli opposition leader, Ariel Sharon, to visit the Temple Mount in the Old City of Jerusalem. This was the holiest site for Judaism but also the third holiest site after Mecca and Medina for Islam and a place of special significance for Christianity. With the status of East Jerusalem remaining to be resolved in an overall settlement, Sharon could not have failed to recognise that such a move would be intensely provocative. The Israeli Government under Ehud Barak attempted to forestall violence by conferring with the Palestinian leadership over the arrangements for the visit, and reactions on the day of the visit were confined to stone-throwing and attempts to break through Sharon's massive armed security. But Sharon further inflamed feelings by publicly proclaiming the Temple area as eternal Israeli territory, in accordance with Israel's official policy since 1980 but in blatant disregard of UN resolutions.

After Friday prayers the next day extensive riots broke out around Old Jerusalem in which several Palestinians were shot dead. The violence quickly escalated and in the first six days of the intifada sixty-one Palestinians were killed and 2,657 were injured. Barak switched abruptly from peacemaker to general and Israeli security measures took on a deliberate harshness. Any effort to restore the conditions for a new negotiation was now doomed. Peace proposals and confidence-building measures continued to be drafted and the Quartet of international negotiating teams – the US, the EU, Russia and the UN – worked hard to produce a Road Map for renewed peace talks. But the Israeli Government refused to consider wider issues until security for their citizens could be guaranteed; and Palestinian militants, whom Arafat could not or would not control, relentlessly continued their indiscriminate killing of Israeli civilians and their attacks on Israeli security forces. Extremist attitudes on both sides fed off each other. The consequent loss of life was immense: in the four years to August 2004 over 2,700 Palestinians were killed and nearly 25,000 injured; and Israel lost 1,001 killed and around 6,700 injured. Yasser Arafat was caged in his headquarters in Ramallah and the Israeli authorities refused to do any further business with him. Only when his life ended and he was succeeded by Mahmoud Abbas as President of the Palestinian Authority did the chance return of replacing violence with renewed dialogue.

Nothing with political overtones happens in the Middle East without a direct or indirect connection with the question of Palestine. Iraq was no exception. The atmosphere in New York, apart from a few short months after 9/11, was poisoned again and again during this period by fierce resentment over the condition of the Palestinians, not just within the great majority of UN Member States but also in large parts of the Secretariat. Through his tactically inept and often brutal behaviour Saddam Hussein marred the few chances he had of gaining greater international sympathy. He never seemed to appreciate what advantages he might have gained if he had played the Palestinian card more adeptly. International perceptions of Israel and the United States detracted from objective consideration of US and UK policy on Iraq and sharpened reluctance among UN professionals and many members of the international community to help with the stabilisation of Iraq, even when it might have benefited the same Iraqi people who had received their sympathy under sanctions. It was against this background that Tony Blair insisted time after time with Washington that the Middle East Peace Process had to be given as much attention as Iraq itself; and the UK remained in no doubt throughout our travails on Iraq that the failure to do this exacerbated our policy problems, raised our material costs and wasted lives.

Meanwhile the containment of Iraq was beginning to slip. The period after the adoption of Resolution 1284 saw little progress in New York. The fundamental issue, the capacity of Saddam Hussein to defy the international community and rebuild his strength, was not effectively addressed. Russia in particular attacked the way in which the sanctions policy was implemented by the US and the UK, criticising the huge number of holds they placed on Oil for Food contracts if they contained any item that could conceivably be of military use. This led in early 2001 to a revision and clarification of the list of 'dual-use' items subject to sanctions scrutiny, a useful piece of US–Russian diplomacy which brightened the gloom for a few months. All this time, however, Baghdad was learning increasingly cunning ways of milking funds out of the Oil for Food programme.

Verbal fisticuffs were the norm when Iraq was on the Security Council. At working level, members of our Missions cut their diplomatic molars on it. Other delegations stood back when Carne Ross, First Secretary at the UK Mission, and his French counterpart Christophe Bigot climbed into the ring. They both defended their corners with aggression, skill and sometimes splendid humour. The Security Council committee overseeing the Oil for Food policy quarrelled regularly over details, with the US and the UK believing that they were on the side of the angels in trying to restrict the amount of money going into Saddam's hands from oil sales and contracts, and Russia and France fighting to dilute the effect of sanctions they saw as unjustified and cruel. The politics overwhelmed any sense of consistent management. The Secretariat's Iraq team was straining to get the Iraqi people fed and supplied while the Iraqi Scylla lunged at them on one side and the Security Council Charybdis tossed them about on the other.

As damaging to the containment of Iraq as any lapse in the Oil for Food effort, but receiving far less public attention during this period, was Iraq's skill at smuggling materials across its borders. The international monitoring system was nowhere near equal to the task of keeping this under control. Increasingly the leakiest route came to be the road and rail traffic through Syria, which was in effect without any controls at all. From time to time London questioned Washington on the wisdom of leaving open this gaping hole. But smuggling through Syria was hard to stop when the massive traffic passing through its neighbours, Turkey and Jordan, whose wellbeing was of greater interest to us, had become an essential part of their economic activity. Stalemate became inertia. Saddam was encouraged: it reinforced his tactical instinct to keep challenging the UN process. Governments grew tired of the perpetual political skirmishing. Other priorities abounded. As the time came for the change of US President, Iraq never seemed to be this week's priority.

Part Two

5

11 September Changes the Equation

The American decision to deal with Saddam Hussein once and for all by force originated in two powerful strands of policy thinking, both born of a national-interest logic which only a superpower could have followed: first, the challenge to US international authority which Iraq represented; and second, defence of the homeland through the extended use of power abroad. For everyone else, including the United Kingdom, the reasoning seemed overblown. When I first realised, quite late on in the development of events in the spring of 2002, that US intentions were serious, I was incredulous. I even took a bet with a senior member of my staff in New York that an American attack on Iraq would not take place before I had moved on to retirement in July 2003. It added an edge to the personal challenge which I rather arrogantly set myself to try to prevent the situation from collapsing into war.

At the start of the new millennium Saddam Hussein was unfinished business, a problem which the Bush 2000 campaign team believed should have been laid to rest a decade earlier. Saddam's survival was a stain on the effective use of US power. Beyond that, his ambition to champion the Arab nationalist cause on Palestine and to bolster his position by acquiring the most dangerous weapons, matching Israel's own, was growing with his increasing sense of durability in office. The Bush team watched Clinton's containment policy gradually losing its grip and despised it as weakness.

If the first policy priority related directly to Iraq, the second had to do more nebulously with the threat of terrorism. Preventing terrorist attacks against US interests meant fulfilling a number of complex requirements, among which had to be included the removal of any threat from hostile rogue states. Iraq was on that list, though not necessarily at the top by the criterion of immediate danger. The 9/11 Commission Report, released in July 2004, underlined how, in the late 1990s and in the first few months of George W. Bush's Presidency, counter-terrorism was just one of a number of policy objectives, with no especial resonance either in government thinking or in the list of US public concerns. It was, in fact, so low on the list of priorities for George W. Bush that he could not make time to meet with Richard Clarke, the man in charge of counter-terrorism in the National Security Council, until September 2001.

The terrorist attacks of 11 September 2001 on the World Trade Center and the Pentagon injected a motivation for action which, although not exclusively concentrated on Iraq, could readily include it. The evidence for this surge of thinking within the Bush White House within days, if not hours, of the 9/11 strikes looks strong, to judge from the accounts of Richard Clarke and the journalist Bob Woodward. The intensification of focus is particularly associated with the input into policy discussion of Deputy Secretary of Defense Paul Wolfowitz, backed up by the group of so-called neocons – Richard Perle, Douglas Feith, Lewis Libby, Elliott Abrams and a number of thinkers and writers outside Government – and given powerful encouragement and cover by Secretary of Defense Donald Rumsfeld and especially Vice-President Dick Cheney. Apart from occasional short meetings on my visits from New York to Washington, I had no direct dealings with these policy-makers: the demarcation lines between the UK's ambassadors in Washington and New York were clear and strong.

Their reasoning was classic superpower thinking. America represented strength based on incontestable democratic values; on 11 September that strength and those values had been directly attacked; Iraq was already a source of challenge to the superpower and to the rule of law and freedom it promoted; Iraq was additionally a supporter of terrorist attacks on Israel and a direct threat to the stability of the world's most important oil-producing region. Iraq therefore became one of the targets in the US response to 9/11. This leap across at least one logical gap could be defended with aggressive justification, so the neocons reasoned because three thousand innocent victims had been slaughtered and because the lessons of passivity could be drawn from the Clinton and George H. W. Bush eras.

The significance of Israel as a factor in all this has received less attention than I had expected in the Iraq commentaries I have read. No foreign country has an unquestionable claim on American favours. The American people and their requirements come first and last. The relationship with the United Kingdom is close and historic, but it is based mainly on pragmatism, not sentiment – even if pragmatism is given a healthy boost by a certain correlation of values and outlook. The US attachment to Israel contains a stronger ingredient of ideology and sentiment and a smaller dose of pragmatism. History, particularly the history of the twentieth century in Europe, plays an important part in that. So does the strength of religious feeling in many parts of the US population. Israel's struggle to create its own place in the modern world contains echoes of the foundation of the American republic, when religious outcasts fled persecution and set their sights on a new promised land. But these historical explanations are insufficient to explain those periods in US policy-making, including under the Presidency of George W. Bush, when the strength of government support for Israel rises above the rationale of overall US interests.

Israel could not have existed in its present form without its relationship with the United States. As an independent and established state in the Middle East, it stands out as a democratic oasis in

79

a politically constrained neighbourhood. Its right to secure existence under international law is a cardinal part of European as well as US foreign policy and is accepted in practice by the larger part of the Arab and Muslim world. But it will not be safe until the Palestinian problem is settled and as a state of eight million people it must eventually reach an accommodation with its Arab neighbours, who number three hundred million and rising.

The Israeli people have an acute sense of being under siege and are determined to maintain a military superiority over any combination of potential enemies in the region. Their success in achieving this since their early days as a vulnerable new nation has reinforced America's loyalty to the idea of Israel's permanent security, even at a substantial cost. But that cost cannot be limitless. So far, the terrorism from which Israel has suffered as a result of the failure to solve the Palestinian question has not struck the territory of the United States. Al Qaida has other priorities. But there is a danger that the situation in Iraq, as it drags on, will change the perceptions of that part of the international community which is angry about both Palestine and Iraq. In Arab and Muslim popular culture, enflamed by subjective and brutal media images of US military action in Iraq alongside Israeli action with US-supplied weapons to quell the intifada in the Occupied Territories, the two are gradually merging. Natural distaste for violence has started to compete with delight at seeing the United States discomforted. The material threat to US interests has grown more serious than at any point since the end of the Second World War.

This has not yet affected the readiness of the United States to help Israel in its search for lasting security and to listen to Israel's assessment of the threats arrayed against it. Iran and Iraq have both raised the deepest Israeli suspicions because of their undoubted hostility to the existence of Israel at Palestinian expense, and Israel has justifiably watched the activities of these two countries with extreme vigilance. Iran has a long history of association with groups such as Hezbollah and Islamic Jihad, whose primary motivation is to inflict damage on the territory and immediate interests of Israel. The thought of an Iran with nuclear capability is anathema to Israel. In the case of Iraq, Israel had already acted on one occasion, in its June 1981 strike against the Osirak nuclear reactor, to deny Baghdad an unacceptable advance in military capability; and on another, during the first Gulf War in 1991, had been on the receiving end of Iraqi missile attacks which Baghdad probably had the capacity at the time to arm with chemical or even biological warheads.

I had seen no direct evidence that the Israelis underlined to the Americans during the 1990s the dangers of allowing the cat-and-mouse game between the UN inspectors and the regime in Baghdad to continue indefinitely. A change in administration in Washington was not required for doubts to be sown about the UN's capacity to ensure that Saddam Hussein never acquired or used WMD. Israel regularly shares its intelligence assessments with its US ally and I knew from my own experience that when its survival was at risk Israel was prepared to make no allowances whatsoever for either Iran or Iraq.

Whether an American assessment of overall US interests has to come out at the same place is a different matter. The stakes for the two nations are not the same. On the whole, from what I have seen close up of American foreign policy decision-making, wise and rational conclusions are drawn in Washington on global security questions more often than extravagant or misguided ones. But Israel's point of view is almost always given fair wind by at least some quarters in the senior administration. This was the case within the Clinton Presidency. In the team preparing for the Bush campaign, loyalty to the protection of Israel's security was even more sharply underlined. Israel's interests were one factor among several in the selection of Iraq for early treatment in a George W. Bush Presidency, but perhaps a factor that helped to tip the scales.

On Tuesday mornings in New York, the fifteen ambassadors of the European Union would gather together in the EU office, two blocks away from the main UN building, to hold their weekly review of events and to plan a coordinated EU approach to UN business. The EU is a powerful player at the United Nations, particularly on economic, social, development and internal management issues. On political and security matters, where in my time EU decisions always required unanimity and where sensitivities about membership of the Security Council crackled across the table, the whole rarely added up to the sum of its parts. I was never quite sure what blowback to expect on Tuesdays.

As my car turned from First Avenue onto 46th Street on Tuesday 11 September, I heard the radio report that a plane had flown into the World Trade Center. 'Had to happen one day,' I said, remembering my low flight down the Hudson River a few weeks previously in a friend's light aircraft, when we had had to avoid several other planes doing the same thing. I still have the photograph I took of the Twin Towers reflected in the polished underwing of the Cessna. Arriving at the EU office, I went straight upstairs to the meeting room. There was no collective discussion of the news flash. The agenda was full of unrelated issues, mostly concerned with the imminent opening of the new season's General Assembly and the speeches our ministers would be making in it. Then someone with a cellphone said that a second plane seemed to have hit the Towers. The atmosphere immediately changed. This was a deliberate attack. I thought al Qaida but did not say it, as no one seemed to be attempting an analysis. Absurdly loyal to our bureaucratic habits, we tried to return to the banal agenda, but half an hour later the news came through of an explosion at the Pentagon. Someone reported that the UN building was thought to be a target and was closing down. The meeting stopped abruptly. I dashed back to the UK Mission office, which was located on the twenty-eighth floor of the Dag Hammarskjold building on the corner of Second Avenue and 47th Street. From our north-facing office in mid-town Manhattan, you could not see the Twin Towers, but smoke was already visible in the sky. We turned on the television in the conference room and the Mission staff stared glumly at the screen as events unfolded. We watched in silent disbelief as the television showed the first and then the second towers collapsing in a huge pile of dust and rubble. It was hard to digest that this was taking place less than three miles to the south of us.

We reached for our telephones and started to check in with family and colleagues. London was already alive to what had happened and reacting with public statements and crisis procedures. Our sister office at the British Consulate-General was beginning to set up emergency arrangements. Knowing that the World Trade Center could hold up to fifty thousand people, we began to contemplate the possibility of British casualties in four figures.

The dreadful day drew on. We all went through our own personal episodes of reaction, locating – or losing – friends who had been closer to the tragedy. My secretary's husband, who was known to be in the vicinity, was not heard from for several hours because he was trapped in the subway, but he survived. John O'Neill, the newly appointed Head of Security at the towers, who had predicted an al Qaida strike on the World Trade Center and who had left the FBI in frustration a few weeks earlier when he could not get his views heard, died after returning to the building to help people. I had held a dinner for him at my apartment only a few months before. My wife, Anne, walked across an eerily quiet mid-town New York to a friend's apartment on Park Avenue and listened to harrowing accounts from a group of grey-faced young executives who had walked there from the financial district.

David Manning, the Prime Minister's Foreign Policy Adviser and a friend from Paris Embassy days in the 1980s, telephoned in the early afternoon. He was stuck at Kennedy Airport en route from a Washington visit – all flights had been cancelled, perhaps for days. I dispatched a UK mission car to ferry him back to Washington. Soon he had teamed up with a group from the UK Ministry of Defence and the Secret Intelligence Service who had been invited across to discuss the implications, arriving on the only incoming transatlantic flight to operate over those seventy-two hours. Of all the British officials involved with the aftermath of 9/11 up to the start of the Iraq War, David was the one most consistently at the centre of things and the regular line of communication to the Americans.

The next few days at the United Nations reflected a changed world. Within twenty-four hours the Security Council had produced a unanimous resolution, led in its drafting by the quick-footed French, which not only condemned the perpetrators but authorised the use of force to deal with them. Everyone was aware by then that this would probably mean an American attack on Afghanistan. Overnight television reports had conveyed flashes and bangs above Kabul, which many took at first to be the start of a US operation. The resolution went ahead nevertheless, virtually without discussion. It was followed the next day by a similar text in the General Assembly, adopted unanimously without debate. However marginal in terms of effective action, these were signals of the world's horror at the attack on the United States and its apprehension that terrorism was getting into regions that threatened any established government. For a period a feeling developed that a new kind of international consensus might emerge.

Capitals competed in condolences to Washington, many of them meanwhile counting the loss of their own nationals in the destruction. Tony Blair came to central New York for an hour, accompanied by an imperious Number Ten logistics team and five bus-loads of the UK media, attended a service at St Thomas's Cathedral on Fifth Avenue and met with British families who had lost relatives. I saw him for a few minutes, but there was no time for any kind of policy discussion before he rushed on to Washington, a day or two behind President Chirac of France, to express British grief and British support. Since these were both genuine enough to earn a high place in American estimation, the assumption began to take shape that the UK would offer material help to the US in any military campaign. The Prime Minister had already that spring, without prompting from the foreign policy machinery in Whitehall, presciently called for a plan of action on Afghanistan to reduce the threat of terrorism, drugs and crime spreading from the failed Taliban state. It was hardly likely that the UK would draw back from involvement now.

At the UN, diplomacy narrowed down to what the United States might do. There was relief that President Bush appeared to be biding his time for a considered rather than an explosive strike against the Taliban. Then we waited for Washington to produce a draft resolution in the Security Council on longer-term action against terrorism. It came the following week, well prepared and reasonable, and negotiating its passage became the first ambassadorial task of the newly arrived John Negroponte, ending the long gap since Richard Holbrooke's departure in January.

Within sixteen days of the tragedy the Council adopted one of the most far-reaching resolutions in the UN's history. It mandated states to take a broad range of actions to stifle terrorism on their territories and cooperate globally to prevent terrorist networks from migrating or linking up internationally. No government could remain passive, whatever their experience of terrorism to date. Normally such a commanding text would have required weeks if not months of negotiation. The other members of the Council suggested barely a word of change from the text presented by the US. The country that caused the most bother in the brief drafting discussion turned out to be the United Kingdom, which had concerns about the effect of one sub-paragraph on the domestically sensitive area of its asylum legislation – when I questioned whether this intervention was really necessary I was quickly silenced by Jack Straw. By 28 September Resolution 1373 was in place. A week later I found myself in the chair of the Council committee charged with its implementation. This was a marked departure from the norm of avoiding Permanent Member chairmanship of any Security Council sub-committee and another sign of the extraordinarily forward response of the UN as a whole. Even in these unprecedented circumstances, I was amazed that the organisation had moved in such a positive way.

The eyes of the world were now on Afghanistan. Well before 11 September 2001 the United States had decided to intensify the pressure on Osama bin Laden, who was widely seen as responsible for the 1998 attacks on the American embassies in Nairobi and Dar es Salaam and whom it suspected of planning further and more dramatic attacks on US interests. Bin Laden's principal operating base had been set up in Afghanistan under the protection of the fundamentalist Taliban regime, the effective controllers of the central and eastern parts of the country after their 1996 coup in Kabul and a government recognised at the UN only by Pakistan and the United Arab Emirates. In October 1999 the UN Security Council had, on a US initiative, unanimously adopted Resolution 1267, imposing limited (by the standards of Iraq) sanctions on the Taliban unless they turned over Osama bin Laden to the authorities in one of the several countries where he had been indicted. Their response had been dismissive. The United States began to prepare alternative ideas for undermining the Taliban's hold on power, focusing on the anti-Taliban forces (the Northern Alliance) in the Panjshir Valley under the ousted government's Defence Minister and hero of anti-Soviet resistance, Ahmed Shah Massoud. These efforts bore no early fruit. On 9 September 2001 al Qaida succeeded in infiltrating agents into Massoud's presence disguised as visiting journalists and assassinated him. The United States, by now receiving interested but not yet well-resourced assistance from the British Government, realised that it would have to start again.

September 11 changed the picture at once. Three days later President Bush named bin Laden and the al Qaida network as the probable perpetrators and issued an ultimatum to all governments, who gave protection to al Qaida or to any other known terrorists to hand them over. Judging that once again the Taliban would take no notice, the Americans launched preparations for a full-scale military campaign in Afghanistan, fortified by the authority contained in Resolution 1368, passed by the Security Council twenty-four hours after the attacks on New York and Washington.

Although the watching world expected an American response within days, George Bush took time to bring together the resources and the planning necessary for a complicated operation in territory that had proved the graveyard for foreign invaders through the centuries. The US Air Force, with some British support in the air and with small deployments of British, Australian, New Zealand and Canadian Special Forces on the ground to direct them, began a sustained bombardment of Taliban and al Qaida targets on 7 October. Pakistan, whose territory was essential for the proper preparation of the ground campaign but many of whose people would, if given the chance, have voted to back the Taliban regime rather than the United States, offered non-military assistance. On 18 November the troops of the Northern Alliance began a sweeping advance across northern Afghanistan, starting with the capture of the key city of Mazar-i-Sharif. By 13 November the Northern Alliance, moving far quicker than their foreign backers had expected, entered Kabul as Taliban resistance evaporated throughout northern Afghanistan. British forces came in swiftly behind them and took control of Kabul's airport at Bagram. On the 18th the Americans caught a Taliban column on its way from Kabul to Tarinkot and annihilated it from the air. That finished the Taliban as a fighting force. By 2 December a 4,000-man International Security Assistance Force (ISAF) under UK command had moved into Kabul to provide support for the new Afghan Government dominated by the Northern Alliance, who had resisted the idea that a UN-organised peacekeeping operation should take on the task.

The United Nations had nonetheless done its homework on the political front. With the full backing of Washington, Secretary-General Kofi Annan had asked former Algerian Foreign Minister Lakhdar Brahimi, one of his most senior and capable lieutenants, to take on the task of preparing for a new government that would represent a much broader spread of the Afghan people than any of its predecessors. In mid-November the Security Council adopted a resolution setting out the principles for this process and calling on the international community to provide security, humanitarian and economic assistance to the country during its transition. Well before the ousting of the Taliban from Kabul, Brahimi had held discussions with a range of Afghan political and military leaders and, with the shrewd argument that essential outside help would otherwise not be forthcoming, had won their agreement to a stable, broad-based government. Before November ended, talks had started in Bonn between the main factions chaired by Brahimi, who had stubbornly resisted the attempts of Washington and particularly London to lead him by the nose. The Americans, British and others sat back anxiously, wondering how long it might take to produce a governing coalition for one of the most fractious countries on the planet.

Lakhdar Brahimi knew what he was doing. On 5 December, only nine days after the start of the Bonn talks, the four main Afghan factions had signed a power-sharing agreement to form a six-month interim government headed not by a representative of any of the ethnic communities that provided the leadership of the Northern Alliance, but by Hamid Karzai, a member of the important Pushtun tribe like most of the members of the Taliban regime. The conditions for a sustainable coalition of the main players in the country seemed to be coming into place. On 22 December Karzai was sworn in as President in the presence of foreign diplomats, generals and the UN. Seventy-five days after the start of the US-led bombing campaign, a new Afghanistan was born, fragile and uncertain, but with the solid support of the international community behind it and a political structure that held out some hope that in the future Afghan governments would be chosen with the participation and consent of the Afghan people. This was how the international community ought to be working, with the power of nations linked to the UN's collective legitimacy.

The Afghanistan campaign had, despite the apprehensions, turned out to be brief and effective. The preparations for the aftermath had brought together the elements for a successful political transition. Only one glaring failure stained the record: Osama bin Laden, the man who had signed a religious edict in February 1998 that 'the killing of Americans and their civilian and military allies is a religious duty', escaped capture.

6

President Bush Comes to the United Nations

I had no privileged view of the immediate top-level reactions to 9/11 in Washington. The Ambassador at the United Nations in New York keeps his nose out of the business of his colleague 200 miles to the south. But Christopher Meyer's reports, and other evidence since, indicate that the question of Iraq's possible direct or indirect involvement in the planning or execution of 9/11 was immediately raised. It was done in a way that suggests that the coiled spring of intention to deal with Saddam Hussein's Iraq had suddenly gone live.

The President, however, kept the impulse within bounds in the early stages. Chapter 10.3 of the 9/11 Commission Report, published in July 2004, carefully examines the sequence of discussions. The Commissioners do not take Richard Clarke's account of his corridor meeting with President Bush on the evening of 12 September, in which the President asked Clarke to look for any shred of a link between Iraq and al Qaida, as an indication that Bush was seeking an opportunity to attack Iraq. The question was fully examined in the first part of the intensive Camp David session on 15 September, in which the top administration planned their response to 9/11. It did not feature in the later part of the discussion, which focused entirely on Afghanistan as the primary military target for planning purposes.

It is right to recall that Washington had to look at two principal issues at this point: what to do about the perpetrators of 9/11 and how to protect the country against any further terrorist attacks. Addressing the second question as a strategic concept, a Defense Department briefing note for the Camp David meeting listed al Qaida, the Taliban and Iraq as priority targets. But that does not mean that they thought Iraq was linked with the first question.

The evidence suggests rather that, with the Vice-President's backing, the neocon group, and especially Paul Wolfowitz, persistently brought up Iraq in the 9/11 context and tried to indicate that there must be a connection. Wolfowitz and the other neocons were predisposed to believe that only states had the capability massively to harm other states. They insisted that al Qaida, even with Taliban support, could not have accomplished the planning and execution of such a sophisticated series of attacks as 9/11. Secretary of State Colin Powell later told the 9/11 Commissioners that Wolfowitz argued at Camp David that Iraq was ultimately the source of the terrorist problem and should therefore be attacked, but he was not able to justify his belief that Iraq was behind 9/11 itself. President Bush, said Powell, did not give Wolfowitz's argument much weight. He saw Afghanistan as the priority and he made this clear to the Prime Minister when Blair visited Washington on 20 September. Clarke's account is also revealing when it describes his team's gobsmacked reaction to the President's instruction to research Iraq on 12 September. 'Wolfowitz must have got to him,' one of them says. It is a picture of a President trying to take account of all the advice coming at him in a major crisis, when he has no personal experience to link his instincts with the real facts. In the event, he appears to have made sensible judgements on the need to put Afghanistan first.

It is clear nevertheless that the hardliners did not give up. Even if the Afghanistan campaign took up the main attention and energies of the administration for the remainder of 2001, those who had long advocated the removal of Saddam Hussein could see that 9/11 had shifted the context. Already by November the administration had begun to suggest that Iraq might be next. The 11 September attacks had brought to life the potential, in domestic political terms, for winning public acceptance for the use of military force against Iraq. Arguments could now be constructed for persuading the President that American security could only be assured by changing things for good in Iraq. George W. Bush appears to have had an instinctive sympathy for regarding Iraq as the enemy of the United States, but he was not convinced in the first months of his Presidency that this deserved urgent attention over everything else. A shrewd political operator, as his 2004 re-election campaign further established, he was not going to go out on a limb for a costly operation that would not attract public support. The transformation of the United States on 11 September into a victim with manifest right on its side turned him into a war President with a much higher level of public sympathy. He quickly became comfortable with that, and stayed comfortable.

Aside from the reasoning that drew the administration into constructing a policy basis for attacking Iraq because they wanted to do it, there was a further rationale for doing it – those involved would of course call it the only rationale: the belief that neutralising Iraq was genuinely necessary in the US's security interests. No one was quite sure what Iraqi capabilities amounted to. Intelligence on Iraq had been thin for several years. Why? Was it because Iraq was such a hard target? Because Iraqi concealment was so skilful? Or because there was nothing to report? The last of these seemed to be the most improbable. Saddam had been up to no good for more than two decades and his rhetoric suggested that his intentions were undiminished. Everything that had gone before produced a heightened tendency to magnify the indications of trouble. After 9/11, with all sorts of questions being asked as to why the Government had failed to spot what was coming, no President could afford to get it wrong again. Of all the scenarios that were then examined by the countries most likely to be the continuing targets of terrorism, WMD terrorism was (and remains) the most terrifying. If risks had to be taken, they should be on the side of over- not under-insurance.

This impulsion came through as strongly on the British side as on the American. Later, in 2004, when giving evidence to Lord Butler's Intelligence Review, Tony Blair is quoted verbatim in a description of his concerns about WMD and terrorism, derived from intelligence reporting and starting well before 9/11:

> There was quite a lot of stuff about bin Laden and his desire to acquire WMD of one sort or another and I was quite often saying . . . 'What are we actually doing about this?' . . . There was a lot to make me concerned about this and actually at the first meeting I had with George Bush in February 2001 I raised it with him but . . . after September 11 it took on a completely different aspect . . . What changed for me with September 11 was that I thought then you have to change your mindset . . . you have to go out and get after the different aspects of this threat . . . you have to deal with this because otherwise the threat will grow . . . you have to take a stand, you have to say, 'Right we are not going to allow the development of WMD in breach of the will of the international community to continue.'

I shall examine later why the conviction built up that Iraq possessed actual weapons of mass destruction, which in theory could be passed on to terrorist groups. For all the political contention between leading states about the policy of the US and the UK on handling the Iraq problem, no one could be sure of the extent of Saddam Hussein's deception and mendacity. It was one of the reasons why the hostility to pre-emptive action in the UN Security Council and elsewhere was not fiercer than it was. This was true after 9/11 and it remained true during the negotiations in New York leading up to the final decision to go to war in March 2003.

Exaggerated as the obsession with Iraq may have been in some quarters in Washington, there were strong reasons for responsible leadership to be worried about Iraq's capability. There is no need here to repeat the story, covered in American books and articles, of the military planning that US Central Command (CENTCOM) took forward from the end of 2001 onwards under the general direction of President Bush. It proceeded below the horizon of my view of things in New York, but that is neither here nor there. The circle of advisers close to Prime Minister Blair in London became increasingly conscious from the start of 2002 that American preparations for conflict were taking on greater shape and detail. This coloured the assurances from Washington that no decisions of principle had been taken to move to a conflict with Iraq, since it grew steadily more obvious that the theoretical option to use force was being gradually honed into a practical one. But everything remained in play from the viewpoint of a UK Government that did not want a war, but wanted the power of the United States to make a difference.

The State of the Union speech which Bush delivered at the end of January 2002 rang alarm bells in a number of quarters with its famous characterisation of Iraq, Iran and North Korea as an 'axis of evil'. 'Iraq', the President said, 'continues to flaunt its hostility toward America and to support terror. The Iraqi regime has plotted to develop anthrax, and nerve gas, and nuclear weapons for over a decade.' But the speech did not carry the message as far as I was concerned that the United States must be preparing a direct attack on Iraq. It seemed much more likely that the principal targets of that rhetoric were Iran and North Korea, and especially Iran. The use of those particular words, so uncomfortable to the ear of any Briton brought up in the tradition of understatement, was carefully calculated in Washington to have an exaggerated effect. Whether or not the pace was picking up towards the invasion of Iraq, Baghdad had pride of place in the list of hostile states spitting in America's face. Comparing Iraq with the other two did not constitute sabre-rattling against Saddam. North Korea largely fell outside the field of subtle or not-so-subtle diplomatic signals: it would have to be handled in its own exceptional environment. Iran, by contrast, was clearly up to this point enjoying the feeling that tweaking Big Satan's tail was relatively cost free. The lumping in of Tehran with Baghdad and Pyongyang in such a public and insulting way delivered a genuine shock. It actually did succeed in changing Iran's behaviour in the weeks that followed, in that Tehran began to take more seriously the need to adjust to the requirements of the International Atomic Energy Authority in the handling of its nuclear facilities and materials. That might have been a tactical rather than a fully substantive move, as later events showed. But it was a move.

So it came as a surprise, which I was reluctant to take at face value, when my Singaporean colleague at the UN, the savvy and well-connected Kishore Mahbubani, returned from a visit to Washington in March 2002 to say that his contacts were assuring him that rumours of deliberate preparations for an attack on Iraq were true. He had been hoping that I could confirm the story, from a position of superior knowledge. I could not; and I could not see that such a policy fitted the real threat. Much later I learnt that David Manning and his team in Downing Street had been made aware of the build-up towards war and were worried that, with regime change as its justification, it might not be sustainable as a politically acceptable policy in the UK. But Number Ten does not tell the Foreign Office everything and neither of them feels bound to fill in the Ambassador in New York unless there is an operational reason or the chance of a private conversation without using the open line. That was why I made sure I regularly came back to London, to keep both my formal lines to the Foreign Office and my more informal ones to Number Ten open. While I was fretting about Africa or involving myself in excruciating negotiations over Middle East resolutions or the International Criminal Court, Singapore stole a march on me over Iraq.

Tony Blair's visit to the United States to see President Bush at his ranch in Crawford, Texas, in the first week of April, with only David Manning, Jonathan Powell and Alastair Campbell with him from

Downing Street, turned out to be the catalyst for the widening of consciousness in the UK foreign policy team of what was at stake over Iraq. At Crawford the two leaders held face-to-face talks for the first time on the live possibility of a joint operation against Saddam Hussein. From that moment on, whatever the general statements of principle that had earlier passed between Blair and Bush on the potential role of the United Kingdom in a military coalition, the precise conditions became a rolling negotiation.

Two fundamental points lay at the heart of UK concerns. The first of these was inescapable. The United Kingdom had to establish a basis in international law for the use of military force. This could not be regarded merely as an item that Tony Blair knew he had to tick off if he was to gather the Parliamentary and domestic support for a British attack on Iraq. The United Kingdom relies upon the proper working of the international system, with the UN at its centre, for the pursuit and defence of our global interests. Cherry-picking when it suits us for short-term reasons leaves us worse off in the longer term. We are not a superpower and we cannot cope with the blowback if we forget that. The Prime Minister had set this out in clear language in public and in private, not least in his wide-ranging and very personal speech in Chicago in April 1999, which proposed rules for the collective handling of dangerous states under the aegis of a reformed UN. 'Any rules', he said, 'will only work if we have reformed international institutions with which to apply them. If we want a world ruled by law and by international cooperation, then we have to support the UN as its central pillar.' No American administration of either political persuasion would have uttered such words. The international and legal rationale for the UK was something the Americans realised from an early stage.

The second condition on which the Prime Minister placed emphasis was progress in the Middle East Peace Process. While this came to stand in the highly desirable rather than the essential category, he felt very strongly about it for two reasons. First, the violent stand-off between the Israelis and the Palestinians continued to poison the international atmosphere more than any other single issue. Second, its costs were piling up: sensible reform in the Arab world, a stable region of oil production in the Gulf, Muslim relations with the rest of the world, international order and justice, the defeat of terrorism, all were held hostage in one way or another by the absence of a settlement. Iraq as a challenge would prove harder to overcome if the temperature remained high on Palestine. The two had to be tackled in parallel.

Blair made this abundantly clear at Crawford. He was listened to by Bush. The other members of the Bush team all saw the point. The meeting led to a well-crafted speech by the President a few weeks later, on 24 June, in which a President of the United States declared for the first time that he supported a two-state solution for the Middle East problem, with Palestine and Israel living side by side in peace and security at the end of a settlement process. But as a condition for the UK's inclusion in a fighting alliance against Iraq, pushing for a solution to the Israel–Palestinian conflict was a less clear-cut issue than legality. As far as I could tell, the precise meaning of parallel action on the Middle East Peace Process (MEPP) was never spelt out. There was a gut feeling on the UK side that the link between the two issues would never provide a block on American action. Nor was it going to become a satisfactory reason for the UK to hold back from participation if the rationale for confronting Saddam Hussein flowed independently from the threat in Iraq.

It is worth looking for a moment at the words used publicly by Tony Blair on 7 April 2002, immediately after his talks at Crawford, in a speech at the George Bush Senior Presidential Library in College Station, Texas. They would have been drafted earlier but revised up to the last minute to take account of the bilateral discussions. They had to find a balance between the American emphasis on regime change in Iraq and the British requirement for a legally convincing case. The two paragraphs, inside a broad-ranging address spelling out the Prime Minister's foreign policy philosophy, read as follows:

As for Iraq, I know that some fear precipitate action. They needn't. We will proceed, as we did after September 11, in a calm, measured, sensible but firm way. But leaving Iraq to develop WMD, in flagrant breach of no less than nine separate UN Security Council resolutions, refusing still to allow weapons inspectors back to do their work properly, is not an option. The regime of Saddam is detestable. Brutal, repressive, political opponents routinely tortured and executed: it is a regime without a qualm in sacrificing the lives of its citizens to preserve itself or starting wars with neighbouring states, and it has used chemical weapons against its own people.

As I say, the moment for decision on how to act is not yet with us. But to allow WMD to be developed by a state like Iraq without let or hindrance would be grossly to ignore the lessons of September 11 and we will not do it. The message to Saddam is clear: he has to let the inspectors back in, anyone, any time, any place that the international community demands.

The passage would have been revealing in a number of ways — and I shall attempt to keep hindsight at bay — to any foreign diplomat used to dissecting the speeches of a political leader in order to fathom what he is trying either to convey or to hide. Most diplomatic services would not on this issue have been delving into every utterance from the British Government, because they would have been focusing on what came out of the American machine. But I can imagine Sergey Lavrov, my perceptive, Soviet-trained Russian colleague at the UN, wondering what pressures the Brits were coming under if they were succumbing to the US momentum on Iraq. The way the passage was presented and drafted suggested that the Prime Minister himself was worried about precipitate action; weapons of mass destruction were the principal concern; the British team had to deal with other arguments for threatening military action, which carried some force; but WMD were what the world should bear principally in mind; the issue was live because of September 11.

But what about the underlying position of the British Prime Minister? As I saw it, he was not ready to make any hard-and-fast decision about using force against Saddam Hussein. He was aware that September 11 had changed the context: the rhetoric against Saddam's brutality had to be stepped up to compensate for the fact that the threat represented by Saddam was not materially different in 2002 from the early 1990s. The UK had to remain within reach of the Americans but keep the focus on WMD, and so the next essential test of Saddam should be to accept the inspectors back in – a substantially weaker demand than would have emerged from George W. Bush if he had spoken on the same day.

Those watching on the touchline would also have been asking themselves why the United Kingdom was associating itself quite so closely with the United States on Iraq. Many might simply have regarded it as a fact of life that where the US went, the UK followed. Certainly on Iraq the pairing was a regular feature of UN debate. Others more familiar with the whole international agenda would have been aware that the UK and the US were by no means on the same side of the argument on every issue and that even on Iraq there were important differences of emphasis and approach.

Tense moments of argument did occasionally erupt. 10 Downing Street, at whatever level, was the usual channel of communication with the Americans, both because the Prime Minister needed to be in control of the overall operational relationship on Iraq and because only he or his immediate advisers could reach the parts of the US system that might act on UK proposals or advice. Of the Number Ten team, I was closest to David Manning, a long-time Foreign Office colleague and friend, and I was often aware of the intensive conversations he would have with Condoleezza Rice, drawing on the full balance of UK credit in the bank, to grind out the implications of a particular action. Other players at the UK end – including me – would often offer items for Number Ten to raise with Washington but have them filtered out as falling below the category of essential on that particular day. Such was the quantity of business across a broad range of political, diplomatic, military and procedural issues that it was rarely possible to have a rounded discussion about how everything fitted with everything else. The fundamental factor that coloured the whole relationship over Iraq – and indeed does so on virtually all US–UK business even where the broad objective is shared – was that the US was in the lead and the UK had to fit in behind.

Why does the UK get into this position with the United States and what does it achieve for UK interests? The question is asked again and again by Parliament, the media and the public in the UK and by diplomatic observers around the globe. The term 'Special Relationship' has an element of truth in it, but it is not used within the Foreign Office or the Diplomatic Service abroad except with heavy inverted commas. Access and influence have to be earned and often paid for. In my experience, from two postings in Washington as well as from regular dealings with the United States in every other diplomatic job, you are much more likely to come across an American with a sceptical view of the UK and all its works than one with a sentimental view. With either you have to prove the worth of the British input to the US in some material way. The frequency with which we do offer something of value suggests both that the American system is a long way from being self-sufficient and that the UK can genuinely fill some of the gaps. But we are constantly reminded of the reality that, in almost every instance, we are small beer compared with the volume and power of the United States. The extent of our influence is constrained and it never does us any good to forget it.

What does the United Kingdom gain from this interesting, mostly rewarding but partly subservient relationship? And why does this question cause such trouble? The predisposition of successive Prime Ministers to spend time, energy and political capital on the relationship with the United States cannot be lightly dismissed as a vanity.

The biggest problem is that the returns from working closely with the superpower appear largely unquantifiable. The UK acquires a good deal of information from the partnership which it would not otherwise collect, not least on security and intelligence matters. A posting in Washington is unusual in a number of ways, but unique in the fact that the UK picks up from its host more useful information than it gives away. Virtually everywhere else it is the other way round. But useful for what? We do not have to play in the same league as the biggest powers. Are we trying to stay up there as a historical habit, when our real profile of affordable interests suggests a more modest self-categorisation? We also keep our skills sharpened in the diplomatic, military and intelligence fields through the incentive to stay within reach of American performance. UK capabilities in these areas, individual for individual, are regarded as high. Finally, we benefit from having the United States as an ally and partner in struggles to implement the world's agenda in our favour against other interest blocs and cultures – nowadays largely non-military struggles, thank goodness, but the outcomes in Europe in 1918, 1945 and 1990 cannot yet be consigned to the shelf of irrelevant history. Nonetheless, the United Kingdom does not completely lack alternatives, primarily in the form of partners and neighbours in the new Europe. Many people in the UK might be perfectly content either to take the risk of lower dependence on the US in a mainly peaceful world or to rely on allies closer to home.

But there is one further calculation that the United Kingdom has to make. How much are we saving in straightforward economic terms by avoiding independent responsibility for our national defence? The decision of the United States to remain a European power from the 1940s through to the 1990s removed our most obvious potential enemy, the Soviet Union, and guaranteed the security of a gradually reuniting and self-obsessed Europe. The peacefulness of Europe is now assured. The size of current defence budgets shows that the nations of Europe have taken a bet on the absence of enemies beyond the foreseeable future. Yet the United States, for all its loyalty to NATO as an alliance, can no longer be safely regarded as a European power. It is a global power with interests in Europe that may be greater or lesser at any one time than its interests in another continent. The US stake in Asia, for instance, has been coming up on the inside track for a while now.

What long-term arrangements are the Europeans going to make in an unpredictable world? To be independent and trust international institutions to preserve a global peace? To be independent and raise defence budgets to the point of reasonable self-sufficiency? Or to be to some extent dependent on the United States? The first two of these options suggest a significant detachment from reality. The third grates. But they are real choices. And whether the first or the third route brings us security – because as sure as eggs are eggs we have not so far chosen the second – stems not so much from where the Europeans have consciously decided to place themselves as from the decisions that might or might not come out of Washington.

It makes sense in these circumstances to invest in the insurance policy which the United States represents and pay a premium now and again. That the United Kingdom should stand out for doing so reflects two things: first, the greater capacity of the UK to relate such an investment to a natural affinity with American values and interests, whereas France, often with support from Germany, has aligned its national identity with a Europe that is distinct from the US; and second, the inclination of many other Europeans to assume that they will have solved the problem of the security gap before they have to call again on the United States. The case for sticking with the only country capable of global power projection when global security is such a tricky business and when the consequences of globalisation are so unpredictable is actually quite strong. Exactly how any particular Prime Minister interprets that incentive, including its limits, is part of his leadership responsibility. Iraq undoubtedly represents an instance when this approach has been truly tested. But that is not a reason to denigrate the national interest calculation behind the general stance.

After the Crawford bilateral summit the momentum began to

gather on Iraq in material ways. The US military planning process took on a life of its own, going through a series of refinements that increasingly clarified who might do what in what strength at a particular time or place. The UK Ministry of Defence had to start doing some hard contingency work of their own in case they fell so far behind that they dropped out of the running. Both exercises were under firm political control. The Americans at one stage thought they might be ready to respond to an instruction to launch an invasion in the autumn of 2002, but early 2003 gradually asserted itself as the most practical timing for a large-scale assault.

The mantra that nothing had been decided and decisions would take account of all the circumstances was true in a literal sense up until quite shortly before military action began in March 2003. But the cumulative weight of the preparations made itself felt. As the spring of 2002 turned into summer, the pressures grew on the United Kingdom to reach a clear-cut position. The senior levels of the administration in Washington understood Tony Blair to have committed himself to active support of the United States – if force had to be used against Iraq – from quite early on in 2002. I know of no moment when the Prime Minister either used words of unconditional support or set out the conditions. When historians are able to pore over the released documents in a few decades' time this may prove to be wrong, but I know that his advisers were occasionally tearing out their hair because he did not draw a line. I gained the impression that the unequivocal gestures of solidarity after 9/11 moved first into natural and readily explicable assistance in Afghanistan. They then mutated into the assurance of 'I am still with you in this, George' when Iraq came so solidly into American sights that it was worth discussing with the Brits. Tony Blair believed in the necessity of removing the Iraqi threat and believed in the primacy of the US–UK security relationship. To stay properly positioned on both he needed to flow with the US current.

The difficulties for the UK in the US presentation of the reasons for striking at Saddam Hussein grew as the summer heated up. I doubt whether Washington's publicly expressed rationale, which changed and accumulated with the passage of time, differed greatly from the US administration's thoughts in private. From one mouth or another, the real thinking tended to come out. Saddam was a threat to the United States that should have been dealt with long ago. He possessed highly dangerous weapons which he had used in the past and he was trying to develop more. In this he was defying the United Nations. He was a brutal oppressor of his people. He supported terrorism and had links with terrorists, some of whom might or might not have had a hand in 9/11. He lived in a fragile region where US interests were numerous. The one policy connection which I do not remember surfacing at the time, and which remains the subject of speculation, is with the sustainability of the American presence in Saudi Arabia. It has been alleged that Washington was beginning to doubt that US troops could long remain in the Kingdom if the internal reaction against such a visible foreign presence continued to grow and possibly feed terrorist motivations. Yet the US could not leave Saudi Arabia vulnerable to Iraqi hostility. The withdrawal of US troops would therefore have to be preceded by the removal of the Iraqi threat. This is a perfectly plausible line of reasoning and I believe it entered into American calculations, but I do not recall it coming up in US–UK discussions and it was understandably not an easy case to present in public.

The UK side was concerned that putting out a long list of reasons for the possible use of force, and particularly building up regime-change arguments, looked too much like special pleading without a clear eye on international law. A gap opened up between the two governments over what their public pronouncements were aiming to achieve. In effect the United States wished to establish in the eyes of the American people that action against Iraq was politically legitimate. The Congressional vote in October 2002 authorising the President to use force against Iraq was of immense importance to the White House. The American system was not especially sensitive or vulnerable to any link between the international position and the domestic one. On the contrary, a suspicion of international institutions runs deep in the United States and the 9/11 attacks infused the nation with a marked impatience with anything but the most vigorous action. For the UK it was different. Parliament would not support an act of aggression that broke international law.

Exchanges between London and Washington through the summer made this point repeatedly. It was received with understanding in some American offices and not in others. London could not be sure that it was gaining traction when a warm breeze from one direction was cancelled out by a cold blast from the other. It became necessary to deliver the argument in a context of sheer pragmatic US interests.

As the debate within the administration gradually squeezed out any hopes of British procrastination, London spent July underlining in earnest that there were limits – not to their courage or commitment, but to the legal scope and therefore the political room for manoeuvre in the UK. David Manning visited Washington at the end of July to go over the arguments in person with his opposite number, Condoleezza Rice. During the course of their conversation the President happened to drop by Condi's office – these coincidences are sometimes arranged – and Manning put the UK position succinctly and emphatically to him. The UK would need an international basis for taking military action if British troops were to be involved. This was not just a matter of the political facts of life in the UK. It was crucial in the British view to have international partners in such an operation and few would materialise unless possibilities at the UN had been tested to the limit. The US ought to be aware that if the UK were to back out, the chances of building a solid international partnership would be significantly reduced.

In early August Secretary of State Powell decided that the argument for wider international backing must be put directly to the President. Bob Woodward describes in his book *Plan of Attack* Powell's unusually long and detailed meeting with Bush on 5 August – the 'You break it, you own it' meeting. A few days later, Jack Straw came across for a long, private discussion with Powell on Long Island, which reinforced the Secretary's understanding of what would be involved in constructing an alliance with, as a minimum, the UK. The US media began to pick up that Powell was arguing that the only way to achieve the US objective was to gather a coalition. Powell's input, on top of but more powerful than the British one, set a policy contest going within the administration for the remainder of the month, as the 'keep it focused' brigade emphasised the disadvantages of expanding the team and losing control and momentum. Certain aspects of the debate were reflected in the inevitable press comment, as unattributable briefings attempted to swing the process. At other moments the hardline attack was public and aggressive. On 26 August, in a bellicose speech to American Veterans in Nashville, Vice-President Cheney directly raised the spectre of an Iraqi nuclear bomb. 'The Iraqis continue to pursue the nuclear programme they began so many years ago . . . We now know that Saddam has resumed his efforts to acquire nuclear weapons . . . Many of us are convinced that Saddam will acquire nuclear weapons fairly soon.' We were startled by the categorical language, which we knew was exaggerated, but at least the focus was on WMD and not regime change for its own sake.

At the end of August, when President Bush was still on holiday in Texas and the senior members of the administration were divided between Texas and Washington, a decisive conference call took place between the senior Americans. It is not covered in the Woodward book, but the British picked up echoes of it later. Colin Powell, at a disadvantage in Washington when the Vice-President and Secretary of Defense were down in Crawford, set out once again the fundamental rationale for taking the UN route in the next stage – the value of having allies. Others put the opposing case that the US would lose more by way of reduced momentum than allies could add. The conference call ended with the President saying clearly and firmly that he did not want the United States to act alone.

The matter did not end there. Vice-President Cheney continued to present his case in public, to the extent of exciting press comment as to whether he was being loyal to the President. Private debate within the administration also continued. The sheer weight of the military planning and build-up exerted its own pressures. The UK team had to sit and watch the ball flying backwards and forwards over the net for several more days.

The date of the President's annual speech to the UN General Assembly, which was set to be the vehicle for a declaration of US policy on the Iraq question, was fixed for 12 September. On the weekend of 7–8 September Blair and his immediate Number Ten team crossed the Atlantic for a meeting with Bush at Camp David. It was at this meeting that the President finally gave an undertaking to the Prime Minister that he would bring the issue to the UN, in the form of a new resolution, as the British side understood it, which would call for the return of the UN inspectors. In return, Bush drew an unequivocal promise from Blair that British troops would participate in any military operation that proved necessary. The Prime Minister used the same phrase as on previous occasions: 'I'm with you.' This time, however, the circumstances and conditions were more clearly identifiable. The United Nations would be given the opportunity to compel Saddam Hussein to divest himself completely and verifiably of weapons of mass destruction. If they failed, military force would be used. The corollary of the arrangement was that if the UN succeeded, force would not be used. It was not spelt out in up-front terms, in part because of the virulent scepticism in some Washington quarters that the UN would be capable of doing any such thing. But that understanding was an important pillar of the British approach for the next few months.

The four days leading up to 12 September produced some elements of minor farce as the British tried to discover the exact terms that the President was going to use at the lectern in the General Assembly. Christopher Meyer's Embassy in Washington went digging, but even their excellent contacts and access did not break through on this one. I had a go in New York with the US Mission at the UN, but John Negroponte had nothing to offer.

Reassuring noises were made that it would be all right on the day, but the detail was being held extremely close. We were finally shown a copy of the text only on the morning of the 12th. The speech was full of fire and brimstone against the regime of Saddam Hussein. It left no one in any doubt that the United States would resort to military force if necessary to see every requirement of the numerous resolutions fulfilled. But it did include the phrase that we had been lobbying for: that the US would come to the Security Council for a fresh resolution.

Only after the speech had been delivered, while we were circulating around to gather reactions, did we learn that there had been a last-minute glitch in the preparation of the text. Unaccountably, as the speech-writing team would not survive long if this happened at all regularly, the text placed on the electronic reader at the lectern turned out to have been the penultimate and not the final version. It was missing the words about the fresh resolution. The President spotted the lacuna as he was speaking and supplied the phrase from his memory: 'We will work with the UN Security Council for the necessary resolutions.' This was a smart piece of filling in, since reading a controversial speech to a thousand people in the room and another several hundred million watching their televisions does not leave huge scope for fast footwork. But Bush's use of the plural – 'resolutions' – set a hare running. The French, for one, had been pressing very hard for a process that would include one resolution to get the inspectors back into Iraq and a second to deliver a judgement on how the Iraqi Government had responded to them. The Americans had been adamant that they would not subject themselves to the delays and equivocation that two resolutions would be bound to entail. The word was supposed to be in the singular in the speech. We – because Brits as well as Americans found themselves rushing round to repair the dyke – had a job to do to bring the French delegation back down to earth by explaining that the plural was a slip of the tongue. Not for the first or last time, the expression of distaste and disbelief on Gallic countenances was an eloquent comment on their limited faith in what they were hearing. A gremlin had struck in the precise spot that was to cause us so much agony over the coming weeks and months.

The 12 September speech set down a fundamental test for Saddam Hussein. He should accept the return of the UN inspectors and deliver up to them all the material and documents on WMD demanded by the UN resolutions or face the military might of the United States. While many members of the United Nations found the aggressive rhetoric of the speech distasteful, few were interested in speaking up for Saddam Hussein and there was universal relief that the US had finally decided to take the multilateral route, even temporarily. Since this important development laid the basis for the negotiations and indeed everything else that followed, it is worth setting out some of the President's precise terms, which followed closely the conditions set out in Resolution 687:

Delegates to the General Assembly, we have been more than patient. We've tried sanctions. We've tried the carrot of oil for food and the stick of Coalition military strikes. But Saddam Hussein has defied all these efforts and continues to develop weapons of mass destruction. The first time we may be completely certain he has nuclear weapons is when, God forbids, he uses one. We owe it to all our citizens to do everything in our power to prevent that day from coming. The conduct of the Iraqi regime is a threat to the authority of the United Nations, and a threat to peace. Iraq has answered a decade of UN demands with a decade of defiance . . . Are Security Council resolutions to be honoured and enforced, or cast aside without consequence? Will the United Nations serve the purpose of its founding, or will it be irrelevant?

If the Iraqi regime wishes peace, it will immediately and unconditionally forswear, disclose and remove or destroy all weapons of mass destruction, long-range missiles and all related material. If the Iraqi regime wishes peace, it will immediately end all support for terrorism and act to suppress it . . . If the Iraqi regime wishes peace, it will cease persecution of its civilian population, including Shia, Sunnis, Kurds, Turkomans and others, as required by Security Council resolutions. If the Iraqi regime wishes peace, it will release or account for all Gulf War personnel whose fate is still unknown. It will return the remains of any who are deceased, return stolen property, accept liability for losses resulting from the invasion of Kuwait, and fully cooperate with international efforts to resolve these issues . . . If the Iraqi regime wishes peace, it will immediately end all illicit trade outside the oil for food programme. It will accept UN administration of funds from that programme . . .

If all these steps are taken, it will signal a new openness and accountability in Iraq. And it could open the prospect of the UN helping to build a government that represents all Iraqis – a government based on respect for human rights, economic liberty, and internationally supervised elections . . .

My nation will work with the UN Security Council to meet our common challenge. If Iraq's regime defies us again, the world must move deliberately, decisively to hold Iraq to account. We will work with the UN Security Council for the necessary resolutions. But the purposes of the United States should not be doubted. The Security Council resolutions will be enforced – the just demands of peace and security will be met – or action will be unavoidable.

Saddam Hussein was cornered. His strategy had for some time been based on the objective of escaping from sanctions without losing his capacity to rebuild his military strength, including his WMD capability. As we now know, he did not possess any stocks of chemical or biological weapons, although the scientific expertise and a few of the necessary ingredients lay within reach. His nuclear programme was years away from a usable weapon even if he had had the freedom to pursue it. His one area of continuing development, on which he was spending a good deal of effort and money, was longer-range missiles. It was a significant part of his make-up and his motivation to retain the image of major military potential, without which he could not present himself as a champion of the Arab masses, a match for Israel and a much too dangerous target for any Iranian attack in the future.

Nevertheless to slam the door on renewed inspections at this point would have been suicide. The body of UN resolutions over the years was crystal clear about his obligations. He had made life as difficult as possible for the previous inspection teams and he had managed to avoid the sole blame, in the eyes of the majority of UN members, for the exit of Richard Butler's UNSCOM in 1998. But he could not afford to block a move that the UN community supported by a large majority. We picked up evidence that, at Kofi Annan's instigation, the UN Secretariat put a strong case to Baghdad for doing what it had been asked. Angry as Saddam was at the scathing and scornful terms of the 12 September speech, he decided to give some ground.

On 16 September a letter arrived at the office of the UN Secretary-General, full of defiant rhetoric but conceding that the inspectors, already constituted for more than two years as the UN Monitoring, Verification and Inspection Commission (UNMOVIC) under Hans Blix as Executive Chairman, could return to Iraq if the appropriate arrangements were negotiated. To emphasise the bad grace with which he had come to this decision, Saddam authorised his Foreign Minister to use Iraq's speaking slot at the General Assembly two days later to deliver a virulent diatribe in his name. He railed against the United States and the international community as a whole for believing that Iraq still possessed WMD and for the suffering the sanctions had caused his people. This speech came close to revoking the Iraqi acceptance of the inspectors' return. But the United States wisely chose to regard the 16 September letter as Iraq's official position and the rest of the UN did not demur.

Having reached the point in the story where the negotiating in the Security Council began in earnest over the detailed procedures for the inspectors' return, it is worth pausing for a moment to re-examine the reasons why the US and the UK, and indeed many others, believed that Iraq possessed weapons of mass destruction. This was the point, mid-September 2002, at which the British Government took the decision to publish their famous dossier setting out the evidence, drawing largely on intelligence sources. The preparation of this document had started much earlier in the year and a form of it had been ready for issue the previous March. It was a measure of my lack of awareness of how far the expectation of an eventual military operation had advanced in London that I argued from New York that publication in March held some serious disadvantages. London had perceived the need to deepen the public's understanding of the Iraqi threat in case a decision to start military action, with British involvement already likely, was sprung on them by Washington. I saw the UN community being startled by the belligerent connotations of such a move and finding it hard to accept the truth of the allegations in the dossier unless objective UN assessors were in place to back them up. The Prime Minister's office decided in the end to postpone the launch, as much because they found themselves out in front of the US administration on public exposition of the intelligence findings as because of the internal debate within the UK team.

The six-month period before the dossier actually hit the news-stands allowed a certain amount of further refinement of the material, to which I was not asked to contribute. The passage of time also brought publication into a different context, that of the President's challenge to the UN and the return of the inspectors. Nevertheless it still made me uneasy that we were revealing to the world both what we knew and what we did not know; and I thought it unlikely that this presentation of the facts would convince the sceptics at the UN or in the capitals that mattered. If we had possessed a crunching block of evidence, surely we would have given a private briefing to those of our allies who were cleared to see whatever level of intelligence was involved. Even the Russians and the Chinese, who might not be in that category, could have been persuaded that we knew what we were talking about. From what I read of the dossier before publication, it did not appear to me to deliver any hammer blows, but the decision was not mine to make. I muttered a couple of times and was then advised by the Foreign Office to shut up.

In summary the facts were these, as I saw them at the time. There was no doubt whatsoever that Iraq had long harboured ambitions to develop a WMD capability and had actually used chemical weapons in the 1980s. Saddam Hussein could have used chemical weapons in 1991 but chose not to. The work of UNSCOM after the First Gulf War confirmed the existence of residual programmes and revealed that work on biological weapons had advanced further than expected up to 1990. A constant drip of intelligence reports from what seemed to be a fair variety of sources indicated that Saddam Hussein's ambitions had not diminished and that biological and chemical materials continued to be concealed by the Iraqi regime. In particular, a long-range missile programme was being actively developed to fit either conventional or WMD warheads. It was clear that no industrial nuclear weapon development was under way inside Iraq: that would have left too many obvious signs, with or without inspectors on the spot. But we had indications – not just from documents that later proved to be forgeries – that Saddam might well be searching for overseas supplies of materials and technology useful for the continuation of a nuclear programme whenever he regained the opportunity. The regime in Baghdad had established a sophisticated concealment operation and they were confident that they could prevent the UN inspectors from finding any incriminating material.

Chapter Five of Lord Butler's Report, published in July 2004, brought an unprecedented amount of reliable detail into the public domain on the intelligence that was available to the British Government in the period from September 2001 to March 2003. The

Report reminds us that Government concerns about proliferation of weapons of mass destruction extended much wider than Iraq, contributing to a sense of what one Butler Review witness called a 'creeping tide' of proliferation and growth in the nuclear, biological, chemical and ballistic missile capabilities of countries of concern. By early 2002, Butler records, readers of intelligence assessments prepared for ministers by the UK's Joint Intelligence Committee (JIC), would have had an impression of:

a. The continuing clear strategic intent on the part of the Iraqi regime to pursue its nuclear, biological, chemical and ballistic missile programmes.
b. Continuing efforts by the Iraqi regime to sustain and where possible develop its indigenous capabilities, including through procurement of necessary materiel.
c. The development, drawing on those capabilities, of Iraq's 'break-out' potential in the chemical, biological and ballistic missile fields, coupled with the proven ability to weaponise onto some delivery systems chemical and biological agent.

By September 2002 readers of the JIC assessments would have had an impression of continuity in this picture, with certain changes in points of detail. Although Iraq was still constrained from developing a nuclear programme, there was strong evidence of continuing work on ballistic missiles, including the development and production of systems with ranges that exceeded the limits set by the United Nations. There was also evidence from one source, supported by one complimentary report, of Iraq having the ability to produce biological agent in mobile facilities, and additional evidence of activity at one site formerly associated with Iraq's biological warfare programme. Finally, there were recent intelligence reports, albeit mainly inferential, that Iraq was producing chemical agent.

Lord Butler's Committee collated this material, and a good deal more, as part of their examination into the quality of the intelligence on Iraq gathered by the British agencies from their own sources. Their report illustrates how much fuel from the intelligence arena was being poured onto the flames of US–UK suspicion about Iraq, flames already stoked by Iraq's past record, the findings of the inspectors during the 1990s and the constant refusal of the Iraqi authorities to cooperate with the United Nations. Until the US investigation teams had delivered a blank return in the months after the conflict, nothing materialised to disprove any of the assumptions that this accumulated corpus of information generated. We were predisposed to assume that there must be something hidden in Iraq, even if the evidence remained thin about solid stockpiles. In the Mission in New York, my Iraq team and I never sat down to examine whether the indications might be wrong, nor did any of my staff voice any doubts to me. The detail might need verification, but surely it could not all be invention.

During the spring and summer of 2003 the Intelligence and Security Committee (ISC) of the British House of Commons carried out their own investigation into the performance of the intelligence agencies and the use that the Government had made of their product. I was interviewed by the Committee while still Ambassador in New York and asked to characterise my reactions to the intelligence material that passed across my desk. I detailed several of the reports later mentioned by Lord Butler and described how firmly I assumed that, whatever the truth of each piece of the mosaic, there could be no question that Iraq was concealing something dangerous. The UK Mission in New York had regular contacts, uninfluenced by our American colleagues, with the UNMOVIC team under Hans Blix while they were going through their long preparation for re-entry into Iraq and we were careful not to stray beyond the limits of what the international experts thought were possible Iraqi holdings. Hans Blix was shown a draft during the preparation of the dossier and did not dispute its contents: he even suggested that parts of the passage on the nuclear element could be strengthened. Thereafter, though a good deal more circumspect in what he was prepared to say in public,

Blix constantly told us, right up to the edge of the conflict itself, that he did not know that the Iraqis did have usable WMD and he did not know that they did not. UNMOVIC's long list of unanswered questions about the Iraqi record on WMD, eventually presented to the Security Council in March 2003, backed up the atmosphere of disbelief that Baghdad's cupboard could be empty. I concluded for the ISC that, given the history, the accounting gaps and the continuing flow of information on Iraq, it would have been a more risky approach for a political leader to ignore the evidence than to act on it.

Confidence that we, the US and the UK, knew what we were talking about because only we were putting the effort into finding out the facts inside Iraq coloured my approach in the Security Council, in public and in private. I spoke up in seminars and on the occasional public platform in and around New York about the danger that Saddam represented through his holding and developing WMD. I can illustrate the kind of pitch I made with a quotation from my intervention, cleared with London, in an open meeting of the Security Council on 17 October 2002:

We remain deeply perturbed by evidence that Iraq believes it can hide its weapons of mass destruction rather than declare them, that it can again fool the inspectors and play games with them. The United Kingdom analysis, backed up by reliable intelligence, indicates that Iraq still possesses chemical and biological materials, has continued to produce them, has sought to weaponise them, and has active military plans for the deployment of such weapons. The United Kingdom analysis, backed up by reliable intelligence, shows that Iraq has in recent years tried to buy multiple components relevant to the production of a nuclear bomb. The United Kingdom analysis, backed up by reliable intelligence, points to the retention of extended-range missiles and to the employment of hundreds of people in projects to develop weapons with a range of over 1,000

115

kilometres that could carry both weapons of mass destruction and conventional warheads.

In informal consultations of the Security Council – the meetings in the side-room behind the horseshoe chamber, which were closed to the media and to other UN Member States – I was even more clear-cut in my contention that there were only two states who were taking the trouble to keep the Iraqi regime under proper surveillance and that therefore the Council should be paying attention to what we two were bringing to the UN. It was all part of the seductive feeling that if you are in possession of information which is available to no one else, you slip into a 'superior knowledge' mode: seductive and dangerous. It took a long time after the conflict was over for the realisation to sink in that the Iraqis had no effective, current WMD programme, had been telling the truth about most (not all) of the areas under UN scrutiny and were not engaged in many of the activities that I had been depicting to my UN colleagues. The extent of the emptiness of that particular locker came as a surprise even to the delegations who were fiercely opposed to our policy in the Council. We have all had to swallow our pride and face up to the conclusions of the US search team eighteen months after Saddam was removed. But the whole collection of perceptions, judgements and second-hand information that we had amassed up to the winter of 2002–3 had taken us to a reasonable human assumption: Saddam had to be lying.

I was obliged to eat my hat in another quarter as well, following a promise I made to my own wife. Anne was in constant contact, as President for several years of the UN Women's International Forum, with the full range of UN and New York opinion and was regularly showered with private questions as to why the US and the UK were quite so adamant that Iraq was guilty. She nobly maintained a UK party line, though in suitably guarded terms. But underneath she was increasingly invaded by doubts as to whether the WMD reasons for a military strike were really so solid. I repeatedly assured her that they were. I was wrong. The WMD story has dumped on my personal credibility right across the public and private spectrum.

I want to make it quite clear that I do not regard the UK's public presentation of the position on Iraq's WMD to have been deliberately dishonest. The September 2002 dossier and its successor in February 2003 have been judged by Lord Butler's Review Committee and there is little to add to that comprehensive examination. The dossiers lacked the caveats that ought to have been applied to particular pieces of intelligence used and the maximum was squeezed out of the available material in order to leave the minimum room for doubt. But the assumption that Iraq was contravening the most important aspects of the UN resolutions was fundamental and went wider than the British Government.

A fair summary of what we had to act on at the time was contained in the 'Net Assessment' of 9 September 2002 of the International Institute of Strategic Studies (IISS), London's leading international security think-tank. Their paper concluded: 'A reasonable net assessment is that Iraq does not have nuclear weapons, but could construct one fairly quickly if it obtained sufficient fissile material. Iraq most likely has a small force of proscribed ballistic missiles with a range of about 650 km, perhaps a dozen or so, which are capable of delivering CBW warheads. It has extensive biological weapons capacities and a smaller chemical weapons stockpile, though delivery means for both are limited and uncertain.' I doubt whether anyone in the British Government system would have had difficulty in signing up to that.

The IISS paper did not, of course, attempt to make a judgement as to whether what was known or deduced about Iraq's WMD capacities amounted to a case for war. That was for politicians to decide.

7

Resolution 1441

With Iraq's agreement to the return of the inspectors lodged at the UN, it was time to turn to the American promise to negotiate a new resolution. The atmosphere in New York was transformed. Security Council delegations started to clamour for information on what a new text might contain. The UN-accredited media shot into overdrive, each journalist desperate to be the first to get hold of a draft. It became difficult to do any other item of business, even though the General Assembly was continuing to meet at head-of-government or ministerial level.

It was not in New York, however, that the essential action on a text was taking place, though that was not immediately clear to us. For some time before Bush's speech was delivered or even sketched out, the US and UK Missions, in close contact with officials in their capitals, had been working on possible formulas for a further resolution in the expectation that they might soon be asked for urgent advice. As the situation evolved, US Ambassador John Negroponte and I burrowed deeper into the detail of what a final text ought to look like, making judgements not just about what our capitals would require as a minimum to create pressure on the Iraqi regime, but also about what it would take if we were to gain the positive votes of most members of the Council. I was concerned that we would meet severe opposition to a text that set out automatic authority – that is, without a subsequent resolution – for the use of force if Iraq committed any kind of new breach, but that Washington would quickly reject a process that did depend on a subsequent resolution. The trick would be to emphasise Iraq's total failure so far to meet UN requirements, reintroduce the inspectors with strict conditions on comprehensive cooperation from Baghdad, underline the consequences if this was not forthcoming, but otherwise keep the language moderate so that the difficult members of the Council were not provoked. The arguments flowed back and forth at official level during August and early September. By 16 September, when Iraq's reluctant agreement arrived, the US and UK Missions had agreed on extensive wording to recommend to our capitals, which we thought would hit the mean between 105 per cent implementation of all the UN's past resolutions and rejection within the Security Council.

Our effort was trumped by the activity in Washington. Negroponte had a close relationship with Secretary of State Colin Powell and a strong following within the senior reaches of the State Department, but it was the National Security Council, with the full and direct involvement of Condoleezza Rice and her Deputy, Steve Hadley, that was trying its hand at resolution-drafting on this occasion. From New York I could not see through the opaque layers of influence on policy-making represented by the different senior offices in Washington, but Christopher Meyer's lucid reporting, together with our occasional telephone calls, kept me abreast of the big picture. Cheney was a prime mover of the drive to deal with Saddam Hussein and he saw this as an American objective which should not be qualified by the need to take account of any outside influence. He was adept at using the media to carry his message, even if it sometimes cut across the more complex positioning of other parts of the American team. He was also a source of encouragement and protective strength to the Pentagon team around Rumsfeld and

Wolfowitz who were transforming the concept into an operational and politically plausible plan.

It was impossible to ignore the disdain felt in these circles for the United Nations as a forum and particularly as an agency for handling Iraq. This sharpened my need to produce analysis and action in New York that both avoided exaggerating what the UN could really achieve and met the UK's essential requirements for dealing with the issue. Condoleezza Rice, who from my perspective appeared to focus primarily on delivering what her President needed in the national security field, took on the task of resolving policy differences within the administration. With little personal experience up to that point of the Middle East but with a sharp understanding of US security requirements, her inclination seemed to be to support regime change in Iraq as an absolute good for American interests as interpreted by her President.

George W. Bush had nonetheless promised first the British Prime Minister and then the UN General Assembly that he would work with the United Nations over this next phase.

The team in the National Security Council were obliged to accommodate the views of the State Department and the US–UN as best they could in order to fulfil this. They were at the same time all too conscious of the rough road travelled by the administration to reach internal agreement on going to the UN at all, and Rice knew there would be strong reactions from the hardliners in the Vice-President's office and at the Pentagon if the text put down in New York was full of compromises. So the approach emerging in Washington was much tougher in tone than ours in New York and proposed a number of measures that were likely to cause trouble within the Security Council. These included the right of the five Permanent Members (P5) to designate sites for inspection; the requirement for UNMOVIC to take Iraqi experts out of the country for interviews; provision for troops from P5 countries to protect the inspectors on the ground; and the establishment of No-Fly/No-Drive Zones wherever the inspectors were operating.

120

David Manning at Number Ten, Peter Ricketts – my successor-but-one as Political Director in the Foreign Office – and I did not need to consult our ministers on the detail to know that the UK had to indicate difficulties with this aggressive approach. We began to work on Washington to sort out a position which both sides could support. Our Security Council colleagues were getting more and more impatient to see something on the table in New York, but more than a week passed by and we had nothing to offer.

It was thus rather galling on 28 September to find what looked like a draft resolution splashed across the pages of the *New York Times*, datelined London, purporting to be the US position. It contained most of the elements of the hawks' approach. There was an immediate cross-fire of questions as to who had let this out, with Washington assuming from the dateline that the British had done so in order to discredit it, and London suspecting that the hardliners themselves were trying to entrench their bottom lines by leaking them. ABC, who also carried an early report of the leak, hinted to us that the original source was indeed American. Within a day or two these extracts were spread about the press and being widely commented on in the UN corridors.

No one in Government circles, either publicly or privately, ever accepted responsibility for the text and it never turned up in New York as a proposal for discussion with other members of the Security Council. But the text became a marker for the other members of the Council, because at that point, with heightened expectations in the air, they had nothing else to go on. Eight weeks down the road, when we eventually reached an agreement in the Security Council, the resolution looked in shape and tone not unlike the draft with which John Negroponte and I had started. The leaked text probably doubled the length of the negotiation. But perhaps it also exerted some leverage on the minds of our opponents in the Council by reminding them how much worse things could be if the full force of the militant line in Washington gained the ascendancy.

Thus began the trickiest textual negotiation of my time in New

York. The production of Resolution 1441 occupied the time and energies of politicians, sometimes up to head-of-state level, to a far higher degree than any other resolution I can recall. The first sign of real trouble in New York came with French and Russian spoiling tactics. They quickly spotted that the US and the UK were taking time to come to a bilateral agreement on how to start the process. There was a lot of transatlantic telephoning, including between President Bush and Prime Minister Blair at one stage. I had strongly recommended to London that the Russians should be fully consulted as we rolled the strategy forward. Igor Ivanov and Sergey Ivanov, the Russian Foreign and Defence Ministers respectively, both happened to be in Washington on 19–20 September as part of their normal bilateral business. Moscow was likely to be less antagonistic in the end, as Iraq's most vocal supporter in the Security Council, if they were brought along as we proceeded, even at a cost, than if they were left behind either to catch up or explode. But internal differences within Washington and between the US and the UK erased the choice of whether to consult potential opponents or not. We had nothing to consult them on.

So France and Russia inserted one of those spanners into the works that make UN negotiating so much esoteric fun. They began to devise their own draft, which took a much lighter approach to the conditions for the re-entry of inspectors and certainly contained none of the provisions that the Washington hawks wanted. When the P5 began to exchange preliminary ideas on next steps, the French threatened to put down their own text if the US–UK tabled theirs. We did not want to get into this game. So we denied – truthfully – that the leaked text had any status and tried another way in, suggesting that the P5 should hold a discussion of concepts. This took place on 1 October.

It is hard to picture from outside the UN system what on earth is going on down the long shadowy corridors of the headquarters building and behind those guarded doors. The Security Council lies at the heart of the UN's intergovernmental system, the forum that nation states use to clear away rivalry and misunderstanding, and the unelected Permanent Five compose the heart of the Security Council. The Member States are advised by the professional Secretariat, the part of the organisation at the command of the Secretary-General and resourced by the Member States, but they are not led by it. If governments collectively decide to handle a subject by themselves, the Secretariat has to stand back and see what results it may be asked to implement. The Secretary-General is in that respect the servant of the nation states, whatever his profile or his international influence.

The familiar public image of the UN is the horseshoe table in front of the Norwegian tapestry in the Security Council Chamber, with Permanent Representatives raising their hands in a vote and their anxious-looking staff clustered behind them. That is the scene of the various dramas over the decades, and of countless meetings of a more prosaic kind (by 2005 the Council was well on the way to its 5,000th official meeting since its inception). But the real diplomacy happens elsewhere. Matters rarely reach the Chamber without several stages of debate and negotiation beforehand, most of it in the side-room for informal discussion. This 'informals' room is the newcomer's introduction to Council life. It is out of bounds to non-members of the Council, to the media and to any other potential interloper. Up until the early nineties, the practice of informal discussion barely existed. Members of the Council had to thrash out their differences in public in the main Chamber, or carry out private corridor diplomacy truly in the corridors or over a drink or a meal elsewhere. As the quantity of business began to expand after the collapse of the Soviet Union and the invasion of Kuwait by Iraq in 1990, the Council began to debate and negotiate in a side-room only a few steps away from the Chamber but ill-equipped for the purpose, with ambassadors and their staff perched uncomfortably on any available chair and with few established rules of procedure. After a while, and with a degree of wisdom that might be questioned given the trend of events in the nineties, the Council asked the Secretariat to furnish the room for permanent and more comfortable informal activity. A U-shaped table was devised, with seven seats down each side of the U and one for the monthly President at the bottom end. There were chairs behind for additional members of staff and for relevant participants from the Secretariat, and one at the table for the Secretary-General or his senior representative, who had a standing right to attend any substantive meeting of the Council in this format. A broad plate-glass window stretched out behind the bottom of the U, almost always closely curtained to keep council minds focused on the job in hand.

The space available in this re-designed room was limited. A good proportion of the original area had to be dedicated to interpretation booths for each of the six official languages of the UN (Arabic, Chinese, English, French, Russian and Spanish). The Secretariat claimed a fifth or so of the seats. Each Permanent Representative had room for three seated assistants behind him. The rest had to stand. At each seat there was an ear-cup, in the unique UN style, through which the interpretation came. A number of overflow ear-cups were positioned on the wall behind, for the standing participants to fight over. People took notes as and how they could.

An abiding memory for any operational member of the Council is this informal consultation room at its most crowded, when the President's pleas for limited attendance have been ignored and the punters are jostling for a few inches of space and an ear-cup. It is remarkable how many human beings can be jammed into a restricted space and yet remain entirely silent when the debate flows. Occasionally – indeed too often, except when the most disciplined Presidents are in the Chair – mobile phones sound with a harsh intrusion and the rustling of a restless audience can indicate that one of the more long-winded members is off on a rant. But the drama of the Council politics has, over the years, been gradually distilled into this stuffy and compelling room. Therein lies the cause of much complaint amongst the wider UN membership about, as they see it, the elitist secretiveness of the Council.

Iraq regularly drew a crowded room. As the struggle to establish or block a route to armed action against Saddam Hussein reached its climax in early 2003, it was barely possible to get through the door into the informals room, let alone listen to the sharp exchanges in any comfort. I increasingly regretted that the Permanent Members of the Security Council allowed so much dramatic action in global diplomacy to take place behind closed doors. The true nature of what we were trying to achieve would have been so much more convincing with a transparent process, and probably no more difficult.

Now, as we began to skirmish on this most sensitive of issues, the cloistered clubbiness of the informals room seemed to be too public. Things could too easily leak: indeed, it was the habit of several elected members of the Council to brief other members of the UN on the inner workings of the Council, having promised to do so in their election campaign. There was too much dirty linen on Iraq for Council operations to be exposed in this way. Moreover, Council members had become impervious to the intended informality of the informals room and regularly read out their prepared Government position as though standing in front of the UN press microphone. What we needed was real private debate to explore the murky depths of possible compromise without having to get our capitals' chop on every word.

What I proposed at the start of the 1441 negotiation was a meeting – or, as diplomats like to term it, a non-meeting – of the fifteen Security Council ambassadors without any assistants or note-takers, at a venue removed from the UN building. I offered my own Mission's conference room. We held our first gathering in this format on 20 September, a sign in itself that the P5 were keen to consult within the Council as a whole. Too often the suspicion ran freely that the P5 would try to keep all the juicy discussions to themselves. The UK and the US briefed the other thirteen Council members on our intentions and tried to allay apprehensions that the decision to come to the UN was a diplomatic diversion. At this meeting I emphasised that Washington's resolve to test whether the UN could solve the

IRAQ: THE COST OF WAR

Iraqi WMD problem was based solely on the disarmament requirements of the Security Council's previous resolutions: this meant that the issue of regime change would sit in the refrigerator for the duration of this approach. Unfortunately the UN media tracked us down before the meeting finished and waylaid a couple of Non-Permanent Members on the way out. The next morning's London *Times* carried a story quoting me as saying that regime change was 'on ice' in Washington, without explaining the context. Eyebrows were raised and another little nail clunked into the coffin of my reputation within the more hawkish reaches of the Washington hierarchy.

We had a second try at this highly restricted format in the US Mission a few days later, after the hardline text had leaked. We underlined the importance of press silence. This text was not the basis on which we wanted the Security Council to proceed. Genuine discussion of fresh ideas was needed among the fifteen if we were to find a way of moving forward by consensus. But the US and UK delegations did not have any firm new language to propose and the Council members could not be sure where they were being led. Two of our developing-world colleagues again made comments to the waiting press. We gave up on the 'informal informals' initiative.

We were not gaining much ground in our occasional P5 discussions either. The Non-Permanents were convinced that the P5 were meeting every other day to drive matters forward. In fact we only gathered as a group five or six times during the whole negotiation of Resolution 1441. On 1 October we began the conversation about concepts, skating round the need to have even a preliminary draft resolution in front of us. We immediately ran into one of the fundamental problems in the whole controversy, destined to plague us until the eve of war. The French were increasingly digging in with their refusal to allow any language that could be taken to authorise the automatic use of force if the Iraqis failed to live up to their requirements. The Americans wanted the resolution to say both that Iraq had already committed a 'material breach' of the previous resolutions and that any further breach, judged by objective

126

fact (in other words, by any Security Council member) and not by any UN arbiter, would lead to 'serious consequences', the euphemism for the use of force. The reader can see from the final text of Resolution 1441 (Appendix 2 on page 436) that both these items are actually there, the first in operative paragraph 1 and the second in the more convoluted language of operative paragraphs 10 to 13. But the earlier formulations of these points, set out in a 'concept paper' to avoid a row about a 'draft', were too clear-cut for the French and Russians and they supported each other in resisting them.

When a negotiating session has taken place in New York, the teams report back to their capitals immediately afterwards, sometimes succinctly by telephone – although this always carries the risk of eavesdropping – and always in protected telegrams or signals. When Washington, London, Paris and Moscow heard of the failure of the 1 October meeting to make any progress, a round of ministerial telephoning started between capitals to try to find alternative ways of getting round the difficulties. Jack Straw happened to be in Paris on other business on 7 October and held a session with fellow Foreign Minister Dominique de Villepin to look at possible reformulations. None of this achieved much. On 8 October the P5 repaired again to the top of the US Mission on First Avenue and, setting aside the stalemate on what the consequences would be for Iraq, tried to concentrate on the question of defining 'material breach' (a substantive contravention of the resolutions) and on proposals for the return of inspectors. John Negroponte patiently went through a set of nine detailed suggestions, after which Sergey Lavrov spelt out Moscow's objections to each of them.

Jean-David Levitte, the Frenchman, shrewd in his arguments but gentler in his methods, attempted for a few minutes to ease the blow, realising that rejection of everything the Americans were offering might snap some threads. He wondered whether 'flagrant violations' might be an acceptable substitute for 'material breach' of the resolutions. But Lavrov would have none of it. Moscow's determination, to prevent unilateral action by the single remaining superpower had been hardened by their experience of the 1998 bombing of Baghdad and the 1999 Kosovo campaign. Stirred afresh by the recent rhetoric from Washington, Russia's emphasis on multilateralism had formed into a formidable obstacle, even though Russia had no particular reason to defend Saddam Hussein's defiance of the UN. Levitte saw that there was no way through and returned to full-scale support of the Russian position. Negroponte and I glared at them. Wang Yingfan of China, sharp and accomplished enough to enter the fray but constrained by Beijing's priorities closer to home, stayed silent. His country's interests were being protected well enough by the two others.

This was a memorable low point. The leaked US language had indicated such a large gap between the two main positions that Paris and Moscow had decided diplomatic niceties could be thrown to the winds. Not only were they spitting out the automatic authorisation of the use of force, they were also resisting quite sensible proposals for reinforcing the capacity of the inspectors to break through Iraqi non-cooperation on the ground. It was difficult to see where on earth we could go from here. Negroponte and I agreed that we would have to try to avoid the P5 format for a while, but there was little else left.

I decided to try a different tack. Over the first weekend of October Anne and I had been staying in East Hampton with Arthur and Janet Ross, great friends and supporters of the United Nations and of the Anglo–American relationship. They held a dinner party in classic Long Island style at which Richard Holbrooke, my colleague from the Clinton era, appeared. On the basis of some fairly accurate reporting by the *New York Times* on the saga in New York, the table started a vigorous discussion of how to get out of tight holes in a stalled negotiation. Holbrooke suggested that it ought to be possible to draft a second resolution, alongside the one we were currently negotiating, setting out the terms for the use of force if the inspectors reported that they had been blocked in their work. This resolution would be provisionally agreed at the time of adopting the first and would come automatically into play without further debate if the trigger was reached. I went back to East Manhattan, worked out a refinement of this idea and sent it to London. The Foreign Office thought it held out some hope.

John Negroponte reacted more doubtfully when I mentioned the proposal to him a day or two after the dreadful 8 October meeting. He thought it might signal that the United States would be prepared to commit itself to a second resolution. I felt that this missed the point: the process was designed to make an agreement on the first resolution, however complex it might be, enough to carry the issue through to completion. Colin Powell told Jack Straw that he would think further about it, but in the end the Holbrooke ploy never gained traction in Washington. My colleagues in London continued to see the point of this approach, but were not going to press it in the face of American opposition. I told them that some such arrangement was going to be necessary if the UK was going to stay within the bounds of legality, which after all was the reason for this whole stressful business.

From this stage onwards ministers started to do an increasing amount of the negotiating. That does not normally happen with UN resolutions. Ambassadors have to accept that there are times when they do not have the fire-power to complete difficult business. But ministerial activity of an operational kind is much harder to keep from the eyes of the media. It can be difficult to test propositions in the course of several exchanges and then back off from them and try another tack when the breakthrough does not materialise. One of the great advantages of the UN as a forum is that it is removed by one degree from the domestic scene. Ambassadors can try initiatives that can then be disowned by the capital – though not too often, for the health of the Ambassador concerned – and compromises that would grate against some domestic position or other if proposed from home can be nobly accepted in the name of the global institution. Ministers who get drawn into the detail and the win-or-lose atmosphere of a major tussle can be taking quite a risk. Iraq had become too big a subject by this stage for that risk not to be chanced.

Jack Straw did not turn a hair: he rather enjoyed big-stake sparring. It was around this time, as best as I can recall, that the UK Ministry of Defence moved into a higher operational gear in preparation for military action, a sign to the Americans that we were indeed serious in our intention to support them on the ground. Jack Straw went to see Colin Powell in Washington. The visit seemed to produce a change in the nature of the US approach in the negotiation towards a more constructive flexibility. Perhaps the UK's credible commitment to total partnership helped.

Powell's input into the textual marathon grew in importance and effectiveness from mid-October onwards. He understood the strengths and weaknesses of the United Nations better than any other senior member of the Bush administration and his decision in February 2001 to make New York his first destination outside Washington as Secretary of State counted strongly in his favour at the UN – as it must have counted against him in other parts of his own system. He was always friendly to the diplomatic foot-soldiers. Iraq in the multilateral context was his subject and this negotiation was his show. He was as aware as anyone that the ground he stood on was unsafe. His President had asked him to take this route, but he could not know how much real backing the White House would give him. He also had to take into account the President's significant domestic achievement on 11 October, when the House of Representatives and then the Senate voted by a wide margin to authorise him to launch an attack if Saddam Hussein remained defiant. From that moment on, Powell knew that the UN represented a desirable but far from essential US instrument for dealing with Iraq. He would not be allowed to raise the cost of securing UN backing too high.

In mid-October the Americans decided to produce new versions of the paragraphs setting out the steps to be taken if Iraq failed to fulfil the requirements. These removed any suggestion that this 'first' resolution should authorise the use of force without a further process and specified that the Security Council would discuss any failure to comply reported by the inspectors. The words 'serious consequences' were removed from this section altogether. The new formulation was given to the French overnight on 16–17 October. The next day Paris returned with a demand that any measures required to bring Iraq to full compliance should be the subject of a specific further decision by the Council. Colin Powell reacted at once. He was not prepared to go back to the President, having spent internal capital getting the White House's agreement to the new version. The United States would adhere to the undertaking to go through a second stage, but not make any commitment to a new Council decision at that point. To our surprise in both London and Washington, the French said quickly that they would not make this a deal-breaker.

This was a significant step forward on a crucial part of the text and the first chink of light on the Russian–French insistence that the Security Council must be in control of every part of the process. It was followed by an immediate reversal. We discovered that the price to be paid within the administration for flexibility in the later section of the text was the re-insertion of 'serious consequences' at the beginning. Because we were unaware, we could not forewarn the French. Paris exploded. Fortunately, they did not withdraw their willingness to continue working on the revised later section, but they said that they would not give their firm agreement to any part of the text until they had seen the complete draft resolution.

Worse was to come. One point of consensus among the P5 was that Iraq should compile a new declaration of their complete WMD holdings as a basis for the returning inspectors to work on. The hawks in Washington now demanded a clause in the resolution stating that if any entry in the declaration was found to be false, this should trigger 'serious consequences'. This was bound to lose us the momentum recently gained. The State Department and the National Security Council, respectively the managers of the negotiation and the guardians of internal peace within the administration, fell into a furious row about it. London threw in its pennyworth and said that the UK would have nothing to do with such a clause. Somehow, as the days passed, this particular firework fizzled out.

All this frenetic activity between capitals and UN ambassadors was accompanied by equally fevered speculation in the media as to what was going on. Flecks of molten lava appearing in the sky were interpreted as full eruptions and wild guesses were made as to the meaning of the deep rumblings underneath. Focused as we were in New York on the word-by-word struggles of the textual exchanges, we found it hard to respond to the frustrated demands for information from our non-permanent colleagues on the Security Council and, even more, from the UN membership at large and from the media. On 16–17 October, giving in to the mounting pressure in the UN corridors, the P5 agreed to an open debate in the main Security Council Chamber.

Some fifty Member States outside the Council put their names down to speak and almost every speaker said with some emphasis that they did not wish to see force used against Iraq, either at all or without specific UN authorisation. A small number expressed virulent criticism of the United States – Iraq itself, together with other usual suspects such as Libya, Cuba, Syria, Iran and Algeria, and the keepers of the Non-Aligned conscience, India and Egypt. But most delegations, including some of these, were prepared to add some balance by calling for Iraq to comply with UN resolutions and for the UN itself to take steps to maintain its authority. This was the occasion on which I made a statement about the sins of Iraq against international law and UN requirements and referred to the evidence of reliable intelligence that Iraq was concealing an active WMD programme. I gave a strong hint that the United Kingdom would wait for a second stage in the Security Council before coming to any decisions about which route to take to compel compliance by Iraq, but made no commitment to a second resolution to authorise force.

France, Russia and others on the Council made it crystal clear that they wanted the UN to stay in control throughout the process. Levitte, for instance, said: 'During the second stage, if UNMOVIC or the International Atomic Energy Authority observe that Iraq is refusing to cooperate fully with inspectors, the Security Council would meet immediately to decide on the appropriate measures to take, without ruling out anything a priori . . . Only a two-stage approach will allow us to preserve our Council's unity; any kind of "automaticity" in the use of force will profoundly divide us.'

Levitte also referred to the suspicions that Iraq was continuing WMD activity: 'Even though France does not possess irrefutable proof, there are several indications that Iraq has used this situation [the absence of inspectors] to pursue or resume its prohibited programmes, notably in the chemical and biological areas. The behaviour of the Baghdad authorities has given rise to strong suspicions in this regard.' Such indications of balance in perceptions of Iraq, spread quite widely through the UN membership, gave us hope that the issue would be judged on reasonably objective grounds, even though we knew that the US and its closest allies were not themselves trusted to take a moderate line. The UK's constant problem was the fierceness of American public statements against Iraq, based on a policy of regime change that we did not share, while we were trying to convince the world that the use of force could only be justified by Saddam's defiance of the resolutions on weapons of mass destruction. The UK too stood on shifting sands. Perhaps, in the intense effort of trying to get others to understand our approach, we underestimated the degree to which they assumed that the United States was going to get to Baghdad come what may.

In London, at around this mid-October point, fine decisions had to be made as to where the UK should place itself on the matter of a second-stage resolution. The fundamental requirement in London was to remain within the bounds of international law. I shall look at that question in greater detail when we lead up to the war itself in early 2003. For now, London knew that it was essential to obtain a first resolution following President Bush's 12 September speech, both to set the basis for the return of inspectors and to bring up to date the risks which Iraq was running if it did not fulfil UN requirements. The United Kingdom was undoubtedly more committed to the concept of collective security through the United Nations than was the United

States. Ideally, we would have wanted specific authority for the use of force. Yet it was not only concern about parting company with the United States that made London reluctant to commit itself to the need for specific authority. It was just as much the worry that the United Nations collectively might never, whatever the circumstances, bring itself to authorise decisive action. The Iraqi regime, after all, had shown time and again that it could manoeuvre within the grey area of partial compliance. The British Government settled for a process whereby, if Iraq showed less than full cooperation after the return of inspectors, the Security Council should meet to express its several views of what was then necessary. But London wished to reserve the option to use military force if UK interests demanded it and would therefore resist being taken to the point of requiring specific new authority. Having determined that this would be the Government's bottom line, the Prime Minister regarded it as appropriate and necessary for military preparations to continue in the meantime.

This whole area exercised me personally. If the United States and the United Kingdom, having come deliberately and with a great fanfare to the United Nations to test the collective approach, failed to secure a new resolution setting out the circumstances for the taking of 'all necessary measures' against Iraq after the return of inspectors, then I could not see that the case had been made for the use of force. A joint military action by the United States and the United Kingdom would have been almost impossible to defend in the Security Council and would have made my personal position untenable. It was at around this time that I made these points clear to the Head of the Diplomatic Service, Sir Michael Jay. I could wear the distinction between the first and second stages in terms of specific UN authority, but I would not be able to stay in my job if the first stage was not achieved at all. The message seemed to meet with a sanguine response, but I was not making the point for effect or attention. It would be a watershed for me.

Four weeks after President Bush's speech the Americans had still not constructed a full text to put down in front of the other members of the Permanent Five. In the week of 21 October things at last began to crystallise. The US delegation presented almost a full text to the P5 for preliminary discussion – we were still playing the game of no formal tabling – and it met with a scratchy reception from the Russians. I launched into a comprehensive rationale for each part of the text, trying from the UK seat to save the P5 from a long and bitter argument about American motivations. Ambassador Lavrov and I often held a duel in these restricted meetings: he knew I was drawing fire intended for the Americans but he could not hold back his irritation that I was trying to play in the superpower league. My intervention was otherwise largely heard in silence.

We met the next day at the Chinese Mission, hotly pursued by the press, and made little progress. Lavrov and I had an unseemly row about the history of Iraq's nuclear file and the involvement of the International Atomic Energy Authority, which featured in the draft text but which Moscow regarded as irrelevant. My French colleague made it clear that Paris was going to have great difficulty with the phrase 'material breach' in the loaded context in which it was placed. Once again, John Negroponte and I realised that we were not going to make much progress within the Permanent Five. We decided instead that we would have to present a text to the full Security Council. Negroponte succeeded over the next forty-eight hours in getting some of the more objectionable parts of the draft removed by Washington. But the aggressive tone of the language remained unaltered.

So the stage was moved back to the informals room of the Security Council, and, lo and behold, not very much appeared to change. Hardly anyone outside the P5 was in a position to comment because the draft was new to them. Sergey Lavrov made a long and telling intervention, slamming most of the text. The Americans and British held off responding, saying that we wanted a fuller discussion when everyone had received instructions. The telephoning between P5 capitals grew more frequent, but none of the fundamental difficulties were being resolved. London started to think that a meeting at ministerial level was going to be necessary, but Colin Powell – wisely, in my view – said that such a public event would not be productive. There was a meeting in Mexico of Ministers of the Asia-Pacific Economic Cooperation, to which both Powell and the Russian Foreign Minister went, but their bilateral discussion on Iraq produced no progress. On the contrary, we heard from the Russians around that time that if the text was unchanged from the one tabled in the Security Council, they had instructions to veto it. None of this was unexpected, but it was depressing.

So far my earlier advice to the Foreign Office that the Russians, if not consulted and squared in advance, were going to be a huge obstacle was proving all too accurate. Things became even more difficult after 23 October when a group of Chechens took a large number of hostages at the Dubrovka theatre in Moscow, immediately making it more problematic for the Russians to consider any kind of concession on Iraq. Negroponte and I held a private session with Jean-David Levitte to test between the three of us what the real possibilities might be of bridging the significant gaps. Levitte said he was about to circulate some proposals for changes to the text, though he pretended that they had no official status; and a day later he did so. Then the Russians came up before the end of the week with a text of their own. Both were out of reach of Washington. For the first time the Americans, British and French started to do some speculative counting of votes in the Council, with the French confident that they could gather more than nine votes for their text and that the US–UK would secure fewer than nine for theirs. The press began to calculate in detail which side might get the three-fifths majority of Council votes necessary to secure a resolution.

I started to worry that the whole negotiation was unravelling. John Negroponte and I decided to show that the US and the UK were serious about taking their text to a vote. On Friday 25 October we announced that we would put our draft resolution into a form known as 'blue', which meant a text ready to vote on with little further notice. Not only was this a sign of hard intent; it also meant that no other delegation could propose a resolution that could be voted on before ours.

This immediately led to a long and informed discussion in the Council. Every delegation asserted their national position and we heard a good deal of criticism of our text. People disliked its judgement of Iraq as being already in breach of the resolutions, the vagueness of its criteria for assessing any further offence and the considerable powers it was proposing for the inspectors to conduct intrusive investigations. The Mexican delegation in particular asked some well-thought-out and tricky legal questions. It was clear to me that the French were closer to the centre of gravity in the Council than the British and the Americans. The unexpected feature of the day, however, was that Sergey Lavrov did not play his usual combative role. He delivered quite a subdued intervention and left us wondering to what extent the Russians were leaving their options open.

We became so taken up at that time with Paris's position as the protagonist for the opposition that I never really analysed why Sergey Lavrov suddenly lowered his profile. There was no talent in New York to match his at attacking an opponent's position. Throughout the negotiations he had been employing all his skills to counter-argue, block, ridicule and disrupt. He was in his element. A decision must have been taken in Moscow for wider policy reasons, bearing on the Russian–US relationship, that Russia should not be in the lead in blowing up the road in front of Washington's Iraq policy. Moscow probably also judged that, having set the pace for the first few laps, French runners could be enticed to take over.

They were right. For the next two and a half weeks Colin Powell and Dominique de Villepin carried the burden of hard negotiation, paragraph by paragraph and eventually word by word. They started that weekend, 26–27 October, entrenched on opposite sides of a significant ravine, with the Americans not wanting to say who in the future would be in a position to judge a material breach by Iraq and the French determined to specify that the Council as a whole remained in control.

*

The WMD experts, though they had no role in the negotiation itself, were not sitting by passively. At the end of October, Hans Blix and Mohamed ElBaradei, the IAEA's Director-General, came to a confidential session of the Council to explain what they needed from the sections of the resolution dealing with the return of inspectors. They did a good job of clarifying that, although not legally necessary, there were good reasons for the inspectors' mandate to be redefined in the new resolution. They wanted strong powers of access. They did not wish to be told exactly how to conduct interviews with Iraqi specialists and they insisted on having control over the choice of their own team – areas where Washington had wanted to intervene. Otherwise they were supportive of the American draft. This took much of the sting out of the Russian and French criticism of the central parts of the text. Blix and ElBaradei went down to Washington at this stage and were given a meeting with the President, which was unusual. It was a clear signal that the United States was going to work with the inspectors and it probably happened because Blix and ElBaradei were judged by Washington to have put up a good show in the Security Council.

During one of these late-October discussions in the informals room, my mind wandered away for a moment from the voices welling up around the table and I began to consider whether there was any hope of surmounting the Franco–American stalemate over 'material breach'. It occurred to me that we should be more specific in saying that the new resolution would give Saddam Hussein one final chance to comply. This would make it much clearer that the US and the UK were not seeking through this resolution to have a basis for attacking Iraq just because it had not complied with all the previous resolutions. That thought had been frightening the horses in the Security Council all the way through. I scribbled out some wording on the back of a scrappy piece of paper: 'Notwithstanding the terms of the first paragraph about Iraq having already committed a material breach, this resolution will afford Iraq a final opportunity to comply with its disarmament obligations and will set up an improved inspection regime to complete the process started by the 1991 resolutions.' I passed the scribble back to my ever-present Legal Adviser, Iain MacLeod, who thought it worth a try. He said he particularly liked the use of the word 'notwithstanding' (such are the thin pleasures of a lawyer in the midst of political mayhem). I did not introduce the idea immediately into the discussion: it was too risky to take such a step until I could be sure that Washington would not object. The Americans and the British try all sorts of concepts out on each other at different levels and in more or less promising political contexts. But eventually the idea did run, with slightly altered wording, which lost the 'notwithstanding' because it sounded too legalistically weasely. The proposal succeeded in dampening down the 'material breach' row and we were able to focus on other fundamental difficulties.

I also felt that we had to address some shrewd questions of the Mexican Ambassador, Adolfo Aguilar Zinser, about the proper legal basis for the use of force even if it was accepted in the Security Council that Saddam had committed a material breach. The implied insinuation that this new resolution would not construct an acceptable legal foundation for military action might do the US–UK position considerable damage. I launched into an explanation of the legal import of the 1991 resolutions. As I did so, I could sense Iain MacLeod going very quiet and still in the chair behind me. I gave a detailed defence of why we needed a reference to Resolutions 678 and 687 of November 1990 and April 1991: Resolution 678 and its call for all necessary measures to be taken against Iraq to reverse the annexation of Kuwait had never been terminated by the Council; and Resolution 687, which would have closed the 1991 military action if all its conditions had been met by Iraq, had not yet been fully complied with. This seemed to have some effect. My Mexican colleague told me later that he now felt able for the first time to explain to his capital the link with the 1991 resolutions, though it would be for his Government to draw from that what political implications they wished. Iain MacLeod and his legal colleague Adrian Fulford, who was visiting to canvass for a place on the new International Criminal Court, told me at the end of the session that they thought I had managed to avoid crossing any of London's legal red lines. But they confessed to having had some uncomfortable moments. That was nice of them: it was my head resting on the block.

There were other risks I had to take with London. The Iraq section in the Foreign Office was beginning to question some of the lines I had used in the Council: the Prime Minister's Office might not wear too strong an emphasis on a second stage. I was clear in my own mind that we would not secure nine votes for a resolution excluding any further role for the Security Council in the judgement of how Iraq was responding to the return of inspectors. We had to show that we had no qualms about a second stage. But I was equally certain it was no use arguing with Washington for a second stage that would leave the decision-making to the Council. I believed that the only way to avoid a later disaster in New York was to have all fifteen members of the Council voting for the resolution. To achieve this, we would have to hit the mean between automatic authority for the use of force, which the French and Russians would veto, and a clear right of decision for the Council in the second stage, which was way beyond what Washington would bear. The best way to do this, I proposed in a telegram to the Foreign Office, was to leave out of this draft any statement of what would constitute a further breach by Iraq after the return of inspectors. We would then rely on the previous resolutions, on which the right to use military force without a new and specific decision of the Council anyway depended. Jack Straw hesitated about proposing such a radical step to Washington, but in the conversations that came thick and fast over the next few days he did in fact put it to Colin Powell, who began to come round to it, and to Condoleezza Rice, who did not. It was eventually dropped when David Manning, the Prime Minister's Foreign Policy Adviser, judged that Rice would never be persuaded. She was again the arbiter of the centre of gravity in Washington, which was a good deal harder than its counterpart in London.

The US and UK Missions were trying to keep up the momentum while our ministers continued to telephone. We wanted to hold a Security Council meeting on Friday 1 November, but the Chinese took over the monthly Presidency that day and it was their New Year holiday. Instead, I invited Jean-David Levitte over for a private meeting. He re-emphasised the depth of the gap remaining between the two sides. While we were talking, Dominique de Villepin came through on the telephone, having traced his Ambassador to my office. Jean-David was too courteous to send me out of my own room, though I got up to go. He told me after the call was over that Paris had moved much closer to a veto if they did not obtain greater clarity on the sole responsibility of the inspectors to declare an Iraqi breach and on the role of the Council in taking a decision at the second stage, both at issue in paragraph 4. This was the precise paragraph of the text which I had advised London to drop because clarity would sharpen the differences. When I reported this to Negroponte, I could not resist repeating my rationale for the omission of paragraph 4. He insisted it would not sell in Washington. He confirmed, however, that the US was becoming increasingly interested in securing a unanimous vote – though he could not explain where the concessions needed for that were going to come from. My advice to London when I reported overnight was that we should stop trying to intervene with new proposals (my particular sin, as it happened); we should leave it to the Americans and French to grind away at their remaining differences and see what transpired.

The weekend of 2–3 November, looked as though it would have nothing to offer. I repaired to the Piping Rock Golf Course on Long Island in a biting wind with my Singapore colleague, Kishore Mahbubani, who naturally wanted to catch up with the story in between putts. I kept my cellphone switched on against the strict regulations of the club and had to hide in a bunker when Jim Cunningham, John Negroponte's calm and very able Deputy, called

141

as I approached the sixth green. He told me Washington had decided to put a revised version of paragraph 4 across to Paris. This in effect gave an assurance that the United States would respect the need for the Council to open up a second-stage debate in the event of a new Iraqi sin, but it did not deliver the clarity Levitte had told me was essential for Paris. Villepin was reported to be very interested in this, which signalled both a clever US move and a willingness in Paris to compromise. I reported it to Jack Straw's office with the comment that I expected the French to extract a price for it elsewhere.

The rest of the weekend remained quiet, but for a little domestic incident. I have a generous-hearted wife and a lazy disposition. My hair gets cut at home. As it was some time since the last shearing and the coming week promised to be high-profile, I asked for a tidy-up. We were spending the Sunday in our rented cottage at Woodstock, in the calm foothills of the Catskill Mountains two hours north of New York. We talked about this and that as the electric haircutters buzzed away. Suddenly there was a pause, followed by a muttered oath. Anne said I had better go and look in the mirror. I did so. My volume of hair might be thin but it was clear that a mini-lawnmower had cut a swathe over the crown of my head. Anne said she was very sorry. The choices were unpalatable: a partial or a total crew-cut. I went for partial, and Anne did her best to even up the lines. The result gave the impression of a no-nonsense armadillo. There was nothing for it but to return to New York and prepare for Monday.

Monday-morning meetings in the UK Mission set the serious business of the week. I made no mention of my crinological adventure and, with a hard look around the room, implicitly dared anyone to speak or even grin. No one flickered. I raced through the meeting and went on down to the Security Council, thinking that perhaps the change of style might be taken as a natural variation. The Chinese had coffee and cakes out for the start of their Presidency. People chatted for the first few minutes without a glance at the offending area. Then up came Kishore Mahbubani, who had last seen me in the clubhouse with maximum thatch. He made a half-comment about Iraq and looked at my head. 'WHAT have you done with your hair?' he yelled. The pretence collapsed and I explained the sequence of events. There was much amusement.

When we regained our offices that morning, I talked to Negroponte and we both checked with our capitals and found that the clouds had not lifted very far. An extraordinary amount of telephoning had taken place between Powell, Straw, Villepin and Ivanov, but the gap had not quite been bridged between the Americans and the French. Powell did not wish to throw anything else into the scales. He had had to clear a number of amendments over the past week with other principals in Washington and he knew that there were limits. Villepin, for his part, had to clear his thoughts with President Chirac. Paris and Washington were each telling the other that the ball was in their court.

That afternoon I heard that Washington could live with the central amendment discussed with the French, but not offer some of the titbits we had been hoping for in secondary areas of the text, apart from a few crumbs in the preambular language. Now this had gone formally through the Washington system, there was very little chance of our gathering any further material to offer. Meanwhile, we heard from Paris that Villepin had not been able to clear the central language with his President. The Russians had several problems in secondary areas and the French were holding out on paragraph 4. The Americans nevertheless put their revised text down on the table in the Security Council on Tuesday and Jim Cunningham and I explained the improvements and asked for support. Sergey Lavrov, firm but not harsh, said he would have to convey the draft to his authorities and he was sure there were still some changes needed. The Syrian delegation, which had by now woken up to developments as this period's spokesman on the Council for the Arab World, began to sound really unhappy with what they saw, but we asked the Ambassador to try his capital before formulating a response.

On Wednesday 6 November the whole Security Council delivered their comments on the text, on instructions from their capitals. Adding them all together, there was considerable trouble still out there. Adolfo Aquilar Zinser of Mexico asked some pointed questions about the whole purpose of the resolution and complained that there was no language in the text offering relief for Iraq if they complied with everything. I gave him a very careful and emphatic reply, saying that the purpose of the resolution was to reintroduce inspections with a chance of their achieving something and to give a clear, last warning to Saddam. We did not have any 'light at the end of the tunnel' language because we had had too much of Saddam's cynical disregard for the UN resolutions over twelve years. It was time for the Security Council to accept that the end of the road had been reached unless Saddam Hussein took this final opportunity. John Negroponte and I did not offer any amendments, but we promised to produce a final version taking this discussion into account, implying that the Council should expect a vote at that point.

Negroponte and I had one last session to decide on our final recommendations to our capitals. Calling round at his office on First Avenue, I found him in the process of e-mailing his advice to his Secretary of State. The French had dug their heels in on the language of paragraph 4: they did not want the trigger for further action against Iraq to be *either* a false account by Baghdad of their WMD holdings in their declaration *or* a failure to comply in any other way: they wanted both. The 'or' had to be changed to 'and'. John and I both agreed to ask our capitals to approve this change. We added in four more points for good measure, judging that we would need them to secure everyone's votes. The and/or change was, however, the most important because President Chirac had hardened his opposition to 'or'.

We began to ask our French and Russian colleagues, because their delegations' votes in the Council would be the marker position for so many others, where their capitals were coming out. This always emerges as a delicate dance between delegations at the end of a negotiation on a draft resolution. Eight weeks of high-level and highly public negotiation now hung in the balance. We learnt that the Russians had decided that they could not abstain on an issue of such importance (even though they had done so in 1999 on Resolution 1284). It would be either a 'yes' or a veto. We knew the French wanted to vote the same way as the Russians (and vice versa); and we presumed they would not abstain either. These exchanges brought us into Thursday 7 November, when the US Mission heard that the White House could finally agree to 'and' instead of 'or' and would allow paragraph 12 to say, as France wanted, that the aim was to 'secure' rather than 'restore' international peace and security. That was all.

I was worried this was not enough. I wanted support from London to try to get two more concessions out of the Americans, because we could not now permit the negotiation to fail. I called Peter Ricketts to ask him to secure permission from Jack Straw for a final try, only to discover that they had both gone to the Queen's annual reception for the London Diplomatic Corps. I managed to track him down and asked him to put down his champagne, straighten his white bow tie and have a go at the Foreign Secretary. I do not know what he had to interrupt, but he called back and told me I could have one more try at the Americans. When I told John Negroponte that I wanted to push these final points, he advised me not to risk it. Washington was at the end of its tether. If I insisted on doing so, I should leave it to the last minute and see whether other delegations still had problems.

His judgement proved better than mine. We had signalled in the Security Council on Thursday morning that we would go to a vote on Friday. The Syrians virulently objected, because an Arab League summit was taking place that weekend and they did not wish to be put in the position of voting, as the only Arab nation on the Council, without checking with their brethren. The US and the UK gave a good impression of considering a delay, but we knew what answer we would get from Washington. We came back and confirmed that a vote was set at ten o'clock on Friday. We then heard that the French were signalling that the 'and' and/or 'or' had done the trick for them. The Russians still had not received their instructions, but Lavrov's body language was calm. We thought we were OK.

When Friday 8 November dawned, I cross-checked with John Negroponte that there was no call for further informal consultations in the Council. No one seemed to be raising problems. We were left with the assumption that the Russians were all right and that the Syrians, out of their depth on the detail but clear in their antipathy, would abstain. A few minutes before ten o'clock I went to meet John Negroponte outside the US Mission and we walked across the road, at 10 a.m. exactly, to the UN building. At that moment his cellphone rang and he was told that the Syrians were voting yes: pressure on them from Arab partners, France and the UN Secretary-General not to rock the boat had brought them round. We entered the building with smiles on our faces, walked together down the long corridor, past the press, briefly answered some shouted questions as to whether we were optimistic, and went into the Council. Kofi Annan was sitting in his private room behind the Security Council chamber and he invited John and me in. He knew by then that the Syrians were voting positively and he gave us his congratulations that we were getting a unanimous resolution, something he had always wanted for the sake of UN cohesion.

We all went into the chamber with the horseshoe table. It was crowded out. Wives could be spotted in the far corners and the press and public galleries were packed. The Chinese Council President had everyone sitting down by 10.15. Iraq chose not to take a seat at the Council table, as the country on the agenda has a right to demand. We went straight into the vote with no speeches. Wang Yingfan of China asked for a call of hands. The photographers were ready. Lo and behold, all fifteen put up their hands and there was an audible stir from the Member States when they realised that Syria was voting yes. It was fifteen to nil. Kofi Annan gave a short, powerful speech of support, praising the Council for finding unanimity and urging the Iraqi leadership to seize the new opportunity to disarm peacefully.

The fifteen delegations then launched into their explanations of vote. The United States and the United Kingdom declared explicitly that there was no automaticity in the resolution for the later use of force, as the matter would return to the Council under the terms of the resolution. But we underlined that the decision did not constrain any Member State from 'acting to defend itself against the threat posed by Iraq or to enforce UN resolutions'. The other members of the Council were much more equivocal. As it transpired, however, and this was something of a surprise, only the Mexican delegation set out in quite unmistakable terms their view that no military action should follow without a further resolution from the Council: 'The possibility of the use of force is valid only as a last resort, with prior explicit authorisation required from the Security Council.' But there was no wording in the resolution's text to bear out this interpretation. All the others were less than specific on this point, including the Russians, French and Chinese, who put round their own joint statement later in the day but without expressly making the Mexican point: 'Failure by Iraq', they said, 'will be reported to the Security Council by . . . UNMOVIC or . . . the IAEA. It will then be for the Council to take a position on the basis of that report.' It was an ambiguous formulation, but consistent with the terms of 1441.

The meeting terminated and we gave ourselves up to the press. I went out into the icy November breeze and did pieces to camera for Fox, Sky and Channel 4. That evening I had a long interview with Charlie Rose, New York's leading talk-show host, in the friendly and positive company of Jean-David Levitte – a clear public signal of no Anglo–French hard feelings. I paid a particular compliment to the central role of Colin Powell in the whole negotiation, all the easier to do because he had come through on the cellphone just as we entered the chamber to express pleasure with the substance of the outcome and to thank the British team for our part in it. He had, moreover, been on his own in the senior US handling of the negotiation. In all these media exchanges there was heavy emphasis on the fifteen-to-nil vote, which really was news. The Prime Minister made a statement immediately after the vote and phone calls started to come in later in the afternoon from the Foreign Secretary, from David Manning at Number Ten and from the rest of the team in London. In the morning the papers on both sides of the Atlantic had front-page photographs of the vote, often featuring Negroponte and me together, my shorn hair so prominent that various friends telephoned to ask whether I was undergoing chemotherapy.

This was the most dramatic negotiation I would go through during my time in New York. Others will help to tell the tale of why the Russians and French decided at the last minute that they could not resist American pressure any longer, but I suspect the difficulty of taking Baghdad's side formed a large part of it. As their public statements implicitly acknowledged, they had been forced to concede their most important point, that there would be no specific requirement for a second resolution giving authority for the use of force. It had been hard for them to let it go in these fraught November days; and it proved even harder for them to recall this as the early weeks of 2003 rolled by. The drama was by no means over.

8

The Inspectors Return

With the adoption of Resolution 1441 a degree of optimism seemed to return to the United Nations. As Thomas Friedman wrote in the *New York Times* a day or two later, 'it was the first hopeful moment I have felt since September 11'. He went on in the same article to wonder presciently whether the mood would last:

> The American public told Karl Rove, and the British public told Tony Blair, that Iraq was a war of choice, and while it may be a legitimate choice, they did not want to fight it without the cover of the UN . . . because there is no war in Iraq that does not end up with a long-term occupation and nation-building, and that can't be effectively pursued alone or under an exclusively US umbrella. Mr Rove, Mr Blair and Mr Colin Powell told that to Mr Bush – who then balanced a threat to go it alone with a diplomatic effort to avoid having to do so.
>
> As I said, all this made for a pretty good weekend . . . But will it last?

This was not a question we asked ourselves in any operational sense. The cracks between positions might be evident, but why disturb the new momentum by trying to address them now?

The inspection team under Hans Blix immediately began to prepare for a full-scale return to Iraq. The Iraqi Government delivered a churlish public statement about Resolution 1441, but it had no choice but to let the inspectors back in. It did not want to hand the US a pretext for war which everyone would support. The resolution gave Blix significant new powers of access and established far more intrusive parameters for future investigation. The hardliners in Washington were hoping that Baghdad would fail the first and immediate test, the requirement to confirm within seven days its intention to comply with all the terms of the resolution. In fact, Saddam Hussein decided to signal his acceptance of the new terms well before the deadline. Blix found it much more difficult to get Baghdad to agree to the precise arrangements for the inspection operation, but he still succeeded in getting an effective team on the ground before the end of November, improving by a considerable margin on his estimate of forty-five days from the passage of the resolution.

Once the inspectors had settled down at their bases in Baghdad, and later Mosul, and begun their work with routine visits to the main listed WMD sites, attention turned to the 1441 requirement for Iraq to produce a full new declaration of its WMD history and residual stocks. It was assumed in both Washington and Paris that the Iraqis would be stuck on the horns of a nasty dilemma. Either they would be caught reproducing the lies and omissions of their formal WMD statements through the 1990s or they would have to deliver a full and truthful account of all their holdings and documentation, which would mean the end of Saddam Hussein's treasured image of Iraq as a state with WMD capability. In Washington there was a growing sense of expectation, as the deadline for the declaration drew near, that Saddam would one way or another supply the grounds for an uncontroversial judgement that he had failed to comply with Resolution 1441.

Again, the Iraqis met the UN deadline with a day or two to spare. On 7 December 11,800 pages in English and Arabic were presented to the inspectors in Baghdad. The document included huge annexes, 3,000 pages of them in Arabic, presenting a monstrous mountain of papers for the inspectors to comb through. Clearly Baghdad believed that this new compilation, patching together vast reams of documents from previous statements with a haphazard collection of confusing and largely trivial new detail, would keep the UN occupied for months. Saddam never abandoned the hope that UN working practices would wrap up the United States in endless complexity.

Blix's team transported the declaration in several heavy boxes from Baghdad to Cyprus and on to New York, where they were offloaded during the first snowstorm of the winter and spirited away into UNMOVIC's offices on the thirty-fifth floor of the UN building, passing for a moment before the full glare of the television cameras. The US administration was desperate to secure an early look at the text, if possible before any other delegation. The declaration, however, was in UN hands and there was no reason to give the United States preferential treatment over the other members of the Security Council. Washington suggested that copies of the documents should first be delivered to the five Permanent Members and put enormous pressure on the US Mission to achieve this over the weekend of 7–8 December. The Council President for December, Ambassador Valdivieso of Colombia, resisted. The ten elected members of the Council were demanding simultaneous access to the text and we could not expect one of them to rule in favour of the P5.

A consideration arose at this point that went beyond privilege and political rivalry: the Iraqi declaration contained so much detailed material on the nature of the regime's past WMD holdings and practices that it presented a proliferation risk. Even the inspectors argued that certain passages should not be allowed to fall into the wrong hands. The Non-Permanent Members, particularly Syria, regarded this as one more pretext for preferential treatment of the P5 and Ambassador Valdivieso was caught in an unpleasant bind. In the end he took the decision, tolerable to all except the Syrians, that the UN should make copies for the P5, whose nuclear status gave them the capacity to judge which parts of the declaration should never be published; that the inspectors and the P5 together should edit the text; and that only then should expurgated copies go to the whole Council. The process lasted a full week, with much muttering and complaining and with little acknowledgement of the miraculous task performed by the UN Secretariat in getting such a vast amount of editing and copying done in so short a time. Saddam Hussein's hope of several months' delay faded quickly.

Eventually the UN turned to examine the substance of the declaration. Public comment began to flow thick and fast. The Americans insisted in official briefings even before everyone had had a chance to read the document that the declaration was full of lies and evasions. They called for a fresh condemnation of the Iraqi regime. Tension rose. Hans Blix and Mohamed ElBaradei came to the Security Council on 19 December to give their first impressions. Their language was more restrained than Washington's, but their assessment was hardly more favourable. Memories of the December 1998 saga were resurrected and the UN membership as a whole began to sense real trouble brewing. The Security Council, however, took the sensible decision that a more considered judgement was needed from the inspection teams and a date was set for a further meeting after the New Year break. This took the sting out of the media comment, as people realised that the declaration on its own was not going to be the basis for immediate military action. Nonetheless, some of the temperature was maintained by continuing statements from the US delegation in the Security Council that the inadequate declaration was in itself a further material breach of UN resolutions. The UK pointedly commented that these statements by the Americans were not consistent with paragraph 4 of 1441 and its famous 'and'.

As it turned out, I had a peaceful Christmas break with the family in Woodstock and we all enjoyed the huge snowfall in the Catskills on Christmas Day. There is nothing like a toboggan and the wet slap of a snowball to put WMD in their proper place. No meetings of the Council were scheduled until the New Year and none on Iraq in the early days of the French Presidency in January 2003. I returned to London at the end of the first week of January for the first-ever global conference of British Heads of Mission and called on David Manning in 10 Downing Street to swap assessments of what lay ahead. My daily reporting from New York was addressed to the Foreign Office and copied around the senior desks in Whitehall Government Departments, but David's position as Tony Blair's professional adviser was the pivotal one and his unusually broad experience – Warsaw, Delhi, Paris, Moscow, the Balkans, and Tel Aviv as Ambassador – gave him a real depth of perspective. His view of the political mood, of the potential to move the Americans to respect our bottom lines, of the requirement for Whitehall to present clear and objective advice to the Prime Minister and of the achievability of the formidable targets Tony Blair was setting himself was absolutely essential to members of the close team working on Iraq. His unfathomable calmness in the handling of this cauldron steadied us all and his accuracy of judgement and disarming frankness exerted an influence on White House thinking as well.

London and Washington were in constant touch throughout this period, the main channel being David to Condoleezza Rice; and Jack Straw and Colin Powell were regularly exchanging views on the declaration and the work of the inspectors so far. These were all close working and personal relationships, cemented by respect and trust and capable of carrying the explosive subject matter. But they did not reach into the offices of the Secretary of Defense, where the British Defence Secretary, Geoff Hoon, found it hard to penetrate, or of the Vice-President, who had no precise opposite number on the UK side. There were few indications coming to London that the United States was contemplating precipitate military action while the principal focus remained on the inspectors and what they might find. Yet we were conscious that Cheney had been arguing for an early-February start to the military campaign and we could never be quite sure whether the lines we were using might snap.

With the inspection team continuing its work on the ground throughout this period, Blix and ElBaradei returned to the Security Council on 9 January having spent three frantic weeks wading through the declaration. Their conclusions were anticlimactic. The declaration turned out to be a hotchpotch of old material hastily thrown together, with a few pages of new but largely uninteresting material inserted to keep up the pretence of cooperation. UNMOVIC and the IAEA judged that the declaration on its own neither proved nor disproved that WMD programmes were continuing in Iraq. They played down the implication that Iraq had failed to do what the resolution required. They said that the large number of questions still remaining to be answered would have to be investigated by the inspectors on the ground before any final assessment could be made. The terms of Resolution 1441 specified that Hans Blix would have to report on the inspectors' findings after sixty days of work in Iraq and Blix set the date for this as 27 January. As with the period before Christmas, the setting of a further date calmed the immediate tension. 27 January became the next crunch date for the United States, according to media comments drawing on Pentagon briefings, to decide whether or not Iraq was cooperating adequately.

For all these short-term postponements, the British Government was becoming increasingly conscious that time was running out on them. London had long known that the momentum behind the American military build-up in the Gulf would make it extremely difficult to keep the UN process going into the early summer, when the weather would turn too hot for a comfortable military campaign. The British objective of keeping the Security Council united behind pressure on Baghdad was also beginning to look forlorn. Up to the beginning of January, Paris had been keen to suggest that continuing cooperation amongst the five Permanent Members would be possible on the basis of 1441. The French were half expecting that UNMOVIC would indeed discover something interesting on the ground. Journalists reporting from Paris were briefed that the French Government believed Iraq still possessed stocks of anthrax and of chemical materials. Chirac had given the occasional hint that, if this proved to be the case, combined military action would not be impossible. This impression of options left open had been strengthened by French contacts with the Pentagon during the autumn to test how a French contribution to an attack might work if things actually turned out that way.

At the end of the first week of January reports appeared in the press that a French aircraft carrier had left Marseilles and was steaming eastwards through the Mediterranean. The French media began to wonder whether French participation in an operation against Iraq was really possible. On 7 January this seemed to strike President Chirac as too forward a position. Perhaps he was becoming increasingly disturbed by the bellicose statements that continued to flow out of the American system even after the success of 1441; or perhaps he sensed that the US resolve to test the UN route fairly was weakening. He made a public statement which stopped all the speculation in its tracks, emphasising the French view that the use of military force had to be a last resort and that France believed it was much too early in the inspectors' task for any such consideration to be applicable. I do not remember what happened to the aircraft carrier, but it was not heard of again.

Action in the Security Council began to pick up. The P5 came to an understanding that, rather than having a constant series of rows about where Iraq was to feature on the agenda, there should be at least one session of informal consultations a week to keep everyone up to date on developments with the inspection regime and other elements of the story. By the coincidence of the alphabet the French and the Germans, newly elected on to the Council from January onwards, held the Presidency for the first two months of the year and so this time the control of the agenda lay in the hands of the opposition, since Paris and Berlin were colluding closely.

The work of the inspectors in Iraq was at this stage starting to turn from the re-examination of known WMD sites to the testing of possible hiding-places of undeclared material or documents. So much political and public recrimination over WMD has built up since the 2003 invasion that the atmosphere of expectation that a significant find might happen any day is hard to reconstruct. But in January 2003 barely anyone was prepared to say with any conviction that there was nothing to be found: neither the inspectors nor our opponents in the Security Council; neither the media nor the political oppositions in the US or the UK. Charles Duelfer, the senior American in UNMOVIC and later David Kay's successor as Head of the Iraq Survey Group, which searched Iraq in vain for WMD after the conflict, was in touch with the UK Mission from time to time and our discussions were focused on the chances of finding the right lead to a WMD cache. The principal British concern during this period was whether there would be time for the inspectors to breach the Iraqis' concealment techniques before the United States lost patience with the process and unleashed their troops. Washington's worry lay more in the direction of mistrust in the competence or the good faith of the inspectors.

As it happened, a find did materialise in mid-January. An inspection team, acting on a Western tip-off, entered and searched the private house of an Iraqi scientist. They discovered that he had hidden there some 3,000 pages of documents on Iraq's earlier nuclear programme. These did not indicate any up-to-date activity on nuclear weapons, but the documents had not appeared in the 7 December declaration, were relevant to Iraq's past activities and should have been handed over long ago under the earlier resolutions. They amounted to a serious misdemeanour, though not quite to a 'smoking gun', in spite of the temptation in Washington to make the claim. In the same week another team re-searched a building thought to be clean and unearthed a dozen shell casings of a type known to have been filled with chemical materials during the 1980s. The newspapers termed them 'missile warheads', but they were more likely to have been designated for artillery use. Eleven of these were found to be empty but in very good condition. A twelfth contained some liquid, which was sent away for examination. The following week four more similar casings were found, totalling sixteen out of the 30,000 or more shells that had not been accounted for by UNSCOM during the 1990s. Again the inspectors did not characterise them as a smoking gun, but the US and UK Governments thought hard about doing so themselves. The casings were definitely usable for chemical or biological warfare. But the nature of the hiding-place was more consistent with the Iraqi claim that they had been overlooked than with the American insistence that they had been deliberately concealed and withheld. Meanwhile, the liquid in the twelfth shell casing turned out to be uninteresting.

Washington and London decided that, without backing from UNMOVIC, they would not convince the world that these developments were a sign of an active and continuing programme. Since the inspectors were now clearly getting into their stride, we felt we could afford to wait a bit longer. UNMOVIC's reputation went up a few notches in Washington, as did the UK's for supplying the information to UNMOVIC. The trend was sustained when the inspectors examined a consignment of Russian-made Volga missile engines which had been imported by Iraq within the previous six months, probably not from Russia itself, and which they suspected were too powerful for the maximum missile range permissible under the resolutions. We seemed to be getting somewhere, but the somewhere was not yet quite far enough.

These were nervous days for me. I could see that the Council's unanimity over Resolution 1441, which had inspired such euphoria at the time of its adoption, was extremely unlikely to be sustained if Iraq scored a few cooperation points with the inspectors and nothing telling was uncovered on or in Iraqi soil. UN headquarters bristled with suspicion that the US and the UK were looking for the slightest pretext to launch an attack on Iraq. The issue was gradually growing into something way beyond the classification of Iraq as a threat to regional peace or to the world's non-proliferation system. In spite of its mixed record, the UN's prime position as the keeper of global peace and security would, in the increasingly sharp view of the French, the Russians and the numerous governments who thought like them, be undermined if the United States and its allies elbowed aside the UN's mechanisms and made their own decisions on war and peace. The division between the two camps – those who put the international system and those who put their own national security concerns at the top of their priorities – could only be bridged if the inspectors caught Iraq red-handed. The UN Member States would not mind if US or UK intelligence led UNMOVIC to a pile of chemical weapons, so long as it was the inspection team that dug them up.

I received personal confirmation of the significance of this issue when my Chinese colleague privately indicated to me that in his view Beijing would not oppose the use of force if Iraq was proved to have deceived the UN over their WMD. Wang Yingfan would not risk misinterpreting his capital on such a matter. I knew that the French and Russian Governments held the same position. A smoking gun would be a priceless political asset for the British Government internationally as well as domestically. Without one, we had thin cover. As the weeks rolled by without a telling development, I went to work morning after morning wondering when we might safely gain this prize, trying not to ask my UNMOVIC liaison team for the latest news and reassuring my long-suffering Iraq desk officer, Adam Bye, that we had to keep going on the Security Council strategy come what may.

It is no use saying now that I advised London that the UK position would be so much more watertight if a smoking gun was discovered. I did so, but any ambassador would have done the same. There would be no great dilemma for the British Government if Iraq was found guilty by the UN's inspectors and condemned by all the members of the Security Council. The Foreign Office hardly needed a wagging finger from their representative at the UN to realise that the UK's position in New York and internationally would be seriously compromised without proof of an unmistakable breach by Iraq. But the point had to be set out clearly for the record because it made such a difference to the UK position. And, within a policy geared to achieving the peaceful disarmament of Iraq if at all possible, I thought it important to underline the high sensitivity internationally of any decision to go to war.

The crux for London lay in the choice between participation in an attack without specific authorisation from the UN and insisting on waiting for the inspection process to be exhausted. So long as the UK could present its policy as falling within the terms of international law, the policy would be judged on its results. For the next two months this exercised the Government deeply from the Prime Minister downwards. The sooner military action was to be launched, the more convincing the arguments would have to be that Saddam Hussein was incorrigibly defiant. That became the fundamental policy and timing dilemma for the British leadership. A great deal depended on it: opinion polls in the UK were showing that some 80 per cent opposed UK participation in a war without UN authorisation. The Labour Party was restless and Cabinet ministers were beginning to mutter about resignation.

I went over this dilemma in guarded terms on the telephone with David Manning and we agreed that I should come back to London on 23 January to discuss the situation in full with senior ministers. I could not afford to leave New York for longer than was absolutely necessary and so it was one of those trips that gave me six hours in central London for eighteen hours of travel. In the discussion at Number Ten I set out my view that the legal basis for the bombing of Iraq in December 1998 served as an important precedent for the basis for military action in the near future, but the decision would have to be taken only after all other avenues were manifestly exhausted and the action would need to be regarded internationally as proportionate to the offence. We went over the possibilities of an UNMOVIC success and the need for maximum UK assistance for the inspectors on the ground. We studied the time factor carefully. These exchanges left me with the impression that no irreversible decision had by then been taken by the Prime Minister that the UK would participate in military action on a particular timing. Securing broad support in the Security Council carried such value that we all agreed that as much time as possible should be devoted to this, though we realised the unlikelihood of holding back the US much beyond early March. While Tony Blair knew that the big decision rested with Washington, and it was clear to all of us in his support team that he was committed to supporting the United States against Saddam Hussein if force proved necessary, a chink of hope remained in his mind that UN pressures on Baghdad, and even Arab desperation to avoid a regional flare-up, might squeeze out a solution before force was actually used.

The clearest public exposition of the Prime Minister's detailed thinking on Iraq came in his extended meeting with the Liaison Committee of the House of Commons on Tuesday 21 January, a few days before the first Blix report in the Security Council and his own visit to Washington for a strategy session with President Bush. The transcript repays reading in full. It demonstrates well the two parameters in his mind at the time on the question of going to war. The first was that Iraq under Saddam Hussein, with its gruesome history and its capacity to develop and use chemical or biological weapons, was a live threat and had to be dealt with: 'If George Bush was not raising the issue of Iraq and weapons of mass destruction, I would be raising it. In fact, I did raise it at the very first meeting I had with him in February 2001, before September 11, before any of the recent events.' Blair's resolute focus on Iraq echoed his up-front determination to deal with Milosevic in 1999 and with the Taliban in Afghanistan early in 2001, before the United States had finally decided what to do about either one. It illustrated a feature of his policy-making much more generally, that when he had accepted within his own mind the rightness of a strategic choice, he would pursue it through any amount of obstacles or counter-argument. This achieved results that a more flexible approach might not have done, but it could also raise the costs to a level that risked his whole premiership.

The second parameter was that war should be avoided if the UK and the US could together find another way of ending the threat. By mid-January, the commitment to support the United States in an attack was well nigh inescapable, but the circumstances making conflict inevitable had not yet, as Tony Blair saw it, closed in on him. As he said to MPs on 21 January: 'When we get to the point of taking the decision, the circumstances will not be the circumstances we have got today, they will be changed by what the inspectors find, by what we are able to tell people, by the circumstances that will exist at that time.' This was not mere prevarication, avoiding a public admission that he had taken a decision to use force. Later on in the hearing, answering a question about the role of the inspectors in the UN process, Tony Blair said:

There are two different sets of circumstances. There is a set of circumstances in which you find the conclusive proof and there is a set of circumstances in which a pattern of behaviour develops of non-cooperation. The first is easy to describe as a category and the second, as you rightly say, requires more considered judgement and I agree with that. Part of the difficulty is that what we are doing at the moment is we are increasing massively the pressure on Saddam and his regime. How are we managing to get the intelligence out of there? How are we managing to see what Saddam is up to, to see the cracks developing in the regime? We are doing it precisely because we are sending troops down there, he knows that the threat is real unless he cooperates, so we are trying to put maximum pressure on him and if I am sometimes coy about speculating what happens after 27 January or if the inspectors say this or say that, it is because I do not want to do anything that weakens that enormous pressure coming to bear on the regime either to cooperate or, frankly, to crumble.

In the same meeting the Prime Minister addressed his intention to go for a second resolution, which by this time was a decided element of UK policy even if the Americans remained to be persuaded. He brought up the possibility of there being 'an unreasonable veto' in the Security Council: 'When I say the preference is for a UN resolution, it is easier in every respect if there is one. All I say, also, however, is we cannot have a situation in which there is a material breach recognised by everybody and yet action is unreasonably blocked. I do not think that will happen but nonetheless you have to have that qualification otherwise the discussion that we have in the Security Council is not likely to be as productive as it should.' And a bit later: 'If they [put down a veto] in those circumstances then I think it would be wrong if we said, "Right, well there is nothing we can do, he can carry on and develop those weapons." Of course it is better if we go down the UN route, and that is what we want to do, that is what I have been striving for all the way through. [But] we must not give a signal to Saddam that there is a way out of this.'

From our confidential discussions I never felt that he held one view in private and pronounced another in public. After this visit to London I took it that my job in New York was to keep the Security Council together in realising the complete WMD disarmament of Iraq by whatever means necessary, but without the use of force if possible. I knew that this would be very hard, but in this last week of January I did not think it would be impossible.

The date of 20 January stands out in my memory as a milestone in the downhill journey of US–French relations. That day was the occasion for a ministerial meeting of the Security Council on the subject of counter-terrorism, inspired by the French January Presidency. For the past fifteen months the UK had been chairing the Council's Counter-Terrorism Committee and I had been expending a huge amount of energy and diplomatic capital in trying to persuade every member of the UN to sharpen their domestic defences, legal and operational, against the possibility of terrorist activity on their soil. The event carried the risk that any meeting of Foreign Ministers would be sidetracked onto

Iraq, but Dominique de Villepin successfully presided over a session principally focused on the subject listed.

Things began to unravel immediately after the meeting broke up. There was no great need for the Council President to come to the microphone outside the Chamber, because the press had attended the whole session. The other Foreign Ministers, including Colin Powell, had already left for lunch at the French Residence. When Villepin faced the reporters, the subject of Iraq did not take long to come up. We knew that the French and German Governments had recently been discussing the imperative need, in their joint view, to prevent the Americans from taking their own decision to attack Iraq. French diplomats had been testing the waters in Washington and had concluded that the United States had firmed up its intention to use force. The French Foreign Minister now launched into a scathing comment on the inappropriateness of military preparations when the inspectors still had so much work to complete. France would, he said, stand resolutely for the primacy of collective action through the United Nations. 'If war is the only way to resolve this problem,' Villepin said, 'we are going down a dead end . . . The United Nations should stay on a path of cooperation. The other choice is to move forward out of impatience . . . towards military intervention. We believe that today nothing justifies military action.'

Powell took immediate exception to this outburst, which he regarded as gratuitous and unnecessarily aggressive. Richard Armitage, the Deputy Secretary of State, later commented: 'He was very unamused. When he's unamused, he gets pretty cold. He puts the eyes on you and there is no doubt when his jaws are jacked. It's not a pretty sight.' When the ministers met on their own for lunch, quite a row broke out. Villepin brought up public remarks Powell had made a few days previously about the high degree of risk Iraq posed to American interests, which he saw as part of a growing Washington emphasis on enumerating the reasons for using force. Powell responded by underlining the ineffectiveness of any measures against Saddam Hussein unless force hung over him as a real threat.

US–French communications, so markedly improved by the 1441 negotiation, took a dive. They were not improved a day or two later when Donald Rumsfeld delivered his notorious aphorism about 'old' and 'new' Europe, comparing the more forthcoming attitude of the Central and Eastern Europeans on Iraq than that of France and Germany.

Something had got to the French over this period. Up until the New Year they had appeared to be keeping their options open. We on the UK side were as genuinely surprised by Villepin's tirade as the Americans; and surprise, particularly between presumed friends, is an indicator of a diplomatic failure on one side or the other. Since Jean-David Levitte's departure for Washington in November, I no longer had quite the same inside appreciation of Paris's thinking and I had not yet got to know his less open successor, Jean-Marc de la Sablière.

Looking back, I think we made an all too common mistake. We interpreted our own position in the light of the most reasonable and accommodating of our ministers' public statements. Those who were suspicious of what we were up to took the truth to be closer to the most unpalatable and disturbing of them. The United Kingdom was repeating ad nauseam the mantra that no basis for war could exist unless Iraq offended against the resolutions of the United Nations on WMD and that all was still to play for, the hard end of the US spectrum of public pronouncements gave a very different impression and it constantly worried London that this was the case. On 20 January Villepin was reflecting French alarm that even Colin Powell, the supposed peacemonger in the US ranks, was now talking up the military option.

Hans Blix's 27 January report now loomed large. Neither Washington nor London was comfortable with the increasing media emphasis on this event as the catalyst for a decision on military action. Although the American press had been speculating that Cheney had been pressing for the start of an Iraq invasion on 1 February, London had been working on Washington for a much more extended timetable and other parts of the Washington system were focused on March rather than February. The US and UK Missions in New York were asked to take some of the weight off 27 January; and we therefore arranged with the incoming German Presidency for February that there should be a further report from Blix on the progress of inspections in Iraq set for 14 February. This was agreed within the Security Council and, when the press was told about it, some of the tension over 27 January eased.

Hans Blix did not reveal his intentions for the 27 January report. The US and UK teams had, between them, been consulting him regularly over the progress of inspections, feeding in what we could by way of information and assistance. Blix kept his thoughts to himself. We therefore had to prepare quite carefully what our delegations would say in the Security Council once he had delivered his report. I told John Negroponte that I was going to ask Blix some very pointed questions about Iraqi uncooperativeness and concealment, and particularly about the lack of progress being made by UNMOVIC inspectors in their interviews with Iraqi scientists.

As I went over my notes during the weekend of 25–26 January at our cottage in Woodstock, the Number Ten switchboard came through on the telephone to say that the Prime Minister wanted to talk. He was due to appear on *Frost on Sunday* and he wanted to bring himself fully up to date on what might come out of the Security Council meeting the next day. These calls, relaxed and businesslike, came through once every ten days or so as the tension built up and Blair wanted to get a feel for the front line. I went over what we knew of the Iraqi performance with the inspectors since the end of November and gave my view that, even though no significant WMD find had been made, Iraq could not be characterised as having cooperated with UNMOVIC in the comprehensive terms laid out in Resolution 1441. It did not seem to me that the complete disarmament of Iraq was going to take place through the process of inspections, but we still needed a significant discovery. The Prime Minister took this on board as, I think, an important consideration in his judgement of what time period he needed to insist on for the inspection process. With a visit to Washington looming, that question of timing was turning into the principal tactical issue.

On 27 January the Security Council met in open session to hear the reports from Hans Blix and Mohamed ElBaradei. No Ministers were present, but the hall was filled with UN delegates, the public and the press in a buzz of anticipation. None of them knew what to expect, but Council members had been given the texts as we sat down and I could see from a quick glance that the UNMOVIC assessment was going to be quite critical of Iraq. I breathed a quiet sigh of relief. We and our opponents knew how important this moment was and we avoided catching each other's eyes. Blix emphasised that the inspectors needed a good deal more time to complete their work. French heads nodded vigorously. But he was equally clear that the nature of Iraq's cooperation with UNMOVIC had so far proved inadequate. In a passage widely quoted from his presentation in the days that followed, not least by the American administration, Blix said: 'Iraq appears not to have come to a genuine acceptance – not even today – of the disarmament which was demanded of it and which it needs to carry out to win the confidence of the world and to live in peace.' The words were double-underlined on the US and UK desks and Negroponte and I exchanged satisfied glances.

Once the reports had been heard in the main Chamber, the Security Council repaired next door to the informals room. Council members had agreed to use the session merely to put further questions to UNMOVIC and the IAEA, but the US delegation surprised me by choosing to set out a full statement of the American assessment to date, which reaffirmed Washington's view that Iraq had committed and was continuing to commit a material breach of the resolutions. I concentrated more narrowly on the questions that Blix and ElBaradei's statements had not fully answered, using the opportunity to emphasise privately for other members of the Council what seemed to the UK to remain highly suspect in Iraq's performance. The rest of the Council were obviously more circumspect in their interventions, but they had to come to terms with the relative severity of Hans Blix's judgement about Iraqi cooperation. On the nuclear side, they were encouraged by the fact that ElBaradei told us in this restricted session that while he needed more time for the complete elimination of Iraq's nuclear capability, he felt elimination through the inspection process was a genuine possibility.

The next day in London, the British Government began to react firmly to what Blix had said. The Foreign Secretary, with little warning to me in New York but feeling the pressure from Washington, put out a statement which said that Blix's report amounted to a judgement that Iraq was in material breach of the resolution *both* because of the inadequate declaration *and* because of its further failure to cooperate with UNMOVIC – the two cardinal points of paragraph 4 of Resolution 1441. 28 January thus became the day when London's assessment moved into alignment with Washington's that, in effect, Iraq now risked the 'serious consequences' that operative paragraph 13 of Resolution 1441 prescribed. This solidified the UK position before the Prime Minister's meeting with President Bush on 31 January. It also left the UK delegation in a different position within the Security Council: even if we were arguing for a way through without force, as we were from time to time, we also had to defend our position that force was already justified.

Later that afternoon I called on Hans Blix and went over the ground very carefully with him. He was grateful for the help the UK had so far given to UNMOVIC but was growing increasingly concerned about the pressure being put on him by the political imperatives in the US and, to a lesser extent, the UK. He refers to this in his own book, *Disarming Iraq*, and is clear there, as he was to me, that while he understood the circumstances, he thought our two Governments were excessively reliant on intelligence that was indicative but not incontrovertible. On the substance, he was sure that Iraq was withholding the high degree of cooperation demanded by Resolution

1441, but doubtful about the likelihood of finding actual WMD. In that respect he had reacted unhappily to the weight Washington was putting on that one sentence from the report. He said he was considering two further moves by UNMOVIC: first, distilling the questions Iraq had still failed to answer satisfactorily and listing them in groups of related items (the concept of what came to be called the 'clusters' document); and second, requiring Iraq to destroy the newly imported Volga rocket motors which UNMOVIC had discovered earlier in January and which the experts had decided could power Iraq's Al Samoud missiles beyond the maximum range allowed under the sanctions rules. Both these measures would increase the pressure on Baghdad and I was encouraged.

When I called on the US Mission to compare notes, I heard from John Negroponte for the first time the plan for Colin Powell to deliver a unilateral presentation of the WMD evidence available to the United States. Washington was thinking of calling for an open session of the Council for that purpose. I expressed my personal doubts. I realised that London would welcome an American move to share the burden of the case against Saddam Hussein – up to then it had only been made in a comprehensive way by the British dossier in September – but I questioned whether new and compelling information could be presented publicly to the Security Council when the US and the UK teams liaising with UNMOVIC had so far been unable to offer anything in confidence to inspire a convincing find. I was concerned that the United States would be using up their ammunition in a single shot when it might not convince the doubters in the Council. Negroponte listened carefully, but told me that the decision had probably already been made in Washington. I realised what that meant, but passed on my doubts to London nevertheless. Their reaction was to steer away from dissuading the Americans from doing something on which they were clearly determined for their own domestic reasons and which backed up the British dossier. Over the next few days the London–Washington lines were humming while the UK side tried to give advice on the areas of intelligence that would form the most persuasive exposition.

On 31 January Bush and Blair met in Washington – Camp David was abandoned at the last minute because of the weather – with only Condoleezza Rice and David Manning present as Iraq advisers. The details of the frequent conversations between these two leaders, and of the almost daily exchanges between their Foreign Ministers or close advisers, will not be available for public consumption for many years. They amount to an extraordinary chain of bilateral consultation and debate, more continuous and substantive than at any other period of US–UK cooperation that I have lived through or read about, including the Churchill–Roosevelt relationship during the Second World War.

The impression I gained after this particular summit was that both leaders still retained the hope, however slim, that some way could be found of dealing with Saddam Hussein without resorting to full-scale military action. There was by now no doubt in their minds that, if this was the only effective route, an allied invasion of Iraq would be pursued together and that no possible alternative would emerge except under the pressure of imminent military action. The domestic foundation and support for the use of force, following the Congressional decision in October, stood clear and strong on the American side. That overshadowed the role of the international community in the eyes of the US administration. The British Government, by contrast, had not yet established the necessary domestic backing, either in Parliament or in public opinion; and this would not be forthcoming unless the use of force was seen as justified in international law. On 31 January the President reaffirmed that he understood the Prime Minister's difficulty in this respect, accepted that the UK needed to try for a second resolution in the Security Council and undertook to support that effort. This did not, however, come out as firmly as the UK had hoped in the press conference that followed. It appeared that the White House team developed cold feet after the meeting about too explicit a statement in support of a return to diplomacy. The President ducked the first question on the issue, and then said: 'Should the United Nations decide to pass a second resolution, it would be welcomed if it is yet another signal that we are intent upon disarming Saddam Hussein.' This was well short of the warm endorsement for which the UK had been hoping. But the two sides understood each other politically: this was to be the diplomatic strategy.

The timing issue came down to three considerations: the minimum reasonable period for the inspectors; time to persuade other members of the Security Council that staying together was the only way of avoiding war; and the momentum of the military build-up. The latter was of course particularly compelling for the Americans. The administration had been intensifying the propaganda war since November and as a result there were two additional factors to consider: the heightened state of US domestic expectations and the downside in any long delay for economic activity and other regular business. It seemed to me at this point that, for all the arguments for flexibility on timing that the British side were constantly putting, it would be very hard to get the United States to wait much beyond the first or second week of March before beginning the military campaign against Iraq. That was all the time we had to make any other approach work.

9

Pitched Battles in the Security Council

I had agreed to give a speech to a forum in Middleburg, Virginia, on Sunday 2 February, and Anne and I decided to spend part of the weekend in Washington. I also made some appointments at the State Department for Monday. We met Jean-David and Marie-Cecile Levitte for lunch on Saturday, anxious to catch up with the couple whom we had come to like best of all our French diplomatic colleagues over the years. Their move to Washington had come just when Jean-David's huge multilateral experience and talent was most badly needed at the UN. He and I settled down to a long chat over coffee to swap impressions of where the world was heading on Iraq.

It was a relief to have a completely frank discussion with this wise, pragmatic man, whose Russian father and Anglo-Dutch mother had left him with no subcutaneous Gallic hang-ups about the Anglo-Saxons, but no qualms either about standing up to them. Levitte, realistic in his appraisal of where the Americans were heading, was as anxious as I was to maximise the chances of avoiding war. He knew that this was a forlorn hope unless some kind of understanding could be patched up between Paris and Washington. The prospects of a rapprochement had taken a turn for the worse since Powell's clash with Villepin at the UN, and Jean-David had already felt the fallout in his daily dealings with the US administration. That morning had brought the awful news of the destruction of the Columbia space shuttle. President Chirac had reacted with instinctive sympathy and telephoned Bush to express his sorrow – as it happened, he was the first foreign leader to do so. Jean-David told me that the two men had talked with greater understanding than they had shared for months. He hoped the conversation might signal the start of a reversal in recent trends, but he also made it abundantly clear that France remained resolutely opposed to US unilateral action against Iraq. He believed that it would do no good at all for the UK to attempt to round up support in the Security Council for a second resolution. France would much prefer each member of the fifteen to be left to react to developments as they thought best. That way the US and, if necessary, the UK could follow their own instincts and policies and others could explain theirs. Why try against the odds to drive all fifteen down the same path?

I explained that the UK's goal was still to disarm Iraq without a conflict. Why could Paris not see that unanimous pressure on Baghdad was our only hope? War was inevitable if we all went our separate ways. Levitte thought that war was inevitable anyway. France was only trying to minimise the effect on international relationships and the UN. We agreed to disagree, but the conversation left me with a lot to think about, because I trusted Jean-David's understanding of the need to deal with the threat posed by Iraq, as well as his commitment to the avoidance of bad blood.

The French approach sharpened the UK dilemma. War was looming and we would be a willing partner in an attack on Iraq if that was the only way to ensure its disarmament. Washington realised that Tony Blair was coming under immense pressure at home. Condoleezza Rice summed it up on one occasion during this period with a succinct quip: 'This is not what we meant by regime change.' The French idea for avoiding outright confrontation in the Security Council would not distress the United States, but we felt that we had no choice, having persuaded the Americans to come with us this far in the search for an alternative route to war, but to press for a second resolution. We shared the French view at that point that the inspectors had not been given enough of a run and we wanted to use as much time as we could to get Saddam Hussein to concede peacefully. But we were in a tight bind and the manner in which French policy was being publicly presented was likely to give Saddam hope that international divisions would save his skin. Both these facets, the shared analysis and the visceral difference over the preparations for war, were aired between Tony Blair and Jacques Chirac during the Anglo–French summit in northern France on 4 February. It did not help to close the gap.

I am sure Levitte did not intend it this way, but the concept of separate paths held another potential trap for the UK. In a crisis where members of the Security Council have sharply differing interests, a vacuum spells danger. France and Russia had already made it abundantly clear that the issue that exercised them more than anything else, certainly more than the fate of Iraq as such, was the US overriding the international order. Both of them, for different reasons, found the rise of a single superpower distasteful. Both wanted to preserve the primacy of the United Nations or make the cost of disdaining it as high as possible. If we initiated an invasion of Iraq without further discussion in the Security Council, I could easily imagine one or the other of our main opponents proposing a resolution condemning our action. They were bound to gain greater support than the Russian draft did after the attack on Serbia in 1999. I wanted the United Kingdom to retain the initiative in New York even if the higher aim of a peaceful outcome proved unachievable.

On Monday I joined Christopher Meyer for a call on Deputy Secretary Richard Armitage in the State Department. This genial, plain-speaking Texan, close to Powell in spirit and a constant bellwether to us of what was or was not achievable in Washington, went through the hard facts with us. He did not think our task was hopeless. We discussed in some detail the prospects for securing nine or more votes in the Security Council for a second resolution, which the State Department saw more favourably than any other part of the administration. We all felt the odds had risen after Blix's presentation on 27 January, but there was a long way to go.

Word came along the seventh-floor corridor that Secretary Powell had returned from a session at the Pentagon, where he had gone to refine his presentation to the Security Council. He was asking to see me for a few minutes. When I arrived in his office, Colin Powell was entirely focused on the details of the text he was scheduled to deliver in two days. I knew that it was much too late to put the case against doing the presentation at all, but I argued for an exclusive concentration on Iraq's WMD programmes, without any mention of the rationale for regime change or the unconvincing evidence of links with al Qaida. I also hoped he would hold back some of the intelligence material that was being considered for inclusion: it was important not to lay out everything we had, because the Iraqis would then be able to calculate how much we did not know. The Secretary, friendly as ever, said he thought my points were valid: he had already weeded out a good deal of material from the more aggressive quarters of the administration. I could see, nevertheless, that the subject had worn down his patience: British instincts were fair enough, but time was short and he had his job to do. The exchange did nothing to ease my feeling that we were all being driven down a path that had not been properly thought through.

The German Presidency started slowly at the beginning of February. Powell's presentation had received such a strong advance billing in the press that there was little point in having further Council discussions about Iraq until we had heard what he had to say. 5 February thus dawned with a marked sense of anticipation. Would this be comparable with the Adlai Stevenson moment, the galleries were asking, when he produced the photographs of the Cuban missiles in the Council and challenged the Soviet Ambassador to deny them?

The Security Council chamber was crowded well before the session was due to start. Several of the Council seats were taken by

Foreign Ministers, including Jack Straw for the UK who had come over to support his ally. Spouses and friends helped to fill the public gallery to overflowing and the press were fighting for space in the balconies. Cameras flashed continually. Not knowing exactly what Powell was going to say, I became caught up in the general mood, refusing to acknowledge the much stronger likelihood that if there was a clinching story to tell I would have heard it by now.

The Americans had set up special screens on either side of the Norwegian tapestry to carry the images backing up Powell's exposition. The Secretary of State sat in the US seat at the table, with the Director of Central Intelligence, George Tenet, and Ambassador John Negroponte captive in the seats behind him. Powell spoke without a pause for seventy-five minutes: we watched the clock with interest because the original estimates of the time it would take to present all the material recommended by the Washington hawks ranged up to three and a half hours. It was a compelling performance, full of the drama of suspicious Iraqi telephone conversations and satellite photographs of loaded military vehicles. He elaborated on the evidence for continuing chemical, biological and missile programmes and interpreted the pictures up on the screens. He was obliged to acknowledge, however, that the weapons of mass destruction themselves did not feature except by inference; and inference in these matters was a skilled job for the professionals. He took us lucidly through the steps that joined up the argument. For the converted it was impressive. I waited for the effect to sink in.

I waited in vain. The unconverted were not bowled over: they saw little here but interpretation. This was the UN and, as a matter of principle, the majority were not prepared to be rolled over by information available only to one Member State. If the UN inspectors came across the line then they would follow. That was a primary and wide-reaching point of which we and the United States perhaps took too little account during these partisan diplomatic skirmishes. On top of that, the debate had in the days after Blix's 27 January report moved on from whether or not Iraq was cooperating with the UN. Blix had clearly said that they were not. Jack Straw's articulate presentation after Powell explaining precisely why they were not was interesting but not new. The question exercising people's minds was rather what the international community should now do about it. Was this really a basis for war in such a fragile region? Would it not be better if the inspectors continued for a much longer period, until they were in a position to assess objectively whether or not Iraq's sins deserved the ultimate punishment? What the hardliners in Washington had predicted from the moment the UN route was suggested was now beginning to happen: the accumulation of UN resolutions and of medium-sized Iraqi sins was not enough to outweigh the judgement of the majority that capital punishment could not be decreed unless Iraq had committed an identifiable and up-to-date capital crime. For all the build-up and the theatre, Powell's speech had not proved that it had.

The French approach cleverly built on this general lack of conviction. Dominique de Villepin was the first speaker at this meeting to make new proposals. He said that the inspection system should be strengthened by the addition of new and higher technology equipment and he offered UNMOVIC the use of specially adapted French Mirage aircraft. The Russians quickly stepped in and said that a Russian spy plane would also be made available. They also proposed the appointment of a new high-level WMD coordinator on the ground. The others did not comment on these suggestions at the table because their speeches were prepared and cleared with their capitals beforehand, but a scrabble ensued for the media stake-out afterwards and Germany, China, Mexico, Pakistan and quite a few others gave the French ideas plenty of wind. The UK, Spain, Bulgaria and, to a lesser extent, Chile pointed to the fundamental block that Iraqi non-cooperation was placing on any UNMOVIC capability. As Jack Straw said at the lunch that followed, a thousand well-equipped inspectors would not do the business if all the Iraqi witnesses had been terrorised into silence. Privately we and the Americans muttered about the sudden conversion of the French and the Russians to tough powers for the inspectors when they had been so resistant to them during the negotiation of Resolution 1441. But we could not escape the sinking feeling that the floating voters on the Council were drifting away from us.

We also had our European partners to contend with. All through the Iraq crisis, and especially after the US administration had decided to bring the issue to the United Nations, the UK regularly had to explain within the EU what it was trying to achieve and why it had thrown in its lot so comprehensively with the Americans. During my career as a British diplomat, much of it concerned with the development of the European experiment and with the re-ordering of the continent after the collapse of the Soviet Union, no foreign policy question divided the United Kingdom from the European mainland quite as sharply as Iraq. The UK Mission in New York came up against constant badgering in our regular meetings with our EU colleagues, over and above their pointed demands for information on Security Council issues. The European Treaties protected the special position of France and the United Kingdom in the Security Council, but that did not dilute the resentment felt for what was generally regarded as an anachronistic and un-European privilege.

Jack Straw, like Robin Cook before him, took his EU duties seriously and was appreciated by his colleagues for that. He did his best to keep his partners up to date on Iraq developments and to keep the pack together on the fundamental elements of policy. I gave as frank a briefing as possible each week to my colleagues in New York, often fuller than the other EU members of the Council, which normally included two elected as well as the two permanent members, but the UK's closeness to the United States on Iraq, resurrecting all the old EU suspicions about the Anglo-Saxon Trojan Horse, and the huge ramifications of the issue for the wider international structures outweighed these tactical responses. Our efforts may have helped most of our partners to understand why we were acting as we did, but we could not hope to win their approval.

The powerful advocacy of France and Germany for avoiding war and upholding European unity always had more impact on the EU majority than the realpolitik arguments of the UK.

Powell's 5 February briefing meeting brought together in New York the British, French, German, Spanish and (as current EU President) Greek Foreign Ministers. Jack Straw came under a severe grilling from the others, with Ana Palacio of Spain, our ally on Iraq but not on marching out of step with our European partners, staying largely silent. Accusations that we were splitting the EU and making a common foreign policy impossible flew thick and fast. Straw defended himself with vigour. The personal friendships within the group were, in the European way, not seriously affected and there were sincere handshakes afterwards. But the political and emotional gap looked very wide.

It would be wrong to conclude from the acerbity of the differences over Iraq at the United Nations and in other international forums that the United States and the United Kingdom descended to abject levels of popularity and influence amongst the membership at large. The US, of course, could look after itself. There was barely a country represented in New York – Cuba, North Korea, Iran and Iraq were really the only long-term exceptions – that did not look for a good relationship, or at least an acceptable modus vivendi, with Washington. In their collective groups – the G77, the Arab League, the Non-Aligned, the smaller ad-hoc collections of developing or Islamic nations – they might put out stinging criticism of US policy and attitudes, but they kept up their personal and informal contacts with the US Mission in the corridors and in private meetings. The United Kingdom did not exert any such magnetism. We had to work for friendship and influence outside, and sometimes within, our normal circles of allies, earn a grudging acceptance in the Security Council and campaign hard for elected positions in other UN committees and councils.

Elections for UN bodies tended to test the general image and popularity of a country as much as the quality of a candidate for a particular office. Between 4 and 7 February, while the Powell briefing was commanding the world's attention, a different kind of international contest was being played out in the basement of the UN building. It was the time for judges to be elected to the International Criminal Court, which had been created by treaty in 1998 but was taking an age to bring into operation, partly because of the high-pitched opposition of the United States. Over a period of four days successive votes were taken to produce an internationally diverse court of eighteen judges. My Jordanian colleague, Prince Zeid bin Raad al Hussein, held the unenviable job of presiding over this political and procedural whirlpool. The UK's candidate, Adrian Fulford, held all the right qualifications but the UK itself might not, in the eyes of many of the voting Missions. By the third day of voting eleven or twelve candidates had been elected from popular countries, by which point it was becoming increasingly hard to ignore the candidates of individual worth. Fulford was elected by a decent margin and the UK Mission, which carried the hopes of an expectant London, breathed a sigh of relief. The French delegation, however, were put through a much more tortuous experience with a candidate of similar quality. It was not until the eighteenth round had gone through several split votes that their man squeezed in. I took this as a sign, which I would never have had the honesty to do if the converse had happened, that Britain could maintain its appeal at the UN despite Iraq.

Hans Blix and Mohamed ElBaradei were due to deliver their next report on 14 February. They decided to visit Baghdad in the days running up to 9 February, to try to secure a more forthcoming attitude to interviews and overflights. UNMOVIC were getting no useful material out of the Iraqi scientists and technicians they interrogated, partly because they were working from lists prepared some time ago and the regime had rung the changes on personnel over the years for security reasons; and partly because the word had gone round that any Iraqi citizen who betrayed information would, with his family, be made to suffer as only Baghdad knew how. Blix succeeded in speeding up the flow of interviewees, but this led to no improvement on substance, as the Iraqi Government insisted that each interviewee should carry a tape recorder to the interview. Much to the annoyance of Washington, when Blix conceded on this practice the regime agreed to pass some necessary legislation and to allow U2 overflights. These items added up to the beginnings of a case, as Saddam Hussein fully intended, for declaring the arrival of a much better Iraqi response on procedure. There were plenty of people in New York ready to capitalise on that.

As 14 February drew near, the US and UK missions came under nervous pressure from our capitals – I even had the Prime Minister on the telephone at one point – to ensure that UNMOVIC and the IAEA delivered as hard a report as possible on Iraq's lack of substantive cooperation. Our problem was that Blix and ElBaradei were becoming increasingly inured to having their arms twisted. They knew who they were working for: the United Nations. They also knew that no governments other than the US and the UK had the capacity to help them in practical ways if they were to do their jobs properly, but they were beginning to jib at the mounting political pressure they were coming under. We had sensed after the 27 January report how much they disliked being selectively quoted to substantiate the case against Baghdad. Hans Blix makes clear in *Disarming Iraq* his strong feelings about being pushed into the seat of judgement on Iraq. Nevertheless, I went to see him to go again over the ground of what was for us the fundamental point: that Iraq was not providing the substance needed to clear up the WMD files. Blix could not disagree, but he remained resistant to the use to which the argument was being put. As it turned out, I did not score highly in London for Blix's product on the 14th.

The French and Germans – we were now halfway through the German Presidency – had planned this as a ministerial meeting of the Security Council. Colin Powell and Jack Straw realised the wind was more likely to blow against them in publicity terms, but they did not hold the Council reins and they could not afford to allow their case to go by default. They sat grimly at the table while Blix delivered a report very different in tone from his previous one. He said that Iraq had made a good deal of progress on process. His visit to Baghdad had produced useful movement. He made no clear reference to the lack of spontaneous cooperation which he had been ready to acknowledge in private. He ended with the assessment that if Iraq were to cooperate immediately, unconditionally and actively (the adverbs of the resolutions), then the inspection process could be completed in quite a short time. But even that was destined to produce a divided reaction: 'they are not, so let's go for it' from one camp; 'so give the inspectors more time' from the other. As a result each became more passionate rejecters of the other interpretation.

There was no doubt in my mind that the 14 February reports were intended to compensate for the spin that had been given on the previous occasion. The US hard sell had backfired. No new finds had come out of the two weeks just past and the effect of the January discoveries had by now worn off. I thought that Hans Blix was beginning to give up on the prospect of uncovering anything really significant. Even he was unsure whether that was due to the cleverness of Iraqi concealment or the fact that there was nothing to find. The more vehemently we tried to insist that it was the first, the more persistently he began to feel that it was the second. The US–UK assumption – and I shared it – that Saddam was guilty made him obstinate. With hindsight we can see that he was right.

The inspectors' reports were followed by one of the more unusual open exchanges in Security Council history. The chamber was again crowded back to the far walls of the public gallery. The order of speakers, after a row some months previously about the (fictitious) capacity of the Permanent Members to fix things, was now arranged by lottery. Jack Straw was somewhere in the middle of the pack, which gave him a bit of time to prepare his reaction to Blix, with scrappy bits of no doubt confusing advice coming over his shoulder from the team of us sitting behind him. Villepin, however, came just

before him and, on top of the expected pitch about the progress the
inspectors were at last beginning to make, he delivered a passionate
peroration about France's mission to save the world from war. He
finished with an ironic reference to the Rumsfeld dig about 'old' and
'new' Europe three weeks previously:

> It is an old country, France, of an old continent such as mine,
> Europe, that speaks before the Council today, that has known
> war, occupation, barbarity – a country that does not forget and
> that is aware of all it owes to the fighters for freedom who came
> from America and elsewhere. And yet France has always stood
> upright in the face of history and before mankind. Faithful to its
> values, it wants to act resolutely with all the other members of
> the international community. We believe in our ability to build
> a better world together.

The audience broke into loud and sustained applause, something
that is never supposed to happen in the hushed and dignified
sanctuary of the Security Council. The Russian Foreign Minister,
Igor Ivanov, also received a brief ovation for an intervention which,
though shorter on winged rhetoric, made the case for extended time
with more compelling logic. Jack Straw and Colin Powell spoke
extempore, Powell in particular setting aside his notes and looking
hard into the faces of his colleagues and opponents. Jack Straw did
not fail to add his own touch of humour, starting with the words: 'I
speak on behalf of a very old country' [pause] 'founded in 1066 by the
French.' Both focused in quite powerful performances on the precise
terms of 1441 and the lack of quality cooperation from Iraq. They
had strict legality and textual logic on their side, but the emotions
were running in the other direction and the majority, borne along by
the wordless support of the onlookers, came down on the side of more
time for the inspectors. There was no way that the US and the UK
could pretend that they had secured any advantage that day.
Afterwards Villepin and Powell sparred for a further few minutes at

the microphone outside the chamber. Straw concentrated on the British press and on several useful bilaterals with Security Council ministers. Thus we salvaged what we could, but the day was not ours.

I had agreed to do an evening interview with Charlie Rose on the Public Broadcasting Service, but first I went in the airport car with Jack Straw to the far side of the East River to wash up the day's events. Straw was phlegmatic about it all, though he had not enjoyed the experience. Our policy had to remain on track. The Council had to be tested for real effectiveness in bringing Saddam Hussein to account and we would go on working for support for a second resolution. I agreed with him that we should not despair, but said I thought it would be very difficult if the trend continued in the Council and amongst the inspectors. I then hopped out into the Friday rush-hour traffic to make my way back to the studio and got completely snarled up at the bridge bottleneck. The lights of Manhattan in the clear, cold air shone their miracle, but they were not what I was there for. I missed Charlie Rose and never had a chance to put my own public gloss on the day. Under the circumstances and for a professional civil servant, it was a blessing and a relief; for someone determined to win the campaign after losing a battle, it was a vanished opportunity.

That weekend brought the first serious snowstorm of 2003. After a Saturday-morning spell in the office to catch up, I dashed up to Woodstock with Anne to try to capitalise on a three-day weekend covering President's Day, but we heard the forecast and hared back to New York to avoid being trapped in the mountains. Monday thus turned into a normal working day as the snow and the papers piled up. The UK and US Missions consulted on how to repair the damage and I took the opportunity for a post-mortem with Hans Blix, to convince him of the UK's continuing seriousness in wanting the inspectors to be the ones to make the assessment on Iraq if at all possible. He accepted this without question, but it did not make him any more convinced from what the intelligence had offered UNMOVIC so far that the verdict was bound to be guilty. And by this point we had boxed ourselves into a corner and needed a guilty verdict.

The run of misfortune continued into that evening. We had invited Jean-Marc and Sylvie de la Sablière, the Levittes' successors in the French Mission, to the Metropolitan Opera to see *The Trojans* by Berlioz. We managed to get to their residence on Park Avenue through the accumulating snow, but came to grief when our office car spun to a halt on 71st Street. We missed the first act, but made it for the second two and a pleasant meal. Diplomats can sometimes switch off, and this was not the occasion for an examination of our respective positions on Iraq. Jean-Marc's body language was quietly confident and I did my best to pretend that my mild tension was meteorologically rather than politically inspired. The evening was all very jolly, but Jean-Marc did manage to mention briskly before we said goodnight that France could not possibly accept a second resolution.

In one form or another Iraq intruded into Security Council business more or less every working day over the next few weeks. A second open debate for the membership at large took place on 18–19 February and the mood generated on 14 February spread out wider. Almost every delegation was for both the absence of war and the full implementation of UN resolutions, without saying how. The Arab speakers insisted that Palestine should receive no less attention than Iraq. I could only bear with it for the morning and went off for lunch with Tom Friedman, the *New York Times* columnist, who was in an apocalyptic mood about the Middle East situation and the long-term implications of invading Iraq. The next day brought a public Council meeting on counter-terrorism and it was useful for me to be seen in the seat of the Chairman of the Counter-Terrorism Committee rather than behind the UK nameplate, to signal that I had other functions to offer than forcing difficult decisions on Iraq. But the clock was ticking. If the United Kingdom was to retain any hope of keeping the Security Council together to apply catalytic pressure on Iraq, which was our first priority, or of finding nine votes to support the use of force, a less attractive way forward, we had to construct an approach with some new and compelling element in it. It was an unenviable position.

The inspection process still held out a slim prospect. We stayed in close communication with UNMOVIC, and UK experts fed in what guidance they could on the areas worth investigating further. On 18 February I went to see Hans Blix for another detailed conversation, to ensure that the arguments we produced in the Security Council were compatible with what he still regarded as theoretically possible in terms of Iraqi capabilities or holdings. This was when he showed me UNMOVIC's work on the clusters document, which I could see straightaway would form a valuable account of why the US and the UK retained such strong suspicions of Iraq. It was a striking illustration of his position, clearer to me from our private conversations than from his public presentations, that there were good reasons to be suspicious of Iraqi activity even if it was going too far to claim proof of active WMD programmes.

I followed this by setting up a secure telephone conversation between Blix and the Prime Minister in my office on 20 February, which Blix describes in some detail in *Disarming Iraq*. He began by briefing Blair on the first glimmerings of cooperation by Iraq: 'Perhaps they are starting to panic,' he said. He asked whether, given the range of questions that the inspectors still had to go through with Baghdad, the UK could secure another two months of time. The Prime Minister promised to get UNMOVIC as much time as he could. The conversation also touched on the strength of the available intelligence, which Blix said was not all that compelling. 'Blair responded that the intelligence was clear that Saddam had reconstituted his weapons of mass destruction programme,' Blix wrote. 'Blair clearly relied on the intelligence and was convinced, while my faith in intelligence had been shaken.' He had been frustrated by the absence of new intelligence in Powell's presentation and disappointed that all the leads so far given him by UK and US intelligence had produced nothing concrete.

The American and British Missions began to examine in detail the possible wording of a second resolution. There were two potential avenues. The first was to highlight paragraph 4 of Resolution 1441 and affirm that Iraq had both failed to produce an adequate declaration and refused satisfactory cooperation with UNMOVIC; this would then lead to 'serious consequences'. This route was favoured in Washington. The trouble was it would probably not be supported by the inspectors and without their support we would have little hope of persuading our colleagues. The second was to stay light on the threat of force and set out a timed ultimatum for Iraq, related to Iraq's failure to take the final opportunity for a peaceful solution offered by 1441. I recommended the latter approach to London and gained the Prime Minister's support. It was the right tactic to have any chance of attracting votes in the Council, but to the Americans it seemed too mild in tone. I could imagine the dismissive asides in certain corridors in Washington about the Brits pussyfooting around. Bush had undertaken to support Blair's need for a second resolution, but underlying scepticism may have diminished the vigour that the Americans brought to achieving a result for us. It was agreed that the US and the UK would co-sponsor a new resolution, but that the UK would be in the lead in promoting it within the Council. With that decision, we were ready for the final round in the Security Council to try to avert a disastrous division over Iraq.

The stakes at home were no less momentous. Over the weekend of 15–16 February London witnessed its largest popular demonstration in living memory against the prospect of an Iraq war. On 26 February the Labour Government suffered its biggest mutiny in the House of Commons when 121 Labour MPs failed to support the motion backing its Iraq policy. Tony Blair knew that Cabinet ministers, most significantly Robin Cook, the former Foreign Secretary and Leader of the House of Commons, might resign if he continued down the track he was on. We felt as though we were bobbing along on the surface of a fast-flowing river, with the water growing colder by the day. But these unmistakable symptoms of popular disaffection with his policy seemed to have no effect on the Prime Minister's determination to see it through to the end.

10

The End of Diplomacy

I tabled a draft second resolution on 24 February. Its elements had been scribbled and cut and re-pasted and discussed in word-by-word detail over the previous few weeks, but it was the timing that was the crucial tactical decision. To have produced it immediately after the 27 January report would have appeared too aggressive: we had been firmly behind the idea of a series of presentations from Blix and ElBaradei and our actions had to fit in with theirs. London was anyway in no hurry so long as their pace of work did not fall foul of American impatience. Waiting until after the 14 February report, however, narrowed our options and our momentum. The core of the political argument at the UN had moved on from whether Saddam Hussein was cooperating or not – in the strictest sense, everybody knew he was holding something back – to whether people believed that this continued defiance merited the death penalty for a regime that UNMOVIC had not caught red-handed with WMD in its cupboards. More strongly after 14 February than before, the two sides of the argument were talking past each other. At the UN, at least, the UK was trapped bang in the middle.

Each January five new elected members come on to the Council for their two-year spell and the character of the organisation changes.

Bulgaria, Cameroon, Guinea, Mexico and Syria had started their two-year term in January 2002. At the end of December 2002 Colombia, Ireland, Mauritius, Norway and Singapore departed, to be replaced by Angola, Chile, Germany, Pakistan and Spain. Each country had its own distinctive qualities and value, but in general the new group proved more polarised than the old, less inclined to listen to the arguments on their merits or to look for a collective solution. They had arrived, of course, in the middle of a top-level crisis, which would have coloured the political stance of their governments. But personal characteristics also played a noticeable part. It was not easy, under the pressure of circumstances, to be sure where any one delegation might be heading.

The core group on which Washington and London thought they could count amounted to four members: themselves, Spain and Bulgaria. The opposing camp comprised France, Germany, Russia and Syria without much doubt; and China was almost certain to stay with France and Russia unless those two could be split. The other six, Mexico, Chile, Pakistan and the three Africans – Angola, Cameroon and Guinea – formed what we termed the middle ground, sceptical, uncomfortable and apprehensive but willing to study the arguments on both sides, perhaps largely out of a desire to avoid offending anybody important. Three of these countries – Mexico, Chile and Angola – had a history of awkward relations with the United States and all of them, as members of the Non-Aligned Movement, were disinclined to be borne along by American strong-arm tactics in a policy branded as an exercise in modern imperialism. Pakistan was a traditional US ally, but its leader, General Musharraf, had taken a hit for his support of the hugely unpopular invasion of Afghanistan. All this was the general perception in the media as well. With a resolution needing a minimum of nine votes to pass, five of these six needed to be persuaded – or, as I reminded London, all six, because no state in a swing-vote position likes to be regarded as the one tipping a controversial draft resolution into adoption. Ten positive votes had to be the target. The US and the UK were going to have to do a miraculous job of persuading and lobbying. So long as we hammered away at the implications of what the Security Council had already agreed, I did not think the task was impossible.

My introduction of the new draft on 24 February concentrated on Iraq's refusal to take the final opportunity presented by Resolution 1441 to come clean with the inspectors. The text was short and free of rhetoric. It did not claim 'material breach' or suggest specific authorisation for the use of force. The key operative paragraph stated that the Security Council 'decides that Iraq has failed to take the final opportunity afforded to it in Resolution 1441'. That on its own, of course, would trigger the consequences set out in 1441, but this was not spelt out. In my explanation to the closed meeting of the Council I set out the areas where UNMOVIC had been unable to account for significant stocks of WMD materials: 8,500 litres of anthrax, 2,160 kilograms of bacterial growth media, 360 tonnes of bulk chemical warfare agent, 3,000 tonnes of precursor chemicals, 1.5 tonnes of VX nerve agent and 6,500 chemical bombs. These volumes were all included in UNMOVIC's clusters document when it was released in early March. I said that the quality of Iraq's cooperation with the inspectors had fallen far short of what was necessary to dispose of these discrepancies. In addition, the Iraqis had been caught developing a missile programme of prohibited range: UNMOVIC had already decided that. No one could be in any doubt that this continued the twelve-year pattern of Iraq's attempts to deceive the Security Council.

The UK draft resolution, I said, sought to keep the Security Council in control of the process through a united judgement that Iraq had made the wrong choice: the choice not to take the final opportunity to disarm voluntarily. We were not asking for instant decisions. The stakes were too significant. There was still time, under pressure from the Council, for Iraq to make the right choice. A proper debate should be held on the proposition that Iraq had failed to cooperate and had triggered the serious consequences forecast in 1441. Anything less than a dramatic change of attitude in Baghdad within the next two weeks would be inadequate. The last chance for peace lay in the Council's saying this formally and unanimously and confronting Iraq with the stark implications. We had to trust that this would finally lead to the complete disarmament demanded fourteen resolutions ago in Resolution 687 on 3 April 1991.

My argument placed the Council on the fine edge of its dilemma. The majority could not accept that they had to make a decision now. The inspectors were beavering away and Iraq did not appear to be about to attack anybody. No WMD had been unearthed. But neither could they argue that Iraq had met the terms of Security Council resolutions. They had agreed in 1441 to a definition of what triggered serious consequences and it would weaken the authority of the Council and the UN if they did not live up to that. All the earlier pressures, bullying, big-power manipulation, sheer hard negotiation, whatever they wanted to call it, had driven them now into this unpleasant corner. The middle-ground six were especially unhappy that their long-awaited two-year spell of work at the elite centre of the UN system should have handed them such a poisoned cup.

France, Russia and Germany, the first two well versed in the rough tactical skirmishing of the Council at the height of a crisis, were not prepared to take this sally passively. They had prepared a memorandum in the form of an open letter to the President of the Security Council (which happened to be Germany), delivered on the same day as my presentation. It fleshed out the Villepin proposal of reinforced inspections, put increased pressure on Iraq at the core of its strategy and set out a time-line for prolonged inspections that would carry UNMOVIC's work well into the summer. The memorandum conceded that the inspections could not continue indefinitely if a peaceful solution was to be found, but it set no specific deadline and left the Security Council in charge of the subsequent decision-making. The memorandum fitted the majority's sense of where they wanted to go. But it was too little too late to bridge the gap with the United States. Washington could barely bring itself to read it.

The intensive process of persuasion now began in earnest, led from capitals and acted out in capitals rather than in New York. There was one last informal meeting of the Council in February, when I set out concisely, in a text cleared with London, the conclusions the UK had come to about Iraq's actual capacities and behaviour. We made no claim about usable WMD weaponry but underlined the threat in Iraq's production capability and pointed to the actions taken by Iraq to hide its evidence and silence its officials. The same arguments were made available to members of the Council individually; and I held meetings with various groups whose attitude would be crucial, including the Elected Ten and the ambassadors of the European Union. In capitals the arguments went wider, particularly when the United States brought up reasons extending way beyond Iraq for each of their target countries to come to heel.

All this was evolving against the gradual crescendo of the beating drum, at the Pentagon, at the Florida Headquarters of Central Command (CENTCOM) and within the forces deployed in the Gulf. The message was now as unequivocal in action as it had long been in rhetoric that the United States was going to finish this off one way or the other. Timing continued to be a principal subject of transatlantic calls, with the parameters of the argument narrowing down to middle or late March, the latter from the UK point of view looking increasingly hard to achieve. An extraneous factor which offered a glimmer of hope for a delay was the difficulty that the United States was experiencing in securing permission from Turkey to invade Iraq from the north. Whether or not that came through made a significant difference to military planning and the Chiefs of Staff were not sounding comfortable with an early date.

I had hoped to persuade the Council to set a date for a third report from Blix and ElBaradei on 14 March, to give us time for a diplomatic blitz on Council members and to leave room for an inspectorial miracle. Washington put their foot down: it had to be no later than the end of the first week of March. This was awkward for me, because I had been planning for months as Counter-Terrorism Committee

191

Chairman to hold a large and significant international meeting on counter-terrorism cooperation, bringing in all the agencies around the world that dealt with any aspect of the defence against terrorism or WMD proliferation. The date for this was firmly set for Friday 7 March. I argued hard for an Iraq meeting on Saturday the 8th, but in both Washington and New York I met reluctance to schedule such an important event during the weekend.

March in the Council began on Tuesday the 4th with the usual consultations over the programme of work for the month. Ambassador Mamady Traoré of Guinea was the incoming President, dignified, gentle and completely unprepared for the storm to come. There was nothing routine about the order of business. We still had to settle the timing of the next UNMOVIC/IAEA report. I had taken the gamble of moving my big counter-terrorism meeting to 6 March to free up the 7th for Blix and ElBaradei. This was how it was eventually arranged. But the discussion aroused the active suspicion of Ambassador Sergey Lavrov, who I think believed that all this juggling of dates was meant to clear the calendar for the start of military operations. I remember having to assure him privately in the corridor that, as far as I was aware, this was not the case.

Behind the formal agenda there was intense analysis and tactical planning going on. Meetings in different casual formats were proceeding the whole time. Colleagues in various groups, not least the EU, had to be briefed and listened to. The US, UK and Spanish delegations were constantly consulting on tactics, partly to share assessments of who might vote how and partly to consider whether the draft resolution needed to be adapted in any way. Should we, for instance, insert an unequivocal ultimatum to Iraq, with a clear-cut deadline? Who might the catalytic players amongst the middle-ground six turn out to be? In and around all this normal life had to go on. I was undergoing a series of dental treatments at the time and poor Dr Mausner's appointments schedule was constantly being messed up – not that she did not benefit from a dentist's natural leverage in extracting a running account of developments from me. There were

National Day receptions to go to, the classic diplomatic duty which also provided constant opportunities to nobble this, that or the other colleague to gain information or get a point across. I could not afford to miss the Bulgarian party that week: Ambassador Tafrov's vote was much too valuable and Sofia was beginning to ask awkward questions.

Other social events threw up chances to hear important viewpoints. On 4 March, having hosted an evening reception in honour of NGOs visiting for the annual Commission on the Status of Women, I arrived late for a dinner given by Bill McDonough, Chairman of the Federal Reserve Bank of New York, and his wife Suzanne. I plonked myself down on the remaining empty chair at the table and found myself next to Henry Kissinger. I began to tell him about my early trials as a First Secretary in the British Embassy in Washington in the mid-1970s, when I had to take the record for Ambassador Peter Ramsbotham's calls on him as Secretary of State. My scribblings had been a mess. Since his mind tended to range over several complex issues at the same time, darting back and forth on the interrelated implications of everything, nothing in the notebook could be broken down into identifiable paragraphs. He also had the habit of lowering his guttural voice just as the punch-line came, leaving the note-taker, stashed out of sight behind him, straining to catch the most important bits. I ducked telling him how often I had had to invent by logical deduction the core elements of my report on US policy during his tenure.

It was not long before our conversation turned to Iraq. Kissinger strongly supported the threat of military pressure on Saddam Hussein and its use if Iraq did not finally respond, but he was puzzled by Washington's insistence on placing so much emphasis on regime change in its explanation of its policy. If the focus of the US–UK pitch had remained exclusively on WMD disarmament, he said, a lot more support would have been gathered from around the world and regime change would have happened anyway. I could not disagree. He was also very interested, and to a degree involved, in enlarging the possibility that Moscow might come round to accepting a second resolution specifying that Iraq was in breach of Resolution 1441 if other foreign policy priorities of theirs could be taken into account. He said bilateral discussions between Washington and Moscow were proceeding at that moment. As far as I could judge, these never came to anything in practice. But it was an illuminating glimpse of a superpower mind at work.

Kofi Annan could not match Kissinger for analysis and power-play, but his determination to prevent another war over Iraq remained a constant driving force and kept him glued to developments in the Security Council, even if he had to remain on the sidelines of the debate. His input on policy was constrained by the lukewarm results of his interventions in 1998 and by his least favourite circumstance, the vehement disunity of the Council itself. I took care to brief him regularly on the struggle between the Permanent Members, both because I trusted him to understand the realities and because I wanted him to see that the UK was still trying to find a way through without the use of force. He felt that the inspectors needed a good deal more time and that the circumstances, even from the US and UK perspective, did not justify conflict. He had always been honest enough to recognise publicly that there were moments when the threat of force was necessary to bring defiant enemies of the UN into line. But the actual use of force was something else; and the imaginable consequences of a US attack on Iraq were beginning to loom very large. The team around him were beginning to voice their alarm in even more forthright terms than he was. It became a distinct possibility that he would state his personal views in public, which would aggravate the difficulties for us in getting members of the Council on our side. It was not my place to try to dissuade him from such a move: Annan had much too independent a mind to accept such direct advice. But he appeared to sympathise with the idea of using a second resolution to keep the Security Council together, even if it was for the purpose of ordaining war.

One of the great worries of the Secretariat at that stage, from the Secretary-General downwards, concerned the possible humanitarian consequences of conflict. The United Nations would have to deal directly with the aftermath and they needed to make preparations. Meetings between Annan, his senior staff and Security Council Ambassadors took place in early March to go over this ground in detail, on the basis of UN predictions that as many as ten million refugees could be created inside and outside Iraq in the event of a war. The anti-war group in the Council seized on this as another reason why military force must be avoided. The UN legal advisers raised the potential requirement for the Secretariat to construct a formal relationship with the occupying power, if the removal of the Iraqi regime proceeded without recognised UN authority. Part of their motive was warning, part of it practical necessity. Either way, it was sobering stuff.

5 March brought me back to the business of considering Security Council tactics. Since the draft resolution I had presented on 24 February did not seem to have attracted much support, we were going to have to think about changing it. The US, UK and Spanish Missions again consulted on the options left to us in what was an increasingly desperate situation. We came up with an amendment that set a deadline later in March (the precise date was left blank) and asserted that Iraq would be assessed as having missed the final opportunity for peaceful disarmament unless the Council decided it was on the road to full compliance. It was important to arrange it that way round because the US–UK would be able to block a Council decision that Iraq was cooperating when it was not. This discussion laid the foundation for the rest of the week's strategy and the three of us agreed to consult our capitals on it.

Other business pressed on the clock as well as Iraq. With ministers expected on Friday 7 March for Blix's crucial third report, I still had to prepare for my major session on the 6th on counter-terrorism. At other times the French invitation to G8 partners for lunch on 5 March to discuss world food security would have been a significant event for our broader UN programme: in the middle of a week like this it was reduced to an arrive-late/leave-early scramble. I dashed on to a bilateral with my Angolan colleague to try to convince him of the evidence on Iraqi non-compliance, reported to London on the day's developments so far and then started to arrange my thoughts for the sixty or so counter-terrorism experts whom I was supposed to be forging into a global coalition the next day. A core group of them came to my apartment for dinner to sort out what the main speakers should be saying.

The actual meeting on the 6th passed in a blur, but we had done so much intensive work in the Counter-Terrorism Committee over the previous eighteen months that I knew where I needed to put the emphasis to encourage a network of security institutions to begin collaborating. It turned out to be the most significant gathering of international professionals on counter-terrorism since 9/11. Resolution 1373 of September 2001 gave my committee the power to require Member States to change their legislation and their practice. If we had been able to have a clear run at the issue, I believe we could have tightened global defences against terrorists in a significant way. Iraq intruded not just by absorbing our time and energies, but by diminishing the willingness of the world to follow our lead. The 6 March meeting nevertheless made a lot of progress and suggested that the effect of 9/11 had not totally lost its momentum. I wound up the session just in time to run from the building to greet Jack Straw, who had arrived by Concorde that afternoon.

We immediately went into a series of engagements to prepare for Friday's open meeting of the Council on Iraq. The Foreign Secretary saw a few of his Security Council colleagues bilaterally, called on the Secretary-General to bring him up to date on our probable next moves, and dropped in on Blix to get an idea of his intentions the next day. Hans had few confidences to offer in that respect. We then sat down to plan a coordinated approach to the meeting with the Americans and the Spaniards, whose solid support for resolute action on Iraq was becoming increasingly valuable in diluting the minority status of the US–UK. The Bulgarians looked firm too, but they were nervous about visibly plotting with the superpower and did not join us in the margins.

Our draft resolution needed tweaking with the latest inputs from Colin Powell and Jack Straw. I was keen to strip the text, thin as it was already, down to the lightest of essentials to declare Iraq in breach of 1441. Neither Washington nor Madrid was much impressed. The fevered atmosphere in New York was the only environment in which I could underline our one tactical imperative: to create a minimum basis for a resolution to be accepted by nine or ten members of the Council. Thursday ended with a chaotic working supper in my apartment as we went through the elements of Jack Straw's speech to the Council, with members of the UK team coming in and out like burrowing meerkats and Straw surprising us all by having read the whole of UNMOVIC's clusters document, which proved to be more than Hans Blix himself had done. I knew from a series of snatched conversations on the telephone and during our rushed visits across the Atlantic that Jack's doubts and loyalties on Iraq balanced out somewhere near where mine did. On top of everything that had gone before, from Saddam Hussein's performance during the Iran–Iraq War to his consistent record of deceit and non-cooperation up to the present day, the clusters document gave Straw renewed confidence that Iraq stood no chance of being judged in compliance.

Friday 7 March dawned on a team of us up early to re-work the Foreign Secretary's speech. Jack Straw and Colin Powell went to see the Mexicans and the Chileans, both of whom were a long way from contemplating any association with our revised resolution. The two men moved on to the main Security Council chamber with very little feeling of comfort. The Guinean Foreign Minister, our former UN colleague François Fall, was in the Chair and the ministers of well over half the fifteen members sat around the table: Chile, China, France, Germany, Mexico, Russia, Spain, Syria, the UK and the US. The lottery-assigned speaking order had placed Jack Straw at the bottom of the list, which was where he wanted to be.

Hans Blix and Mohamed ElBaradei went first as usual. Blix did not declare Iraq in compliance, but the impression he gave was one of gradually improving cooperation: 'While the numerous initiatives, which are now being taken by the Iraqi side with a view to resolving some long-standing open disarmament issues, can been seen as "active" or even "proactive", these initiatives three to four months into the new resolution cannot be said to constitute "immediate" cooperation. Nor do they necessarily cover all areas of relevance. They are nevertheless welcome and UNMOVIC is responding to them in the hope of solving presently unresolved disarmament issues.' The tenor of this went against the US–UK case. I decided that it needed a quick public response and obtained Jack Straw's permission to slip out while the meeting continued to make a point at the press microphone outside the chamber: if Iraq was cooperating as the resolutions specified, it would be blindingly obvious; if Iraq was avoiding full cooperation, this too would be blindingly obvious.

Most ministers focused on the need for time and support for the inspectors. When his turn came, Dominique de Villepin described the work of UNMOVIC as effective, re-presented the French proposals for prolonged and reinforced inspections and declared the need for a summit meeting of the Council before coming to any vote on the resolution. He ended with the assertion that the essential choice for the Council lay in disarmament through war or through peace. He left no doubt as to which his country would choose. The hall was again packed, but the mood this time seemed more apprehensive and the Frenchman was heard in silence. Colin Powell then read his speech from the page, elaborating on the details of the unanswered WMD questions but giving a more downbeat impression than in his previous performances.

Jack Straw had been taking notes energetically through these interventions, his prepared text gradually filling with red ink glosses. Occasionally he thrust small bits of paper behind his back with phrases for me to comment on or fill in. Once or twice Adam Bye beside me had to dive into his pile of reference documents to dig out a fact or a quote. Straw started his intervention from his prepared text, but then began to look up and develop his points spontaneously, House of Commons style. He said that he had been struck by the fact that not a single minister speaking before him, whatever their political position, had suggested that Iraq was now fully, actively and immediately in compliance with Resolution 1441. Iraq had not so far taken the final opportunity afforded to it. If anyone had any doubt about that, they should study the details of UNMOVIC's clusters report, all 167 pages of which he had read (the team behind him worried a bit about that one, because the clusters report had not at that point been publicly released and our obtaining it for him had been a minor coup).

Straw then launched into a forceful rejection of the French arguments, addressing Villepin across the table by his first name, more in the style of an EU Council of Ministers than a formal meeting of the Security Council. Many of the UN Ambassadors looking on were shocked by this untraditional political directness. 'Dominique,' he said,

> also said that the choice before us was one between disarmament by peace and disarmament by war. That is a false choice. I wish it were that easy, because then we would not be obliged to have this discussion; we could all put our hands up for disarmament by peace and go home. The paradox we face is that the only way we are going to achieve disarmament by peace of a rogue regime that all of us know has been in defiance of the Council for the past twelve years – the only way that we can achieve its disarmament of weapons of mass destruction, which the Council has said pose a threat to international peace and security – is by backing our diplomacy with the credible threat of force . . . The choice is not ours as to how this disarmament takes place; the choice is Saddam Hussein's.

In his final paragraph Straw declared that, on behalf of the three sponsors of the current draft resolution, Spain, the US and the UK, he was introducing an amendment specifying a further period beyond the adoption of the resolution for Iraq to take the final opportunity to disarm and to bring itself into compliance. The key paragraph read:

> OP3: Decides that Iraq will have failed to take the final opportunity afforded by Resolution 1441 unless, on or before 17 March 2003, the Council concludes that Iraq has demonstrated full, unconditional, immediate and active cooperation in accordance with its disarmament obligations under Resolution 1441 and previous relevant resolutions, and is yielding possession to UNMOVIC and the IAEA of all weapons, weapon delivery and support systems and structures prohibited by Resolution 687 (1991) and all subsequent relevant resolutions, and all information regarding prior destruction of such items.

Jack Straw concluded: 'The Council must send Iraq the clear message that we will resolve this crisis on United Nations terms: the terms that the Council established four months ago when we unanimously adopted Resolution 1441.'

The audience in the hall was hardly sympathetic to the substance of what the UK Foreign Secretary had presented, but the United Nations is nothing if not responsive to style. A ripple of applause echoed around the chamber as Straw came to his close. Its volume and extent did not match Dominique de Villepin's on 14 February, but on 7 March it was the only applause of the day. Someone's mobile phone rang a few minutes later and it was a message from the Prime Minister, who had been watching on C-Span all the way through, to say what a fine performance he thought it had been. He was not the only one. The UK Mission was amused to receive a number of e-mails over the next twenty-four hours from Americans who had watched the debate live. Someone called Donna Canfield, for instance, wrote: 'Bravo Jack Straw! I have not felt such passion about a British person since I fell in love with George Harrison in 1964! You were perfection, and really stuck it to old Dominique, he looked like he got a bad snail!'

It was a searing performance in a forum unused to the cut and thrust of live debate. But we still lacked an Adlai Stevenson moment. We were in need of a miracle if the doubters were to be brought across. Once the Council meeting was finished and the media had been fed, ministers and ambassadors went up to the thirty-eighth floor for lunch with the Secretary-General and ran another lap of the track. The French proposal for a summit was seized upon as a new item, procedural of course, and the real substance of the deep division was left to bubble underneath the surface. Those who backed hard action against Iraq opposed the summit idea; those who did not liked it. The middle ground did not seem to see any salvation in it. The Mexican Foreign Minister pointed out that such an event would need to be supremely well prepared or the Council would find itself washing the same dirty linen under brighter lights. No conclusions were drawn. Jack Straw then left for the airport under a snow-filled sky. I did the round of the news channels camped out on First Avenue, guided as always by my superb but now freezing Press Officer, Catherine Mackenzie, who through this whole saga probably did more than any member of the UK team to keep UK policy sounding relevant and sensible to the ever-growing packs of reporters descending on the UN.

The fifteen ambassadors repaired to the side-room for informal consultations, rather disrespectfully, I suppose, to see what we could salvage from the ministerial exchanges. Decision-making and leadership at the political level are indispensable for diplomacy, but divisions become entrenched when ministers are asked to defend their country's line in public. The constant insistence of our opponents in the Council on high-level meetings was intended to make the context as difficult as possible for agreement on a forceful approach to Iraq. This time the members of the Council held a really good debate behind closed doors, talking directly to each other's points in the way originally intended by those who invented the informal format. The main items of contention were how to keep up the threatening pressure on Baghdad without killing the work of the inspectors, and how to give time to the inspectors without bringing comfort to Saddam Hussein. The Americans and the British concentrated once more on the wording of Resolution 1441 and the essential requirement for Council not to think it could start from another point of departure. The French, Germans and Russians countered that if the inspections were beginning to produce something – anything – useful, then how could war be justified? It was convenient for them to overlook the point – which even the Secretary-General acknowledged – that the inspections were only gaining minimal Iraqi cooperation because of the palpable and imminent threat of force. Everyone in the room knew that without the American military build-up there would be no inspectors in Iraq at all. On the strict item of our business, the revised draft resolution, the stand-off remained as pronounced as ever. Ominously for us, the Chileans started to sound as if they were drifting away from us and were not at all taken with our idea of a renewed ultimatum.

The morning of Saturday 8 March threw up one of those intensely bright early spring skies which made my inevitable trudge into the office that much more unwelcome. It was time to plan the details of the end-game in close coordination with London. The draft resolution would not have a chance unless we made it clear what exactly Iraq was being asked to do to escape the ultimate punishment. I began to work up the fine print of possible benchmarks. We had to stay within reach of UNMOVIC's perceptions of what Iraq might still be holding back. In speeches and seminar appearances during this period I was regularly referring to Iraq's probable holdings of growth media for biological weapons and laboratory samples of anthrax, aflatoxin, botulinum toxin and ricin. All featured in the British dossier as items unaccounted for from Iraq's known past activities, but none of them had been incontestably shown to be still part of a live programme. The benchmarks would have to be composed from more convincing and up-to-date evidence. The list narrowed down to intimidation of Iraqi interviewees, cheating on missile ranges, suspicious work on unmanned aircraft (UAVs) and serious lacunae in their accounting for anthrax and VX nerve gas experiments. I thought about mobile laboratories, a chief American preoccupation, but Hans

Blix was coming to the view that they did not exist for WMD. I added in a sixth area of potential pressure, the failure by Iraq at any point in the whole story to state publicly and convincingly that they recognised the requirements of the UN, had no intention whatsoever of dealing in WMD ever again, and would assist the inspectors in every way possible.

Washington did not sound very interested in benchmarks. This was unsurprising, as the idea to them suggested further delay and weaselly half-responses from Iraq. Both Powell and Rice preferred to think, if the business of securing another resolution had to be pursued at all, that the necessary votes could be rounded up by some friendly diplomatic conversations in the six middle-ground capitals, calling in some favours from Pakistan, Mexico and Chile and suggesting benefits in development assistance for Angola, Guinea and Cameroon. At this stage the Americans were particularly interested in the prospect of understanding reactions in Mexico City and Santiago. They had harboured similar hopes of a top-level deal with the Russians, but these had foundered the previous week on Moscow's angry response that the Americans had not lived up to their promises to consult and could not be counted to deliver their side of an arrangement. From this moment onwards, Washington–Moscow relations gradually became more difficult.

London was prepared to commit time and effort to supporting US approaches in such quarters, but we did want to test the benchmark idea to its limits as well. I fed in some thoughts for a series of telephone calls at head-of-government level and stood back. The choices seemed to me to be very narrow. It was now almost inconceivable, unless there was a Damascene conversion somewhere significant, that we would not be facing a veto from Paris or Moscow or both. In theory, a veto could be explained away in political terms, if the majority in the Council supported a certain course of action. But if the nine votes were not going to appear there would be nowhere to turn. I was much more sanguine than the Americans about the chances of finding these votes and that was the message I left with London. I also underlined the merits of keeping the initiative in our own hands: it would be very hard for anyone else in the Council to set down antagonistic proposals while ours was running.

Anne was away on a visit of Security Council spouses to the Arab Gulf and so I took myself up to Woodstock alone on Saturday afternoon to try to gather some last drops of inspiration from the mountain air. The two-hour drive was a welcome contrast to the relentless pressure of mid-town New York, but the cost of absence from the office began to bear down on me as Sunday morning drew on. I decided to abandon the white-tailed deer and the pileated woodpeckers in the woods beyond our garden. I had to obtain Hans Blix's final word on the benchmark proposal and compose as watertight a list as possible of what we would ask Baghdad to do over the coming ten-day period. Responding to UNMOVIC's advice, I took VX and mobile laboratories out of my draft list and inserted an extra requirement: that Saddam Hussein should make a televised declaration of his intention swiftly to settle all outstanding questions with the inspectors.

Still in my office late on Sunday afternoon, I received an unexpected caller. The President of the Council and current spokesman for the middle-ground group, Ambassador Mamady Traoré of Guinea, arrived at the twenty-eighth floor of our Second Avenue building and asked for a private word. It transpired that the Six – Chile, Mexico, Pakistan and the three Africans – had met the previous day and had begun to work out their own benchmark proposal. This was based on a forty-five-day ultimatum within which Iraq would be set a list of tasks, to be judged by Blix and with the Security Council taking the final decision if his verdict was negative. In truth, this was a non-starter on at least three counts: the time period, the judge and the final arbiter of action. But the approach in itself indicated that the Six were looking for a way of solving the problem and I promised to report his approach to London and recommend that the initiative was taken seriously. I did not give him the details of the UK's own imminent benchmark proposal, preferring to preserve the slim chance that the Six might be prepared to run it themselves.

Monday 10 March was spent in consultations with London and UNMOVIC and then with the Americans, who were becoming increasingly nervous that we would set the bar for Iraq much too low. I returned to the idea of dropping the paragraph in the draft resolution that was frightening the Council horses, because it asked them too explicitly to declare Iraq in breach. Off the New York stage efforts were proceeding to try to convince the Latin Americans that the US–UK ideas were the only remaining hope of keeping the United Nations in the game. The Prime Minister was fully in the picture, closely involved in the detail and personally at the centre of the telephoning, including several times to me in New York to check the prospects of movement. Only he could secure the understanding of the Americans that our initiative required more time if it was to have a chance of bringing the doubters over in the Security Council. I felt that, just possibly, a few members of the Council might look over the edge of the abyss and decide that maintaining the authority of the UN was preferable to opposing but being unable to stop the war. We had to give it a try.

We held back from introducing our benchmark concept in the Council on 10 March, as I wanted to see where the Six were heading. The agenda was dedicated to a second round of comments on Friday's ministerial meeting and Jack Straw had, after all, proposed an amendment to our draft resolution only the previous working day. The opposition stuck their knives into the apparently automatic authority for the use of force in our approach and we had a job to do to hold it there. Benchmarks were only worth turning to when we had cleared more undergrowth.

Tuesday morning was spent in an effort to settle some further nervous questions from Washington, but gradually we were starting to convince them that benchmarks were worth an effort. Tuesday afternoon had been given away to a public Council debate on Iraq, so that the UN membership at large could express their apprehensions. I skipped most of it, deciding instead to keep to a promise to address a couple of hundred American schoolchildren and their teachers, gathered by the Institute of Civic Leadership, for a briefing on the issue of the moment. It turned into one of the fiercest grillings I received from any American audience during this whole period. Everyone in the hall appeared to be anti-war and anti-Bush. I wished the White House and the Pentagon had been present to witness my stout, though no doubt unavailing, defence of their policy.

After a quick pass through the UK office I went on to a Charlie Rose interview, as good an opportunity as existed in the American media system to get points across in depth to a thinking US audience. As we came to the end of the recording, Charlie received a message through his ear-piece that Tony Blair was trying to get hold of me. The Ten Downing Street switchboard are famous for their ingenuity in digging people out of strange places, but this was the first time they had hauled me off a television set to discuss refinements to a Security Council draft. My instructions were clear: keep going with the preparation of the benchmark proposal in New York while all the other diplomatic avenues were being simultaneously covered. Minister of State Valerie Amos was visiting African capitals at that moment; Pakistan, for all the benefits they had gained for supporting the US in Afghanistan, was starting to row backwards; and the Western Hemisphere was awash with complex manoeuvring. I had to warn the Prime Minister that it was proving very difficult to be sure we had middle-ground votes on our side. 'So how many can we count on?' he asked. 'Four,' I said, 'the US, the UK, Spain and Bulgaria.' 'Crumbs' was the word I think I heard down the line. It did not leave me feeling particularly proud of what we had achieved in New York over the previous two months.

For a short while there seemed to be some hope that another member of the Council – the Latin Americans would have been ideal – might take over the job of leading on benchmarks, a real sign that the US–UK were gaining broader support. But as we moved into

Wednesday 12 March that prospect began to fade again. We could not afford to wait any longer, or the time we had at our disposal to put against the ultimatum would dwindle into nothing. Washington was giving us nothing for sure beyond 17 March, but it seemed to me that we might squeeze them to 24 March if things started to go our way. Before the scheduled afternoon session of informals I found a moment to gather the Six together and explain to them what I was likely to propose in an hour's time. This seemed to go down well, though they were a long way from being able to indicate any support in substance. I also looked in on Kofi Annan to give him a private indication of what we were trying to achieve with our last throw. I did not ask him directly for support, nor did he offer it. We understood each other on most parts of the UN agenda, but the gap on Iraq was just too wide.

The session was scheduled to begin at six o'clock. At a quarter to six the Foreign Secretary came through on the telephone with a clear and undebatable instruction to change the basis of the UK presentation. The United States had got cold feet about the degree of editing I was proposing on our draft. The benchmark concept was to be described to the Council in restricted format, but the UK was not to propose it formally unless several others indicated that they thought it worth detailed discussion. That was a minor shock; but no experienced diplomat should be too distraught at the idea of putting a non-proposal to a non-meeting. The substance can be made the same. The real issue is whether or not it is going to work.

Luckily for this occasion, the UN's appalling record of starting meetings on time played in my favour. My Mission team had prepared a written text that could, with a different oral introduction, serve the purpose as before. When the meeting began, Ambassador Traoré turned to me to lead off. I introduced my non-paper illustrating the kind of benchmarks that could reasonably be set for Iraq. The ultimatum date was not filled in, but Council members would need to understand that very little time remained for Saddam Hussein to make a convincing change of attitude. I said that if an approach of this kind gained traction in the Council, the UK would be prepared to amend our draft resolution so that the wording threatening an 'or else' for Iraq would be removed (it would remain there implicitly, of course, in the references to Resolution 1441). I hoped that such a presentational change would make a difference to those Council members, like Pakistan, who wanted to avoid both crossing the United States and enflaming their domestic opinion.

The Six recognised that I had made a genuine attempt to produce a benchmark proposal and thanked me for my efforts, but they did not like the residual, implied ultimatum and everyone was trying to analyse the degree to which it could be used to trigger the use of force automatically. Mexico and Angola, with some support from Hans Blix, attempted to turn the idea into a down-payment by Iraq, which, if it was judged to have been delivered, would permit a further period of testing to continue. I suggested instead the metaphor of a ship with a hole in it needing a repair kit, and threw in an approaching iceberg for good measure. I was amused when the Spanish press later leaked a report from the Spanish Mission which described the UK as presenting its case with vigour, though some parts were long-winded and confused. Fair strike. But we had succeeded in getting the concept out in the open and I suggested that further discussion should await the next day, when people ought to have received detailed instructions.

Thursday 13 March was the day, perhaps inevitable with hindsight, when the hostility to what the US and the UK were trying to construct came spilling out. I was still receiving stalwart moral and political support from my phlegmatic Spanish colleague, Inocencio Arias, whose chairmanship of Real Madrid earlier in his career must have convinced him that a late goal was always possible. But I was losing the Americans, who saw this last-minute UK activity as neither one thing nor the other. With a session of informals due in the afternoon again, I went over the ground privately with the Six. Their disappointment that the UK effort had failed to live up to their hopes, especially where the short timing and the disguised ultimatum were concerned, came through sharply. For the first time we began to get clear indications that several of them, not least the Latin Americans who had earlier been the real promoters of the benchmark idea, were moving out of reach.

In the afternoon's informal consultations the UK Mission awaited with some apprehension the considered views of our Council colleagues. We thought it might be possible to curtail a full table-round of comments by suggesting a break for detailed discussion in smaller groups, but my Bulgarian colleague, whose Government was increasingly in the public firing-line at home, had instructions to set out his national position in detail. That opened the floodgates. Our critics focused on the short time-line and on automatic authority for the use of force. This prompted the French, Germans and Russians to renew their cry of 'What's wrong with continuing inspections?' All the divisions resurfaced. As the succession of interventions played through, it looked as if we were indeed left with no more than the four votes we had to hand at the beginning of the exercise. Traoré compounded our difficulty by re-stating the Six's idea of forty-five days of tests judged by the inspectors and we ended in a most uncomfortable position. It was not the easiest reporting telegram I sent to London that night.

The next morning, Friday 14 March, saw the UK Mission in a deeply apprehensive mood. Our options were alarmingly thin. President Chirac had famously declared at the beginning of the week that he was convinced war was always the wrong answer and that he would veto a UN resolution authorising the use of force 'whatever the circumstances' – something which we knew would probably be the case in practice but which, pronounced in public, was a gift to Saddam Hussein. Our strategy had now to be based on finding a text that the Council majority could support and testing the French determination to veto in that situation. If the Six were to table a fresh proposal of a prolonged period of benchmark testing under UNMOVIC and the Council's control, the US and the UK would be forced to veto and everything we had gained with Resolution 1441 would be lost.

As it happened, London took the news of Thursday's setback with surprising equanimity, given what was at stake in the UK domestic context. Although each of the six governments whose votes we needed had indicated a favourable response at one point or another, they had never all come on board at the same moment. When they touched base with one another they reinforced their collective doubts. The WMD arguments they felt bound to take into account, particularly if the UN inspectors backed them up, but regime change worried them as a policy dictated imperiously by power. If Iraq now, who next? London was coming to terms more quickly than I was to the implications of the vanishing votes. I gained the impression of an almost fatalistic calmness in ministerial offices: this was going to be played through to the end whatever the consequences, because it seemed the right thing to do.

Nonetheless, the risk of a counter-proposal had to be faced. Whispers wafted in about the quiet hand of the French and the Russians at work on one. The telephones rang non-stop across the Atlantic and between Security Council capitals. The US, UK and Spanish Ambassadors in New York compared assessments and aligned their reporting to home base. John Negroponte eventually gave it to me straight, superpower style: 'We can't go on like this. The benchmark approach has got to stop.' I realised that he was right. 'The US has got to switch off the Six,' I told him. We looked at the draft proposal the Six were now circulating, which was leaking out into the press. It included an absolutely unacceptable paragraph specifying that the Council would hear the judgement of the inspectors as to whether or not Iraq was cooperating and then take a decision on next steps. We began to contact representatives of the Six to say that any movement away from 1441 would destroy any hope of keeping the Security Council together. More significantly, Washington started to speak its mind at high levels in capitals, suggesting to the Latin Americans in particular that US disappointment at the low degree of support would take a long time to dissipate. We discovered that the Chilean Government, in an angry reaction to this, had published the Six paper without consulting the others. Cohesion was beginning to crumble.

Suddenly, like a mist lifting off the mountainside, their initiative faded away. No one came back to us to ask for further discussions; no one put in a bid for informal consultations. The five Permanent Members had scheduled a meeting in the middle of the afternoon to discuss the draft of the Six. We were preparing for an unpleasant exchange, but I sensed that delegates in New York were beginning to lose interest in further negotiation while their capitals were still so far apart. The news broke that the leaders of the United States, the United Kingdom and Spain were going to meet in the Portuguese Azores over the weekend. I telephoned round the P5 and no one objected to a cancellation. The talking stopped.

There seemed to be no reason to stay in New York that Friday night, so Anne and I took the late-evening road up to Woodstock. The Number Ten switchboard woke me early on Saturday to ask me to brief the Prime Minister on the implications of the previous day. I was struck by his continuing interest in a diplomatic solution, perhaps with a final ultimatum from the allies or even from his Arab brethren for Saddam Hussein to leave Iraq. But there were limits to a discussion of strategy on an open line.

We got up and went for a bicycle ride in the early-spring sunshine and then the telephone began to ring again. My Mission told me that Hans Blix was about to submit his clusters document and UNMOVIC's future programme of work and the Iraqis had seized the opportunity to invite him and Mohamed ElBaradei to Baghdad. The UNMOVIC and the IAEA teams were apparently rather excited by the prospect. Our machine went into action and we explained why a visit to Baghdad was a thoroughly bad idea. Whichever way events now went, the last thing we wanted was hostages of that seniority in the Iraqi capital.

We returned from Woodstock at the end of Sunday morning. We had originally been planning on leaving that day for a week's skiing in Aspen; instead the office beckoned. There were preparations to make for the aftermath of the Azores summit and for an explanation to the Security Council. The traffic was unusually busy on the FDR expressway for the middle of Sunday and I began to realise I had left myself too little time to consult London.

The south-bound carriageway ground to a halt and I braked too late. I clipped the car in front and the car behind crunched into ours rather harder. Luckily we were able to drive on, but summoning the police and exchanging insurance details took more time out of the day. What a moment to choose for my only road accident in five years in New York!

When I reached the office, feeling increasingly numb as events stripped away my options, instructions were starting to come in for the withdrawal the next morning of the UK–US–Spanish-sponsored draft resolution. Adam Bye, my Iraq desk officer, was already preparing the text of a statement. I exchanged e-mails with Jack Straw to confirm the nuances not just of the text but also of the timing, because what happened in New York had to be carefully aligned with Government statements in London, where a major debate on Iraq was due to be held in the House of Commons on 18 March.

At around 5.30 p.m. I met with Negroponte and Arias to finalise tactics for Monday. It was agreed that the British, as the first promoters of the draft resolution, would lead off with the public announcement that we were not pursuing it. This would have to be calibrated with an expected informal session of the Security Council, designed partly to follow up the vacuum created by Friday's collapse into silence and partly to respond to UNMOVIC's request for a meeting to discuss their work programme. By Sunday evening Blix and his team were aroused on a much more immediate point: the Americans had warned them that UNMOVIC and the IAEA would be well advised to start moving out of Iraq altogether within the next twenty-four hours. Memories came back of UNSCOM's hurried departure from Iraq in December 1998 and Blix was determined not to appear subservient to US instructions.

I searched for Hans, but discovered that he had already left for a dinner to which Anne and I had also been invited, the annual fundraising event for the Metropolitan Opera on the stage of the Lincoln Center. I found him on his cellphone there and told him that the 10 a.m. Council meeting would be accompanied by a UK–US statement ending negotiations at the UN. He was resigned to having to bring his teams out of Iraq and was by now mainly concerned for their safety, as talk of hostage-taking was rife. I reported all of this to London and then we dashed of to join the Met dinner, apologising profusely, not for the first or last time, that Iraq had trampled on my time-keeping. I found myself sitting next to the eldest daughter of the King of Spain and we talked about anything but our two countries' alliance in the coming conflict.

Early on the morning of Monday 17 March I re-checked the fine print with London. The text needed a final tweak, but the main elements, including the side-swipe at the French, stayed the same. The timing had become more awkward. The meeting of the Cabinet, which was to precede the announcement to Parliament, and at which Robin Cook was expected to resign from his position as Leader of the House, had been brought forward from 5 p.m. to 4 p.m. London time, 11 a.m. in New York. This meant that I could not wait until after an informal meeting of the Security Council, the proper sequence, before making a public announcement that the UK–US–Spanish draft resolution had been set aside. With the Council set to meet at 10 a.m. and the clock now approaching 9.30, I had no option but to make my statement as the Council gathered for their session.

John Negroponte, Inocencio Arias and I quickly assembled at the US Mission on First Avenue, while our press teams went over to marshal the crowd of eager journalists now pouring into the UN building. At a couple of minutes to ten John thought that we had better make our way over the road. My feet felt leaden. I just managed to avoid a joking reference to the scaffold. As we entered the main door, ready for the long walk past the assembled flags of the

191 Member States and down the central second-floor corridor, our staff suddenly pulled us aside and diverted us down the basement staircase. The informals room was closed for repairs and the Council was being temporarily re-housed. By another of those happy little ironies, this was the day on which the seats were to be replaced, thanks to the generosity and I suppose the sensitive posteriors of the German delegation.

Down in the basement a microphone had been set up in a corner behind the Viennese café, facing a jostling mass of reporters and cameramen. There was no dignified backcloth to give the occasion a symbolic colouring. The statement had to be read, text in hand, no time to memorise it, though I tried to look up for half-sentences at a time:

I would like to make a statement on behalf of the three sponsors of the 7 March Draft Resolution. As you know, we have worked very hard in the last few days in a final effort to seek a Council consensus on Iraq. In an effort to reunite the Council, the United Kingdom proposed last week an ultimatum which would challenge Iraq to take a strategic decision to disarm.

There were three key elements to the compromise we proposed. First, tough but realisable tests, including an unequivocal commitment to disarmament by Saddam Hussein. Second, a realistic but tight timetable for completion of those tests, given the urgent need for Iraq to comply after twelve years of prevarication. And third, an understanding that if Iraq failed the tests serious consequences would ensue as set out in Resolution 1441.

Having held further discussions with Council members over the weekend and in the last few hours, we have had to conclude that Council consensus will not be possible in line with Resolution 1441. One country in particular has underlined its intention to veto any ultimatum 'no matter what the circumstances'. That country rejected our proposed compromise before even the Iraqi Government itself and has put forward suggestions that would row back on the unanimous agreement of the Council in Resolution 1441 and those suggestions would amount to no ultimatum, no pressure and no disarmament.

Given this situation, the co-sponsors have agreed that we will not pursue a vote on the UK–US–Spanish resolution in blue. The communiqués and press statements that issued at the Azores summit explain the position of our governments on the way forward. The co-sponsors reserve their right to take their own steps to secure the disarmament of Iraq.

I cannot claim that this will ring down the years as the most eloquent of declarations. But it made the necessary bare points. We were looking for united pressure on Iraq. We warned you that this was the only way to avoid conflict. You signed up to 1441 and then slid away from it. Alternative proposals missed the point. Diplomacy is over. We shall now take our own decisions.

Negroponte and Arias then made shorter parallel statements. The cameras flashed incessantly. We had little idea how far the sound of our voices was carrying and it was all a crowded, messy occasion. When I watched the news bulletins later, I saw that throughout our period at the microphone the other members of the Security Council were wandering like lost sheep backwards and forwards behind us, looking for the basement conference room which was supposed to have been reserved as the Council's home for the day. To uninitiated viewers it appeared that they were walking out on our statements. They would have not have been misled by the symbolism.

The informal consultations that followed proved something of an anticlimax. Hans Blix and Mohamed ElBaradei talked in surreal fashion about their future work programme and, more to the point, briefed the Council on the withdrawal of their staffs from Iraq. Strangely in the view of some, but with a logic geared to denying the allies any justifiable pretext for an invasion, the Iraqis had allowed UNMOVIC and the IAEA to leave without a hint of obstruction.

The Council agreed to take note, because Russia would not permit a warmer verb, of the Secretary-General's responsibility to take decisions on the security of UN staff in Iraq and so that item, so contentious in 1998, was settled without too much acrimony. The atmosphere was very charged. Attention was starting to flow towards the expected televised address by President Bush at 8 p.m. that evening and the Council business rather faded away. The President in due course announced a forty-eight-hour final deadline for Saddam Hussein to comply with the terms of Resolution 1441 and the media focus switched to that. The ashes of the Security Council's work were left to swirl unattended in the UN basement draughts.

11

Collapse into War

In the United Kingdom the focus immediately shifted to the House of Commons debate, scheduled for 18 March. The moment the Blair Government had been preparing for more than a year had arrived: it was time to gain the approval of the British Parliament to end the threat posed by Saddam Hussein through UK military action. If this debate had been held without any new UN resolution, it would have been unwinnable. But Resolution 1441 had reinvigorated the argument that Iraq was in breach of international law and had given the Security Council the opportunity to implement a solution. A majority in Parliament now had to agree to the proposition that the UN was not capable of completing the job of disarming Iraq and that the US–UK alliance would therefore have to do it themselves.

The debate had to settle two fundamental questions. Was the use of force legal? And was it justified? These two questions have become fused and confused in the arguments that have raged ever since the decision was made to commit British forces to combat in Iraq. Both have been the subject of intense controversy and both have engaged at some level the subjective judgements of those involved. But they are different questions.

There is no final arbiter of a case in international law as there is in

217

a domestic legal system: a sovereign state can refuse to accept the jurisdiction, for instance, of the International Court of Justice. Public opinion, therefore, has more scope to make its weight felt. For the UK Government, what mattered was that there should be a judgement by its law officers that the action contemplated was not going to break the law. The Attorney-General, Lord Goldsmith, in a written statement to Parliament on 17 March 2003, set out his interpretation of the combined effect of Resolutions 678, 687 and 1441 and determined that the use of force against Iraq would be legal. The statement, the Attorney-General's final word on the matter, is set out in Appendix 3. It explains why the authority to use force under Resolution 678 continued to be valid; and it declares in paragraph 9 that 'Resolution 1441 would in terms have provided that a further decision of the Security Council to sanction force was required if that had been intended. Thus, all that Resolution 1441 requires is reporting to and discussion by the Security Council of Iraq's failures, but not an express further decision to authorise force.'

Lord Goldsmith's judgement has been the subject of argument ever since, not least because his earlier and fuller advice to the Prime Minister, dated 7 March and classified secret, went into greater detail on the difficulties of proceeding without a second resolution. The 7 March document was leaked shortly before the May 2005 General Election in an attempt to cause damage to the Government by insinuating that the judgement was forced out of Lord Goldsmith by political pressure. But despite the headlines, Tony Blair's opponents had to concede that the Attorney-General had not stated that war without a second resolution would be illegal. His point was that a second resolution would be far preferable. Lord Goldsmith asked for my advice in January 2003 about the negotiation of Resolution 1441: I pointed up the significance of the failure by our opponents to keep the Security Council in control of the decision-making on a further breach by Iraq and I underlined the parallels with the justification for the December 1998 bombing. It did not surprise me that it took time for the Attorney-General's team to get right inside the sequence of resolutions, their negotiating history and their legal implications. Many of us had doubts about the use of force against Iraq on a March 2003 timing, but they were mainly on the policy aspects and the practical implications.

The fact is that Lord Goldsmith delivered his legal judgement on 17, not 7, March; and he has not changed it since. People have wished to claim that British participation in the conflict was illegal and they have a number of unofficial legal opinions on their side to back them up, but they have not, so far, been able to make the charges stick. The Government's opinion has not been formally challenged either in the UK Courts or by the UN Security Council. The Deputy Legal Adviser in the Foreign Office, Elizabeth Wilmshurst, resigned over the issue, but she had taken no such stand over the bombing of Iraq in December 1998, when the legal case rested on the same sequence of resolutions. Her resignation letter, later published, stated that the legal team in the Foreign Office were of the view that going to war against Iraq without a second resolution would have been illegal under international law. If that was the case, they never told me in New York. Their very able colleague in my Mission, Iain MacLeod, who sat at my shoulder throughout the drama of those final weeks in early 2003, interpreted the resolutions as I did: I would not have continued with our line of approach if he had advised me of a fundamental legal problem.

The difficulty for those who opposed the use of force has been that the basis for the attack on Iraq was contained in Security Council resolutions that remained valid. The difficulty for Washington and London has been that those resolutions had, for a lay audience, lost their teeth with the passage of time. If a government is obliged to defend its actions by going back twelve years to the aftermath of a war that has become political history, then inevitably scepticism will be voiced. But the strict legal case resides there. Saddam Hussein never satisfied the UN's terms for the finalisation of the first Gulf War. Resolution 687 of 3 April 1991 required him to cooperate with the UN in eliminating and accounting for all of Iraq's WMD. He did not cooperate, and he offered no verifiable evidence for the full elimination of his WMD. As a result, he left himself liable to the continuing use of force authorised by Resolution 678 of 29 November 1990. That was the legal basis for the bombing of Iraq in December 1998, explained by me in the Security Council at the time, on instructions from London. The legality of that action was cleared with the Government's legal advisers and was never challenged in the Council or in any relevant court of law. The effect of Resolution 1441, even if it revised the terms of Iraqi compliance, was to reconfirm the validity of those resolutions.

Much attention has been focused on the claim by the British and American Governments after the adoption of 1441 in November 2002 that there was no 'automaticity' contained in their interpretation of the text of 1441: in other words, that the two governments could not unilaterally judge that the time had come to use force against Iraq, without any further reference to the Security Council. People ask: was that not exactly what happened? The correct answer, which is 'no', is widely regarded as unconvincing. But the fact is that the US and the UK did fulfil the strict terms of the resolution. 1441 stipulated that anyone who judged that Saddam Hussein had breached the resolution – and France never succeeded in removing the implication in paragraphs 4 and 12 of 1441 that *either* the inspectors *or* a Member State of the UN could make the judgement – should bring the matter to the Council for further assessment. France, Germany, Russia and several others had wanted 1441 to state that only the Council could then take a decision. But the resolution they voted for did not say that. The Security Council thus adopted a resolution that gave them first refusal on the responsibility to act, but which did not address the consequences of their not taking it up. That vacuum was filled by the earlier resolutions, which had not been repealed or supplanted.

These interconnecting UN texts leave opponents of the war frustrated, since they regard the lines of connection as thin and unclear for a full-blooded debate about war and peace. But their effect is to leave the main issue one of justification rather than legality. That is much more a matter of subjective opinion; and it appears from polls and media comment that the majority of people in the United Kingdom who have a view on the subject did not and do not see the attack on Iraq as justified. Political leaders have to live with the consequences of unpopular decisions, but they are not compelled to follow the will of the people except at election time. The result of the UK General Election of 5 May 2005 reflected popular opinion on Iraq, among other things, but it still saw the Blair Government returned with a substantial majority. For the Prime Minister and his Government, what mattered on the eve of the invasion of Iraq was that the House of Commons supported them by a margin that both delivered a significant majority and saved the Parliamentary Labour Party from being regarded as disastrously split.

The speech delivered by Tony Blair at the opening of the 18 March 2003 debate is considered one of the best of his political career. How he collected himself from the disappointment of the collapse of diplomacy at the UN is hard to explain. I heard convincing evidence of the depression in the offices of 10 Downing Street the weekend before. Sceptics may claim that Blair had been mentally ready for that moment from way back, but that was not how it looked to those of us involved in trying to find a peaceful route out. The assumption that war was inevitable and right would have been reflected in quite a different psychology in the final weeks of diplomacy; and it would have led to a different approach to the preparations for the post-war period, which were almost entirely left to the Americans.

Tony Blair's case to Parliament rested on two principal arguments. First, that Iraqi WMD capability and Saddam's brutality combined represented an urgent threat to world peace, which would have to be dealt with if national security and international order were to be maintained. As the Prime Minister put it:

. . . Because the outcome of this issue will now determine more than the fate of the Iraqi regime and more than the future of the

Iraqi people, for so long brutalised by Saddam. It will determine the way Britain and the world confront the central security threat of the twenty-first century; the development of the UN; the relationship between Europe and the US; the relations within the EU and the way the US engages with the rest of the world. It will determine the pattern of international politics for the next generation.

The second plank of his argument was that lack of action to implement UN resolutions was as dangerous for the health of the international system as action in current circumstances:

What would any tyrannical regime possessing WMD think viewing the history of the world's diplomatic dance with Saddam? That our capacity to pass firm resolutions is only matched by our feebleness in implementing them. That is why this indulgence has to stop. Because it is dangerous. It is dangerous if such regimes disbelieve us. Dangerous if they think they can use our weakness, our hesitation, even the natural urges of our democracy towards peace, against us. Dangerous because one day they will mistake our innate revulsion against war for permanent incapacity; when in fact, pushed to the limit, we will act. But then when we act, after years of pretence, the action will have to be harder, bigger, more total in its impact. Iraq is not the only regime with WMD. But back away now from this confrontation and future conflicts will be infinitely worse and more devastating.

And later:

I have come to the conclusion after much reluctance that the greater danger to the UN is inaction: that to pass Resolution 1441 and then refuse to enforce it would do the most deadly damage to the UN's future strength, confirming it as an

222

instrument of diplomacy but not of action, forcing nations down the very unilateralist path we wish to avoid.

The force of the Prime Minister's argument rested in part on the Government's conviction at the time that Saddam Hussein possessed and was further developing WMD. 'We are now seriously asked to accept', he said, 'that in the last few years, contrary to all history, contrary to all intelligence, he decided unilaterally to destroy the weapons. Such a claim is palpably absurd.' I have analysed earlier why this belief was so strong in the American and British Governments and why Saddam Hussein kept up such a dangerous pretence. But a belief it was. Tony Blair has had to live with the surprise that no one subsequently has been able to locate WMD stockpiles in Iraq. That does not alter the fact that Iraq was in breach of UN resolutions. But it does magnify the accusation that the punishment was out of proportion to the offence.

The belief in the existence of WMD was widely enough shared in the House of Commons on 18 March 2003, and the rhetoric of the Prime Minister was sufficiently powerful, that a large majority of MPs, making their judgement on the merits of the argument as well as their party loyalties, voted for the motion that military action should be pursued. The British Government had finally caught up with its American counterpart in having both national and international cover for the use of force.

In New York the three days before the actual start of the military campaign passed in a state of glum resignation. Everyone knew from President Bush's broadcast on the evening of 17 March that war was inevitable within days or perhaps hours. Bizarrely, the Security Council held an open meeting on Iraq on 19 March, attended by the Foreign Ministers of France, Germany, Russia, Syria and, in the Chair, Guinea. I suppose they wanted to show that the unilateral decisions of a minority ought not to disrupt the normal business of the UN. For a moment Colin Powell and Jack Straw contemplated joining them, but the timing and the risk of an unpleasant scene deterred them.

The French were fuming about the sideswipe against them in my 17 March statement and the Germans, though constantly more worried than the French about the effects of a transatlantic split, were too close to them, and too far away from Washington, to have anything soothing to say. I did not expect to have a happy time in the chamber. Jean-Marc de la Sablière reminded me every time I passed within earshot what the line-up of votes would have been for our draft resolution: he was not feeling isolated, he said; he had plenty of good company.

I decided to tackle the German and French Foreign Ministers directly as we began to gather for the meeting. I said how sorry I was that we had had this fallout and suggested that we Europeans should plan to work together more closely on the whole area of WMD proliferation in the future. Both Joschka Fischer and Dominique de Villepin were polite enough to say that this was worth considering, but they did not wish to talk about Iraq. Gunter Pleuger, my German colleague, made a genuine attempt to paper over our differences and we rather formally complimented each other on the handling of our opposing cases in the Council. Otherwise the atmosphere was frosty. The actual Council meeting was insubstantial, concentrating unrealistically on the future work of UNMOVIC and the IAEA, and only a few mournful comments were uttered about the collapse of diplomacy. No lunch was held afterwards, to everyone's relief.

That night the Americans launched their bombing campaign, jump-starting it by a day in an attempt to kill Saddam Hussein at one of his family farms. He escaped unscathed, but we did not know that for certain until days later. This first sign of military action came as a shock: it had always been so theoretical up to this point, so postponable. Now that it had started, the world became a different place. No one knew whether the conflict would go on for months, with casualties mounting up and all the humanitarian consequences the UN had predicted.

Rather than sit and wait for news of the campaign to dictate the reactions of the watching community in New York, I decided we had to persuade people to think about the operational implications of what had happened. On 19 March we had begun to consider the role of the United Nations in caring for the Iraqi people after the conflict: there was nothing to be done while the fighting continued. The Secretary-General had been asked to submit proposals for a mandate for the Secretariat and a continuation of the Oil for Food programme, which was feeding more than half the Iraqi population. This put Kofi Annan in a dilemma; he wanted the UN to remain engaged in this major crisis, but he was at the same time receiving advice from his team that the Secretariat should keep its distance from what they saw as unjustified interference in the sovereign affairs of Iraq. Annan wisely judged that a UN role could be constructed while respecting Iraq's theoretical independence and he agreed to make some suggestions. Worried that these might be framed in such a way as to criticise our position, I started preparing a British version.

Against the background of huge, sometimes hysterical, specu-lation in the media and in the drawing-rooms of East Manhattan about the collapse of the UN system and the emasculation of the Security Council, the willingness of the Permanent Five to get together to discuss next steps emerged as a pleasant surprise. In the late afternoon of 20 March, as the television screens were beginning to fill with images of the 'shock and awe' bombing campaign around Baghdad, the P5 agreed to meet to see what could be salvaged from the mess. It helped to have a concrete operational question to ponder and outright recrimination was avoided. The Russians, under-standably enough, could not resist underlining that any involvement of the Secretariat must be organised on a basis that did not stain them by association with an 'illegal occupation'. But we were negotiating again.

That same day, I telephoned Jean-David Levitte in Washington to express my regret that all our joint efforts to find a way through without war had come to nothing. The next day he sent me a note to reassure me that it would not make a difference at a personal level, but he could not resist attaching a section from a W. H. Auden poem, a pointed reference back to the casual way in which the diplomats, as the poet saw it, allowed the First World War to gather pace:

But in the evening the oppression lifted;
The peaks came into focus; it had rained;
Across the lawns and cultured flowers drifted
The conversation of the highly trained.

The gardeners watched them pass and priced their shoes;
A chauffeur waited, reading in the drive,
For them to finish their exchange of views;
It seemed a picture of the private life.

Far off, no matter what good they intended,
The armies waited for a verbal error
With all the instruments for causing pain:

And on the issue of their charm depended
A land laid waste, with all its young men slain,
The women weeping, and the towns in terror.

They carry terror with them like a purse,
And flinch from the horizon like a gun;
And all the rivers and the railways run
Away from Neighbourhood as from a curse.

They cling and huddle in the new disaster
Like children sent to school, and cry in turn;
For space has rules they cannot hope to learn,
Time speaks a language they can never master.

We live here. We lie in the Present's unopened
Sorrow; its limits are what we are.
The prisoner ought never to pardon his cell.

Can future ages ever escape so far,
Yet feel derived from everything that happened,
Even from us, that even this was well?

Levitte left me to ponder the connotations of this passage on my own. No comparison with the start of the First World War could be made to stand up for long, but the suggestion of obstinate positions held in defiance of a collective logic, of the military build-up creating a momentum of its own, of the suppression of any honest analysis of what horrors war might bring to those who were not lucky enough to observe it from a distance, even the hint of the later futility of the League of Nations, were all rather chilling.

Despite the hard feelings, our colleagues and opponents on the Security Council did not turn their backs on their practical responsibilities. The need to deal with the real-world consequences of the breakdown of diplomacy laid a basis for the slow, grudging and sometimes painful process of bringing Iraq back into the UN's normal business agenda. Kofi Annan played his part in this process. As the conflict started and the Secretariat building filled with bitter reproaches over the sidelining of the UN, he took an extremely cautious position. I went to see him four days into the war. In his quiet, calm way, with never a hint of reproach in his voice and only momentarily in his eye, he said he wished to see how things developed on the ground before making any decisions about UN involvement. He was clear that he did not wish the UN to take over responsibility for administering the country once the fighting had died down: the political and practical minuses were too manifest. I suggested that the United States was in any case most unlikely to offer the UN such a role. Annan said he was reluctant even to appoint his own Special Representative at this stage, as London and

Washington wanted. I could nevertheless see that the situation presented an opportunity for renewed UN involvement in Iraq and that Annan was alive to this.

The next day the Secretary-General invited the Permanent Five up to the thirty-eighth floor for a working lunch, the only time he did so during my five years in New York. The conversation was notably constructive. Short of doing anything that implied legitimisation of the war, the Russians, French and Chinese wanted to pick up some of the shattered pieces. We agreed on a way to continue the Oil for Food distribution programme after the conflict, to avoid the risk of starvation for the 70 per cent or so of the population who depended on it. Annan set out his preferred architecture for a later UN role: three equal pillars – the Coalition, the Iraqis and the UN – working in harness. The previous day he had been over the ground with Condoleezza Rice, who had gone to see him privately in New York, and the idea seemed to be within negotiating distance of the Americans. All five of us accepted this approach as a sensible potential framework for the next steps, but the non-Americans had not been consulted on it and we could not be sure what would happen in practice.

The Prime Minister and Jack Straw decided to pay a lightning visit to UN headquarters late on 27 March, following a council of war they had just held with President Bush at Camp David. They helicoptered in from JFK Airport and, contrary to the usual protocol, I met them only when they reached the entrance to the building. The thirty-first floor had been cleared for Blair to do a number of media interviews and while that was going on I held a gloomy conversation with Jack Straw about the breakdown at the UN and the mountain we would have to climb to remedy it. The Prime Minister then had a long discussion with the Secretary-General, most of it tête-à-tête. As I understood it, nothing specific was agreed, but the visit helped to convince Kofi Annan that the UK could accept the three pillars structure, would do its utmost to create a politically protected space for the UN in Iraq, and would help limit the humanitarian effects of the conflict.

As for the conflict raging 5,000 miles away, little was said. None of us knew how long it might drag on and that exercised the Prime Minister more than anything else. He was not ready to focus on the precise arrangements for the post-conflict phase and it was not for me to ask about it in a one-and-a-half-hour visit. It was a glum and unproductive evening. It reinforced my feeling that events had moved on beyond anything I could offer, that the whole British machine was being carried along on the tide and that we would have to wait for it to turn.

The Security Council nevertheless plodded ahead with the bits and pieces left to us. Before March was over, with the military campaign in full swing, when we had absorbed the full force of Russian resentment and after some constructive work from the German delegation under Gunter Pleuger, the Security Council unanimously adopted a resolution (1472) ensuring the continuation of the Oil for Food programme. For all the public hammering of the use of force in the corridors and in the international media, this decision had a calming effect on the internal UN system and suggested to delegations and Secretariat alike that they were going to have a purpose in the context of Iraq. Kofi Annan did decide in early April to appoint a Special Adviser for Iraq, Rafiuddin Ahmed, underpowered for this stormy territory but an experienced UN hand and an important symbol of UN involvement. Unlike Brahimi in Afghanistan, Ahmed did not have the authority and independence of a Special Representative and was never allowed to stray far from East Manhattan. The arrangement left the impression that the Secretary-General was only going through the motions.

Then the military campaign began to eat up Iraqi territory and some of the British gloom lifted. Too used by now to finding the next thing to worry about, we wondered whether the real crunch was going to come in Baghdad, where an urban guerrilla resistance had long been predicted. We began to enjoy the ludicrous expostulations of the Iraqi Information Minister, 'Comical Ali', that all was well for Iraq's defence and the invaders would be ejected soon enough. The leading American column cut through to the centre of the city on 6 April and it seemed that the end of the fighting might be only days away. I had nothing on my desk to indicate what the next steps were going to be. It was all happening elsewhere.

The vacuum started to be filled when President Bush and Prime Minister Blair met on 7–8 April for a bilateral summit in Hillsborough, Northern Ireland. Only then were we able to get a sense that top-level planning for the post-war phase had become the priority, although the military details were never conveyed to us in New York. The important thing to come out of Hillsborough for us in New York was that the place of the United Nations in post-war Iraq, over which London and Washington had been at odds for quite a while, was given a push forwards. The President and the Prime Minister together declared that they wished the UN to play a 'vital' role in the construction of a new Iraq.

The Anglo–American skirmishing over that adjective 'vital' is worth touching on in a little more detail, because the part that the United Nations was later to come to play in Iraq, selecting the new Iraqi leadership and adding legitimacy to the political transition, illuminates the variable attitude of the United States towards the global institution. The Hillsborough meeting was preceded by a careful public exposition by the British Government of their vision for the administration of the country. This had been set out by the Foreign Secretary in a speech to the Newspaper Society Annual Conference on 1 April. There were four key commitments: first, the provision of emergency relief, for which the Government had already allocated £240 million; second, a medium-term international aid programme overseen by the United Nations; third, the long-term redevelopment and rehabilitation of Iraq, under a new UN Security Council resolution to endorse an appropriate post-conflict administration – the UK believed that the UN should take a leading role in organising a conference to bring together representatives from all sections of Iraqi society and to place decisions about Iraq's political and economic future firmly in the hands of the Iraqi people;

and fourth, ensuring that Iraq's oil wealth would be used exclusively for the benefit of the Iraqi people.

This prescription went beyond what was considered wise or acceptable in the United States. Even Secretary of State Colin Powell, the senior member of the administration most likely to countenance a US partnership with the UN, poured cold water on a leading role for the UN. Speaking at a NATO meeting on 3 April, Powell said: 'It was the Coalition that came together and took on this difficult mission at political expense, at the expense of the treasury . . . but at the expense of lives as well. When we have succeeded and when we look down the road to create this better life for the Iraqi people to rebuild this society . . . after these decades of devastation wrought by Saddam Hussein, I think the Coalition has to play the leading role in determining the way forward.' London was concerned that this was missing the point: it would surely save a lot of treasure and lives if there was the widest possible support from the international community in helping Iraqis to get back on their feet. The UK made the hard calculation that the UN was going to be needed in the aftermath of the war, both to form the foundation of an international effort to reconstruct Iraq and to bring skills and experience to bear in the technical administration of the country. The UN possessed these skills in greater abundance than Washington or London. At the same NATO meeting, Jack Straw said that the top priority was to put the country quickly back in the hands of its own people: 'Iraq has to be run by Iraqis, not by people parachuted in from outside.' Reporters were amused to spot that, as he was talking to them, two booklets slipped out of his pocket onto the ground, a map of Iraq and the Charter of the United Nations.

The UK and the US argued out these points in the final stages of the military operation. As the Hillsborough summit approached, Washington gave a little ground. The joint statement of the two leaders at Hillsborough included the following passage:

As the coalition proceeds with the reconstruction of Iraq, it will work with its allies, bilateral donors and with the United

Nations and other international institutions. The United Nations has a vital role to play in the reconstruction of Iraq. We welcome the effort of UN agencies and non-governmental organisations in providing immediate assistance to the people of Iraq. As we stated in the Azores, we plan to seek the adoption of a new UN Security Council resolution that would affirm Iraq's territorial integrity, ensure rapid delivery of humanitarian relief and endorse an appropriate post-conflict administration for Iraq. We welcome the appointment by the UN Secretary-General of a Special Adviser for Iraq to work with the people of Iraq and Coalition representatives.

In the end it was the President personally, in spite of some tugging on his coat-tails from his team, who insisted that the UK's requirement for an adjective at least as positive as 'vital' should be met. During the question-and-answer session with journalists after the summit, President Bush deliberately repeated the word several times. Asked point-blank what it meant, he defined a possible role for the UN: 'A vital role as an agent to help people to live freely. That's a vital role, and that means food. That means medicine. That means a place where people can give their contributions. That means suggesting people for the interim Iraqi administration. That means being a party to the progress being made in Iraq.' What Bush did not say was that he could see a leading political role for the UN.

For those in New York who wanted to see the bare realities of what had occurred reversed, this was not enough. They wished to have the UN in charge, with the Charter setting the principles, the Member States providing the resources and the Secretariat leading the implementation. For the UK, the result at Hillsborough was more than we had expected to secure from Washington. The Americans, however, were not going to cede central control. Kofi Annan knew this and he was not asking for anything different. Aware from his more than thirty years of inside experience of the true strengths and weaknesses of the UN, he realised that a large and deeply disturbed territory like Iraq was beyond the capacity of the world body to administrate. There had to be a phase where a coalition of capable states established security and laid the foundations for a new political structure. Then the United Nations could coordinate the input of resources and expertise and take over the transition process when the situation had settled down. This is what had recently happened in East Timor, with the Australians providing the early steel and a UN administration under Sergio Vieira de Mello running the transitional machinery. It was also the pattern in Afghanistan under Lakhdar Brahimi, though the UN's political role was more closely confined to the capital. In both places UN resolutions had set the framework for political change. In Iraq the change of regime itself was highly controversial. Annan was wiser about the UN's limitations than his staff and he was not going to overreach. Where he and his Secretariat did agree was in leaving the United States and the United Kingdom to handle the political and administrative consequences of their own decisions, echoing Colin Powell's advice to President Bush in August 2002 about going it alone: 'You break it, you own it.'

Even at Hillsborough the allies could not be sure that the end of Saddam Hussein's regime would come rapidly. Baghdad could be hiding a surprise. The absence of a second front in the north because Turkey had stayed out of the conflict meant that Iraqi forces could re-form north of Baghdad and continue to cause trouble. But 7 and 8 April passed without any sign of a counter-attack or of organised urban resistance. The worry that our armies would get bogged down, or that Saddam Hussein's crack troops would defend Baghdad street by street and raise the casualty levels on both sides to an unacceptable horror, began to lift. There was no sign of the millions of refugees and the starving civilian population predicted by the UN Secretariat. The campaign had delivered the best-case scenario: a brilliantly conceived and executed military strategy, US troops operating with impressive speed and accuracy, British and Australian units performing their subsidiary but significant roles courageously and the Iraqi resistance melting away to nothing. On 9 April, as American armoured columns reached the centre of the capital, the people came out onto the streets in a spontaneous outburst of delight, just as Ahmed Chalabi had predicted to the Pentagon. Iraqis, with help from American soldiers, brought the statue of Saddam Hussein tumbling down from its plinth in Fardus Square. It was all over.

The precipitous collapse of Iraq's defence led to much speculation about Saddam's planning. Perhaps it had been his intention all along to have his best forces fade away and save themselves for guerrilla warfare later. The evidence from both military and intelligence sources pointed rather to a deep reluctance in the Iraqi ranks to fight for a lost cause and for a dictator who had miscalculated. Saddam himself appears to have been surprised and disappointed by the speed of his regime's demise. When his statue crashed to the ground, his standing and his image evaporated. From then until his capture on 12 December, he was on the run with minimal support and unable to reconstitute any of his military units. The Baathist and Sunni extremist resistance was able to draw on financial reserves secreted away by the regime over the years and members of the security forces undoubtedly joined the anti-Coalition ranks. But we never found clear indications that it all followed a pre-ordained pattern. The strategy and operational effectiveness of the insurgency had to be generated from a collapsed system and from whatever opportunities the handling of the post-conflict phase presented.

12

The Occupation Starts Badly

By 10 April Baghdad lay in the hands of the American forces and the guns had stopped firing. It was time to turn to the requirements of a Saddam-free Iraq. I would be leaving the United Nations on 26 July, the day before my sixtieth birthday – the mandatory Foreign Office retirement age – but it was clear there would be plenty of work to do over those three and a half months in New York. I shall briefly describe the parts that affected the setting up of an occupation administration in Baghdad with UN authority and a degree of UN participation, but the next stage of this account is mainly about the creation of a political structure for Iraq's transition, which I witnessed at first hand in Baghdad between September 2003 and the end of March 2004.

The United Kingdom held limited discussions with the American team responsible for planning the aftermath of the war. The Foreign Office and the Ministry of Defence consulted with the State Department, but that was not where the operational work was being done. UK planning at the beginning of 2003 had largely been concentrated on setting up a Joint Forces operation in Turkey, which the Americans assumed would be playing a major northern flank role in the whole enterprise. When that prospect vanished on 1 March with Turkey's refusal to be drawn in, the forces moved to the south-east. It was not until mid-February that we learnt that retired Lieutenant-General Jay Garner would lead the civil administration in Baghdad. At the request of the Pentagon, the UK Ministry of Defence (MoD) appointed Major-General Tim Cross to act as Garner's deputy, assigning him a small team to help plan the British role in the reconstruction effort in Baghdad. The MoD did devote time to learning from the Pentagon and from US Central Command (CENTCOM) how the British Army's new role in Basra and the south-east would link in to the overall post-conflict structure and what lesser part we might play in security arrangements at the centre. We ended up with around 12,000 troops in the south under a Major-General, and in Baghdad we provided a two-star deputy to the US military commander in Iraq, with a unit of fewer than 100 soldiers to back him up. On the humanitarian side the UK's Department for International Development (DfID) under Clare Short had made their largely independent preparations to contribute to civilian relief efforts, mainly in the south, but the total preparation effort did not amount to a fully articulated plan. London had been too absorbed with the challenge of whether and when a conflict would erupt to enter into the detail of what next. It might also have been politically awkward to get into precise planning discussions when the Government was regularly asserting that no decision to use force would be made until it was clear that there was no alternative. The consequences of the UK's failure to insist on adequate preparation were to prove costly.

As it happened, a significant amount of work had been done in various departments in Washington to assess the probable reactions of the Iraqi people to the removal of Saddam Hussein's regime and to predict what might be required by way of security control and civilian administration. The Central Intelligence Agency wrote their own paper, pointing out the divisive tendencies in Iraqi politics and the risk of sustained violence. A State Department team under Tom Warrick from the Bureau of Near Eastern Affairs, including some experienced American Arabists and drawing on the input of over 200 Iraqi exiles, had been putting a huge effort over more than a year into a project called 'The Future of Iraq', a paper that has stood the test of time in its assessment of the difficulties any new administration would face. It went into the detail of Iraq's violent history, indicated the scale of the challenge the United States would face after regime change and made proposals for the early transfer of power to a new Iraqi leadership.

It was the Pentagon, however, that was in charge. There had been a great deal of discussion among senior members of the administration in the months leading up to March 2003 about the post-war phase, but the short-term priority was the invasion itself and the talk led to few decisions. In the end, Donald Rumsfeld took the reins into his own hands. He argued that only the Pentagon had the capacity to act and that the military would be left with the problem in practice. The Pentagon had after all been responsible, under the Office of the Secretary of Defense (OSD) and with the energetic General Tommy Franks in operational charge, for the whole war-planning process from late 2001 onwards, and the Pentagon budget was bearing the cost of the operation through the invasion and beyond. Rumsfeld was determined to retain control of the post-conflict arrangements despite the greater expertise available in the State Department. Eight weeks before the start of the conflict an 'Office of Post-War Planning' was established in the Pentagon in accordance with a specific Presidential Directive for that purpose (PD 24) and Garner was brought out of retirement to head it.

Jay Garner was a strange choice for such a high-profile assignment. He had a distinguished military record and had, in the early 1990s, headed the effort to protect the Kurds after the first Gulf War, Operation Provide Comfort, but he had little knowledge of the region beyond that and no experience of political institution-building. He had retired from the army several years earlier and was running a profitable private-sector company in Washington. Douglas Feith, the Under-Secretary at the Pentagon responsible for Iraq planning, telephoned him on Rumsfeld's behalf in January 2003 and asked him to drop what he was doing and come to help on Iraq. Garner resisted for a day or two but eventually gave the loyal response and agreed to set aside his business interests for a period.

On arrival, Garner found that the Pentagon was prepared to supply him with almost no serving officers and he had to appeal to fellow retired officers to staff his planning office. He tried at first to bring in the State Department people involved on the Future of Iraq Project: at a brainstorming meeting at Fort Myers on 20–22 February Tom Warrick asked some highly pertinent questions about the tasks the unit would have to perform and the resources they had at their disposal to do so. Yet within a week Garner was ordered by Rumsfeld to let Warrick and his colleagues go. It was assumed in Garner's team that this was because they might not be loyal to the Pentagon's approach – a striking symptom of the competitiveness between the two departments and perhaps also of the personal rivalry between Rumsfeld and Powell, which had featured constantly throughout the Iraq saga. Garner did his best to pull the strings together, but he was not in a position to fill the strategic vacuum that Warrick and his team had warned might develop: there was too much to do at the tactical level. Neither he nor Major-General Cross had large teams to back them up, and neither even had a political adviser.

Two considerations in particular influenced thinking at the Office of the Secretary of Defense as the Pentagon prepared for the conflict. The first was the ongoing development of a military concept for the United States which combined huge technological and mechanical capability with restraint on the size of military manpower. This suited the objectives of protecting vital US interests, surgically eliminating direct threats and minimising the impact of war on US domestic opinion. It was a philosophy that Defense Secretary Donald Rumsfeld had inherited both from his own previous experience in government and from the Pentagon itself, where significant modernisation work had been initiated under the Clinton administration. Its effect had already influenced the way in which the

Afghanistan campaign had been managed: the expulsion of the Taliban Government had been implemented with supreme efficiency, in partnership with local forces opposed to the Taliban. Yet Bush and Rumsfeld, scorning the Clinton administration's predilection for peacekeeping operations, refused to deploy sufficient numbers of American troops outside Kabul after the war to ensure country-wide security, even though their NATO allies and the United Nations repeatedly asked them to do so. This diminished the coherence and effectiveness of the post-Taliban administration of the country.

The second consideration was the advice the Pentagon was receiving from Iraqi exiles, which seemed to mesh with its own assessment of the likely response of the Iraqi population to the fall of Saddam Hussein. Prominent in this category was Ahmed Chalabi, the leader in exile of the Iraq National Congress, who insisted that Iraqis would rejoice at the overthrow of the regime and welcome their liberators with open arms. Chalabi had a close relationship with both Rumsfeld and Cheney and was being groomed by the Defense Department, despite loud protests from State, to lead Iraq's transitional government after the war. The primary tasks of the US military once the conflict had come to a halt would be to ensure provisions and security until an Iraqi administration could be put in place: a matter of a few months, perhaps. This reliance on one channel only of Iraqi exile advice, together with the failure to examine the conflicting forces inside Iraq itself, with all the American expertise available, led to the decision to commit the post-conflict administration to such a small team, one that had no experience of political planning and did not attract the respect and attention of the US military hierarchy.

The reality was that the end-state for Iraq was never clarified in strategic terms from a coordinated American perspective, either for their allies or for themselves. The emphasis lay on what the United States military did best: war. No one really knew what would happen in the aftermath. The title chosen for the administrative effort under

Garner, the 'Office of Reconstruction and Humanitarian Affairs' (ORHA), indicated its limited objectives. It never filled its modest complement of less than 300 staff. CENTCOM did not take it seriously or establish a connected infrastructure for it. In circumstances without any clear precedent or historical example, the Office of the Secretary of Defense took a gamble that the best-case scenario would emerge. That was the basis on which the team under Jay Garner was established, with the instruction to tidy up the place as quickly as possible and to hand over power to an Iraqi Interim Authority (IIA). Military leaders foresaw an early drawdown of American troops, trusting that one or more of three scenarios would come about: the Iraqis would quickly take over, the international community would contribute higher numbers, or the coalition's civilian structure would assume control. When General Franks arrived in Baghdad on 16 April, with the conflict phase finished, he told his field commanders, according to a well-researched article by Michael Gordon in the *New York Times* in October 2004, that combat forces should be prepared to start pulling out within sixty days: by September the more than 140,000 US troops in Iraq could be down to little more than a division, or 30,000 troops.

The UK Government saw no particular problem with this approach. In his message to the Iraqi people on 4 April, Tony Blair laid out the strategy for the reconstruction period.

Coalition forces will make the country safe, and will work with the United Nations to help Iraq get back on its feet. We will continue to provide immediate humanitarian aid, and we will help with longer-term projects. Our troops will leave as soon as they can. They will not stay a day longer than necessary. We will make sure deliveries of vital aid such as food, medicine and drinking water get through. Our aim is to move as soon as possible to an interim authority run by Iraqis. This will pave the way for a truly representative Iraqi government, which respects human rights and the rule of law; develops public services; and

240

spends Iraq's wealth not on palaces but on schools and hospitals.

Blair's goals fitted well enough with the remit given to Jay Garner. The conundrum for planners affected the United Nations as well. The calculations of the UN Secretariat and UN agencies that a vast humanitarian crisis would be created on the heels of a US-led invasion turned out to be wide of the mark. If such a scenario had actually transpired, the international system would never have been able to cope with it: and the gaps and deficiencies would have been laid at the door of the Coalition. As for Iraqi reactions, we all hoped for the best. But I remember my Egyptian colleague, Ahmed Aboul Gheit, subsequently Foreign Minister of Egypt, telling me in the main corridor of the UN building as the conflict began that the violence and brutality of those Iraqis who would decide to resist a foreign occupation would shock us to the core. I thought that he was exaggerating in order to express his own deep distaste for what was happening. He proved to be spot on.

No sooner was the conflict over than the unexpected started to occur – unexpected, that is, in the offices that mattered. Released from the shackles of a brutal and efficient regime, a large number of Iraqis took to the streets in a wave of looting and destruction. As far as it was possible to tell, this explosion of spontaneous violence was not directed at the Coalition as such. The huge majority of Iraqis were overjoyed that Saddam had been removed and his machine shattered. But after their long experience of oppression, mal-treatment and sanctions, Iraq had lost its sense of communal purpose and national pride. Individuals and close families had for too long been narrowly focused on their own survival. Now at last they were free, and everyone was out for what he could get. Mixed in with these confused emotions of release and desperation came a strong element of criminality, stimulated not just by the disappearance of recognised forms of law and order – so inescapable under Saddam – but also by the opening created for the tens of thousands of convicts whom Saddam had released from prison the previous year.

The Coalition forces were unprepared for this outburst of criminality. They had been trained and briefed for a different kind of hostility. Images of Iraqis carrying off spoils from the National Museum in Baghdad, while American troops stood by, filled the news bulletins. Comparisons were made with the efficiency with which the military guarded the Ministry of Oil and the oilfields, stoking speculation – in the view of the UK team, wholly inaccurate – that the US was only there for the oil. One thing that the Pentagon had taken precautions against was an attempt by Saddam Hussein to set fire to the well-heads, as he had done in 1991. They were caught by surprise on both fronts.

Perhaps commanders believed that the looting would quickly die away as the people adjusted to their new circumstances. When the situation extended into the second week, they realised that they were facing a more deep-rooted problem. There were too few soldiers in theatre to take up full-scale police duties, when the priority remained to ensure the security of the Coalition itself and of the principal areas and buildings of government. Haphazard attempts were made to stop attacks on public property and to arrest the perpetrators, but the effect was partial and the high-level instructions did not change. The American Army again insisted that it did not do police work, but there was no one else to do it for them. Jay Garner had not yet arrived in Iraq – General Franks did not regard it as safe for ORHA to deploy until 21 April – and there was no line of contact to the old Iraqi police force. The looting continued.

The effect of this setback was threefold. First, the Coalition was rocked back on its heels after the splendid achievements of the campaign. The transition to the next phase faltered, physically and psychologically. Second, the impression the liberators had made on their Iraqi constituency was significantly tarnished. Underlying the delight that the removal of Saddam inspired in the majority of the population was a feeling of resentment and humiliation that it had taken foreigners, Americans no less, to achieve what they had long wished to do for themselves; and they began to worry about the absence of law and order. Third, those who genuinely planned to do the Coalition mischief were encouraged to see signs of an ineffectiveness on which they could capitalise.

As Donald Rumsfeld famously remarked, 'stuff happens'. As the second week turned into the third, however, and symptoms of respect for the new administrators failed to materialise, Washington itself began to conclude that enough stuff was happening to threaten the US strategic position. If this was going to be the reaction of the Iraqi population to their new-found freedom, changes would have to be made to the American approach. Jay Garner, who through no fault of his own had been allocated a role in one assumed set of circumstances only to be confronted by another, was telephoned by Rumsfeld within a week of his arrival in Baghdad to be told that he was being replaced. By the time President George W. Bush had declared 'Mission accomplished' on 1 May on the decks of the USS *Missouri*, ORHA was history and Ambassador L. Paul Bremer III had been selected to head the Coalition Provisional Authority (CPA). Given even less time to prepare himself than Garner, Bremer arrived on 16 May with no proper administration in place in Baghdad. Apart from the fact that the Secretary of Defense stood at the apex of both the civilian and the military operations in Iraq, his relationship with the US military structure trying to keep order in the country was unformulated. Yet he came out with instructions to change the policy fast.

Instead of the objective of turning the country over to a selected Iraqi leadership and drawing down US forces as quickly as possible, Bremer was asked to assert Coalition control and bring Iraq to national elections for a transitional government only after order had been restored and the principles for a new, democratic Iraq established. He abandoned the plan to construct an interim Iraqi government with significant powers and cancelled arrangements for local elections, which provoked further violence on the streets in some Shia areas. He also brought with him two decisions, issued as decrees four days after his arrival, that could only have been taken at the top level before he left Washington and which were, at the time and subsequently, widely criticised. He rejected the Iraqi Army, some 400,000 strong, as a source of security manpower; and he barred anyone with a Baathist connection from holding a job in the new Iraq. Before the invasion began, Douglas Feith and the Office of the Secretary of Defense had, in concert with Jay Garner, been developing a policy in exactly the opposite direction: to retain and retrain the middle and lower ranks of the existing Iraqi security forces and put them to work for the new order. This approach had been agreed in the National Security Council, backed by the senior American commanders and explained to the President in early March. It fitted with the expectation that the Americans would be welcomed by the Iraqi population and with the desire to hand over power quickly to an Iraqi transitional government. The collapse of law and order immediately after 9 April and the realisation that the Garner model was not working led to these hastily taken decisions and the loss of strategic coherence. The decrees on the army and the Baath Party let slip an opportunity for asserting control which the Coalition was never able to recover.

In New York the controversy over the decision to attack Iraq continued to dominate the politics of the Security Council and the mood of the wider membership. Beyond the immediate resentment, many governments worried that the principle of primacy for the sovereignty of individual states had been infringed. The tension between sovereign rights and the upholding of international standards has always been, and continues to be, one of the deeper fault lines in the UN system. An early article of the UN Charter – Article 2, paragraph 7 – stipulates that the United Nations must not intervene in matters that are essentially within the domestic jurisdiction of any state. Security Council resolutions regularly reaffirm respect for the sovereignty and territorial integrity of a particular state and this mantra, while it has its proper place in the Charter, has become a comfort blanket for weak or oppressive governments. Article 2.7 is equally clear that this principle should not stand in the way of enforcement measures taken by the Security Council if international peace and security is threatened. But the Security Council is perceived as being dominated by powerful states, each with an agenda of their own. The dilemma of the modern age in global security lies in the increasing number of cases where conflict or wide-scale abuse of human rights is taking place within the boundaries of a Member State. As globalisation magnifies the ripple effect of internal strife, so the tension between national and international prerogatives becomes more acute. We tried to ease this clash of principles during my time in New York with an attempt to fashion guidelines for outside intervention in internal catastrophes. It foundered on the refusal of many countries to re-open or even discuss what Article 2 of the Charter really meant.

The second instinct amongst those most troubled by the American decision to use force in the name of the international community was to limit the damage. The superpower was big and rich and was dangerous to those it chose as its enemies. More than that, the superpower had a point about Iraq. Invasion might have been an overreaction, but Iraq had defied the United Nations and got away with it for twelve years. If any value was to be salvaged from the wreckage of collective diplomacy over Iraq, the sooner the instruments of the UN were reconnected to the handling of the situation, the better.

These conflicting motivations produced a constant swing between eruptions of indignation and reluctant cooperation. The Russians in particular were determined that nothing should be done by the Security Council that legitimised or excused the unilateral use of force, as they saw it, by the United States with the United Kingdom in tow. Tony Blair suffered a particularly difficult moment when he visited Moscow on 29 April and was scornfully questioned in public by President Putin as to where Saddam Hussein and the weapons of mass destruction were now to be found. China shared this hostility to unilateralism, though they were more subdued in their expression of it. Both of these countries had live domestic concerns which made their defence of the sovereignty principle imperative. France and Germany continued to produce flashes of high-voltage resentment at US–UK behaviour, responding more to their concern that the whole Middle East would be destabilised and to their wish to tie down Gulliver with the threads of multilateralism. But all of them gradually came to realise that the UN had to be reinserted into the management of Iraq or multilateralism would be further set back.

The United Kingdom was once again caught between the currents. US patience was in short supply. The UN had, in the American view, failed to deal with Saddam Hussein's defiance. It did not have the strength or the organisation to take responsibility for a transformed Iraq. Americans were going to have to do the job, alone or with whatever allies decided to help. A 'vital' role for the UN was one thing, a lead position quite another. It should either become an ally or remain at arm's length.

The UK saw in that approach a missed opportunity to broaden international support for the effort in Iraq and hankered after the dose of extra legitimacy that the UN would inject. We were where we were and the job had to be done one way or the other, but we felt more exposed to the political and cultural backlash in the Arab and Islamic worlds, and indeed in Iraq itself, if we and the US were left with the sole responsibility. I well remember a mid-April discussion at a dinner in my apartment, when the House of Commons International Development Committee was visiting the UN to assess how aid for Iraq should be organised. A selection of my ambassadorial colleagues gave their personal views on what had happened. The larger-than-life figure of the South African Permanent Representative, Dumisani Kumalo, thrust himself into the exchange: 'I cannot possibly support the decision which the United States and the United Kingdom have taken to use force against Iraq. But thank goodness the Brits are there to provide a bridge back to the UN. We would otherwise all be out of reach of the Americans for a long time.' He had articulated one of Tony Blair's primary considerations.

Such perceptions did not necessarily instil confidence in Washington that the UK, and particularly its team in New York, placed the same priority as the US did on absolute control for the Coalition in Iraq. But we were unrepentant. The UK's international profile and set of interests differ from those of the United States even while many of our values and objectives remain the same. We could not afford to distance ourselves from the international community, nor could we do without the proper functioning of the global institutions and their collective resources.

The Iraq saga illustrates more clearly than any other issue of its generation the struggle the United Kingdom has taken on to knit together the hard and soft elements of international action, dealing with the most corrosive cases of illegitimate behaviour while sustaining trust in collective legitimacy. This approach underlay Tony Blair's decision to tackle the civil strife in Sierra Leone head on: he was widely praised at the UN for doing so and he acted at the invitation of the Sierra Leone Government – no resolution was needed to give international authority for military action. It lay behind the Prime Minister's tough insistence on the use of force to confront President Milosevic of Serbia. It formed a large part of the British Government's determination that the Middle East Peace Process should not be ignored while Iraq dominated the headlines. Even while the Iraq campaign was proceeding, the Quartet of international negotiators was working on the question of Palestine, finally achieving the formal transmission of the road map document to the Israelis and Palestinians on 30 April. But this was a long way from being enough. The United Kingdom remained highly uncomfortable on Iraq without warmer support from the international community.

These political and psychological differences played themselves out in New York and between capitals. Slowly, however, the practical need to pick up the pieces and get on with life reasserted itself. By the end of April the US and the UK had thrashed out between them the main elements of a draft resolution establishing a legal basis for the

Coalition's continuing activity in Iraq. In an echo of the way Resolution 1441 was conceived and born, there was for a while a debate between London and Washington over how brazen the language should be on Security Council approval for the current state of affairs, with London nervous about too aggressive an approach. But the text was ready for discussion with Security Council colleagues by 9 May. It called on UN Member States to support the needs of the Iraqi people, asked the Secretary-General to appoint a Special UN Representative for Iraq and set out a mandate for the involvement of the UN machinery. At the beginning of the two-week negotiation it also asked the Council to 'endorse' the establishment of the Coalition Provisional Authority in Iraq, with a broad list of administrative and security functions. But this quickly proved too much for the most sensitive members of the Council to swallow. The references to the occupying powers as an 'Authority' had to be modestly tucked away in the preamble of the draft; and the operative section highlighted instead the primary requirements of the Iraqi people and the role of the UN and other international institutions. Sanctions were terminated, with the exception of weapons supplies, and a Development Fund for Iraq was set up under quite strict conditions to ensure the spending of available finance on the needs of the population.

The political conditions for transferring power to the Iraqis inevitably took up a high proportion of the time and effort in this negotiation. The Americans wanted maximum freedom of action and no time limit. The Russians, French and Germans, still with the sympathy of the majority of Council members behind them, wanted the Iraqi people in the lead as soon as possible, with the UN holding the ring in the meantime. The UN Secretariat wanted to be central and independent but not to take responsibility for the administration of the country. Within this triangle of positions the emotions and resentments were rekindled.

In the end, however, we all wanted a resolution. The operative paragraph in the political area finally stated that the Council:

Supports the formation, by the people of Iraq with the help of the Authority and working with the Special Representative, of an Iraqi interim administration run by Iraqis, until an internationally recognised, representative government is established by the people of Iraq and assumes the responsibilities of the Authority.

The ambiguities, or shall we say the subtleties, of this passage are clear even to the unpractised eye. It suggested that the Iraqis would be forming an interim administration that they could happily run. But the actual responsibilities of governing rested with the 'Authority' until a different form of representative government was established. The precise role of the UN Representative in all this was unspecific but – and this was the unspoken challenge – it could be earned. This final text had moved a long way from the assertive clarity that the Americans wanted at the beginning and it avoided foreclosing on a tolerable degree of flexibility. The facts of life underlying the arrangement were more telling. This was an occupation, as the light reference to 'occupying powers' in the preamble made clear. The Authority was going to be in charge until it decided otherwise.

The reference to an occupation caused some grinding of teeth in Washington. Many thought that it was a mistake, and a year later still thought it was a mistake. I argued firmly for it. The straight fact was that it reflected the truth: there was no other basis to explain the presence of Coalition troops in Iraq and there was no other body of law to determine the proper behaviour of those troops under international norms than the Fourth Geneva Convention, which sets out the duties of an occupying power. If we had resisted, we would have had the concession wrung out of us by the rest of the Security Council as a condition of their agreeing to a resolution. My second reason was a touch more devious. I believed that it was essential to make the period of Coalition control in Iraq as brief as possible, or we would be drawn down into a swamp of complex hostility in the country and in the region and find it difficult to extract ourselves with honour. Facing up to how the rest of the world perceived us was going to form an important part of getting that judgement right. The rhetorical comparison in the Arab and Muslim worlds between the occupations of Palestine and Iraq delivered a continuous rain of propaganda blows on our subsequent work on the ground. These hurt, but the admission helped to dispel early on the myth that the United States and the United Kingdom were welcome in Iraq. This, at least, was the UK perspective.

Resolution 1483 was adopted on 22 May by fourteen votes to nil, with no abstentions. The negotiation always had the potential to rival the eight-week battle to produce Resolution 1441, but virtually all Council members wanted to restore the basis for collective action on Iraq. Washington, eager to establish some international legitimacy and pushed by some well-judged recommendations from John Negroponte in New York, made significant concessions during the course of the discussions. Our usual opponents were impressed by what they were able to squeeze out of the negotiations and decided to make a positive story of it. As Ambassador Sergey Lavrov of Russia said in the Security Council after the vote: 'The significance [of the resolution] is primarily that it creates an international legal basis for joint efforts to be made by the entire international community to deal with the crisis and outlines clear guidelines for those efforts.' That sentiment did not post-legitimise the conflict itself, but it undoubtedly conveyed Russia's acceptance of the legitimacy of the post-conflict structure.

Only Syria was left in a troubled state of mind. Damascus did not want to concede a scintilla of legitimacy to the occupation. Such a precedent looked far too dangerous in the light of Israel's hold on the West Bank and the Golan Heights and of their own vulnerability should the United States find itself in the mood to move on elsewhere. It was only too easy for the Syrians to imagine from the aggressive public statements of the Secretary of Defense that they might be next on the list. We could not get them to agree to the final concessions accepted by the others. The Syrian Permanent Representative was recalled to his capital for consultations, a sign of both displeasure and panic, leaving his Deputy to plead repeatedly with the sponsors of the resolution for extra time. We gave him a full day but then asked for the text to be put to the vote, apprehensive that any further delay would lose us the other Council members. Syria was absent from the chamber, hence the 14-0 score. Six hours later instructions arrived from Damascus authorising a positive vote, predicated on the lifting of sanctions on their Iraqi brethren even though they disliked much of the rest of the text. That did not change the score in the record, but it allowed us to present the Council as being once again unanimous.

In many ways this uncontested result was an even greater negotiating achievement, again primarily for US diplomacy, than Resolution 1441. The decision to go to war generated immense anger and concern at the UN and in the region and the strain on relationships in New York and around the world was intense. We had thought that the refusal of most Council members to concede any kind of legitimacy might leave us no room for manoeuvre at all, but somehow everyone got enough out of the outcome for their purposes. The UK was encouraged to think that the troublesome start to the occupation, which was beginning to worry us deeply, could be remedied with a high degree of international involvement. With 1483 under our belts, all we had to do was get the administration of the country on a steadily upward curve. Surely, with most Iraqis enthusiastically supporting the opportunity for a changed life, that should not be so hard.

13

Sent to the Front Line

With the framework for international action on Iraq secured and Paul Bremer up and running, diplomacy at the United Nations moved on to some of the world's other priorities, neglected during the crisis. The Security Council had for some time been planning to send a visiting mission to West Africa. We resurrected the idea for the end of June and, now that I had passed responsibility for the Counter-Terrorism Committee on to my Spanish colleague, I agreed to lead the mission because of the UK's strong interest in Sierra Leone and its troubled neighbourhood. That and other regular business occupied my remaining weeks in New York.

Beyond that, retirement beckoned. In the spring of 2003 I had been asked to become the next director of the Ditchley Foundation, a conference centre in the Oxfordshire countryside that specialises in private, high-level discussion of issues of interest to policy-makers in North America and the United Kingdom. It seemed to me to be the perfect combination of intellectual challenge and calm living environment. I was not due to start at Ditchley until July 2004 and so Anne and I decided that we would take a sabbatical, something a crowded career had never allowed. UN friends had offered to lend us their house in central France for the autumn and then we thought we might spend two or three months in Cape Town. It all began to look extremely inviting, not least the thought of vanishing from the media circuit and retreating into traditional civil servant obscurity.

Then, in early June, Alastair Campbell came to stay for a night. He had given tremendous support to the UK Mission over the tough period behind us and had been a constant source of advice and encouragement to me in my enforced exposure to the public eye. Something he said on the telephone before he arrived, however, made me wonder whether he had a further motive for looking in. Over a glass of wine looking out across the East River, with the lights of the Queensborough Bridge and Roosevelt Island shining reassuringly in the distance, he told me that Iraq was 'a mess' and asked if I would be prepared to move to the rather less civilised environment of Baghdad. I quietly cursed my idiocy in leaving such an apparent vacuum in my programme for the next twelve months. I explained the post-retirement decisions I had made, declared that I was not going to back off my agreement with Ditchley, suggested that the Foreign Office had plenty of talent to deploy – John Sawers, the Ambassador to Egypt now working with Bremer in Baghdad, was a case in point – and asked him, with apologies and regrets, to tell headquarters that I was not available. He did not press unduly and promised to convey the message.

His question nevertheless changed the equation. I had never set foot in Iraq in my life and my Arabic had receded to some antediluvian stratum in my memory. I was quite tired. But the other relevant boxes all had ticks in them: Middle East experience, three postings in the United States, familiarity with the UN and the EU, knowledge of the saga to date. There might be something I could contribute. After a few days of procrastination and family discussion, I gave David Manning a call at Number Ten and asked for his private advice. We went over the various factors quietly and sensibly and he ended by telling me to expect a telephone call from his boss.

Nothing in fact happened for several days. The line to and from London returned to its customary semi-activity. Then the Number Ten switchboard found me at the quiet beginning of a New York summer's day and put the Prime Minister through. He told me he wanted someone to succeed John Sawers in Baghdad who was used to the ways of a crisis and with whom he was accustomed to dealing. There were serious hurdles to be overcome and he wished to put together the most experienced UK team possible. I knew I could not turn down a request of that nature and at that level, but I said I could only go to Baghdad until the end of March 2004, when I would need to start preparing for the move to Ditchley. Tony Blair accepted this at once and he never went back on it. A few days later the public announcement was made and that was that. It caused some amusement among my colleagues in New York that I was being sent out to Iraq to implement the terms of the resolution I had sponsored not many weeks earlier.

We cancelled the house in France and put aside the Cape Town brochures, and I started to read the detailed telegrams from Baghdad more carefully. Life again took on a sharp short-term/long-term contrast. The intensive process of saying farewell to New York took over. I declined to go straight out to Baghdad at the end of July, when John Sawers was leaving to take up his new position as Foreign Office Political Director, and secured August as a necessary recuperation period. With all of that, September seemed a long way off.

Not that Iraq faded away entirely from UN business. The members of the Coalition had to report from time to time on the progress being made in implementing Resolution 1483: Council members remained suspicious about the conduct of affairs, particularly the continuation of the Oil for Food programme and the management of oil revenues through the Development Fund for Iraq. Public meetings were held for the wider UN membership to hear reports from the Secretariat on its work on the ground. The Iraqi staff on the food-distribution programme continued to perform their essential role in keeping more than half the population fed and agencies like UNICEF and the World Food Programme braved the awkward and increasingly dangerous conditions in the country to try to look after the most vulnerable sectors of society.

Nor had the WMD question gone away. Members of the Security Council continued to query the absence of UNMOVIC from Iraq, but they knew that the United States was not going to allow the inspectors back in. UNMOVIC continued with its quarterly reports even though it no longer had a team on the ground, and on 5 June Hans Blix said his farewell to the Security Council. His businesslike report reflected what have increasingly come to be seen as the facts and it hit the precise line of division in the Security Council. 'In the period during which it performed inspection and monitoring in Iraq', Blix wrote, 'UNMOVIC did not find evidence of the continuation or resumption of programmes of weapons of mass destruction or significant quantities of proscribed items whether from before 1991 or later, with the exception of the Al Samoud 2 missile system.' Then he put the boot in, as he had long been wanting to do. 'As I have noted before, this does not necessarily mean that such items could not exist. They might – there remain long lists of items unaccounted for – but it is not justified to jump to the conclusion that something exists just because it is unaccounted for.' On Iraq's level of cooperation he said: 'From the end of January 2003 the Iraqi side, which until then had shown cooperation on process but not in equal measure on substance, devoted much effort to provide explanations and propose methods of inquiry into issues such as the production and destruction of anthrax, VX and long-range missiles. Despite these efforts, little progress was made in the solution of the issues during the time of UNMOVIC's operations in Iraq.'

So there it was. As far as the official international inspectors were concerned, there was not much there. But neither had the Iraqis helped to clear up the missing pieces of the puzzle. Those who believed that war could only be justified if Iraq was caught red-handed saw that their line had not been crossed. Those who were focused on the strict sense of all the previous resolutions knew that Saddam Hussein had not met the conditions. Take your pick. Media comment, however, was already beginning to move on. On the day after this final Blix presentation, Philip Stephens wrote in the

Financial Times on the WMD furore: 'History, I suspect, will be indifferent. Much more important will be its judgement of how Mr Bush deployed American power after Baghdad had fallen. Did he have the stamina to rebuild Iraq and install representative government? Did he use its authority to bring peace in the Middle East?' The implication that successful handling of the aftermath could put the war itself into a fairer perspective seemed to me to be apt.

Soon after the adoption of Resolution 1483, Kofi Annan managed to persuade Sergio Vieira de Mello, by now well ensconced in Geneva as the High Commissioner for Human Rights, to take on the additional role of Special Representative in Iraq. Sergio, a clear-minded and charismatic Brazilian who had been an employee of the UN since 1969, had long experience of field work with the UN High Commission for Refugees. He was, with Lakhdar Brahimi, one of the two most capable UN professionals of his generation. His recent work as Special Representative in Kosovo and then in East Timor had been a model of UN political and administrative management. He was extremely reluctant to make the move from Geneva, where he had counted on restoring his strength after all his travails in conflict-torn areas. Annan was insistent, knowing that the UN could not hope to recover its authority on Iraq unless the best people were available on the ground there. Sergio eventually conceded, on condition that the secondment was limited to a four-month period and that he could return to the High Commissioner post thereafter. I was sorry to realise that, with my arrival in Baghdad timed for mid-September, I would only coincide for two weeks with this supremely accomplished and ingenious UN diplomat.

Shortly before my departure the Security Council held a public meeting to hear the first report from their new Special Representative and speeches from members of the recently formed Iraqi Governing Council. Sergio de Mello had prepared his report very carefully. It was a long and, in the UN style, rather formal document. He paid tribute to the people of Iraq and was quick to emphasise the primacy of Iraqi interests. He praised the work of the Coalition Provisional Authority so far, but in a way that seemed to emphasise the separate and adjudicating character of the UN presence in Iraq: it was the UN Special Representative, rather than a spokesman for the Coalition, who was reporting to the Security Council and detailing the progress made so far. Towards the end of his presentation he drew attention to the worsening security situation: 'The potential impact of this violence must not be under-estimated. It threatens to undermine confidence in the transition and to shake the resolve of Iraqis committed to leading their country through this very delicate period in its history.' He continued: 'The United Nations presence in Iraq remains vulnerable to any who would seek to target our Organisation. Our security continues to rely significantly on the reputation of the United Nations, our ability to demonstrate, meaningfully, that we are in Iraq to assist its people, and our independence.' We later returned to those words and saw in them Sergio's elevated but ultimately tragic vision of the United Nations standing above the world's troubles.

Adnan Pachachi, a former Iraqi Foreign Minister and UN Ambassador from pre-Saddam days, then spoke for the Iraqi Governing Council (IGC), a group of twenty-five Iraqis appointed on 13 July by Paul Bremer, with the help of Sergio de Mello and John Sawers, to be the senior Iraqi input into the new administration. Pachachi was a natural elder statesman and the most widely acceptable representative of his country for this meeting; he had come to New York with Ahmed Chalabi and one of the three female members of the IGC, Akila al Hashemi, a senior member of the Iraqi Foreign Service. Pachachi had close ties to the State Department – some speculated that, given a chance, he would be their choice of leader. In his speech he set out the primary goal of the new Iraqi leadership: 'To shorten the duration of the interim administration period and put together an elected government under a constitution to be endorsed by the population in free elections.' De Mello and

Pachachi together gave the impression, since Bremer was not present, that they were the authentic voices of the new Iraq in this first link with the international community. It was an image neither we nor the Americans wanted to dispel. When his turn came to speak, John Negroponte highlighted the leading role of the Iraqi Governing Council in the coming phase and did not once mention Bremer's name.

Afterwards I had a long talk with Sergio de Mello and tried to gain a sense of what was really happening. His manner was friendly, with just a touch of reserve to indicate his distaste for what the UK had gone and done. He described the difficulty of finding suitable representatives from all the Iraqi communities and his concern that the Baathists still presented a significant threat, but he was holding something back. He made no specific suggestion on what the UK might do to help and said little about the experience of working with Bremer. I could not help but feel his growing frustration that, for all his recognition that the Americans were in the lead, his formidable capacity for solving these kinds of problems was not being fully used. He was starting to wonder what he could really contribute in this role. I told him how much I was looking forward to cooperating with him and privately hoped that, between us, we could do something about that.

As it happened, I had arranged to travel down to Washington the next day, my third to last as Ambassador, to talk to the Iraq team in the State Department (I could not get in to the Pentagon) and to meet Paul Bremer, known to family and friends as Jerry ever since he converted to Roman Catholicism and took St Jerome as his patron saint. He and I had had no contact for almost twenty-seven years, but we had worked quite closely together in the mid-1970s, when I was in the Washington Embassy during Henry Kissinger's tenure at the State Department and he was one of Kissinger's executive assistants. I had badly needed his help, which he had willingly offered, to interpret the deeper intricacies of Kissinger's policies. I had liked him a lot, and had wondered whether we would ever work together again.

Since then our paths had deviated. He had served as Deputy Ambassador in Oslo, as Executive Assistant to Secretary of State Alexander Haig and as US Ambassador to the Netherlands. After a Reagan administration appointment as Ambassador-at-Large for Counter-Terrorism, he retired from the Foreign Service in 1989 and became Managing Director of Kissinger and Associates, the consulting firm founded by his former boss. In the period leading up to his Baghdad assignment, he was Chairman and CEO of Marsh Crisis Consulting, a risk and insurance services company in New York. With a concurrent Congressional appointment from 1999 as Chairman of the National Commission on Terrorism, Bremer had an impressive and varied record. But he had little direct experience of the Middle East.

We met in his temporary Washington office and he greeted me without a smile. He looked amazingly fit and young for his sixty-one years, full of bustle and serious energy. After a few reminiscences about the 1970s – I seemed to remember our relationship rather better than he did – he briefed me on the progress thus far in the Iraqi political process. He had firm ideas about his two principal objectives: the creation of a political transition that would bring Iraq by stages to complete independence over the next eighteen months; and the economic and social reconstruction of the country. Both would require a secure framework, and here his optimism had been boosted by the recent elimination of Saddam Hussein's two sons, Uday and Qusay. The route the Coalition Authority would have to take to get to a free and stable Iraq was clearly shaped in his mind. It would shortly be announced as the Seven Steps plan, which he summarised for me: (i) establishing an interim Iraqi government; (ii) deciding the mechanics for drawing up a new constitution; (iii) setting up new ministries and central institutions; (iv) getting the constitution written; (v) ratifying it; (vi) holding elections for a new government, and (vii) transferring power to it.

Conscious of the turmoil on the ground and of the growing concern in London that the handover process risked becoming dangerously protracted, I opened up the thought of fallback plans. Were there not bound to be unpredictable developments as Iraqi political emotions and rivalries welled up out of the huge new fissures in their landscape? To what extent were we going to have to flow with the currents? The Iraqis were agitating for a faster transition and we could not be sure that the plan he had outlined would be acceptable.

I received a sharp reply. The most important thing the Coalition could provide, Bremer said, was a well-marked-out road to elections. There would be no deviation from that, or we would all be in chaos. It would be the job of the British team to support that process and make it work. I did not argue, nor did I take up with my interlocutors elsewhere in Washington the possible need to adapt to circumstances as events unrolled. We covered a few more areas, including his inclination not to ask me to become his formal deputy – with which I agreed – and I left, disappointed that it had not been a warmer start to our new partnership. I sensed trouble.

It was only later that London sent me as part of my briefing the paper setting out the CPA's 'Vision for Iraq'. The introduction stated: 'The plan describes the six core elements that will need to be woven together to rebuild Iraq. From these core elements flow a series of key tasks, milestones and targets. Nonetheless, we should consider this plan as a living document, suitable to a dynamic reality that will require innovation, flexibility, and revision.' Quite. I deduced that the message Jerry Bremer was passing to me was more directly related to his view of my role in the system than to the realities on the ground.

I returned to New York to complete the last stages of packing up. One of the hardest parts of leaving was saying goodbye to our cottage in Woodstock. Anne and I had never once spent a continuous week there, but for weekend after weekend, often over only a single night, we had repaired to the quiet clearing down Bellows Lane to breathe in the clean air of the Catskills, play a round of golf, shut the door on a turbulent world, light the fire, listen to music and be ourselves. We decided to spend a good part of August there. I hauled out my old Arabic books and sorted out the dusty vocabulary cards from my Lebanese education of thirty years before. We tuned in to the news of events in Iraq and I asked for briefing papers from the Iraq Unit in London. If ever there was calm before the storm, this was it.

On the morning of 19 August, our peace was shattered. CNN began reporting the news of a huge explosion at the Canal Hotel in Baghdad, the headquarters of the UN in Iraq. We sat glued to the television screen while the increasingly awful news filtered through. The pictures showed a whole corner of the hotel blown away, a gaping hole where the Special Representative's office had been. The reports suggested that Sergio de Mello remained alive: rescue workers had been talking to him in the rubble. Other members of his team, several of whom we knew, were missing. The telephone started to ring as the family of Nadia Younes, Sergio's Chief of Staff, who were old friends of ours, sought desperately for news of her and asked whether we could help. I checked with everyone I could think of, but Nadia could not be accounted for. Fiona Watson, with whom I had been sitting not long ago in the office of Rafiuddin Ahmed at the UN, had been killed. It was soon confirmed that Sergio had bled to death in the ruins. Nadia's body was found the next day. Twenty-three people in all lost their lives.

The suicide bomb attack of 19 August 2003 was the UN's 9/11. The organisation had suffered losses all too regularly over the years in peacekeeping operations, criminal attacks and brave action too close to wars. But the Canal Hotel disaster removed at a stroke the UN's sense of invulnerability, the assumption that the world understood the UN's unselfish mission and would allow it to operate above the fray. When former President Ahtisaari of Finland later conducted an inquiry into the attack, he concluded that the inadequate defences around the hotel, and the refusal of the UN team to accept an offer of Coalition protection, stemmed largely from this assumption. The lesson of 9/11 itself, when the UN building had been evacuated after a report that it was a target, had failed to get through. Nor had Sergio's own warnings, clear enough in his words to the Security Council twenty-eight days earlier, translated into a real understanding of the risks. The world had changed again and what was beginning to take shape on the soil of Iraq was a bitter symbol of that change.

The bombers had chosen their point of attack for maximum effect. Their truck had smashed through a flimsy and unguarded gate at the back of the hotel and detonated a 500-pound aerial bomb, packed with explosives, against the inner wall. Their objective was plainly to make it far more difficult for the US-led Coalition to gather broad support for the reconstruction operation. The blow did more than wipe out some of the best individual talents in the UN's service: it deeply demoralised the United Nations as an organisation and doubled the distaste within it for the war. Kofi Annan had lost his best lieutenant, someone who might have been a candidate for his own job one day, a man widely revered for his courage, judgement, commitment and charm. With Nadia's death, one of the most compelling characters in Annan's senior team had vanished. She was sharp, shrewd and funny, with a cigarette and a glass of something never far from her hand and a throaty chuckle that we can all still hear in our memories. For Kofi Annan himself, it was the darkest single moment of his extensive UN career. It would be a long time before the UN's full capabilities could again be deployed in the service of the new Iraq.

Ten days later, suicide bombers struck again, exploding a powerful device in the square outside the mosque in Najaf, killing not only the intended target, Ayatollah Mohammed Baqir al Hakim, but close to a hundred of his fellow worshippers. That attack removed the senior Shia cleric most likely to lead Iraqis to a stable independence, with his advocacy of cross-community cohesion and non-violence. Saddam Hussein had been trying to eliminate him for years, in Iraq and in exile in Iran; it took the liberation of the country from his grasp to create the lethal opportunity.

Those ten days in August radically changed the nature of what I was being asked to do. I had been looking forward to working with Sergio de Mello even for the short period we were to have been together on the ground. His depth of experience and acute political judgement would have helped immeasurably to fill the gaps in the American approach to handling Iraq. The triangular relationship between the US, the UK and the UN, and the interplay of all three of us with the Iraqis, would have given me something to work with. It was now extremely doubtful that the UN would be able to maintain a presence at all. I was facing a much lonelier task.

I had set aside the first two weeks of September to call round Government offices in Whitehall and discuss in detail what I was expected to do in Baghdad. Everyone was returning from the holiday break, hoping that the period they had needed to restore their own depleted energies might also have brought improvements on the ground in Iraq. Instead the headlines gave them an indication of the trend. There was little to set on the progress side of the ledger.

The Prime Minister called a meeting on 2 September to hear the plans for the next stage. John Sawers and I soon realised that he was less than impressed by the achievements made so far and he was not in a mood to sit through a long briefing. 'We have got to get this sorted in a different way' was his introduction to the discussion. He homed in on the security situation, unconvinced that the need for more Coalition troops was demonstrated and much more intent on the swift Iraqi-isation of the security sector, especially the police. He said we could not afford to wait twelve months for 70,000 new policemen. If necessary, the intensive programme to remove Baathists and other servants of the Saddam regime would have to be reversed. The situation required a war-level sense of urgency. 'If we fail,' I recall him saying at one point, 'we set back prospects everywhere. If we succeed, we change the whole environment in the Middle East.' We were asked for a plan within forty-eight hours.

In this and other discussions around Whitehall we also focused on the political framework. John Sawers, now in his new job as the Foreign Office's Political Director, had been intimately involved in the selection of the Iraqi Governing Council and understood as well as anyone in the British system how difficult it would be to generate the unifying national leadership that Iraq now needed. Tony Blair and Jack Straw insisted that the IGC must be the visible government. This conformed entirely with the consensus of the July debate at the UN and with the public pronouncements of the US administration in international gatherings, but it did not appear to square with the CPA's approach in Iraq itself. The Prime Minister set the target of a handover of power to Iraqis by the summer of 2004. I had earlier expressed to him my private objective of achieving this by the time of my expected departure in March, but in reality Sawers and I could see that, with Bremer planning an eighteen-month transition, the summer was ambitious enough.

The other issue that aroused Tony Blair's impatience was the Coalition's media efforts. He could not understand why the world's most sophisticated media nation could not put together an operation that both kept the Iraqi people informed of the policies and actions of their ruling Authority and presented an image internationally of a competent administration. If that meant the immediate injection of resources to establish three or four new satellite channels, then the cost would be worth it. A thousand other things needed attention and urgent solution: electricity generation, oil production, infra-structure security, employment, disbursement of funds, Iraqi public-sector training, human rights protection, judicial arrangements and so on. The specific British role in the south had to be staffed and organised and the International Development funding allocated to it had to be disbursed and accounted for. I have mentioned the principal areas of emphasis at the top level because they were correctly identified as the essential items. The power to achieve these goals did not, however, rest with the British Government machine.

During these days of rapid preparation, I needed one fundamental question to be settled: what would my status be in Iraq? The United Kingdom had willingly slipped into a position of co-equal responsibility with the Americans under Resolution 1483 for the proper administration of the country during the occupation period. In practice the United States was way out in the lead both as decision-maker and as provider of staff and resources. For a short while London had toyed with the idea of becoming the 'occupying power' in the south of Iraq, bringing the Australians with them, as the next most committed and effective contingent, and leaving the Americans to take the sole responsibility for the remaining and larger portion of the country. Washington was unhappy with that idea and it was dropped. Orders from the Coalition Provisional Authority therefore issued in the name of the US and UK jointly (the term used was 'the Coalition'); the thirty or more other nations involved offered their services unburdened by any share of the international accountability.

I talked the issue through with John Sawers. Full of restless energy and highly tuned politically, he had served in Washington with me in the mid-1990s and later as the Prime Minister's Foreign Policy Adviser. He was familiar with American ways and vigorously supportive of a close relationship. As Political Director, he would be my principal London manager. He had clearly got on well with Jerry Bremer and believed I should continue as his partner rather than his deputy. Others in the Foreign Office thought I should have a clearer operational role. Partnership was what Bremer himself preferred since it would not affect the US chain of command. I was content with this, as it meant I could offer an alternative UK perspective when it was needed. I would, however, be at one remove from the line of responsibility and I wanted London to understand that. In legal and political terms, this meant that the UK's involvement in the administration of Iraq was delegated on the ground to Bremer and not to me. I pointed all this out before I left and ministers accepted it as the correct description of the position. The problem was that the UK had had no hand in the appointment of Bremer and the US documents setting out his official appointment made no mention of his responsibility to the British as well as to the American Government. Beyond that, the international framework for what we were attempting to do remained deeply unsatisfactory, in that no precedent existed for an ad hoc group of nations taking over a country and guiding it through to a new stage of freedom and development. It was certainly not what the Fourth Geneva Convention was designed for. The Government team at home was deeply concerned about the task we were taking on and was relying on me to make a difference on the ground. Yet they were almost fatalistically tied to following the US lead. It was unsettling.

During my last few days in London the leaden feeling of being carried off from wife, family, friends and a secure and comfortable life began to intrude on me physically. The irony of returning to the Middle East to help rule a whole country, when I had thought that my task in Dubai thirty years before as the last Assistant Judge of the Trucial States Court was an amusing vestige of a passing era, did not seem quite so funny now. At the same time there was a job to be done and I wanted to get on with it. In this split frame of mind I said a difficult goodbye to Anne and our two daughters at Heathrow and walked off to board the British Airways flight to Kuwait.

Part Three

14

Early Weeks in Baghdad

The 11 September British Airways flight into Kuwait dropped me into a typical Middle East visa vacuum, with Kuwaiti immigration refusing to recognise my carefully assembled papers from London and leaving me sitting in a steamy office for an hour. It was a bracing reminder of the petty Arab bureaucracy I thought I had left behind for good with my last posting in Saudi Arabia in the mid-1980s. I suppressed my irritation and donned an air of infinite patience. The British Embassy in Kuwait eventually sorted out the problem, but then I learnt that a broken-down C130 meant the military flight into Baghdad had been delayed. Time took on an oriental shape and I settled down in a corner of the Embassy with a book. Before an hour had passed, an RAF flight suddenly materialised and I had to hurtle over to the military airport to catch it.

And so I entered Iraq for the first time. I was invited to sit in the cockpit of the Hercules, eager for a glimpse of the landscape, but the wind had been blowing and the dust and haze obscured everything. The RAF crew were well versed in the avoiding tactics required for a landing in Baghdad, but as we corkscrewed down towards the airport ominous warning pings – an indication of a possible missile attack –

started to sound in the cockpit. There was a moment of tension, but we landed safely.

I was met by my Royal Military Police close-protection team and by David Richmond, Acting UK Representative since the end of July, who was staying on as my deputy. I had come to rely on his shrewd observation and effective management of business when he was my Security Council section head in New York; I would need both qualities again now. A mixture of fellow travellers poured out of the plane behind me. It was only when David moved across to introduce me that I discovered the new Iraqi Foreign Minister, Hoshyar Zebari, had been one of the passengers squished into the functional seats in the belly of the aircraft. Zebari did not seem to have taken offence, but it was an early signal of how the military viewed the relative pecking order.

The track away from the south side of the airport bumped and snaked across the sand until it reached the beginnings of a decent highway, which ran for about eight miles. As we approached the outskirts of the city, we passed gardens and palm groves growing right up to the side of the road with occasional glimpses across open ground hinting at the shape of the city. Palm trees mingled with tall mosques and dusty slums. This was a capital of potential dignity. Only government buildings appeared to have suffered damage from the war and there was no sign of any repair effort. Entry into the headquarters of the Coalition Provisional Authority, known as the Green Zone, started with a heavy security check from behind large concrete barricades, with the giant crossed swords of Saddam Hussein's parade ground visible on the left. We drove along inside the ugly new concrete walls – 'Bremer walls' the Iraqis came to call them – which insulated the heart of Iraq's new administration from danger and from the people they had come to govern, and soon arrived at the Republican Palace, a vast, sprawling complex which Saddam Hussein had used as his seat of power until ambition drove him to construct grander palaces elsewhere. Built of sand-coloured stone, with a pale blue dome over the central block and great curling wings on either side, it looked imposing and crummy at the same time. Four massively sculpted heads crowned the parapet of each section – supposedly representing the conqueror Saladin, but with a striking resemblance to Saddam. A few palm trees gave the gardens character and shade, but the grass was thin and the blue-tiled fountain dry and grimy. Inside, marble-lined corridors struggled to achieve grandeur; cracks had appeared everywhere and the wood trimming looked tawdry.

The Coalition's intrusion had not helped. Concrete blocks, barbed wire and sandbags filled the entrances. Makeshift huts, trailers, tents and military kit were spread about the grounds. It could have been a scene from M*A*S*H but for the incongruous features of the palace, heavy reminders of the man we had come to replace. The interior was strewn with temporary wiring and building materials, and the more impressive rooms were gradually succumbing to plywood partitioning as the numbers of administrative staff grew. I was led straight through internal security controls into the poorly lit central section, where Paul Bremer had set up his office in the room in which Saddam had once worked. The large rectangular reception room beside it held the American outer-office staff, who spilled over into the windowless corridors to leave space for the British team. At the other end of the rectangle from Bremer's inner sanctum, David Richmond and I shared an office that had once belonged to Saddam's Chef de Cabinet. There was dust everywhere.

I was not expecting to find the American and British civilian staffs so completely integrated at the heart of the building, with not even a screen to separate their desks or the papers on them. This was encouraging: it spelt access and easy lines of communication. My two Private Secretaries, Simon Shercliff and Raad Alkadiri, who had flown out twenty-four hours ahead of me, were trying to sort out their desk space from the scattered furniture and the boxes on the floor. They were both positive spirits, but just at that moment they were finding it hard to smile. Simon represented the classic Foreign Office First Secretary, just into his thirties, one posting in Tehran behind him, sharp, resilient and ready for anything. His job was to hold my whole office together and we came to depend on him more than we cared to admit. Raad had come from the private sector. He was a British citizen with an Iraqi father who had spent his early years in Baghdad and then completed his education in the UK. In his late thirties, full of passionate exuberance, I had met him through friends at the UN and had recruited him to be my Iraq adviser and unofficial interpreter. He was to become an indispensable source of informed advice. Helen Brodie, our magical administrator and office mum, was sitting at the huddle of desks opposite, regaling them with descriptions of what it had been like at the outset, with no air-conditioning in the 120-degree heat and only packing cases for furniture.

The dirt, discomfort and inventive arrangements were bound to be part of the experience, but at the same time I could not help wondering whether the Coalition was sending the right signal by taking over the hated dictator's official residence in this zone of seeming privilege. Having bombed most of the other large govern-ment buildings, the Americans must have felt they had little choice, but it was not difficult to imagine how the Iraqi people viewed being ruled from such a place. Apart from anything else, and for all its external grandeur, the palace did not appear to have enough room for the civilian controllers of a country of Iraq's size. It would take time to learn how everything fitted together, but first impressions left me uneasy.

Members of the wider UK team joined me in my office for a discussion on the state of play. A few of them had been there from the early days of General Garner's operation, but the turnover had been rapid and everyone seemed to be on a learning curve. The UK had sixty or so non-military staff, with an average age way below mine – this was a boost for enthusiasm and resilience, but the team was short of administrative and Middle East experience. I described my talks in London, set out some thoughts on our role over the next few weeks and moved on to the issue of security. Pessimism prevailed.

I had taken the Foreign Office's earlier description of the CPA as 'dysfunctional' to be a junior partner exaggeration, but the British experts out there were seriously concerned. They saw too many gaps in the Coalition's coverage and felt the CPA were failing to grasp the wider picture. The infrastructure was fragile and there was no new national leadership in sight. Yet the Americans seemed to harbour no doubts that a new Iraq was achievable.

Before the light had entirely faded, I walked across the office to say hello to Jerry Bremer. I received another businesslike greeting. He was sitting behind his large, uncluttered desk, wearing a tailored suit and his trademark desert boots. I immediately noticed the sign at the front of his desk: 'Success has a thousand fathers.' Jerry came round and sat in his chair in the centre of the room, putting his feet up on the low table in front of him, his vigorous body language contrasting with my brief memory of Garner's. He dispensed with personal enquiries and gave me a quick sketch of the current picture. He said he was beginning to doubt the capacity of the Iraqi Governing Council to take on genuine responsibility for the administration of the country, even though a new cabinet of ministers had just been appointed to report to it. The IGC was too cumbersome and inexperienced to be productive. I held myself back from insensitive questioning: all these senior Iraqis on the IGC had, after all, been hand-picked by de Mello, Sawers and Bremer himself and should have been as well qualified as any. I wanted to ask whether he thought they might need more power to show their potential, but chose to be diplomatic.

I asked him instead what he wanted from the British in the system, as he had never described a clear role for me. He ducked the question, as though there was no substantive answer he could usefully offer. Perhaps he felt it would have been too impolite to give his real view, which my team and I concluded later was that my appointment threatened his own freedom of action and his pre-eminent status in Iraq.

I went to survey my living quarters and to unpack. I was luckier than most. My room in a trailer cabin would normally have been allocated to two people. I spent a raw hour unloading my bags into the plywood cupboard and onto the spare bed, disobeying the instructions on the wall and stringing up a washing line to take extra hangers for my suits and shirts. Then I swept up some of the dust and made the narrow bed, mentally thanking my daughter-in-law, Jo, for her canny advice to pack a good feather pillow. I pulled out a book to read but the long journey caught up with me and I soon fell asleep.

So began a routine that intertwined the desperately important with the trivial and the surreal. We quickly learnt that what mattered was the American system. They were the leaders, the providers, the breakers of moulds and the builders of hope. The CPA was their instrument and their culture. The other nations represented within it were accepted and appreciated, but only to the extent that they fitted into the American approach. Tony Blair's stance alongside the US brought us real privileges on the ground and we were considered as first ally and theoretical co-equal, but all was relative to US control in practice. 'Brits get tolerance-plus,' ran the CPA aphorism, 'the rest tolerance-just.' Everyone had to earn American respect the hard way – and unquestioning loyalty was expected to be the first ingredient.

I quickly learnt in Baghdad that the British might have developed a system and an administrative ethos to handle the projection of power, but we no longer possessed the power to put it to use. The Americans had the physical and the psychological voltage, but lacked the structure and the experience to deliver it accurately in a new environment like Iraq. In each other's eyes we were only half-qualified, but the Brits had to show they knew it or they would be cut out. This affected the approach of the senior players in London as well. David Manning and, when David moved on to become Ambassador in Washington in the autumn of 2003, Nigel Sheinwald at Number Ten conveyed consistently relevant advice to the White House and the National Security Council in Washington. Yet they and their teams had to calculate how much they could load onto any one conversation, in case the door slammed shut. I believe that the same consideration influenced the way the Prime Minster handled his input to the President.

By coincidence, Secretary of State Colin Powell visited Baghdad on my second day and Jerry Bremer invited me into his office for a private word. Powell gave me a hug and a warm expression of thanks for being there, but he did not give the impression of owning the scene, or wanting to. Although Bremer had served half his career with the US Foreign Service, his appointment in Iraq had been at the suggestion of Henry Kissinger, most recently his boss in the private sector after retiring in 1989, and fell within the responsibility of the Defense Department. He reported to Donald Rumsfeld, not to Powell.

We started to discuss how to implement the Seven Steps. The first three stages – establishing an interim Iraqi government; deciding the mechanics for drawing up a new constitution and appointing ministers – Bremer considered achieved. His problem now was how to ensure that the constitution came before elections when some leading Iraqis were insisting on the opposite. Bremer made clear his belief that his chronology was the only way democracy could safely be introduced to a new area. Powell listened and asked the occasional question, but I did not sense he was really speaking his mind. I decided to talk again about fallback plans, as I had done at my earlier meeting with Bremer in July. Since there was no calendar attached to the Seven Steps, I questioned whether there would be time to implement them in the right order. Should we not be considering a quicker transfer of power and a possible Plan B on the timing of national elections, perhaps holding them before the drafting of a constitution? This got short shrift from Jerry: 'I've told you before, Jeremy, and I am telling you again, the way forward is set, it is agreed by the President and we are not going to change it.' Colin Powell listened to this reprimand in mildly embarrassed silence and the conversation soon broke up. I did not see the Secretary again in Iraq until my last week in the job.

The next day I began to set up appointments with the Iraqi Governing Council, giving priority to the nine members who had been established as the monthly rotating Presidents. The IGC had been designed as an embryonic Iraqi Government, partners of but for the moment subservient to the Coalition Provisional Authority. From the start – and contrasting with Afghanistan, where the United Nations held the central role – the IGC suffered from a deficit in legitimacy for having been selected by the occupying power. The members numbered twenty-five in all, divided on sectarian grounds at the insistence of the Shia: thirteen Shia, five Kurds (the two main party leaders and three independents), five Sunni Arabs (one established Islamic party leader and four independents), a Turcoman and an Assyrian Christian. The Shia were by no means a monolithic block: they divided into groups holding strong religious or secular leanings, six and five respectively, with two – including Ahmed Chalabi – ready to see which way the wind blew. Only the six religious Shia and the two senior Kurds had party affiliations with significant support on the ground. The former had close ties to and great respect for the religious hierarchy in Najaf, at whose apex stood the powerful but, by his own assertion, non-political figure of Grand Ayatollah Ali al Sistani. The five Sunni Arabs had been the most representative individuals Bremer, Sawers and de Mello could find, but most of them had lived abroad as exiles and did not speak for more than a small proportion of the disorganised and demoralised Sunni community.

Those selected to share the IGC Presidency had been chosen for their political weight, actual or potential. There was no magic about the number nine, except that it allowed the CPA to get the sectarian proportions right: five Shia, two Sunnis and two Kurds. There would otherwise have been a Shia blowback. Two of the Shia were senior clerics with little experience of the international arena: Mohammed Bahr al Uloom, the father of the Council in age and the recipient of the most formal respect, who was independent and influential but without a natural political constituency; and the suspicious and reserved Abdul Aziz al Hakim, the leading voice in the Supreme Council for the Islamic Revolution in Iraq (SCIRI), a group close to

Iran from its exile years. Ibrahim al Jaafari, leader of the mainly Shia Dawa Party, a rival but also a potential ally of SCIRI, was the politician with the greatest media appeal to the Iraqi population. Ahmed Chalabi and Iyad Allawi were secular Shias, the most active of the exiles during the Saddam era and the two IGC members with the deepest understanding of modern international politics. They were related to each other and had collaborated in opposition until they fell out in the 1980s. Ahmed Chalabi's immediate family had been landowners and community leaders before Saddam and he had developed strong business interests in Jordan and elsewhere, sailing close enough to the wind to have incurred a Jordanian indictment against him, which remained active. I shall come back to Allawi, but his most notable difference from Chalabi was his refusal to be drawn into alliances just to further his own ambitions. His concept for a cross-sectarian party, the Iraqi National Accord, was well judged in principle but slow to attract a following.

The four others sharing the IGC Presidency were the two Kurdish leaders Masoud Barzani (Kurdish Democratic Party) and Jalal Talabani (Patriotic Union of Kurdistan), political rivals until they put down their weapons in 1996 and became brothers in the resistance to Saddam, and two Sunnis: Adnan Pachachi, elder statesman and Foreign Minister from the mid-sixties, and Mohsen Abdul Hamid, the founder and leader of the devout Iraqi Islamic Party, the only organised political grouping among the Sunni Arabs but too narrowly based to carry weight across the country. None of the three women on the IGC were included in the Presidential nine.

My first interlocutor turned out to be Ibrahim al Jaafari, a complex, thoughtful man with a strong religious commitment and an almost perverse determination. He was at heart an Iraqi nationalist, which was what gave him his appeal, but his policy programme was hard even for Iraqis to understand, since he both recognised and resented the importance of what the Americans had done. He was virulently anti-Saddam and criticised the Coalition's slowness in finding the fugitive dictator and bringing him to justice. Like all the religious

Shia politicians, he was adamant that there would have to be elections before a new constitution, partly because the Shia majority could not accept US control over the drafting process, but also because only with the Shia properly installed as a majority government could they be sure of controlling the future character of Iraq. I argued hard for work on constitutional principles first: elections could not possibly be held until the country was much more stable and progress needed to be made soon on a basis for transferring interim power to Iraqis. But I quickly realised I was not making an impression. Jaafari and those who thought like him were more concerned with control than order of events and deeply aware of the legitimacy deficit in being so closely associated with the Coalition.

My next call was on Iyad Allawi. He had begun his political career as a Baathist, but rebelled against Saddam's growing power in the early 1970s and took himself and his family into exile. I had met him in London and liked his bluff, frank manner, his air of authority and his recognition of the problems ahead. Here was a man, I felt, with pragmatic understanding of the compromises required. Sitting with him in his party offices was his brother-in-law Nouri Badran, the Minister of the Interior, normally one of the most powerful operators in any Arab government, but in this set-up all the ministers were protégés or placemen of IGC members. He said hardly a word throughout. Allawi talked first about the security situation, criticising the American decision to disband the army and worrying that funds were not being disbursed nearly fast enough to re-form the Iraqi police. He pointed to the strategic confusion sown by having both an American and an Iraqi government structure, not to mention the autonomous Kurds in northern Iraq, and argued for greater responsibility to be given to the Governing Council if Iraqis were going to learn how to run their own country. Allawi said he hoped the British would help resolve some of these problems and play a leavening role with the US, whose insensitive style of command was already grating with him. I told him that this was dangerous territory for me: my first responsibility was to support what the Americans were trying to do. Silently, I recalled that the Iraqi press were speculating that certain IGC members were already beginning to flex their muscles against Coalition control and I realised that Iyad Allawi must be one of them.

I spent much of the rest of this first week calling on the heads of the CPA sections and left off further meetings with IGC members until I had seen the Council working as a group. It was a struggle trying to discover how the whole administration fitted together. The Americans provided 90 per cent of the staff and kept close hold on the more sensitive areas of business, particularly oil and finance. From seven thirty onwards Bremer was holding meetings in his office from which the UK team was excluded. Discussions of the security situation, the latest intelligence reports, the availability of money, the movements of visitors, were all-American. My team was finding it very hard to make inroads. The juxtaposition of our two central offices was, I began to recognise, more apparent than real. Nevertheless, I talked to as many people as I could and tried to take stock.

I had two other important visitors in those first days: General Sir Mike Jackson, Chief of the General Staff, who was trying to link the work of British troops in the south with overall US strategy; and General John Abizaid, Commander of the whole US Central Command operation in Afghanistan and Iraq, who understood the intricacies of the Middle East better than any American in the current hierarchy. Both men were sensitive to the risk of strategic failure in Iraq if the security situation was not quickly controlled and a strong political momentum established. True to form, the American was more focused on what was going right and the Briton on what was going wrong, but they were not so far apart in their assessments. Both thought we were facing severe threats, and both believed that we could overcome them if we played our cards right.

The overwhelming problem for the Coalition was the lack of legitimacy inherent in the occupation. Internationally it deprived us of partners to share the burden and diminished respect for the new

Iraq. Internally, however, we faced a bigger problem. There was confusion and equivocation in the minds of the Iraqi population. They rejected the idea of American control in principle, but in practice they appreciated that the US-led Coalition had rid them of Saddam Hussein and was now all that stood between them and chaos. Unconsulted on their views, they saw the establishment of a Governing Council of so many exiles and unknowns as American manoeuvring for its own ends. On most days in most places, neither the IGC nor the Coalition had much effect on people's daily struggle to survive. They wanted control over their own lives as quickly as possible.

It was essential for the Coalition to implant two things in Iraqi minds early on: belief that their situation was going to get better; and confidence that US policy was aimed at empowering them to run their own affairs. In mid-September we could not identify visible progress on either front. The UK contingent did not for a second believe that Washington wanted the CPA to remain there in the long term: everyone was for getting the business done and moving on. But five months into the post-war phase, where was the real momentum? Were we fussing excessively? Would American power pull off one of those astounding breakthroughs that we had witnessed before – not just in two world wars, but more recently in the Bosnia negotiations, in removing Milosevic from Belgrade, in Afghanistan, in the invasion of Iraq itself? Iraqis wanted jobs and respect, electricity and normal family life, books in their schools and peace to drink coffee in the street cafes with their friends. They did not need a crash programme for privatising the economy and establishing a stock market, which was the assignment in the CPA of Tom Foley, a friend of George W. Bush and an ideological proponent of free enterprise. They did not want the country flooded with American contractors, which seemed to be the Pentagon's approach, when they believed that Iraqi firms could handle all but the high-technology aspects of reconstruction.

Central to all our problems was the security situation. The conflict had created losers but had not eliminated them; and it had brought freedom. Both developments are bad for law and order in the early stages of a massive transition, because the defeated and the criminal have a higher motivation to exploit opportunity than the ordinary law-abiding citizen. After Saddam's regime fell, no security structure existed to assert state control. The Iraqi Army fell apart and, even after the false start with Garner, the Americans appeared more concerned to eradicate all vestiges of the regime than to fill the security vacuum. The police force existed in theory but could not operate without resources or a direct top-down system of detailed instructions. The other, more shadowy security organisations, which had exercised the most effective hold over the population under Saddam, had broken up into subversive cells or just faded away like the army. These two elements had amounted to some six or seven hundred thousand men in the pay of the previous regime. Not only were some of them bound to cause trouble, but something had to replace them as a capable structure. It was unnerving to see many other activities of the CPA being energetically organised without this central requirement being effectively addressed.

In addition, there were the non-Iraqi infiltrators. Abu Musab al Zarqawi, generally regarded as holding the al Qaida franchise in Iraq, was present in the country before the invasion, though probably not in league with the regime. Once the repressive atmosphere was lifted, his organisation had room to grow, with a determination and capability greater than that of the police and with a knowledge of the environment deeper than that of the Coalition. Other factors played to Zarqawi's advantage. My staff came to caricature my head-shaking disbelief at the US military's refusal to deal with the open Iraqi borders and Saddam's unguarded ammunition dumps. In fairness, neither problem was straightforward. Iraq's frontier comprised thousands of kilometres of inhospitable territory, which any well-organised unit could penetrate. Vast piles of weapons and ammunition were lying around in military areas and it would have taken several thousand soldiers or militia to protect them. Yet the first full-scale US operation in the Western Desert near the troublesome Syrian border did not take place until May 2005. The result of leaving borders and weapons stores virtually unguarded for such a long period after the Coalition took charge was to feed the opportunity for sustained violence by Iraqis and non-Iraqis alike. Inaction on these fronts contributed to a security vacuum and enormously raised the cost of the Coalition's task.

It would be simplistic to object, though it was true, that the Coalition, and especially its lead nation, did not have enough soldiers on the ground. Secretary of Defense Donald Rumsfeld's well-documented antipathy to raising the number of troops caught up in Iraq grew organically from his rejection of a nation-building role for the United States. Rumsfeld could see, especially once the insurgency had confounded his expectations and grown roots, that more US troops meant more US targets. The crux of the American miscalculation lay in their decision neither to use more US troops nor to engage parts of the Iraqi Army, and in their failure to understand that it can be a more straightforward task to win a war than to handle the aftermath. Most forces, particularly US forces, are trained for the first and not for the second. In the mid-1990s, after the Somalia debacle, the then British Army Chief, General Sir Charles Guthrie, offered his US opposite number the assistance and experience of the UK armed forces if they wanted to designate part of the American military to handle post-conflict or peacekeeping scenarios. He was not especially surprised when the offer was politely turned down. US military philosophy was predicated on the hard defence of US national territory and interests and on the projection of massive destructive force wherever in the world it might be needed. Collective 'soft' tasks such as peacekeeping and post-conflict reconstruction could be organised by other countries whose military profiles and capabilities were more attuned to such responsibilities.

The fact is that in Iraq, where the United States made the choice to go to war, there were not enough security forces of one sort or the other to handle the peace. The issue had come to a head in a very public way before the invasion when the retiring US Army Chief of Staff, General Eric Shinseki, who himself knew a thing or two about the Middle East environment, told the Senate Armed Services Committee in February 2003 that 'several hundred thousand' soldiers would be required both to win a war with Iraq and then to maintain control over the country. 'We're talking', he said, 'about post-hostilities control over a piece of geography that's fairly significant, with the kinds of ethnic tensions that could lead to other problems.' At the same hearing, the other Service Chiefs referred to the overstrain that their commands were already suffering, causing them to draw too heavily for comfort on the National Guard and the reserves. Shinseki's testimony was subsequently ridiculed by other parts of the Pentagon and within the Washington hierarchy. Deputy Secretary of Defense Paul Wolfowitz called it 'wildly off the mark' and said that it was difficult to understand how someone could predict that the occupation would require more troops than the invasion itself. Yet he and his colleagues were constantly trying – with only rare success – to enlarge the number of countries contributing to the Coalition.

Shinseki proved wrong about the conflict but right about the post-conflict period. The military were ready for the war and the momentum was right, in American military and political terms, for a March attack. But they were not ready for the consequences, nor did they recognise – perhaps because modern wars can be won in short, hugely powerful strikes directed from an impersonal distance – that the aftermath would require preparations of the same quality as the battle plan itself. It is interesting that Jay Garner was assigned the immediate task of arranging the administrative and humanitarian requirements of the country and then of handing back control to suitable Iraqis as soon as he could. The UK Government thought this was the right strategy. It was only when that approach hit a barrier that not just a new administrator but a new policy, on which London was not consulted, was brought in: to assert American control in a much more comprehensive fashion and only hand back power when a far higher standard of political and infrastructural development had been achieved. Frustrated at the looting and sabotage after the war, the United States decided to take a firmer grip, yet found itself in control of a foreign territory without the resources, the training or the will to perform effectively.

The second great challenge was political. It became very clear to us that the catchment area for politicians capable of national leadership was very narrow. Unlike Afghanistan, where Hamid Karzai was installed as a figurehead widely enough accepted to steer the transition, none of the IGC politicians would be allowed by the others singly to represent the Iraqi people. If they all had their own priorities and antagonisms, who was going to form the apex? Before the conflict the Office of the Secretary of Defense thought the answer would be Ahmed Chalabi. But that choice was not only hotly contested by other parts of the US administration, it flew in the face of the White House's ambition to bring Iraq to a condition of democratic stability and make it a beacon for change in the wider region. Chalabi would have been no more capable of winning a fair election on Iraqi soil than any of the other political exiles: in fact he consistently came at the bottom of the popularity polls. We were locked into a vicious circle. Bremer found himself disappointed with the quality of the Iraqi Governing Council, while at the same time the IGC chafed at the comprehensive control emanating from the CPA and made no attempt to raise their game. I could see that the prospect of an early handover to an Iraqi government was receding while the security problem was only likely to deteriorate if Iraqis took against the occupation.

It was difficult to know how to deal with it all from a UK perspective. There was very little hope of a massive injection of reinforcements, given American constraints and wider international reluctance to be drawn in. I knew that Bremer and the military commanders had got nowhere on this issue and there was no point in hammering away at them. The Prime Minister was hoping for the rapid training of new Iraqi forces rather than higher allied numbers and I was unlikely to get support from him or his close advisers in London for an appeal to Washington. I made a nuisance of myself on this issue throughout my six months in Iraq, but essentially it was already too late when I arrived. The US decisions, uncontested at the time by the UK, not to reconstitute the Iraqi Army and to exclude from authority any Iraqi with a Baathist record, left only two alternatives: to upgrade the Coalition or wait and hope.

I tried to voice these apprehensions in a second private chat with Jerry Bremer before my first week was over. The Americans – CPA and Combined Joint Task Force 7 (CJTF7 – the US military arm in Iraq, commanded by Lieutenant-General Ricardo Sanchez) working together as separate units – were at that stage working on the details of CENTCOM's Joint Strategic Plan for the next few months, which seemed to be taking a long time to mature. Bremer was prepared to give away very little information, which frustrated me, but I could see he was worried. He was also irritated that CJTF7 held different views from him on where military tasks ended and where civilian affairs began. General Abizaid was under pressure from the Pentagon to draw down the number of US troops in Iraq by as much as a division (30,000 troops) by spring 2004 and transfer the role of the US Army in the less disturbed provinces to the CPA or the Iraqis. The CPA was hideously understaffed for such a function and the Iraqis disorganised and unpredictable in quality and loyalty. Some of the best people in the Coalition effort, largely unrecognised back in the United States, were the Army civilian affairs officers, exposed, courageous and imaginative. The reconstruction effort could ill afford to lose them.

Bremer opened up rather more to me on his philosophy for the nurturing of a new Iraqi society. He had set out his 'Vision for Iraq' in a mission statement in early July, listing the perfect outcome in each sector of activity without addressing the route or the resources to get there. In this discussion he produced a simpler, interconnected set of objectives: a political transition founded on new constitutional principles, an economy led by a vibrant private sector and a renaissance of civil society activity, an area where Iraq had once shown a lead in the Arab world. He said that he hated to see arrangements develop on sectarian lines when the longer term interests of the Iraqi people would be much better served if shared horizontally rather than vertically. The Iraqis had insisted on sectarian percentages in the IGC and the ministries, not the Coalition. I said I supported this approach, but I wondered how we were going to achieve it in practice. I looked at Bremer and wondered whether he really trusted his own drive and energy to surmount these problems or whether he recognised that the pieces were not likely to fit together. He said nothing to indicate any depth of concern and, as in our first conversation, made no mention of a particular role for me to play alongside him.

We walked out of the office with our separate security teams and got into our separate cars to go to the weekly meeting of the Iraqi Governing Council, my first. In the early months of IGC activity, these gatherings took place in a single-storey building just inside the Green Zone, which seemed more like a modest gentleman's club than the decision-making centre of a nation of twenty-five million people. A meeting-room, a waiting-room, a single office for the overwhelmed staff and a dining-room were its only assets. This formed the setting for the strange, evolving partnership between Americans and Iraqis for the first nine months of the occupation. The British were the only other nationality present. I suppose that the United Nations would also have been allowed to participate; but that hope had been buried in the rubble of the Canal Hotel bomb in August.

On 17 September the agenda proceeded haphazardly, with decisions on major subjects such as the nationality and foreign investment laws interspersed with complaints about the rough handling of IGC members by US security at the entrance to the Green Zone. It was Bremer's meeting and he was in control. It was remarkable to see a US diplomat telling the leaders of an ostensibly independent country what they could or could not do. The loss of national dignity under the forceful swagger of the American presence, which some of the IGC members felt very keenly, was for the time being offset by their recognition that they would not have been in Baghdad or in that room but for the United States. I was introduced graciously by the President for the month, Ahmed Chalabi, and said enough in reply to indicate that I was sensitive to their temporary powerlessness, but otherwise I kept my counsel.

After the main meeting I sat in the waiting-room and talked to the most approachable of the three female members of the IGC, Akila al Hashemi, who had been a senior career member of the Iraqi Foreign Service under Saddam but had been blocked from the top jobs because she was not, and refused to become, so she told me, a member of the Baath Party. She had participated in the July meeting of the Security Council in New York and this was my second extended conversation with her. I remembered her telling me, in her engaging mixture of French and English, how she had never been aware in her youth of her sectarian origins. When asked by a fellow Arab during a spell at Grenoble University in France whether she was a Shia or a Sunni, she had had to telephone her father to find out. Commenting now on the transformation of her country, she seemed confident that the Iraqi majority would stick with the CPA transition. Yet she was surprisingly sharp on the need for a speedy transfer of power to Iraqis.

As these early days passed at the Republican Palace, the unfamiliar gradually metamorphosed into the routine: meetings, e-mails, calls on the CPA sections, brainstorming with David, Simon and Raad, more meetings, a dash to the Convention Centre or the IGC headquarters (both located in the Green Zone), chats with the UK military and intelligence wings in Baghdad, a snatched plastic meal in the featureless CPA cafeteria, report-writing and telephone calls to London. The official day started with Ambassador Bremer's 8 a.m. meeting with the senior CPA staff. It was always a very top-down affair. British team meetings are full of political context and indiscreet comment, which ensure that everyone working on a particular project has a feel for its relative place and for the pressures on the decision-makers. The CPA meetings were much more clipped and one-way. Sitting on the Administrator's right and therefore last to be called in the clockwise table round, I could not resist – habit rather than insubordination – occasionally adding a brief analysis of what London thought of a political development, or of the latest saga at the UN. My team was amused to watch Bremer's expressionless face as I did so. The feedback from other participants was more positive and I decided not to be deterred. In my restricted meetings with UK staff at 9 a.m. each morning I tried to be more forthcoming.

Friday morning brought the weekend, CPA-style, with no eight o'clock meeting, no tie, and an extra two hours downtime. I swabbed out my trailer room, calculating the plus points for my soul after several years of domestic inactivity. I took a quick dip in the pool among the graceful palm trees and wrote a letter or two, after which I set off through the sand and dust, past lines of cabins and piles of building materials, to the office fifty yards away. From then on it was just another normal working day.

I soon learnt that, for all my acceptance of a hard day in sparse comfort, I could not match my American counterpart for stamina. Bremer's day rarely ended before midnight – and often later, if Washington (at eight hours' time difference) still had concerns. By seven thirty in the morning, when his first office meeting began, he had already been to the gym and taken an Arabic lesson. Fridays seemed to be no exception. I recalled him telling me in the 1970s of Kissinger's shuttle diplomacy missions, when his boss would for days on end retire to bed at two in the morning and get up at six, leaving Bremer to close down the office after him and open it up before him. He was not averse now to putting his office staff through the same test. He followed this routine for months on end, barring the occasional and no doubt exhausting overseas visit. No one in Iraq during those fourteen months of the occupation could claim that they worked harder than the boss.

*

Saturday 20 September started like any other day. I was becoming seriously disaffected with the artificial milk, which was all there was to pour over my breakfast cereal. Bremer was away on a Washington visit and the morning meeting was short. Clay McManamy was Bremer's deputy in those early months, an old and trusted colleague of his from his days as Counter-Terrorism Coordinator in the late 1980s, a quiet, decent man and no threat to the Administrator's sole authority. Then the news came in that Akila al Hashemi had been shot in her car as she left her house in the suburbs. Clay and I dropped everything and raced round to the field hospital, just in time to see her being wheeled in from the ambulance, covered in blankets, tubes dripping into her, unconscious with her head back, grey. It was desperate to see that expressive, curious face so lifeless. She was said to be stable, but tests soon showed that a single bullet had penetrated several of her abdominal organs.

Ahmed Chalabi, at that moment Council President, came into the hospital and we formed a mournful cavalcade up to the medical library for a talk. We expected emotional fireworks from Chalabi over the attack on Akila, but he remained serious and rational, making a number of requests for immediate security improvements for Governing Council members. Since McManamy was hesitant, I took the lead in the reply, trying to balance the need for reassurance with a reminder of the reality that we could not protect everybody all the time. Julie Chappell, a young British diplomat seconded to the CPA political team who had grown particularly close to Akila, sat tearfully at the back of the room. Raad Alkadiri took the note efficiently, showing a remarkable ability to adapt to Foreign Office bureaucracy in extreme circumstances.

The next day Iyad Allawi chaired a meeting of the Security Committee of the IGC. Clay McManamy listed the difficulties in guaranteeing Green Zone security. I proposed the creation of a sub-committee to implement new security measures. It was accepted at once as a double opportunity, for proper follow-up action and for increased Iraqi responsibility in an important area. I also offered the loan of a British armoured car for whoever was currently President, which went down well with Allawi, who was now acting President in the absence of Chalabi on an overseas trip.

These partly practical, mostly bureaucratic responses made little difference to the real threat to IGC members and could do nothing for Akila al Hashemi. For a day or two the doctors remained hopeful. Then on Wednesday the news came in that she had taken a dramatic turn for the worse. We prepared despondently for the weekly Council meeting, at which I was due to take the main CPA role for the first time in Bremer's absence, and decided that we would scrap the routine agenda and offer as much practical help as possible on IGC personal security. As it turned out, Akila rallied slightly and held on throughout the day. I wrapped up the meeting with an appeal for partnership between the CPA and the IGC that required some rhetoric from UN Security Council days. The underlying apprehension of the Iraqi politicians – that they had put themselves in the hands of an administration that might not be able to look after them – came through very clearly.

The next morning we woke up to the sound of an explosion in the middle distance. It turned out to be a bomb at a hotel on the other side of the river where a number of American journalists were accommodated. It had sounded close enough to be a mortar round dropping inside the Green Zone. You cannot spend your time thinking about unexpected and instantaneous oblivion and continue properly with your work, but neither can you completely ignore the dangers. That morning I set myself the objective that none of my team should be killed or injured by a preventable or avoidable attack – no one could do anything about being in the wrong place at the wrong time. We set up our own British security committee, making our own decisions where we felt that the American approach, which was a shade more fatalistic, was not meeting the circumstances. This more proactive approach was important in keeping the British contingent together in Baghdad for longer than most of them felt it was sensible to stay.

Akila died that same morning. It was a brutal waste of a talent her people desperately needed. She would not have become a great leader, but her modesty and her articulate enthusiasm for a free Iraq made her very special. Iraq needed such a role model.

Her funeral took place the next day, Friday 26 September, and the complex series of Islamic ceremonies included a short service at the IGC headquarters. The coffin was slowly carried in by Akila's family, their faces stained with tears, and a dignified, Western-dressed lay reader chanted the funeral prayer in a melodious voice. Iyad Allawi delivered a eulogy in Arabic, his head down and his voice not carrying well. He then pulled me forward to speak for the CPA in Bremer's absence. I offered the appropriate Arabic greeting at the beginning and read my piece slowly in English. At the end I added the Arabic condolence '*Al-baqa fi Hayatkum*' – 'May her memory live on with you' – which drew a murmured response from her relatives. There were no women present.

We moved outside to hear the equivalent of the Last Post, offered from a quavering trumpet in the police band, and then followed the coffin, perilously balanced on the back of a pick-up truck with Akila's brothers and cousins perched on the sides, moving slowly down the Governing Council drive. Informal, dignified, communal and quiet, this deeply sad farewell was disturbed only by the crunch of a badly driven car trying to do a U-turn and then by an incongruous change of musical style as the police band broke into something close to 'Jingle Bells' while the hearse left the compound. When it was over, we were all left hollow with the sense of a bad omen.

15

Pessimism Is Unpopular

Two weeks after my arrival in Baghdad I paid my first visit to Basra, where the main British military contingent was based. Hilary Synnott, recently retired from his Ambassadorship in Islamabad and an old and trusted colleague, had just taken over the running of the CPA office for the south of Iraq. Raad travelled down with me, chuffed to be sitting up in the Hercules cockpit. The flight offered us a clear view of the southern desert, with the Tigris and Euphrates rivers coming together in the marshes and the Shatt al Arab estuary shining clear in the setting sun.

The CPA headquarters in Basra was temporarily sited in a ramshackle old building in the city suburbs, manifestly vulnerable to any would-be car-bomber. The largely British CPA team in the city had settled down well, equipping themselves with rudimentary offices, sparse living quarters and an expat bar which was noticeably absent from the Republican Palace in Baghdad. After an evening's discussion of current business, we repaired upstairs in time to catch the final stages of a goalless draw between Arsenal and Manchester United, complete with a fight on the pitch. I spent the night in a bare room with questionable washing facilities, saved from sleeplessness by a surprisingly comfortable mattress.

Hilary Synnott and I ranged through the city the following day. Our call on the UK's 19th Brigade at the old Governor's Palace on the Shatt al Arab was enlivened by a noisy demonstration at the gates, which swallowed up the security car ahead of us and smashed its back window. Their appetites satisfied, the demonstrators allowed us through quite politely. Our calls on the university chancellor and the deputy governor of the province provoked strong statements of concern about security and funding. Even in Basra, where the mainly Shiite community was much more cohesive and law-abiding than the population in and around Baghdad, looting and crime had become the main bugbears. British troops, barely 12,000 strong in an area that encompassed around 4 million people, had done a remarkable job in restoring some semblance of community life and in supplying the provisions necessary to maintain it.

We went on to the port at Umm Qasr, still only barely working but showing a huge potential for expansion. Two dhows and a tramp steamer were unloading into colourful Iraqi lorries – these were everywhere, with legal or illegal contents spilling out of them. Road transport was already becoming the biggest private-sector business in Iraq. With proper security, we would have had this place humming in no time, but looters were coming in over the southern wall every night and undoing the previous day's repair work. I took up these questions later with the Commander of the Coalition's Multinational Division (South East), Major-General Graham Lamb, who feared that a surge of attacks inspired from further afield was about to hit the south. The British military and intelligence professionals in the sector were just beginning to get through to some of the grey areas of community and religious leadership there, including the two main religious Shia political parties, the Dawa Party and the Supreme Council for the Islamic Revolution in Iraq (SCIRI), whose organisations had survived the Saddam era by staying underground and by taking refuge in Iran. The concern of local Iraqi politicians that their community would increasingly be invaded by insurgents and terrorists from the north was beginning to bring in some useful real-time information.

Iraq had never been a single state until the British forged the three

Turkish provinces of Mosul, Mesopotamia and Basra into a unit of empire after the First World War. From then on the Iraqi people had experienced colonial, monarchical and despotic rule and the Shia community, whose heartland stretched from south of Baghdad to Basra, had suffered from all three. Now the chance of freedom lit them up; they were determined not to be cheated again. SCIRI and Dawa had depended for their survival partly on their ties to Iran, and partly on the capacity of their tightly formed and devout communities to keep strangers out of their affairs. Basra and the people of the lower rivers psychologically faced southwards: they were well placed to benefit from maritime trade and the growing wealth of the oil-producing Gulf countries. They were also conscious of the oil beneath their feet and ready if necessary to defend it as their own. Nonetheless they were Iraqis, wary of too tight an Iranian stranglehold and prepared to experiment with a new Iraq so long as it created a new opportunity for the Shia majority.

CPA headquarters had agreed that the British should take on more or less entirely the task of governing the south-eastern sector of Iraq. Bremer and Sanchez rarely visited. The Deputy Administrator in Basra, who reported directly to Bremer, and the British Commanding Officer travelled to Baghdad every month or so, but very little American money filtered through to the British area and Basra and its surrounding provinces developed largely into a separate administrative area. The fact that there were so many fewer violent incidents in the south-east than in the centre and north – the British area suffered around 2 per cent of the incidents occurring in Iraq as a whole – was due to the nature of southern Iraqi society as well as to the more open style of the British in charge. The southern Shia had suffered more than any other group under Saddam and they remained very suspicious of links with Baghdad. As the insurgents grew in strength further north, the south held together and managed to keep them at bay. The visit entrenched my feeling that this was not where the main test would come. I returned to the capital convinced that Baghdad was where I should concentrate my effort.

*

For quite a period in the second half of September Bremer was absent from Iraq. The reason for this was money. One of the most difficult areas of CPA business for the uninitiated to penetrate was the management of Iraq's finances. The arrangements agreed in the Security Council in May 2003 for the establishment of a Development Fund for Iraq had been complicated and it was not until several months after my arrival that the United Nations transferred to the DFI the nearly $3 billion that had accumulated in the Oil for Food programme accounts. The continuing proceeds from Iraq's oil production also passed through the Fund before being allocated to ministries under the rudimentary budgeting procedures evolving at this time, but the total could not possibly cover all the requirements of the next year. Bremer and his budget director, David Oliver, worked miracles to make ends meet. There just was not time, given the interconnected demands of security and daily Iraqi living standards, to construct a sophisticated process of estimates, allocations, disbursements and audits. No attempt was made to consult Coalition partners on financial issues beyond exhortations to encourage our Governments to donate aid to Iraq. Oliver briefed me privately a couple of times on the economic assumptions the CPA was using. They appeared to have little more than back-of-envelope quality and depended almost entirely on massive US funding.

The UK asked once or twice to supply a Treasury official to the CPA financial team, but the offer was turned down. Nor did Bremer allow me into his internal discussions in these areas. Contract decisions were even more carefully protected: the UK was as frozen out as any other non-American contributor. From time to time London reminded Washington that it would not be understood in the UK if British contractors were not allowed to compete fairly. Over the first year of the Coalition's life UK companies in fact obtained some 12 per cent of available new business – a fair result from a national viewpoint when we were contributing less than 3 per cent of the overall funding, even if the lion's share came in the south where our own aid programme was running. I found what opportunities I could to remind the CPA that Iraqi companies had to be given a chance to win business and employ Iraqis or the blowback would wipe away any progress in reconstruction. The message got through to the extent that Tom Foley's ambitious and wholly premature privatisation and modernisation plans were gradually pushed to one side, but no attempt was ever made to start a national employment programme.

As for Iraq's budget, no amount of fast-footed financial planning would make up for the revenue gap. At current oil prices Iraqi revenues might reach $12 billion in a full year. Oil for Food funds and other remaining sources of income might bring the total to $15 billion. On the debit side, the cost of continuing the UN-type food distribution programme, without which most Iraqis would have risked starvation, came to at least $5 billion a year. Fuel subsidies, with petroleum products and electricity virtually free to the population, amounted to a similar sum. Barely $5 billion remained to run the rest of the public sector. Bremer knew as well as anyone that the success of the post-conflict operation would rest on the recognition by the Iraqi people that things had improved. He set his sights on the provision of a further $20 billion from the US Congress for the development of Iraq in 2004. This was in addition to the vast bills coming in for the maintenance of the US military machine.

I doubt whether Jerry Bremer had any more time to sleep during his days in Washington in September than he had in Baghdad. He is said to have attended more meetings and paid more calls on Congress within the space of a single week than any other member of the Executive in US history. He had prepared his case well and he had support from nearly all the members of the Congressional Delegations who had visited Iraq at his invitation over the previous four months. The cost of the President's Iraq policy was starting to raise serious questions in Congress and within American public opinion more widely: the knives were out, not just amongst

Democrats, to cut down the staggering sums being put about in the media. When Bremer returned to Baghdad on 30 September from his two-week expedition, he was confident of an outcome close to what he had requested. In the event the total agreed for appropriation came to $18.7 billion. It was inevitable that concessions should have been made and ironic – in the light of later events – that one of the funding cuts should have been to the overhaul of the prison system and the building of new facilities for holding captured insurgents. But this was a considerable achievement.

With Bremer back and the miserable symbolism of Akila's funeral behind us, the pace of activity in the CPA picked up. My office was starting to bed down well. Simon managed to instil some bureaucratic order into the turmoil – even into Raad – and we were joined by a Military Adviser, Lieutenent Colonel Simon Plummer, known to us all as Plum, whose dazed look on his first day was soon replaced by pertinent advice on the security situation and some skilful contact-making with the US military. These three quickly formed a bond of remarkable strength. The financial future was looking rosier and the security forces were beginning to score more consistently against the insurgency in the Sunni heartland. The pessimists were in the minority again.

At the first Governing Council meeting of October Bremer asked me to make a pitch to the IGC about the need to accelerate its work on the constitutional process. The ministries were now up and running and the next function for the Iraqi leadership was to establish a Preparatory Committee to consider a new constitution, without which there could be no movement on elections under the current plan. I encouraged them to take up this responsibility. There was much sage nodding of heads around the table at this expression of practical good sense from their occupation overlords. Yet effective action failed to materialise. This stemmed partly from the divisions in the Council about the chronology of the transition process, with the Shia members heavily influenced by Ayatollah Sistani, and partly from the raw emotions lying beneath the surface of everything we were trying to shape in this formative period. National pride had taken a beating and individual political ambitions were growing. The religious Shia parties saw the advantages of having a political organisation in place and wanted to preserve them. SCIRI and Dawa had after all taken the risk of keeping their parties alive during the Saddam Hussein era and now felt it was payback time. The Kurds were self-contained and similarly organised. Only the Sunnis had no political base outside the Baath Party. Throughout my time in Iraq the Americans and we tried to stimulate Sunni political initiatives and to convince them that they had a stake in the new Iraq. David Richmond and I went out to speak to political gatherings and arranged with Iyad Allawi to meet groups of Sunni tribal leaders, but the great majority in the Sunni heartland refused to see regime change as positive and set no store by the politicians we had found to represent them.

The controversy over whether to allow the participation of previous members of the Baath Party, which extended to hundreds of thousands of civil servants, teachers, doctors, judges and other public-sector professionals, as well as to members of the security forces, all of whom had needed to sign up as Baathists in order to practice their profession at any senior level, had developed into a bitter rift, pitting ideology against pragmatism. Bremer had appointed Ahmed Chalabi as Head of the IGC's De-Baathification Committee and – as Bremer must have known he would – Chalabi carried out his work with a passionate efficiency. Those who recognised the implications, such as Iyad Allawi, were just as fierce in their opposition. At the early October IGC meeting the Turcoman spokesman launched into a sudden diatribe against the excesses of the Saddam era and proposed the 'physical removal' of all known Baathists, together with their women and children. For a moment there was an embarrassed silence. No one at the table quite knew whether he meant exile or execution; the uproar that then ensued did not leave room for an explanation. The incident starkly reminded us of the depths of hatred within this traumatised people.

The other reason for the loss of effective traction in the IGC was more pervasive. The levers out to the population were not working. This had little to do with the Coalition's selection of community representatives to form the IGC or the Ministerial group under it. Two years on, the principal candidates for high office in Iraq's transitional institutions are nearly all the leaders chosen by Bremer, Sawers and de Mello in July 2003. Ayatollah Sistani and the renegade cleric Muqtada al Sadr apart, the public voices affecting the politics of the occupation period came from the original IGC. Our problems had more to do with the occupation's legitimacy deficit and with the lack of structure connecting the administration and the political leadership of Iraq with ordinary people. Autocracy and harsh security had functioned as a system under Saddam. The introduction of freedom and the removal of fear were welcome, but were not enough on their own. In the early weeks after the war, army commanders and political officers started to organise a few local elections, some of which worked well. Bremer closed down these initiatives, which he saw as inconsistent with the chronology of his Seven Steps. This was a pity. The people who personified government to the millions struggling to find food, water, jobs, law and order, medical attention and education for their families were the provincial governors and municipal leaders, the police chiefs, university professors, doctors and judges who were recognised in the streets and who could be appealed to in their sitting-rooms, and these people, crucially, were not yet part of a national political process. The foreigners had performed the supreme task of ridding them of Saddam, but since then, except when the US Army turned up on an operation or a town-hall meeting drew a few hundred local people into contact with a CPA representative, the Coalition seemed to have little impact on daily life.

This lacuna could have been partly remedied by two things: an effective media operation and steady improvement in the provision of major public services. I still cannot explain how the US, the nation with the greatest experience of modern communications, with a free press and with no difficulties in conjuring up resources when the will was there, delivered such a shambles on the media side. The main CPA effort seemed always to be dedicated to briefing the US press and too little attention was paid to America's new constituency in Iraq. By the time, well into 2004, that an effective media team had been created and the funding found for television stations to reach the majority of the population, the CPA's credibility as a trustworthy provider of daily information for the Iraqi people had evaporated. I think Tony Blair blew more gaskets on this one subject, because it was remediable, than on any other. But even he could not get the point home in Washington, or at least not in a way that penetrated the operating machinery even when the President agreed with him.

The provision of services centred round the supply of electricity. When the conflict began, electricity was being generated country-wide at the rate of around 4,000 megawatts, enough to keep the lights on in most major cities for eight or ten hours a day. Oil production averaged 2.2 million barrels per day. By spring 2005 oil production was stuck at 2 million barrels a day (a successful Iraq could produce 6 million), and electricity generation at 4,100 megawatts (demand could by then have risen to 9,000). With the lights on for three hours and then off for another three, the reminder of no progress was a constant throb. That in itself was a measure of the effectiveness of insurgency sabotage and intimidation.

It was not as if the American system was not capable of achieving the most remarkable successes when everything clicked into place. The CPA set itself the daunting target of replacing the whole of the Iraqi currency within a period of four months from mid-October onwards. The logistics of this exercise were mind-boggling. Thousands of tonnes of old dinars with Saddam's face on them had to be collected and destroyed and the same volume of new notes had to be ordered, printed, delivered to Iraq in ninety-seven jumbo jet flights and distributed to banks, on a timescale that had never before been attempted in a country of twenty-five million people, even in a stable and smooth-running environment. The UK company De La Rue carried out their fastest-ever currency printing programme. The progress reports and homilies coming out of the highly motivated currency exchange team read like the records of revivalist meetings and we guardians of British understatement smiled when we read them. But by early 2004 it was clear that the programme was on track, that the threat of sabotage or criminal attack had been kept at bay, and that the change was going to be of immense benefit, economically as well as symbolically, to the transition process. I and my team ate humble pie and sent our congratulations. The dinar rose steadily in the foreign exchange markets for the following few months.

This was an example of American power delivery at its best. If the same effort had been directed at the electricity sector, and oil production, and the media, and most critically at police training, perhaps the security deficit would have righted itself more quickly as the Iraqis gained confidence and took on more responsibility. But the CPA was not large enough an organisation to grapple with all these sectors at the same time. Bremer's decisiveness and drive could fill some of the gaps, but he did not delegate and he could not focus on everything at once. The CPA civilian complement in the final months of 2003 numbered around 1,300 people, of whom close to 90 per cent were American: an embassy, not a government. This included the civilian advisers in the ministries and the teams in the provinces coordinating – and in some places holding together – the local administrations. We were not reaching far enough into the substrata of Iraqi life to make a difference. Nor, significantly, were we empowering Iraqis to take over the job themselves.

Every few weeks the provincial teams, civilian and military, were summoned to Baghdad to consult together on their experience to date and to learn best practice from the centre and from each other. The first meeting I attended was held in Bremer's absence and, although I held no rank in the CPA itself, I was encouraged by several senior voices in the system to grasp the political discussion and try to mould it into a real debate. There was a risk involved. In our private brainstorming sessions, the UK team was beginning to find holes in the CPA's approach. We could not attempt to address them all, or even raise them for discussion, without endangering the relationship with our senior cousins.

Three interlinked issues beyond security were emerging as the key problems: the constitutional process, which would determine not only the future structure of the country but also the duration of the occupation; the place of the Sunni Arabs in the new Iraq, whose disaffection with the process so far threatened to overturn the whole project; and the guidelines for the provinces and the governorate teams, who had to create new local administrations and find new leaders in each of their areas, but in such a way as to promote the unity of Iraq rather than fragmentation into individual communities. The CPA's Governance Section, as the political department under Ambassador Bremer was termed, were writing detailed papers on all these areas, which were models of clear thinking and good political theory, but which lacked the essential ingredient of transplantability into the real Iraq.

I made a bid to chair the political session of the end-of-September Regional Coordinators' Conference. A sharp reaction from Scott Carpenter, the Head of Governance Section, signalled that I had overstepped the mark. I launched into my points anyway, underlining the need for the CPA to understand that time to get things right had to be earned from Iraqis by improving their lives; that winning Iraqi hearts and minds involved style and manner as well as substance; and that we had to intensify our outreach programme to solve the Sunni and the national leadership deficiencies. I was interested to see that these themes were immediately taken up by the military commanders in the hardest areas, Major-General David Petraeus in the North-West Division and Major-General Ray Odierno in North-Central, who had regularly encountered the same issues in their daily grind and were determined, when they saw the absence of a CPA lead, to use their own initiative to solve local problems.

A number of concerns were put on the table: the implications for security if the Sunnis were not given a stake in the future of Iraq; the lack of coordination and guidance from the centre; the building of Iraqi links between the different parts of the country; and resources, the perennial complaint. Petraeus had, through his own initiative, put 12,800 Iraqis on his local payroll and wondered how long he could go on affording them. Many of these issues were already being addressed within the CPA, but the wires to the provinces were not carrying the message, nor was the centre absorbing the lessons that were being learnt at the coal-face by those in everyday contact with our real customers. Iraqis were desperate for jobs, but nearly all the larger CPA contracts were going to foreign firms and imported contractors. This discussion quenched a thirst for debate but indicated a longer-term communications problem. It was noticeable that at least 50 per cent of the talking had been done in British accents, without raising visible hackles. I remember wondering what Bremer would think of it all when he returned, if indeed anyone on his office staff gave him a fair description of the day. I never heard him refer to it; and we never again held such a spirited discussion of what was going right and wrong in Iraq.

By early October it was time for a foray into Kurdistan, my first experience of what was to become a very familiar journey. Simon Shercliff and I piled into a Black Hawk helicopter with a few American minders and we set off over the northern plains. We refuelled at a desert airbase near Kirkuk and then climbed up into the fresh green foothills, flying low to avoid trouble and terrifying flocks of sheep and goats hidden in the small eroded valleys.

The Kurdistan Democratic Party headquarters on the mountain ridge of Salahaddin welcomed us in. The Kurds had done well for themselves in the period between the two Gulf Wars when, with US and UK protection from the air, they kept Saddam Hussein at bay, capitalising on their portion of the Oil for Food programme as the rest of Iraq was never able to do and attracting other forms of Western investment on top of that. Since full independence for the

Kurds remained a pipe-dream with Turkey so hostile, these twelve years had conditioned them to the autonomy they had always wanted: a Kurdistan Regional Government and Assembly, their own language, their own right to scrap with each other. We knew it would be hard to pull them back into an integrated Iraq. Masoud Barzani, the longstanding Kurdish Democratic Party chieftain, was away but his nephew Nechirvan, who held the title of regional Prime Minister, led us into a discussion of the contribution the Kurds could make to a united Iraq. He assured me that independence, though inextinguishable as an ambition, could be treated as a long-term aspiration, provided they were left with a sufficiently strong system of autonomy. Getting that concession out of the Iraqi Arabs was going to be a challenge.

The next morning we drove down the escarpment to the internal Kurdish demarcation line, picked up a mad escort of Patriotic Union of Kurdistan police and hangers-on and careered off to Lake Dukan. As we clung to our seats round the hairpin bends and over the narrow passes, we could see dotted along the boundary line with Arab Iraq to the south the perfectly still figures of single Peshmerga border guards, standing every few hundred yards as the first defence of Kurdish territory. At Dukan, Jalal Talabani greeted us with expansive bonhomie. He was a little more nuanced than his KDP counterparts about the prospects for inter-Kurdish unity in the tussles to come, but just as sure as they were that Kurdistan had to start by testing Baghdad for the federal system the Kurds wanted. Lunchtime brought us our third huge meal in fifteen hours, at which point diplomatic training had to cut in. We left in the helicopter for a Ride of the Valkyries back down the escarpment, with the doors open and loose possessions flying out into the ether, blue lakes and green valleys clear in the sharp mountain air.

Back in Baghdad a row was brewing over Turkey. Washington was growing increasingly desperate to recruit other national contingents into the Coalition and Ankara's recent offer to send 10,000 soldiers to central or northern Iraq looked like a godsend. Bremer was left to wrestle with the practicalities. Washington had only two days previously reacted with 'incredulity and anger' – so Bremer told me – at his suggestion that there might be no net gain in allowing the Turks into Iraq if they then intervened in Iraqi politics and created a precedent for Iran. The US Army had already put three deployment options to Ankara; the prospect of finding militarily competent reinforcements had speeded up the Joint Chiefs' proactivity. The IGC meeting on 9 October made Bremer's position even more difficult: every Iraqi present opposed Turkish involvement. No one could claim that the objections came only from the Kurds. Whatever the differences between them, the Iraqis were determined that the independence they had not yet gained from the United States was not to be compromised by their neighbours – any of them.

I supported Bremer's approach and encouraged him to hold out. On my way back to London in mid-October I arranged to pass through Ankara, where the UK Ambassador, Peter Westmacott, an old friend from Washington days, took me in to see the Deputy Chief of the Turkish General Staff and the Permanent Secretary at the Foreign Ministry. General Basbug was defiant, warning me darkly about the risks of rejecting a generous offer of help where it was needed. I told him what was actually going on in Iraq: it was not just a matter of what the United States might want; the Iraqi view had to be taken into account as well. This was a neighbour with whom Turkey would have to live into the indefinite future. I wondered whether the long-term consequences had been fully considered. Basbug grew more thoughtful, but said little. As soon as we had left, he moved straight on to a pre-arranged press conference and announced that the Turkish Government was considering the three options offered by the Americans.

In the Ministry of Foreign Affairs, Ambassador Ziyal seemed to understand the strategic downsides better, but said the issue had travelled so far down the road to implementation that it was hard to see how it could be reversed. I pointed out that the legitimacy of the move could be assured only by an invitation from the Iraqis. Would it not be better to wait for one? Ziyal did not answer. Nonetheless, in the way of these things, the seeds of doubt had been sown in Turkish minds. Ankara gradually began to back-pedal and a day or two later signalled to Washington that a Turkish contingent was willing to come if invited by Iraq. That was where it stayed. It was the right decision, saving endless trouble later. But Bremer lost points with Washington as a result because of the primacy of keeping US troop numbers down.

It was a relief to find myself back in the familiar streets of London. I had only been gone a month, but felt as though I had been away for an age. Whitehall was not unduly concerned about the Turks, who only really responded to the United States and were therefore Washington's problem. The home team's main focus in Iraq was the south, where British troops were beginning to make progress in their independent way and violence remained spasmodic. As I traipsed round the offices with my Baghdad-oriented apprehensions, I realised that I was not delivering a very welcome message. People understood that the security situation in the centre and north of the country was gradually deteriorating, but that was surely for the Americans to fix. I responded sharply that Iraq would be won in the centre or it would not be won at all. This struck home at the mid-week gathering of Chiefs of Staff at the Ministry of Defence. The Chief of the Naval Staff, Admiral Sir Alan West, asked: 'If you are saying that security will get worse before it gets better, where is the evidence that it is going to get better?' I said that there was none yet, only hope. The meeting turned sombre.

I was getting used to the role of unpopular messenger. In New York, with no further career job to compete for, I had developed a certain immunity to the snap of London's fingers on tactical detail. In Baghdad my independence of position was even more pronounced. I wanted to be sure that I was painting an accurate picture when so many UK interests were at stake. Nevertheless, I was working to policy lines that I respected. My daily guidance came from John

Sawers, my predecessor in Baghdad and now, as Foreign Office Political Director, Jack Straw's senior adviser on Iraq, and from Nigel Sheinwald, recently brought back from Brussels, where he was the UK's highest-ranked Ambassador, to succeed David Manning as the Prime Minister's Foreign Affairs Adviser – a position filled from the Foreign Office. We three knew each other well and talked regularly on the telephone; I always spent time with them in London. On this visit, I made sure that Nigel, in particular, because he was now the channel of constant communication with Condoleezza Rice in Washington, knew why I felt that the administration of Iraq was running into serious trouble. Because my account did not square with Rice's, it put him in an awkward position, not least in having to work out in his own mind which of us was closer to the truth.

Nigel took me in to see the Prime Minister, who was sitting on the sofa in his small inner office with his core team around him. It was the first time I had been there without the focused presence of Alastair Campbell in the chair beside the desk. Simon Shercliff, my Private Secretary from Baghdad, whom I had smuggled into the meeting to brighten his day, received a nice warm welcome for braving the front line. Blair asked me to lead off and I launched into an edited version of my concerns. I described the long-term prospects for improvements in Iraq's infrastructure, now that Congress had agreed to release new money, with tactful praise for Bremer's achievement in instilling a sense of dynamism into the CPA operation. I set out the plan for the political transition as it was emerging at the Baghdad end, but underlined the need to be prepared for changes. I warned that there was no improvement in prospect for the security situation. The Coalition was not going to be able to cope with the combination of growing Sunni disaffection and terrorism while men, materials and motivation remained endlessly available.

Blair took all this quite calmly, though I was hardly describing the progress that he had demanded in early September. In these meetings in his inner office, with his close family of advisers around him, I was there to fill in the details of my particular area. He sat on the sofa with Jonathan Powell, his Chief of Staff, silent beside him and put a series of questions, but he gave little away of his own thinking after I had answered. I came to the conclusion that he was resigned to a certain amount of bad news: this was what Iraq had come to mean. His thoughts seemed focused on what he would need to say next to George Bush, how many suggestions for changes he would have room to put to him, what adjustments he needed to make to immediate policy and its presentation. It was hard to get into the strategic questions.

At the end of the meeting the Prime Minister unexpectedly asked me for a paper with practical recommendations to put to Bush. If things were not going well, he needed a basis to explain why the UK felt that. Encouraged, I submitted this a day later, including all my old favourites: dealing with the borders and the ammunition dumps, bringing aid projects into the Sunni areas, creating jobs and devolving local responsibilities to the Iraqis, accelerating Iraqi-isation of the security services and searching for wider UN and international input. The most important element, however, had to be rapid progress towards creating an interim Iraqi government to take over from the occupation, because the Coalition's shelf life was beginning to shorten. Washington must be asked to firm up a timetable. I knew that the Prime Minister was particularly sympathetic to this central point, which had featured in his thinking from the start.

I was never told what the American reactions were to this list or even how it was put to them. My London colleagues were unhappy that there was still so much to be done and, as far as I could tell, fed these elements across to their US counterparts in what they judged were digestible chunks. With such thin lines into the Pentagon, and with our excellent relationship with the disconnected State Department so redundant, the channel from Sheinwald to Rice had to carry the burden but avoid overload. It seemed that the British had still not earned the right to engage with Washington in a comprehensive strategic debate.

At that week's meeting of the Cabinet Ad Hoc Committee on Iraq, which Defence Secretary Geoff Hoon chaired in Jack Straw's absence, I brought out the same menu of concerns. The ministerial team was no more thrilled to hear my pessimistic assessment than anyone else and asked whether the British should not be making a stronger input into policy formation in Baghdad. I said we were doing our best, but London should not imagine that the UK could exercise 50 per cent of the influence in Baghdad when we contributed only 2 per cent of the resources. There was a momentary hush. Hoon pointedly reminded the meeting, with the Treasury representative nodding vigorously, that the Chancellor of the Exchequer had just shut the door on any increase in Government spending, full stop. Two per cent it would remain.

This became the pattern of my regular exchanges with my London colleagues, whether in person during my monthly return visits or in the flow of telegram and telephone traffic from Baghdad. There was a limit to which I could convince Ambassador Bremer that the current approach was not working and it was my job to report this and see whether higher political voltage could achieve more. Downing Street was acutely conscious that the Prime Minister could only complain to the President for so long that the trend was worrying without producing concrete suggestions for a remedy. It seemed to me from quite early on that we were going round in circles and gradually losing the American ear. I saw no easy way out.

16

Two Chickens, Two Eggs

In Baghdad apprehensions were growing that the approach of Ramadan would bring a deterioration in the security situation. US military activity had started to constrain the capacity of the core insurgency to inflict more than occasional local damage on Iraq's infrastructure. As Coalition troops developed a more sophisticated knowledge of the terrain, and as intelligence operations began to form a web of sources and contacts producing real-time information, the number of 'Former Regime Elements', as the Iraqi insurgents were dismissively termed, being killed or captured steadily increased. Nonetheless, the insurgents were learning as well; and they began to make up in accuracy and lethality for what they could not achieve in numbers. The rate of casualties was gradually creeping up – in the streets, within US forces, among new Iraqi recruits and around the activities of foreign contractors trying to mend the infrastructure.

Saddam loyalists were not the only enemy within the Iraqi population. As the realisation grew within the population that it would take far longer than they had expected for standards of living to improve and for foreign troops to leave, patience started to wear thin. The Sunni Arabs, close to 20 per cent of the population, had by no means all benefited from Saddam Hussein's rule, which dealt ruthlessly with any sign of opposition or disloyalty beyond a very narrow core, but they saw no advantage in the democratisation of a state with a 60 per cent Shia Arab majority. Bremer tried to address Sunni disaffection from early on: the CPA set up a special operation to form new political contacts and inject project money and for a while, until the Americans pulled the job back into their own ranks, David Richmond was assigned a special role in constructing overtures to local Sunni leaders. It was not enough to stimulate the Sunni community as a whole to reorganise themselves for the new circumstances. Political frustration, nationalist pride and the sense – with the Palestinian intifada running hard – of a wider Arab grievance pushed a growing number of individuals and groups to take up weapons and have a go at whomever they saw as responsible for their humiliation. Some joined the ranks of the Saddamists; others teamed up with hardened criminals, who themselves were finding the climate fruitful; many just came out hunting when they felt their anger rising and set up a trap for a passing patrol or a civilian car with a foreigner in it. The risks grew for all foreigners out and about on the roads and ordinary Iraqi civilians often became caught up in the violence.

The least numerous of the violent forces confronting the Coalition, but becoming gradually more lethal in their methods, were the non-Iraqi terrorists inspired by al Qaida. Abu Musab al Zarqawi, a middle-class Jordanian who is thought to have started his terrorist activity with the aim of dislodging the Hashemite dynasty in his own country, appears to have crossed into Iraq before the US invasion to develop his own brand of Islamic extremism under the al Qaida franchise. He began to organise and train tiny cells of suicide bombers to attack targets that would do the greatest damage to the Coalition's capacity to run a smooth administration. New recruits came in a steady trickle across the frontiers and were put straight to work. One suicide bomber in October, a Yemeni, was identified as having crossed the border only two days previously. Zarqawi's strategy included direct attacks against Coalition patrols and facilities, the killing of prominent Iraqis supporting the occupation authorities and more general attacks on the Shia or Kurdish population aimed at inciting intercommunal violence. He was reckoned to have been responsible for the bombing of the Jordanian Embassy, the attack on the UN headquarters at the Canal Hotel and the assassination of Mohammed Baqir al Hakim in August 2003, all of them significant indirect blows against the Coalition, aimed at denying us allies and raising the cost for Iraqis who chose to support us. Later he moved on to the high-profile kidnapping and beheading of foreign workers in Iraq with the objective of slowing down the implementation of reconstruction contracts. The effects were tangible and cumulative.

As the months went by, the ability of terrorists and insurgents to avoid detection and develop new methods of attack kept pace with the growing effectiveness of Coalition forces and intelligence in tracking them down. The firmness of the US military reaction caused huge problems for the insurgency. The prisons started to overflow with captives. But at the same time this escalation in the use of force and the sometimes-indiscriminate use of fire-power by the Americans swelled the numbers of the disaffected. Within the Iraqi population an increasing amount of cover or indirect support was offered to the front-line resistance, as the insurgents came to be seen. The net result for the Coalition was a steady draining of sympathy just when our political and economic objectives required the support and trust of the population.

We speculated constantly about the role of the neighbouring states. Surely Iran would not be able to resist fomenting the opposition? With their American arch-enemy now entrenched on their borders, the regime in Tehran had real cause to make life as difficult as possible for them. The Iranians were concerned that the United States might reactivate the Iranian dissident movement Mujahideen-e-Khalq against them. They had proxies in Iraq, such as the Badr Corps (the SCIRI militia), Iraqi Hezbollah and a number of Iranian subversive units and agents directly or indirectly on their payroll. Basra was full of them. They also harboured designs on the religious centres of Najaf and Kerbala, where they began to buy up property at a disconcerting rate. Iranian pilgrims crossed the border sometimes at the rate of many thousands a day to visit holy sites long barred to them: it was all too easy to infiltrate agents at almost any time.

On the other hand, Tehran did not want to create a completely chaotic Iraq or it might throw up another Saddam Hussein. Towards the end of my time in the country, I coordinated a CPA assessment of Iranian involvement, which concluded that Iran's long-term aim was a stable, Shia-led neighbour, free of foreign interference, rich enough to offer good business and friendly enough not to present a threat. Did Tehran want a mirror-image government of Shia clerics in Baghdad? I saw no clear evidence of that. The Iranian leaders are more cautious in nature than they are normally perceived. We judged that they wanted to influence but not to dominate, and would take care not to provide the United States with a pretext to attack them. Iran wished to see a weak but not a turbulent Iraq, with the Americans thwarted and then removed, and would use its levers to turn the temperature up or down in line with developments. I believe that this has remained their approach ever since.

Our other bugbear was Syria. We had good evidence that the Syrians were happy to allow Islamic extremist recruits to cross Iraq's western frontier. Possibly unknown to President Bashar al Assad, who often tried to assure us – as he did with me when I called on him in November – that Syria would keep its hands off Iraq, the more unpleasant corners of the Syrian security forces contributed money and materials in moderate amounts to the Sunni insurgents. But they too had to ensure that they did not give the United States an open reason to turn on them and this kept their interference within limits. Because the Coalition never dominated the full extent of Iraqi territory, both Iran and Syria found it reasonably easy to remain undetected in their calculated encouragement and manipulation of both Shia and Sunni resistance to the foreign presence.

*

Shortly after my return from London in the last week of October General John Abizaid paid one of his regular visits to Baghdad. I never really understood how, in a situation where American lives were being lost every day and where the global prestige of the United States was at stake, the American machine could afford to have its most able military mind on Middle East matters devoted only part-time to the Iraq theatre. As Commander of CENTCOM, he had the Horn of Africa and Afghanistan, not least the elusive Osama bin Laden, to worry about as well. Abizaid's Lebanese origins gave him the advantage of a deep understanding of the psychology of the region. On 24 October I had a long one-on-one conversation with him, in which I set out my concern that violence could not be controlled under the current set of circumstances. It struck a chord with Abizaid – 'and I am not normally worried', he said. He was gearing up for a full-scale examination of next steps with Donald Rumsfeld in Washington in a few days' time. Abizaid wanted much more urgent action to bring the Sunni Arabs in to the political arena and to develop Iraqi security capability; and he favoured taking a risk with the early transfer of power to Iraqi political leadership. I knew that this tied in with the assessment of General Sanchez, who told me he was raising dust to try to unjam the present security stagnation. Both were guarded in what they said, but I believed that neither thought that the Coalition had enough troops on the ground to achieve US objectives. The President and the Defense Secretary had both said publicly that they would commit the number of soldiers to Iraq that their Generals requested. But both Abizaid and Sanchez knew that the US Army had no spare troops: if they asked for the level of reinforcements that would enable them to complete the task they risked their positions. I gained the distinct impression that they hoped the UK channel would try to wake up the Washington system to the threat of failure.

Was Bremer immune to such apprehensions? It was not easy to get to his inner thinking. His policy approach was grounded in his loyalty

Barrow library

Customer ID: *********86208

Items that you have renewed

Title: Iraq :
ID: 38003046864682
Due: 12 August 2021

Total items: 1
Account balance: £0.00
22/07/2021 04:15
Borrowed: 1
Overdue: 0
Hold requests: 0
Ready for collection: 0

Free computer help
at Barrow Library

Ask

to the President and, at least when he began, he was ideologically comfortable with his instructions. Up until the end of 2003 he reported primarily to Donald Rumsfeld, through regular telephone conversations, occasional team video conferences and rare visits back to Washington. I could not imagine that these exchanges were focused on the nature of Iraqi society or on his lack of tools to do the job. He brainstormed privately with Abizaid every two or three weeks and consulted with Sanchez more or less every day. In none of these exchanges, I believe, and probably not even to himself, did Bremer admit any doubt that Iraq would respond to an imposed vision. It was a leading reason why he disliked the sceptical leaning of the British approach, to which our low-grade power and resources did not in his view really entitle us. If success had a thousand fathers, they all had to have an unquestioning faith in the outcome. He and his core staff, including the Governance team, saw Iraq as an American project in every sense that mattered and only Americans – and the right Americans at that – were qualified to conduct it. Bremer and Abizaid understood each other well, but they each had their separate lines to the Defense Secretary, who was the first point at which responsibility for the civilian and military operations in Iraq came together, and they could not afford to show any weakness that might get back to headquarters. Below the strategic level, there was tension in Iraq between the CPA and the Army, and between different parts of the military structure – central command, the commanders in the field, military intelligence and the civilian affairs officers – about, for instance, the right mix of hard and soft operations and about the responsibility for political overtures in rough areas.

What Jerry Bremer brought to Iraq was a sense of positive drive and control, which the American system needed to ride over the difficulties. This suggested an assumption that the difficulties themselves did not require deep analysis and could not in the end resist American power. One of the most striking memories of my time in Iraq is of the regular stream of American players, from the civilian and military teams in Iraq and from visitors on influential desks in

Washington, sometimes at the instigation of Donald Rumsfeld himself, who came to my room to hear a no-holds-barred analysis of what was going right and what was going wrong in Iraq. Almost without exception they entered into the spirit of these discussions with real understanding. Somehow, when they returned to a collective American debate about next steps, they clicked back into the reveal-no-weakness mode, with no one clearly accountable for the actual results. It did not just frustrate us Britons; I believe it worried many competent and perceptive Americans.

As for the political process, time was ticking by. A Constitutional Preparatory Committee had been established under the Iraqi Governing Council, but by mid-October it and the IGC itself were going round in circles. I never saw any concrete product from the Committee. The passage of time with no progress was widening the loss of Iraqi popular confidence. In reporting to London, I drew a direct link between the security stalemate and the next stage of the political transition. I pushed for elections to be the focal point for 2004 rather than the writing of the definitive constitution. I did not believe that we would be able to circumvent the objections of important Iraqis, including Grand Ayatollah Sistani, the most powerful voice in the country, to the production of a constitution before elections. Sistani had made this precise point the subject of a religious edict, a fatwa, before I arrived in Iraq, but the Americans were hoping that its effect would fade with time and the passage of events. Bremer, right in theory but not in practice in this vital area, remained determined to establish the underlying principles of democracy before elections. Some of his closest advisers in Baghdad thought at this stage that it might become a resignation matter for him. The Governing Council was supposed to be resolving this question of sequence through the work of the Constitutional Preparatory Committee, but they seemed incorrigibly reluctant to take the initiative. This was partly because of the vigour with which American policy was presented, even if most of them saw it as going in the wrong direction.

My theoretical independence from the CPA as the co-equal British partner in the occupation authority was of no practical use unless I supported the American lead. I was not bound by Bremer's instructions, but I was not in a position to strike out on my own. From the beginning I made it clear to him that I was there to back him up and I stuck to that, especially in public and in our regular sessions with visiting Congressional delegations. His appreciation of this kept us together through the disagreements on some of the detail. But I had to try where I could to influence the advice going in to him and I had to use my own judgement with our main Iraqi interlocutors.

On 25 October Bremer asked me to go back up to Kurdistan to broach the need for political compromise with Masoud Barzani, the leader of the Kurdistan Democratic Party, whom I had not yet met. Barzani rarely attended the meetings of the IGC in Baghdad: he disliked debate around a table of a hundred shifting views. His single-minded mission was to defend the way of life and autonomy of the Kurds and, to his mind, this was best done by remaining among them. When I called on him at his headquarters at Salahaddin, he was wearing his signature outfit of fatigues and a rather untidy headdress, Arafat-style. Short in stature and laconic in Arabic or Kurdish, he took time to appreciate. Before I had finished my work in Iraq I came to recognise that he was a pivotal personality at this stage of Iraq's history.

I delivered a message that had been carefully scripted with the Governance team in the CPA, one of whose members accompanied me, as did Simon Shercliff. I said that the British Government remained a firm ally and protector of the Kurdish way of life, but the framework had to be a united Iraq. We needed his help to make the political process move forward. The IGC must now start to make progress with the Constitutional Committee and, in general, must begin to work more efficiently on government business, with better attendance from its senior members. He looked at me unsmilingly. I said he had an important role to play in demonstrating that the

317

Kurdish nation would contribute to our purpose: there was now no alternative. Barzani took all this calmly, and countered with a request for more secure accommodation in the Green Zone in Baghdad if he was to spend time there. I was then treated to an exposition of Kurdish bottom lines in the negotiation to come over constitutional arrangements: the retention of the Kurdish National Assembly and Government, the continuation of the Kurdish language and culture and the maintenance of their security force, the Peshmerga. I glanced over to where Simon was taking the notes to ensure that he wrote down the words carefully: Barzani was not closing the door on some kind of autonomy arrangement. This was significant, given the pressure the Kurdish leadership was facing from their people for an outright break with Arab Iraq.

After a generous lunch at the guest-house, we took our leave for the return helicopter flight down the mountain, only to discover that the Black Hawk that had ferried us up had disappeared. The crew apparently had better things to do than to hang around for four hours for a civilian, and a non-American one at that. I telephoned my office and set them the challenge to bring me back to Baghdad by bedtime. Before long they called me back to say they had been told that there were no helicopters available. I asked them to sort it. Plum and Raad told me later that they looked at each other when I put the phone down and decided for once to put aside the demeanour of junior cousin. They raised the temperature, with Plum obliged to cash in the brownie points he had been amassing with the US military.

Two hours later there arrived at Salahaddin the three 'Little Bird' four-seater helicopters that normally flew noisily as security above Bremer's convoy whenever he travelled outside the Green Zone. He had left for Washington for the strategic security discussions Abizaid had mentioned and the Little Bird crews had been spending the day practising their live firing in the desert. With Simon and my bodyguard in the two Birds behind me, I took the single spare seat in the lead helicopter, so cramped that the only place to put my right foot was through the door-less gap and onto the strut outside. The sun had just set and we winged it down the escarpment through the blue-black dusk, never more than a hundred feet off the ground, the first-hint-of-winter wind buffeting into our faces and nothing but a thin seat-belt holding us on board. We passed like nighthawks through the oil flares of Kirkuk and over the evening activity of various surprised villages out in the fields. Luckily, when I made my dishevelled re-entry into what was left of the Baghdad office day, it did not take too long to un-knot my few remaining strands of hair. My son Nick telephoned almost as soon as I got in: a Black Hawk had gone down in northern Iraq and there was mild concern at home even though I never told them in advance that I was travelling by helicopter. I rang Anne and confirmed that I was all in one piece. She was pretty appalled at the Little Birds story.

The next morning the telephone got to me before the alarm clock. Simon gave me the news that the Rasheed Hotel, where our largest group of colleagues was accommodated, had just taken a full-scale rocket attack. Rockets – crude projectiles fired from tubes in the back of a van, with the explosive force of a rocket-propelled grenade – had grazed the hotel before, but this time the planning was more audacious: the launch position was later found to have been just outside the Green Zone wall, a mere 270 metres from the hotel. A US Army Colonel had been killed instantly and fifteen people wounded, including Jacob Nell of the UK Treasury, a member of the currency exchange team. I rushed into the office and took stock. The hotel was a mess and would need to be evacuated, and we had to find our people new quarters. After the standard morning meetings I called the British contingent together in the bizarre venue of the CPA chapel, formerly Saddam's formal reception hall, complete with a red throne and murals of Al Hussein missiles roaring off to destroy the Zionist enemy. I praised everyone for their professional calmness and reported on the facts so far. John Simmons, our Security Officer, took everyone through the new sleeping arrangements. Miraculously the British Army had come up trumps with a dormitory for thirty-five in their quarters near the river. We arranged for the displaced to be moved across for the few days necessary to sort out something else. They were there for four months.

Later I went to see the damage at the hotel. The American Colonel, Chad Buehring, a member of the CPA Psychological Operations team turned out to have been one of those inspirational figures, forty, married, two sons, who put everyone else's troubles before his own and believed in the invincibility of the good guys. At the first sound of an explosion he had jumped out of bed, grabbed his rifle and run to the window to see what defence he could improvise. The next rocket hit him full-on. Jacob Nell in the floor below had been in his bed when a rocket flew in over his head and struck the back wall of his room. He had been lucky to escape with severe lacerations.

The team's confidence in Green Zone defences took a dive and those who wanted a break were encouraged to go home. I cannot recall anyone who decided to pack it in for good: they all came back again – even Jacob Nell. That says something about the collective determination, the courage or perhaps the plain foolhardiness of a remarkable set of British volunteers, as well as about the compelling nature of the work in which they were engaged. Nevertheless, I told London that another explosion like that might see the end of the UK presence in the CPA. This sobering message at least helped to ease budgetary problems over security and accommodation from then on.

In the middle of this turmoil I slipped out for my first solo call on one of the most influential and – for the CPA – difficult members of the IGC, the Shia cleric Abdul Aziz al Hakim, the political leader of the Supreme Council of the Islamic Revolution in Iraq. He had taken up the mantle of his elder brother Mohammed, the Ayatollah assassinated in Najaf the previous August, and thus carried the prestige of a family that had defied Saddam for years, losing over seventy of its members in the process. He could not immediately project the political acumen of his brother and, since he shared

Grand Ayatollah Sistani's strong suspicions of the US agenda, was prickly in his dealings with us. Nevertheless, he represented a constituency that we had to convince if we were to make progress with the transition: SCIRI was the best organised of the Shia religious parties, with close – though not subservient – ties to Iran and an associated, partly Iranian-funded militia, the Badr Corps, which was all too capable of intimidation but which the Coalition was never able to disband.

It did not take long after the initial courtesies for Hakim to inform me, half disdainfully because I was new to him, that the Governing Council, over which he was presiding that month, would break off communication with the CPA for a week in protest at its refusal to acknowledge the majority preference for putting elections before the constitution. The Council was drafting a number of new proposals, which they wanted implemented on a take-it-or-leave-it basis. Some of them concerned the IGC's security, which he said was a cardinal point for everyone not only because of the threat but also because of the undignified handling of senior leaders by the Coalition military. He wanted SCIRI and the Badr Corps to take over all the security arrangements for the IGC in the Green Zone. I told him none too gently that this last demand was way over the line. I would answer the other items when I saw them.

Later in the day I teamed up with Meghan O'Sullivan, the feisty and imaginative heart of the Governance team, to visit Ahmed Chalabi in his well-fortified villa, known as the Pagoda because of its Chinese trimmings. Chalabi had by this stage lost most of his support in the Pentagon, which had at last recognised the extent to which he was following his own agenda. We realised that he had set aside none of his ambition to come out on top in the new Iraq and we were watching for his next move, suspecting that he would attempt to team up with the religious Shia, the least susceptible group to US influence. Chalabi was also the most westernised of Iraq's leading politicians, the most skilful at adapting his style to his audience. He could be disarmingly frank in discussing his perceptions of what was developing. He told us not to over-react: the IGC were unlikely to cut off discussion entirely, but they were angry over the personal risks they were taking for little political return. As we talked, news came in of further bomb attacks, as well as of one or two significant arrests, around the city. Chalabi pulled me aside to give a private warning that his own intelligence network – he too had a small militia to protect him and keep him informed – was predicting an imminent series of well-planned ground attacks against the Green Zone. We drove back through the poorly lit back-streets of the Al Mansour district in a thoughtful mood. The sum of what we had heard from these and parallel conversations during the day made me think that, with Bremer away in Washington, members of the IGC were trying to flex their muscles while the B team was in charge.

At the next day's Council meeting Chalabi's prognosis proved close to the mark. Without saying anything to me, the CPA Governance Section had issued some stern warnings on the limits of its patience. It transpired that Chalabi himself had been advising his colleagues not to force the issue: this was not the time. Abdul Aziz al Hakim introduced the subject of greater authority for the IGC and circulated some points in Arabic, but he remained vague as to how he wanted them followed up. Responding for the CPA, I set out the conditions and a rough timetable for their earning real power in due course. I stuck to Bremer's policy lines on all of this – I was in no position to do otherwise – but wrapped them in diplomatic language, which the IGC was not accustomed to hearing. I left them with a commitment that we would gradually grant them more responsibility. This satisfied the Council for the moment and they decided to leave the real fight for Bremer's return. I had avoided the indignity of a breakdown on my watch, but the fundamental problem remained.

Bremer returned from his security talks in Washington and called me in for a solo discussion on 1 November. We agreed that we were entering a hard series of negotiations for the transfer of power. He did not offer me a briefing on his trip, a sure sign that agreement on the way forward was proving elusive in his capital. He said he realised that stagnation meant security as well as political problems: he had to keep up the momentum. I asked what this meant in practice – telescope the Seven Steps or alter them? I was back on the thin ice of fallback plans. Bremer said he was extremely reluctant to do the latter because it risked diluting the principles that the United States had come to Iraq to promote. But he agreed that we had both a growing insurgency and a dysfunctional IGC to contend with. He hinted that he might prefer to stomach an interim constitution rather than concede early elections, but he would not wish to stay on in Iraq just to usher in an appointed provisional government, which was the common denominator between the IGC members who wanted early elections (the Shia) and those who did not. This was the first time I had heard him voice the possibility of adapting the planned process. An interim constitution seemed to me to offer a way through the stalemate. We left it that we would go through a round of consultations with the leading Iraqis and then review where we stood.

I stayed in the background in the subsequent round of CPA–IGC skirmishing. The Iraqi side had to feel the force of American views and only Washington could judge the red lines. But I kept privately in touch with the more communicative Iraqis and I brainstormed behind closed doors with the Governance team. The latter were beginning to feel the pressure from their boss and, while they resented having to come down to the UK office, they seemed to find it useful to bounce new ideas around. We started to work through the options for solving the elections dilemma and devolving power. Early elections might have been possible to organise using the UN's food distribution cards as identity documents for some 70 per cent of the population. The problem was in part their logistical complexity, but also the advantage that the organised religious Shia parties would gain over the secular Shia and Sunni parties who had no firm following and had not had time to build a constituency. The Kurds were a separate issue. The Governance team was beginning to come back to the idea of elections at the local level, already tried in the early stages by a few of the CPA's provincial coordinators, who had been stopped in their tracks when Bremer arrived. It was important to give the Sunnis in particular an incentive for coming on board.

On 6 November Bremer invited the nine Presidents of the Iraqi Governing Council to his residence, a substantial villa close to the Republican Palace, for a decisive discussion. 15 November had been set as the deadline for agreeing on the political process and he told them that he could not wait much longer for them to make up their minds. This led to the most interesting IGC political discussion I had witnessed to date. Abdul Aziz al Hakim, Jalal Talabani, Ahmed Chalabi and Adnan Pachachi were present and Ibrahim al Jaafari appeared for some of the time. Iyad Allawi sent a message that he was unwell, but I knew from my recent private discussions with him that he was half thinking of bowing out of the debate altogether. The other members of the nine, Barzani (KDP), Bahr al Uloom (independent religious Shia) and Mohsen Abdul Hamid (Sunni Islamic Party) were represented by deputies. I cannot remember a meeting where all the principals were present at the same time: some of the deputies, such as Adel Abdul Mehdi, al Hakim's number two and later a candidate for Prime Minister, and Roj Shaways, Barzani's lieutenant and later Deputy President in the Transitional Government, became significant players in their own right.

Jaafari intervened early on with an insistence on full elections at the beginning of any process. Talabani countered this with a plea to his colleagues to recognise that time was too short to allow this. He did not specifically refer to the CPA idea of starting with local elections, which Bremer had now put on the table, but seemed to suggest devolution to a transitional government after popular consultations. Pachachi presented some ideas he had been working up for an interim constitution. None of them persuaded the others. Chalabi painted an elegant picture of an indefinite impasse and, with support from Pachachi and Talabani, insisted that early transfer of power to an Iraqi government was the only way out. I decided at this point to intervene. I suggested that when there was a chicken-and-egg problem, it was sometimes possible to get around it by creating two chickens and two eggs. Laid out in sequence, it was a matter of subjective perception as to which came first. An electoral law would be needed at the start, then a first round of elections. This would enable the constitution to be written by an elected body and then full elections could be held under that new constitution. The Americans listened in stunned silence but did not contradict me, and Jerry Bremer never told me afterwards that he disagreed with my approach. The event went down in the record as the two chickens, two eggs meeting. At least it left the Iraqi side with something to think about.

Abdul Aziz al Hakim spoke, as so often, right at the end. He underlined that Ayatollah Sistani's fatwa on elections before a constitution could not be circumvented. But he added, significantly, that this did not preclude other variations. Bremer had the last word, reminding them who made the ultimate decisions and pointedly asking them not to propose something that they knew he could not accept. He made it clear that he expected the next move to come from the Council.

The Iraqis were left to get on with their own business as we entered into a welter of internal discussions on the Coalition side. Nigel Sheinwald from Number Ten and Lieutenant-General Rob Fry, the Deputy Chief of the Defence Staff responsible for Iraq, came through to sound out Bremer's thinking at first hand and to try to force the pace on decision-making. This was the first direct support I had had from London for my effort to turn the Americans towards a practicable programme. General Abizaid was also back in town and we could have done with his pragmatic input, but he remained invisible because he was concentrating on military reorganisation. Word had begun to get round that Washington was growing more worried about the clock than the niceties of the political evolution in Iraq – 2004 was, after all, a Presidential election year – and was starting to consider a wider range of alternatives, including giving in to Sistani. This put Bremer under increased pressure to deliver results, but he was hard to shift from his chosen course and, in these circumstances and on this timing, close to immune from being replaced. From the UK point of view, he was also the one senior American operator who, for all his inflexibility, was beginning to learn the realities of Iraq.

I briefed Sheinwald and Fry on the latest tussle with the IGC and repeated my firm view that we must tie the Americans down to a decision on as early a transfer of power as made practical sense – perhaps in the early autumn of 2004. We then went in to see Jerry Bremer and went over this ground. He stuck to his red line on constitutional principles before elections, but he indicated that he might be prepared to contemplate an interim constitution if a permanent one was truly blocked by the Sistani fatwa. This seemed to us on the UK side to be the one chance to break the stalemate.

It was at this point that Ambassador Robert Blackwill, one of Condoleezza Rice's deputies in the NSC in Washington with significant Foreign Service and Pentagon experience, appeared for the first of a series of influential spells on the ground in Baghdad. He and Bremer knew each other as colleagues of old, but I never worked out how both of them were able to operate on the political detail in Baghdad at the same time. Blackwill symbolised Washington's impatience and pragmatism. Bremer undoubtedly had the President's support on the principles and – his most significant asset – George W. Bush's personal confidence. Neither gave me an explanation of how their roles fitted together, beyond a comment from Blackwill that senior people in his capital were keen to accelerate the political process and he had come out to lend a hand. This had to indicate some dissatisfaction in Washington with Bremer's performance, but as far as I could tell Bremer had cleared his lines scrupulously with both the Pentagon and the White House as he went along. If Blackwill's arrival suggested that Bremer's team in Baghdad did not have the experience and the voltage to deal with the enormous problems facing them, then this was understandable. Yet it hardly created an atmosphere of clear and confident American leadership.

Blackwill pulled me aside for a private discussion, clearly wanting to know whether I had my own separate views. I explained my twice-round-the-track approach and Blackwill said he had already reached the same conclusion. He thought that Bremer was beginning to come round to it – a comment that indicated that there was no thought in Washington that Bremer could be overridden: the Administrator's authority was a cardinal point. He produced a series of detailed questions about timing, sequence and Iraqi reactions, which were very much to the point and to which I gave answers that stayed within Bremer's lines of tolerance. He indicated that the time-line for a political transition would have to take account of the US election calendar. He thought a process could be devised which set the Governing Council to work on drafting a basic law by May or June 2004, with elections before the end of September (he wanted it earlier than that, but I said that the summer would be too hot) and a handover to an interim Iraqi government by 1 October. This first transitional government would be committed by the basic law to a census, to elections for a constitutional assembly and to the drafting of a permanent constitution by the end of 2005. After that, new elections would take place and Iraq would emerge from the transitional process, fully independent and democratically structured, by the end of 2006. I said that this was something worth discussing with the Iraqis, although I thought that three elections were too many. I told him Jack Straw was due to visit Washington the following week and said I would probably go with him. Blackwill thought this would be a good opportunity to settle the final details of the process.

I met Jalal Talabani later in the day and he told me he had some news. In his position as monthly IGC President, he believed he had brought the Council round to unanimous agreement on an approach consistent with the most flexible variation of the CPA's position, an interim constitution before elections. The Governance team checked with some of the other IGC members and it seemed broadly right. I encouraged Talabani to set the seal on this quickly, if he could, and gave my view that it was probably within reach of the American bottom line. I warned him to be very careful about public presentation, as Blackwill had been emphatic that Washington's reaction could be difficult if they were not in control of any public announcement. Even allowing for the probability that there were still people, including Bremer, who were not yet entirely on board, it seemed that the logjam might have been broken.

I now had to prepare for my visit to Washington with Jack Straw. It was difficult to leave Baghdad while these negotiations were proceeding, especially as a series of insurgency rocket attacks on the Green Zone was further unsettling the team's mood and casting doubt on our security and accommodation arrangements. As soon as I arrived in Washington, I rang for a report from my office in Baghdad and discovered that the latest rocket attack had damaged cars just outside the Republican Palace. A US Marine guard had frightened people for a short while by announcing that the Palace was under attack from infiltrators.

Jack Straw's meeting with Paul Wolfowitz gave us an opportunity to raise the issue of Green Zone security. I knew Wolfowitz slightly from my previous Washington postings and had admired his powerful, questioning mind. From Baghdad, where my information was mostly second-hand, I could see that he was far more attuned than the Defense Secretary or the Vice-President to the need to adapt American decisions to real life in Iraq. At the same time he was so ideologically committed to the rightness of asserting US power and eradicating Saddam Hussein's legacy that he appeared to under-estimate the real threat of strategic failure. The Foreign Secretary tried to engage him in a proper policy discussion but Wolfowitz remained rather stiff and formal. I doubt whether he set much store by the British contribution. I had a go at him on CPA security. I said that the system was still, from the British point of view, taking too long to reach firm decisions on better Green Zone defence. UK civilians were all volunteers and, unless they chose to stay, the United

States would start to run out of allies. With the news just breaking of sixteen Italians killed in a bomb attack in southern Iraq, we could not afford to be anything but proactive in looking after our people. Wolfowitz said he understood this and would follow it up. Over the next few weeks the CPA was indeed more energetic in patrolling the edges of the Green Zone and closing possible approach points. But the underlying philosophy never really changed: there was only so much that could be done and a certain number of casualties were inevitable.

After a very lively session at the CIA, where Jack Straw and George Tenet, the Director, agreed on almost every point in a fairly pessimistic analysis of developments, the Foreign Secretary called on Vice-President Cheney for what he regarded as his most substantive meeting with him in his experience so far. Again we went over the political options and again I sensed that the American side was becoming more concerned about timing than principles. The Vice-President asked what we thought of the new ideas under discussion, partial elections in the summer of 2004 and a transfer of power in the early autumn. Jack Straw underlined the UK's wish to see the Iraqis taking up greater responsibility as soon as possible and asked me to comment on the detail. I said that the new time-lines struck me as an improvement on our earlier policy. Iraqi tolerance was draining away. Security in Iraq could not be achieved unless people saw their lives improving. Taking something of a risk, I pointed to the need to make legitimacy in the eyes of both Iraqis and the international community a more central criterion for our transition plan. We had to accelerate the transfer of power and the creation of new security forces. The Vice-President did not contest these points. He even listened politely to my contention that direct US communication with Syria was worth considering if it brought a more forthcoming approach from them on the Syrian–Iraq border (nothing came of it). Meanwhile Jack Straw took the opportunity to argue for a coordinated US-European dialogue on Iran, a subject that was beginning to occupy his attention almost more than Iraq.

This was the only time I was involved in a discussion of Iraq with the Vice-President. A twenty-five-minute slot was not enough of a basis to make any lasting judgement. I did not gain the impression in Baghdad that he was brought into the detailed operational discussions between the CPA and Washington, but in this conversation he appeared thoroughly familiar with the background. He played well the game of wanting to hear what we had to say and checking that the British, as junior partners, were on board for imminent US decisions. Otherwise he kept his counsel.

Jack Straw went on to see Condoleezza Rice the same morning and the pace picked up. We had discovered that morning that Bremer had taken a snap decision to come back to Washington to be part of this round of discussions. He then went straight back to Baghdad after twenty-four hours in Washington, without pausing to see us along the way. I wondered for a while whether he could not countenance my presence in his capital while he was in Baghdad. This was probably unworthy, as he needed to clear his lines with his principals on the deal to be struck with the Iraqis, but he made no attempt to link in with the British Foreign Secretary or to alert me to his presence in Washington. Condi Rice did not appear to have an agreed transitional plan to present to us. We went into the details of a possible package, containing two sets of elections straddling the writing of a new constitution, and I described the difficulties of arranging elections on a crash timing or in the summer heat. Finally she sought our agreement for a transfer of power to an interim Iraqi government as early as 1 July 2004 in order to move it well clear of the Presidential election campaign. Jack Straw thought that this might just be possible, so long as we avoided elections for the interim government. I said that even indirect elections, with local consultations on candidates for a national assembly, would pose severe problems. Rice's response showed that the calendar was the administration's most important concern. She said she would have the details set down for us shortly. I suspected that we were going to be given a fait accompli.

By the time Jack Straw met Colin Powell for lunch on 13 November, the State Department was able to give us a written timeline for the political process. The objective would be to produce an electoral law, with some constitutional principles in it, before the end of February 2004; to bring in a CPA-selected interim government by July, together with some form of national council chosen on the basis of consultations in the eighteen provinces; to organise a census in Iraq in early 2005 while also holding a mini-election for a constitutional assembly; to place the writing of a new constitution in the first half of 2005; and then to have full elections in late 2005 or early 2006. Powell showed no signs of owning either the process or its outcome. He and Jack Straw were close and they used this occasion to share their frustrations over the twists and turns of US policy. They agreed, however, that the US plan held a prospect of progress.

Colin Powell was distinctly worried about the escalating violence and he was critical of the slow progress the Coalition was making on the ground in training up the Iraqi security forces. He believed that the Pentagon was exaggerating the number of Iraqis capable of performing a security function and therefore over-complacent about the date by which the interim Iraqi administration could take over responsibility from US forces. Straw and Powell also discussed arrangements for President Bush's State Visit to Britain the following week, which they expected to attract large and hostile demonstrations. Richard Armitage, the Deputy Secretary, warned us of possible terrorist attacks on the UK in Iraq aimed at embarrassing the President before or during the State Visit.

So, by the tortuous process of argument behind closed doors, which American administrations often undergo on the way to making difficult decisions, a compromise had been reached between Bremer, with his resistance to early elections, and the White House and the National Security Council, which wished above all to avoid a stalemate. The British input was incidental. I could see Bob Blackwill's hand in the blueprint that had emerged, exploiting my concept of two sets of elections, but grinding out an agreement between Washington and Bremer was a classic intra-American affair. Yet we knew that the legitimacy of an interim government selected by the Americans was likely to be contested in Iraq and internationally. The Governance team in Baghdad had been working hard on a complex system of popular consultations at the municipal and provincial level, termed 'caucuses', to produce locally proposed candidates for an interim assembly without broaching full-scale elections. The problem was that caucuses would be immensely complicated to implement but were unlikely to satisfy the religious Shia. The plan was left on the table and was to cause a good deal of anguish in the weeks to come. At least the approach we heard in Washington had the virtue of giving everyone a part of what they wanted. Bremer had kept at bay the concept of early elections; Ayatollah Sistani and the religious Shia politicians would get elections before a permanent constitution; and Washington had set a timetable for the end of the occupation well before the Presidential elections.

The result left Bremer with a difficult assignment, as he had to square both Washington and a divided IGC. Back in Baghdad, while I was still absent in the UK, he moved quickly to sell Washington's decision to the Iraqis. After all the infighting, there was no room for further adjustments. He was fortunate to have Jalal Talabani as current President. He turned up the pressure on his colleagues to accept that other options were closed and after a contentious discussion the IGC adopted the plan on 15 November by twenty votes to four (the four members closest to Sistani). It was a thin victory and it left scars. The two main poles of influence, the Americans and the religious Shia, had made their weight felt equally. Because his voice resonated like no other with the Iraqi people, Sistani's resistance to American control of the long-term process had proved to be insurmountable. Because the IGC knew that they could not survive on their own in the short term, they gave way grudgingly to their American mentors. As it turned out, the transition plan that emerged from the principles of the 15 November Agreement, for all the difficulties we would meet in its implementation, was a good one. Even against the pressures later in 2004 of the constantly deteriorating security situation and the opposition of Muqtada al Sadr and the militant Shia, the plan held. It gave Iraqis enough of a vision of their future for the majority to remain faithful to it and to that extent it was a solid achievement.

Thinking back on this visit to Washington, the only one I made during my time in Baghdad, I realise that at no time did either side raise the question of weapons of mass destruction and the failure of the Iraq Survey Group, the US investigation unit under David Kay and later Charles Duelfer, to unearth any residual weapons or relevant materials. At that point I was still convinced that hard evidence would somewhere be found that Saddam had concealed small stockpiles. From time to time there were moments of suspense. Soon after I arrived we heard news of the discovery of several fighter aircraft which had been buried in the desert – no mention of how the satellite cameras had missed such an operation – and only came to light when the wind blew away the sand. How much easier to hide barrels of chemical or biological substances! On another occasion the US Army located metal canisters on the bed of the Tigris which they then unaccountably failed to guard. When they returned the next day they had gone. For all the prominence the subject achieved in both our countries because of the enquiries into the intelligence failures, the issue formed no part of the operational purpose of constructing a new Iraq. Even at the UN it was water under the bridge.

The Iraq Survey Group, more than a thousand strong for much of the time, was under the control of the Pentagon and based away from the CPA. While I was briefed once or twice by my team on the lack of progress, I never came across its personnel while I was in Iraq. Bremer received periodic reports of its activities, but kept his distance. He and I did not mention the ISG to each other. The whole area fell increasingly into that category of issues that felt like weights round our ankles but about which nothing could now be done. The politicians would have to do the explaining. The real test now was whether the outcome in Iraq could make the whole effort seem worthwhile.

George Bush's State Visit to the UK the following week passed off without great embarrassment. The Prime Minister took the opportunity to put to the President, after a hard round of preparatory discussions on the British side, which I had gone back to London to join, a hard-hitting paper on security, which was in his view the only real threat to the fulfilment of a respectable political process. The Prime Minister had asked me to put into the paper recommendations for filling those gaps on the ground I had constantly been raising – Sunni disaffection, borders, weapons, security training – which had generated frequent transatlantic telephone calls over the previous weeks. The Blair team was conscious, as I was, that arguments put to the White House were not being translated into action on the ground and the Prime Minister wanted other pressures to weigh on them. He decided that this private paper should reach the President at the same time as a public blast from the Iraqi leadership on the brutality of terrorist tactics in Iraq, to indicate that our Iraqi partners were feeling the pain of poor security. We groaned inwardly, as these things were difficult to produce at the drop of a hat and an initiative of this kind could too easily be traced back to a British source. But Simon Shercliff and I managed to discover where Jalal Talabani was over the following few hours and I persuaded him, halfway through a visit to Ankara, to speak up publicly the next day.

I returned to Baghdad on 20 November as the news filtered through that the religious Shia members of the Iraqi Governing Council were beginning to rebel against the 15 November Agreement. Having voted against it, they felt entitled to continue resisting it. Bremer held an immediate meeting of the Presidential Nine in his villa. True to predictions, Abdul Aziz al Hakim, Ibrahim al Jaafari and Mohammed Bahr al Uloom began to complain vigorously about the plan for caucuses. With telling inconsistency, given their previous demand for early national elections, they now wanted the Governing Council to continue to run the country through the early part of the transitional process. Bremer pushed back but more gently than usual. In this he followed the advice of his newly appointed Deputy for Policy, Dick Jones, a career Foreign Service officer who was concurrently the US Ambassador in Kuwait, that we should reject any changes to the agreement but play things long. I described to the Iraqis the enthusiastic reaction of President Bush and Prime Minister Blair in London to the achievement of the 15 November plan and suggested that their concerns on the detail should be dealt with in the implementation. The Presidential Nine decided to go into a huddle amongst themselves and Bremer asked me to find Jalal Talabani, bring him back to Baghdad and persuade him to take his place in the chair. Otherwise, by the rules of rotation, Abdul Aziz al Hakim would be presiding.

After the others had left, Hakim stayed behind in the villa to talk to Bremer. I was not invited to stay but neither was I asked to leave, so I sat in. There then emerged, more clearly than before, the real reason for his hesitations. He asked Bremer for private guarantees that the proposed transition process would not deny the Shia community their natural majority in Iraq. Bremer politely explained that this majority was what a democratic process was likely to produce. Hakim remained uncomfortable: this was not what he meant. With some degree of circumlocution he conveyed that he was asking for a pre-ordained fix. He would rather not abandon the IGC process if he could avoid it, but he wanted the Americans to give him a basis for explaining to his own community that they would not have power stolen from them by American manipulation. In other words, the religious Shia wanted elections with pre-ordained results. The exchange bore out Bremer's concern for entrenching the principles of democracy before elections. He left Hakim and his colleagues with the clear implication that if they tried to reverse the decision the IGC had taken on 15 November, the US would no longer be able to work through the IGC. That seemed to do the trick, at least for the time being.

17

The Shia Resist

So it was that the Coalition Provisional Authority entered a long period of debate, negotiation and agony over the implementation of the 15 November Agreement. Ayatollah Sistani and the religious Shia did not let go of their antipathy to the appointment of an interim government that might then be hard to remove, or to any electoral process that they believed could be influenced by the United States. Scott Carpenter and his Governance team toiled away in the far reaches of the Republican Palace, making up with ingenuity for their lack of experience of the real Iraq, in an effort to create a system short of actual elections that would ensure that the incoming government would reflect the wishes of the Iraqi people. I knew they wished the British would leave them alone to try to satisfy Bremer as they saw best, but we kept on intruding with reminders of the raw ingredients they were working with: this was a proud and humiliated people who would not accept a system presented from outside unless they felt some ownership of it. The complexity of the proposed caucus process they were proposing defeated their purpose because it aroused the suspicions not only of the Shia politicians but also of ordinary Iraqis, as malicious rumours began to circulate. We went through endless discussions trying to bring the various pieces together in some new adaptation of the plan. But somehow we could never get the polarities of the magnet right. Weeks went by without any real progress being made either on the mechanics for creating a transitional administration or on the drafting of a basic law. The 15 November Agreement held, but its implementation was going nowhere. The shadow of the Grand Ayatollah hung over it.

During this whole period the CPA had to contend with a separate political influence, the only one in this period besides Sistani to make an impact on the political process from outside the Iraqi Governing Council. The renegade Shia cleric Muqtada al Sadr, the son of an important and popular Ayatollah killed off by Saddam several years earlier, had gradually been gaining a following among the poorer and more disaffected urban Shia. Picking up on the growing Shia dissatisfaction with the postponement of national elections, he went so far as to declare himself leader of a provisional Iraqi government. Bremer had wanted to have him arrested back in August, when his potential for trouble had emerged. When he consulted the British, whose responsibility for the south-east of Iraq would have been affected, the Ministry of Defence in particular decided that the situation was too fragile to risk a confrontation. They assumed that the cleric's influence would fade with time. For months after that Bremer complained that the British had prevented him from dealing with the problem when the cost would have been relatively low. It was a difficult call. A direct confrontation might have excited the poor Shia community in Baghdad, together with the combustible societies in the intensely religious cities of Najaf and Kerbala, into a resistance to the occupation that would have matched our problem with the Sunnis. After the events of 2004, when Muqtada al Sadr had to be confronted militarily but was never satisfactorily contained, we had to accept that Bremer had been right.

What made our task all the more difficult was the threatened emergence of a new and powerful militia. An important focus of Bremer's policy for the creation of a stable Iraq was his insistence that the centre should be in proper control and that it should operate on well-established principles. Throughout his time in the saddle, Bremer pushed for solid rules and audit systems to prevent corruption in the ministries. He worked hard to establish lines of control from the centre to the provinces. He removed police chiefs whose venality or disloyalty could not be ignored. In particular, he stipulated that the State alone must be responsible for security and that private militias should be disbanded. The last of these was particularly tricky. For a start, the Kurds refused to integrate their own fighting forces, the Peshmerga, without whom they would not have survived Saddam's constant hostility, into the new Iraqi security forces. The main religious Shia party in the south, SCIRI, took a similar approach to the Badr Corps, whose history was partly heroic, since they had resisted Saddam's rule as best they could, and partly suspect, since their ties to the regime in Tehran and its security apparatus were strong. The Sunnis had never developed a community militia, as they normally had representatives in power in Baghdad in both the political and the military spheres. Part of our trouble during this period was that the Sunnis felt marginalised by developments and were now casting around to fill the gap, feeding both the Baathist insurgency and localised support for al Qaida. Even individual politicians, such as Ahmed Chalabi, collected their own private security units around them and ran their own intelligence machines. Without strong central control, Iraq could easily have relapsed into a mosaic of local baronies, awash with weaponry. Bremer's instincts in this case were spot on.

It was thus a considerable surprise to the CPA when, in November 2003, General John Abizaid, the CENTCOM Commander, suddenly proposed that the militias should be formed into a security force in support of the central authority. He wanted to bring unofficial armies in off the streets, but he was taking a risk in appearing to legitimise them and thus encouraging others to form. He called together some of the senior members of the Iraqi Governing Council and put his idea to them. The Kurdish leaders and Chalabi looked like cats with the cream. Iyad Allawi, who understood the murky depths of Iraqi security tensions better than anyone, could not believe his ears. Ibrahim al Jaafari, who had not been invited, was livid when he discovered that the Dawa Party militia had been ignored.

Bremer himself had severe doubts, but Abizaid – perhaps with pressure building on him from Washington to speed up the establishment of a capable Iraqi security sector – had decided that the threat of an unstoppable deterioration in security required a proactive response from the US military. Bremer was not in a position to overrule him when the civilian and military wings of US action in Iraq held equal status under the Secretary of Defense. Abizaid had a detailed paper written, which set out the procedures and rules for amalgamating the militias into a parastatal structure and more or less told us to get on with it. The basic idea was fair enough: the recruiting area for the new Iraqi Army and police should be enlarged and the militias denied their independent capability. The rules were carefully written to prevent particular groups from taking over a unit. Iraqi politicians, however, saw it differently: they spotted the opportunity for a double game, whereby the militias would be given a more authoritative status while preserving their sectarian loyalties. The tension between the two, in the months that followed, was never dissipated.

Then there was Saddam Hussein. We had by now begun to assume that, like Osama bin Laden, he might evade capture indefinitely. It seemed increasingly unlikely that he was in a position to give orders to the insurgency or to rally a powerful resistance around him again, but the fact that he was at large remained a blot on the Coalition's record. General Sanchez had devoted a considerable force of special troops to hunt him down and on several occasions they had come close to catching him. But Saddam knew the terrain too well from his early years of evading the authorities when he was out of favour.

In mid-December I travelled back to New York to catch up with my UN contacts and call on the Secretary-General. Waking up one morning in the guest-room of my old apartment in Beekman Place, I switched on the radio and caught the middle of a press conference. It was Bremer's voice, with that distinctive note of satisfaction in it: 'Ladies and gentlemen,' [pause] 'we got him!' My first thought was selfish: as with the 15 November Agreement, I had missed a seminal Baghdad moment. Then I allowed in a huge feeling of relief that this stain on the Coalition had been wiped clean. It restored invaluable momentum to our efforts after November's depressing slew of ambushes and suicide attacks. Unfortunately, in spite of the useful intelligence that came from the contents of Saddam's briefcase, the capture had no long-term impact on the strength of the insurgents. They had by now learnt to generate their own energy.

While in New York I wanted to report back to the Security Council on the progress being made by the Coalition. This was scotched by the Americans, who did not want a British voice taking on this task. My successor at the UN, Emyr Jones Parry, arranged a private lunch instead and I managed to get into my usual sparring match with Sergey Lavrov, who was indignant that the Security Council had been left so short of information. He was right, of course. I had the peg of Saddam's capture on which to hang a more upbeat report than would have been the case a day earlier. My former colleagues were not inclined to be aggressive: they just wanted to know what was going on. For their part, they confirmed that the UN remained racked with grief over the loss of Sergio de Mello and his team and anger over the war, and were most unlikely to have any contribution to make for the foreseeable future.

That afternoon I took the long elevator up to the thrty-eighth floor and sat in the little waiting-room gazing at the clear view out to the sea and wondering how to describe my Baghdad experience to Kofi Annan. Once in the familiar dark-panelled office, its desk still bare of papers, I was given as warm a greeting as ever, but I could see the strain of the past few months in his eyes. It would have been good to talk about something other than his least favourite subject and I knew that the UK's partnership with the Americans had widened the distance between us. I said straightaway how much I missed Sergio, not expecting – and not getting – more than a look of anguish in response. I then went over the implications of the 15 November Agreement and suggested how the United Nations might most easily re-insert itself into Iraq. Note-takers were present and I had to be careful how I described the risk of stalemate between the CPA and Ayatollah Sistani. Kofi Annan had a brief in front of him but left it unopened. He was in a firm mood about what he wanted from the coming period. Fortunately his requirements were modest and I did not have to argue against him. He accepted that it would be hard to get a UN team into Iraq in the first few months of 2004 and recognised that an external team making occasional visits could not be the same thing. His goal was to have a full group on the ground by the beginning of July 2004, when an Iraqi interim government was likely to be in place. I suggested it might be an idea to call a meeting in New York in January, with both the IGC and the CPA present, to relate the drafting of the new basic law to the requirements of recent Security Council resolutions. I said I did not know whether the Americans would agree to it, but it was one way of showing that the UN remained in play. It was encouraging to hear that he thought the agreement a good one under the circumstances. He was much more sceptical, however, about the Coalition's real capacity to control events through the coming year. We were both skirting round overt criticism of the handling of the post-conflict period and I did not try to change his view.

Back in Baghdad I saw few signs of progress. David Richmond had been trying to persuade the CPA to initiate a process of popular consultation on the implementation of the 15 November Agreement, but Bremer decided he could not afford to risk the unravelling of the tense compromise in the IGC – understandable in the short term but a dangerous postponement of the real issue of what the Iraqi people would stomach. I supported David – I thought this a cardinal issue – but we made no impact.

Things began to slow down for the Christmas break. I had been trying hard to persuade the Foreign Office that Anne should be allowed to join me in Baghdad for the Christmas period onwards. She had been involved with women's issues at the UN and I had received a warm request from the CPA section dealing with civil society and democratic initiatives to recruit her for their next stage of work. The Foreign Office, however, saw her primarily as a spouse and decided that it would be wrong for the boss to have his wife out for Christmas if the others could not. Anne's capacity for maximising the fun when festivities were due would have gone down well in Baghdad, but there it was. She eventually came out in January and spent six weeks helping the enthusiastic but disparate women's organisations sort themselves into some kind of effective operation.

In December, after seven months non-stop on the job, Bremer finally decided that he needed to take a proper break. Most of the senior Americans followed his example. The place virtually closed down for the week of Christmas and under those circumstances it was deemed safe to leave me officially in charge of the country. Of my team, David Richmond returned for a well-earned family holiday and I sent Simon Shercliff after him for a very necessary escape, given that he was beginning to fall asleep at meetings in the middle of taking the record. Raad Alkadiri drew the short straw. He had lasted longer than almost anyone else in Baghdad without respite but remained open to exploitation with his cheerful enthusiasm for the job in hand. We settled down to a sparse Christmas, buoyed up by warm messages from the Foreign Office and the prospect of a consignment of Christmas goodies (which arrived sometime in the New Year). Maybe the surroundings put me in a petty mood, but I thought it a bit rich that I was asked to pass the Prime Minister's greeting cards on to members of the Iraqi Governing Council without a single card or word for the UK team.

Having wondered so many times in the three previous months what I would do differently if I were running Iraq, I found myself in a curious predicament. I did not hold the levers for activating the American system and would probably make a fool of myself if I tried.

What could be done anyway in a mere week? Raad and I had some private fun with the symbolism of a British proconsul in Iraq eighty years on from Sir Percy Cox and T. E. Lawrence, but we did not move far from the Green Zone and no surprise edicts emerged from the Republican Palace that week. I enjoyed running the CPA morning meeting in the more transparent British style and felt I was getting a response from the American section heads, who opened up with their thoughts on how to sell Coalition objectives more proactively to ordinary Iraqis. But my primary responsibility was to ensure that nothing went wrong and I spread the warning that no one was to think of celebrating the holiday out in the streets of Baghdad. Christmas dinner comprised tough steak and East European wine from the culinary desert of the Rasheed Hotel.

When Bremer returned on 30 December, the melancholy lifted with the sudden restoration of dynamic activity. He ran straight into an escalation of Shia resentment over the time it would take to reach national elections. I had kept in close touch with senior members of the Governing Council, and knew that something was brewing. Bremer was not pleased to discover that, the day before his return, the Governing Council had agreed to send a letter to the UN Secretary-General asking him to intervene in the political process. This was a religious Shia initiative to undermine the American timetable and the idea of appealing to the UN had come out of the blue. I felt badly let down because I had made it clear to them that they were to make no moves until the Administrator had been consulted: they had no independent authority without his say-so. The letter asked for an opinion from an expert UN team about the possibility of conducting elections for a provisional national assembly. Only if the UN declared this to be impracticable would the Governing Council look at alternatives such as caucuses or an appointed interim government.

The CPA team immediately tried to stop the letter, but it had been faxed through to the Iraqi Delegation in New York and delivered with unusual efficiency. Washington was asked to take action to nullify its effect. Scott Carpenter and Meghan O'Sullivan sardonic-ally pointed out that it was probably better this time to let the Governing Council stew for having acted without consultation. Bremer, however, immediately summoned Abdul Aziz al Hakim, the Council President responsible for pushing this decision through while most of his senior colleagues were absent, and took him to task. I joined in, asking why he had deliberately gone against my advice the previous day. Hakim blustered that we were making too much of it. Why should the UN not be involved? Bremer responded that he had been misusing his position to serve a minority view: Washington was livid and had already approached Annan with a request for him to ignore the letter. After the meeting I telephoned Jack Straw and asked him to put in his own call to Annan, which he immediately did.

New Year's Eve brought the weekly Governing Council meeting. After a brief reference to his visit to Washington, where the President had reiterated to him his firm support for the 15 November Agreement, Bremer launched into a tough criticism of the Council's letter to Annan. Not only had the Iraqis failed to consult the CPA, but what they had done was incompatible with the 15 November Agreement. The Council began to divide. Adnan Pachachi, as the senior Sunni voice, asked pointedly what all the rush had been over the letter and why the full Council had not been consulted. The Shia members supported Abdul Aziz al Hakim, with Ahmed Chalabi particularly prominent in his defence as he gradually began to build his alliance with the organised Shia parties. Ibrahim al Jaafari and Mowaffaq al Rubaie, an active but lay religious Shia, tried to underline the importance of respect for 'the religious authorities', meaning Sistani, who had been agitating for months to dilute US control of the political process. Hakim kept on asking what all the fuss what about. Hadn't it always been agreed that the UN should play a role? The other non-Shia stayed silent, not quite sure what was going on and timid about opposing the voice of Sistani.

Bremer and I refused to retreat. Angrier now than we had ever been, we emphasised that the only way forward was for the

Governing Council and the CPA to work together and for the 15 November Agreement to be implemented. Bremer said firmly that he would make no further proposals. It would be up to the Council to propose the next steps when they had sorted out their differences. The meeting broke up in a cold atmosphere.

When we arrived back at the Republican Palace, a telegram awaited us reporting on Jack Straw's call to Kofi Annan. The Secretary-General had made it clear that he did not wish to be caught between the Iraqi Governing Council and the Coalition Provisional Authority. I sent a copy to the other end of the office for Jerry Bremer to read. He then came along to my office – for the first and last time in my six months there – for a quick and good-natured discussion on what we should now do. We came to the conclusion that the Secretary-General should be asked to send a brief and anodyne reply, reconfirming his view that early elections were impracticable and making no reference to the sending of an expert team. That was in fact the way the incident ended. What we had not achieved was any reduction in the strength of Shia resistance to the 15 November Agreement.

We then remembered that it was, after all, New Year's Eve. I began the evening at Maude House, the residence of Major-General Andrew Figgures, the senior British officer in Baghdad. He had set up a table of roll-a-dice horse-racing and I immediately lost ten dollars. Then, going against my own strict instruction that no one should leave the Green Zone on such an obviously vulnerable date, I crossed the city to Adnan Pachachi's house where we nibbled on an assortment of Arab goodies and listened to an Iraqi trio playing Egyptian music. It was not long before we heard the news of a bad bombing at a Christian-owned restaurant not far away. No Coalition personnel seemed to have been involved: sadly, it was again Iraqis who suffered. My Royal Military Police team drove me back to the Green Zone at breakneck speed through increasingly deserted streets. Finally I joined the party at the British Villa, where I now had a much more comfortable room to myself. We consumed the requisite amounts of booze and amazed the CPA Governance team with a loud and unmusical rendering of 'Auld Lang Syne'. Finally, collapsed on my bed upstairs in the villa, I telephoned round the family to wish them a Happy New Year. I found Anne at a house-party in the South of France, in the middle of a five-course dinner. They were impressed that I had managed to get to three parties in one evening, less so with the description of my recent eating habits, and we exchanged the hope that 2004 would produce a more peaceful life for the semi-retired.

As the year turned, I decided that it was time to give London a forecast for the last six months of the occupation. Every discussion table I had so far attended was stacked with half-full and half-empty glasses. The determinedly optimistic reports of the Americans seemed to all of us to clash with the trend, while the UK's regular harping on what could still go wrong meshed better with the realities but was uninspiring. Bremer was adept at keeping bad news in its place and tenacious in his regular presentation of the bright spots to the US media and to Congress, whose representatives arrived in Baghdad every three or four weeks to examine the scene. He nevertheless seemed to me to have learnt over the eight months of his administration that creating a new Iraq would involve more than the expression of US willpower and the delivery of vigorous action. Because his incisive mind focused so sharply on the areas he selected for attention and because he tended to close down discussion on the darker regions beyond, it was hard to define the extent to which he was adjusting to the impact of new Iraqi politics. But I could see that he was gradually parting company with the ideology he had carried out with him at the start. Paradoxically, as his capacity to adapt to circumstances grew, his stock in Washington began to fall. This was partly because his earlier predictions of steady progress were not being borne out, but partly also because the Sistani problem threatened to disrupt the White House's election planning.

I wanted my 1 January assessment to stand the test of time without succumbing to gloomy prognostications. I listed the principal obstacles still confronting the Coalition. The insurgency was by now entrenched. The opposition possessed men, materials and motivation in ineradicable quantities and would not be defeated within the transition period, even if their impact was greater at the tactical than the strategic level. While most of the ministries were beginning to get into their stride under IGC and CPA supervision, there was still no sign of a credible political leadership for a united Iraq, nor of an effective command capability for the nascent security forces. Donor money, including US funding, was flowing in too slowly. The implementation of the political process was at risk. The provision of essential utilities and services was far behind target and the shortages, added to the perception of poor security, were costing us support and consent. Jobs were scarce. The Coalition was fundamentally unpopular. Because the CPA's public voice in Iraq was so weak and the idea of popular consultation on the new political process had been rejected, we could not claim to be in touch with the Iraqi people. Most of the neighbours were unfriendly. Turning all or even some of that round in the remaining six months would present an enormous challenge.

At this point in my draft, I wondered what I could possibly offer on the other side of the ledger to compensate for that formidable string of downsides. I had to dig deep. I said it was a plus that the Coalition retained forward momentum. The military had had a good few weeks and the insurgency was faltering. The Coalition – or, more precisely, US public opinion – had learnt to absorb losses. No political opposition of broad appeal had emerged to challenge the Iraqi politicians we had selected and Sistani was a net plus because he opposed violence and advocated a unified Iraq. The new Iraqi currency was appreciating and commerce was starting to flow internally. There was a platform here for eventual success. But – and this was the point of the telegram – there would have to be one more heavy investment of effort. Neither Washington nor London should expect a reduction in the number of forces on the ground during 2004. The Iraq theatre remained a security crisis and all our people needed daily protection.

I asked for an acceleration in the disbursement of funds. Filling the gaps now was more important than keeping money back for later stages. Bremer could do with help from London in getting this message across in Washington. The CPA itself needed reinforcement: it could no longer afford to shape itself as a brilliant cowboy operation (I hesitated over this phrase, but left it in: how better to describe both the resourcefulness and the inadequacy of 1,300 foreigners, many of them young, idealistic and inexperienced, trying to run the civil affairs of an unmalleable population of twenty-five million?). We had now to broaden out the competence of our effort: not just pummel the insurgency but reach out and persuade suspicious Iraqis to rethink their opposition; invest in a new justice system; treat political compromise as a strength not a weakness. The enterprise could go right and it could go wrong. Too much was at stake to duck the costs of pulling the odds a little further our way.

In one sense my New Year's Day message was poorly timed. On 4 January, the Prime Minister paid a brief, unannounced visit to Basra with a party of UK press photographers to see the British troops there and Bremer and I were asked to go down and brief him on developments. Blair had come straight from a family holiday in Egypt and my round-up had not passed through the London bureaucracy quickly enough to reach him. In fifty minutes of discussion in the dimly lit guest-room of the Basra airport building, the British Forces HQ, we were unable to get into the depths of the issues. It was in any case Jerry Bremer's show: I could not contradict his efficient no-notes assessment, sober but not alarmist on the security situation, robust on the Sistani problem, open-minded on bringing the UN back in, rather too rosy on the economy and infrastructure. The Prime Minister asked a few questions, but clearly decided that this was not the moment to push for answers on the difficult issues. I kicked myself later for missing an opportunity, but I felt at the time that this

348

was one of those moments when his self-protection mechanism cut in to insulate him from the painful realities of the Iraq saga.

Adnan Pachachi was the incoming President for the month of January. As our first action of the New Year, Bremer and I went to see him about the drafting of the new Transitional Administrative Law (TAL), as the new set of interim constitutional principles was to be called. This time I drove through the streets with Jerry in his convoy – two Humvees with open machine-gun nests in the lead; a look-alike, blacked-out Suburban swerving back and forth across the street just ahead of us; then the second Suburban for the 'Principal'; another Suburban behind; and then another couple of Humvees. Overhead, two Little Bird helicopters scoured for ambushes. Any unsuspecting Iraqi driver meandering along on his own side of the road, minding his own business, was swooped upon and pressed – without physical contact, just – into the gutter. Traffic at intersections was held up in advance by more Humvees. To the Iraqi eye, the whole business could not be so very different from Saddam's time. But I remembered that Bremer's car had been raked by gunfire on the road to the airport not long before and the violence confronting us was not a joke.

Pachachi understood without needing to be told what his task would be that month. As both President of the IGC and Chairman of the Drafting Committee for the Transitional Administrative Law, he had to take the lead in steering between the two most prominent rocks on the road: Sistani on the one side and the Kurds on the other. Bremer laid heavy emphasis on the implementation of the 15 November Agreement as it stood. Pachachi wanted to go and see the Ayatollah himself, to work out a deal, but as a secular Sunni he was unlikely to carry the necessary weight. We persuaded him to wait a while longer, to see whether the religious Shia had learnt a lesson from their failure to get away with the letter to Kofi Annan. That initiative had not been the only one attempted by Abdul Aziz al Hakim while Bremer was absent over Christmas. He had also driven through a proposal (Resolution 137) that the women of Iraq should be treated strictly according to Islamic law, causing widespread horror amongst the enthusiastic liberals of Baghdad and the north. Maysoon al Damluji, as Deputy Minister of Culture one of the rare women ministers and a close associate of Pachachi's, was pleased to hear in that same meeting that Bremer, without whose approval no government decision could be made, would refuse to sign any such legislation if it came to him for approval.

Bremer next decided to take on the Kurds, who still had to be persuaded that a united Iraq was in their best interests. 2 January was chosen as the day for our first round with the Kurdish leadership and Bremer's team in one Black Hawk and the British and other hangers-on in the second set off for the northern city of Irbil. Flying with the boss was an aerial version of the drive through Baghdad. A third, decoy, Black Hawk full of security men flew alongside, while two heavily armed Apaches circled around at a distance like sheepdogs in the sky, swooping over villages ahead of us to check them out for trouble and exposing themselves bravely in the process, as they flew low enough to be attacked by rocket-propelled grenades. Sheep, goats, donkeys and birds scattered in panic beneath us as we roared along, while people stared up in sudden surprise. I was interested to see that most Iraqis in the countryside waved at us, but two or three smallholders leapt forward and grabbed a few stones to hurl bad-temperedly as we passed over. I took the gesture as deep-felt concern for their chickens.

Once we had reached the hilltop hotel outside Irbil, beyond the northern foothills, which looked amazingly green after the recent rains, Jalal Talabani and Masoud Barzani soon appeared, the first time I had ever seen the two men together. The contrast in their personalities – avuncular charm on the one hand and mountain grit on the other – came through even more plainly than when we saw them separately. But the substance this time was deadly serious for us all. Bremer had prepared a hardline approach and warned them they could not dictate their version of the TAL's federal structure. Neither one tried to argue for a separate Kurdistan. They knew that this was unrealistic in the present circumstances, with Turkey breathing over them and support from the US and the UK most improbable. But they did press their arguments for minimal interference from Baghdad and embellished them with a long history of the reasons why, which Bremer had to bring to a halt to preserve our chances of getting back to Baghdad before nightfall.

We went carefully through the various points that would need to be settled in the TAL negotiation, saying very firmly that all the long-term issues, such as the status of Kirkuk and the detail of the federal relationship, would have to be left to the new permanent constitution. The two Kurds fought back with determination, until Bremer and I jointly unveiled our trump card: they could not expect the protection of the US and UK Governments, which had served them so well over the previous twelve years, if they did not recognise the limits at this stage of the transition. I had no idea whether London would actually back this up if it came to the test, but a line had to be drawn or we would never find a way forward. Jerry then threw in a nicely timed sweetener: the United States would ensure that Arab Iraq would not be in a position to reverse the degree of devolution granted to the Kurdish region once it was agreed within the IGC. Barzani and Talabani breathed an audible sigh of relief. We decided to deliver one last warning. We told them that their henchmen's behaviour in Kirkuk, where the Kurds were now in a majority and throwing their weight around, was unacceptable. The minorities in Kurdish territory had to be respected or the Kurdish minority in Iraq would not deserve the same treatment. We would not tolerate the correction of Saddam's abuses by Saddam's methods. They took the point. Our group flew back down through the wintry sunset and on into the dark, satisfied with the afternoon's work.

Now that we had secured the basis for the Kurds' cooperation, the principal obstacle to a transitional law was Grand Ayatollah Sistani. This remarkable Iranian-born Shia cleric, who had barely left the precinct of the Najaf mosque and his adjoining house for thirty-seven years and yet filled the need of virtually all Iraqi Shias, indeed most

Iraqi Arabs, for paternal guidance in their public affairs, showed an extraordinarily perceptive understanding of the real political battle lines. I always felt that his influence on developments in this unprecedented period of Iraq's history was, on balance, positive. He preached for an Iraq united in justice and against violence. He kept the Shia community as calm as he could in the face of bitter provocation from extremist Sunni terrorism. He understood the need to protect Iraq's independence from neighbourly interference, including Iran's. Rejecting the temptation to take on a political role, which he realised most Iraqis wanted to see separated from religious duty, he steadfastly refused ever to meet a representative of the Coalition. He was deeply suspicious of American motives and determined to prevent the Shias of Iraq from being robbed of their natural majority. But he also realised that without the Americans Saddam Hussein would never have been removed and that the presence of Coalition forces was necessary for a while to stop Iraqis from tearing their country apart.

These considerations held Sistani back from issuing a fatwa against the 15 November Agreement. But he did not like it. He did not accept the American contention that early elections were impracticable, believing that this was their excuse for hanging on to power through their appointed proxies. The US-proposed alternative, local caucuses to produce popular candidates for a transitional assembly, seemed to him no less complex or vulnerable to violence than full elections. He disliked the idea of an American-shaped law for the transitional period, fearing that principles would be established that were alien to Islam and the Iraqi way. He never abandoned his judgement that national elections should precede any other step in the political process. Hence the end-December appeal to the UN from Abdul Aziz al Hakim, which we read as probably a genuine if mishandled attempt to square the circle and bring Sistani on board. The Grand Ayatollah rejected the UN Secretary-General's reply to the Hakim letter, which upheld the UN's doubt about early elections, as over-influenced by the US.

Bremer's frustration grew. He was not going to give in to Sistani on elections and he put his Governance team through seemingly endless variations of the caucuses concept. I supported him on the first and remained agnostic on the second, expecting it to collapse under the weight of its own impracticability. The pressure from Washington for a solution steadily increased as the implications of a long stalemate sank in. The National Security Council had gradually taken over the management of the politics of Iraq from the Pentagon over the previous few weeks, responding to President Bush's insistence that there should be better coordination within the administration after an autumn of growing fractiousness between the various departments. I only picked up odd hints of the full story, as I realised that Bremer's telephone calls to Washington were increasingly going to Condoleezza Rice rather than to Donald Rumsfeld and as press stories commented on the Defense Secretary's attempts to separate himself from responsibility for the lack of progress. The immediate symptom on the ground in Iraq was that Ambassador Robert Blackwill's pragmatic but, in the context of Iraqi politics, heavy-handed influence increasingly made itself felt.

The State Department began to come more into the picture as the prospect of the end of the occupation period advanced and Bremer was irritated to find Secretary Powell telling the UN Secretary-General that the United States might well invite the UN to play a more active role. But there did not seem to be any alternative route that offered progress. Once UN headquarters realised that Washington was unlikely to reject the idea, Kofi Annan did indeed take up my proposal to call a meeting in New York of Iraqi, CPA and UN representatives. However strong the Administrator's reluctance, meeting Sistani's appeal for a UN judgement on when elections might be possible seemed to be the only way to break the impasse.

As these pressures built up, I took myself away from Baghdad for a spell. The British Embassy in Tehran had finally arranged a day's programme for me there, overcoming the resentment I had caused a few weeks earlier when the *Guardian* newspaper highlighted a remark

I made about the Iranian inclination to meddle in Iraq's affairs. I knew that I would not achieve any change of heart in Tehran, but I had set myself the task of offering a briefing from the coal-face to each of the six neighbouring capitals. So colourful were the circulating rumours about the Coalition's intentions to use Iraq for their own nefarious purposes that I think it helped, in my long conversations with Foreign Minister Kharazzi and other senior Iranian officials, to go over the reasons why we wanted to hand over power as soon as possible and why the best sort of Iraq for Iran would be a stable, economically prosperous neighbour interested in trade and a peaceful life. London's approach, which I thought eminently sensible, was aimed at creating relationships all round that would promote that outcome. Passing back briefly through Baghdad, I reported these thoughts to Jerry Bremer, who was not in the slightest bit interested. To him Iran remained a source of trouble and little else. I had to admit that it was difficult to argue with him when reports of Iranian machinations in Iraq were coming through regularly. But this did not exorcise my instinct that in the longer term it was better to engage Iran than to threaten confrontation.

After an idyllic few days skiing in Switzerland it was time to catch up with London's assessment of where we were heading. Since things did not seem to be going too badly around Basra, the Foreign Office was inclined to believe that it must be possible to turn round the security situation further north. They did not really know whether to accept my judgement that without Coalition reinforcements violence would continue, even escalate, into the indefinite future. Most people thought I was right, but since the political and economic areas were so interconnected with security, higher troop numbers were not necessarily going to solve the problem on their own. In any case, they appeared to be ruled out by the United States. I decided to stop bashing my head against that particular wall. The US and the UK had to stay and finish the job: to depart defeated was unthinkable. Together, we had chosen to do the task this way and we had to bear the costs. From then on, my line in public and in private was that perseverance would in the end be effective, so long as both the Coalition and the Iraqi people could tolerate the worst days of violence. My overt message was that it was doable, with pain. Privately, I could not be sure that we were not heading for failure.

In London I heard that the date for a UN meeting had now been fixed for 19 January. In Number Ten Downing Street, Nigel Sheinwald wanted to know whether the Sistani problem could be circumvented: perhaps the Prime Minister should try for direct contact with the Grand Ayatollah to convince him that our publicly expressed aims were genuine. I advised against: a rejection was too likely, Washington would be cross and the press would make a meal of it. We had no alternative but to leave the Americans in the lead and make the most of UN involvement – if it happened: I thought the UN Secretariat would resist being drawn back into action inside Iraq just to dig the United States out of the deepening pit.

18

Growing Anxiety in Washington

Before taking the flight to New York for the UN meeting I decided to risk a telephone call to Kofi Annan from London. Always approachable but never easy to advise, the Secretary-General would, I knew, be trying to avoid two undesirable outcomes: risking more UN lives on a US problem and seeing the UN left on the sidelines of the most significant security issue of his tenure. The 19 January gathering would be his first direct and public involvement on the details of Iraq since the Canal Hotel bombing in August. When I reached him, he seemed glad to go over some of the sensitivities in bringing together the CPA and the Iraqi leadership on his own home ground. He told me that he was not ready to decide whether the UN should help out over the transition timetable, but he accepted that a team should prepare for a role in Baghdad once the Iraqis had taken back responsibility for governing themselves and he saw that this could be linked with assisting the selection process for the proposed national assembly and government. I pointed out the opportunity presented by Washington's need for help at this precise moment: they genuinely wanted the UN to play a vital role now in the political process. He took the point, but I could tell that, unsurprisingly, his instinct was for caution.

John Sawers travelled with me to New York to represent the Foreign Office and we sought out our US and UN Secretariat counterparts for a round of preliminary skirmishing. We knew the Americans were at last serious about bringing the UN in when Robert Blackwill started to talk about the possibility of engaging Lakhdar Brahimi for the task. Brahimi, who was coming to the end of his remarkable stint as UN Special Representative in Afghanistan, was well known for his independence of mind and his capacity for making uncomfortable proposals. Washington's desire to capture his credibility and authority was a clear sign it was now prepared to pay a price for the legitimising involvement of the United Nations. On the UN side, Kieran Prendergast, the British Under-Secretary-General for Political Affairs, predicted that Annan would remain reserved about next steps, and that Brahimi would be extremely reluctant to be dragged into Iraq when he had so firmly opposed the invasion. We would be in for a difficult time if, when the Americans had finally brought themselves to accept a genuine role for the United Nations, the latter turned them down. We failed to hold any preparatory meeting with the IGC delegation. Adnan Pachachi, Ahmed Chalabi, Abdul Aziz al Hakim and Mohsen Abdul Hamid, accompanied by the Ministers of Foreign Affairs and Planning, passed us in the corridor as we each attended our separate meetings with the Secretary-General. The choreography was telling: it looked as though the UN was bringing two warring parties together to try to broker a solution. No wonder Bremer looked so uncomfortable with it all.

Down in the bowels of the UN building in cramped Conference Room 8, selected no doubt because it was the only meeting-room with a circular table, Annan led off the main meeting with a brief and judicious introduction, asking to hear whatever assessments people had to offer. Pachachi and Bremer followed with unorchestrated but consonant appeals for the UN to send a team to Iraq to assess options for choosing the transitional assembly. The Secretary-General missed my bid to speak immediately after Bremer and brought in Abdul Aziz

al Hakim, who starkly distanced himself from the 15 November
Agreement and his Iraqi colleagues by expressing an explicit
preference for early direct elections. I countered this by underlining
the series of elections agreed on 15 November and suggested that we
should all be able to agree on steps short of elections in 2004 that
were as representative, transparent and inclusive as possible under
the circumstances. With a mildly hypocritical but loyal nod to
current CPA policy, I proposed that the parties represented around
the table should arrange to hold a detailed discussion of the caucus
concept, which could be seen as introducing an advance element of
democracy into the process; but I said that early national elections
were not going to be practicable. This provoked a hastily penned
note from Blackwill reprimanding me for hinting that the US was
prepared to discuss alternatives to the caucus system – an
intervention that I could not understand when he had, the evening
before, made a very explicit distinction between partial and direct
national elections, the same point that I had just made. I scribbled a
reply saying that I had not suggested any such thing.

The meeting went through several more laps of the table, covering
security, the economy, a whole host of things, but skirting round the
critical question of whether the UN would be prepared to offer help
in the short term. John Sawers passed me a slip of paper with
suggestions for a more direct approach. So I intervened again to ask
Kofi Annan whether he could clarify the Secretariat's position. Was
he willing to plan for an eventual UN presence on the ground and, if
so, could the preparations for this eventuality begin with immediate
advice on the right sequence of steps and the appointment of a
Special Representative to handle it? Would it not make sense to send
out a security assessment expert to see what might be done? The
Secretary-General eventually acknowledged the CPA request for an
early UN assessment and undertook to follow up with technical
discussions amongst his own people before giving a full reply.

After a hurried press conference, during which Bremer and I
pointed up the wide area of agreement between the IGC and the

CPA on almost everything except the detailed procedures for creating a national assembly, John Sawers accompanied me to the top of the building to find Lakhdar Brahimi. John had not met Brahimi before, but I had grown to know him well during my years in New York, as Kofi Annan turned to him frequently for wise and independent advice, as he had with Sergio de Mello, and to help him on the hardest issues. Now seventy, his wiry features were beginning to show his years, but his mental energy was undimmed. I liked his directness and, since we found it possible to talk to each other about the most difficult issues, constantly learnt from his formidable experience.

John and I briefed him on the exchanges downstairs and listened to his account of developments in Afghanistan – all relevant and interesting as evidence of what the UN could achieve when properly mandated and resourced, but he was not getting to our real issue. I threw a direct question at him: would he be prepared to help in Iraq? He said he had barely had a day off in two years and could not at his age move on to such an intensive assignment without a proper break. But he betrayed his interest in the substance by criticising the CPA's approach on municipal and provincial caucuses to produce a national assembly, which he said would not work, after which he suggested that he would be too inclined to give the Americans a hard time to be useful. He launched into a critique of all the main Iraqi parties, wondering – as we had been doing for months – where the right leadership was going to come from. John was impressed by this evidence that Brahimi would be his own man: Kieran Prendergast's predictions in that respect were borne out. We were left with the feeling that if Kofi Annan decided the UN had to take up the opportunity on offer, Brahimi would in the end be persuadable, both because he was a loyal UN servant and because Iraq was the great issue of the day.

That meeting in New York turned out to be the catalyst we needed for renewed momentum. Two weeks later Lakhdar Brahimi was appointed Special Representative and came out to Iraq alongside a team of UN electoral experts led by Carina Perelli from the Department of Political Affairs. Despite some vicious Shia propaganda against Brahimi for his alleged Sunni bias, Ayatollah Sistani decided to hold direct talks with him, as he had never done with any CPA representative: for all his suspicion that the United States might seek to control the UN agenda, Sistani saw greater legitimacy in the UN than he ever did in the CPA. Brahimi eventually produced a report in the spring which, to Sistani's irritation, argued that national elections would not be sensible before the mid-2004 transfer of responsibility and would require at least eight months' preparation once the interim Iraqi structures were in place. The caucuses were consigned to the back-burner and the Governing Council, some of whose members were hoping that they would come through these disputes as the only acceptable de facto government, was assigned no significant role in the next stage. Everyone lost something. It was a compromise of considerable artistry, fulfilling the expectations of those in Washington who valued movement over principle. It certainly caused London very few problems and indicated what Sergio de Mello might have achieved if he had survived.

Immediately following our trip to New York, John Sawers came out to Baghdad to take the political temperature at first hand. Our Diplomatic Service boss, Sir Michael Jay, accompanied him because difficult and expensive decisions now needed to be taken on the security and accommodation of the British team as well as on policy. Both for the Americans and ourselves, the cost of establishing a protected presence over the coming period was to amount to more than the rest of our Middle East embassies combined. With the count of rockets that had landed in the Green Zone now reaching well into three figures, I had decided that every Briton should sleep under hard cover. Michael Jay's visit led to a decision to put everyone in portable cabins under the firmly built but unattractive car park of the Green Zone Conference Centre.

John and I went to call on Iyad Allawi, the often disaffected member of the Governing Council with whom I kept more closely in touch than any other. He was at his gloomiest: Sistani was polarising the communities; the IGC and the CPA were losing their grip; the Iraqi street was dismissive about the UN initiative, which they read as CPA desperation and weakness. He believed that matters were going to deteriorate badly. He responded to our entreaty to step up his efforts to build bridges to the Sunni community, but he felt there was a limit to what he could do. He asked us to consider postponing the handover date beyond the end of June. We said there was no chance of this. John came away rather depressed. We went on to other calls where the mood was lighter: Ibrahim al Jaafari, Nasreen Berwari (the impressive female Minister of Municipalities and Public Works) and Masoud Barzani, who was on a rare visit to Baghdad. All thought that deals were possible, but there was no doubt the tensions were rising.

From late January onwards the hard pounding on the text of the Transitional Administrative Law began in earnest. Three main issues, rooted in the depths of Iraq's disturbed history, had to be addressed over and above the arrangements for the transition. The first was the relationship between the various communities of Iraq, who in long generations had not been able to develop freely or to protect themselves. No accurate figure existed of their numbers, since the last census had been taken in 1979 and even that was contested. The more reasonable claims made by each (usually 65 per cent for the Shia Arabs, 30 per cent for the Kurds and 25 per cent for the Sunni Arabs) were exaggerated but passionately defended. The CPA assumed that the real figures stood somewhere in the region of 60 per cent for the Shia and 20 per cent for the other two, with the Kurds slightly ahead of the Sunnis. 1 or 2 per cent had to be reserved for the much smaller minorities of Turcomans, Assyrians, Chaldaeans, Jezzidis and others, of whom only the first two were represented in the Governing Council. Minority rights obviously had to be protected, but the central issue was whether both the Kurds (mostly Sunni Muslims) and the Sunni Arabs could come to terms with a democratic system that would almost certainly place them under

Shia rulers. If they could not, the Kurds retained the option of retreating into an autonomous region in the mountains, as they had done for the last twelve years of Saddam's rule. The Sunnis, whose main numbers were to be found west and north of Baghdad but whose tribal areas would be hard to coalesce into a viable separate territory, were more fearful of what change would bring. Because they had learnt better to accommodate Saddam, they were also less well organised politically now that he was gone.

The second issue was religion. Iraq is often described as a largely secular state and it is true that a majority of Iraqis, probably even a majority of Shia Iraqis, would reject an Islamic political structure comparable with Iran's. But we probably underestimated the effect of religious feeling in the country. Most Iraqis are practising Muslims and feel keenly (95 per cent in one poll taken during the CPA period) that Islam forms an essential part of their identity. Given the mixed success generally of the combination of Islam and democracy and, in Iraq, the polarised attitudes towards the religious Shia parties, the way Islam would feature in the TAL and later in the new constitution was bound to raise passions.

The third issue was the relationship between the central power of the state and its constituent parts. Commentators frequently refer to the risk of civil war in Iraq and, if relations between the main communities break down, the possibility of conflict cannot be dismissed. But CPA analysts regarded such a development as less likely than the failure of the central system to hold the loyalty of the local communities and the fragmentation of Iraq into many more than three parts. Even the Kurds, left to their own devices through the 1990s, spent as much time fighting with each other as keeping Saddam Hussein at bay. The PUK and the KDP remained uneasy partners in this negotiation. A united Iraq, the only honourable outcome from the US–UK intervention, would have to be founded on the attachment of all three large communities to the centre; and therefore all three would have to agree to any constitutional arrange-ment. The Shia majority developed strong views about minority vetoes, but their future depended on the three groups sticking together.

These were big questions for foreigners to negotiate among peoples whom no power in history had ever forged into a stable unit on this territory. Bremer faced one further problem: Washington's extreme anxiety as the days and weeks passed that the handover date should be met with Iraq in a passable state. To his mind, I was not making his job any easier. When John Sawers, with whom his relationship had been smoother, came out to Baghdad in late January, Bremer appealed to him to get me to adhere more faithfully to US policy lines. He was tired of absorbing contrary advice and comment from his UK partners. Normally I would go into Jerry's study to sort out any differences, convincing him I think, because it was true, that I was fully supportive of his targets even if I held my own views on how to get there. John and I had a word about the problem and I went across to Bremer's office to repeat the message: I was there to help, even if I sometimes saw things from a different angle.

Jerry said he accepted this and hinted that his larger problem was Washington. I think he recognised that at least I understood something about the intricate make-up of Iraq and his need to forge a delicate balance between its myriad pieces. Washington micro-managed from a distance without that understanding. I distinctly remember the 29 January morning meeting being aroused from its routine ritual by an injunction from Bremer that Washington was to be ignored if it attempted to set strategic targets directly with any part of the CPA: only objectives agreed by him were valid. He had enough on his hands cementing the separate paths of the civilian and military wings of US power in Iraq without the sorcerer's apprentice playing havoc in his own system.

Once my visitors had left, I rejoined Bremer for the intensifying negotiations over the Transitional Administrative Law (TAL). He chose to concentrate first on the Kurds. We continued through a series of tussles with Barzani and Talabani to draw them to a point where they would be committed to a united Iraq without losing their traditional way of life. Everyone understood that the Kurds would never renounce their long-term aspiration to independence, but that was not a choice for now; nor could they make no choice at all. They wanted a clear designation of Kurdish territory, including the city of Kirkuk; the continuation of the Kurdish National Assembly, with local government structures responsible to it; and the maintenance of the Peshmerga as a fighting force for the defence of the Kurdish homeland. The first and third of these were unobtainable from the Iraqi Arabs. The CPA decided to leave all questions of internal boundaries for the constitution proper in 2005. Bremer decided to play hardball on the Peshmerga. Although to Kurdish minds it was not a militia, he insisted that it should be brought within the framework of national security forces or disbanded. He felt he would otherwise be laying the new state open to the continuation of all the other private armies.

The IGC had established a drafting committee for the Transitional Administrative Law, chaired by Adnan Pachachi and served by a cross-section of skilful Iraqi lawyers. The twentieth century in Iraq was dotted with attempts to design the definitive constitution, none of which were respected by the executive from the time of British rule onwards. But the experience left behind a talented legal profession. The world imagined that the CPA, or at least some shadowy group of American lawyers, was guiding the Iraqi pen through every clause of the new draft, but Pachachi kept his independence, conscious that this was Iraq's business and that he had to sell the product eventually to the people around Ayatollah Sistani. He realised he would have to leave the Kurds to the Coalition, as that was where the leverage lay. The tension rose as Masoud Barzani dug in against the draft wording on security forces and on the nature of the federal structure. For one interminable early February session, trapped by a snowfall up in the Salahaddin fastness, Bremer and I ground through the text word by word, trying to invent formulae to express the precise median line between independence and weak autonomy. It was a strange place to dredge up echoes of Security Council drafting habits. We eventually hit on an approach that might work and slithered back down the icy roads to relocate in our helicopters. Only when we were back in Baghdad did we discover that the compromise we had lit upon might not be acceptable to Washington because it went against their idea of the precise federal arrangement needed to satisfy Sistani. Bremer set aside for a few days any thought of re-opening the text with the Kurds. It would have brought the whole TAL negotiation to a halt.

My frustration deepening that the CPA was being overruled by Washington just when Bremer was getting to grips with the realities on the ground, I took myself off for a day down the shabby roads of east-central Iraq to the poorest provincial capital, Al Kut. There I saw just how vulnerable the local British team's headquarters was on the banks of the Tigris (it was later attacked and almost overrun) and heard the bitter complaints of struggling independent politicians about the corruption and intimidation practised by the larger political parties. How were we ever going to make a stable democracy out of this place?

Anne was now out in Baghdad and came with me on this trip, travelling in a separate car as a precaution. With the experience of her recently completed SAS training course in the Brecon Beacons, she was rather more aware of the security risks than I was, having long ago handed myself over to the care of my top-class Royal Military Police bodyguards. Visiting women's groups regularly in the centre of Baghdad, she was more often exposed to the chance of an attack than those of us whose daily routine unfolded on safer ground. But in her six weeks out there she only once had a weapon raised against her in anger. Walking with a female colleague the safe hundred yards from the Green Zone Convention Centre to the Governing Council compound, she was told to stop and retreat by the American guard at the gate, gun raised. Explaining that her pool car had disappeared and waving her pass to show that she had CPA work to do, she advanced a few more steps. There was another shout and the sound of a trigger being cocked. She decided that the future of the women of Iraq could be put on hold for a little longer and she backed off. We only later discovered that the security rules about pedestrians had been changed, without anyone bothering to give notice to mere civilians.

Bremer by now had his own lines out to Ayatollah Sistani and the inner core of political clerics who surrounded him, sometimes through carefully drafted letters and occasionally through intermediaries. From these he developed an accurate view of what might or might not set off the fuse for a public rejection of the TAL by the religious Shia. A Sistani fatwa would be fatal, and it worried Washington. But bowing to the Shias would lose us the Sunnis and the Kurds. I thought that Bremer had the trade-off about right. Although the Sunni community featured less in our diplomacy than we would have liked, we were constantly looking for ways of reaching out to them and of bringing aid projects into their area. IGC politicians such as Pachachi, Allawi, al Yawar, al Rubaie and al Sumaidaie, who was the most liberal of the independent Sunnis, tried hard to bring Sunni local leaders in to their coalitions. I occasionally joined Allawi's meetings with Sunni tribal leaders and I once made a speech to a Rubaie-inspired conference of cross-community dignitaries. Somehow the various streams of activity never coalesced into a river. History had not prepared them for the necessary compromises and we in the Coalition failed to motivate them politically.

Ahmed Chalabi also had a clear view of the need for bridge-building. His political future depended on it. He recognised but was not deterred by his low popularity as an exile: it meant that he would need powerful allies. Before the war and in the early stages after it, he tried to hitch himself to the United States. Each side then realised that it was not going to work, though the Americans in Baghdad, like the British, continued to talk to him because he could be revealing and perceptive about the constantly swirling movement of political forces. Next he planned to create a faction from the great land-owning families of Iraq, drawing on his father's connections, but came to see that the time for such an elite hierarchy had passed.

Gradually he began to move across to the strongest single camp within the IGC, the religious Shia, because they possessed what he did not, a significant political organisation, and he could offer what they lacked, financial backing. He also saw the advantage of staying on the right side of Iran. I well remember one moment during these TAL negotiations when he arrived at the Republican Palace with a Shia group led by Mohammed Bahr al Uloom and Bremer received them in the main CPA meeting-room. Uloom, a political independent, delivered a sharp homily on the need to respect the natural Shia majority and Chalabi came in behind him. As he started, he uttered the devout Muslim's preamble to a formal speech: '*Bismillah ar rahman ar rahim*' – 'In the name of God, the Compassionate, the Merciful.' Jerry Bremer leaned my way and whispered, 'That's a first.' Chalabi's final choice of partners proved a telling one and he reaped the benefits in the January 2005 elections. The legitimacy these ties bestowed on him and his alliance, combined with his personal effectiveness as an Administrator, convinced the Americans that they would have to start dealing with him again if they wanted the central government to work.

In early February Paul Wolfowitz came through on a visit (making it necessary for the CPA to hide another visitor, Tom Warwick, the chief author of the 'Future of Iraq' paper, from his view). Wolfowitz asked me straight out how I thought Sistani would react to the evolving negotiation. Governance Section and the British team had been brainstorming that week on exactly this question. I said the CPA should be allowed to follow its own sense of where the balance lay between the communities. If we constantly took the Iraqis' view on what they regarded as acceptable we would invite an escalation of bidding. So long as the United States remained convincing about its intention to leave Iraq to the Iraqis as soon as possible, Sistani would be satisfied. His first consideration, judging by his words and his actions so far, was to bring about a working democracy for all Iraqis and not just a Shia majority. If Iran had more malign objectives in mind it still had not found the strategic levers to impose them; and Sistani, as an Iranian exile and rival to Iran's religious hierarchy, was largely independent from Iranian influence in setting his priorities. I suggested that it would be better to leave Sistani to draw his own conclusions about the risks of dividing Iraq than to run after him as each objection to a drafting point emerged. The fine judgement that needed to be made was when to schedule the first full set of elections. If, as seemed increasingly to be the case, Bremer was inclined to fuse together the early 2005 elections for a constitutional assembly and late 2005 elections for a new government promised in the 15 November Agreement, this might be enough to persuade Sistani and the religious Shia not to mutiny – all the more so if the UN delivered a verdict that elections could not safely be held earlier. Wolfowitz offered no argument against this analysis; but then most American players held back on definitive opinions in private conversation when they were uncertain where the authoritative view amongst principals in Washington might come out.

A day or two later I checked privately with Bremer to see what continuing pressure he was under from Washington to fine-tune the details of the federalist structure. He said that, following his resistance to the Pentagon's attempts to deny the Kurds the continuation of the Kurdish Regional Government, because they feared it would prolong the Shia resistance to a TAL settlement, there appeared to be a temporary lull. He mentioned that he had exchanged letters with Ayatollah Sistani offering a US guarantee of elections within a certain period and constraints on the independent powers of the Transitional National Assembly – moves I certainly supported from the UK viewpoint but of which we would not have been informed if I had not put the question. The interesting development, however, was that Sistani had implicitly accepted that early direct elections were unlikely to be condoned by the UN team, which had now started its work. The realities were beginning to weigh on him too. Jerry subsequently showed me, on strict terms of confidentiality, the text of this written exchange. When I then held another brainstorming with Governance Section, I discovered that they were not up to date with the latest Bremer–Washington interplay and I swapped my assessment for their read-out of the next steps in the negotiation. I do not think the Iraqis had any idea that the negotiation that Bremer was conducting with them was only half as intensive as the one he was engaged in within the swirling ranks of his own administration.

Embroiled as we were in the TAL negotiations, we were not insensitive to the growing toll from violence. Everyone now had to assume that he or she was a possible target. CPA workers on women's rights in the south were shot in cold blood at a roadblock. Suicide bombers began, as I had always feared, to attack the entry points of the Green Zone and early one February morning we held a sad memorial service for the Iraqi staff killed at Assassins' Gate three weeks earlier. On 1 February in Irbil two bombers entered the line of well-wishers at the KDP's Feast of the Sacrifice celebration and blew themselves and 105 others to oblivion. I accompanied Bremer on a low, cold flight up to Kurdistan to express our condolences to Barzani and Talabani. He could not resist using the contact to try out some late suggestions from Washington on a crucial part of the text. It did not go down too well, but perhaps the CPA team was not looking for the most propitious moment to inject proposals that they did not regard as constructive.

At the end of the first week of February Robert Blackwill returned to Baghdad accompanied by Lakhdar Brahimi. The UN elections team had been examining the options on the ground for a few days, confident of their considerable experience in this field and firmly resistant to any outside influence. These arrivals multiplied by three or four the number of cooks in the front kitchen and it quietened for a while the voices in the back one in Washington. Blackwill was careful to take the UK view as he became more deeply involved in the small-text calculations of each stage, both out of genuine interest in our assessment of a theatre we knew well and as a running check on our conformity to US guidelines. Our problem at any one moment was to fathom which US loyalty test we were being subjected to.

As for Brahimi, he immediately called me in to present my opinions. In a not-unfriendly way he signalled that he needed to keep his political distance. He emphasised the UN's autonomy by conducting the hearing in the style of a parliamentary select committee. He gave little away at this point of his own impressions, but I lodged with him my firm view that direct elections in 2004 were neither practicable nor politically wise. Three days later he told me he was moving towards a recommendation that the June date for the end of the occupation should be adhered to, that elections should not be attempted until early 2005 and that they should be for a double-function assembly, which would have both legislative and constitutional responsibilities. He had no opinion on the method of choosing the interim government for July. These views of his never changed, despite American pressure on him to produce an alternative to the caucuses system. I concluded that he had arrived with his mind more or less made up and nothing he heard on the ground in Iraq inclined him to change it.

Throughout these interwoven discussions with outside administrators and advisers I kept up a running series of private exchanges with the most accessible senior Iraqis – the devout Shia, Mowaffaq al Rubaie, who kept close to the goings-on around Sistani; Mohsen Abdul Hamid of the Iraqi Islamic Party, the only political organisation in the Sunni area with an identifiable personality; Ahmed Chalabi as he ranged across the spectrum looking for an opening; and occasionally Abdul Aziz al Hakim as the back-marker on the religious Shia side. We were all gradually getting used to each other as partners. I also continued to touch base with Iyad Allawi, who held the most forthright views on the practicality of what we were attempting, had ideas on how to defeat the insurgency, and was independent to the point of insouciance as to the eventual outcome for himself. In the second week of February he presented me with an apocalyptic forecast: Sistani was adamant about early elections and would not compromise; Brahimi would not survive the virulent Shia criticism of him as a Sunni Arab Nationalist; Iran was interfering outrageously and drawing the political opportunists, whom he did not have to name, towards them; and the insurgency and terrorist violence was unstoppable. He did not regard the CPA as having the momentum or the impact on Iraqi public opinion to cope with these threats. He said he had decided to travel to Washington within the next two or three weeks to ask the administration to delay the transfer of sovereignty.

When I went over Allawi's concerns with Bob Blackwill he reacted calmly. The intelligence did not support this assessment of Sistani's position. In the other areas the Coalition had no choice but to soldier on. Later I showed him the record of my exchange with Allawi, for transparency's sake and to give him the detail. It contained a passage on a separate issue over which the UK was temporarily in dispute with the United States: the need for a security cooperation agreement with an independent Iraq so that Coalition forces could remain in the country by invitation. Washington was reluctant to open up this area of potential trouble, but London had more exacting legal requirements and was eager to normalise the status of our military operation. Knowing that Allawi would take a close interest in the area, I sought his view on the likelihood that an independent Iraqi government would approve such an agreement. He thought they would. Blackwill seized on this snippet and took me to task for washing dirty Coalition laundry with an outsider. I later received a handwritten note from him, asking me in the name of the White House to adhere strictly to CPA policies in every respect. He seemed to have missed the point that this particular item was not CPA policy, because London and Washington had not yet reached a common position, nor for that matter was it always easy to know what was.

As always throughout this saga, I shared an account of our daily struggle with London. I think they sometimes wished that I would rock the boat a little less vigorously, but I knew what they wanted on the substance and was ready to be judged by results. Unlike Bremer, I was never micro-managed and I was happy to keep it that way. Yet tensions were growing as the February days lengthened. The Prime Minister telephoned at one stage for a first-hand read-out, clearly worried that another stalemate might develop, and I was asked to find a date to come back to London to go over the details of what we were getting ourselves into.

Meanwhile the spectrum of conditions for the people of Iraq continued to widen. Security worsened, with two separate incidents on one awful day in February when fifty Iraqi recruits were killed by suicide car-bombs. Electricity generation remained sluggish. Day-long queues formed at gas stations and taxi drivers turned into gasoline smugglers. It was easy for the media to paint a constantly gloomy picture. On the other hand, the streets swarmed with business; cars, washing machines and TV satellite dishes were being imported at an unprecedented rate; schools and universities were running and oil production was creeping up. There was progress and there was carnage. Almost everyone we met – Anne put the question to a good variety of women's groups – expressed gratitude to the Coalition for having rid Iraq of the Saddam regime. They then asked why we had to take so long to restore law and order. It was from these indications that we increasingly realised that the prospects for success no longer rested with the Coalition: it would depend on the tolerance and stamina of the Iraqi people.

There were even moments of passable normality. On 19 February the Iraqi National Symphony Orchestra put on a concert in the Green Zone's Convention Centre. Proud of their heritage but short of rehearsal time, they settled themselves on stage and waited for the expected audience of a thousand to turn up. With two or three hundred in their seats and the clock ticking, Maysoon al Damluji, the Deputy Minister of Culture and their paymaster, marched on to the stage and instructed them to get going. Silence was demanded and they launched into their overture. Barely twenty bars into it a mobile phone started to ring. The conductor stopped and glared round at the audience, ready to punish this mark of disrespect. The phone rang again and the first cellist sheepishly fished his phone out of his pocket. There was huge amusement in the audience, but the incident did not diminish the poignancy of Fauré's *Elegy* later in the programme.

By 23 February the CPA's tortuous negotiations with the Kurds were far enough along to fix a wider discussion within the Governing Council. A meeting between Lakhdar Brahimi and Ayatollah Sistani eased some of the Shia tension over early elections: the two wily old foxes apparently got on better than either of them had expected. Sistani's recognition that he was unlikely to obtain UN backing did not mean that he would accept whatever the IGC concluded, but Bremer decided that, with the end-February deadline less than a week away, the textual negotiations would have to go into almost continuous session. Washington remained in a state of heightened anxiety. Fed by Blackwill's reports from Baghdad on the lack of progress, they were beginning to suggest that, if the Iraqis could not make up their minds on the next steps, the best arrangement for July would be to turn the Governing Council into the interim government. This seemed perverse to me. After all our concern about Sistani's capacity to block a reasonable solution, this would have fulfilled his worst expectations. When I heard that Number Ten were wondering whether they should not humour Washington on this, I decided I would have to intervene. The Governing Council would have no legitimacy. The image of an occupation would remain, while the CPA would no longer have the authority to control the political process. The decision would play directly into the hands of the insurgency. I ran this analysis by Jerry Bremer, who agreed.

At this point, Bremer called all nine Presidents to his villa to go through the draft text of the Transitional Law that Pachachi's committee had produced. Little progress was made, not least because Bremer himself was distracted by a visit from Rumsfeld the same day and had to absent himself to deal with a new Pentagon initiative to take over control of the Iraqi police, as well as the armed forces, on the grounds that their budget was providing the funding. Bremer's deputy, Dick Jones, and I pushed painfully through the main areas of difference, trying to avoid textual discussion by thrashing out eight major 'concepts' that were still causing trouble: the role of Islam, the powers of the Presidency, devolution to the provinces, the Army, the number of official languages (not just a Kurdish but also a Turcoman point), the promotion of women candidates for the Assembly, the judiciary and the conditions under which the TAL could later be amended. We partly solved the language issue, but the rest lived on to trouble us. As I left central Baghdad to catch a flight for London, I sank into a feeling of helplessness. Everything the CPA had learnt over these grinding months about the unique characteristics of Iraq was being overridden by the imperative of capitals' immediate interests, and the UK government appeared not to want to argue with Washington when the downsides of the Americans' preferred course of action lay several months away. My imminent visit to London was going to be timely.

I was luckier than most of my colleagues in being allowed the use of an RAF HS125 from Baghdad airport to Damascus, where I usually managed to catch a direct flight to London. The standard route for everyone else ran through Basra or Kuwait and was plagued by hours of waiting or by suddenly cancelled schedules. The penalty for the more fortunate resided in the style of take-off from Baghdad. Because of the ever-present danger of missiles we could not risk a conventional departure. Once airborne, the plane flew low along the runway and then turned on its side, the wing appearing to clip the tops of the bushes below. When some arbitrary angle had been achieved, it righted itself and climbed in a few seconds to ten thousand feet, leaving stomachs flipped sideways at ground level. On this particular day I had to go via Amsterdam, where the connecting desk for the London leg attempted to turn me away on the grounds that I had not left enough time between flights. I bad-temperedly pointed out that my presence at the check-in counter disproved them, that I had nothing but hand luggage and that they were about to lose me my job. Against odds lengthened by my poor tactics, I was allowed onto the flight and made it to Downing Street just in time.

The Prime Minister's first question was 'So how is it?' On such occasions you give the short answer, but it strengthened my motivation to tell the full story at a later date. I argued for visible change in the present arrangements when an Iraqi government took over, and explained why. I suggested that if there were short-term considerations in capitals, which I accepted were a fact of political life, they had to be set against the importance of bringing Iraq to a respectable state in the end. I commended the shape and substance of the TAL we were trying to achieve, said my piece about the need to protect UK interests in the security field after handover, expressed frustration about the Pentagon's attempt to take over the police, and spoke up for an enlarged UN role as soon as possible. Jack Straw was there and backed me up: he had throughout been handling the wider diplomatic context, including a series of Security Council resolutions, and recognised that, now we knew the security situation was unwinnable in the short term, the most important step was to obtain consensus on the structure and timetable for the transition. To my surprise, there was no argument. The Prime Minister wanted to know that what I was describing was achievable. I took a deep breath and said yes. He told us to get on with it.

We did not in this conversation touch on the reasons why we had failed to make more progress. A backward-looking discussion was never going to restore lost time or reform the American way of doing things. I had not so far attempted, and was not going to initiate now, an appeal to the Prime Minister to produce changes that I could not secure for myself in Baghdad. It would close down any relationship with Bremer and it would place too much strain on the London–Washington link. I did, however, ask Nigel Sheinwald to mention to Condoleezza Rice my view that Bremer was managing the TAL negotiations in the right way and should be left to engineer a result as he thought best. I was not sure whether this message got through, but the final days of the TAL struggle seemed, with the odd exception, to flow better.

I slept little on the return journey. The blacked-out HS125 dropped me down into Baghdad airport at 4 a.m. and the close-protection team drove me in through a deserted city. It was spooky travelling down the empty highway past the palm groves where Bremer, Sanchez and most recently Rumsfeld had had ambushes planned against them. We had scored a minor coup with the Americans in picking up a whisper of the Rumsfeld threat, enabling him to divert. As I arrived back at the British Villa, Anne was just getting up to begin her return journey to London and on to New York with the Iraqi women's delegation to the UN. I was too tired to be of much help with her packing and was upset that she was leaving. She had made such a contribution in her six weeks, not just to the morale of the women she was working with but also to the sanity and good humour of the British CPA team. I fretted about her dawn exit down the same stretch of insidious road, but she e-mailed me from Kuwait at teatime to report that, apart from the interminable waiting on each leg of the journey, all was well.

It was hard to keep my eyes open for the rest of the day's business. By now the TAL negotiations had shifted to the renovated government offices next to the original IGC headquarters and, when I rejoined it, the Council was creeping at an agonising pace through each paragraph of the text. After three and a half hours they had reached the seventh out of 160 articles, becoming increasingly stuck for a formula to describe the role of Islam in the state. Mohammed Bahr al Uloom, the senior cleric on the IGC but not the world's most practised chairman, started to lose patience. Bremer, who wisely if uncharacteristically stayed silent throughout the session, wanted to continue through the night, which would have done me in, but Uloom adjourned before 10 p.m. We discovered that the religious Shia members were planning to travel down to Najaf the next morning, 26 February, to consult Ayatollah Sistani. That would scotch another day and we realised that the end-February deadline was becoming impossible to meet. We had no choice but to accept that keeping the most important off-stage participant briefed was an essential step.

While the remaining Council members continued their desultory work on the text, I took myself off for a tour of Saddam Hussein's underground bunker beneath the nearby 'Believers' Palace', as the Baath Party headquarters was known. This pseudo-Islamic monstrosity had been bombed to pieces in the first Gulf War, rebuilt through the 1990s and then destroyed again in March 2003. A group of Yugoslav companies had been engaged by Saddam to construct three floors of living and working quarters deep below ground. Several metres of layered rubber and reinforced concrete had been inserted between the floor of the upper building and the ceiling of the bunker. The blast-proof metal doors, manufactured in Germany, we were told, stood three feet thick. The palace itself had been torn to shreds by fourteen American 2,000-pound bombs, but the bunker was completely unscathed. The lower two floors were now flooded from the Tigris water table and millions of mosquitos were breeding there in the pitch dark. Apparently Saddam did not use the place much during the conflict, fearing that the US Air Force might have more powerful penetration bombs or that nuclear or chemical weapons might come into play. We found packets of chemical weapon antidotes lying around in the bunk-bedrooms. The machinery rooms were full of air-filtering and electrical back-up equipment. The emptiness of the place was eery, a powerful symbol of psychotic isolation.

In the evening Jerry Bremer and I, with Raad Alkadiri as interpreter, travelled across the city to dine with the Ayatollah of the Khadimiyah mosque in Baghdad, Hussein al Sadr, who was one of our allies in trying to bring Iraq back to peaceful unity. He was close to Mowaffaq al Rubaie on the IGC and communicated regularly with Ayatollah Sistani, though he could not claim to have a decisive influence on him. The evening had been planned to celebrate the launch of a remarkable ecumenical initiative by Canon Andrew

White of Coventry Cathedral. Orthodox, Armenian, Catholic and Shia clerics were present, but their Sunni Muslim counterparts, although part of the initiative, never showed up. At the after-dinner tea-drinking stage, a plate of baklava was brought round by a young boy, who was asked by the Ayatollah to greet the Administrator with a kiss. He then stood alongside to have his photograph taken. I whispered discreetly to Andrew White: 'Remember the pictures of Saddam and the young British captive in 1990?' Andrew roared with laughter and repeated the question to the whole company in his booming voice. Bremer glowered. Raad could hardly contain himself.

19

Agreement at Last on the Political Process

On 27 February, with the whole Council back in session, the negotiations restarted in earnest, but the IGC could never last long without some kind of a distraction. Adnan Pachachi, now back in the chair, allowed the senior female member, Raja al Khuzai, to introduce a motion repealing the infamous Decree 137 on Women and Islamic Law which Abdul Aziz al Hakim had pushed through the depleted Council in December. It was passed by fifteen to ten. Immediately the meeting-room door was flung open and an ululating group of women poured in to celebrate. Adel Abdul Mehdi, Hakim's deputy in the Council, rose abruptly and summoned the religious Shia group out of the chamber. End of session. I took the opportunity to telephone London and ask them to have a go at Washington about their constant attempts to insert textual changes as the negotiations proceeded, despite Bremer's resistance. Number Ten called Condoleezza Rice, but it turned out she had already backed off. The rest of the day was spent trying to entice the Shias out of their sulking tent, but to little avail.

The next morning Bremer decided to call the Council to work in a series of different groups scattered about the government building. He, Dick Jones and I took turns leading them through the more difficult parts of the text, and runners carried suggested fixes from room to room as we went on. Bremer then pulled representatives of the main parties together in one room: Pachachi and Sumaidaie for the Sunnis, Rubaie and Adel Mehdi for the Shia, and Shaways, Barzani's deputy, for the Kurds. We ground through a paper of hard-rock issues and tried to sort them out. I was sent off to a side-room with Rubaie and Sumaidaie to work out a passage on devolution to the provinces and after a couple of hours of hard grind we produced something quite presentable, establishing the principle that any region of at least three adjacent provinces, not just Kurdistan, could form a collective structure, though not explicitly with the kind of advanced autonomy that the Kurds enjoyed.

The fundamental obstacle remained Islam. The discussion went on for a long time while we passed from one group to another, trying to leach away the effect of the Shia walk-out the previous day. The religious Shia group, with Adel Abdul Mehdi of SCIRI as their most passionate spokesman in this round, saw their opportunity to shift the Iraqi State away from its historically secular leaning. They began to use quite threatening language about the consequences of Shia disappointment in this fundamental area. They proposed a text for the TAL that would make the tenets of Islam the main determinant of state legislation. The Kurds countered by pointing out that this could only apply from now on to new legislation, not retroactively to what already existed in Iraqi law, which the occupation authorities did not have the power to change.

With the temperature rising and despite the thinness of the ice, I decided to step forward. I suggested that the TAL should specify that no new legislation should violate the universally agreed tenets of Islam: in other words, Islam should not be the proactive model, and sectarian interpretations of Islamic law should be excluded. I knew that the Americans would be able to live with this and I began to get some firm support in the Council, most of whose members wanted a result. Rubaie went down the corridor to telephone Sistani, through the Ayatollah's son and office-keeper, Mohammed Ridha, and came back with some encouragement for this approach if the word 'new' was dropped. The Sunnis now entered the fray to pour cold water on this. Brimming with apprehensions of an extremist Shia takeover, they pulled out of their memories a whole host of modern rights and freedoms, the Universal Declaration of Human Rights for a start, which would be impossible for the new Iraq to legislate on under such a clause. We pressed on into the small hours, hopping between the meeting-rooms and the dining-room downstairs. My protection team called me out into the cool air to share a box of Kit-Kats at one point, before I piled back in for more punishment. We had embarked on the last day of February and sleep was not high on the agenda.

Eventually the sessions came to a close and we retired for three or four hours. The next morning we found that the Iraqis could not face an immediate return to the arena. My compromise language had in any case suffered some wounds during the break, not least from a Washington intervention attempting to steer away from an outcome entrenching Sharia Law, which would in their eyes devalue the whole enterprise. There was a certain amount of desultory skirmishing during the day. Finally Bremer managed to call a full plenary at 6.30 p.m., the first since the Shia walk-out over women's rights. The IGC started to go through the whole text from the beginning. It was very slow. Over supper, which witnessed small, tired groups silently chewing away at the standard product of the Rasheed Hotel kitchen, we tried to have another go at Islam. I got into a huddle with Mowaffaq al Rubaie and suggested a few changes not wholly consistent with Washington's ideas, which were not going to work. At one point Ahmed Chalabi came up and glared threateningly at the two of us, before hissing at Mowaffaq that he had told him not to attempt any redrafting. Mowaffaq whispered to me that it was clear that Chalabi was trying to prevent the TAL from coming into effect at all, because he preferred to have an empty political space to work in. I spread that round, but in the end it did not turn out to be true.

The Kurdish problem was by no means settled either. We were

beginning to lose Masoud Barzani on the provision for bringing the Peshmerga under state control. Washington's insistence that the strength of Kurdish autonomy be limited so as not to threaten the future unity of Iraq was proving too much for him. He walked out of the side-negotiation and looked as if he was intending to leave Baghdad altogether. Raad was alerted by his Kurdish contacts and he ran to fetch me. I caught Barzani in the corridor and had a hard conversation with him about the true implications of the TAL. It did not set anything in concrete for the new Iraq: that would be for elected Iraqis to settle later, free of foreign interference. But to destroy the chances of reaching the next stage was not in the longer-term interests of the Kurds. The United Kingdom would not back an independent Kurdistan, but neither would we let the Kurdish nation be dissipated within an Arab Iraq. I suggested some language for him to propose as a final compromise. He went back in and tried it, and it worked. The Americans, who were not aware of my intervention, did not contest it.

As midnight passed and March arrived, the pace started to pick up on the article-by-article textual discussion. Now the issue of devolution to the provinces began to turn sour, with the Kurds this time leaving the rhetoric to the Sunnis, who saw the need for a barrier to stave off the Shia majority but had no easily identifiable territory to amalgamate. The debate became highly political and articulate, with short, telling speeches from Pachachi and Sumaidaie on balance between the communities and with Adel Mehdi questioning why the Council should sow the seeds of Iraq's division in the future with a weakening of the centre now. The CPA team listened quietly. Then Chalabi began to criticise the proposed language on the post-handover security arrangements, a far more neuralgic subject for both the US and the UK, and a sensitive one between us given our differing approaches on the need for fresh UN cover. But we managed to preserve our previously constructed compromise. And on and on it went. The atmosphere was hard but remarkably courteous. Jalal Talabani delivered two expansive and good-humoured offerings, one of them shadowing his friend Chalabi's slide towards Shia positions on Islam, the other cheerily promoting Iraqi unity; and I realised that the game of political alliances for future elections was starting to be played. Barzani, who was present, and Allawi, through his deputy – he could never bring himself to appear for any of this US-refereed business – were moving in the other direction, with deep apprehension about a Shia-dominated state influenced by Iran. But none of that could be settled now.

The Islam text suddenly went right. The Shia group had kept in touch with Sistani's office and thought that they had sufficient cover to settle. Bremer left the intercommunal tensions to work themselves out. The text in the draft stayed close to my earlier proposal with the addition of a reference to 'democratic principles' as a guideline for legislation. The Sunnis seemed to cave in on the prominence of Islam, knowing that they would regret it later. The insertion of a 25 per cent quota for women candidates in the legislative election arrangements somehow squeezed through, having been the subject of a bitter row at an earlier stage. The end finally came at 4.20 a.m. on Monday 1 March, with exhaustion and some concern that we had patched over swamps that remained to be drained. There were short, cheerful speeches from Bremer, Mohsen Abdul Hamid, Pachachi, Talabani and even from the laconic Barzani. Everyone was taking photographs of each other and of the oval table surrounded by rows of deputies and staff who had increasingly crowded in on the climax to watch a small piece of history in the making.

We snatched another brief rest before returning to the office to report to Washington and London. I rang Nigel Sheinwald in Number Ten, Jack Straw and John Sawers in the Foreign Office, and later Kofi Annan and Lakhdar Brahimi. They were all hugely relieved that we had at last cleared the TAL hurdle. I suggested some possible press lines to the Secretary-General and received a mildly gruff response, but he was pleased with the overall development and impressed that we had missed the original deadline by only four hours. The Prime Minister later sent a warm message to Bremer and me and our teams.

I wandered along to Jerry's office to show him the message and offered him my own congratulations for holding the ring between Iraqi tensions on the one hand and Washington's anxieties on the other. He in turn thanked me as warmly as he had ever done to date. We sat and talked through the next stages: his mind was already moving on to election preparation and enacting legislation. There was a huge amount to do. He pointedly asked whether I was going to do a press conference: his media people had clearly expressed concern to him that I might try to steal some of the limelight or run off-message. In fact, I had already decided to stay off the air and leave it to him.

My office then settled down to drafting a longer analysis for London. It had been a remarkable negotiation, well managed in the final stages by Bremer, and the document the Iraqis had produced was unprecedented for the Middle East region, full of clarity about the duties and limitations of the State and packed with authoritative clauses on the primacy of individual and minority rights. The debates had maintained an atmosphere unsullied by personal animosity and marked by an unusual degree of compromise. They indicated the capacity of the Iraqi people to manage a democratic system if only they could continue to talk to each other and recognise their mutual interest in a united country. I described the British input as ancillary: I had kept to the background as I owned neither the text nor the process, but the UK presence helped to calm the underlying tensions and to edge the nastiest rocks to the side of the road.

The play, however, was not yet done. This was the first day of the Shia religious festival of Ashura. As we started to pick up the CPA's routine business the next morning, the unmistakable thud of a bomb rattled the palace windows. It was a suicide attack at the Khadimiyah mosque, which killed more than sixty people on top of the eighty-five who we soon heard had been slaughtered by several suicide bombers in Kerbala. This was very clearly an attempt by Sunni extremists to provoke the Shia community into rejecting the TAL result. The international media went into overdrive on the disruptive power of the insurgency and the terrorists. The Governing Council met and declared three days of national mourning, which postponed the official signing ceremony for the TAL until 5 March.

In the early evening Bremer and I, against the strong recommendations of our close-protection teams, drove through the city to the house of Ayatollah Hussein al Sadr to express our condolences. Mowaffaq al Rubaie was there and described how, immediately after the bombs had exploded, a hothead had grabbed the mosque loudspeaker and started to broadcast hate messages against the Americans. Rubaie had told the security people to close him down at once. He said that the atmosphere out there was highly flammable. We returned to the Green Zone through streets that now appeared even more threatening, as the locals would have known that the Administrator had been to see the Ayatollah for a ninety-minute call.

Early on 3 March Bremer took stock of the situation with General Sanchez. The casualty toll had reached 180 dead and 550 or more injured, with 70 of the dead and 280 of the injured Iranian residents or pilgrims. Bremer said that the Coalition could not just express its sorrow and move on. There had to be a show of force or the Authority would be seen as incapable of asserting control. Sanchez asked testily whom he should hit and where. Bremer suggested picking up Muqtada al Sadr for a start, and the Badr Corps in the south needed to be dealt with. Sanchez asked whether he had full political cover for a hard operation. Bremer said he did. I intervened, asking whether the first Coalition action after several hundred Shia had been killed or injured should be an attack on the Shia. Sanchez nodded but said nothing. Bremer was unhappy. I proposed that the CPA should quickly approach the senior Shia clerics and ask them what further security they needed. Bremer said that the US military had already done that. It was left that Sanchez would consider the options and come back with a proposal.

*

On 4 March, the last day of the mourning period, the Governance team suddenly appeared in my office to report that Ayatollah Sistani was now dead-set against the TAL signing ceremony that had been rescheduled to the following day. Abdul Aziz al Hakim had sent his son down to Najaf to detail the deficiencies he saw in the Law and Sistani had now pronounced that he could not accept Clause 61(c), which specified that ratification of the new constitution could be blocked by any group of three provinces together (a clear reference to the Kurds). Sistani had queried why this proposal had appeared so late, without proper discussion. Within the CPA we knew that the Kurds would reject any concession. We touched base with some of the senior Iraqis and discovered that a lot of caucusing was going on amongst the Shia, largely organised by Chalabi, it seemed. Suspicions of a sabotage operation grew strong.

As luck would have it, the CPA's monthly conference of Regional Coordinators had been arranged for the morning of Friday 5 March. We decided to go ahead with it in spite of the uncertainty about the holding of the TAL signing ceremony. I prepared to say my farewell piece to my colleagues from the provinces and encourage a discussion on the real political implications of what we were trying to do in Iraq. This kind of collective brainstorming was alien to the American way of doing things and only British voices from the provincial capitals added anything substantive. I tried to broaden the discussion during the second session, but then Simon Shercliff entered in a rush and hauled me off to an emergency meeting of the Governing Council. I never found another chance to say goodbye to the regional teams, whose physical courage and imaginative contact with the Iraqi people achieved so much.

When the Council reassembled with just three hours remaining to test for ways through the blockage, the religious Shia members were nowhere to be seen. Masoud Barzani, who would have to agree to any compromise solution, had now arrived to keep a personal eye on developments. No discussion ever got going. The Shia were apparently collected at Hakim's house and the other Kurdish leader,

Jalal Talabani, a long-time ally of Ahmed Chalabi, was with them. The minutes ticked by and we hung around in listless groups, trying out ideas on each other and discussing generalities with the Iraqis. Finally, Talabani appeared and I persuaded him to give me a hint on what the Shia wanted: he said they were demanding excision of the offending Clause 61(c) giving the Kurds a veto. He knew that this would be impossible for Barzani. I suggested that ratification might be changed from a referendum to a vote in the proposed Transitional National Assembly. He went to try that out on Barzani.

At around 4 p.m. Chalabi and Rubaie came in and it was clear that no solutions were going to be proposed on the Shia side. By now the Convention Centre next door had filled up with the world press, the Baghdad Diplomatic Corps, an orchestra and choir and the British MP Ann Clwyd, the Prime Minister's Special Envoy for Human Rights. The CPA press office was going insane. There was nothing we could do. I tried to persuade Bremer that we would have no signing today and that cancellation now was the best option, but he felt that this was something the Iraqis would have to conclude. Rubaie asked me to try some of my textual compromises, but I told him I had agreed with Bremer to leave the ball in the Iraqi court. At that moment, Sistani's son came through on his cellphone and I sat there looking in the other direction but trying to pick up Rubaie's end of the Arabic exchange. He attempted to persuade Mohammed Ridha Sistani that the ratification of the constitution could be controlled by the National Assembly, but Ridha kept cutting in on him. Then he lost the connection.

Five o'clock, then six o'clock, passed. The Shia migrated into an upstairs room and I wandered up there and found the American Governance team with them. Dick Jones and I took turns at trying to convince them that some compromise was necessary. They seemed to be preparing to go down to Najaf the next day to talk directly to Sistani. The atmosphere grew tense. I asked why a change in 61(c) was so essential when the Assembly had the right anyway to amend the TAL with a 75 per cent majority, which came to more or less the same thing. Chalabi smiled knowingly, as though that argument had already come up and failed. Ayatollah Bahr al Uloom lost his temper and called my question an insult. The temperature dropped further and Jones and I got up and left. Eventually, around 7.45 p.m., the IGC gathered together with Bahr al Uloom, as it happened, in the chair. He asked whether anyone had any advice on how to proceed. The non-Shia, who had been expecting some news from the Shia side, started complaining about the discourtesy of being left waiting for so long. Uloom took offence and tried to walk out, but was caught by his son and by Chalabi and encouraged to re-take his seat. There then ensued a long round of mutual recrimination. Finally, Uloom called a halt with a ruling on a forty-eight-hour delay. I did not see what it would achieve.

The next day we could do nothing but wait for Najaf. Bremer asked the team to go through the remaining options. Someone suggested that perhaps the recalcitrant members of the IGC should be expelled. I proposed instead that we should force a majority signing. We divided up lobbying duties and I went off to calm Barzani as best I could, because we could not afford to lose him through appearing to be focused only on the Shia. I repeated to him that the UK would not allow anything to be imposed on the Kurds so long as they remained committed to a unified Iraq. He relaxed a little bit.

On 7 March a rumour began to circulate that the Shia group that had been to see Sistani in Najaf had found a way round the problem. We did not give it much credence, but rather than sit around and wait, David, Raad and I decided to go off and tackle Ibrahim al Jaafari, the most religious and impermeable of the non-clerical members of the IGC and, as the principal spokesman for the main wing of the Dawa Party, one of the better known politicians in the country. He gave us the outcome. Virtually all the religious Shia group would sign the TAL, but they would then issue a statement of reservations making two principal points: first, that the TAL, a piece of temporary legislation produced by an unelected body, could not be used to impose conditions on a future Iraqi Assembly; and second, that they objected to the right of three contiguous provinces to veto the constitution. Jaafari offered a long explanation as to why the history and make-up of Iraq justified these arguments. But the conversation was gentle and good-natured.

Later we went out in the dark through the eery back entrance to the Green Zone and tried to persuade Abdul Aziz al Hakim that the TAL, very little of which he had negotiated personally because of his dislike of doing direct business with the Americans, presented the right balance between the communities. I got myself into tangled metaphors about compromises and bridges and gave Raad a hard time with the interpretation. Hakim was unyielding; but he appeared to hint that he might sign the document himself. We stayed too long to make it back to the CPA cafeteria for supper and had to make do with a bag of Iranian pistachios from our host. When we returned we heard that the Rasheed Hotel had been hit by another salvo of rockets from a car parked even closer to the Green Zone wall than in the October attack. Luckily no one had been hurt. We were also told that the Governing Council was to reassemble the next morning.

At 10 a.m. on 8 March we gathered in the government office building and milled about, trying to find out what was likely to happen. Everyone appeared to be there, but the meeting did not start. Ahmed Chalabi worked the room like a professional diplomat, as if he had a strategy that he was reminding people to follow. We later learnt that it had been his idea in Najaf to recommend the sign-with-reservations tactic, after pointing out in an emphatic speech the dangers of destroying the TAL altogether and inviting American wrath. With the clock ticking towards a signing ceremony now theoretically re-scheduled for 11 a.m., I asked Bremer what was going on. He said he had agreed with Bahr al Uloom, as President, that they should not start until the last minute, to prevent people from raising further issues and pushing the whole thing off track again.

At 11 a.m. on the dot Uloom tapped on his glass and started the meeting. He could deliver a fine broadside when he felt like it. He let fly for five minutes on the subject of togetherness, order and compromise and that should have been that. But Ahmed Chalabi flashed his grin and launched into his own sermon. That unleashed a table round, with characteristic contributions from Talabani (five minutes and plenty of political knock-about), Barzani (twenty-three seconds), Jaafari (serious and rather obscure), Rubaie (briefer than usual, and to the point) and a few more all trying to outdo each other in mutual congratulation. Fortunately, nobody wanted to raise anything controversial, though we could not be sure of that at the start. Abdul Aziz al Hakim and Iyad Allawi, as so often, were not present. Mahmoud Othman, the independent Kurd who held the record for speaking at length off the point, strangely did not ask for the floor. Samir al Sumaidaie, the most gentle and liberal of the Sunnis, did so repeatedly and was studiously ignored by Uloom. Finally Uloom gave the microphone to Bremer, who delivered a well-judged homily on the rule of law and democratic civilian control, and time was up.

The CPA team walked over to the Convention Centre, leaving the security men to herd the Governing Council members into a waiting bus to ensure that none escaped en route. A good crowd had turned up for the ceremony. The Governing Council members were seated prominently at the front and the Coalition principals were tucked away tactfully in the third row. The orchestra had been disposed of this time, but a group of schoolchildren had rehearsed some songs and were not going to be denied. They were followed by a diminutive young boy, half the height of the microphone, who delivered a poetic monologue in an ear-splitting yell. After one verse his teacher tried to ease him off the stage, but he slipped her grasp and unburdened himself of his next poem. Our audio translation system had failed and we caught nothing of the meaning, but the Governing Council members were doubled up.

Speeches came and went and the twenty-five Iraqi leaders, four of them represented by deputies, walked up and signed the document. Everyone was warmly applauded and there was plenty of laughter, with Jalal Talabani again playing the comedian. When all was done, the massed press took endless photographs and some heckling began. Our hearts sank, as this could well have been the time for some Islamic opposition to be voiced. But the yelling all seemed to be supportive and no one turned a hair.

So the deed was done. We all repaired for coffee and brownies in the bare canteen next door. The religious Shia had prepared a list of objections, as forecast, but did not produce it until the following day, accompanied by a hard public statement from Sistani. In this way the Ayatollah's sting was drawn, for the time being. It would have been much worse if the TAL had been signed on 1 March and he had announced his opposition afterwards. We had cleared a significant hurdle, but we were a long way from finishing the course.

That, in effect, was my last substantive piece of business with the Governing Council. I would not leave Baghdad until the end of March, but the next week was taken up with a signing-off visit to London. In my final days in the Green Zone I made many sad farewells, but there was little further work I could undertake on a continuous basis and I asked David Richmond, as my successor, to take up the reins.

In London I spent a good deal of time with the media and with Parliament, trying to convey the message that an extraordinary amount had been achieved since April 2003, but the threat from continuing violence remained too great for us to expect anything from now on but a hard, agonising slog. To my colleagues in Whitehall I presented my gloomiest assessment so far. I pointed to the ineradicability of the terrorist threat within Iraq – the awful news of the bombings in Madrid just before the Spanish elections, which we all suspected was the work of al Qaida, had forcefully reminded us that Iraq might become a source of ideas and experience for international terrorist cells. I described the scheming amongst sectarian politicians now beginning to emerge and threw in the difficulty of tactical coordination with the Americans for good measure. John Sawers asked a question or two and I could see some of them wondering whether the experience out in Iraq had got to me, but no one challenged my pessimism outright.

I then went to deliver my final report to the Prime Minister. He appeared relaxed and cheerful on the back of the TAL achievement, delighted to have some good news for a change. I was not able to meet his mood. I said that while I conceded that the UK's sector in the south remained relatively free from the problems further north, security in the centre was deteriorating. There was little prospect of the violence fading away or responding to hard military action while the local population in the worst areas remained even passively sympathetic. I told him I thought the transition period would see some degree of confrontation between the three main communities. We had managed to push through the TAL, but only because we had persuaded the Shia that none of it was irrevocably binding. We had a long way to go before we could bring back our forces from Iraq. The Prime Minister took this calmly. He asked a number of detailed questions, but he knew that I was no longer in a position to influence the situation on the ground and the conversation did not get into strategy. As in every exchange I had with him on Iraq, I was struck by the firmness with which he accepted that there would be a long series of difficult passages to be surmounted. There was no question of giving up for that reason. The costs were not and could not be calculated: the greater they had proved in the past, the more reason there was to continue until a worthwhile result could be achieved. He took what I had to say on board, kept his broader thoughts to himself and thanked me warmly.

On the way back to Baghdad I accompanied Jack Straw in a quick pass through Riyadh to brief the Saudi Foreign Minister on the latest developments. Prince Saud bin Feisal was deeply concerned not just about the Sunni extremist violence, some of the instigators of which had moved into Iraq from Saudi Arabia, but also about the implications of democracy in a neighbour with a Shia majority. I could give him no comfort on either front, except to say that an Iraq governed with the consent of its people should ultimately contribute to the stability of the whole region. I do not think he was persuaded.

Once back in the Green Zone it was packing-up time. On 22 March I went down to the Governing Council to say farewell. Ahmed Chalabi was in the chair. I explained why I was leaving and delivered my unified Iraq lecture. This time my metaphor was built around the river, the most evocative geographic feature in the region: staying on opposite banks was bad; meeting on the bridge good. They knew what I was getting at, but it was too late for a deeper conversation about the difficulties I was leaving them to face.

Not long afterwards I held a last meeting with Jerry Bremer, who was in his friendliest mood. We chatted about the political trend, Chalabi's ambitions, whether the Shia could rise to the needs of all Iraq, the rightness of our prescription for the transition, his reluctance to see the UN taking over, the role of the Brits. Although he had sometimes had his doubts about specific parts of the UK effort, he did not want, or did not choose, to raise them now and he expressed satisfaction with the close relationship overall, which we agreed was truly unprecedented. I told him I had valued his leadership and his patience with the second-guessing with which he had been plagued throughout. The things that grated were left unsaid. I suspect he was relieved to see me go. My departure would release him from a voice regularly coming at him from the side and questioning his one-way style of management. Loyalty in his eyes meant 100 per cent conformity. I felt that I had little left to offer when the room for policy debate remained so narrow.

Throughout the whole Iraq saga the United Kingdom never had a significant impact on US policy formation. The arguments and rivalries in Washington and between the civilian and military machines on the ground were too intrusive; and Bremer's jealous guardianship of decision-making shut out the kind of brainstorming discussion in which the British make the best contributions. This was not necessarily an American prejudice against us or against foreigners in general: Americans in the CPA fortress who had long experience of the Arab world were likewise under-utilised if they did not have the right political credentials. Nor, without risking a break with Bremer, could I appeal to London to compensate in Washington for the power that I lacked in Baghdad. The Blair–Bush line of communication remained strong and constant, but whatever strategic agreement they might have reached rarely fed down to the tactical level when it was so closely controlled from the Pentagon. Jack Straw and Colin Powell kept just as regularly in touch, as they had in the months leading up to the war, but Powell's understanding and wisdom seldom won through in Washington. The power of the United States in Iraq had been delivered down a hard and narrow channel.

If the British made any contribution to policy in Baghdad it was more indirect. We managed to exert an influence on political thinking in the CPA Governance team through regular tactical sessions of a kind they seemed disinclined to hold with their own Arab world experts, and there was a grudging recognition that we were sometimes ahead of them in identifying trends. Nevertheless, Scott Carpenter and his vigorous young group generally wrote their papers for Bremer without reference to us and we often had to fight our cause after these had reached his desk. If I was able to add value, it was perhaps within the Iraqi Governing Council itself. Iraqis set much store by style and manner and in these troubled circumstances they particularly wanted to feel understood. They respected power, like anyone else, but they were not pushovers and they disliked being dictated to. They looked to me to smooth the rougher edges of American presentation, to offer a way forward that they could accept without humiliation, to apologise for tough handling and always to show respect for the sovereign dignity of a people still on the floor. I never abandoned the CPA-agreed policy line, but I was often frank with my Iraqi interlocutors about what it meant and how it had been put together.

At times it was important just to have been there. The

negotiations over the Transitional Administrative Law might have provoked more firestorms if the British had not been in the room, as some of the story of Iraqi intercommunal politics since the CPA period has indicated. The Americans are not widely trusted in that part of the world and the Iraqis wanted my reassurance that they were not being led down an impossible path and that promises would not later vanish into thin air. So I was involved in a good deal of political hand-holding, to the point where even my silent presence could be helpful. This role was reinforced in the Iraqis' minds by the part they saw me as having played at the United Nations in the construction of Saddam's downfall. The credibility, affection and respect accumulated over the months, and the interpreting of events and the sugaring of the medicine appealed to them in their uncertainty and helped persuade them in some instances to follow their better instincts. But my role was never decisive.

As I packed my bags for the last time, somehow finding a wrapping for the huge, leaking tin of Kurdish honey that had come to me from Jalal Talabani's cupboard, I had to acknowledge regret at leaving when I felt I still had something to offer. It was a wrench to abandon an experience so extraordinary and so intensive in its human relationships. For all our failings, laying the foundation of a new Iraq had caused us all to raise our professional game to the highest possible pitch, to feed off each other's talents, to change our priorities and to take decisions that had enormous consequences for our countries and for our lives. For most of us, children of the longest period of peace in the West's history, the Iraq experience had brought us as close to war as any of us were ever likely to come. Going home was necessary, but it was not easy.

20

A Free Iraq

On 31 March 2004 my career with the British Diplomatic Service came to a close. My valedictory assessment from Baghdad did not try to make a drama out of the situation the United Kingdom found itself in. It concluded unexcitingly that the US and the UK had to keep slogging on and bear the costs. The 8 March Law had created a satisfactory framework for the rest of the transition. The cardinal fact to report was that the majority of the Iraqi people remained tolerant of the Coalition – just – but only because they had no alternative. While they did not want their country to be occupied by foreigners, they were glad to be rid of Saddam and understood the opportunity they now had for a better future. The hardest part was still to come: casting the Iraqi state loose on its own in an atmosphere of intercommunal tension. The genuine democrats remained disorganised; the best organised were not the most democratic. If effective political parties did not come into being soon to represent the mainstream views of the secular communities, Shia as well as Sunni, the Islamists, with the momentum behind them, would attract a majority in any poll. I said it seemed highly unlikely that the security threat would disappear with the end of the occupation in mid-2004. Because of the abject preparations for the post-conflict

396

phase and the failure to address mistakes immediately, violence had been allowed to entrench itself. The insurgents and terrorists were comparatively small in number but lethal in effect, with weaponry and planning capability to last for a long time. They would continue to operate until and unless a significant majority of Iraqi society turned actively against them.

David Richmond, my immediate predecessor and then my deputy, took over as my successor for the remaining three months of the Coalition Provisional Authority. He had known Iraq at first hand far longer than I had and his sharply accurate observations had brought depth to our reporting. Bremer worked more easily with him than with me, perhaps because he saw him as less likely to be a rival or a threat, but David continued to find it hard to inject the UK's policy preferences at the opportune moment. He was witness to the further deterioration of the relationship between the Coalition and the Iraqi people as resentment against foreign occupation grew and American sensitivity to this made the US–UK relationship on the ground more tense at times.

The final period of the Coalition Authority achieved its primary purpose, the handing over of a viable state to the Iraqis, with difficulty. The apprehensions of all three major communities grew that their interests were not going to be served within an independent state. The religious Shia parties, determined to oversee the writing of the permanent constitution and thus to dominate the character of the future Iraq, fumed over the clause in the Transitional Administrative Law that obliged them to secure the agreement of the other main communities to the new structure. The Sunni Arabs, accustomed to rule, saw only an endless future of subservient minority status. The Kurdish leaders, torn between making the most of a united Iraq and striking out for independence as their people wanted, settled for keeping their options open and maximising their tactical leverage. Armed resistance to any undesired development remained an option for everyone, not least the legion of unemployed young men. Muqtada al Sadr and his Mehdi Army of impoverished and resentful Shia caught the imagination of all those who wanted the foreigners driven out and Iraq's humiliations redressed. The most important functions for the CPA to perform in its final weeks were to promote the attractiveness of cohesion and magnify the feel-good factor in daily life.

In these they failed. The targets of increased oil production and electricity generation were not met. Jobs were scarce. The larger contracts went to foreign firms. After a tolerable winter, the number and intensity of terrorist attacks began to grow again in the spring. The daily count of American casualties rose. Insurgents and foreign terrorists, sometimes separately and sometimes in tandem, increasingly targeted the new Iraqi security forces, the most sensitive infrastructure and the people and places most likely to foment intercommunal resentment. Their callous disregard for innocent lives crossed new boundaries. US forces decided to raise the aggressiveness of their response, particularly in the most hardline areas of the Sunni heartland such as Fallujah, but the result of tactics that showed no respect for ordinary citizens was almost invariably to motivate more insurgents than they killed or captured.

In April the story broke of the abuse of Iraqi prisoners by US soldiers in Abu Ghraib prison, with catastrophic consequences for the image of the United States in the country, the region and the world. The International Committee of the Red Cross report detailing these abuses had been delivered to the CPA in February, but the story only emerged in the world media when photographs of acts of maltreatment and torture were released. My legal adviser had been shown a copy of the ICRC document at a moment in February when I was away. He immediately drew the attention of the Ministry of Defence in London to the passages about possible maltreatment by British soldiers, and told me he had done so. These cases were rapidly investigated and dealt with, we were told, though the MoD kept us in the dark about the unacceptable abuses committed by British soldiers in Basra, which later led to courts martial in the UK. The ICRC never directed a separate copy of their report to me – I was at a loss later to understand why, when they knew that the UK's human rights experts, and occasionally I myself, were regularly raising with the US military the need to process arrestees and prisoners more quickly and sensitively. Not realising that such explosive material was contained in the rest of the report and preoccupied with other things, I remained personally unaware of the Abu Ghraib abuses until the news broke in April with the release of those shameful photographs.

The Coalition had to grit its teeth and keep going, even as the realisation deepened that its presence in Iraq was as much the problem as the remedy. Since the establishment of the original grouping of over thirty nations on the ground in the spring and summer of 2003, very few new applications to join had been received. Japan and the Republic of Korea were notable exceptions. The intimations we had earlier had from France, Germany and Russia that they would consider what assistance they could give once the political framework was clearer had not led to anything more tangible after the adoption of the TAL. The tragedy of the Madrid bombing in mid-March and the new Spanish Government's decision to withdraw their troops from Iraq underlined the unlikelihood of broader international burden-sharing. It was going to be a struggle just to keep the participants we had. The twelve months that followed saw the situation deteriorating in this respect rather than improving.

As the weeks passed in the spring of 2004, the CPA concentrated increasingly on constructing a successful transition to an interim Iraqi government and a satisfactory basis for the continuation of the Coalition military assistance under Iraqi sovereignty. Badgered daily by Iraqi politicians inside and beyond the IGC to revise the transition process in their favour, Bremer insisted on the sanctity of the TAL and its implementation. With the date and format of the interim incoming government agreed, the options boiled down to the selection of the best Iraqis to assume the top positions. Bremer possessed the theoretical power to appoint them, but he had a number of constituencies to satisfy if Iraq was to have a chance of holding together, and they were not just Iraqi ones. An acceptable division of responsibility between the main communities was essential, but Washington, the region, the wider international community and the UN would all need to buy into the outcome if the new-born Iraq was to receive the positive backing from outside that would be necessary for survival.

Bremer was again helped in his task, as in the effort over the winter to rescue the 15 November Agreement, by Robert Blackwill and by Lakhdar Brahimi in his continuing capacity as UN Special Representative. With Brahimi in this role, the expectation that the United Nations would play a 'vital' part in the construction of the new Iraq was at last being fulfilled. The requirement for any result to be accepted internally and internationally as legitimate gave Brahimi pride of place in this triumvirate: the two Americans would in the end have to accept his choice if there was disagreement. The recognition that they could not contest the UN's decision on such a crucial matter was a remarkable indication of how much the Americans had lost the initiative.

In practice, all three saw the sense in close collaboration, although Brahimi insisted on his independence of action throughout. The challenge was to select a government and an assembly with credibility. Ayatollah Sistani had now reluctantly conceded that the real transition would not begin until elections were held in early 2005. Sistani's primary concern was to ensure that those who held key interim appointments between July 2004 and January 2005 could not extend their hold on power or disrupt the subsequent stages of the transition. This meant that the three would need to satisfy Sistani on the form of the interim administration and the Iraqis chosen to lead it.

The process came to a climax as May turned into June. The interim government needed to be appointed well before the end of June so that the departure of the US-led Authority could be made as seamless as possible. Brahimi was ready with his selection, with

American approval, but the IGC had a surprise in store for him. His choice for Interim President fell on Adnan Pachachi, the veteran Sunni statesman who had been Foreign Minister in the 1960s and had become a leading member of the IGC. His seniority and lack of overt political ambition would have made him widely acceptable. Pachachi must have intimated that he was prepared to take on the position or Brahimi would not have been on the point of nominating him. At the last hour, as the Council was about to gather to make the formal appointments, Pachachi decided to withdraw his name from the running. The news did not surprise me when I heard it, as Pachachi was already showing signs of weariness before I left Iraq and was under pressure from his expatriate wife to avoid the limelight. There were also machinations going inside the IGC that indicated to Pachachi that he would not have broad support across the community divides. Then a second blow struck Brahimi's plan. His first choice for Prime Minister, Hussain al Shahristani, a religious Shia with close connections to Ayatollah Sistani but a political moderate, likewise ruled himself out at the last minute.

A frantic scrabbling ensued to find replacements. This was not the way it was supposed to happen. The Sunnis, despite constant and sympathetic prodding from the CPA since the previous summer, had still failed to organise themselves and the range of available presidential candidates with appeal at the national level was narrow. Brahimi and the CPA turned to Sheikh Ghazi al Yawar, a member of the IGC, who had been working in the background to pick up support and may have been undermining Pachachi. He was a senior member of Iraq's largest tribe, the mainly Sunni Shammar, although not recognised by them as a leader because he had lived abroad as a businessman for most of the Saddam era. His contribution to the workings of the IGC had shown him to be independent-minded and moderate, but he was critical of the Coalition and its way of doing business. Bremer and Blackwill recognised the internal credibility that these qualities conferred on him; he was offered the position by the IGC formally, and he accepted.

As for the Prime Minister slot, the collective second choice was a much more likely figure for the Americans to have selected from the start. Iyad Allawi had kept his distance as a member of the Iraqi Governing Council and was critical of the Coalition effort, despite his close ties to the American and British Governments. He had rarely turned up in person for the most significant events or discussions. For all that, he had been my private choice for chief executive for the transition. He possessed an expert knowledge of the security sector and clearly understood Iraq's need for cross-community cohesion. While his strongest alliance was with Masoud Barzani, the Kurdish Democratic Party leader, he made as great an effort as any of the Iraqi politicians in this period to build bridges with the Sunni tribes and with the other secular forces in Iraq, both because he understood Iraq's need for Coalition politics and to broaden his own narrow following. But he found it difficult to maintain communication with the Shia religious parties and his suspicion of Iran ran deep.

Brahimi and the Americans had assumed, as I had, that Sistani would not accept the nomination of Allawi as Prime Minister. Their selection of Shahristani indicated the priority they placed on accommodating Sistani. But when they had to turn as a matter of urgency to their real preference, they were surprised to learn that the Grand Ayatollah would not object. Allawi's name, with al Yawar's, was rapidly submitted to the IGC for approval and we were able after all to keep to our schedule for the interim government's appointment.

As the midsummer date for the handover drew near, the insurgency grew bolder and terrorist attacks increased in intensity. The world wondered what kind of state was coming into being. But no force short of a popular insurrection could deliver a strategic defeat to the Coalition and no political leader offered a vision to unite Iraqis in a general uprising. Bremer persevered. The handover ceremony was set for 30 June and the CPA prepared to pack its bags and head home, leaving the Coalition forces to stay on under a resolution produced in late May by the UN Security Council setting out the conditions for international support of the newly independent state.

Early on 28 June Bremer, with no more than a few hours' notice to his British partners, suddenly announced that the ceremony would be advanced to that morning. The necessary documents were signed, the flag of the new republic was raised and Bremer was into his helicopter and off to the airport almost before the news had reached the outside world. There was no doubt that the manoeuvre had helped avert a day of planned bloodshed on the thirtieth, but the image of the occupying power cutting and running before its due departure date was the one that the international media chose to promote. Most Iraqis were not concerned. This was their beginning.

The history of the brief period of interim government under Iyad Allawi will be told elsewhere. The violence continued unabated and the growing power of Muqtada al Sadr, a threat to the orthodox Shia hierarchy as much as to the new state, had to be confronted on its home territory in the holy cities of Najaf and Kerbala. Allawi learnt the limitations of his inexperienced security forces and was compelled to rely upon the Coalition a great deal more than he wished. Fallujah, part symbol of the insurgency, part base for non-Iraqi terrorism, finally felt the full wrath of the US military in November, by which time the violence had so sickened the majority of the Iraqi population that their sympathies rested with the forces of law and order even if they were still foreigners. The principal service that Allawi performed for his country through this phase was to deliver elections on time at the end of January 2005. He found himself unable to make daily life much better for the majority of the population and his political credibility suffered for his association with the Coalition throughout his premiership. But on this vital issue he held firm, burnishing his credentials more internationally than at home.

The prospect of genuinely free elections concentrated people's minds. Voters were bound to be the target of as much violence as the opposition could muster against them and the elections threatened to bring out all the intercommunal suspicions and rivalries kept in check first by Saddam, and then by the occupation. There were loud calls for their postponement. The Sunni Arabs, still unable to find convincing community leaders to represent them at the national level and reluctant to face the inevitability that their number would be the measure of their power in a democratic Iraq, flirted with the idea of a boycott and then left themselves no time for anything else. The international media began to predict a disaster. The UN Secretary-General, unwisely choosing a moment just before US election day, wrote an open letter to the US administration suggesting that the time was not right. He was not forgiven for it.

In the early part of the election campaign, which began in earnest in November, there was violence and it was awful. Hundreds of Iraqis died in bombings and assassinations in the last few weeks of 2004 and the toll of American soldiers killed in Iraq passed the 1,500 mark. Polls in the United States and the United Kingdom showed the lowest public support for Iraq policy since the invasion. Criticism of the timetable continued, but postponement of the election would have presented a victory to terrorism and time would not have made the choices any easier. It was much the better policy to keep to the timetable of the Transitional Administrative Law and exemplify the kind of perseverance on which the whole transition depended.

As the year turned, the accumulated experience of the Iraqi and Coalition security forces working together gradually began to limit the reach and power of the violence. Allawi arranged deals with municipal leaders to reassert control in the more troublesome towns in exchange for higher local funding, provided by the United States. Muqtada al Sadr's supporters in the poorer areas of Baghdad laid down their arms for $500 million. The clearing out of Fallujah in November proved to have disrupted the liaison between Iraqi and non-Iraqi cells and broken the lines of communication between Zarqawi and his groups. US intelligence homed in on some of the more sophisticated bomb-makers and the frequency of the most lethal attacks went down. On polling day, as those of us observing from a distance nervously turned on the news programmes, we heard that there had been eight rather than eighty or eight hundred suicide-bomb explosions around the country and fewer than thirty deaths – a miserable comment for one of the most significant days in Iraqi history, but a comparative relief against the background of what we had stirred up over the previous twenty-two months.

The lasting image of election day conveyed something completely different from the chaos predicted: lines of voters queuing peacefully for hours to play their part; citizens swearing that they would vote whether or not it killed them; ballots being tallied as in a practised democracy, with no accusations of stuffed boxes or double-counting; Iraqi women voters proudly holding up their indelibly stained fingers for the world's photographers. The turn-out, 58 per cent overall despite the very low figures in Sunni territory, was well above the average forecasts and higher than the Coalition's own predictions. I felt not just relief but pride in a people whose quality of determination I had never seen so clearly demonstrated. When it came to the comments from Coalition capitals, however, I found the claims of victory and vindication distasteful. Certainly, Saddam Hussein would never have been consigned to prison and this election would never have taken place without the invasion of Iraq. But it seemed to the rest of the world that the people of Iraq had gone out to vote in January 2005 in spite of what had happened to them since 9 April 2003, not because of it. The principal credit for the day was earned by the Iraqi people themselves.

21

Adding Up the Cost

The Iraq story remains unfinished and my account tells only of those parts I witnessed. Historians will have to piece together from a number of different perspectives, particularly of those closest to the action, the full story of how and why things were done as they were. From my viewpoint, it was right to have removed Saddam Hussein, but the next stage should not have been so expensive.

Regime change in Iraq began as an item of unfinished business with a dictator who challenged the superpower. It was then brought through to the planning stage by a group of neo-conservative thinkers who believed that American strength had to be used or lost. It mutated into a response to the events of 11 September 2001, not because Iraq was clearly responsible but because the rationale and the opportunity for asserting power was suddenly magnified. Apparent spin-off benefits in the region – affecting Israel, Saudi Arabia, Iran, oil and the need for reform in the Middle East – added enough to the positive side of the ledger to make the risks seem tolerable.

The risks themselves, however, were never accurately assessed. Once the planned approach reached a successful conclusion on 9 April 2003 and the unplanned took over, as happens more often than not in war, the process developed into a series of reactions to events. The impression that remains with me from the stormy period of the occupation is of a series of apparently vigorous but often remote and wrong-headed decisions, considered adequate at the time but then overtaken by realities that should have been more carefully analysed. Choices were made which depended on the best-case scenario, with no insurance policy in place for a worse outcome. Gradually, as the American and British authorities showed that they could not control developments, Iraqis moved from a passive to an active state while the Coalition headed in the opposite direction. We lost the initiative in the early weeks when we failed to secure the country. The new Iraq has not yet recovered from that mistake.

The question of control, central to this whole story because the United States tried to control the international approach to Iraq and the Pentagon tried to control the internal American handling of it, introduces a paradox. We are seeing US objectives in one sphere cause US headaches in another. To the benefit of many non-Americans, the United States promotes and defends freedom and democracy in the world. But when introduced into other cultures with different histories and values, democracy does not necessarily lead to choices and policies that are immediately compatible with the interests of the United States. That is the whole point of free choice. The policy would not be worth pursuing unless democracy carried in the longer term a collective global value, a stronger mutual interest between peoples in stability and peace. It takes time for all the ingredients of democracy to settle into place. A strategic patience is needed while the J curve, bringing downsides before benefits, works itself through.

Americans are not naturally patient in adversity. They tend to treat resistance to their chosen path as unfriendly and often confront it by turning up their diplomatic and economic power. The resistance is either overcome or entrenches itself more deeply. If that deeper opposition continues to cause direct damage to US interests, then they will turn to the threat and then the use of military force if necessary. In those cases where this approach does not resolve the problem, the situation has to be re-thought. A marked shift in US attitudes may follow and the damage can be considerable. American involvement in Vietnam followed this pattern; so did their intervention in parts of Central America. Korea remains unresolved. On the other hand, the history of twentieth-century Europe would have been quite different without the massive contribution of the Americans, once Europe's interests were defined as theirs. In the case of the Cold War confrontation with the Soviet Union, where military power was threatened but was ultimately unusable without unacceptable cost, American reliance on economic strength, diplomacy, alliances and patient pressure produced one of history's most remarkable geopolitical victories. These examples illustrate the importance of making a correct calculation about the likelihood of force succeeding before the die is cast.

The Cold War is over and the United States is unchallengeable in conventional terms. Fortunately for the rest of the world, the American people harbour no sustained imperial ambitions and no wish to harm others so long as they are able to pursue their preferred way of life. But successive US Governments have not found it easy to develop the long view, this sense of strategic patience. In a democracy, it can be unpopular not to use the nation's available strength to dispose of a perceived problem. What makes Iraq, Iran and North Korea so interesting as major geopolitical issues is that they stand on the dividing line between problems that respond to forceful action and those that do not. Of these three, Iraq came to a head first because dealing with it seemed to offer the greatest benefit at the most affordable cost. If it can easily happen that the spread of democracy leads to a short-term loss of control, then the implications need to be factored in. In Iraq, where Donald Rumsfeld declared during the conflict 'we don't do empire' and then the United States sent its proconsul to run the country, the work necessary for keeping the costs down was never properly done. As Condoleezza Rice acknowledged in a *New York Times* interview in 2004: 'The assumptions we were working on turned out to be wrong.'

If the British Government was more nervous about the implications of taking over Iraq, which it was, why did it fly blind with the United States? I have tried to bring out the three principal reasons: that the British Government, and in particular the Prime Minister, were convinced that Saddam Hussein was a threat to the UK's wider interests that had to be removed; that there were solid grounds for staying close to the United States on a security issue of primary importance; and that it was in Tony Blair's nature, reinforced by his experience in Government, to persevere through the difficulties on a subject on which he instinctively felt he was right.

With the political decisions made, including on the legal framework, and with the policy supported by a majority within the Government and in Parliament, it was the job of the British military and civil service professionals to implement it as effectively as possible. For these teams too there was no going back, and I cannot think of a single individual who bailed out mid-course. Nevertheless, it was awkward to share responsibility with our American counterparts while being assigned a subsidiary role, at best, in the policy-making. Partnership with the United States in top superpower gear involves accepting secondary status. Not only on Iraq but on many occasions during my diplomatic career, I have had to recognise that straight talking with US colleagues, presuming an equal rank, has its limits. You sometimes have to wait until power works, or until the stark realities impose themselves. With such a partner, you have to share the larger perspective, the belief in freedom and an ordered world, to make it worth holding on through the bumpy ride.

It will take longer than a year or two to make a final judgement on whether or not the invasion of Iraq was worth the cost. Iraq and the wider region will have to pass through several stages of change before any of us can come to a fair conclusion. The costs along the way have already been shown to be high, not only in human and financial terms, but also in the loss of credibility and trust in Government. So far, neither the American nor the British Government have succeeded in convincing the majority of people with a stake, however indirect, in the outcome in Iraq that they had good practical reasons for taking the action they did and that good practical results were achieved. This has only partly to do with the failure to find weapons of mass destruction, which both President Bush and Prime Minister Blair were assured by their advisers existed in Iraq. On that issue, I have come to the conclusion that both leaders made an honest mistake in accepting that Iraq was pursuing an active WMD programme.

This does not, however, remove the trust problem. After all the confused and varied explanations for the origins of the Iraq invasion, the majority of people have concluded that WMD were not the real reason for the American decision; and that the UK, for whom WMD were the reason, went along with that decision even when it knew that the American rationale for the use of force was not the British rationale. The real American reason was to trigger change in the American interest by removing an inimical and threatening regime. The objective was in one sense laudable, but the explanation lacked transparency and the method lacked legitimacy. The British Prime Minister tried hard to make up for both these deficiencies, but he was not able to bridge either gap before he finally had to decide whether to abandon the American approach or stay with it. He stayed with it because he saw the removal of Saddam Hussein and the cementing of the US–UK alliance as valuable benefits for the UK. In doing so he had to accept the consequences for his credibility of switching to the American basis for using force.

If things turn out well in Iraq, the final judgement may not be as harsh as it now seems in the middle of 2005, when the outcome is uncertain and the costs look high. The consequences of not invading Iraq might also have been damaging. The Iraqi people were in deep distress and the US and the UK were increasingly being held responsible for the humanitarian situation. The UN sanctions regime was rapidly eroding and Saddam Hussein was finding the resources to rebuild his armed forces, with or without weapons of mass destruction. He was already providing financial incentives for

Palestinian terrorism. Kuwait and the oil-producing regions further to the south would have remained vulnerable and the arguments for political reform in the Middle East would have lost momentum. Writing out a balance-sheet is not a simple matter. With Saddam gone and the United States a presence in the immediate region, the stagnant relationship between governments and peoples in the Middle East has been shaken. It is quite possible that more stable and dynamic societies may evolve, but the intervening phases are likely to be fraught with trouble. By the time an evaluation of the long-term impact of the Iraq war can be made, perhaps the pain and cost of the mistakes in the catalytic early stages will be set in a different context.

What about the consequences in international security terms? Have terrorists gained the greater benefit from the Iraq experience? The CIA think-tank, the National Intelligence Council, issued a report in January 2005 which concluded that Iraq had replaced Afghanistan as the training-ground for the next generation of terrorists and was providing them with an opportunity to gain operational experience and enhance technical skills. Iraq, in the current phase, was described as a 'magnet for international terrorist activity'.

Whether sucking non-Iraqi terrorists into Iraq has turned the world into a more dangerous place remains to be seen. They have certainly made the reconstruction task far more difficult. But will international terrorism itself become stronger? The worst outcome would be the creation of a new generation of terrorists who had gained operational experience and renewed motivation from Iraq and who were left free to migrate to other theatres and even more sensational targets. The best result would be the defeat of violence in Iraq by the people rejecting not just the brutality of terrorist action but also its nihilistic political message. The outcome in Iraq is important for all of us

Security forces cannot beat this kind of enemy on their own. Even during my brief involvement on the ground in Iraq, the balance of advantage swung back and forth between the international terrorist cells at work there and Coalition forces. In the early months of the post-conflict period the failure of the United States to impose a solid security structure encouraged the al Qaida franchise under Abu Musab al Zarqawi to bed down, draw in reinforcements and plan a long campaign. The chance of having a go at the United States, such a prominent and apparently vulnerable enemy, motivated hundreds of fanatics from the Islamic world, many of them with a Sunni extremist background, to offer themselves as terrorist foot-soldiers and suicide bombers. This influx raised the lethality of the attacks against Coalition troops and law-abiding Iraqi citizens alike and sharpened the impression internally and internationally of a country out of control. Over the winter of 2003–4, however, American forces and the intelligence agencies began to regain some ground. Large numbers of activists were killed or captured and the cells were forced to keep their size and profile down. This did not prevent them from carrying out lethal attacks, but they could not gather the strength to mount a strategic challenge to the Coalition. They began to look for more consistent support from the Saddam loyalists and from the growing numbers of disaffected Iraqis, whose motives and style of operation had, until that point, been different. The purposes of the various groups gradually began to merge around the objective of causing chaos, of turning a majority of the Iraqi population against the foreigners and the government they had introduced. It became a struggle for hearts and minds.

As 2004 drew on the Coalition made further mistakes: they neglected to establish effective communication with ordinary Iraqis; they bungled the handling of Fallujah in April and May; they failed to deny Muqtada al Sadr room to develop a demagogic platform of hostility to the foreign presence; and the awful images of American and later British soldiers abusing Iraqi prisoners were plastered across the world's television screens, made worse by the loaded, bloodthirsty coverage of the Qatari news channel, Al Jazeera. The test became not whether the Coalition could survive the constant series of direct terrorist attacks on the security forces and the Iraqi Government but whether the people of Iraq would wish to keep going with the transition. The stakes involved in the holding of national elections steadily rose. The violent opposition realised this and threw everything into disrupting the election campaign.

The elections therefore assumed a double importance. They had to create a legitimate transitional government; and they had to signal that Iraqis would not be deterred from voting by violence. 30 January 2005 achieved both these aims. Iraqis defied both insurgents and terrorists and lined up to vote, discovering in the process that the capacity of the violent opposition to bring society to a halt was much less formidable than they had feared. From then on, for all the propaganda to the contrary, the principal target of violence became the Iraqi State and not the foreign occupier, a psychological shift that has diminished the legitimacy of the bombers and made the majority of the population more determined to defeat them. There is no doubt that the violence will continue, perhaps for a long time. It will not be eradicated from Iraqi society until the people in each locality cooperate to remove it with a government and security forces they trust. Sectarian differences, the culture of violence and the massive number of armaments available in Iraq make this a formidable task, but so long as the main communities can be persuaded to work together, terrorism will not have the power to destroy the prospect of a new Iraq. It remains the case even now that most Iraqis, if asked whether they would rather go back to the days of Saddam Hussein, will say no.

The other danger is that terrorists trained and hardened in the Iraq theatre will move elsewhere with an enhanced capacity to harm Western interests. American and British defences have learnt a great deal about their enemy. It was noticeable in the run-up to the January elections that the sophistication of the suicide and planted bomb attacks diminished because the security forces had picked up or disrupted many of the more experienced bomb-makers. International terrorists will need to work in small cells and to hide their cross-border cooperation cleverly to avoid being detected. Yet it is hard to believe that some of them will not succeed at some stage, using weapons that can combine small size with terrible lethality.

The essential requirement is to reduce their motivation to try. This is a much broader agenda than a security operation. One of the greater long-term costs of the invasion of Iraq has been the loss of respect in the Islamic and developing worlds for Western principles and values, including for democracy. Terrorism is not an ideology; it is an instrument. Declaring war on it without weakening the reasons for using it will not make us safe. The picture that the Arab media were able to paint, distorted as it was, of a brutal occupation – matching Israel's occupation of Palestine – enlarged the reason for young radicals in the Islamic world to join al Qaida or its derivatives.

The principal aim of al Qaida was, and remains, to bring down the Saudi Government and replace it with an Islamic fundamentalist successor. Most modern terrorist groups have come into existence within a domestic political or ideological context. The Palestinian organisations internationalised their support and their activities but Israel has always been their focus. The IRA in the United Kingdom, ETA in Spain, various groups in South-East Asia, the FARC in Colombia, all want to force political change inside their national territory. But globalisation has influenced their methods and the pervasive presence and political impact of the United States has broadened their choice of targets. Al Qaida, in particular, for all the un-Islamic cruelty of its methods, has developed a cultural hallmark which appeals to millions of Muslims concerned about their identity, their religion and their helplessness in a Western-dominated world. Bin Laden's original political and ideological motivation may have been narrowly focused on the Saudi regime, but his example and his effect have produced something more widespread and international: violent resistance to the effects of globalisation and to the power which drives it.

A link has thus been formed between ideological terrorism and the anger of the have-nots. Poverty itself is not a root cause of terrorism. The brutal desire to kill indiscriminately and cause chaos arises surprisingly seldom from the ranks of the deprived and the oppressed. Sympathy for terrorism does, however, if that is a way to challenge the perceived causes of their deprivation. Desperate people look for a champion and there are parts of the world, a world polarised between the winners and losers from globalisation, where Osama bin Laden and others who claim to have taken up his mantle have filled that need. Terrorism thrives if it finds popular support, but it can also survive on passive popular acceptance. Eradicating terrorism within a specific territory is only possible where both government and people want that to happen. We have to create the conditions for that outcome on a global basis.

The decision by the American and British Governments to bring change to Iraq lacked a broader strategy while the future of Palestine remained unresolved and international development policies were failing to bite. We have not yet addressed the larger questions in a systematic way. Tony Blair recognised the connections and tried to persuade the United States to deal with them more directly, but he remained loyal to the US position even when his arguments failed to make sufficient impact. The overall effect has been to enlarge the political, economic and cultural divides within which the feelings of alienation and desperation grow. The United States and the United Kingdom cannot afford to ignore this trend or fail to engineer at least some policies that inspire sympathy in the Islamic and developing worlds.

Such policies will work best if they attract support within the framework of the United Nations. The UN cannot do what its members will not empower it to do, especially on a tough security issue. I have been repeatedly impressed by the quality of the UN's capacity to help disturbed territories back to long-term stability, when the environment is secure enough to allow it. What we required on Iraq was a partnership with the UN, not a challenge to it. Making only minimal use of Sergio de Mello in the summer of 2003 was a mistake; so was the failure to recognise that creating the conditions for a full UN role thereafter would have brought greater legitimacy to the political process that followed. By the time the Coalition half-turned to Brahimi in early 2004, it was too late.

I do not accept that the United Nations has been irreparably damaged by Iraq. It was derided for some weaknesses which were its responsibility and for some which were not. The WMD inspection system came closer to the truth than its principal critics. The controls on implementation of the Oil for Food programme were inadequate, but the programme was under the policy control of the Member States, not the Secretary-General. Brahimi developed a more acute understanding of Iraqi politics than the CPA. Nevertheless, the UN could not cope with Saddam Hussein. Member States have to face realities more honestly. The wide programme of reform proposed for the UN Summit to consider in September 2005 can lead to improvements, but only if political leaders decide to pool their longer-term international interests. Ignoring the potential of the UN to make a difference will hurt us all.

With or without the UN's contribution, the result in Iraq matters. If Iraq succeeds in its transition to a more stable, prosperous country, governed with the consent of its people and living at peace with its neighbours, perhaps history will assess the decision to go to war more generously. The outcome, however, no longer rests primarily with the powers that took the initiative. After the rows at the UN, the secretive planning, the huge deployment of resources and the appalling loss of life, the mistakes and the sometimes-heroic achievements of the Coalition, after all the bitter controversy the elections of 30 January 2005 brought the saga back to where the test really lies, with the Iraqi people. No one could say at the start of the conflict and no one can safely say now whether Iraq will end by constructing something worthy out of the fractured half-opportunity it has been given. Iraqis do not know themselves. They have had to pay a high cost for the chance of freedom.

Epilogue (2016)

The final chapter of my original 2005 book remains unrevised. I hope there may still be a value in recalling how things appeared only a year after the Coalition period terminated. But now that the world has moved on and the Chilcot Inquiry has reported, the reader of my postponed offering sits in a different environment and deserves a more up-to-date assessment.

Anyone sitting down in the summer of 2016 to assess the consequences of this forceful Western intervention in the affairs of another region has to think first about the condition of Iraq itself. The US-led Coalition claimed to be giving Iraqis a new opportunity, but the last twelve years have seen unending violence and few improvements in most people's standard of living. Would the continuation of Saddam Hussein's repressive dictatorship have benefited the Iraqi people more than the chaos of a new start and an open political system?

A judgement on this still has to be provisional. The Middle East has become the archetypal troubled region of the early twenty-first century because the high potential of its talented peoples has in most places been held back by distressingly low standards of governance. Whether or not outside powers intervene – and they intervened constantly during the twentieth century without much care for indigenous interests – time is needed for cohesion, stability and economic dynamism to come through. The British, after all, are still arguing over their identity and political structure eight centuries on from the Magna Carta.

Iraq had never consensually governed its own affairs within its current borders when Saddam was ousted. At the end of June 2004 its people were given a choice by the CPA, but in circumstances that should have been more favourable. The fundamental error of the Coalition was to have lost control of security almost immediately after the invasion was over. President Bush in effect set the wrong mission for CENTCOM Commander General Tommy Franks: he needed to deliver not just an Iraq without Saddam, but a secure and functioning Iraq without Saddam. This would have required pre-invasion planning for at least a full year after the Iraqi forces had been defeated, with detailed estimations of the resources necessary to lay the foundations for the next stage. Secretary of Defense Donald Rumsfeld was determined to avoid the commitment implicit in such an objective, and rejected or buried any analysis that showed it might be the wisest course. The 'Mission accomplished' celebration of 1 May 2003 on the USS *Missouri* sits heavily in the historical record as one of the greater moments of hubris in US post-Cold War policy-making.

Regime change in Iraq in a sense foreshadowed the Arab Spring, because the people were ready to end Saddam's oppressive tyranny. In contrast with Tunisia, Egypt, Syria and Libya, Iraq's political upheaval was generated by military intervention. But it shares with those other Arab states struggling to shake off tyranny the syndrome of post-regime change vacuum. Not only did the US Government, or subsequently the Coalition Provisional Authority (CPA) in Baghdad, fail to identify a leadership structure for the aftermath of the invasion, they never seriously set about analysing and creating the ingredients for forming one. Where had the lessons of the two calamitous world wars of the twentieth century vanished to? The care with which Roosevelt, Truman, Churchill, Marshall and MacArthur planned for and administered the recovery of Germany and Japan after 1945 (a comparison to which Ambassador Paul Bremer constantly referred) was rooted in the mess the Allies made of the Versailles peace in 1919. Iraq was of course on a different scale, but no war is too small for its consequences to be left to luck. Libya and Afghanistan are still teaching us that.

During the CPA year we saw how much the people of Iraq wanted to make the new opportunity work. Grand Ayatollah Sistani repeatedly voiced the aspirations of a majority of Iraqis in calling the nation to order, compromise and unity. The mixed group of semi-leaders the CPA assembled in the summer of 2003 as the Iraqi Governing Council wanted order and unity to emerge. But they choked on compromise. So bloody and divisive had Saddam's rule been – carrying a Sunni Baathist label, but in reality the project of a Tikriti sub-group brutally pursuing their own interests – that the Shia majority became determined never to allow a Sunni minority to dominate again. Then the Shia turned out to be sub-divided themselves, and no unifying personality has emerged with both the strength to forge consensus and the integrity to put the people first.

With hindsight, perhaps the only figure left standing by Saddam who might have been capable of doing this was Mohammed Baqir al Hakim, the Shia Ayatollah who headed the Supreme Council of the Islamic Republic of Iraq. He survived Saddam's purges by taking refuge in Iran, but was assassinated by al Qaida in August 2003 in a double strike – the other victim that August being Sergio Vieira de Mello, the UN Special Representative in Iraq – which did as much to diminish the prospects for success of the Coalition as any other post-invasion event. Unlike Ayatollah Sistani, Hakim would not have declined to assume a political position. He did not want to be considered for the Iraqi Governing Council in the weeks before his death, leaving it to his brother to fill that role, but that could have proved a wise judgement in the light of later developments. The important factor was his status as a leader who had borne the heat and burden of Saddam's rule, as opposed to the Westernised expatriate dissidents such as Ahmad Chalabi and Iyad Allawi whom the Americans had favoured. Whether he could have achieved more for Iraq than the Prime Ministers who followed the CPA period has to stay hypothetical. But it remains an important lesson for any policy of intervention that trouble comes from the absence of a visibly capable leader to assume power after the dirty work has been done. Iraq remains a country whose future within its UN-approved borders is not yet assured.

The shock waves from the implosion of security in Iraq hit other countries too. The rebellion in Syria might have happened anyway, following on from the turnovers in North Africa. But the predatory emergence of al Qaida and then ISIS at the heart of the Syrian opposition was made far more likely by the survival of Abu Bakr al-Baghdadi under al Qaida in Iraq and by the battle-hardening experience of the resistance there. Research will show in due course how strong an interplay developed between the Iraqi and Syrian theatres, perhaps including the transfer of some chemical weapons before the invasion, and continuing with the failure of the Coalition in 2003–4 to control either the border between the two countries or the flow of weaponry from Saddam's conventional arsenals into the wrong hands. The collapse of the Soviet Union, and then of Yugoslavia, has demonstrated for modern Europeans how malign forces exploit a vacuum much more quickly and effectively than the law-abiding majority of the population. The risk of that happening is close to a certainty in an uncontrolled situation. The Coalition, and the Iraqi leadership that followed, should have placed the rule of law as the highest policy priority in the period after the invasion. Both preferred to pursue narrower interests, and have left the people of Iraq to suffer as a consequence, dragging the people of Syria after them. If Jordan, Lebanon, Saudi Arabia and others were also to be drawn into the continuing storm, historians would be even less kind to the instigators of the Iraq adventure.

Nevertheless there are other reasons why the West's attempts to open up the region to opportunities for better governance and higher standards of living have fallen on stony ground. We are observing in the tragic struggles in Syria, Yemen, Iraq, Libya and elsewhere, including Egypt, a disappointing incapacity in these societies for striking internal compromises for the sake of the larger nation. The Arab World has suffered bitterly from outside interference since

Ottoman times, but still seems unable to shake off the assumption that only a hard man in power and a top-down system can achieve stability. This is not the place to start a lecture on Arab and Islamic culture, and others are far better qualified than I am to give it. But the infertile political environment may have something to do with the hallowed precepts for living in a harsh desert climate, where a deterministic outlook, strict rules for daily life and the widespread exclusion of women from public involvement sap innovation and adaptability. Circumstances of constant insecurity, not solely the region's fault, also change the nature of social and political interaction and increase the probability of tribal and sectarian differences. I hope the twenty-first century will give these talented peoples space to think through the systemic challenges and evolve a more peaceful way forward. It has to be their responsibility in sovereign independence to make the choices.

What is evolving in the Middle East is anyway part of something bigger. Let's call it global regime change, to underline the irony of what is happening on the American superpower's watch. I wrote at the start of this book in 2005 that the story of Iraq was the story of the projection of American power. It still is. The passion that Americans feel for freedom, a passion generated by the colonists' escape from poor governance in Europe and their rejection of the rule of George III in 1776, has brought about two great consequences: the spread of freedom much more widely throughout the world than would have happened without great-hearted US involvement in the twentieth century defeat of fascism and in the encouragement of democracy everywhere; and, alongside that, the unrealistic belief in the minds of too many Americans that freedom is an unqualified and self-sustaining blessing with a uniquely American stamp on it.

A freer world is by nature a more disordered world, unless the investment in consensual order is as strong as the investment in freedom. If other things are equal, freedom of choice leads human beings to return to their comfort setting of a tribal identity. For people of a distinct identity to combine in a larger political grouping of many identities, there have to be powerful reasons. For much of human history where this has happened, the reason has been brute force: conquest, or defensive alliances against conquest. With the advance of civilisation (in certain respects), economic effectiveness and economies of scale have become important new grounds for cooperation. But if a community believes that it can maintain or improve its quality of life without compromising on its identity, it can readily see the costs of wider cooperation as excessive. Leading politicians in the advanced democracies consistently underestimate the importance of re-emphasising for their electorates the vital reasons for sticking together in larger units.

So our world of greater openness and opportunity is, paradoxically, moving towards fragmentation, as communities react to the costs of globalised cooperation and resent the intrusion of other cultures. Iraq has accelerated this trend in two important ways. The perception of American exceptionalism has diminished the authority by example of the principal advocate of democratic freedom; and the concept of justified intervention to keep global order has been knocked back. To most people on the planet now it is unacceptable to allow the United States on its own to interpret international legitimacy.

This is quite a high price to pay for the failure to keep the United Nations membership onside for the invasion of Iraq. The UN, as we all know, is not the automatic route to international peace and security that its founders imagined it might become. The forces of nationalism and the resistance to globalisation have proved too strong for that. But in an era when no imposed system of international authority or discipline is ever going to be accepted, the UN stands in the eyes of most global citizens as the repository and guardian of international legitimacy. Losing your audience in that theatre carries a cost for the influence and leadership aspirations even of the greatest powers.

So the circumstances for the maintenance of global order are now very different from the days following the end of the Second World War. The 193 members of the UN have a treaty, a set of principles and a forum, all of them immensely valuable, but they lack an acceptable leadership structure and a credible enforcement system. This puts a high premium on compromise and on a compatible understanding between nations of their mutual interests. The eighteen months between 9/11 and the invasion of Iraq will, I believe, be seen as a watershed moment in modern history when acceptance of US leadership in a shared global enterprise might have materialised if the Americans had shown any lasting interest in the sharing bit.

As it was, the Pentagon saw it differently. 'Stuff happened,' said Donald Rumsfeld, but the people who predicted that stuff would happen, principally Secretary of State Colin Powell, were sidelined. President George W. Bush never acquired a vision of the right end-game in Iraq and so the resources required to reach it were never allocated. The British had serious qualms about the post-invasion planning, but they were sitting in the second carriage, not driving the engine.

President Bush's successor has demonstrated that he understands the downsides of proprietorial intervention. The Obama doctrine of withdrawal from places where the US has little right to be has a lot to justify it when contrasted with the neocons' focus on using power when and where you think you have it. Yet this refusal to engage in messy regional conflicts has led to criticism of US passivity in Syria, Libya and indeed Iraq itself. Some of this has struck home. Just as the Chilcot Report finally emerged in the summer of 2016 with its trenchant judgements on the 2003 intervention, Washington was stepping up its military involvement alongside the Iraqi security forces to a level of 4,500 personnel. US objectives were more related to counter-terrorism than to propping up a chaotic Baghdad, but the ungoverned space that ISIS exploited to set up its notorious caliphate was enlarged by the failure of the US-led Coalition to settle a post-Saddam Iraq. Afghanistan is similarly slipping into deeper trouble because the groundwork for a new state was never properly done.

So the US is damned if it acts and damned if it doesn't. The perceptions of withdrawal from proactive engagement in the Middle East have fed into calculations by competitor states such as Russia and China that the US can be challenged more assertively. This certainly formed an element of Moscow's decision to enter the Syrian theatre in 2014 and has played a part in Russia's actions in Ukraine and China's in the South China Sea. The cumulative effect of American miscalculations in Vietnam and Iraq can be seen as having exercised a greater impact on the redistribution of global hard power than respect for their comparative successes in the Balkans and in the maintenance of NATO as a powerful defensive alliance. Yet action to support global order cannot be totally abandoned because particular campaigns ended badly. Compromises are necessary even between countries that are suspicious of each other; and the dialogue over Syria developing in mid-2016 between the US Secretary of State and the Russian Foreign Minister takes a significant step in this direction. The UN and its principles exist to provide an objective framework for such initiatives, and stands as one of the few exceptional instruments this generation possesses for avoiding the kind of great power war that has wrecked every previous era. As Secretary-General Kofi Annan so clearly put it at one stage in the Iraq saga, despite his deep-rooted distaste for war, sometimes the threat of the use of military power has to be present to induce leaders to follow international rules. And, some would add, it cannot be a bluff.

We have to continue to look to Washington to get the judgement right in these respects. It is noticeable that US involvement in the East Asia security field, where the need to assess very carefully the interaction with another potential superpower has led to more nuanced approaches, feels quite different from that in the Middle East, where the Americans can deploy overwhelmingly superior strength where they wish. Similarly, the handling of Russia after the US knew it had won the Cold War has lacked the finesse and the comprehensive strategic mastery of US Cold War policy-making. It seems to require the challenge of an almost equal power centre to bring the best out of American superpower capability.

That is one reason why Iran has been able to draw such advantage from the US involvement in Iraq. American disrespect for Iran's strategic capability, as well as for the nature of its regime, led Washington to underestimate the degree to which Tehran might benefit from the removal of Saddam and to misjudge the higher importance of Iran to US long-term interests. In Baghdad in 2003–4, Ambassador Bremer was totally uninterested in the work the UK team initiated within the CPA to assess the true effect of Iranian meddling in Iraq. The Coalition's fumblings left scope for Tehran to turn their interference tap on or off at will, to produce just the right amount of chaos in their neighbour: enough to scupper the establishment of an American power base there, but not so much that another Saddam might be able to rise from the ashes and threaten his neighbour. While the crucial US relationship with Turkey is quite different, it is noticeable how freely the Turks under President Erdogan have been determined to pursue (not always wisely) their own nationalistic interests, whether or not that offends their most powerful ally.

Can the rise of terrorism in its latest forms be laid at the door of our Iraq policy? Two factors in particular have enabled the capabilities of groups like al Qaida and Islamic State: first, the availability of ungoverned space (both physical and virtual) within which to grow and weaponise concepts of religious perversion and hate; and second, the recruitment appeal of resistance to the system of unequal global power distribution which has left certain types of people behind. Iraq played a part in each of these trends, though events in Afghanistan after the Soviet invasion exerted a strong influence and in recent years the North African desert and Syria have become much more troublesome. A rebellion on the Syrian model could have happened in Iraq under Saddam, though he was a more efficient repressor than Bashar al Assad. The degree to which al Qaida in Iraq, under Abu Musab al Zarqawi and later Abu Bakr al-Baghdadi, was able to grow and mutate into ISIS was enlarged because of the removal of Saddam and the success of the insurgency against the US-led Coalition. The interplay between the situations in Syria and Iraq has proved significant and damaging, just as much as between Iran and Iraq, and developed from the poor control of the security theatre in Iraq after the invasion. The growing reach and lethality of the ISIS franchise in Western Europe especially, but also in the US, have some of their roots in the failures of administration in Iraq. Nonetheless, it would go too far to claim that the phenomenon of extremist jihadism would have failed to emerge without the Iraq invasion.

Then there is the United Kingdom. The Chilcot Report sets its criticism of Tony Blair's judgement primarily in the context of British interests and administrative principles. The wealth of detail in the Report about internal UK processes tends to underplay the constant elephantine presence in the room of American power projection, but it was a strong reality at the time and I have made it a cardinal theme of this book. Blair fell from political grace only partly because the argument that Saddam was a real and present WMD-laden danger proved to be an exaggeration. I have always had some respect for the Prime Minister's contention that it might have been a greater mistake to assume, on the evidence at the time, that Saddam possessed no WMD. Surely the larger Blair sin in the eyes of the British public was to move his criteria for going to war from British to American foundations. There were honourable reasons for standing by our first ally after the 2001 attacks, but this shift enlarged the perception of menace from Saddam and reduced the importance of the international rules-based approach which Blair himself had promoted in his 1999 Chicago speech. It was this policy element that disturbed the advisers around the Prime Minister more than any other, as well as losing him public sympathy. It appears paradoxical that this was the politician who in his three general election campaigns routed the opposition by the greatest margin in more than a century.

The effects of this particular divorce between the leadership and the common citizen in Britain have been far-reaching, given that the trend in popular disaffection has anyway been accelerated by social, technological and economic changes in a freer and more open world.

The linkages can be traced from the protests over Iraq in 2003 to the vote in the June 2016 referendum to leave the EU: 'The people up there in charge just do not seem to be taking our views into account.' The lines of cause and effect here are of course very complex. It is ironic that the Europeans who appeared to share the British public's distaste for the use of force in 2003 were roundly rejected as alien in 2016. The invasion of Iraq and the vote to leave the EU have both had a marked effect on the UK's image and impact abroad. They bring back with some force the Dean Acheson aphorism that the UK has yet to find its post-empire place in the world. But the principal political error lay in the fact that the domestic interests of the British people just did not seem to be the primary criterion.

The Iraq saga has also left its mark, sadly, on the relationship between the British and American peoples. It is conventional to say that we are joined together by shared history, values and culture, but the way the world is currently heading in diverse directions has rendered this less true than even twenty-five years ago. Barack Obama has eased some of the glaring incompatibilities of the George W. Bush era, but the Atlantic is still widening socially and politically. Growing insularity in the UK is as responsible for this as American subjectivity. The two societies are identifiably different.

Iraq contributed to this distancing because the pretexts for involvement rang far hollower with most Britons than with most Americans. We are rightly proud of our armed forces, but we feel that something has failed if they are sent into violent action. The British bar is set higher. Brits are less overtly passionate about patriotism, religion, power and wealth. Perhaps we are also more exhausted by our long engagement with the outside world and by the loss of the factors that used to tip the international playing field our way.

Yet the ledger is full of entries on the other side. Americans have created the most dynamic and technologically advanced society in history, and have remained open and generous in doing so. The British legacy in parliamentary democracy, in sport, the arts, science, and medicine, has been almost as distinguished. We are the principal investors in each other's economies and first allies when it comes to a big crunch. We must not lose faith in each other.

I have been quite critical of American mistakes in this account of the Iraq story, but I am not anti-American. Having spent most of my diplomatic career either in the United States or closely involved in projects with it, I remain full of admiration for both the achievements and the continuing potential of this remarkable republic, and for the open-hearted spirit of its people. Iraq, however, is not to be counted amongst its more glorious moments, and I wanted to set out the reasons why. A world without an America on top form is always going to face a poorer and more threatened future.

Appendix 1

Resolution 687 (1991)

Adopted by the Security Council at its 2,981st meeting, on 3 April 1991

The Security Council,

Recalling its resolutions 660 (1990) of 2 August 1990, 661 (1990) of 6 August 1990, 662 (1990) of 9 August 1990, 664 (1990) of 18 August 1990, 665 (1990) of 25 August 1990, 666 (1990) of 13 September 1990, 667 (1990) of 16 September 1990, 669 (1990) of 24 September 1990, 670 (1990) of 25 September 1990, 674 (1990) of 29 October 1990, 677 (1990) of 28 November 1990, 678 (1990) of 29 November 1990 and 686 (1991) of 2 March 1991,

Welcoming the restoration to Kuwait of its sovereignty, independence and territorial integrity and the return of its legitimate Government,

Affirming the commitment of all Member States to the sovereignty, territorial integrity and political independence of Kuwait and Iraq, and noting the intention expressed by the Member States cooperating with Kuwait under paragraph 2 of resolution 678 (1990) to bring their military presence in Iraq to an end as soon as possible consistent with paragraph 8 of resolution 686 (1991),

Reaffirming the need to be assured of Iraq's peaceful intentions in the light of its unlawful invasion and occupation of Kuwait,

Taking note of the letter sent by the Minister for Foreign Affairs of Iraq on 27 February 1991 and those sent pursuant to resolution 686 (1991),

Noting that Iraq and Kuwait, as independent sovereign States, signed at Baghdad on 4 October 1963 "Agreed Minutes Between the State of Kuwait and the Republic of Iraq Regarding the Restoration of Friendly Relations, Recognition and Related Matters", thereby recognising formally the boundary between Iraq and Kuwait and the allocation of islands, which were registered with the United Nations in accordance with Article 102 of the Charter of the United Nations and in which Iraq recognized the independence and complete sovereignty of the State of Kuwait within its borders as specified and accepted in the letter of the Prime Minister of Iraq dated 21 July 1932, and as accepted by the Ruler of Kuwait in his letter dated 10 August 1932,

Conscious of the need for demarcation of the said boundary,

Conscious also of the statements by Iraq threatening to use weapons in violation of its obligations under the Geneva Protocol for the Prohibition of the Use in War of Asphyxiating, Poisonous or Other Gases, and of Bacteriological Methods of Warfare, signed at Geneva on 17 June 1925, and of its prior use of chemical weapons and affirming that grave consequences would follow any further use by Iraq of such weapons,

Recalling that Iraq has subscribed to the Declaration adopted by all States participating in the Conference of States Parties to the 1925 Geneva Protocol and Other Interested States, held in Paris from 7 to 11 January 1989, establishing the objective of universal elimination of chemical and biological weapons,

Recalling also that Iraq has signed the Convention on the Prohibition of the Development, Production and Stockpiling of Bacteriological (Biological) and Toxin Weapons and on Their Destruction, of 10 April 1972,

Noting the importance of Iraq ratifying this Convention,

Noting moreover the importance of all States adhering to this Convention and encouraging its forthcoming Review Conference to reinforce the authority, efficiency and universal scope of the convention,

Stressing the importance of an early conclusion by the Conference on Disarmament of its work on a Convention on the Universal Prohibition of Chemical Weapons and of universal adherence thereto,

Aware of the use by Iraq of ballistic missiles in unprovoked attacks and therefore of the need to take specific measures in regard to such missiles located in Iraq,

Concerned by the reports in the hands of Member States that Iraq has attempted to acquire materials for a nuclear-weapons programme contrary to its obligations under the Treaty on the Non-Proliferation of Nuclear Weapons of 1 July 1968,

Recalling the objective of the establishment of a nuclear-weapons-free zone in the region of the Middle East,

Conscious of the threat that all weapons of mass destruction pose to peace and security in the area and of the need to work towards the establishment in the Middle East of a zone free of such weapons,

Conscious also of the objective of achieving balanced and comprehensive control of armaments in the region,

Conscious further of the importance of achieving the objectives noted above using all available means, including a dialogue among the States of the region,

Noting that resolution 686 (1991) marked the lifting of the measures imposed by resolution 661 (1990) in so far as they applied to Kuwait,

Noting that despite the progress being made in fulfilling the obligations of resolution 686 (1991), many Kuwaiti and third country nationals are still not accounted for and property remains unreturned,

Recalling the International Convention against the Taking of Hostages, opened for signature at New York on 18 December 1979, which categorizes all acts of taking hostages as manifestations of international terrorism,

Deploring threats made by Iraq during the recent conflict to make use of terrorism against targets outside Iraq and the taking of hostages by Iraq,

Taking note with grave concern of the reports of the Secretary-General of 20 March 1991 and 28 March 1991, and conscious of the necessity to meet urgently the humanitarian needs in Kuwait and Iraq,

Bearing in mind its objective of restoring international peace and security in the area as set out in recent resolutions of the Security Council,

Conscious of the need to take the following measures acting under Chapter VII of the Charter,

1. *Affirms* all thirteen resolutions noted above, except as expressly changed below to achieve the goals of this resolution, including a formal cease-fire;

A

2. *Demands* that Iraq and Kuwait respect the inviolability of the international boundary and the allocation of islands set out in the "Agreed Minutes Between the State of Kuwait

and the Republic of Iraq Regarding the Restoration of Friendly Relations, Recognition and Related Matters", signed by them in the exercise of their sovereignty at Baghdad on 4 October 1963 and registered with the United Nations and published by the United Nations in document 7063, United Nations, *Treaty Series*, 1964;

3. *Calls upon* the Secretary-General to lend his assistance to make arrangements with Iraq and Kuwait to demarcate the boundary between Iraq and Kuwait, drawing on appropriate material, including the map transmitted by Security Council document S/22412 and to report back to the Security Council within one month;

4. *Decides* to guarantee the inviolability of the above-mentioned international boundary and to take as appropriate all necessary measures to that end in accordance with the Charter of the United Nations;

B

5. *Requests* the Secretary-General, after consulting with Iraq and Kuwait, to submit within three days to the Security Council for its approval a plan for the immediate deployment of a United Nations observer unit to monitor the Khor Abdullah and a demilitarized zone, which is hereby established, extending ten kilometres into Iraq and five kilometres into Kuwait from the boundary referred to in the "Agreed Minutes Between the State of Kuwait and the Republic of Iraq Regarding the Restoration of Friendly Relations, Recognition and Related Matters" of 4 October 1963; to deter violations of the boundary through its presence in and surveillance of the demilitarized zone; to observe any hostile or potentially hostile action mounted from the territory of one State to the other; and for the Secretary-General to report regularly to the Security Council on the operations of the unit, and immediately if there are serious violations of the zone or potential threats to peace;

6. *Notes* that as soon as the Secretary-General notifies the Security Council of the completion of the deployment of the United Nations observer unit, the conditions will be established for the Member States cooperating with Kuwait in accordance with resolution 678 (1990) to bring their military presence in Iraq to an end consistent with resolution 686 (1991);

C

7. *Invites* Iraq to reaffirm unconditionally its obligations under the Geneva Protocol for the Prohibition of the Use in War of Asphyxiating, Poisonous or Other Gases, and of Bacteriological Methods of Warfare, signed at Geneva on 17 June 1925, and to ratify the Convention on the Prohibition of the Development, Production and Stockpiling of Bacteriological (Biological) and Toxin Weapons and on Their Destruction, of 10 April 1972;

8. *Decides* that Iraq shall unconditionally accept the destruction, removal, or rendering harmless, under international supervision, of:

(a) All chemical and biological weapons and all stocks of agents and all related subsystems and components and all research, development, support and manufacturing facilities;

(b) All ballistic missiles with a range greater than 150 kilometres and related major parts, and repair and production facilities;

9. *Decides*, for the implementation of paragraph 8 above, the following:

(a) Iraq shall submit to the Secretary-General, within fifteen days of the adoption of the present resolution, a declaration of the locations, amounts and types of all items specified in paragraph 8 and agree to urgent, on-site inspection as specified below;

(b) The Secretary-General, in consultation with the appropriate Governments and, where appropriate, with the Director-General of the World Health Organization, within forty-five days of the passage of the present resolution, shall develop, and submit to the

Council for approval, a plan calling for the completion of the following acts within forty-five days of such approval:

(i) The forming of a Special Commission, which shall carry out immediate on-site inspection of Iraq's biological, chemical and missile capabilities, based on Iraq's declarations and the designation of any additional locations by the Special Commission itself;

(ii) The yielding by Iraq of possession to the Special Commission for destruction, removal or rendering harmless, taking into account the requirements of public safety, of all items specified under paragraph 8 (a) above, including items at 'the additional locations designated by the Special Commission under paragraph 9 (b) (i) above and the destruction by Iraq, under the supervision of the Special Commission, of all its missile capabilities, including launchers, as specified under paragraph 8 (b) above;

(iii) The provision by the Special Commission of the assistance and cooperation to the Director-General of the International Atomic Energy Agency required in paragraphs 12 and 13 below;

10. *Decides* that Iraq shall unconditionally undertake not to use, develop, construct or acquire any of the items specified in paragraphs 8 and 9 above and requests the Secretary-General, in consultation with the Special Commission, to develop a plan for the future ongoing monitoring and verification of Iraq's compliance with this paragraph, to be submitted to the Security Council for approval within one hundred and twenty days of the passage of this resolution;

11. *Invites* Iraq to reaffirm unconditionally its obligations under the Treaty on the Non-Proliferation of Nuclear Weapons of 1 July 1968;

12. *Decides* that Iraq shall unconditionally agree not to acquire or develop nuclear weapons or nuclear-weapons-usable material or any subsystems or components or any research, development, support or manufacturing facilities related to the above; to submit to the Secretary-General and the Director-General of the International Atomic Energy Agency within fifteen days of the adoption of the present resolution a declaration of the locations, amounts, and types of all items specified above; to place all of its nuclear-weapons-usable materials under the exclusive control, for custody and removal, of the International Atomic Energy Agency, with the assistance and cooperation of the Special Commission as provided for in the plan of the Secretary-General discussed in paragraph 9 (b) above; to accept, in accordance with the arrangements provided for in paragraph 13 below, urgent on-site inspection and the destruction, removal or rendering harmless as appropriate of all items specified above; and to accept the plan discussed in paragraph 13 below for the future ongoing monitoring and verification of its compliance with these undertakings;

13. *Requests* the Director-General of the International Atomic Energy Agency, through the Secretary-General, with the assistance and cooperation of the Special Commission as provided for in the plan of the Secretary-General in paragraph 9 (b) above, to carry out immediate on-site inspection of Iraq's nuclear capabilities based on Iraq's declarations and the designation of any additional locations by the Special Commission; to develop a plan for submission to the Security Council within forty-five days calling for the destruction, removal, or rendering harmless as appropriate of all items listed in paragraph 12 above; to carry out the plan within forty-five days following approval by the Security Council; and to develop a plan, taking into account the rights and obligations of Iraq under the Treaty on the Non-Proliferation of Nuclear Weapons of 1 July 1968, for the future ongoing monitoring and verification of Iraq's compliance with paragraph 12 above, including an inventory of all nuclear material in Iraq subject to the Agency's verification and inspections to confirm that Agency safeguards cover all relevant nuclear activities in Iraq, to be submitted to the

432

Security Council for approval within one hundred and twenty days of the passage of the present resolution;

14. *Takes note* that the actions to be taken by Iraq in paragraphs 8, 9, 10, 11, 12 and 13 of the present resolution represent steps towards the goal of establishing in the Middle East a zone free from weapons of mass destruction and all missiles for their delivery and the objective of a global ban on chemical weapons;

D

15. *Requests* the Secretary-General to report to the Security Council on the steps taken to facilitate the return of all Kuwaiti property seized by Iraq, including a list of any property that Kuwait claims has not been returned or which has not been returned intact;

E

16. *Reaffirms* that Iraq, without prejudice to the debts and obligations of Iraq arising prior to 2 August 1990, which will be addressed through the normal mechanisms, is liable under international law for any direct loss, damage, including environmental damage and the depletion of natural resources, or injury to foreign Governments, nationals and corporations, as a result of Iraq's unlawful invasion and occupation of Kuwait;

17. *Decides* that all Iraqi statements made since 2 August 1990 repudiating its foreign debt are null and void, and demands that Iraq adhere scrupulously to all of its obligations concerning servicing and repayment of its foreign debt;

18. *Decides also* to create a fund to pay compensation for claims that fall within paragraph 16 above and to establish a Commission that will administer the fund;

19. *Directs* the Secretary-General to develop and present to the Security Council for decision, no later than thirty days following the adoption of the present resolution, recommendations for the fund to meet the requirement for the payment of claims established in accordance with paragraph 18 above and for a programme to implement the decisions in paragraphs 16, 17 and 18 above, including: administration of the fund; mechanisms for determining the appropriate level of Iraq's contribution to the fund based on a percentage of the value of the exports of petroleum and petroleum products from Iraq not to exceed a figure to be suggested to the Council by the Secretary-General, taking into account the requirements of the people of Iraq, Iraq's payment capacity as assessed in conjunction with the international financial institutions taking into consideration external debt service, and the needs of the Iraqi economy; arrangements for ensuring that payments are made to the fund; the process by which funds will be allocated and claims paid; appropriate procedures for evaluating losses, listing claims and verifying their validity and resolving disputed claims in respect of Iraq's liability as specified in paragraph 16 above; and the composition of the Commission designated above;

F

20. *Decides*, effective immediately, that the prohibitions against the sale or supply to Iraq of commodities or products, other than medicine and health supplies, and prohibitions against financial transactions related thereto contained in resolution 661 (1990) shall not apply to foodstuffs notified to the Security Council Committee established by resolution 661 (1990) concerning the situation between Iraq and Kuwait or, with the approval of that Committee, under the simplified and accelerated "no-objection" procedure, to materials and supplies for essential civilian needs as identified in the report of the Secretary-General dated 20 March 1991, and in any further findings of humanitarian need by the Committee;

21. *Decides* that the Security Council shall review the provisions of paragraph 20 above every sixty days in the light of the policies and practices of the Government of Iraq,

including the implementation of all relevant resolutions of the Security Council, for the purpose of determining whether to reduce or lift the prohibitions referred to therein;

22. *Decides* that upon the approval by the Security Council of the programme called for in paragraph 19 above and upon Council agreement that Iraq has completed all actions contemplated in paragraphs 8, 9, 10, 11, 12 and 13 above, the prohibitions against the import of commodities and products originating in Iraq and the prohibitions against financial transactions related thereto contained in resolution 661 (1990) shall have no further force or effect;

23. *Decides* that, pending action by the Security Council under paragraph 22 above, the Security Council Committee established by resolution 661 (1990) shall be empowered to approve, when required to assure adequate financial resources on the part of Iraq to carry out the activities under paragraph 20 above, exceptions to the prohibition against the import of commodities and products originating in Iraq;

24. *Decides* that, in accordance with resolution 661 (1990) and subsequent related resolutions and until a further decision is taken by the Security Council, all States shall continue to prevent the sale or supply, or the promotion or facilitation of such sale or supply, to Iraq by their nationals, or from their territories or using their flag vessels or aircraft, of:

(a) Arms and related *matériel* of all types, specifically including the sale or transfer through other means of all forms of conventional military equipment, including for paramilitary forces, and spare parts and components and their means of production, for such equipment;

(b) Items specified and defined in paragraphs 8 and 12 above not otherwise covered above;

(c) Technology under licensing or other transfer arrangements used in the production, utilization or stockpiling of items specified in subparagraphs (a) and (b) above;

(d) Personnel or materials for training or technical support services relating to the design, development, manufacture, use, maintenance or support of items specified in subparagraphs (a) and (b) above;

25. *Calls upon* all States and international organizations to act strictly in accordance with paragraph 24 above, notwithstanding the existence of any contracts, agreements, licences or any other arrangements;

26. *Requests* the Secretary-General, in consultation with appropriate Governments, to develop within sixty days, for the approval of the Security Council, guidelines to facilitate full international implementation of paragraphs 24 and 25 above and paragraph 27 below, and to make them available to all States and to establish a procedure for updating these guidelines periodically;

27. *Calls upon* all States to maintain such national controls and procedures and to take such other actions consistent with the guidelines to be established by the Security Council under paragraph 26 above as may be necessary to ensure compliance with the terms of paragraph 24 above, and calls upon international organizations to take all appropriate steps to assist in ensuring such full compliance;

28. *Agrees* to review its decisions in paragraphs 22, 23, 24 and 25 above, except for the items specified and defined in paragraphs 8 and 12 above, on a regular basis and in any case one hundred and twenty days following passage of the present resolution, taking into account Iraq's compliance with the resolution and general progress towards the control of armaments in the region;

29. *Decides* that all States, including Iraq, shall take the necessary measures to ensure that no claim shall lie at the instance of the Government of Iraq, or of any person or body in Iraq, or of any person claiming through or for the benefit of any such person or body, in connection with any contract or other transaction where its performance was affected by

reason of the measures taken by the Security Council in resolution 661 (1990) and related resolutions;

G

30. *Decides* that, in furtherance of its commitment to facilitate the repatriation of all Kuwaiti and third country nationals, Iraq shall extend all necessary cooperation to the International Committee of the Red Cross, providing lists of such persons, facilitating the access of the International Committee of the Red Cross to all such persons wherever located or detained and facilitating the search by the International Committee of the Red Cross for those Kuwaiti and third country nationals still unaccounted for;

31. *Invites* the International Committee of the Red Cross to keep the Secretary-General apprised as appropriate of all activities undertaken in connection with facilitating the repatriation or return of all Kuwaiti and third country nationals or their remains present in Iraq on or after 2 August 1990;

H

32. *Requires* Iraq to inform the Security Council that it will not commit or support any act of international terrorism or allow any organization directed towards commission of such acts to operate within its territory and to condemn unequivocally and renounce all acts, methods and practices of terrorism;

I

33. *Declares* that, upon official notification by Iraq to the Secretary-General and to the Security Council of its acceptance of the provisions above, a formal cease-fire is effective between Iraq and Kuwait and the Member States cooperating with Kuwait in accordance with resolution 678 (1990);

34. *Decides* to remain seized of the matter and to take such further steps as may be required for the implementation of the present resolution and to secure peace and security in the area.

Appendix 2

Resolution 1441 (2002)
Adopted by the Security Council at its 4,644th meeting,
on 8 November 2002

The Security Council,

Recalling all its previous relevant resolutions, in particular its resolutions 661 (1990) of 6 August 1990, 678 (1990) of 29 November 1990, 686 (1991) of 2 March 1991, 687 (1991) of 3 April 1991, 688 (1991) of 5 April 1991, 707 (1991) of 15 August 1991, 715 (1991) of 11 October 1991, 986 (1995) of 14 April 1995, and 1284 (1999) of 17 December 1999, and all the relevant statements of its President,

Recalling also its resolution 1382 (2001) of 29 November 2001 and its intention to implement it fully,

Recognising the threat Iraq's non-compliance with Council resolutions and proliferation of weapons of mass destruction and long-range missiles poses to international peace and security,

Recalling that its resolution 678 (1990) authorized Member States to use all necessary means to uphold and implement its resolution 660 (1990) of 2 August 1990 and all relevant resolutions subsequent to resolution 660 (1990) and to restore international peace and security in the area,

Further recalling that its resolution 687 (1991) imposed obligations on Iraq as a necessary step for achievement of its stated objective of restoring international peace and security in the area,

Deploring the fact that Iraq has not provided an accurate, full, final, and complete disclosure, as required by resolution 687 (1991), of all aspects of its programmes to develop weapons of mass destruction and ballistic missiles with a range greater than one hundred and fifty kilometres, and of all holdings of such weapons, their components and production facilities and locations, as well as all other nuclear programmes, including any which it claims are for purposes not related to nuclear-weapons-usable material.

Deploring further that Iraq repeatedly obstructed immediate, unconditional, and unrestricted access to sites designated by the United Nations Special Commission (UNSCOM) and the International Atomic Energy Agency (IAEA), failed to cooperate fully and unconditionally with UNSCOM and IAEA weapons inspectors, as required by resolution 687 (1991), and ultimately ceased all cooperation with UNSCOM and the IAEA in 1998,

Deploring the absence, since December 1998, in Iraq of international monitoring, inspection, and verification, as required by relevant resolutions, of weapons of mass destruction and ballistic missiles, in spite of the Council's repeated demands that Iraq provide immediate, unconditional, and unrestricted access to the United Nations Monitoring, Verification and Inspection Commission (UNMOVIC), established in resolution 1284 (1999) as the successor organization to UNSCOM, and the IAEA, and regretting the consequent prolonging of the crisis in the region and the suffering of the Iraqi people,

Deploring also that the Government of Iraq has failed to comply with its commitments pursuant to resolution 687 (1991) with regard to terrorism, pursuant to resolution 688 (1991) to end repression of its civilian population and to provide access by international humanitarian organizations to all those in need of assistance in Iraq, and pursuant to resolutions 686 (1991), 687 (1991), and 1284 (1999) to return or cooperate in accounting for Kuwaiti and third country nationals wrongfully detained by Iraq, or to return Kuwaiti property wrongfully seized by Iraq,

Recalling that in its resolution 687 (1991) the Council declared that a ceasefire would be based on acceptance by Iraq of the provisions of that resolution, including the obligations on Iraq contained therein,

Determined to ensure full and immediate compliance by Iraq without conditions or restrictions with its obligations under resolution 687 (1991) and other relevant resolutions and recalling that the resolutions of the Council constitute the governing standard of Iraqi compliance,

Recalling that the effective operation of UNMOVIC, as the successor organization to the Special Commission, and the IAEA is essential for the implementation of resolution 687 (1991) and other relevant resolutions,

Noting that the letter dated 16 September 2002 from the Minister for Foreign Affairs of Iraq addressed to the Secretary-General is a necessary first step toward rectifying Iraq's continued failure to comply with relevant Council resolutions,

Noting further the letter dated 8 October 2002 from the Executive Chairman of UNMOVIC and the Director-General of the IAEA to General Al-Saadi of the Government of Iraq laying out the practical arrangements, as a follow-up to their meeting in Vienna, that are prerequisites for the resumption of inspections in Iraq by UNMOVIC and the IAEA, and expressing the gravest concern at the continued failure by the Government of Iraq to provide confirmation of the arrangements as laid out in that letter,

Reaffirming the commitment of all Member States to the sovereignty and territorial integrity of Iraq, Kuwait, and the neighbouring States,

Commending the Secretary-General and members of the League of Arab States and its Secretary-General for their efforts in this regard,

Determined to secure full compliance with its decisions,

Acting under Chapter VII of the Charter of the United Nations,

1. *Decides* that Iraq has been and remains in material breach of its obligations under relevant resolutions, including resolution 687 (1991), in particular through Iraq's failure to cooperate with United Nations inspectors and the IAEA, and to complete the actions required under paragraphs 8 to 13 of resolution 687 (1991);

2. *Decides*, while acknowledging paragraph 1 above, to afford Iraq, by this resolution, a final opportunity to comply with its disarmament obligations under relevant resolutions of the Council; and accordingly decides to set up an enhanced inspection regime with the aim of bringing to full and verified completion the disarmament process established by resolution 687 (1991) and subsequent resolutions of the Council;

3. *Decides* that, in order to begin to comply with its disarmament obligations, in addition to submitting the required biannual declarations, the Government of Iraq shall provide to UNMOVIC, the IAEA, and the Council, not later than 30 days from the date of this

resolution, a currently accurate, full, and complete declaration of all aspects of its programmes to develop chemical, biological, and nuclear weapons, ballistic missiles, and other delivery systems such as unmanned aerial vehicles and dispersal systems designed for use on aircraft, including any holdings and precise locations of such weapons, components, sub-components, stocks of agents, and related material and equipment, the locations and work of its research, development and production facilities, as well as all other chemical, biological, and nuclear programmes, including any which it claims are for purposes not related to weapon production or material;

4. *Decides* that false statements or omissions in the declarations submitted by Iraq pursuant to this resolution and failure by Iraq at any time to comply with, and cooperate fully in the implementation of, this resolution shall constitute a further material breach of Iraq's obligations and will be reported to the Council for assessment in accordance with paragraphs 11 and 12 below;

5. *Decides* that Iraq shall provide UNMOVIC and the IAEA immediate, unimpeded, unconditional, and unrestricted access to any and all, including underground, areas, facilities, buildings, equipment, records, and means of transport which they wish to inspect, as well as immediate, unimpeded, unrestricted, and private access to all officials and other persons whom UNMOVIC or the IAEA wish to interview in the mode or location of UNMOVIC's or the IAEA's choice pursuant to any aspect of their mandates; further decides that UNMOVIC and the IAEA may at their discretion conduct interviews inside or outside of Iraq, may facilitate the travel of those interviewed and family members outside of Iraq, and that, at the sole discretion of UNMOVIC and the IAEA, such interviews may occur without the presence of observers from the Iraqi Government; and instructs UNMOVIC and requests the IAEA to resume inspections no later than 45 days following adoption of this resolution and to update the Council 60 days thereafter;

6. *Endorses* the 8 October 2002 letter from the Executive Chairman of UNMOVIC and the Director-General of the IAEA to General Al-Saadi of the Government of Iraq, which is annexed hereto, and decides that the contents of the letter shall be binding upon Iraq;

7. *Decides* further that, in view of the prolonged interruption by Iraq of the presence of UNMOVIC and the IAEA and in order for them to accomplish the tasks set forth in this resolution and all previous relevant resolutions and notwithstanding prior understandings, the Council hereby establishes the following revised or additional authorities, which shall be binding upon Iraq, to facilitate their work in Iraq:

– UNMOVIC and the IAEA shall determine the composition of their inspection teams and ensure that these teams are composed of the most qualified and experienced experts available;
– All UNMOVIC and IAEA personnel shall enjoy the privileges and immunities, corresponding to those of experts on mission, provided in the Convention on Privileges and Immunities of the United Nations and the Agreement on the Privileges and Immunities of the IAEA;
– UNMOVIC and the IAEA shall have unrestricted rights of entry into and out of Iraq, the right to free, unrestricted, and immediate movement to and from inspection sites, and the right to inspect any sites and buildings, including immediate, unimpeded, unconditional, and unrestricted access to Presidential Sites equal to that at other sites, notwithstanding the provisions of resolution 1154 (1998) of 2 March 1998;
– UNMOVIC and the IAEA shall have the right to be provided by Iraq the names of all personnel currently and formerly associated with Iraq's chemical, biological, nuclear, and ballistic missile programmes and the associated research, development, and production facilities;

- Security of UNMOVIC and IAEA facilities shall be ensured by sufficient United Nations security guards;
- UNMOVIC and the IAEA shall have the right to declare, for the purposes of freezing a site to be inspected, exclusion zones, including surrounding areas and transit corridors, in which Iraq will suspend ground and aerial movement so that nothing is changed in or taken out of a site being inspected;
- UNMOVIC and the IAEA shall have the free and unrestricted use and landing of fixed- and rotary-winged aircraft, including manned and unmanned reconnaissance vehicles;
- UNMOVIC and the IAEA shall have the right at their sole discretion verifiably to remove, destroy, or render harmless all prohibited weapons, subsystems, components, records, materials, and other related items, and the right to impound or close any facilities or equipment for the production thereof; and
- UNMOVIC and the IAEA shall have the right to free import and use of equipment or materials for inspections and to seize and export any equipment, materials, or documents taken during inspections, without search of UNMOVIC or IAEA personnel or official or personal baggage;

8. *Decides* further that Iraq shall not take or threaten hostile acts directed against any representative or personnel of the United Nations or the IAEA or of any Member State taking action to uphold any Council resolution;

9. *Requests* the Secretary-General immediately to notify Iraq of this resolution, which is binding on Iraq; demands that Iraq confirm within seven days of that notification its intention to comply fully with this resolution; and demands further that Iraq cooperate immediately, unconditionally, and actively with UNMOVIC and the IAEA;

10. *Requests* all Member States to give full support to UNMOVIC and the IAEA in the discharge of their mandates, including by providing any information related to prohibited programmes or other aspects of their mandates, including on Iraqi attempts since 1998 to acquire prohibited items, and by recommending sites to be inspected, persons to be interviewed, conditions of such interviews, and data to be collected, the results of which shall be reported to the Council by UNMOVIC and the IAEA;

11. *Directs* the Executive Chairman of UNMOVIC and the Director-General of the IAEA to report immediately to the Council any interference by Iraq with inspection activities, as well as any failure by Iraq to comply with its disarmament obligations, including its obligations regarding inspections under this resolution;

12. *Decides* to convene immediately upon receipt of a report in accordance with paragraphs 4 or 11 above, in order to consider the situation and the need for full compliance with all of the relevant Council resolutions in order to secure international peace and security;

13. *Recalls,* in that context, that the Council has repeatedly warned Iraq that it will face serious consequences as a result of its continued violations of its obligations;

14. *Decides* to remain seized of the matter.

Appendix 3

The Legal Opinion of the Attorney-General

Baroness Ramsay of Cartvale: To ask HMG what is the Attorney-General's view of the legal basis for the use of force against Iraq

Answer: The Attorney-General (Lord Goldsmith):

Authority to use force against Iraq exists from the combined effect of resolutions 678, 687 and 1441. All of these resolutions were adopted under Chapter VII of the UN Charter which allows the use of force for the express purpose of restoring international peace and security:

1. In resolution 678 the Security Council authorised force against Iraq, to eject it from Kuwait and to restore peace and security in the area.
2. In resolution 687, which set out the ceasefire conditions after Operation Desert Storm, the Security Council imposed continuing obligations on Iraq to eliminate its weapons of mass destruction in order to restore international peace and security in the area. Resolution 687 suspended but did not terminate the authority to use force under resolution 678.
3. A material breach of resolution 687 revives the authority to use force under resolution 678.
4. In resolution 1441 the Security Council determined that Iraq has been and remains in material breach of resolution 687, because it has not fully complied with its obligations to disarm under that resolution.
5. The Security Council in resolution 1441 gave Iraq "a final opportunity to comply with its disarmament obligations" and warned Iraq of the "serious consequences" if it did not.
6. The Security Council also decided in resolution 1441 that, if Iraq failed at any time to comply with and cooperate fully in the implementation of resolution 1441, that would constitute a further material breach.
7. It is plain that Iraq has failed so to comply and therefore Iraq was at the time of resolution 1441 and continues to be in material breach.
8. Thus, the authority to use force under resolution 678 has revived and so continues today.
9. Resolution 1441 would in terms have provided that a further decision of the Security Council to sanction force was required if that had been intended. Thus, all that resolution 1441 requires is reporting to and discussion by the Security Council of Iraq's failures, but not an express further decision to authorise force.

I have lodged a copy of this answer, together with resolutions 678, 687 and 1441 in the Library of both Houses and the Vote office of the House of Commons.

Acknowledgements

A number of people had to show forbearance over the production and then the postponement of the 2005 book text. My Random House editor, Joy de Menil, gave me tremendous support in writing the original copy, with a keen eye for the compromise between revelation, readability and good sense. My literary agent, Natasha Fairweather, bore the brunt of the to-ing and fro-ing in 2005 with constant equanimity and has remained a marvellous help in re-setting the target in 2016. My William Heinemann editor, Jason Arthur, worked wonders to reset the text and achieve an early publishing date in 2016. I tested the tolerance of several close friends in the early stages as authorship cut across events and arrangements: they know who they are and will remember having to dig deep for patience. And working colleagues in the Foreign and Commonwealth Office and Cabinet Office were put to a great deal of trouble to no purpose when I withdrew the 2005 text from publication. I am grateful to them all.

No one has had their lives more disrupted, though, than my family. I am very grateful to my children, Katie, Nick and Alex, and their families for their consistent encouragement and tolerance, whatever their misgivings. But I owe my biggest debt to my wife Anne, whose life was also affected by the Iraq saga, and who has been my keenest editorial adviser throughout.

I will not be making money out of this book. I shall be donating any money I receive from this book to charity.

Index

White, Andrew, 377–8
Wilmshurst, Elizabeth, 219
Wolfowitz, Paul, 78, 90, 120, 283,
    328–9, 367
women's rights, 69, 116, 193, 342,
    349–50, 365–6, 369, 372, 374, 376,
    379, 381
Woodstock, New York, 142, 152–3, 165,
    183, 204, 211, 260
Woodward, Robert 'Bob', 78, 104, 105

Y

al Yawar, Ghazi, 366, 401
Yemen, 311

'You break it, you own it' meeting
    (2002), 104, 233
Younes, Nadia, 261–2
Yugoslavia SFR (1945–92),
    377, 420

Z

al Zarqawi, Abu Musab, 281, 311–12,
    404, 412, 425
Zayed bin Sultan, Emir of
    Abu Dhabi, 20
Zebari, Hoshyar, 270
Zeid bin Raad, Prince of Jordan, 179
Ziyal, Ugur, 305